Unholy Child

Also by Catherine Breslin

The Mistress Condition: New Options in Sex, Love, and Other Female Pleasures

UNHOLY CHILD

A Novel by

Catherine Breslin

The Dial Press
New York

Published by
The Dial Press
1 Dag Hammarskjold Plaza
New York, New York 10017

Manufactured in the United States of America
First printing

Design by Francesca Belanger

Library of Congress Cataloging in Publication Data

Breslin, Catherine.
  Unholy child.

  I. Title.
PZ4. B8423Un [PS3552.R388] 813'.5'4 79–17219
ISBN 0–8037–9261–1

To Ding, Gus, Pepi, Sasha and the Parker

For very special help rendered at different points along this odyssey, I offer grateful thanks to Tom Berman, Wendy Weil, Lucian Truscott, Roberta Ashley, Tom Moskalewicz, and my prodigious editor, Joyce Johnson.

This novel is a work of fiction, of imagination. Any coincidental resemblance to persons living or dead is only that.

Unholy Child

One

As Ambulance 54 pulled up at 3:42 P.M. at the emergency entrance of Parkhurst General Hospital, the attendant in the rear ripped the oxygen mask off the face of the young woman lying on the stretcher. From the front seat Sister Julia O'Gorman gasped, "Oh my God. Is she dead?" The last blast of sirensound swallowed that question as the two attendants sprang from the small green vehicle and yanked the wheeled gurney onto the blacktop. They rolled it toward the electric-eye doors of the emergency entrance, rolled it so rapidly that the aluminum edge of the gurney banged against the wide doors as they opened.

The emergency team was already clustered, waiting, at the end of the long hospital hall, with Martha Hopkins, the head nurse, pointing into GYN One. The gurney hurtled into the examining room. The young woman lying on it was so blanched her freckled skin had a greenish tinge. Her short red-gold hair was streaked with what looked like smears of brown paint; her fuzzy pink bathrobe was soaked with blood from the waist down. Her facial muscles hung flaccid, utterly without form—the look of death or coma, not sleep.

As the attendants lifted the body and dropped it onto the high steel-wheeled examining table, Hopkins slapped a blood-pressure cuff around the patient's left arm. "Okay, what've we got?" she asked as she pumped up the cuff, her eyes on the large black-and-white dial mounted on the wall above the examining table.

1

"Sister Angela Flynn, age thirty-three," said the ambulance driver. "From the St. Rose of Lima Convent in Cambridgeport. Found bleeding in her room from unknown causes."

Hopkins watched the dial; the needle was stuck on zero. "Get two IVs going, fast," she snapped. "And get Kovaleski down here stat." The surgical resident and the medical resident each grabbed an arm to insert intravenous needles; a nurse slashed a scissors up the length of the pink robe.

Hopkins reached for a pulse in the left wrist. "Anything else?" she asked the driver.

"Yeah. When we picked her up off the floor we found a pair of scissors underneath her."

"Okay, thanks." No pulse in the cold, clammy wrist. As the attendants rolled the empty gurney out of the room, one resident said, "Shit! This vein's completely collapsed."

"Try an ankle cutdown," the other said.

One last slash in the robe, and the nurse flipped it away from the body. In one quick glance Hopkins assessed the bloated belly and legs, the blood-soaked pubic hairs. *GYN, sure enough,* she thought as she looked back at the unmoving BP dial.

A quiver went through the patient. As if sensing her nakedness, she stirred, moaned, her limp facial muscles reshaping into a look of bewildered pain. "Cover this woman up," Hopkins ordered the nurse. As a small white draw sheet fluttered down over the nun's upper body, Hopkins bent down toward her face, stroking the matted red hair. "Sister? Sister, can you tell us your name?" she asked loudly.

Sluiced from the blackness into bright white light. Strange noise all around her. Strange hands touching her skin. Woman in white shouting.

Cold. So cold. Cold like death.

Daddy cold like this when he was dying. Fear strong as the

2

cold pressing her chest. So hard to breathe. People all around, touching her, hurting her.

"That's right, that's all right, you're awake now. Can you tell me your name?"

Daddy cold like this when he died. Jesus help me help me. Not now. Not like this.

"You're all right, you're in a hospital. We're going to help you now."

Danger. Danger. Fear like sparks in the huge darkness of her mind.

"Can you just tell us who you are?"

She was trying to make her mouth shape her name when the long slide into nothingness began again.

In the front seat of the ambulance, Sister Julia O'Gorman, the thirty-four-year-old local coordinator of the twelve nuns living at the St. Rose of Lima Convent, sat numbed and waiting. Waiting for someone to come and tell her what to do, where to go.

But no one came. No one was *going* to come, Julia realized. She must go in there herself, where they had taken Angela. She was Angela's religious superior. Her duty was clear: to be with Angela.

Yet that last sight of her kept flickering like a slow-motion replay in Julia's head. She realized that her body was quivering, trembling. She pressed her hands against her knees to still the motion and closed her eyes. *Jesus Mary and Joseph, be with me now. Give me strength. Give me—*

She moaned, a small, wounded sound. Sweet Jesus, she could not even pray right. *Be with Angela,* she amended the thought. *Let Your grace and power see her through this time of trial.*

Enough. Go. Julia picked up her black purse and stepped out of the ambulance. As she neared the hospital entrance the wide doors swung open, and the ambulance men rolled the empty stretcher out. Julia nodded mutely to them and walked into the long, dim hall. At the other end there were lights, bustle; that must be where they had taken Angela.

Outside the examining room, she could see a glimpse of her, lying on a high table. People in white were moving, hovering all around her. Suddenly one of them yanked a white curtain around the table, cutting off Julia's view. She turned away from the door, blinking, bewildered.

A nurse behind a desk twenty feet down the hall smiled and beckoned. Julia walked unsteadily up to the desk. The nurse asked, "Are you a relative of the patient?"

"No. I'm—yes, I guess I am."

"Very good," the nurse nodded. "If you'd like to help us out, you could go talk to the admitting desk. Give them the information we need on the patient." As Julia stared blankly the nurse added, "When they come in by ambulance we need a family member to process them through."

"Oh, yes!" Julia clutched at her black purse. "Thank you. Of course I could do that. Thank you very much."

The nurse pointed around a corner of the hall. "Just follow the blue line in the floor."

At 3:47 Dr. Lawrence Kovaleski, Parkhurst Hospital's chief resident in obstetrics and gynecology, was in the staff room catching his first coffee of the afternoon when his pocket beeper went off almost simultaneously with an emergency page to ER over the PA system. Kovaleski muttered, "Fuck, one more of those afternoons," and pitched the plastic cup into a waste container on his way to the Emergency Department. When he saw the running and commotion outside GYN One, Kovaleski froze for one moment, sucking in a deep breath. In a reflex motion he pulled his stethoscope from the pocket of his white coat as he walked rapidly into the treatment room.

The patient was pale, unconscious, obviously shocky; clothing bloodstained, dried blood covering anterior thighs. Evident mass in abdomen. Cavello, the medical resident,

4

said rapidly, "Sister Angela Flynn, age thirty-three. Severe hemorrhage, unknown cause. No pulse, no BP."

Kovaleski tried for a blood-pressure reading himself; no nudge on the dial. He asked Hopkins, "Did you call Talbott?"

"Not yet."

"Well, get him down here stat." In the rush of possibilities Kovaleski was fielding, cardiac arrest seemed paramount. As he weighed ordering the crash cart, the nurse murmured, "No arrest. She's just not registering."

Goddam Hopkins, always two jumps ahead of him. Kovaleski snapped back with, "Why isn't she catheterized?"

"Calm down. We haven't had a chance to get in there yet," Hopkins said.

The medical resident working on the left arm said suddenly, "Aha, got it! Jeff, let me try her other arm."

"Pour a liter of normal saline into her until we get some crossmatched blood down here," Kovaleski said as he busied himself with drawing a small tube of blood from this woman who had already lost more than she could spare.

Again the sharp slide back into the light.

Man bending over her. Glasses. Black mustache. "Sister Angela, I'm Dr. Lawrence Kovaleski, the chief resident of the gynecology service. Can you tell me what happened to you?"

She turned her head away from the face. Gray-haired nurse smiling. *Don't talk. Don't talk. Danger. Don't talk.*

"You're at the Parkhurst Hospital Emergency Department and we're trying to help you. But we need to know what happened."

Strong lights spinning slowly around her body. Inside her head a large, dark space lit only by cracklings of danger. Cold, so cold. So afraid.

"Sister Angela, we only want to help you. But we need *your* help. Can you tell me how this started?"

She turned back to the face. Suddenly one thought

5

moved out of her terrified confusion: the danger was in this place. If she told them what they wanted to know, they would let her go back home, to safety.

She whispered, "Bleeding."

"Okay. Can you tell me how long you've been bleeding?"

"All day."

"What do you mean, all day? Can you tell me when it began?"

"Nine thirty. Maybe ten."

"All right. How much did you bleed?"

"I don't know. A lot. Am I dying?"

"No, no. You have a serious medical situation, but we're going to help you now. What caused the bleeding?"

Faint shake of the head. "I'm so cold," she whispered.

"I understand. You'll feel better soon, when we get some fluid into you. Can you give me any estimate of how much blood you lost—a quart? A couple of quarts?"

"I don't know. Just a lot." She closed her eyes. She did not want to see those faces floating like balloons above her, slipping in and out of focus.

Something had happened. Something bad. Why couldn't she remember?

All she remembered was the blood.

"Have you had any pain?"

"Yes." Yes, yes. Body so sore. So hurting. Not like her own. This sore, strange body.

"What kind of pain, where was it?"

"Stomach."

"Is it sharp, dull, constant, intermittent? Can you give me some description of the pain?"

"I don't know. It hurts."

Now he was lifting her eyelid, shining a small light into her eyes. Face so close she could see the prickly hairs of his mustache. "Did the pain precede the bleeding?"

"Yes."

"But you don't know what caused it?"

"No."

Hands on her neck, pressing, kneading. "Sister, when was your last menstrual period?"

Sparks flickering, flashing in the dark space. "Six weeks ago."

"Have you missed any periods?" The sheet over her body moved aside. Cold metal pressed over her heart.

"No. I'm always regular."

"How often do you have them?"

"Every—" *Think. Yes.* "Every twenty-eight days."

Now he was touching her where she had never been touched before—pressing, squeezing her breasts. She caught her breath. Mother of God, what were they doing to her in this place?

"How long do you flow?"

"Four or five days," she gasped.

Sheet pushed farther down. "Is there any possibility that you're pregnant?"

That bizarre question came at her like a slap in the face. She rolled her head back and forth on the thin white pillow. Strongly: "No. That's not possible."

Sheet moved again. He pushed his fingers deep into her side. "Does that hurt?"

"No." A metal disc pressed on her stomach. She felt the cold roundness.

"How did the bleeding start?"

"I don't know. It just came."

Now he was squeezing her belly. Suddenly the pain came at her again like an ocean breaker, pitching her without warning back into that terrifying trough.

"Does that hurt?"

Like a sharp hand clawing, tearing at her insides. *Don't scream. Don't scream.*

"Sister, does that give you pain?"

Whisper: "Yes."

7

"Is that the pain you've been experiencing today?"

"Yes. Hurts."

Now he was touching her legs, pressing sharply into her skin. "Sister, how long have your legs been swollen like this?"

"Two days."

"Can you be any more specific about the quantity of your bleeding?"

Faintly: "Just lots of blood. And clots."

Hands pressing on the inside of her knees, trying to push her legs apart. The cracklings of danger very bright now in her head. With her eyes pinched shut, she concentrated all her strength in her lower body.

"Sister, we just want to examine the site of your bleeding. This isn't going to hurt you; I'll be very gentle. But we have to examine you."

The words seemed to come at her from some far-off place. She let them roll past without touching her. Only the danger was real. That and this thing they were trying to do to her.

Another pair of hands pulling on her thighs. Their touch hot, burning on her skin. Mind blank. Dark. Body shaking. Hard to breathe. *Help me. Help me.*

"Okay, leave it alone." The hands came off her legs; the sheet back over her body.

Tired. So tired. Want to sleep. But the voice came at her again: "Sister Angela, have you noticed any changes lately in your breasts?" No answer. "Did they change in size? Have the nipples changed in color?"

"Yes."

"Well, Sister, that's a physical change that is usually associated with a pregnancy."

The voice strong yet distant: "No. No. I *could not* be pregnant."

Sergeant Michael Leighton, the tall, lean young cop in charge of the Cambridgeport Road Patrol, paced the lawn

8

outside the St. Rose of Lima Convent, his hands jammed into the back pockets of his blue uniform. Several nuns dressed in skirts and sweaters hovered uncomfortably on the front step, their arms folded across their ribs, watching him like furtive sentries.

Fact was, Leighton felt almost as uncomfortable with this situation as those nuns did. Speeding tickets, parking tickets, DWI—that was what Leighton was used to handling in this tranquil, tree-lined, fat-cat suburb of St. Paul, Minnesota. This thing here this afternoon, it shaped up first like one more routine ambulance call. Leighton handled it himself because he happened to be patrolling the neighborhood a few blocks away.

He knew these nuns wanted him the hell out of here. He saw a couple more of them peeking out the front windows, giving him the once-over. He could just about lip-read the prayers they were tossing up to get him out. Well, let 'em pray. Leighton was no goddam Kojak, but he was enough of a good cop to know he wasn't leaving this place till he got some answers.

A maroon Ford pulled up to the curb. Sergeant Robert Paige, a plainclothes cop in the Detective Unit, stepped out and slammed the door. Paige—why the hell was he here? Leighton nodded curtly to him and said, "I thought Lieutenant Vance was coming. I called in for Vance to come."

"Yeah, well, Vance's busy." Paige ran his eyes over the blank face of the four-story, red-brick convent. "What you got?"

"I dunno. See what you think."

The sentry nuns slipped inside as the two policemen approached the door. "Thanks, Sister," Leighton said awkwardly to the one holding the door open for them. He led Paige through the dreary convent parlor with its plastic-covered chairs and overstuffed maroon velour couch, past the brooding three-color lithograph of the Holy Family.

In the upstairs hall Leighton pointed to the rust-colored prints—apparently made by bare feet, approximately size six

—visible on the orange carpeting. "First off, I saw these. So I followed them down here to the bathroom."

At the doorway of the bare communal bathroom, Leighton swallowed. All that stuff pooled and splashed on the white tile floor, splattered on the beige walls, smeared in handprints around the doors—Leighton had never in his goddam career seen so much blood.

But Paige seemed unimpressed as he stepped delicately around the puddle. "There's more in there," Leighton said, nodding toward the tub enclosure. Paige opened the door and peered into the tub. Two towels floated in six inches of mixed blood and water. "When I saw that I figured we might be dealing with an abortion here. Maybe a self-abortion. I looked for a fetus in the water, but I couldn't find anything. Then I checked out the johns. There's blood all around but the water in the bowls was clean. I figure she probably flushed it down."

Paige glanced into a toilet cubicle, noted that the roll of paper was empty and red handprints were visible on the cardboard core. "Hmmmph." He hitched at the belt of his badly fitted brown suit. "What else you got?"

Leighton ignored the two nuns hovering at the end of the hall as he led Paige to Sister Angela Flynn's small, spare bedroom. The pool here was larger, but less visible against the brown linoleum floor. A half-dozen things that looked like cloth—towels and scatter rugs, maybe—were so saturated with blood that Leighton couldn't tell their original color. The rest of the room looked fairly clean, except for a small red smear on the sheet at the edge of the narrow unmade bed, and another on the brown bookcase kitty-cornered by the window.

Leighton pointed to the steel scissors in the middle of the floor. "Those were under her when the ambulance guys picked her up."

Paige grunted noncommittally as he moved into the room.

Okay, so maybe he'd overreacted, hit the panic button. Leighton still wished Tim Vance had answered his call instead of this jerk Paige. "I asked the nuns in the hall if they'd noticed her having any problems with swelling, and one of them said yes, in her legs and here." He tapped his stomach.

Still no response from Paige.

Leighton finished lamely, "Anyway, I figured somebody ought to check it out."

Paige nodded, sucking noisily on a tooth. "Well, I tell you, Mike—I seen female hemorrhages this bad had nothing to do with an obstetrical situation."

"Oh, yeah?" Leighton reminded himself that Paige had worked seven years as an ambulance attendant before he joined the Cambridgeport force; he should know what he was talking about.

"Sure. Cancer, fibroids, superficial wounds—a lotta things could produce this kind of result." Paige opened the closet door and glanced into a half-filled laundry bag lying on the floor.

Leighton stepped around the blood-pool. "But she didn't have any open wounds I could see. It all seemed to come from down around the vagina."

"Yeah, well. Maybe she was trying to get herself straight with a coat hanger." Paige slid open a bureau drawer. "Whatever it is, the doctors are gonna find it out soon enough. There's no way she can hide it once she gets to the hospital."

"Okay, you're the boss." Leighton joined in the cursory search of the bare little room—checked the plastic wastebasket under the sink, and the dustless space under the single bed. A brown purse was sitting on the small maple desk; Leighton snapped it open, fingered through the contents. Hmm. Funny. He hadn't realized nuns carried around that kind of money.

"Is there anything we can help you with, Officers?"

A brisk, mannish nun in her mid-forties was standing in

the bedroom door, glaring at Leighton and the open purse. Her voice was as controlled as her carefully folded hands, but there was no mistaking that outrage in her eyes. Leighton snapped the purse shut and replaced it on the desk as Paige said, "No, thanks, Sister, we're just about finished up." He slammed the bottom drawer shut. "Have you got any idea what happened here?"

Firm shake of the head. "No. We didn't even know Sister Angela was sick. When the sisters came home from school they just—found her."

"Well, don't you worry yourself about it. I'm pretty sure she's going to be okay," said Paige.

As he was stepping into the hall, the nun asked, "Officer, is it okay if we clean up?"

Leighton shook his head. He was about to say *No, better leave it alone* when Paige turned, looked at the floor and said cheerfully, "Sure, Sister, go ahead. If you use hot water and a strong detergent you'll get it up pretty good."

As he followed Paige down the stairs of the dim, silent convent Leighton reminded himself to write this one up as a "CYA" report. *Cover your ass, Mike,* he thought angrily. *Let this one be on Paige.*

In the ladies' room of the emergency reception area of Parkhurst Hospital, Sister Julia O'Gorman scrubbed her stockings clean with wet paper towels. Her skirt was also stained from kneeling beside Angela on the floor, but fortunately the navy wool material didn't show the spots.

That feeling of nausea was still strong, but she couldn't throw up; she'd already tried. She picked up her purse and walked back outside, trying to order her fluttering thoughts, decide what to do next.

Two St. Rose nuns were standing by the reception desk —Sister Claudine Schneider, a forty-eight-year-old regional supervisor of the St. Benedictine Order who lived at the St.

Rose convent because it was out of her own district, and Sister Dorothy Grier, the tall, soft-spoken twenty-eight-year-old who taught sixth grade in the parish school. Feeling an astonishing flood of relief, Julia ran toward them. "Claude! Dot! Oh, I'm so glad to see you."

They hugged her briefly, in an awkward triple embrace. Claudine said, "Julia, how is Angela?"

"I don't know. In the ambulance she— A lot of them are working on her, back there." She nodded toward the Emergency Department doors. "I don't know if she— I think she's very bad."

Claudine scanned the large waiting room, looking for a private space. A dozen people were lounging on scattered chairs; several of them were already staring at the nuns. Hardly the place to hold this conference, but there seemed no other choice. "Julie, come over here." Claudine steered her toward the far corner of the room.

The molded yellow fiberglass chairs were bolted together in a straight line. They sat, Julia in the middle, and leaned toward each other with bent heads, making a small confessional triangle of privacy.

Claudine said quietly, "Julia, I was just coming home when they took Angela out. I need to know what happened."

The shaking was back in her legs. Julia pressed her hands against them, opened her mouth to answer. But all that came into her head was that sight that would live with her always now—Angela lying on the bedroom floor. She tried again to speak, then shook her head, covered her face with her hands.

Dorothy fished a Kleenex from her purse and passed it to Julia as she whispered, "Margory and I came home first from school. We had a glass of pop in the kitchen. When I went upstairs to leave my books I saw the footprints outside the bathroom. I looked in and it was—my first thought was somebody's been murdered. I went downstairs to get Margory. She was screaming, she didn't want to come up, but then she did." Julia was dabbing at her cheeks, breathing deeply, trying to control herself.

Claudine asked, "Where was Angela?"

"We didn't know," said Dorothy. "I said, 'We've got to look for her' but Margory said no, we should phone the school for help. And then we saw Julia through the bathroom window, walking over from the school. So we went down and told her please come upstairs, something is terribly wrong."

Julia folded the Kleenex tightly between her fingers and picked up the recital. "When I saw the bathroom I told Dot to look for Angela in by the tub. I went down to her room. I think I knocked—there wasn't any answer. I opened the door." She swallowed. "I thought first she was dead. I knelt down beside her and I think I said something like 'Angela, can we help you?' At first she didn't answer, so I told Dot to call an ambulance. And then Angela said, 'No, don't. I called the doctor and his nurse told me just to keep my legs elevated.' "

Claudine straightened sharply in the chair. "That doesn't make any sense," she murmured.

Julia nodded. "I know. So I signaled Dot to call it anyway, and when I told Angela it was coming she said, 'I'm too messy for the ambulance. Please clean me up.' So we got a basin of water and I was trying to wash off her legs, only I couldn't because they were just covered with blood."

"What else did Angela say?"

"Just—to please close the door to her room and she'd clean it when she got home. And then once—I guess she fainted. But I thought she was dead. I slapped her face—three or four times. And then she came to again and I told her it was all right, the ambulance was coming to take care of her." She paused. "They took *so long* coming and the policeman got there first, but finally they came. The men kept asking her what happened, was she shot, was she stabbed, but Angela wouldn't answer—she just kept shaking her head back and forth. And then I guess they realized how really sick she was, and they took her out."

Claudine gave Julia's arm a quick, comforting squeeze. "Well, now it's in the hands of the Good Lord."

"Oh, yes. I'm *sure* she's going to be okay," murmured Dorothy, who was not sure at all.

Julia blew her nose into the sodden Kleenex. "One more thing—when I told her I was coming with her to the hospital she said, 'Okay, but only you. Nobody else.' So I won't tell her that you're here. But oh, Claude, I'm so *glad* you are. It's so hard waiting like this."

There was one question Julia had been dreading to hear since this ordeal began, and Claudine asked it now: "Did anyone know Angela was sick?"

Julia's stomach muscles tightened into a spastic knot. She pressed one hand over her abdomen. "Yes. *I* knew. She came to my room around seven this morning and said she couldn't go to school because she had the flu so would I please tell Virginia to drive on without her."

The word snapped, whiplike, from Claudine: *"Flu?"*

Julia nodded, a rapid bobbling of her head. "She said she had stomach cramps but she'd taken some Bufferin and she thought she'd be better soon."

At the words "stomach cramps" Claudine's body stiffened.

"So I went down to breakfast and spoke to Virginia and when I went back up for my things I stopped by Angela's room to tell her everything was taken care of."

Taken care of. Claudine stared coldly at the opposite wall.

This was the part that was so painful, now, for Julia to remember. "When I walked in, Angela was kneeling down by the sink, bending forward with a towel in her hands. I thought maybe she was vomiting. So I asked if I could help her and she said no, no, she felt much better. She got up and said she'd probably take a taxi to the school later that morning, when she was feeling better."

She took a breath. "So I told her I'd check on her at noon and I went over to school."

From Claudine: "How was she at noon?"

There were few times in Julia's adult life when she had told a conscious lie, but this one came effortlessly. "I never got a chance to check. I had such a busy morning with the vocabulary testing and—I just never had a single moment free, and I thought probably she'd gone on to school anyway, like she said."

Claudine's lips were pressed into a tight, grim line. "Well, never mind. What's done is done," she said shortly. "Angela is in good hands now, and the rest is up to the Lord. I think we might say a prayer for her right now."

They bowed their heads and murmured a ritual Hail Mary. But Claudine's thoughts were fixed on two things blurted out in Julia's agitated confession—*stomach cramps.* And *policeman.*

Julia's were fixed, numbly, on those burned-in images of blood and death.

Two

Now there was another doctor. Thin. Gentle. His voice very soft. Calm. This man did not frighten her like the other.

He told her he was Dr. Keith Talbott, the chief of the gynecology service. Chief. So he was in charge.

"I just wanted to reassure you, Sister, that you're making good progress. All your vital signs are good." Smile. A kind smile. "I don't want you to worry. We're going to take good care of you."

She tried to echo the smile back. Whispered: "Thank you, Doctor."

She stiffened as she felt the sheet come off again. But this man touched her more gently, more quickly. She was stiffened against the questions, too. But he only asked, "Sister, these bruises on your legs—can you tell me how you got them?"

"No."

"Have you seen a doctor lately?"

"No."

He asked a few questions about the bleeding, about the pain. She told him the same things she told that other doctor. Then: "Is there any chance you could be pregnant?"

Didn't they *know* she was a nun? "No. I already told them. No."

"All right, Sister." He tucked the sheet up around her shoulders. "You try to get some rest. I think we have everything pretty much under control."

Faintly: "Thank you."

Every part of her wanted to sleep. But Angela knew she must stay awake, alert to what they were trying to do to her.

A nurse smoothed the sheet. "Sister, is there anything I can do for you?"

"Yes," Angela said slowly. "Could you clean me up?"

As he crossed the hall to an empty examining room Dr. Keith Talbott gripped the head nurse by the elbow. "Hopkins, I want a tight lid on this. You understand? *Nothing at all goes out.*"

"Okay. Done."

Kovaleski followed him into the room. As Talbott closed the door Kovaleski slumped into a chair, his legs sprawled wide. "Jesus Christ, what a case!" He ran one hand distractedly through his black hair. "A nun, for crying out loud."

Talbott leaned against the green-tiled wall, arms folded

across his chest, looking at Kovaleski with faintly concealed distaste. He had never much cared for this high-pitched, exuberant little man, but at this particular moment Kovaleski's Polish emotionalism was almost more than Talbott could take. Forcing a deliberate flatness into his voice, Talbott said, "Okay. The question is, why has this patient had a recent episode of profuse bleeding?"

"I guess it could be a lot of things. Maybe a fibroid uterus. But when I saw those glandular breasts, expressed the fluid—I think it's gotta be a pregnancy-related hemorrhage. Okay, I know that's not the first diagnosis you go for with a young nun. But it fits the rest of the clinical picture —the four-plus edema, and the contracting uterus—"

Sharply: "That mass isn't necessarily the uterus."

"Yeah, sure, okay. But when I was manipulating it, it felt like it was contracting. That's when she complained of pain."

Talbott looked down at the floor and recited a roster of possible alternative diagnoses, like a lecturing professor: Ectopic pregnancy. Aborted fibroid tumor. Cervical cancer. Dysfunctional estrogen-related bleeding. Trauma—possibly a forcible rape.

"Or attempted abortion," added Kovaleski. "The scissors could figure in either of those. But I keep coming back to those breasts. I couldn't pick up any fetal heartbeat, but you don't get glandular breasts from a rape. Not a recent one, anyway."

Talbott grunted in reluctant agreement. "What kind of a history did you get out of her?"

"Bleeding, pain. Not many specifics. And nothing reliable. She's very lucid, considering her condition—a hematocrit of *twenty,* for Lord's sake. But withdrawn. You can see, she doesn't want to talk." Talbott nodded. "Christ, I don't wonder why. A *nun.* Criminee."

Dryly: "Well, they're human too. Didn't you do a pelvic?"

"I tried, sure, but she wouldn't *let* me. Half dead, and she's got those legs nailed together like she was on a cross."

Talbott found the offensive tastelessness of that last remark intolerable even from Kovaleski. Yet he realized from his own brief examination of the nun that there were special circumstances operative here that might impede the indicated course of treatment. He glared angrily, reproachfully at Kovaleski's white socks as he said, "Well, it's got to be done. I'll give it a try myself and if I don't have any luck we'll do it in the OR if we have to. Did somebody bring her in, somebody we could get a better history from?"

"I understand there's a couple of nuns outside. I haven't talked to them."

"Okay. I'll handle that, and you go take another look at the patient. We're still wide open on possibilities with this thing. And keep in mind, Kovaleski—you can't diagnose a condition you haven't considered."

When the policemen finally left the house Sister Mary Luke collected the six nuns who were home in the community room. They clustered by the wide arched door, each one taking refuge from the unnatural violence in their midst in the close presence of the others.

Since Julia and Claudine were absent, Mary Luke took charge. "Okay. This has been a pretty upsetting experience for us all. Has anybody got any questions?"

Roxanne said, "Just—what happened?"

"Nobody seems to know," said Mary Luke. "Is everybody here okay?"

Nods of agreement. Someone asked where Margory was, and Joan said in the chapel. *Just as well, and let her stay there,* Mary Luke thought grimly. If there was one thing she expected of any nun, it was a reasonable control over her emotions. That was what nuns were trained to, like teachers in a fire drill. And the way Margory had been crying and moaning and carrying on since they got back to the house —well, it only made her appreciate how well the rest of them were responding to this distressing situation. Of course they

19

were shocked, upset—anyone would be. But what Mary Luke read on their faces was calm and concern. Above all, control.

She felt proud of the whole bunch of them.

The next topic, inevitably, was cleaning up, restoring the usual order of the house. When Mary Luke asked for volunteers, Joan said hesitantly, "But—didn't Julia say we should close the bedroom door and leave it alone till she came back?"

"Yes, she did," Mary Luke said calmly. It was no simple thing for her to deliberately disobey the order of a superior, but in this case she had to assume Julia was temporarily unhinged, didn't know what she was saying. Luke couldn't believe Julia actually meant for them not to undo that—*mess*, that was the only word she could think of to describe it. "But the policeman told me it was all right to clean up. I'll take the responsibility."

The relief of the others was palpable. Roxanne volunteered for the bathroom; Mary Luke said she'd take the bedroom. Irma had to go out to a Spanish lesson, but Joan and Priscilla would pitch in until the others came home to help.

The doctor who finally came into the lobby to talk to them at 4:15 was a tall, handsome, grave-looking gynecologist. He introduced himself as Dr. Keith Talbott, and assured them that Sister Angela was responding very well to treatment.

"Oh, thank the Good Lord for that!" Julia exclaimed.

"She's suffering from an acute blood loss, as you know, but she's tolerating the transfusions well, and her blood pressure is coming up quite rapidly."

The nuns murmured their gratitude for the good news. Julia said, "Doctor, could I see her? Talk to her?"

"Perhaps, for a few minutes. When she's a little more stabilized. I'll let you know." He paused, seemed to be weighing his words. "What concerns us most is the cause of this onset of severe bleeding. Sister Angela hasn't been able to give us a medical history that would explain it, and we were wondering if you could shed any additional light."

Julia told him about the flu that morning. Prodded by the doctor's questions, Claudine said she had first noticed the swelling in Angela's legs quite a few weeks before. "We knew she had some kind of medical problem, but Sister Angela told us that she was seeing a doctor, that the problem was nothing serious."

The doctor was looking sharply at them, seemed to be searching for something in their faces. "There seems to be. an abdominal mass of some sort that has caused her severe bleeding," he said carefully. "We're looking for the cause." Silence from the nuns. "Okay, thank you, Sisters. We'll let you know as soon as we have any further developments."

When he went back through the wide swinging doors Julia went limp with relief. "Oh, thank God. Thank God, Claude."

But Claudine's expression was remote, preoccupied. She had a pretty fair idea of what was on that doctor's mind, even if Julia—naive, prissy Julia—did not. Claudine looked at the bank of phones on the lobby's opposite wall and said, "Julia, did anyone notify Angela's family?"

Julia reacted with a start. "No, I don't think— Of course, they ought to know." The color, the liveliness, was flowing back to Julia's face. "I could do that right now. I could call her mother. Now that there's good news to tell her." She gathered up her purse, fairly babbling in her relief. "I'm sure I've got a dime. She's in the phone book, I think. Or else Angela's brother. Oh—and the Motherhouse." She looked at Claudine. "Should I call someone at the Motherhouse?"

Claudine suggested she hold off on that until they had more definite news. *Let's see if you can do this right, at least,* Claudine thought grimly as she watched her move toward the telephones. The matter of Julia's earlier, astonishing negligence, which had led directly to this emergency, would be dealt with later in the appropriate manner—Claudine would see to that.

Right now she was more concerned with keeping Julia calm enough to deal with the present situation. So she waited until Julia was out of earshot before she said, "Dorothy, do you remember that conversation we had about Angela last Sunday in the community room?"

"You mean—when she didn't come back from the weekend on time?"

Claudine nodded, tapping her fingernails on the chrome arm of the chair. "I said it then, and I'll say it again —when this thing is over, I won't be surprised if it turns out she's having a baby."

When Father Earl O'Neill, the Catholic chaplain at Parkhurst Hospital, got a call at 4:28 that a hemorrhaging nun from Corpus Christi Convent had been brought into the emergency room, he assumed it was one of the old, retired sisters with a GI problem. In the ER hall he ran into the mustached young resident on the case, who agreed it might be a good idea if Father O'Neill talked to Sister Angela: "Might help calm her down some."

O'Neill's first shock inside the examining room was that the nun was so *young*. And so pale, so distraught. A sweet, frightened girl with reddish-gold curls and transfusions going into each arm. O'Neill was already wondering whether he should be intruding here when she saw him, spotted the Roman collar, and her green eyes suddenly went live with panic.

"Sister Angela? I'm Father O'Neill, the hospital chaplain," he said with a hearty assurance he didn't feel.

The question came out in a gasp: "Am I dying?"

"No, no, merciful heaven, certainly not. The doctors tell me you're responding very nicely. No, I just make it a point to drop in on our new patients. Especially when one of them is a sister. Purely routine, I assure you."

Her eyes rolling like she was a trapped animal. "If I'm not dying, why are you here?"

Damned idiotic doctors anyway, sending him in here like this. O'Neill began backing toward the door, covering his confusion with professional balm. "Please, no, Sister, I promise you—you're doing very well. No cause at all for alarm. I'll drop by tomorrow, I think that would be better. Now don't you worry about a thing, Sister. You're coming along just fine."

Out in the hall O'Neill looked around for that young doctor to chew him out. Whatever was wrong with Sister Angela Flynn, his visit sure hadn't helped—the sight of him seemed to scare the daylights out of that poor girl.

Well, if she didn't need him, somebody else probably did. After twenty-eight years on the job O'Neill knew that he would probably find an anxious little bunch of nuns waiting for news of Sister Angela in the waiting room.

He spotted them as soon as he walked in—three of them, dressed in civvies, huddled like wet birds on those damned uncomfortable yellow seats along the far wall. Two of them pretty young things, one middle-aged, sitting there like the chairman of the board. Even without their gold crosses, O'Neill would've known them anywhere as nuns. Something about the careful tightness of their bodies, the blankness of the expressions, always tipped him off.

They exchanged introductions. St. Rose of Lima, not Corpus Christi—ah well, that explained *that.* O'Neill delivered ritual reassurances and offered them the loan of his private office as a waiting room.

"Oh, thank you, Father. If that wouldn't put you out," said the young black-haired one, Sister Julia, who seemed to be the Mother Superior. Damnedest thing with the nuns these days—nothing turned out the way you expected.

"Not at all, not at all, Sisters. In fact you'll have it all to yourself. I'm due for dinner shortly at Blessed Sacrament, and Father Leonard always likes it served right on time."

Such a busy morning. Never a moment free.

Lord forgive her for that thin, miserable lie, Sister Julia thought as she walked along the blue line on the hospital floor that led back to the examining room. She hadn't *meant* to lie. It just came out that way.

What she should have said was, *I forgot. I just forgot.* But then Claudine would have asked how Julia could possibly forget such an important thing, and that was the part Julia felt so helpless to explain.

The truth was Julia was in the middle of what she called one of her "brown times." Julia did a lot of forgetting then, and a lot of doubting. The strength of her commitment to the religious life just seemed paper-thin, dissolvable. Even dissolving.

She'd come through those "brown times" before, so they didn't frighten her now as much as they used to. What was scary about this one was how long it seemed to be lasting. For five, six weeks now she'd been going through the ritual motions of Masses and prayers, community life, even schoolwork, without any feeling of *validity.* The old routine seemed simply—routine. Under the thin skin of her surface serenity, she felt restless, constantly irritated. Sometimes she caught herself daydreaming, spinning strange fantasies about things that had no place in a religious life—things like family. And children. Wondering how that would have been, to have children of her own instead of that borrowed stream of second graders.

Sometimes she wished there was someone she could talk to. Someone to . . . listen. But when you tried to talk about something like that, people—even other nuns— seemed to think what you meant was leaving the convent, getting married. They read something *nasty* into what were really just wandering thoughts. Not even thoughts, just— questions. Scary questions.

It wasn't like they thought. Not at all. It wasn't *sex* Julia was missing. But they never understood that.

The blue line zigged around a corner of the hall. Julia followed it very precisely, walking close to the line. She couldn't talk to anyone at St. Rose anyway; she was the Superior, after all. She had a position, a leadership, to maintain. She had to point the way, by her example, for the rest of them.

So she'd learned to tough out these "brown times" alone. It helped to remember how the other ones had ended —with a renewed, even stronger, sense of dedication. A satisfaction, even a *gratefulness,* for her commitment.

Probably in another week or so she would have been through this one. The worst would've been over then, at least. If only this awful thing hadn't happened to Angela right *now.*

But it *had* happened, it had. And there was no way Julia could see to explain to Claude or any of the others why she'd failed Angela so badly. Not now: it was too late.

The blue line stopped near the room where they had taken Angela. Julia hesitated at the door, but the nurse standing beside the bed nodded her inside.

Julia forced her face into a reassuring smile as she approached the bed. But her relief when she saw Angela was genuine. Angela still looked pale and distressed; bags of blood were hanging above the bed, running into tubes taped to both her arms, and under the sheet her left leg was propped up on some kind of pillow. But she looked *alive* now, at least.

"Oh, Angela!" Julia patted the limp hand lying on the white cotton blanket. "You're looking so much *better.*"

Another strange face. Angela blinked up at it.

No. Not strange. As she murmured Julia's name Angela grasped her hand, gripped it. In this nightmare that was happening to her, Julia was something real. "You're here."

"Of course I'm here, dear. I'm waiting right outside."

Julia, from that place where she was safe.

No. Not safe. Relief and confusion swirled slowly in her dark head. Something she must tell Julia. Something important.

Julia talking about the doctors, what the doctors had said to her. Angela pushed away that talk with, "They cleaned me up."

"I knew they would. They're taking very good care of you. I just want *you* to take good care of yourself and get better very soon."

Murmur: "I'm so sorry for all the trouble I made."

"Don't be silly, it's no trouble at all. *I'm* sorry I didn't come to check on you at noon."

The room. Something about the room. "My room must be a mess. Just close the door because I'll be home tomorrow and I'll clean it up."

"All right. Whatever you want." Julia smiling with her mouth, not her face. "I tried to call your mother. I forgot she was visiting your brother in Arizona."

Another swirl in the confusion. Angela's eyelids fluttered. "My mother won't have to come, will she? Because I'm okay. I'll be home tomorrow."

"Okay, if you don't want her. You don't think I should call your brothers?"

So hard to think. "Maybe tomorrow. So they won't worry. Let's wait and call them tomorrow when I'm home."

"All right. And you can tell me what to say to them."

Breathing still hard. Thinking so muddled, so confused. She said again, "I never meant to make all this trouble. I'm so sorry." Julia was protesting, patting her shoulder, when the next pain-wave came at her.

Angela closed herself into the pain. Distantly, she heard the nurse say, "Sister, I think you'd better go."

At 5:10 Dr. Talbott told Dr. Kovaleski that they were going to have to check on Sister Angela's kidney function, to eliminate the possibility of renal shutdown.

Kovaleski made a low whistle. "Foley catheter?" Talbott nodded. "She's not gonna like it."

Talbott snapped, "We're doing it anyway."

The doctors again. Tall one talking about her kidneys —long, complicated sentences she couldn't understand. "So we must insert a catheter into your bladder. This is a completely painless procedure, but it is very important, very necessary to your treatment."

She turned her face to the green-tiled wall. Someone pulling up the sheet. Someone trying to pull her legs apart.

A perception of imminent, urgent danger exploded in her head, exploded into a ferocious strength. Words rolled past her: "Please relax, Sister. . . . Absolutely painless, I promise you. . . ." In some dim way she understood that if this was lost, everything was lost.

Strong hands. Hard to fight. Other hands, touching her near that private place. "Almost . . . a little more. . . ."

Angela fought.

The grim struggle lasted five, six, seven minutes. Hopkins and another nurse applied a steady pulling pressure on the left leg; Kovaleski pulled on the right. But the patient's silent, powerful resistance belied all the figures on her chart.

Talbott felt whipsawed between loathing and anger— loathing for what he was having to do, anger at the nun for making this simple procedure such a barbaric invasion. When the legs finally began to give, the patient reached down to protect herself. Kovaleski pulled her hand away, and held the right leg firm as she tried to heave her body out of their grip.

When the legs finally came apart enough to give access to the urethral opening, Kovaleski muttered, "Wow." Talbott was concentrating on inserting the tube, but he also saw what Kovaleski saw.

Something—someone—had ripped this woman open from the vagina to the rectum.

Three

Talbott held a vial of deep amber urine, the net result of the grim struggle, up to the fluorescent light of the examining room ceiling. Then he passed the glass container to Nurse Hopkins and leaned over the patient.

Calmly: "Good news, Sister Angela." Reluctantly, she turned her face away from the tiled wall, looked up at him. "Your urine specimen looks clear. There's no blood in it. What we'd like to do now, as soon as your condition is more stabilized, is take you up to the operating room so we can get a better assessment of those kidneys."

She nodded, did not protest.

Talbott walked out feeling drained, defeated. Even nauseated. And now he had Kovaleski to contend with.

He crossed to the examining room across the hall and found Kovaleski pacing, palming his fist, clearly bursting to talk. As Talbott closed the door Kovaleski said, "Okay, that's it, then. She's already delivered." He prodded Talbott's silence with, "Did you see that perineal tear?"

"I saw it." Talbott pushed his hands into the pockets of his starched white coat, clinging determinedly to the roster of medical possibilities. "That could be the result of trauma. A violent rape could do that."

Kovaleski's assessment of that likelihood showed in his hiked eyebrows. "Well, assuming a delivery, I can tell you pretty exactly when it took place. Because when I did that year of GYN residency in South Africa it happens we saw a lot of results of home deliveries in the Zulu and Khosa women. In fact they only came into the hospital if they had complications—previa or abruptio, or a bad perineal tear like this one. A botched-up home delivery like this—that's one thing I never expected to see again back here in St. Paul, boy, I can tell you. Especially not on a— Anyway, I saw so many of them over there, probably a couple hundred, that I learned to fix the time of birth pretty accurately from the distinct time-related changes in the tear."

Talbott was feeling a quick, invigorating jolt of clinical curiosity. "Very interesting. What are they?"

"Up to six hours the edges are pinkish, healthy-looking. From six to eight hours they get a distinct grayish coloration. The change is so pronounced, so reliable, it's really something to go on. I'd look at the color of the tear, and ask when the baby was born. The Zulus all had watches—the men do, anyway, because they need them to get to their jobs on time. They mostly work about one, two hours away from—"

Talbott cut him off. *"Larry!"*

"The edges of Sister Angela's tear were distinctly pink." Kovaleski looked at the wall clock, which read 5:25. "I'd say with reasonable medical certainty that she delivered a child around noon."

This startling nugget of fact put an abrupt end to Talbott's dogged, narrowing search for alternative diagnoses. His eyes followed Kovaleski's to the clock. "Okay. The lab results on the hormone test should be back in about ten minutes. If it checks out positive for pregnancy I'd like you to come with me to talk to the other nuns."

When Sister Roxanne called down the hall from the second-floor convent bathroom, suggesting they take a break in the cleaning, Mary Luke tried not to show her relief. She even made several more passes with the mop until Priscilla said from the bedroom door, "Come on, Luke. Come while the coffee's still hot."

"Okay." Mary Luke squatted and scraped one final clot from the floor with her fingernails. When the edges were pried loose she could pinch the gelatinous mass between her fingers and drop it almost whole into the mop bucket.

The five nuns involved in the cleanup were sitting, awkwardly scattered, on the hall rug. Mary Luke stepped around the smaller pieces of furniture moved out from Angela's room and slid down against the wall, her knees drawn to her chest. Priscilla handed her a mug of coffee, which Mary Luke wasn't sure she could drink. She said, "Thanks, Pris," and set it on the rug beside her.

Margory was still whining, sniveling. "Oh, Luke, you're so strong. I wish I could help you in the bedroom, I really do, but I just—" She shivered.

Like a fat rabbit, Luke thought. *A fat, stupid rabbit.* "It's not so bad," she said shortly. "I think the smell's the worst part. How's the bathroom coming?"

"It's almost done," said Roxanne. "But it was very— What I can't figure out is if Angela was that sick, why didn't she call somebody for help?"

Mary Luke shrugged, and made herself sip from the mug. "Who knows? She's a strange one, Angela is." An uncharitable thought, put into words, but she let it stand.

"She probably couldn't make it to a phone," said Priscilla. "I mean, *look* how she was bleeding."

They talked briefly about what could possibly be wrong with Angela. Someone mentioned something about a tumor, but that hardly seemed to explain the bloodbath they had spent the past several hours trying to obliterate from the convent.

Margory was staring at the footprints she had been trying to scrub from the hall rug with cold water before they set. "I saw them when I came home at noon," she whispered, for what Mary Luke reckoned was the seventh time. "I walked right past them and I didn't realize. If I'd just *seen* what they were I could have gotten help for her right then. I could have—"

"Forget it, Margory," Mary Luke said sharply. "What's done is done." The coffee was going down better than she'd expected. "I'm supposed to go out at seven. It's my mother's birthday, and I said I'd pick her up for the party. But I could call her now, tell her something's come up."

"No, no, Luke, you go," Roxanne insisted. "Virginia will be back soon and she can finish up. You mustn't disappoint your mother."

"Especially on her birthday," Margory added.

"Okay. If it's all right with you guys I'll go. I can still work for twenty minutes before I have to change." Mary Luke stood up and replaced her mug on the tin tray. Back in Angela's bedroom she picked up the mop bucket and carried it down to the bathroom to replenish the hot water· and suds. As she went down the hall Margory was back on her knees at the scrub brush, still sniveling, wiping her nose on the back of her hand.

After a brief, quiet conference with Roxanne and Priscilla in the bathroom, Mary Luke stopped on her way back to the bedroom. "Margory, there's something you could do for us, if you don't mind."

Margory looked up from the carpet, blinking, pushing the hair away from her eyes. "Of course, Luke, anything. I really want to help. Except I can't go into that room. I wish I could, but I just—"

"Mrs. Kelly is downstairs to serve dinner, and we'd just as soon she wasn't in the house tonight, all things considered. Do you think you could drive her home?"

Mary Luke caught the relief that flashed in Margory's eyes before she dropped them back to the rug. "Of course, Luke. If you think that would really help."

"Thank you, Margory," Mary Luke said dryly. "That would be a *great* help."

When Julia got back to the chaplain's office she told Claudine and Dorothy that Angela was "much better. Oh, much." She didn't mention that strangeness, that wounded animal wildness in Angela's face. It wasn't anything they needed to know, or anything Julia wanted to think about.

Instead they talked, distractedly, disjointedly, about things like Dorothy's math tutoring and the M.A. courses in

Special Ed that Julia's married sister was taking. Then, finally, Dr. Talbott was back, with another doctor.

He countered their anxious questions with, "She's responding very nicely. When we get some more blood in her we'll be taking her up to surgery." He paused, added carefully: "As I already said, she seems to have some kind of bleeding mass in her abdomen. We're still trying to ascertain the cause."

Softly, Claudine broke the long silence. "We were wondering if it could be a pregnancy."

As Julia heard that astonishing word her hands flew up, an involuntary gesture. She turned toward the doctor, waiting for him to rebuke Claudine. But instead he said firmly, gratefully, "You said it, Sister. That possibility is very high on our list to be eliminated."

As Julia stared, open-mouthed, Talbott exchanged a glance with the other doctor. "In fact, I must tell you, Sisters, that the lab tests have already confirmed that as a probability. Right now I would say we are ninety-nine percent positive that the medical situation we are dealing with here is pregnancy-related. The main question we have is how far advanced the pregnancy might be."

Julia turned away from the others, pressing her hands against her mouth. After a brief silence Dorothy murmured, "She's had that swelling for quite a while. I think I noticed it first around Christmastime."

Talbott said gently, "All right. Thank you, Sister, that's helpful." He waited. "There is a possibility that the child may already have been delivered. Do you know if the other nuns may have found—anything at the convent when they were cleaning up?"

Julia bent her head over her hands. Claudine said, "We don't know."

"It would help a good deal if you could find out. We'll have more answers when we get her up to surgery. But if you could call the convent— Sister Angela's medical condition is still causing us some concern. Any information you could get for us would help us in determining the proper course of treatment."

Claudine nodded curtly. "All right, Doctor, we'll find out." The short, brutal conversation apparently terminated, she turned toward Julia.

But at the office door Talbott looked back and said hesitantly, "There's one more thing, Sisters, if you don't mind." The three nuns looked numbly toward him. "If you have no objection, I'd like to have the psychiatrist on call talk to Sister Angela when she gets out of surgery."

Claudine voiced the question: "Psychiatrist?"

"Sister Angela is denying any knowledge of any pregnancy. I think this—amnesia is genuine. It's clear to me that she is not lying, that this is truly her perception of these events. But I'm concerned about her psychological status. I think once her medical condition is stabilized, it would be advisable to have her speak with a psychiatrist."

Claudine said, "Of course, Dr. Talbott. Whatever you think best."

When the doctors left, Claudine put her arm around Julia. "Come on, Julia. It's all right, it's all right."

Julia said tremulously, "But it's *not* all right. Claude, I swear I never—I never even thought . . .''

Gently, Claudine prodded her into a gray cushioned chair, her hand moving comfortingly over Julia's back. "I know. Come on, sit down. I could tell you hadn't thought about that, Julie. But I have, for quite a while. I wasn't sure, of course, but I'm not so surprised."

Julia looked at Dorothy. A faint edge of accusation: "Dot, did you . . ."

Dorothy nodded, staring at her knitted fingers. "Well, just lately, I thought maybe. But not really. I thought it must be—something like a tumor."

Claudine said, "Julie, do you want me to make the call?"

The call.

Julia pulled the shredded robe of her authority around her shoulders as she said, "No, no. It's my responsibility. I'll do it."

Sister Roxanne answered the community-room telephone. "Oh, thank goodness, Julie, we've all been waiting for you to call. How's Angela?"

"Much better. She's going to be all right."

"Well, thank the Good Lord for that."

Julia twisted the telephone cord around her finger. She knew from the level tone of Roxanne's voice that these were useless questions, but she had to ask them anyway. "Rox, I was wondering—did you clean up?"

"Oh, yes. I know you said not to but then the policeman said—"

"No, no, it's all right."

"Well, we got most of it up. We'll have to go over some of it again tomorrow but the worst of it's up."

How to put the question? Julia asked, "Did you find anything?"

"What d'you mean?"

"Oh, I don't know. Just—anything."

Puzzled: "Just towels and rugs, with clots of blood. And some tissues on the floor."

"Okay. Thanks, Rox. Just leave the rest alone, and we'll be home as soon as we can."

It can't be true, Julia was telling herself as she walked the blue line again. *They must be mistaken.*

The doctors seemed so sure. And Julia knew so little about pregnancy and childbirth. But none of what she knew squared with the silent horror-scene in Angela's room. Pain, yes, Julia knew there was pain. Even screaming, crying out. But not that bleeding, not that deathly silence.

No. No. They must, somehow, be wrong. *They must be wrong.*

The trembling was back in her as she neared the room where they had Angela. Julia didn't want to frighten Angela, didn't want to make this terrible thing any harder for her to bear. And she was so afraid Angela would see the accusation of what those doctors had said written on her face.

Oh, not to go back into that room. Julia would give anything not to have to go back into that room. *Jesus Mary and Joseph, make me strong.*

As she came up to the door someone was rolling a huge green machine out of the room. So much strangeness in this strange place. Julia mouthed a question toward the gray-haired nurse standing beside Angela's bed. The nurse said, "It's all right, Sister. We just needed an X ray."

"Oh." Julia walked up to the bed, her hands pushed deep into the pockets of her cardigan. She stood a short distance from the bed and said, "Goodness, Angela, you're looking better every time I see you." That wasn't true, but Julia said it anyway, in a nervous singsong voice.

"Oh, Julie. Hi." Angela's face bent into something like a smile. She seemed glad to see Julia. "Yes. I know. I'll be all better tomorrow." Her voice so weak, gaspy. "They're taking me up to surgery. They think it may be something with my kidneys, that's why I was bleeding so."

"Oh, that's good. That's very good." Julia made herself take one step closer to the bed. It was easier if she didn't look at Angela's face. She looked at the plastic tube taped to Angela's left arm, at the blood running down through the tube, as she said, "When was the last time you had your period?"

Sweet Jesus, she hadn't meant to ask that, hadn't meant to ask anything like that. But Angela didn't seem upset by the question. "Two months ago," she was saying. "I missed a month and maybe that's why I was clotting like that."

Julia nodded energetically. "Well, they're very good doctors. I'm sure they're going to fix up whatever it is just fine."

Another nurse came around the curtain, holding out a clipboard with the surgical consent form for Angela to sign. The gray-haired nurse lifted Angela up, but still she had trouble holding the pen. So Julia moved in closer and propped Angela from the other side. She felt damp, heavy. Floppish.

The signature came out a wild, indecipherable scrawl, but apparently that would do. They laid her back down, and Julia took a small step back from the table. "I just hope you aren't feeling worried, Angela," she said in that ridiculous singsong voice, "because Dr. Talbott is really a very good doctor and he said as soon as they get more blood into you everything will be all right."

Angela murmured, "They took the X ray to see if I had any air inside. So maybe it could be the air, too, but Dr. Talbott thinks it's my kidneys."

Then the pain-wave hit her. Julia backed away from the table, watching, terrified, as Angela's body closed like a clenched fist. The nurse said loudly, *"Breathe,* Sister! Take a deep breath." But Angela was thrashing, fluttering, not even gasping now. The nurse chided, "Don't hold your breath. That only makes it harder, Sister."

As Julia watched Angela fighting off this silent attack she realized—Sweet God, how could she possibly have thought all this had nothing to do with childbirth. So blind, *so blind* not to see, not to understand.

Julia had no idea how long the spasm lasted. But she could tell it was over when Angela went loose again, went limp on the table. Angela whimpered softly, as much from embarrassment as from the pain. She turned her face toward Julia, and Julia saw the shame and confusion clouded in with the frightened wildness in her eyes.

And something else—an appeal. A mute appeal for help.

Angela murmured, "Oh, Julia."

Suddenly Julia felt very strong, very sure. She moved

back to the table and gripped Angela's right hand. "It's all right, Angela dear, it's all right. I'm here and you're going to be fine." She smoothed back Angela's damp, filthy hair. "I'm right here and I'm going to stay with you and keep you safe. You don't have to be afraid, Angela."

Angela so moist, so weak. But the talking helped a little. Julia could read that on her face. She she kept talking, soothing—it didn't matter what she said; Julia could see that now —and she kept touching Angela, pressing her hand, patting her shoulder, reassuring her with her touch.

When the nurse said that she had to go do something, Julia said, "That's fine, you go. I'll stay here with her." She squeezed Angela's hand and smiled—a wide, real smile. "We'll be okay, dear, won't we?"

Angela whispered, "Yes. Sure." So the nurse left and Julia kept talking, kept soothing.

When the next pain came—Julia felt it in Angela's sudden-tensed hand, in her crumpled, twisting face—she froze. For one terrified moment the impulse to run was very strong.

But the moment passed almost immediately, and Julia echoed loudly what she'd heard the nurse say before: *"Breathe,* Angela! Breathe deep, it will help." And she let Angela's clawing fingers cut into her hand, took as much of the pain from her as she could, chanting, "Breathe, breathe. That's right, *deep.* Don't fight it, *breathe."*

When the wave was finished, Angela was panting like a frightened child. That Julia understood. That Julia could deal with. She said calmly, "There now, you're all right. You're going to be fine. That wasn't so bad, was it?" Angela made a slight shaking motion with her head. Julia wiped her damp forehead with a towel lying near the pillow. "Don't worry, dear. You've got very good doctors. They're the best. I know they're going to help you and I'll help you too."

Julia realized now that what she was doing here was

filling the space between the pains. *Talk, talk.* "You know, I think before you come home we'll get you a new plant. For the hanger in your room."

Angela nodded exhaustedly. "It died. The one I had."

"I know, when you went away on vacation. So we're going to get you a new one, a present from the house, to let you know how glad we are to have you home again."

Stronger now: "I kept meaning to throw it out. I kept watering it."

"I always liked the way it looked, so green in the window. So we'll get you another, and you should tell me what kind of plant you'd like, and then all of us can have the pleasure of seeing it through the door when we come by."

She felt very strong and ready for the next wave. The pain didn't seem so bad, now that she knew what to do, knew how to talk Angela through it, like a chanted prayer, like a lover's promise: "Don't be afraid. *Breathe.* I'm here, I'm here."

When Angela came out of that wave she murmured, "Oh, Julie, I'm glad you're here."

Julia said, "Well, I'm glad too, dear." And realized that she meant it. In some way she could never have anticipated, she felt closer to Angela right now than she ever had with any person before. Anyone. In this strange, cold bright-lit room anything was right, everything was right. And Julia was not afraid.

But the next pain came very quickly after the other, and this one was something different—violent. Angela gasped, "Oh! It hurts so bad."

Julia kept talking, chanting her ritual commands to breathe, but suddenly Angela wrenched out of her hands, jackknifed her body into a strange, broken shape on the bed, turned away from Julia. Julia could not see her face, but she could hear those low growling animal sounds coming from her.

"Oh God, it's starting again!"

The bleeding. Angela must mean the bleeding. Julia said, "It's all right, I'll get help. I'll get help, Angela."

Fighting the pain like she had fought the hands.

Now this this so bad bad bad ripping up into her tearing into her tearing out this thing squeezed between her clenched legs.

She yanked herself away from the thing. But she could feel it still. Against her skin. Touching her skin.

Some thing.

From the examining room door Julia saw the gray-haired nurse behind the desk down the hall. She signaled frantically, and the nurse came running. As she came in the door Julia said, "I think she's bleeding again."

The nurse ran up to the table, Julia right behind. Angela was still curled in that bent shape, face angled to the wall, knees pulled against her chest. The nurse lifted the sheet, looked under it. Muttered: "She's passing more than blood. I'll get the doctor."

Sudden calm: only the two of them again. But Angela so far away, not in reach. Julia patted her shoulder, felt the tightness of it. "Don't worry, please, Angela dear. They'll help you. The doctors are very good. They'll fix whatever it is."

Angela so silent except for the panting, so tight. She didn't seem to know Julia was there. Didn't seem to need her now.

"They'll know just what to do to help you. You're going to be all right, you're going to be fine. And I'll stay with you, I'll be here all the time."

No words from Angela. Only those strange, panting, terrified sounds. But still Julia was not afraid. Angela so broken, so alone. Julia wanted only to hold her, calm her, give her comfort.

Then the nurse back with the doctor, moving very

quickly, pulling things out of cabinets, closing around the table. The nurse said, "Sister, you better leave."

So Julia left.

Nurse Hopkins pushed the large reddish-purple mass into a stainless steel basin. Dr. Kovaleski took the basin from her hands, examined the contents. Then he looked at the table where the patient was lying on her side, silent, tensed, curled like a question mark.

Well, somebody had to do it. Kovaleski approached the table and said firmly, "Sister Angela."

Forced by the tone of his voice, she turned her head. "Sister Angela, you've just passed a placenta, an afterbirth." He pushed the basin up toward her face. "And that is always preceded by one event. Can you tell me anything about that?"

Forced, Angela glanced at the huge, ugly thing in the silver bowl. Like some monster fished up from the sea. Mother of God, what were they doing to her?

She flipped her face back to the green-tiled wall. In a flat, very faraway voice: "No. I don't know anything."

Dr. Talbott was on the telephone, confirming arrangements with the anesthesiologist, when Nurse Hopkins tapped him on the shoulder. "Bingo," she muttered.

Talbott glanced at the stainless-steel basin covered with a small towel. He said into the telephone, "Okay, so you're all set?"

He hung up the receiver and took the basin from Hopkins as she lifted off the towel. An apparently normal term placenta, with a four-inch stump of sharply excised umbilical cord attached. Hopkins said, "She just passed it spontaneously."

Wordlessly, Talbott lifted the membrane, turned it over. No gross abnormalities or torn vessels evident.

So. That was it, then. All other possibilities denied.

Feeling a grief he hoped he did not reveal, Talbott said, "Okay, Hopkins. You stick with the patient, get her as calm as you can. I'll go talk to the other nuns."

They read it on Dr. Talbott's face as he came through the door of the chaplain's office. But still it had to be said.

He pulled up one of the gray chairs, the first time he had sat in the nuns' presence. Pushed away Claudine's choked question with, "No, no, she's all right."

He stared at the rust-colored carpet, looked for a way to make this easier. Then said simply, "Sisters, I'm sorry to have to tell you this, but Sister Angela has just passed a placenta. That means the child must have been delivered sometime this afternoon, back at the convent."

Claudine and Dorothy reacted with slight movements of their bodies. But Julia sat very straight, upright, hands tightly folded on her lap, looking at the doctor. Talbott said, "Her bleeding was caused by an incomplete placental separation—by the fact that she failed to deliver the placenta herself." Silence. "It would be very helpful to us if we had the baby. Is there someone who could search for it?"

Julia and Claudine looked at each other. Julia murmured, "We can't ask them to do that. I think we should go back home and look."

Claudine said, "Yes, of course."

"Thank you, Sister," Talbott said. "That would be a big help." Silence. Then, in a quick burst of words: "There has to be a baby somewhere. Look in the bathroom, look in the bedroom. Look on the window ledges. There has to be a baby somewhere. If it's alive when you find it, call an ambulance. Otherwise bring it back here. I'll come pick it up when I've finished in surgery."

Talbott stood, awkwardly. At the door, he said, "I'm very sorry, Sisters."

When he closed the door behind him Julia leaped, propelled, from the chair. "All right. All right." Pacing, pacing.

41

So much to think of. "We'll go home. We'll go right home. But first—I think I should call Sister Philomena. I think she's got to know."

Claudine touched Julia's arm. "I'll do that. You two go back home." She pulled the car keys from her purse and put them in Julia's hand.

Julia shook her head. "No, Claude, I should call her. It's my responsibility. All of this."

"No, Julie, let me do it. It's all right. Really, it is."

Julia looked sharply into Claudine's face. She did not want Claudine to think that she was shirking even now, shirking this painful call. But Claudine smiled sadly, shook her head. So Julia let it go. "Okay. Thanks. Tell her—"

"I know what to say." Feeling a warm burst of forgiveness for Julia, Claudine hugged her briefly, fiercely. "I'll do that much. You two go do the hard part."

Four

Sister Philomena Levesque, the Superior General of the Congregation of the Sisters of St. Benedict, was working at the massive walnut desk in her paneled Motherhouse office when the call came from Sister Claudine. The nun on the switchboard said, "I told her you were working and didn't wish to be disturbed, Sister Philomena, but she says it's important."

"That's quite all right, Marianne. Put her through."

Claudine related her news in five or six terse, difficult sentences. Philomena asked only where Angela was now, and how many other people knew about this.

"Just us, and the doctors, I think." She hesitated.

"There was a policeman who came to the convent earlier with the ambulance, but that was earlier this afternoon."

"All right. You did quite right to call me, Claudine. Thank you. I'll meet you at the hospital as soon as I can get there."

Quietly, calmly, Philomena hung up the telephone. She fingered the heavy gold cross around her neck, betraying no outward sign of the thoughts thundering through her head.

She looked at the pile of unanswered correspondence that had seemed so important a few minutes earlier and pushed it to the far side of the large polished desk.

How odd, that it should be Angela Flynn. So many of the hundreds of nuns in the order Philomena barely knew, even by name. This monstrous thing might have been easier to comprehend if it had happened to one of the sisters Philomena did not know. But tiny, gentle Angela Flynn, always the "good nun"—

Incredible.

Philomena remembered the day she first met Angela—she was Gayle Flynn then, a timid waif of a girl transferring into the fifth grade of Blessed Sacrament parochial school, where Philomena was the Head Girl of the eighth grade. Philomena had discovered her that February morning, creeping down the school hall, looking for the principal's office, afraid to ask directions. She still recalled the surge of protective warmth she had felt then for Angela—so much smaller than the other girls, so much more vulnerable. Such a tiny sad girl, trying so hard, always.

Then later Angela had trailed her through the Benedictine Academy and the St. Benedict novitiate, so of course their paths had crossed occasionally, mainly on ceremonial occasions. Now—this.

Philomena allowed herself a brief moment of compassion for Angela, a quick thought for the pain she must be suffering. But her concern then moved very quickly to the

723 other nuns she was shepherding through these difficult transitional times.

They must do right by Angela, of course. They *would* do right by Angela. They would do what they could to help her for as long as she was still a member of the congregation.

But the 723 others must also be protected.

Philomena reached for the Rolodex on her desk and flipped it to the number of Dermott Hallihan, the lawyer who handled most of the order's business affairs.

Her call intruded on a chess game between Hallihan and his son. Philomena apologized for the interruption, and relayed in brief, unemotional sentences the import of Claudine's message.

"I see." Hallihan paused. "And where is the child?"

"The doctors sent two of our nuns back to the convent to find it."

"I see," he repeated. "And that's all the information you have?"

"For the moment."

Hallihan flipped briefly over the bizarre range of possibilities, and came to an instant judgment. "Sister, I may be jumping the gun on this, but it's better to be safe than sorry. I think you might consider calling in Benjamin Haverty. He's one of the best lawyers in this town, in my book."

A brief pause. "You think that's necessary, Dermott? Calling in someone from outside?"

"Sister Philomena, I won't pull any punches with you here. Haverty's specialty is criminal law, and in *that* department he's the best you could get anywhere. Now, on what you've got so far I certainly wouldn't say this was *necessary*. But just to be on the safe side, I think Ben Haverty might prove a great help in dealing with a situation as delicate as you've got here."

Philomena was finally beginning to digest this wholly unimagined situation. She remembered what Claudine had said about the policeman, and realized for the first time that this unfortunate event might not be kept entirely private. "Very good, Dermott. I appreciate the suggestion. If you could get in touch with this Mr. Haverty, you can reach me for the next while at the chaplain's office of Parkhurst Hospital. And Dermott—"

"Yes, Sister."

"You'll forgive me for saying this, but I'm sure we can rely on your complete confidentiality in this matter."

"But of course, Sister Philomena, say nothing more. I'll be in touch with you shortly."

She'd seen this so many times on television. Patient rolling down the hospital hall.

Strange. How it felt so different. When it was really happening.

Helpless. So helpless. Some strange man pushing her like a skinned dead beef on TV. Lights flashing overhead. Walls in and out of her vision—some curved, some flat, some sharp.

Kidneys. Fix the kidneys. But where were they taking her, what were they going to do?

That paper they brought her to sign. She remembered only one word from it: *hysterectomy.*

They must be taking her to cut her open, take out her insides. Her sick insides.

Different lights, different walls now in the elevator. Going up. The dark little man who was pushing her bed standing beside it now, not looking at her, not speaking. She didn't want to talk anyway, not to this strange man. But wished someone was with her. Like Julia. Or Dr. Talbott.

Another hall. Big doors swung open. The man lifted her to another table. Another nurse, strange nurse in a wrinkled green robe. "Hello there, Sister. How are you feeling?"

"Okay." She twisted her head, looking around this big room with the huge lights suspended over her. "Where's Dr. Talbott?"

"He'll be right with you. In just a minute."

Tiles to the ceiling. Steel and glass cabinets with bottles and instruments, shiny big silver instruments.

Hysterectomy.

Now Dr. Talbott bending over her, smiling. A warm smile. Green robe. White mask around his neck. "Sister Angela, you're looking much better." She nodded, tried to give back the smile. "Your vital signs are coming up very nicely. I think we'll have you back on your feet in no time at all."

Whisper: "I hope so." She wanted to believe him. But so hard, in this terrifying place.

"Now I'd like you to understand that this procedure isn't going to hurt you at all, Sister." Voice calm, reassuring: "We'll just put you to sleep, and when you wake up I'll be there. You just leave the rest of it to us."

Yes. *Yes, to you.*

Another doctor at her other side. "Sister Angela, we're just going to give you a little something to put you under." Touching, poking at the tube in her left arm. "I'd like you to count backwards from one hundred for me."

"One hundred. Ninety-nine. Ninety-eight. Ninety . . ."

Whoosh. Something hit. Hit hard. Swirling. Sucked down. To the dark place. Like so many times before.

She fought the fall. "Ninety-nine. Nine . . ."

Don't go. Danger. "Ninety. Ni . . ."

No escape. No rescue. *Don't go.* No way back. No . . .

"Ni-seven. N . . ."

She sank.

When they let themselves in the kitchen door of the convent at 7:13 they could see four of the nuns—Margory, Irma, Virginia and Roxanne—through the half-open door of the community dining room, sitting over a cold supper. Julia nodded toward the basement stairs, and Dorothy slipped down them to get the plastic bags from the storage closet.

Forcing a smile, Julia put her head through the dining room door and said, "Hi, everybody." She countered the barrage of greetings and questions with, "Angela's much better, thanks. Much better. She's going to be okay."

"Are you home to stay?" Margory asked. "Because we can set another plate."

"No, no, Dot and I just came home to get something. Angela's up in surgery now and I want to be back there when she gets out." Julia hesitated. "Is anybody else in the house?" Shakes of the heads. "All right. Dot and I have something we must do, and I'd like you all to stay here while we do it."

When Dorothy came up the basement stairs she sent a few cheerful words through the dining room door. Then Julia closed the door on the four nuns, and she and Dorothy walked upstairs.

Dorothy went to her own room and took a white flowered towel from the rack beside her sink. Julia waited for her by the pieces of furniture in the hall outside Angela's closed door.

When Dorothy came back with the towel Julia pushed the door open. That strange, sweet smell of blood was still heavy in the air. In the dim twilight coming through the window, the room looked very bare, very small.

Julia switched on the overhead light. Ah. The blood all washed away. Just the smell of it still there.

So bare, so ordinary, this room. With the small furniture out in the hall and the rugs gone and the iron bed stripped down to the mattress, the room seemed as naked as a person.

The doctors must have made a mistake, Julia was thinking. It couldn't be here, not in this small, scrubbed bare room. But she made herself say aloud, "Dot, it has to be here."

Julia opened the closet door on the left wall. Pushed through the clothes hanging on the rack. Dorothy pulled out the laundry bag sitting on the floor, loosened the drawstring and felt inside it. "It's just laundry, Julie."

"Okay." As Dorothy pushed the bag back into the closet, Julia walked to the open window. The doctor had said *look on the ledge.* But the cement ledge was only a few inches wide, and bare.

Julia turned, leaned on the sill, trying to collect her flying, rushing thoughts. Dorothy was opening the bureau drawers on the right wall, patting the neat piles of clothes. Julia looked at the small maple desk, but it had only a three-inch drawer, too small for—

She was deciding the doctors *had* made a mistake, it could not possibly be here, this thing they had been sent to find, when she noticed the three-foot-high wooden bookcase kitty-corner by the window.

Odd. It should be flat against the wall. The way Angela always had it.

She took one step to the bookcase, looked over it. She could see a basket behind it, and something in the basket.

Julia said very quietly, "Close the drawer, Dot. I've found the child."

Five

Dorothy closed the drawer and came over to the bookcase, saw the green straw basket behind it. Without speaking, they pulled the bookcase away from the wall, bumping it against the wooden rocking chair. When Dorothy slid the basket out along the floor, Julia could see a small puddle of blood underneath it.

The child was head down in the basket, curled, folded, closed. In the cruel overhead light Julia could see dried red splotches on the bluish-gray skin of the feet, the buttocks and part of the back. A boy-child, Julia could see that. The way it was lying, tipped into the half-filled wastebasket, that was almost all she could see.

The room was so still she could hear the humming of Angela's electric clock. Dorothy looked up, her eyes very wide, and whispered, "Should we . . ."

Julia shook her head violently. So Dorothy folded the white flowered towel and laid it over the top of the basket. Then she pulled a white plastic garbage bag down over the thing.

Gripping the edges of the wicker basket through the plastic, Julia lifted it enough for Dorothy to slide the second bag underneath. As Dorothy pulled up the bag and fastened it with a wire tie Julia stepped back, stepped away.

That trembling was back in her. Julia knew she must be strong, must come through this. She *would* come through this.

But it was not possible for her to pick up that basket. She said, "All right. Listen, Dot. I'll drive the car around to the front. When you see me out there, bring the basket down and come out the front door."

Dorothy nodded. Julia slipped down the stairs and let herself out very quietly through the kitchen door.

Dorothy waited by the window in Sylvia's room, with her raincoat folded in her arms. When she saw the blue Chevette come around the corner she went back to Angela's room, wrapped the raincoat around that bundle and lifted it into her arms.

She carried it against her chest, as stiffly as she could. But the thin weaving of the basket had so much give that Dorothy could feel the shape of that lumpy thing inside.

She had to set the basket down to open the locked front door. Then she carried it across the lawn. Julia had already opened the car's rear door; Dorothy put the basket down on the floor, and sat in the front seat.

While they were driving back to the hospital—it helped

that Julia had to drive, had that to concentrate on—Dorothy asked, "Julie, when did you think—that's what it was?"

"Never. I never did." After a sharp moment of silence Julia said, "If I'd thought that's what it was, of course I would have done something to help her."

They drove the rest of the way in silence.

Sister Angela was already under when Dr. Kovaleski came in from the scrub at 7:34. With the patient immobilized in stirrups and the surgical site well visualized, Kovaleski said, "See what I mean? It's grayish. Distinctly grayish. Compatible with six to eight hours post delivery."

When Talbott looked at the site framed by the green surgical drapes, what he saw was a woman ripped apart. A ragged fourth-degree perineal tear was slashed through the posterior vaginal wall, through the perineal flooring and the rectal muscle into the lining of the rectum itself.

The anesthesiologist had flipped the sheet forward from her chest, exposing her swollen breasts. Talbott said sharply, "Please keep her covered. As much as you can." Respect, this woman was so damned needful of respect. Talbott wanted her to get as much of it asleep as awake.

The anesthesiologist adjusted the drape so he could still see the movement of the upper chest. Talbott turned his attention back to the tear. His gloved hand moved into the tissues, found another tear high in the vagina—this one straight-edged, approximately an inch and a half long. When Talbott murmured this finding Kovaleski said, "Sure, that's how she got that short stump on the placenta. She stuck those scissors clear up her wazoo and nicked herself some doing it."

"That's *enough*," Talbott said angrily. "Just watch your damned mouth, Kovaleski."

In the sudden silence around the operating table, Talbott proceeded with his careful exploration: cervix well visualized, relaxed by general anesthetic. He moved his gloved hand through the jagged opening of the cervix. The uterus was approximately the size of an eighteen-week pregnancy, compatible with seven hours postpartum. Very carefully, his fingers explored the surface of the uterus, checking for tears. He could feel the knobby site of the placenta, two inches above the cervix, two o'clock position.

No perforations, no lacerations. Talbott withdrew his hand. "Larry, do you want to check this out?"

"Okay, thanks." Kovaleski used both hands to explore the uterus. Talbott barely listened to his confirmation of Talbott's findings.

So it was basically simple. So much more simple a case than Talbott had suspected when he first saw her on the examining table.

For them, only thirty minutes of careful stitching through the four layers of muscle and tissue torn open by the unattended delivery of her child.

Simpler for them. Harder, so much harder for her.

The parking garage of Parkhurst General was located a long, cruel distance from the chaplain's office.

Dorothy carried the coat-wrapped bundle as inconspicuously as she could, and Julia walked slightly in front of her, blocking the view. Still, the dozen people they passed seemed to look directly at the strange lump in Dorothy's arms.

When they got behind the door of the chaplain's office, the dam of their composure broke. Dorothy dropped the bundle on the floor in a corner by the door. Then she walked as far away from it as she could get in the narrow office and crumpled into a chair, hugging her thin arms, crying, finally, without restraint. Julia paced back and forth on the carpeted floor, wiping the palms of her hands on her sweater, saying over and over, "It was in a wastebasket, Claude. Upside down in a wastebasket. In the room all the time. All the time we were there."

Their pent-up grief was noisy, with an edge of hysteria to it, but Claudine let it come. She did not, in fact, know how to stop it.

Suddenly, Sister Philomena's large, solid presence filled the office door. In an abrupt silence the three nuns stood at attention. Philomena lumbered slowly into the room, acknowledging the three by name. She set her brown purse on the chaplain's desk and pulled out the large swivel chair behind it. Sat, heavily, arranging her folded hands in her lap.

Her assessment of which sister needed the most immediate attention was already made. She looked sharply into Julia's face, commanding calm as she said, "Julia, how is Angela's condition?"

Obediently, Julia retrieved that calm from somewhere in herself. "We don't know, Sister Philomena. She's still in the operating room. We're waiting for Dr. Talbott."

Philomena nodded. "Well, Sisters, I know this is a difficult time for us all. But we must find the strength to come through it with grace and faith."

The frozen emotions in the room thawed, and flowed toward Philomena. Philomena's eyes moved around the cheerful, modernly furnished room, and rested on the coat-covered bundle by the door. "Is that—"

Claudine said faintly, "Yes."

Philomena's eyes moved on, and they did not come back to the bundle again. "I must say, this is a very pleasant place they have given us to wait in."

From Claudine: "Yes, it is. Father O'Neill was going out, and he said we could use his office."

Philomena glanced at the brightly colored religious posters taped to the brick wall. One of them, yellow letters on a red background, read, "Some Things Have To Be Believed Before They Can Be Seen." Philomena pointed to it, nodding: "Now that's a coincidence. I believe they have the same poster up in the community room of our novitiate."

Julia felt a sudden, urgent need to speak. "Sister

Philomena, the doctor asked us— He'd like our permission for a psychiatrist to talk to Angela."

Philomena had not shown one flicker of outward physical reaction to the rockslide of news that had come at her since Claudine's call. And she did not show one now as she repeated calmly, "A psychiatrist?"

Julia twisted the gold ring on the third finger of her left hand. Rapidly: "The doctor said Angela doesn't seem to know anything about a pregnancy. I think she doesn't, either. When I saw her— I don't think she's lying. She just really doesn't seem to understand."

Philomena absorbed this new catastrophe and decided, "Of course. I think that's an excellent suggestion."

They talked quietly, harmlessly, of different things until Dr. Talbott finally came. Afterward, Julia could not remember anything that was said.

Keith Talbott changed back into his whites without taking time to shower and loped back to the chaplain's office. Inside the door he briefly acknowledged the introduction of a fourth nun and assured them that Sister Angela's surgery had been uneventful, that she came through it very well. His eyes dropped to the bundle by the door; he looked inquiringly toward Julia, who nodded.

Talbott crouched in front of the bundle, shielding the view of it from these women. When he pulled off the plastic bagging and towel he saw that the child was cold and still, obviously dead. Behind him Julia said faintly, "We didn't touch it. We found it just like that."

"Okay." Talbott pulled the plastic covering back into place, pushing the towel inside. "Thank you, Sisters. I'll—" He stood. The women were all looking, fixedly, at other spots in the room. "I'll see you later." Talbott lifted the basket and carried it out.

In the hospital morgue, at the far end of the Emergency Department by the ambulance entrance, he set the basket on the steel autopsy table. Talbott knew that the human mind tended to work peculiarly in moments like this. What was on his own mind, now, was a realization that for the first time since this ordeal began he was finally alone.

He peeled back the plastic bag, set the towel aside. The male infant was in a fetal position, head down. Some pink material seemed to be twisted around the neck.

Talbott took hold of the infant's feet and lifted him carefully out of the basket. As the head came above the wicker rim he saw that the pink material was a nightgown. And something else, something white, was protruding from the mouth.

Every detail of this intensely private moment printed like slow-motion film in Talbott's brain: the handsome unwashed newborn with the full head of brown hair, the jagged umbilical cord dangling down by his chin. The wicker basket partially filled with waste papers. And sections of umbilical cord. And a pair of worn brown shoes.

The facial expression so peculiarly peaceful. But the mouth stretched, stuffed with that cloth material.

Very carefully, Talbott lowered the infant back into the basket. In the silence of the morgue room he turned away from the table and bent over a desk on the opposite wall, gripping the back of his neck.

Since this nightmare began, Keith Talbott had been looking for a clarified moment. For an illumination.

Now, finally, he had it. But it was not what he expected, not what he needed.

Whatever Talbott had been looking for in this event, it was not the unspeakable truth inside that wicker basket. Clarity: yes, that was clarity. But right behind that clarity was turmoil, and right behind the turmoil, fear.

He rocked his knees against the desk. Ah, now he understood it all—the remoteness, the lack of affect. The brutal catheter battle. The haunting, piercing pain in those green eyes.

For one brief moment Keith Talbott allowed himself the fantasy that he could save her, protect her. Keep the secret safe. Bring her to refuge from this unbearable truth.

But the moment was very brief. Talbott straightened, stiffened. Looked around this clinical room constructed to pry the final scientific answer out of mystery.

The wall phone was mounted above the desk. Beside it, taped under a plastic sheet, was a list of phone numbers.

Talbott dialed 9 for an outside line, then dialed the number for the Ramsey County Medical Examiner's office. At 8:55 he told the man on the other end of the line, "This is Dr. Keith Talbott at Parkhurst General. I want to report a suspicious death."

Six

She was swimming underwater. Toward a warm light.

"Wake up, Sister. That's right, you're waking up. Come on, you're awake."

She opened her eyes. Another nurse bent over her. Strange nurse. Fat red face.

"Okay, it's nice to have you back with us. How are you feeling, Sister?"

She felt—slow. Empty. Sore. What had they done to her?

She whispered, "Where's Dr. Talbott?"

"He'll be in to see you in a little while. Your operation went fine. I don't think we'll have any problems with you. How are you feeling?"

She turned her head away from the voice.

Promised. He promised to be here when she woke up.

"I'll tell Dr. Talbott that you're awake. I'm sure he'll be in to see you soon. Are you feeling any discomfort?"

Wall blank. Yellow. Paint. Not tile.

She closed her eyes.

When the square blue rig from the Medical Examiner's office pulled up at the Parkhurst General emergency entrance at 9:05, a tall, tired-looking doctor in hospital whites was waiting for the blue-uniformed officials. The three men walked without speaking through the wide steel-plated doors of the hospital morgue, just inside the entrance.

Joseph Brooks, the investigating officer who took the call, did not immediately notice the green basket at the end of the autopsy table. He glanced quizzically at the doctor; the doctor nodded toward the bundle. Brooks's partner, Gino Lefante, was standing closer to it. Moving very carefully, Lefante removed the body by its feet from the straw basket and laid it on the steel table.

Fucking right this one's suspicious, Brooks thought as he eyed the pink and white cloths around the neck and in the mouth. He cleared his throat and asked, "Did the death occur in the hospital, Doctor?"

"No, no. Someone brought him in here after the mother was treated in the Emergency Department for postpartum hemorrhage."

"Do you have an identity on the mother?"

The doctor hesitated briefly, then said, "Angela Flynn." He folded his arms across his chest. "Sister Angela Flynn."

"You got an address?"

"I don't know the street. It's the St. Rose of Lima Convent in Cambridgeport." Brooks wrote the information without comment on his sheet. Talbott watched the pen move across the clipboard.

"Can we interview the mother?"

"No, not right now. She just got out of surgery."

"Do you have any identity on the father?"

"No. No."

"Okay. Where was the body found?"

"At the convent."

"By yourself?"

"By two nuns. I asked them to go back and look for the baby."

"Anybody call the police?"

The guy appeared startled by the question. "No, I don't believe so. I called your office when I saw the body. As soon as I saw the—cloth material."

"These two nuns. Are they available for an interview?"

"I guess that could be arranged. They're waiting in the chaplain's office."

"Anything else you can tell me, Doctor?"

"No. Nothing I can think of."

"Have you fixed a time of death?"

He lifted one hand helplessly. "I have no idea."

"Okay. You know what time the body was discovered?"

"I think about eight thirty. Something like that."

"Okay." Brooks made another entry on his sheet. "Anybody else have contact with the body?"

"No. I brought him down here, and called your office as soon as I examined him." The guy looked down the table at the body and said, almost to himself, "The strange thing is, I was a Catholic seminarian myself once. For six years."

Stick with this job long enough, Brooks thought, *you get to see anything.*

Confession seemed about finished. The guy looked right at him. Eyes blanked out, trying to focus.

Connecting. "All right, Mr.— Is there anything else you need to know?"

"Not right now. I'm calling the Medical Examiner now, and he may want to talk to you."

"Okay, fine. Of course."

"Then I'd like to talk to the other nuns."

Nod. "Do you mind if I talk to them first, tell them you're coming?"

Brooks was not without his own sensitivity. "Not at all, Doctor. After we've talked to Dr. Rhoades."

There was one more question Julia had been pushing out of her mind since they found the child, and it answered itself as Dr. Talbott came back through the door of the chaplain's office. He sat, exhaustedly. Said, "Sisters, I don't know any gentle way to put this."

"Just say it, Dr. Talbott," Sister Philomena said.

Haltingly, with his lean face pulling into grimaces, he told them that the baby had some material in its mouth. That he himself had called the Medical Examiner's office, as required by law in these cases. That two men from that office were now at the hospital and would like to talk to the nuns who brought the baby in.

So. It was the worst, then.

"He'd like to see you now, if that's convenient. If I might make a suggestion—have you considered calling an attorney?"

From her chair behind the desk Sister Philomena said, "Yes, that has been taken care of. I'm waiting now to confer with Mr. Benjamin Haverty."

"Ah, well. Very good."

"In fact I'm expecting him here momentarily. Could the sisters speak to this officer in another place?"

"Of course. There's a meditation room down the hall. It's probably free."

"Claudine, if you could go with them . . ." Claudine nodded.

Julia asked, "Doctor, could I see Angela again? Just for a minute?"

"I'm going to check on her now. I'll let you know, Sister."

Sister Philomena nodded a dismissal. "Thank you, Dr.

Talbott. We appreciate that courtesy. As we appreciate everything you've done tonight for Sister Angela."

Julia said, choking, "Oh, yes, Doctor. We thank you so much."

He shook his head, his face heavy and sad. "Not at all, Sister. I only wish it could have been more."

After an awkward silence: "If you don't mind—I could show you to the room. It's just down the hall."

Sister Philomena was taking a rosary from her purse as the doctor led the three of them to the meditation room.

Sister Philomena Levesque wasn't sure what she expected in a top-grade criminal lawyer, but it wasn't this tall, fat, untidy man with rumpled hair and cigar ashes spilled down the front of his extraordinarily baggy suit. In fact, She was appalled by his appearance. But Dermott Hallihan had said he was the best, and Philomena realized by now they were going to need the best.

She ran through a crisp recital of the situation for him, finishing with, "Now, I'd be grateful to hear your opinion on this, Mr. Haverty."

The way he chewed on the stump end of his cigar was really quite disgusting. After a moment's thought he took the stump out of his mouth, swept the ashes down his shirt front. "I have no opinion yet, Sister. Where is Sister Angela now?"

"Upstairs. Do you want to see her tonight?"

"I think not. Tomorrow will be soon enough. But I don't want anyone else to see her either."

"I believe Dr. Talbott has asked a psychiatrist to see her. Is that . . ." She lifted her brows questioningly.

He said dryly, "I was thinking mainly of the police."

At the mention of the word "police," Philomena felt her stolid control finally give way. "I see. You realize, Mr. Haverty, that this is a most—unfamiliar situation we find ourselves in. I'm afraid I—have few guidelines on how to proceed."

He smiled. A warm, surprising smile that rearranged his pouchy face into a look of—reassurance. "Not to worry, Sister. That, fortunately, is what you have hired me to provide."

"How are you feeling now, Sister Angela?"

Dr. Talbott standing over the bed. His face serious. Not smiling.

"Better," she whispered.

"Good. The surgery went very well. We've discovered the source of your bleeding, and taken care of the problem."

She turned her head away. "Did you take something out?"

"No, no. We only stitched up some lacerations that have been giving you discomfort. I think now we have your medical situation under control. Your vital signs are still responding nicely."

Waiting. Seeming to want her to talk. But she didn't want to talk.

He had promised; he was not there.

"Is there anything else troubling you? Anything you'd like to talk about?"

"No." She closed her eyes. "Is it all right if I sleep?"

"That's just what I'd like you to do." His finger touching her shoulder. Soft finger. "And I'll see you tomorrow. Sleep well, Sister Angela."

Lieutenant Timothy Vance, the thirty-three-year-old chief of Cambridgeport's Detective Unit, was lying on a leather couch in his barnwood-paneled basement playroom, drinking an Amaretto and listening through stereo earphones to a Willie Nelson record, watching the wall of colored lights blink in synchronization to the music. When the telephone rang at 10:54 Vance pushed off the earphones and groped for the extension phone on the end table behind his head. "Yeah. Hi, Chief. What's up?"

As he listened Vance snapped upright on the couch, slapping at his trouser knee. "Goddamit, they say it happened early this afternoon," Marwick was saying. "Why the hell didn't we get this sooner?"

"Well, I guess we did. Leighton was over there covering a routine ambulance call, and he called in for me to take a look at it. I had an appointment at Suburban Savings to check out that possible embezzlement so I sent Paige over. He said there didn't seem to be much to it."

"Well, there fucking well is now," Marwick said angrily. "I've got to meet the D.A. at the morgue. You get your ass over to that convent and see what we can salvage from this thing."

"Check. I'm on my way, Chief."

"And Tim—make sure everything's done right. There's going to be plenty of goddam fallout from this thing, and I don't want it falling on us."

"Right, right." Vance dropped the phone on its cradle, snapped off the electric switches and took the basement stairs three at a time. As he loped down the hall he pulled his gun and shield from the top shelf of the front closet. He was backing the Pontiac out of the driveway before he realized he hadn't told his wife he was going out.

Screw it—Alison was used to these night calls anyway. The traffic was light enough that Vance could make good time without his siren. He should be there in twelve, fourteen minutes.

That was still about seven hours too late.

Strong shot of light pushing her out of her groggy sleep. She opened her eyes, blinking.

Man standing over her. Frizzy red hair. Eyes big through thick glasses. "Sister Angela, I'm Dr. Bruce Heilbron, a staff psychiatrist at Parkhurst Hospital. Dr. Talbott has asked me to speak with you. I'd like you to answer a few questions for me, if you don't mind."

She turned her face away. So sleepy, confused. Why didn't they leave her alone, let her sleep?

"What is your understanding of why Dr. Talbott asked me to see you?"

"I don't know." She swallowed. Mouth so dry. "I don't feel well."

"I understand. That's a normal reaction to your surgery. You'll feel better in a while."

"Could I have some water?"

"In a while. But if you'll just bear with me now, I'd like to discuss a few things with you. Do you know why you're in the hospital?"

"I was bleeding." Voice faint, distant, flat.

"Do you know what the cause of the bleeding was?"

"No."

"Do you remember what kind of treatment you had in the emergency room?"

Long stillness. Then: "They gave me blood."

"That's right. Had you noticed any changes lately in your physical state—an increase in your belly size, changes in your breasts?" She nodded slowly. "What did you make of that?"

"I don't know. Nothing."

"Did you think that might indicate that you were pregnant?"

She blinked.

That strange word again. "No. I told them that already."

"My information is that you passed a placenta when you were in the emergency room. Can you explain that, what it might mean to you?"

"No. I don't know anything about that."

.   .   .

Julia was so unnerved to discover that the hospital meditation room was a kind of chapel, with a bare altar and a lighted imitation stained glass window, that she was not quite able to speak when the man in the blue uniform came in to interview them.

He sat on the bench in front of theirs, sat sideways, writing what they said on a clipboard.

At first Dorothy did most of the talking. Then Julia took hold of herself and told him what happened after she looked behind the bookcase.

When the man finished with his questions he thanked them and said it was all right for them to go. Sister Philomena was still conferring with the lawyer in the chaplain's office, so the three nuns sat on chairs outside in the hall. Claudine murmured something about going home, but Julia said, "I've got to see Angela again, if they'll let me. I've got to see if she's all right."

So they waited. Finally someone sent Julia up to the third floor, where they had taken Angela, but the nurse at the desk said she was sorry, but the patient could have no visitors tonight.

So that part was done. In the Chevette going home, with Claudine doing the driving, Julia's mind finally detached from Angela and moved ahead, to the other nuns at St. Rose. She looked at her watch. "Eleven o'clock! Claude, it's eleven o'clock."

"I know that, Julie," Claudine said quietly.

"But the man said the police would be coming to the convent. They must've come by now. Did anybody call home to tell them?"

"I don't think so."

"Oh my God." She rocked forward urgently on the car seat. "Claude, can't you drive any faster?"

"It's okay, Julie. You had to take care of Angela. That was the right thing to do."

"But if they had to hear it from the *police* . . ."

63

"Please try to relax, Julie. We'll be home in a few minutes. We did the best we could."

She knotted her hands in her lap, trying to pray, looking out the side window of the car. It seemed to move faster that way.

When the blue Chevette pulled into the convent's back driveway, she leaped out and ran, stumbling, for the kitchen door. As she threw it open Roxanne looked up, startled, from the stove, where she was pouring a coffee.

Julia knew instantly that they had come in time. *Oh, thank you, thank you, Lord Jesus.* She pushed away the questions with, "Roxanne, I want to see everybody who's home in the community room. Right away, quickly, please."

In the community room Irma, Virginia and Mary Luke were watching the large portable TV. Julia said, "Turn it off, please. I have an important announcement to make." Irma turned the switch; Mary Luke asked, "Julia, what's wrong?"

Julia made a gesture that translated as *later, later* and sat in the blue chair by the arched door. Claudine and Dorothy sat on the couch. As the other nuns came into the room, their faces tight with questions, Julia pushed her black purse into the arm-crack of the chair, trying to still her trembling hands.

When they all seemed to be there she said, "Angela's all right. The doctor said she's going to be okay."

Over the murmur moving around the room she said, "But I have very bad news to tell you." Time so short, already run out. "I'm sorry to say that Angela gave birth to a child earlier this afternoon. Here in the convent. Dorothy and I took it to the hospital and the doctor said it died under suspicious circumstances so he— So the police will be coming here soon. I wanted to tell you all before they came."

Margory started to cry, but the rest just looked at Julia. What she saw mostly were those wide, disbelieving eyes.

"Of course we should cooperate with the police in any way we can. We have nothing to hide. Any of us."

She wanted to explain, soften it somehow, if she could. "We all knew Angela had a medical problem. She could have told us about it. But she didn't. Of course we would have helped her, helped— She never told us. Never asked. I know this is a very terrible thing that happened, a very terrible thing for you to have to hear, but you must understand we would have helped her if we could. All of us. But she never let us."

Now they were moving, turning toward each other, talking. Julia kept saying in a high, shrill voice, "Of course we would have helped her. She should have come to the community. But she never, ever did. You all know how she was. How she—didn't let anyone help. None of you must feel you're to blame. If anyone was to blame it was me. But Angela didn't let us help her. Of course we would have. We—"

The sharp ring of the front doorbell cut her off. In the sudden silence Claudine got up from the couch, moved to the door.

Two uniformed policemen were standing on the stoop. One of them said, "Sorry to bother you, Sister. But we're here to secure a crime scene."

Seven

Dr. Heilbron asked her, "Can you tell me what you did last week?"

"I taught school. Same as always."

"And on the weekend?"

"I visited friends of my family."

"Out of town?"

65

"Yes."

"And yesterday, Monday?"

"I came back late. By plane. I went right to school. I never missed a day until today."

"Do you remember what you did last night?"

"I think I watched TV for a while. With some of the sisters."

"When did you go to bed?"

"About ten. I was tired from my trip."

"And this morning? Do you recall what you did this morning?"

Groggily, obediently, she searched her mind. But there was only the dark space. "No," she said finally. "I don't remember."

When Lieutenant Tim Vance pulled up at the convent at 11:14, one squad car was already parked outside. Corporal Tarrenton let him in the front door. "What's happening?" Vance asked.

Tarrenton gestured with his head. "Crime scene's upstairs. Nobody else's here yet."

"Okay." Several women Vance assumed to be nuns were clustered in the front parlor. "Evening, Sisters. I'm Lieutenant Tim Vance of the Cambridgeport Police."

A pretty young black-haired nun moved forward. "Good evening, Lieutenant. I'm Sister Julia, the local coordinator." She seemed, if possible, more nervous than Vance. "Where would you want to start—upstairs?"

"I believe so, Sister." In his twelve years as a cop Vance couldn't remember feeling more awkward than he did right now.

Julia said, "Roxanne, would you please show him around?"

Vance followed the plump, bow-legged nun up the stairs. One piece of luck here—he'd have a few precious moments to work alone before the swarm descended, quiet moments when he could think straight. Vance was damn well going to make the most of them.

The nun showed him the scrubbed, bare bathroom, described where the blood-pools had been. Vance asked sharply, "Who cleaned it up?"

The nun started guiltily, murmured, "We did. The sisters did. We asked the officer who came by this afternoon, and he said it was okay." She hesitated. "He told us to use hot water and a heavy detergent."

Vance's reaction showed only in the grim tightening of his face. To the nun he said, "Okay, Sister." She took him to the bedroom—bare and clean as a bone, with the wooden bookcase pulled away from the wall. "Thanks, Sister. Is there anyplace else Sister Angela might have been today, someplace she did her work, maybe watched TV or something?"

"Well, her office is the room across the hall. I don't know if she used it today."

"Okay. And is there something she used to carry her personal effects—I don't know, would you call it a purse?"

The reaction that flicked across the nun's face was too small to be called a smile. "Yes, Lieutenant," she said dryly, "I'd call it a purse. It's over there on her desk."

She took Vance's nod for a dismissal, and retreated to the hall. Vance was already pulling in information in huge, undigested gulps.

Bedroom approximately eight by fifteen feet, one window, facing south. Tan walls, brown lino floor. Large brownish water-leak stain in the ceiling's acoustic tiles. Single iron bed, closet and bookcase along the left wall; desk, bureau and white enamel sink along the right. Bureau and desk plain maple, almost G.I. issue. Wooden rocking chair abutting the wooden bookcase. Empty string plant hanger on its orange cushion. Empty hook on the ceiling above the chair.

Wooden crucifix above the head of the stripped bed. Brown lithograph of Jesus figure on the right wall. Family

67

snapshots in a plastic cube on the cluttered desk. Some kind of handwritten prayer jutting up from the desk in an angled plastic frame. A paperback of *Dark Fires* by Rosemary Rogers, marked with a bookmark, lying on the desk on top of a personal letter headed, "Dear Gayle," signed "Love, Gary."

Two calendars taped inside the closet door. Second week of May circled on one, with the notation, "Week of the child." Small furniture—nightstand, wooden footstool—out in the hall. Brown shoes on the lower shelf of the nightstand.

Larger wooden desk in the office across the hall. Large bookcase holding papers and books, mostly academic-type. Cartons stacked in two corners. Vance opened the top carton: wooden nursery-school blocks and forms, brightly painted. Black telephone on the office desk. Vance lifted the receiver, heard a dial tone.

He crossed back to the bedroom. Vance had already realized that if Sister Angela had a halfway competent attorney the police would never get a chance to interview the nun herself. This brief moment alone in her room was probably the best shot he was going to get at unraveling the mind of this mysterious lady.

What struck him most, here and in the bathroom, was the starkness, the absence of personal statement. Even the college dorms Vance had once briefly inhabited gave off more personal clues than this place. Here was a whole bunch of women sharing a bathroom with not a hair blower or a pair of drying panty hose in sight.

And this room was even colder, even more self-denied. A crinkled toothpaste tube on the ugly little white sink. Aspirins, cold creams, a few pill bottles and cold remedies in the mirrored cabinet screwed to the wall above the sink. But no makeup, no perfume or hair spray. None of what Vance considered normal female clutter.

He realized, grimly, that part of this unnatural neatness was courtesy of the Cambridgeport Police Department. In

68

the two other murders he'd handled—a homosexual high school teacher stabbed to death by a teen-age kid he'd picked up downtown, and a nagging wife dispatched by her husband's World War II souvenir Luger—there'd been bodies, blood, weapons. Plenty of evidence.

Now this—a drab, tidy little convent, clean as a witch's tit. Only evidence of a body was a small puddle of blood behind the bookcase. All the massive hemorrhaging that had freaked Leighton into calling him earlier that day—all of it gone, scrubbed away. On the instructions of his own man.

Vance muttered quietly, savagely, *Goddam cocksucking fuckup Paige.* Here he was smacked into what looked like the most important and sensitive case he'd ever have to handle, and his own man had told the nuns it was fine to go ahead and destroy the evidence.

Okay—there was nothing for it but to retrieve what he could. Vance opened the brown plastic shoulder bag on the desk. He found a bundle of cash—several hundred bucks, he estimated without counting. And a plane ticket from Milwaukee to Minneapolis made out to FLYNN, GAYLE MS. Vance walked to the door and asked the nun hovering down the hall, "Gayle Flynn—is that Sister Angela?"

"Yes, that's her family name."

More letters in the desk drawer, some of them in the immature scrawl of the guy who signed himself, "Love, Gary." A red plastic address book. Time later to find Gary in it.

Sergeant Jerome Edge, the head of Cambridgeport's Physical Evidence Unit, was standing in the bedroom door, carrying two large black cases. "Hey, Lieutenant. What've we got here?"

Vance closed the desk drawer. "Possible homicide, Jerry. Very touchy, very sensitive stuff. I want you to give it the best shot you got."

"I always do," said Edge, who was something of a fa-

69

natic perfectionist at his job. "Where d'you want me to start?"

Vance showed him the two pertinent rooms. "Go for the blood. Anything you can get."

"You want fingerprints?"

"Nah, no point. Not now, anyway, if there ever was."

Edge looked at the bright-lit white-glove-clean bathroom and commented dryly, "Not much of a crime scene."

Vance slapped the doorframe, hard. "Much, hell. It's *no* crime scene. See what you can get up from the cracks in the bathroom floor. There's one good smear on the bedroom bookcase, and a good spot behind it. And check out the garbage good. The best blood samples we can get here are probably in the garbage pails by now."

For the life of her she could not understand why, after this terrible day, this man with the glasses and red cheeks was making her tell her life story. In brief answers to his prodding questions she told him that she had three brothers, two of them married. That her father was dead. That her mother shared an apartment in St. Paul with her unmarried brother. That she was the principal of Benedictine Kindergarten School in Paxton. That she liked teaching, especially preschool children. That she still taught one class herself. That she had college degrees in history and education. That she entered the order at age seventeen and lived at the St. Rose convent for twelve years. That her health was generally very good, except for several allergies.

"I'm very thirsty," she said finally. "Can I have some water?"

He poured a glassful from the carafe on the nightstand, held it so she could drink through the plastic straw.

"Thank you," she murmured. But didn't mean. Cruel man. Why didn't he go away, leave her to sleep?

But still those questions. "Do you think you could do

some mathematics for me? I'd like to have you subtract backwards from one hundred by a decrement of seven."

It took her a while, but she finally managed to find ninety-three, eighty-six and seventy-nine.

"Thank you, that's very good. Now can you tell me who's buried in Grant's tomb?"

Her eyes came wide open at that one. She said almost angrily, "President Grant."

"Mm-hmm. Very good."

Enough of this madness. Enough.

She rolled her sore, pained body away from that punishing voice. "Now can I sleep? I'm very tired."

The convent doorbell was ringing steadily now. Julia stayed by the door like a good hostess, admitting a stream of strange men, some in uniform, some not. Julia was trying her best to respond appropriately to this bewildering invasion.

It was Claudine who thought of the other nuns. Some were still hovering in the background, trying to be helpful; others had taken refuge behind the closed doors of their own rooms. Claudine realized that all of them were wounded, hurting. They needed a chance to vent their feelings, to deal with this crisis as a community.

So when Julia had a free moment, Claudine suggested that she send the nuns who weren't needed by the investigators to the community dining room. "I think they need to talk, Julie. They need to be together, away from—this."

For a moment Julia made no reaction. Then: "Of course, Claude. Of course. That's a very good idea. Could you—"

"Yes, sure, I'll take care of it." Quietly, Claudine spoke to Virginia, who was standing uncertainly at the far end of the parlor; Virginia left to collect the others. The next time the doorbell rang, only Julia, Dorothy and Claudine were there to do the receiving.

At first the talk in the dining room was halting, difficult. Then it tumbled out of them like flow from an unplugged drain.

Margory admitted she'd actually suspected a pregnancy as early as January, when she was kidding Angela about both of them losing weight, joining a slimnastics class. Mary Luke said she'd thought it must be a tumor—the lump seemed so *high up* to be a baby.

Sylvia said one reason she didn't think it could possibly be a baby was that she'd never seen Angela with a man. It wasn't as if she went out to dinners or meetings with men like some of the sisters did. (*Virginia and Joan, for instance,* she thought.)

All of them were stunned, appalled at the idea they could have lived right here with her every day and not realized what was happening. But Angela had done so much to hide it anyway, Virginia reminded them—all those bulky shirts and sweaters she wore, and the way she pulled a sofa cushion or a newspaper over her lap whenever she sat down to watch TV.

Even those who admitted now that they may have suspected a pregnancy said they hadn't mentioned it to anyone else. They hadn't thought it was any of their business—"not the kind of thing you talk to other people about," as Mary Luke put it—and anyway they'd thought Angela must be taking care of it herself.

The one thing they all agreed on was that whatever Angela's problems had been, she hadn't invited—even allowed—anyone in the house to help her deal with it. "I know for a fact different people in the house were concerned about her medical condition. Even alarmed about it. I heard a lot of talk," said Irma. "But Angela was so—unapproachable."

They talked a little about what a secretive, distant kind of person Angela was—always smiling, sure, as Roxanne pointed out, but it was like a phony smile, something pasted on. She never really let her hair down, never confided anything about herself. Especially in the last school year she'd been increasingly remote, even demanding—"Ever since she got that new job as principal," said Sylvia. "I think maybe that kind of went to her head."

Joan said, "You know this is a house of very caring, very concerned people. It isn't as if we aren't a real community." Nods around the table. "Angela just wasn't part of us. She didn't let herself be part of us. Maybe that's why—" Joan left that last remark unfinished. "Anyway, I just mean maybe she never really belonged to our community. She obviously wasn't willing to share, and that's what a community's all about."

Around the dining room table that night the sense of shared feeling, of comforting and fortifying each other, was very strong. Not until the next day did they discover that this extraordinary moment of pooled, undammed confidences had also been a dry-run rehearsal for the police interrogation each of them would undergo.

Upstairs, the second floor was filling up with law-enforcement technicians, among them a State Police inspector, Stuart Nevelson, who was shooting off flash pics of the scene, focusing on the residual bloodstains, and an assistant D.A., Andrew DaSilva, who was wandering around the hall, about as helpful as a lap dog. Tim Vance realized now that this thing was bigger than he had originally anticipated—a lot bigger than a suburban possible homicide. But he still had his own job to do, and he damn straight was going to make sure it got done right.

Sergeant Robert Paige came up the stairs, looking about half as rattled as Vance figured he ought to. Time later to ream out Paige like he deserved. Vance asked him if anything significant was missing from the scene, and Paige remembered the bloody scissors he'd seen on the bedroom floor. Vance sent him downstairs to find out what the nuns had done with the scissors.

73

Sergeant Edge was down on his knees in the bathroom, rubbing moistened Q-Tips into the cracks in the tile floor. "How's it going, Jerry?" Vance asked from the door.

"Not so good. There's always something left, but the nuns used a lot of detergent cleaning up."

Goddamned idiot Paige. "Well, get everything you can. Did you get a shot of the footsteps in the hall?"

"Yes, sir." Edge got up off his knees and walked to the hall. "And Inspector Nevelson did too. He's shooting in color, and I sure wish we could switch over to that. A shot like this, blood on an orange carpet—it just won't come out worth a damn in black and white."

Vance smiled slightly at the deft way Edge had worked in a plug for his pet project. "Okay, Jerry. Just do the best you can."

Paige came back with Sister Joan, who located the scissors where she had put them, under the brown shoes on the nightstand shelf. Vance glanced at the shiny eight-inch instrument and asked, "Is this the way you found them, Sister?"

She blinked. "Oh, yes. Except they were all bloody. I dunked them into the bucket to wash them off."

"Okay. Thanks, Sister." No help for it now. He said to Paige, "Give 'em to Edge. Tell him to mark them for evidence."

"The chief's downstairs, with the D.A.," said Paige.

"Okay, thanks."

Vance found Chief Marwick sitting in the front parlor with District Attorney Abrams and a couple of nuns. He took the men aside, briefed them on what he had found—and not found.

Marwick winced when he heard about Paige's cleanup order, but Abrams didn't seem to care. "Okay, Tim," Abrams said. "Is Andy DaSilva upstairs?" Vance nodded. "Get him down here, would you? I'd like to start debriefing a few of the nuns tonight."

. . .

When the men asked if there was a private room where they could ask the nuns a few questions, Sister Julia took them to the small office at the end of the community room. The district attorney said that would do fine if they could bring in a few more chairs, and the police chief carried them in himself from the community room. As Julia was helping them arrange the chairs around the wooden desk a balding young man came in and was introduced by the district attorney.

Julia murmured, "Very nice to meet you, Mr. DaSilva."

As they stood awkwardly around the office the district attorney called Claudine and Dorothy into the room. "What we'd like to do now, Sisters," he said, "is just ask you a few questions about what happened today while it's still fresh in your minds. This isn't a formal interrogation, you understand—just a preliminary interview. Your initial impressions may be very helpful to us in pursuing this investigation."

The three nuns nodded their agreement. "Well, then, if it's all right with you, Sister Julia, we might as well begin with you."

Claudine and Dorothy left the room; the police chief closed the door. Julia sat on a straight-back chair pulled up to the desk. DaSilva sat opposite her with a yellow note pad laid on the desk.

Julia's face had a blank, madonnalike look, except around the mouth, where a nervous habit was printing premature lines. And her upper lip was pinched into tight vertical creases as DaSilva opened: "You understand, Sister Julia, that you are in no way required to speak with us. That this statement is entirely voluntary on your part."

She nodded. "I understand, Mr. DaSilva."

She handled the questions fairly well until he got to the part about her coming home from the school. Julia said faintly, "Sister Dorothy told me something was terribly wrong. So I walked upstairs and I went to my room—"

"Is that the room next to Sister Angela's?"

"Yes. And I put my coat and books down on the bed and I walked back out to the hall. Dorothy said—"

"Did you then see the footprints in the hall rug?"

She shook her head. "I saw them when I first went upstairs." She felt the brimming start in her eyes, tried to stop it. "I stepped over them because I had to put down my coat and books." Then she lost control.

If they'd taken her down to the police station and shined lights in her eyes and shouted threats at her, Julia could not have felt more beaten, more anxious to confess. The criminal they were after, supposedly, was Angela. But as she faced these intimidating men, answered their painful questions, Julia knew very well which one was really guilty.

Dr. Keith Talbott had already finished off one and a half Scotches by the time Heilbron got to his house. "Bruce, come on in. I really appreciate your coming by like this. Can I get you a drink?"

"Yes, thanks. I'll have whatever you're having."

Ginny said she would get it and went to the kitchen. Heilbron sat on the couch, but Talbott kept walking around the room, pacing, pacing, rubbing the heel of his hand over his chin. "I really wanted to talk this thing over with you, Bruce. I'm damn worried about her mental state, about the balance of her mind."

Heilbron said carefully, "I think that's certainly an area of concern."

"Did you get much out of her?"

"Not much. Her cognition seems intact. But her affect is inappropriately bland, unconcerned. She's not demonstrating any degree of the emotional distress appropriate to her situation. She did fairly well on the perceptual tests, but she wouldn't talk about any pregnancy. She's still denying any possibility of that."

"I honest to God think she doesn't remember it, Bruce."

Heilbron nodded. "That's entirely possible. When the human mind is subjected to information it can't digest, for whatever reasons, it sometimes goes into dissociative reaction. In other words, it blocks out the information that threatens the psychic integrity of the individual involved."

Talbott sat heavily in a chair. "You mean she doesn't remember it because she can't bear to remember it?"

"That's a rather crude way to put it, but it captures the idea."

Talbott suddenly wished he had someone else to talk to besides this twenty-nine-year-old on-call psychiatrist. "So what happens now?"

"That part is unpredictable. Either her mind will find a means of digesting the information, or it won't."

"What do you mean, *won't?*"

"I would say there's a possibility here of a total retreat from reality, a psychic disintegration."

"You mean she'll go over the edge for good?"

"Well, for an indeterminate period of time, at least."

Talbott jumped up and began to walk again. "Jesus, Bruce. We can't let that happen."

"It certainly couldn't be considered a favorable development."

"I mean, she got through the pregnancy. She got through the birth. She went all the way to full term without cracking. Doesn't that mean something?"

"Given the subsequent events, those facts in themselves have no definitive bearing on the psychiatric prognosis."

Almost to himself, Talbott said, "She's so frightened, so hurt. So *alone.* When I think of the hell she must have gone through . . ."

Ginny came back carrying a small tray with three glasses on it. Heilbron said, "Thank you, Mrs. Talbott," as he took his. Talbott switched his empty for a full one without comment as he asked, "What else did she say to you?"

"Not much. She's quite detached and reluctant to talk. I don't see any strong evidence of psychotic or suicidal tendencies. But the fact that she exhibited no incredulity about the questions I was asking her—I find that significant. She didn't ask me, for instance, why you had asked me to see her."

"Okay." Talbott was concentrating fiercely on everything this man was saying. "That doesn't surprise me. She's very—helpful. As much as she can be."

"I understand you ordered some analgesia to reduce her local discomfort."

"Yes, sure. That isn't the area of pain that concerns me."

"My tentative diagnosis would be hysterical neurosis, dissociative type. That's a psychiatric syndrome that can easily occur in a situation of major stress resulting from shame and guilt. In effect, she's separating those portions of her experience from the rest of her mental function in order to keep her overwhelming stress at a tolerable level."

"Yes, sure. I can see that."

"This has some effect, of course, on her total mental function. During the dissociative state she will tend to isolate certain functions from her mental control, which gives her the ability to perform certain acts out of—or at least, isolated from—her conscious volition. And those acts may be so thoroughly repressed that they're not consciously remembered."

Goddam psychobabble. "Okay. So what's your prognosis? And how do we treat this?"

"The major risk is more widespread deterioration of her mental function. She might possibly harm herself. I understand you've ordered special nurses."

"Yes. Yes. I don't want her left alone."

"Fine. I would concur with that order. As long as the

specials are with her, immediate help would be available in the event she reached a critical, more disturbed state of dissociation. I think it's also desirable that she not be interrogated by anyone not directly concerned with her medical condition. This might have a very destructive effect on her precarious mental state."

"Okay. Very good." Talbott's hand roved from his chin into his hair, making it stand peculiarly on end. "But what happens if she starts remembering on her own?"

"Then we'll deal with that reality in progressive stages, as she can handle it."

"Okay. That sounds right." He paused. "I've got to see her, I've got to treat her. I think I've got a pretty good rapport with her. I think she trusts me. But how should I proceed?"

Heilbron considered. "I think I'd avoid further talk about a pregnancy, about a baby. She'll come back to that when she can handle it."

"All right. That sounds right."

"Let her give you the clues. She'll talk when she's ready. But if she's pushed too soon, she may retreat completely."

"That's just what I'm afraid of. She's so close right now to the edge."

"I'm quite willing to continue treating her, Keith, if the various parties involved are willing. But right now, I think, we are in a critical period. The form of ongoing treatment will have to be determined by her response to the present critical period."

Talbot's face pulled into a tight grimace. "In other words, if she can handle this part of it, there's some real hope for her?"

"Very possibly. Very possibly."

"Oh God, I hope so."

Heilbron left after he finished his drink, but Talbott had two more. His body was past exhaustion, but his mind needed blotting, needed unraveling before he could sink into the sleep he craved.

At one point Ginny came and stood behind his chair, kneading at the steel-tight muscles in his shoulders. "Ahhhhh, thanks. That feels good."

"Keith, I know it's hard. But don't let it get to you."

That was Ginny. That, maybe, was one of the reasons he had married her. But for once he wanted to try to explain. "How can I tell you about today?" he said slowly. "It was like every nightmare about the absoluteness, about the *certainty*, was lying there in the ER waiting to be pulled back. Pulled back to life."

Her hands came off his shoulders. "I know that part of you is still tied up in that—that priest thing." Her voice came out sharper than she intended. "But you have a good life now. You have a family, you have work you like. Can't you ever leave that behind?"

He didn't answer her for a while. Then he said, "I'm really very tired. Why don't you go up, and I'll be there soon."

When she hesitated, hovering, mutely anxious, he said, "Right now I think I'd like to be alone."

In her hospital room she moved and cried out in her restless sleep. A gray-haired nurse got up from the chair where she had been quietly knitting and moved toward the bed.

But the patient never woke. The nurse smoothed the sheets, checked the flow of the tubes. Then she went back to her chair and took up her stitches.

Lieutenant Tim Vance came into the small convent office near the tail end of the black-haired nun's interview, when she was telling them about putting the baby into the plastic bags. She was crying pretty heavily, blowing her nose a lot. This Sister Julia—the local coordinator, whatever that was—seemed to be taking this thing harder than most of the other nuns.

Vance listened for a few minutes, then slipped quietly back out the door. He asked the two nuns sitting in the parlor about Sister Angela's whereabouts on the previous weekend. One of them went to get the logbook where Sister Angela had written the name and phone number to contact in case of an emergency.

Vance thanked her, noted them on his pad and went back upstairs, where Sergeant Edge had finished collecting the blood samples. "Okay, Jerry, go for the garbage. And check it real good."

Edge wrinkled his aquiline nose. "Want to bet there's a dumpster?"

Vance smiled. "There's always a dumpster, Jerry. But at least it's not a Chinese restaurant. The stuff's probably all clean and plastic-wrapped, like the rest of the place."

Looking out the window of his study, Monseigneur Stephen McCloskey, the pastor of St. Rose of Lima parish, saw the strange buzzing of nocturnal activity at the convent—cars coming and going, some of them police cars. He waited for someone to phone or drop by, for someone to explain. When no one called by midnight the monseigneur swallowed his pride and walked across the grass.

His first shock came when a uniformed policeman opened the door. McCloskey walked into the parlor saying, "Excuse *me*. I see all this coming and going and I was wondering if someone would care to explain."

A group of men was sitting in the parlor with some of the nuns. One of them stood and extended his hand. "Father, I'm Mark Abrams, the Ramsey County district attorney. Would you care to sit down?"

McCloskey sat. The feeling in the room was quiet, muted, pained—like a death in the family. McCloskey said, "What's going on here?"

Abrams looked over at the nuns. Sister Julia ducked her head and made a gesture with her hand. Abrams looked back at the priest. "Father, I'm afraid we have very sad and tragic news." Haltingly, he told him.

Almost immediately the priest began to cry. "Oh, merciful heaven, I can't believe it." He pulled a large handkerchief from his pocket and blew his nose. "That dear, sweet little woman. Who could believe it?"

"All of us here would rather not," Abrams said quietly, "but I'm afraid those are the facts before us."

McCloskey kept on crying.

When one of the nuns hesitantly offered him coffee, he said, "I think I could use a drink." She brought him a stiff, sweet brandy.

Lieutenant Vance was packing up his own selection of evidence when Sergeant Edge came back upstairs. "Find anything?" Vance asked.

"Not in the dumpster, Lieutenant. There's some stuff in the bags in the basement trash cans—bloody paper towels, and an empty Comet can with bloodstains on it. I took some photos. You want me to collect the stuff?"

"Nah, leave it till tomorrow. We're going to have to come back and toss the place more thoroughly anyway. Let's wrap it up here for tonight, but before you come back to the office I'd like you to go by the morgue and photograph the body, and pick up the nun's clothes from the Parkhurst Hospital ER. There should be a bathrobe anyway, and maybe something else."

"Okay, check."

Vance took his evidence bag downstairs. After he conferred briefly with Abrams and Marwick in the small office, it was decided to post no police guard in the convent that night. The possibility that Sister Angela had an accomplice among the other nuns had not been definitively foreclosed, but Sister Julia had promised nothing more would be touched or thrown out, and neither Marwick nor Abrams was willing to risk the suggestion implicit in posting an all-night male guard in this convent.

The relief that came out of these nuns as the investigators finally took their leave was so strong Vance could almost smell it.

The team reassembled at 1:45 A.M. at the Cambridgeport Police Station. At that time of morning the station was normally as dormant as a tomb, but tonight some dozen men were moving urgently in and out.

In the small staff room past the dispatch office, D.A. Abrams took off his suit jacket and laid it over the back of a wooden chair. Vance, Marwick and DaSilva sat near him around the seven-foot Formica-topped table. "All right, what have we got here?" Abrams asked.

"One hell of a mess," Marwick grunted.

No one disputed that assessment. Abrams loosened his tie, tipped back on his chair legs. Christ, it was a relief to be out of that convent, that frozen, overpolite kind of museum. To be able to talk and think again—finally think.

Abrams opened with: "What gets me, what I just can't get any handle on, is how a dozen mature, intelligent women could live right there with her for nine months and not see this is a pregnant woman. I just can't see that at all. If they were high school kids, all right, maybe. But these are all educated women."

"I'm having some trouble with that myself," said Marwick.

"Yeah, well, sometimes you see what you want to see," said Vance. "For sure none of those nuns wanted to see any baby."

DaSilva was shaking his head. "Yeah, but it was right in front of them every day. My wife—boy, you can't miss *her.*"

Abrams said dryly, "I think I should explain, Greg, Tim, that Andy's wife is pregnant for the fourth time in five years.

Okay, this isn't getting us anywhere. What have we got to work with here?"

Vance spilled the contents of a plastic evidence bag onto the table: The brown purse. The letters. The address book. An appointment calendar. He opened the purse and pulled out the contents, which included the packet of cash, the airline ticket, a card listing seven physicians' names and phone numbers, and a container of prescription pills issued to Sister Margory Montecito. Without comment, the investigators scanned the various items, passed them back and forth.

Finally Chief Marwick tapped his pipe into a large glass ashtray. "Okay, to repeat: what have we got here?"

"It's a pretty strange picture," said Vance. "Apparently Sister Angela is an exemplary teacher, the principal of a kindergarten school run by the order, and she generally sticks pretty close to home. But last weekend she flew over to visit family friends in Milwaukee. She didn't make it back until Monday afternoon. And she's got an unusual, according to the other nuns, amount of cash in her purse." Abrams riffled the stack of greenbacks lying in front of him on the table. Vance continued, "The nuns have no idea where she got the money."

Silence around the table. Abrams cleared his throat: "All right. Assuming that what we have here is a prosecutable unlawful death—which, by the way, is by no means established yet—I think the key question would be, did she act alone?"

The talk went back and forth. Vance came down fairly strongly on the probability of a second person being involved. "Look, there's a chance she did it alone, sure. But after delivering her own baby? Have any of you guys been in the delivery room when your own kids were born?"

Abrams and DaSilva nodded. Vance continued, "Well, my wife took all the training for that natural childbirth stuff.

She did months of exercises, she even had some shots to help her through it. Even so, Alison could no more have climbed off that table— Not to mention all that hemorrhaging Sister Angela was obviously doing. But when Sergeant Edge moved that bookcase tonight to shoot the blood behind it, it took the two of us to budge it." He broke the heavy silence around the table with, "Hey, I just find it real hard to believe that this woman, in the state she must've been in, could've moved that bookcase by herself, let alone make it look so natural stuck against the corner that nobody spotted it for four hours."

"But then you've got the question, who else would leave the body behind the bookcase?" Marwick pointed out. "Any able-bodied person would've got that baby out of the house, and that probably would've been the end of it."

"Maybe. Maybe. But there's a lot of loose ends here," said Vance.

"One thing I was wondering about," said DaSilva. "Whoever took that plant hanger down from the ceiling— one of the nuns who was cleaning up, I assume—apparently stood on the rocking chair to do it. They could've looked right behind the bookcase and seen the baby. In fact, they could hardly've missed it."

"Yeah, but they did," Abrams said wearily. "Look, this is still getting us nowhere. Assuming the possibility that she *did* have an accomplice, who's the likely candidate?"

There was general agreement around the table that the other nuns in the house were not good prospects. "First off, they were all present and accounted for on their jobs," Vance pointed out.

"We'll check that out more thoroughly tomorrow, of course," interrupted Marwick.

"Right," said Vance. "But anyway, the bug those women have for cleaning up—I think there's no way any one of them would've left the scene—not to mention the body— like it was."

"Which comes back to my point: who else might have been involved?" said Abrams.

Silence. Then Marwick said, "I'd have to go for the father."

When the word that had been on the minds of these men all night was finally spoken aloud, a certain tension around the table dissipated. "There's an element of logic here," Marwick continued. "Who else had a stake in concealing the evidence? Say it was just an outside friend of hers—what kind of friend wouldn't have called a doctor or an ambulance—would've left her for dying on the floor?"

"And the baby still in the room," Vance pointed out. "It just doesn't add up. Unless that person had as much interest as Sister Angela did in keeping this thing covered up."

"Which leaves us with . . ."

"The daddy," said Vance.

Abrams shook a Marlboro from his pack. "That's about the way I see it, Tim," he said evenly as he lit up. God, it felt good to finally be able to reason this nightmare through aloud. "It could have been a married man, somebody who had a powerful motivation for concealment. Maybe he panicked, ran out on her before this thing was finished right." The scenario Abrams had just unwittingly drawn for himself was so vivid it pulled a grimace to his face. He went on speaking, urgently: "I'd like to get one thing straight right now. The only reason any of our offices should be concerning themselves with the identity of this man is because he's the only likely accomplice we have to go for. We're pretty much working purely in the dark on this thing so far, and we've got to look for some answers wherever we can find them—fast. Now, I don't want anybody at this table or anywhere else to get the idea we're going after this man for any prurient reasons like idle curiosity. We're going after him because he's all we've got, period."

Murmurs of acknowledgment, agreement around the table.

Suddenly Marwick felt compelled to mention the possibility that had been haunting his mind. "I'll tell you one thing that concerns me, Mark—we've recently had a couple of attempted rapes, assaults, down around that part of town. Teen-age kids accosted, that kind of thing. Now, if it should turn out that this woman was the victim of a rape, which might explain why she never went for help with her pregnancy—just too shocked by the attack to handle it—well, if that should turn out to be the case, this police department is going to look mighty bad. Mighty bad."

"Well, Greg, I can appreciate your concern in that direction," said Abrams. "But I don't see it supported by any evidence, not a shred of it, so far. Let's assume the father was someone known to her. With knowledge of the pregnancy. Repeat: Who does that leave us with?"

DaSilva said, "Boy, that could be like looking for a needle in a haystack. I guess the first idea most people would go for is a priest. But geez, it could be anybody."

"Not necessarily." From the pile of evidence on the table Tim Vance plucked the letters he had taken from her desk. "She's had correspondence with two males that indicates some degree of personal involvement. One of them's a guy in Boston who apparently makes educational films. But the dates there don't seem to fit. The most recent ones are from one Gary Tucker. Tucker looks to me like a pretty good bet."

"You got any idea when they met?" asked Marwick, who had already done a nine-count back from April.

"Apparently sometime last summer." Vance hooked his arm over the back of his chair. "If you're going for Daddy, I suggest we start with Tucker."

"Hmmph." Marwick rubbed his pipe against his cheek. "What do we know about this guy?"

"Not much, except that he's apparently the son of the family she went to Milwaukee to visit last weekend." The men listening around the table reacted to that news with a stir of their bodies. From the correspondence he appears to be a pretty naive kid. I've only flipped through the letters, but they sound kind of like what a college kid might send to his high school girl friend—'real good to see you last time, thinking a lot about you, glad to hear you're okay.' That type of thing.''

"Okay." Marwick glanced at the wall clock, which read 2:36. "Get on that first thing in the morning, will you, Tim?"

"Done," said Vance.

The dreams were so powerful, so vivid, she almost thought she was awake.

Yet when she was surely awake, feeling those strange crisp sheets, those needles and tapes, she remembered nothing of the dreams except the feeling.

Trapped. Trapped. Someone chasing, closing in on her. Helpless. Trapped.

She tried to stay awake, to keep hold of these real sheets and real pains, but then the feeling floated back on her, heavy, pushing her back down into those drugged, hellish dreams.

Eight

Julia realized when she opened the convent door at 7:30 A.M. and saw Angela's older brother Edwin standing on the stoop, tight-faced and irritated, that she had never liked this man. Never liked his arrogance, his condescending. And she didn't like him now as he flashed his quick salesman's smile at her: "Ah, Sister Julia? I believe you're the one who called me?" Always so full of himself, so patronizing of their nun ways.

Julia nodded: "Yes, I called, Edwin. Thank you for coming. Come in, please."

He followed her into the parlor where Claudine and Dorothy were already waiting, saying, "I must say I was pretty surprised by your call, Sister Julia. You weren't too specific on the phone, but I figured it must be something important to get me out this early."

Julia introduced Claudine and Dorothy. Flynn tossed them a throwaway smile and perched on the edge of a wooden armchair, jiggling one leg impatiently. As he glanced at the painting of St. Benedict hanging above Julia's head he said, "Is Gayle—Sister Angela—okay? Is she in some kind of trouble?"

Even the few hours of sleep she'd managed to get had helped her, Julia realized as she looked at this man and said calmly, "I'm afraid we have very bad news to tell you, Edwin. I tried to get to you with it last night, but with everything that was going on I never got the time."

His leg wasn't jiggling now. "Well, gosh, I figure Sister Angela must have done something, got herself in the soup somehow, you calling me down here like this, but I can't see —just what did she do, anyway?"

"Angela's in the hospital right now, Edwin. Parkhurst Hospital." Julia lifted her hand, interrupting the question coming out of him. "No, no, she's all right. The doctors say she'll be fine. Although there was a time yesterday when we truly didn't know whether she was going to live or die."

He clutched the front of his checkered suit jacket. "Well, my gosh, what happened? Was she in a car crash or something?"

"No. She was found hemorrhaging here in the convent. But we got her to the hospital in time and as I told you, Edwin, the doctors say she's going to be fine. Thanks be to God for that." She paused. "That isn't why we called you down here."

The question his whole face was framing was anxious, angry. So Julia looked right at him and told him about the baby, and what the doctor had said about the death being suspicious, and the police being called in.

Flynn had lurched forward in the chair. "What—what do you mean? I don't understand." So Julia went through the story once again, quite methodically. When she finished, Claudine said gently, "I know this is very difficult for you to understand, Ed. It was for us too."

"Ouff." He looked like he had just been kicked in the stomach. "My God. My God. I just can't believe it. You're telling me she had a baby? My sister Gayle?" His face was as bleached as his white shirt. "Her of all people. I just flat can't believe it."

Claudine said, "Ed, you must have noticed all that weight she'd put on."

Bewilderedly: "Well, sure. In fact we kidded her about that when she came for Sunday dinners. Asked her when she was going to go on a diet, that kind of thing. I remember her —laughing about it. Like it was some kind of joke."

"Her legs were also very swollen," said Claudine. "Did you notice that?"

Blankly: "As a matter of fact, we did. The last time she was out at the house I remember my wife remarking on her ankle being puffed up something fierce. But she said she'd turned it coming downstairs."

Claudine nodded. "She told us the same thing. But it was both ankles. She said she'd been to see your mother's doctor, Ed. Do you happen to know whether or not she went?"

"Gosh, I don't know. I don't think so, but I can sure find out."

Julia said, "The police would like to know the name of that doctor, Edwin."

"Well, sure." Flynn was slowly beginning to react, to connect this stunning news to the rest of his life. "Speaking of my mother, Sister Julia, I'd like— Now, my mother is a pretty elderly woman and not at all well. Not at all well. I'd sure like to spare her from having to hear about all this."

Julia glanced at Claudine, who made a head-shaking motion. Julia said, "I appreciate your concern in that direction, Edwin, but I don't believe that will be possible. The Cambridgeport police chief and his men were here very late last night, with the district attorney. They seem to feel there is definitely—foul play involved here. And they said if that turns out to be true there's no way they could keep Angela's name out of the newspapers."

"Oh, my God." Flynn was rocking on the wooden chair, clutching the front of his suit coat. "I just can't believe it. Her of all people."

Claudine said, "Ed, the police were asking us last night if Angela was close to any particular men friends. We were wondering if perhaps you'd know . . ." She made a questioning gesture with her uplifted palm.

"What, Angela? My God." He made a choked sound that came out something like a laugh. "Good Lord, no. Excuse my language, Sisters, but I'm pretty thrown by this thing." He shook his head. "Men friends—no, of course not. I always got the impression that when she wasn't out with us on family outing kind of things she pretty much stuck around the convent, doing her work. She was always talking about how busy she was with the school. We saw her once or twice a month at least and I sure don't think she spent much time outside with anybody else except maybe a few good old friends like Ron and Margaret Hogan. I always figured when she wasn't out with the family she was here at the convent, doing her nun things." He paused. "Phewff. Boy, this is really something to take in."

"That was our impression too, Ed," said Claudine. "But the police will probably want to talk to you further about it. . . . They've been asking us where Angela was last summer. We understood she went on a camping trip with some of your family in August."

He nodded, scowling with concentration. "Yes, sure, I think she did. With my cousin Mary Alice Russell and her family."

Claudine said, "Well, the police will probably want to speak with them, too."

Flynn's eyes roved blankly around the room as he muttered exclamations to himself. Julia said, "Edwin, we thought you would probably want to notify your family yourself. The sisters could do that for you, if you prefer. But we presumed you would—"

"Yes, yes, sure. Of course, Sister. Thanks, I'll take care of that."

Julia passed him a slip of paper. "These are the names of her doctors at Parkhurst Hospital. The gynecologist and the psychiatrist. I think you'll have to speak with them before you can see her."

"All right, thanks. Gosh, I wasn't even thinking of— How *is* she?"

"They say she's doing very well, considering. They expect her to make a full recovery." She hesitated. "But as of last night she couldn't remember anything to do with a baby."

Flynn put one hand over his mouth. Claudine said, "Ed, I believe the Superior General, Sister Philomena, has already talked with an attorney. I'm sure you'll want to talk to him too."

"Of course. Thanks." He was staring at the piece of paper in his hand as if it were the only real thing in the room.

In the blue Chevette, driving over to the police station a little later, Julia couldn't resist saying, "Oh, Claude, did you *hear* what he said?"

"Hear what?" Claudine asked dryly.

"I mean, that was Angela's own brother, right? And he saw her all the time. He said they saw almost as much of her as we did."

"Yes, he did."

"And he had *no idea.* No idea at all. His reaction was just like ours—incredible. I've felt so guilty that we didn't see it but he's a married man, her own brother—he never saw it either."

"No, he sure didn't."

"They saw almost as much of her as we did and they never suspected it at all." Julia lifted the hands she had clenched on her lap. "Oh, God forgive me, Claude, but that does make me feel a little better."

"Time to wake up, Sister Angela."

She surfaced from a groggy sleep to find a nurse pushing a tray on a wheeled table over her body. A nurse with blotchy skin and wiry brown hair that looked like a dish-scrubber they used in the St. Rose kitchen.

Cheerfully: "Good morning there, Sister. It's your breakfast time." The nurse touched a button that pushed the head of her bed upward with a steady metallic whine. "I let you sleep late because I thought you needed it, but it's time for your breakfast now."

Angela looked at the plastic bowls and cups on the plastic tray and shook her head. "No. I don't want it." She pushed the table with her hand; it rolled a few inches away.

"Now, Sister, couldn't you eat just a bit? You need it to get your strength back."

She shook her head again, exhaustedly. "Can you please put me back down?"

"Well, all right then." Again that metallic whine. As soon as she was flat enough she turned on her side, looking toward the windows. "But I'll just leave it over here. In case you change your mind."

The nurse rattled the tray onto a dresser across the room and came back to the other side of the bed, looking right at Angela this time, her mouth bent into a crooked hook of a smile. "How are you feeling, Sister?"

Curtly: "Better."

Not better. Sore all over, sore and aching. Weak. Oh, so weak. She'd promised Julia she would come back home today. But she felt so sore and weak.

"Wouldn't you like me to freshen you up a bit? Wash your face, comb your hair?"

"No thanks. I'd like to sleep." She rolled away from the nurse, toward the wall of closets.

"All right. That certainly won't do you any harm."

Not sleep. Think.

Think and remember. Yesterday so muddled, so confused. So much happening that she didn't understand.

Now she must remember. Sort it all out. So they would let her go back home. This hospital—what was she doing in a hospital?

A rattle of paper cut into her rush of thoughts. She turned her head and saw the nurse sitting over by the windows, flipping through a magazine.

Angela watched her for a startled moment. Then asked, "Why are you here?"

"Oh, I'm just here in case you need me." The woman put down the magazine. "I'm your special nurse, Mrs. Langton. I'm here to get you whatever you want."

Silence. Then: "I want to be alone."

"Oh, now, Dr. Talbott wouldn't like that." The nurse got up, smoothing her white Dacron skirt, and walked toward the bed. "He's assigned special nurses to stay with you in case you need anything."

"But I don't. I'd rather be alone."

"Well, dear, why don't you talk to Dr. Talbott about that when you see him. But right now we have to follow his instructions, now don't we?"

Angela turned back to the wall of closets.

Strange. So strange. All of it. Everything upside down.

How could she think, get it all straight, with that strange woman sitting right across the room, watching her?

She tried to clutch at the thoughts anyway. But within a few minutes she drifted back into restless, troubled sleep.

A dozen men, all of them investigators of one official agency or another, sat in on the eight A.M. meeting in the Cambridgeport Police staff room. Chief Gregory Marwick ran through the facts of the case for the benefit of those off duty the night before. "Now we want to know everything we can get on Sister Angela Flynn—and I mean everything," he said. "We want to know her contacts, her activities. Especially in the week before the incident. Family background. Work profile. Anything you can get. You all know the routine." He turned to the district attorney. "Mark, you got anything you want to add?"

"I think that about covers it, Greg," Abrams said carefully. "Except I'd like it clearly understood that the normal confidentiality goes double in this case."

"Right. I don't want any goddam press leaks coming out of this office," Marwick agreed. "Okay, get busy."

As the meeting broke, Abrams signaled to Andrew DaSilva and Dominick Scotti, his thirty-year-old chief investigator, and asked them to take the depositions from the three nuns coming over from the convent.

A uniformed policeman at the desk showed Julia, Dorothy and Claudine to the cramped two-desk five-by-nine-foot office off the staff room where someone had already set up a stenotype machine. DaSilva greeted the three nuns with an embarrassed friendliness apparently designed to set them more at ease, and introduced Investigator Scotti, a big man with a black mustache.

"Sisters, I'd like you to understand what's happening here," DaSilva continued. "Basically, I'll be asking you about the same points we covered last night, in a little more detail, and Mr. Scotti here will transcribe our conversation. What we'd like from you is any information pertinent to our

95

investigation—what you did, what you observed. I know this isn't an easy experience for you, but I'd like to assure you that we're only interested in what pertains directly to this investigation. This isn't meant to be a fishing expedition."

Julia didn't like to look at these men. So she looked instead at the small black machine on the spindly legs that would take down everything she said. For anyone to read.

"The interviews should take about forty-five minutes," he was saying. "Are there any questions you'd like to ask me, Sisters?"

Julia sniffed quietly. Claudine said, "I think you're quite clear, Mr. DaSilva."

"Thank you, Sister Claudine. Now if it's all right with you I'd like to interview you separately, starting with Sister Julia."

Julia sat on the straight-back chair that DaSilva pointed to, feeling calm and strong. This place didn't frighten her. One office, another office—they were all really the same. And she'd already been through the story so many times before.

This time Julia was determined to tell it calmly, strongly. She was fed up, fed up, *fed up* with baring her most private feelings in front of these strange men.

One hour into the morning Lieutenant Tim Vance was wishing he'd put in more time as a traffic cop. Heavy traffic —that was the name of the game today. DaSilva and Scotti interrogating. Another A.D.A., Bloom, checking out the Boston filmmaker. Leighton and Paige filing depositions.

Every available man on the Cambridgeport force, plus a couple borrowed from neighboring Paxton, was working on this thing—typing up search warrants for the convent, out questioning the nun's doctors, questioning her contacts in and out of the school. A Cambridgeport town judge was wandering in and out, activating court orders. Plus, plus.

All of it Tim Vance's responsibility. And if it wasn't all

done right, the Cambridgeport Police were going to come out of this thing looking like a bunch of clowns. Small-town Keystone Kops.

It was 9:04 before Vance got a moment free to dial Wisconsin information and ask for the number of the police department in Oak Creek, a Milwaukee suburb.

In the Oak Creek Detective Division Sergeant Frank X. Sullivan was about to leave the office to check out a stolen-car report when the secretary asked him to take a call on line four from a Minnesota police lieutenant.

"Sure." Sullivan punched a button on his phone and said into the receiver, "Sergeant Sullivan. Can I help you, sir?"

"I sure do hope so, Sergeant," said the voice on the other end. "This is Lieutenant Timothy Vance, Chief of Detectives over here in Cambridgeport, Minnesota. That's a suburb of St. Paul–Minneapolis, in case you can't find it on your maps."

Sullivan chuckled dryly. "What can I do for you, Lieutenant?"

Vance ran through the basic facts of the case. "We understand the woman in question was down in Oak Creek last weekend visiting some friends of hers. We'd like any information you can get us on that visit."

Sullivan flipped open his black notebook. "Very good. You got a name on that?"

"Ralph Tucker. Address, forty-eight Cedarview Lane in Oak Creek."

Sullivan's hand froze. No need to write that name; he knew it as well as his own.

"We'd like to nail down the identity of the father involved here," Vance continued, "and from certain evidence in our possession it seems the man in question might be Gary Tucker. I guess that would be the son."

Another thunderbolt. "That's right, Gary is Ralph's

97

son. Well, this is quite some news. How do you want me to proceed?"

"We'd like you to interview the Tuckers, check out how they might be involved. We're also interested in the circumstances of the visit last weekend—her frame of mind, activities, and so forth."

"Very good."

"We're pretty much swimming in the dark over here, and it looks like we may not get access to the suspect. We'd sure appreciate any leads you could work up from that end."

"I'll get right on it, Lieutenant."

Sullivan hung up the phone. Pensively, he tapped his index finger against the receiver.

This thing made no damn sense at all. Frank Sullivan knew Ralph Tucker as a fellow Rotarian on the Oak Creek chapter, a fellow Knight of Columbus and former Boy Scout leader. He was real active in the local Laetrile organization and served on about a half-dozen civic committees, youth programs, that type of thing. The idea that Ralph Tucker could be mixed up in a St. Paul murder— Why, Sullivan would as soon suspect his own mother.

When Superior Court Judge Samuel Aaron walked into his office at 9:20, his secretary looked up from the telephone and said, "Judge Flanagan calling."

"Okay, I'll take it in my office." Aaron crossed the large beige carpet, sat behind his teak desk and said into the phone, "Bill? What's got you going so early in the morning?"

"Listen, Sam, I'm concerned about this case over in Cambridgeport. Did anybody fill you in on it?"

"Not yet. What have you got?"

Flanagan filled him in.

"Well, I'll be damned," said Aaron. "You hang around this place long enough and I guess you see just about anything."

"The word is they may go for a murder-two indictment," Flanagan continued. "Under normal circumstances, of course, this would go into the assignment lottery. But I've already talked to Joe Grimaldi and Chuck McNamara, and we pretty much agree these can't exactly be considered normal circumstances."

"I don't think anyone could give you an argument on that, Bill."

"The point is, Sam, I don't think any of the Catholic judges would feel comfortable handling this case. If you're agreeable, we'd like you to take it from word go."

"I see. Well, I can appreciate the problem you guys have with this one, Bill. If it's agreeable to the rest of us, I have no objection to handling it."

"Thanks, Sam, I appreciate that." The relief in Flanagan's voice was fairly naked. "I'll get back to you later."

"Right. Later, Bill." Aaron hung up the phone and swiveled his chair to stare out the plate glass window at the landscaped expanse of the Civic Center Plaza. "A nun murder, whew!" He stroked the thinning hair over his ear.

When Sam Aaron first got involved in Republican politics, an old pro had told him that one newspaper article was worth five thousand dollars in campaign contributions. But a nun on trial for murdering her baby—now what would *that* be worth?

Driving over to the morgue with Marwick for the postmortem examination of Baby Boy Flynn, D.A. Abrams allowed himself the bleak hope that this thing might turn out to be a stillbirth after all. Considering the circumstances of the delivery, that wouldn't be surprising. The kid might very well never have breathed at all.

Okay, that left the cloth material to be explained. But she might have panicked, put it there when he was already dead. Might have, might have.

One year earlier Mark Abrams had been a moderately

successful thirty-five-year-old civil lawyer in St. Paul, specializing in contracts. Successful but restless, more than slightly bored. He'd gone after the Republican nomination for D.A. more for self-advertisement and diversion than any realistic ambition, since no Republican D.A. had been elected in the county within living memory.

For a number of reasons, only a few of them calculable, Abrams won the election. Now, four months into a job which he had scant background and training to handle, he was daily astonished at how tough it had turned out to be—how overwhelming the case backlog was, how slowly the antique wheels of justice moved. But all his previous problems had shrunk to insignificance with the news that a Roman Catholic nun might have murdered her baby, and that he, the Jewish D.A., might have to prosecute.

Abrams was holding on to that "might have" as he and Marwick walked in through the garage entrance of the old Ramsey County Morgue, walked through the large tiled receiving room, past the wall of square steel doors that made up the refrigeration unit, into the autopsy room.

The Medical Examiner, Dr. Kenneth Rhoades, was over by the telephone, wearing a baggy white surgical uniform. "Ah, Mark, Greg. Thanks for coming," Rhoades said. "I've got something to show you."

He led them to the lighted screen on the west wall where two X ray films were already mounted. The bones showed up light-colored on the film, the body tissues darker. Rhoades ran his index finger around some oddly shaped patches of lighter color. "This clearly indicates the presence of air in the lungs, stomach and upper intestinal tract," he explained. "That pretty much confirms my preliminary findings."

"Okay. Thanks, Ken," Abrams said glumly. "I think we may be headed for rough water on this one. Give it your best shot, will you?"

"Of course. As always," Rhoades snapped curtly. He

100

strapped on a large rubber apron, pulled on skin-tight rubber gloves. "You want a gown?"

"No thanks," said Abrams. "I'm not planning to get that close."

The crowd assembled in the autopsy room was something of a record for a Ramsey County postmortem: Dr. Rhoades and his denier plus three staff pathologists and a toxicologist, two police chiefs, the district attorney, and two police photographers. All of them clustered around the long steel table where a small white sheet covered the eighteen-inch-long body of Baby Boy Flynn.

Mark Abrams attempted to distract his mind from the realization that this was the first autopsy he'd had to witness. He made a catalog of observations: microphone suspended in the air midway above the table. Two large steel trays, one of them spread with an array of surgical instruments, angled over the lower end of the table. Steel gutters running along the table sides. Water already running into the steel sink bolted to the table foot.

Large sunlit room. Walls light-brown ceramic tile. Glass cabinets with bottles, jars—pickled specimens, it seemed—along the walls. And—weirdly—a headless skeleton standing by the windows. Bones wired together, Abrams supposed. Where the hell was the skull?

That question became abruptly irrelevant as Dr. Rhoades lifted the sheet away from the body, and Mark Abrams forced himself to look.

Strange. So strange. A still-curled naked newborn boy with a jagged-edged string of umbilical cord, and the gunk of childbirth dried in patches on his skin.

The only times Abrams had seen a baby like that was when his wife delivered—three times, natural childbirth. He still remembered the feelings he'd had then. Kids didn't turn out to be an unmitigated blessing. But that moment—nobody could take it away from you.

Now this pathetic, unwashed child, with those clothes

wrapped all around his neck. Rhoades was saying, "Gentlemen, if you want to photograph the body, now is the time."

Sergeant Jerome Edge and Inspector Stuart Nevelson shot off their strobe lights, then stepped away from the table.

Rhoades dictated into the suspended microphone, "The body is that of an apparent full-term, well-developed male infant, identified here as Baby Boy Flynn." He was lifting and moving the body now, slipping a flexible steel ruler over its surface as he dictated the dimensions: "Crown-rump length is twelve and one quarter inches. . . . The head circumference is thirteen and one half inches. . . ."

Now he was describing the physical aspects of the green straw basket and its various contents, including the "body partially covered by a light-pink bloodstained nightgown which surrounds the neck; one end is stuffed into the infant's mouth. Involved in the superficial knot around the neck are a pair of bloodstained white panties which also extend into the infant's mouth."

Rhoades reached into the green basket that had been placed on the table behind the infant's head. "Present in the wicker basket is a portion of umbilical cord measuring eight and one half inches. One end is cleanly severed, the other severed in a ragged conformation. Also present in the basket is a seven-eighths-inch portion of umbilical cord. Other contents of the basket are numerous pieces of bloodstained papers and a pair of worn brown loafers."

Rhoades lifted his foot from the recorder pedal. "All right, gentlemen, I'd like to have some good photographic documentation on this." He unwrapped the pink nightgown from the neck. Gripping the top of the small skull with his left hand, he pulled the jaw open with his right, giving a maximal display of the panties. "Get me a close-up on this, will you?"

As the strobe lights flashed, Rhoades pushed his right fingers into the oral cavity, feeling for the back edge of the cloth material. With his right foot activating the recorder pedal, he dictated: "The pink shortie nightgown is removed from around the neck. It was folded, not knotted, around the neck with a small portion of one end sticking into the infant's mouth. The pair of white cotton panties extends into the oral cavity, extending all the way back to the nasopharynx."

Rhoades pulled the panties out of the mouth. Watching carefully from the foot of the autopsy table, Mark Abrams made a mental measurement of the material as it came out. Astonishing—five or six inches of thick cotton knit seemed to have been crammed into that newborn mouth.

Rhoades went on dictating an external description of the body. "Vernix caseosa is present in the external auditory canals . . . the lower extremities are folded and cyanotic . . . conjunctivae and sclera are injected . . . there is fixed posterior purple lividity . . ."

Now he was lifting the large reddish-purple placenta from a plastic container, weighing it, describing it into the microphone. Slicing it open, with a half-dozen slashing cuts, on the towel-covered surface of the steel tray just a few feet away from where Mark Abrams was standing.

Now Rhoades was lifting a scalpel from the upper tray. As he said, "We make the usual Y-shaped incision . . ." Abrams turned abruptly away from the table and walked out of the room.

Chief Marwick walked out after him. Abrams leaned against the tile wall of the morgue receiving room. "I don't know about you, Greg," he said wearily as he shook a Marlboro from his pack, "but I figure some of the things that go with this job, nobody pays you enough to have to watch."

103

Nine

At 9:23, on Ralph Tucker's fifteenth lap around the indoor track of the European Health Spa, large patches of sweat were appearing on his gray sweatsuit. A gym instructor intercepting his path called out, "Ralph, there's somebody here wants to talk to you."

Tucker jogged on, calling over his shoulder, "Tell 'em to wait."

"Guy says it's important."

Reluctantly, Tucker slowed to a walk. He picked up a white towel, mopped his sweaty face and wrapped the towel around his neck. "Okay. Where is he?" The instructor nodded toward the building lobby.

Tucker found Sergeant Sullivan pacing in the lobby. "Well, Frank!" Tucker said heartily, extending his hand. "What can I do for you?"

"Sorry to break up your workout, Ralph, but I've got a bit of a problem."

"Well, I figure it must be pretty important." Tucker sat on a plastic-upholstered blue chair. He was a short, wiry stump of a man who gave off a tight-muscled energy that belied his cropped gray hair. "What can I do to help?"

"Matter of fact, Ralph, they've had an incident over in Minnesota, and the police have reason to believe either you or Gary may have some knowledge of it." Sullivan cleared his throat. "Are you acquainted with a Sister Angela Flynn?"

The look of puzzlement on Tucker's face appeared to be genuine. Sullivan added, "I understand she's a nun someplace up around St. Paul."

"Oh, you must mean Gayle." Tucker rubbed the towel vigorously into his damp hair. "Yes, sure, Sister Gayle is a friend of the family. Matter of fact she was down here visiting us last weekend."

Sullivan nodded. "That's what I've been given to understand." Then he delivered the rest of Vance's message.

Nudged by a mild curiosity about Ralph Tucker's unexpected interruption, the gym instructor glanced through the glass window of the swinging door leading from the gym to the spa lobby. He could see Tucker sitting, quick-freeze-like, with his towel held up by his head.

Then Tucker snapped the towel off his neck, stood up and started pacing around the lobby. Looked at the floor, looked at the ceiling, smacking the towel against his leg. A couple times he pulled up his shoulders, like he was blocking a punch. Whatever news Tucker was hearing, the instructor could tell he was getting it in a wave of zingers.

And the small guy who was delivering it didn't look any too happy either, hunched over with his elbows dug into his knees, watching Tucker like the guy'd just drowned his dog.

Finally, his curiosity no longer mild, the instructor pushed open the gym door. He heard Tucker saying, ". . . if that's the case, Frank, if my boy Gary was responsible, we'll do the right thing, of course. But I tell you right now I don't believe it. Not for one minute. Gary's not that kind of boy."

Ah yeah, sure thing, pops. The instructor said, "Hey, Ralph, the weights're free if you want 'em."

"What?" Tucker looked over, blankly. Took a minute to focus. "Oh, thanks, Bud. Nanh, I'm finished for today." He looked back at his visitor. "What can I do now to help, Frank?"

"I'd like you to bring Gary around to my office for an interview."

"What time?"

"Soon as you can make it."

"Okay. Let me get out of this damn sweatsuit, and I'll see you there in about an hour."

The gym instructor stayed out of Tucker's way as he steamed back through the gym to the shower room.

On the stroke of 9:30 Sister Philomena Levesque walked into the large oak-paneled council room on the Motherhouse second floor where the eight other nuns who served on the St. Benedict General Council were already assembled and waiting. (For this extraordinary meeting only Claudine Schneider was absent.)

Philomena sat in the high-backed brown-leather-padded chair at the head of the table, and opened the black leather folder stamped with a stylized gold cross in which she carried the papers pertinent to a meeting. "Good morning, Sisters," she said.

Greetings were murmured back at her. "You all know the reason for this very important meeting," Philomena continued. "Before we make any deliberations or decisions, let us pray to the Holy Spirit, that He may give us wisdom and charity, and guide our deliberations. Let us take a few moments to pray silently."

Philomena bent her head over her folded hands; the other nuns did the same. The heavy stillness inside the room was broken only by the sound of a lawn mower buzzing and backfiring on the convent lawn past the vaulted open window.

When Philomena crossed herself, signaling the end of the prayer period, she cleared her throat and said, "All right. I have no recent news on the situation to convey, except to say that Sister Angela's doctors have told me she passed a fairly comfortable night. They do not anticipate any further aggravations of her medical condition. I know we are all very grateful for that fact, and of course we will all be praying for her rapid and complete recovery."

Nods, murmurs around the table. Philomena looked down at the paper on which she had neatly outlined the points to be covered at this meeting. "There are, however,

106

a number of aspects to this unfortunate tragedy that will not be so easily resolved. I have called you all here this morning to hear your collective thoughts on how we should best proceed." She paused. "Are there any questions?"

After a brief silence Mary Christopher asked, "Has the bishop been notified?"

"Yes, I spoke with him last night," said Philomena. "He of course expressed great concern for everyone involved, particularly Sister Angela. It was his judgment that this matter could best be handled as an internal concern by the sisters of the order."

What Bishop Paul Roche had actually expressed was irritation at being awakened, and a polite horror at the news, so eloquent that Philomena perceived it very well over the telephone lines. But Philomena was still grateful for his instinctive hand-washing response. So the priests who ran the Church were choosing not to shoulder this particular cross. Very good: it was quite enough right now that the sisters must contend with the lawyers, the doctors and the police.

As she had expected of this meeting, the voices were calm, the thoughts well considered. No one at that table was indulging herself in any untoward display of emotion.

Elaine showed some reaction when she realized that this private tragedy the nuns were enduring would most likely be reported in the public press. But the discussion moved on very quickly to practical considerations. Corrine suggested that a request be made in the letter of notification, to both the kindergarten parents and the other St. Benedict sisters, that they should not divulge any information about Sister Angela or the order itself, any part of it, to reporters.

That idea was approved by general agreement around the table. Then Mary Christopher suggested that, particularly if the event did become public knowledge, a series of meetings—both for the sisters, and for the school parents—might be arranged, in which they could openly discuss the impact this tragedy would have on their communal lives.

"An excellent suggestion, Mary Christopher," said Philomena. "I think the older nuns in particular may have a great deal of difficulty understanding this. Our great challenge now as a religious community will be to surmount this tremendous tragedy in a way that our faith and commitment will be strengthened by this adversity."

"Oh, yes, Sister Philomena," murmured Elaine. "That's what we must all try to keep sight of."

Philomena nodded acknowledgment of that lone vote of confidence. Then her eyes moved down her agenda. "I am particularly concerned about the impact on the children in Sister Angela's own class. It might help if we gave the school parents a phone number they could call, in case they wanted to discuss the matter personally with a representative of the congregation. Corrine, could you handle those calls?"

"Yes, of course, Sister Philomena."

"I feel we have a clear moral responsibility to offer whatever guidance and help that we can," Philomena continued as she folded her hands over the open leather case. "Further than that, I think we should avail ourselves of some professional guidance in dealing with this exceptional situation. It is, after all, something none of us have any experience in dealing with. So I would suggest that we arrange a meeting between the parents and some psychologist or psychiatrist, some professional person on whose discretion we could absolutely rely."

The sense of solidarity around the table suddenly fragmented. Marilyn voiced the bewilderment most of them were feeling: "A psychologist?"

"Yes," Philomena said firmly. "I believe such a person could offer valuable guidance. It might also be beneficial to arrange counseling sessions for the sisters as well—especially the sisters at St. Rose, who will be the target of much of the police investigation."

Now she had lost them. Looking down the long polished table, she saw the confusion and resistance they were feeling, clearly evident on their faces.

Quietly, urgently, Philomena began to talk about how many times they themselves had acknowledged around this very table that they lived in turbulent and changing times—for better or for worse. About how painful and incomprehensible this present tragedy was, for all of them—herself as well as the other sisters. About how what was needed now most of all was faith and understanding.

Yes—understanding. And if some of that could come from psychological experts they must make themselves open to it. Even welcome it.

She could still feel the disquietude, the doubts, as she looked down the polished table.

But the decision to arrange psychological counseling for the parents and the sisters was agreed to without further debate. The rest of the council meeting was devoted mainly to organizational details concerning the letters, the meetings, and so forth.

At 10:28 the assignment desk editor at WKCB-TV, the ABC affiliate in Minneapolis–St. Paul, took a call from an anonymous male offering a "hot tip."

The editor listened. "Oh, yeah?" He scrawled on a scratch pad, *C-port—nun.* "Have you got any details on that? Any names?"

He listened awhile longer, slouched in his chair, snapping at his metal watch wristband. Then said, "Well, thanks very much. We'll check it out."

He dropped the receiver on its cradle and looked at the two words on the paper. Then he tore it from the pad, crumpled it and lobbed it toward a wastebasket as he remarked to a secretary across the room, "Jesus Christ, you don't have to tell me it's spring. The nuts are out in the full bloom of the season."

At 10:31 another anonymous call to the newsroom of WRCY-TV, the CBS affiliate, was fielded by reporter Kevin Corrigan. Corrigan jotted a few notes, asked several unproductive questions and said, "Thanks. We appreciate the tip."

"Just check it out. You'll see it's good stuff," the male caller said.

Corrigan walked across the hall to the office of assignment editor Ted Markowitz. He said from the door, "Hey, Ted, I just got a pretty interesting tip. That some nun over in Cambridgeport had a baby last night, and killed it."

Markowitz paused in midswing from his typewriter. Then he pitched his swivel chair backward, reaching with his left hand for the back of his head. He looked at Corrigan.

For a moment neither spoke. Then Markowitz said softly, "Well? What you think, Kev?"

"I dunno. It's a wild one, all right, but the guy sounded possible."

"Okay." Markowitz slapped the arm of his chair. "Then check it out good. Try the M.E.'s office, and the D.A. Check with the Cambridgeport Police. If this one's good stuff there's no way they're gonna be able to keep it wrapped up."

At 10:44 Meg Gavin, a thirty-six-year-old reporter, was sitting at her desk at the *St. Paul Eagle-Bulletin,* shuffling the notes of her two-week inquest into the suburban tax-rate structure of metropolitan St. Paul–Minneapolis. Son of a bitch if this wasn't worse than a college term paper. So much more fucking *dull,* all of it nothing she ever wanted to know anyway. *Time to move on, Meg-o,* she reminded herself again. *Time to hit the road, Jack.* Whatever was out there couldn't be any worse than this.

Someone called, "Meg." She looked across the room and saw city editor Dick McAlpine beckoning her to his horseshoe-shaped desk.

Meg walked up to the desk. "Dick, dear old Dick. If you're about to tell me, please God, that the world can do without understanding the suburban tax rate I think I might even spring for lunch."

"Well, maybe they can wait on it awhile." McAlpine

looked at the paper in his hand. "I don't know, I don't think there's anything to this. But we just got a tip that a nun out in Cambridgeport maybe had a baby yesterday, and maybe killed it."

Meg Gavin froze, her breath caught in her throat. McAlpine peered up at her over his horn-rims and murmured in demurral, "Like I said, I doubt there's anything to it."

Her reaction was slow coming. Then, with a rush of exhaled wind, she smacked both hands on the horseshoe desk. "Dick! That's *mine*. Nobody else. This one's mine."

McAlpine smiled. "What's yours? I'm telling you, it's probably a crock of shit."

"Or maybe not. Where's she supposed to be now?"

"Parkhurst, the guy said. Frankly, this thing sounds off the wall to me. It would be a nice little yarn if it worked out. But I wouldn't hold my breath on it, Gavin."

"Hold your own. I'm telling you, Dick, I've got a feeling about this one. But just remember—it's my story, *right?*"

McAlpine sniffed. "Good little Catholic girl. You *want* it to be live is all." But Meg Gavin was already running toward her desk.

The nurses kept interrupting, kept disturbing her. Once every hour they took her temperature and her blood pressure. They brought her juice and pills—such a lot of pills, different assortments every time they came. And they changed the blood-bag that was still running into her right arm, and emptied the other bag hung under the bed, the bag that drained that other tube.

Angela didn't want them bothering her. She didn't want to talk to these nurses, didn't want to acknowledge them. She only wanted to be left alone.

But she still wondered why *they* didn't talk to her, except for that special nurse, Mrs. Langton, the one with the brown-bush hair. She wondered why they, all of them, avoided looking at her face.

Like she wasn't there, almost.

Now one of them was coming in with a bouquet of flowers. Mostly daisies and blue irises, in a white basket tied with a pink bow. The nurse read the card aloud to her: " 'Best wishes and get well soon. Father McCloskey.' Now isn't that nice, Sister."

She murmured, "Yes. Thank you."

Flowers. How strange to get flowers.

She had never in her whole life, except on the day of her profession, had flowers sent to her. And even then they were only for the main altar.

Probably it felt so strange just because she'd never been in a hospital before. All kinds of people got flowers in hospitals. Even nuns did. So that was really very nice of Father McCloskey to send them, even though she was still a little embarrassed to get them.

She lay turned toward the closets in a way that she could still see the flowers on the dresser. They were almost out of her line of vision, so she wasn't *enjoying* them, really. But she still liked to look at them, just a peek now and then.

That pink bow. Something about the pink bow.

Ah yes, sure, she remembered now. That day when the family went on a picnic to pick blueberries at Spofford Pond.

That was probably the happiest day she could remember, that Sunday when Daddy took them all to pick berries at Spofford Pond. The whole family was together then, all of them living together. And such a beautiful day it was, all sunny and gold, the air humming with bugs. She filled her berry pail faster than anyone else. And when Daddy came over to look at it he saw the old surveying stake there in the field with the pink ribbon tied to it. Pink faded from red by all that sun, Daddy said. And he took the ribbon off the post and wove a garland of wild flowers around it, flowers that were just blooming all around them in the berry field. And then he put it on her head, saying, "Here's a crown for my princess, my number one girl."

She could still remember the spilling rush of happiness she'd carried in her, that day at Spofford Pond.

Just for one moment she allowed herself to feel that old wish, that Daddy was still alive today.

But she let go of the wish as she realized that if he were still alive he would probably come to see her in the hospital, and ask her how she was feeling, ask her about what happened to her. And she wouldn't know what to tell him.

So maybe it was better, really, just for now at least, that Daddy was dead.

In the autopsy room of the Ramsey County Morgue, Dr. Kenneth Rhoades extracted the two small reddish-pink lungs and carried them to the autopsy table on the window side of the room, where the denier had placed a stainless-steel pail filled with cold water. Looking around him, Rhoades realized that the district attorney was missing from the room. "Get Abrams in here, will you?" he asked one of the pathologists as he laid the lungs on a towel next to the pail. "I don't want him to miss this."

When Abrams and Marwick came back into the room Rhoades managed not to show his irritation as he lifted the right lung and placed it into the water. The small organ slipped from his gloved hand and floated. "I'd like some photographic documentation of this, gentlemen," Rhoades said as he stepped away from the pail.

When the strobes were finished he immersed the left lung. "As you'll observe, gentlemen, they float." More strobe-flashes. "This isn't a conclusive test of the degree of aeration involved here, but it's a good indication."

When the photographers were finished, Rhoades carried the lungs back to the autopsy table and dictated, "All five pulmonary lobes are expanded. No visible or palpable lesions. The visceral surface of both lungs, anterior and posterior, are covered with numerous petechial hemorrhages." He slashed apart both miniature lungs with his knife. "Representative sections of the expanded pulmonary lobes are taken for microscopic studies."

113

As Rhoades severed and removed the heart, Abrams left the room again.

One by one, the various organs and glands of Baby Boy Flynn were removed, weighed, examined and dissected. It did not occur to some of the observers around the table to be grateful, but in fact this postmortem was in at least two respects less unpleasant than most to witness. One, the bowels that were stripped and washed at the wall sink contained only a small amount of fluid and fetal fecal material.

And two, the cranial bones did not require sawing. After the denier made a single incision through the scalp and, grasping the infant's longish brown hair, pulled it forward over the face, he was able to penetrate the soft fontanel at the top of the skull by pushing a surgical scissors through the tough membrane.

Once the membrane was cut, he pushed his thumbs through the fontanel and bent the soft skull bones outward. They came apart along the jiggly suture lines, and the denier was able to hold most of the brain in his left hand as he severed the brain stem from the spine.

At 11:05 Rhoades dictated a final sentence for the PM tape: "The brain will be retained and preserved in formalin for further study." As he lifted his foot from the recorder pedal he stripped the rubber gloves from his hands. "All right, that concludes it, gentlemen. Thank you for your attendance."

He unhooked the rubber apron, pulled it over his head and went looking for Abrams and Marwick. Those two didn't look like cherries to an autopsy room, but their absence spoke louder to Rhoades than their tough exteriors. He was already planning to check out the men's room when he found them in a staff office behind the receiving room.

As Rhoades walked in, Abrams looked up from his glum examination of the cracked linoleum floor and asked softly, "So?"

"A satisfactory PM," said Rhoades. "I'd fix the cause of death as asphyxia due to gagging."

"No question about it?" asked Marwick.

Rhoades shook his head. "You saw for yourself the aeration of the lungs, the air in the X rays. The petechial hemorrhages on the lungs and right kidney are also consistent with asphyxiation."

"Okay," said Abrams. "Well, that's it, then."

"One more thing you might be interested in, concerning the segments of umbilical cord. Mind you, this is just medical hypothesis. Nothing I could testify to in court. But the ragged end of cord attached to the body—that wasn't cut with any instrument."

Abrams was already wishing he didn't have to hear what was coming next. "The cord is a thin membrane, but it's slippery, and remarkably tough," Rhoades continued. "It would be very difficult to sever manually. Maybe not even possible. My hunch is that she delivered the baby someplace where scissors were not available to her, and bit the cord free with her teeth. That would account for the seven-eighths-inch fragment found in the basket."

"Jesus H. Christ," said Marwick.

Rhoades was so caught up in his unraveling of an unusual piece of physical evidence that he seemed to have no consciousness of the actuality of what he was describing. "The idea's less bizarre than you might think, given the circumstances of an unattended birth," he said cheerfully. "She was probably functioning on a highly instinctual level. Severing the cord in that manner—that's instinctual with a good many animal species. Monkeys, for instance."

Abrams swallowed hard. He looked with great attention at the pattern of lacing on Ken Rhoades's dirty white shoes as Rhoades was saying, "My conjecture would be that she bit the child free of her at the time of delivery, and then carried him back to the bedroom and cut away the rest of the cord with scissors she had available there. As I said, this is nothing reliable enough to testify to in court. But I thought it might be helpful to you in putting the pieces together."

115

Fighting an overpowering weariness, Mark Abrams said, "Okay, Ken. Thanks for a good job. I guess we can take it from here."

It seemed to Ralph Tucker as if the drive to his business had never taken so long. Immobilized at red lights, he pounded the steering wheel, pounded off the suspicions crowding his head.

Goddam kids. They could break your heart these days. Not that his Gary wasn't a good, clean boy. Ralph Tucker would've just about sworn to that. Never had a moment's cause to doubt that boy yet.

But these police—well, they must know something. And they were saying it was Gary.

Goddam kid. If those police turned out to be right, Ralph Tucker was personally going to take that boy apart.

As he charged through the back entrance of his store at 11:14 he bellowed, *"Gary?* In my office. On the double!"

Tucker was throwing himself into his desk chair when Gary appeared in the office doorway, the sleeves of his navy work uniform rolled up over his muscular arms. Puzzled, he asked, "Dad? What's up?"

"Gayle Flynn had a baby last night, that's what's up." Tucker looked at his beefy, healthy young son, at the alarm signaling in his usually blank eyes. "And the police think you're the father."

Gary blinked. "Police?"

"They think she may have killed the baby. And they want to know if you're the father."

Bewilderedly: "Killed? She killed the baby?"

Tucker hunched tensely forward in his desk chair. "Gary, I want the truth. I'll stand behind you but I have to know the truth. Is there any chance you're mixed up in this thing?"

"You mean did I—no. No. God, no."

In the doorway behind Gary his thirty-five-year-old

116

uncle Brad made a snorting sound. "You think the kid did it? Not a chance."

Tucker snapped at Gary, "You sure about that?"

Gary lifted his hand helplessly. "Yeah, Dad. Sure, I swear it."

Tucker felt the choking knot in his gut begin to loosen. He slumped backward in the chair. "All right, Gary. If you give me your word on that, it's good enough for me."

Brad pushed his way into the cubicle office, stood with his hands thrust on his hips beside his brother's desk. Gary was still standing numbly at the door. "*I* knew she was pregnant," said Brad. "I told Gary. I told him to stay the hell out of it."

Tucker said slowly, "Well, that was right. As long as he wasn't involved."

Gary asked, "What do you mean, 'killed'?"

"I don't know. Suffocating or something. Frank Sullivan got me out of the health spa, said he'd had a call from the St. Paul Police. He said they'd appreciate any help we could give them in the investigation."

Brad was counting off on his fingers. "August to April, that's eight months, right?" Nobody contradicted him. "So she probably did get knocked up at the lake. And if it wasn't Gary, who else was up there?"

The first random thought that sprang into Tucker's head was the husband of Gayle's own cousin, Walter Russell. But Brad continued: "Who was it turned up at your campsite without any invitation? Who hung around for two weeks mooching? Screwed up your vacation and you couldn't even get rid of him?"

With a mixed rush of relief and dread Ralph Tucker knew he was probably naming the guilty man: "Ziggy. Roy Danziger."

117

Ten

Now it was that fat-cheeked, red-haired doctor from the night before coming through the hospital-room door. He walked right up to the bed before he said, "Sister Angela. How are you feeling today?"

"All right. Much better." She didn't think she'd have to see this one again. All those dumb, pointless questions—she'd thought that part was finished.

"Very good." As he pulled a chair up to her bed he signaled with his head to the nurse by the window, who got up and walked out of the room. "And how is your frame of mind?"

"What?"

"What are you thinking about?"

Angela considered for a moment. "I'm very tired."

"That's quite understandable. I'm Dr. Heilbron, if you recall. Do you remember me?"

"Yes."

"We had a brief conversation last night. Do you recall where we talked?"

"Yes." It was probably those glasses with those fat red cheeks made him look so much like an owl. "Here, in this room."

"That's right. And do you recall what we talked about?"

Pause. "You made me do mathematics. And asked me about Grant's Tomb."

"That's right, Sister. I'd like to know if you've had any new recollections since we talked."

Oh, why couldn't they leave her alone? Just leave her alone. "What about?"

"About the events that brought you to the hospital."

"No." She stirred in the sheets, moved a little closer

toward him. "Doctor, that nurse—I don't want her sitting in here. Can you just ask her to go?"

"Well, Sister Angela, your special nurses have been ordered by Dr. Talbott, for your own benefit." She was beginning to shake her head when he said, "I'm afraid you'll have to talk to Dr. Talbott about that, when you see him."

"Oh." She subsided a little, turning her knees toward the window.

"You haven't had any new thoughts, any recollections since we talked?"

She shuffled her anxious thoughts. "No. When can I go home?"

He took a while answering, seemed to be counting the freckles on her face. Then he said, "I think, Sister, when you're ready to leave the surgical ward in a few days we'd like to transfer you for a while to Ward Five. So we can continue to aid and observe your recuperation."

She looked at him with wary alarm. She understood that he was saying that this strange punishment they were doing to her wasn't finished yet, would go on, would not stop yet. That they were not going to let her go home to St. Rose, where she would be safe. "No, no. I just want to go home to the convent."

He was talking very smoothly, very calmly. "I understand how you feel. But you must understand that you have undergone some very stressful, traumatic experiences. Physically, we expect you to mend quite rapidly. But your psychological recovery may take a little longer. That's why we'd like to keep you with us for a short while in Ward Five —a very pleasant place, I assure you, where you will have the privacy and tranquillity to complete your recovery."

Sweet Jesus, what were they doing to her? She shook her head vehemently. "No, please. I just want to go home. I'll be all right again as soon as I get home."

"Sister Angela, please trust us. The judgment of your physicians is that your best interests would be served by a

119

transfer to Ward Five. We feel you will need a little more time, a little more care."

In a bewildered cry: "I don't understand. Why won't you let me go home?"

He didn't answer her right away. Just watched her in his cold, owlish way. Then: "Sister Angela, you must understand that you have experienced some quite severe psychic traumas. Now, Ward Five is the hospital's psychiatric unit. A very private"—her head rolling back and forth on the pillow, her hands fluttering in protest—"very pleasant environment, I assure you. A place where you can feel at ease and secure, where we will be able to assist you in making your full recovery."

Psychia—crazy. They wanted to put her in a place for crazy people.

She stirred toward him again, tried to put her whole self into what she was saying, to make him understand, "But I don't need that, Doctor. I'm not—I don't need that. I'll be well again as soon as you let me go home." When he shook his head she said urgently, "I have to get back to my job. I have a whole school to run. And I never missed a day, ever, until yesterday."

He kept on talking in that flat voice, saying she should not trouble herself about this right now, they could discuss it again later. That she should get her rest, that he would be in to see her again soon. That Dr. Talbott would be in to see her shortly. That she should now just rest and collect herself, not burden her mind with concerns about the future.

She pulled at the sheet, barely listening, making no response. When he said he would see her again tomorrow she dismissed him with a curt nod.

She rolled back toward the closets as the wire-haired nurse came back into the room.

Let that man come back all he wanted, talk till he was blue in his fat face. She was sure of almost nothing except one thing: she would never, never let them send her to that Ward Five, that place for crazy people.

. . .

Meg Gavin made it out to the yellow brick Cambridge-port town hall in eleven minutes flat, and saw that the white station wagon of the WRCY-TV remote crew had beaten her to the parking lot. A couple of radio news cars too. Bastards. Meg whipped her Camaro into a parking slot and ran toward the basement entrance of the police department.

Inside the hall, chaos. A uniformed cop guarding the buzzered gate of the office waved her off: "Sorry. No entry."

Meg scanned the newsmen scattered down the hall, and decided to go for Kevin Corrigan. "Hey, Kev. What's going on?"

"Hey, Meg. I see your ear is still nicely tuned to the jungle drums."

"Nice, hell. You beat me to it. What are you getting out of them?"

"Nothing much. I got Chief Marwick on the phone and he pretty much confirmed the tip but wouldn't say anything more. I assume you got the same one we did."

"Yeah, I guess. A little mind-blowing, isn't it?"

"Well, us good ex-Catholics might say so."

"You think they're going to make a statement?"

Corrigan shrugged. "Who knows? I hope to hell they do —I need something on film to run besides a scenic view of this rat-ass P.D."

"Oh, tell me."

"I'll tell you one thing—there's a real tight lid on this thing right now."

Meg grunted, and drifted alertly down the basement corridor of the 1920's-vintage town hall. This place may have been adequate to the civic needs when it serviced a bunch of milk farmers, but now that the pastures were sliced up into expensive subdivisions, the Police Department had to share the basement with the Parks Department, the Water Department and the town library.

She noted in her reconnoiter that the Detective Division was shoehorned behind a door at the far end of the hall, sharing space with Juvenile and Identification. The wooden door was locked, but might be more easy to infiltrate, in due time, than the goddam buzzer gate.

Meg would have kicked in two weeks' salary to see and hear what was going on right now behind that locked door. Christ alive, this Cambridgeport was the kind of suburb where a big story was that a 3M vice-president got drunk and passed out in the golf-club locker room. And now these East Podunk cops were fielding the smoking potato of a murder like this. Wire-service stuff, national news for sure.

And all Meg Gavin could do about it was wait them out.

She wandered back to the vending machine in the hall by the main door and punched out a can of Diet Pepsi. Rationing it into small sips, she scanned the faces of the fortunate bastards hustling back and forth through the buzzer gate, in and out of the locked Detective Division door.

Damn, son of a bitch. She couldn't recognize a single one of them.

When the Tuckers walked into the Detective Unit of the Oak Creek P.D., Sergeant Frank Sullivan noted that both of them were dressed in blue work uniforms. Sullivan had already checked on the availability of the small interrogation room down the hall, so he took them to it without any small talk.

As soon as they sat around the folding metal table Ralph Tucker said, "Frank, my boy Gary gave me his word he didn't do it. And I believe him."

"Well, Gary, I'm pleased to hear that." Sullivan looked right at the big, good-looking kid, who ducked his head in embarrassment. "And if that's good enough for your father, it's good enough for me."

"Thanks, Frank," the elder Tucker said. "You just tell us what we can do to help."

"All right, Ralph, let's begin at the beginning. How did you people become acquainted with this Sister Flynn?"

"Why, it was up at summer camp in Menominee," Tucker said. "Tess and I took our trailer up there for four weeks last August, and we met these people in the trailer parked at the next campsite—Walter and Mary Alice Russell and their three little boys. Mary Alice had her cousin visiting with them, and that was Gayle Flynn. They were just vacation acquaintances, so to speak."

"What kind of people were they, Ralph?"

"Nicest folks you'd ever want to meet, Frank. Walter Russell is a substantial businessman with Frigidaire out in California—a very successful one, I can tell you that. So we had that in common. Exchanged our business cards and so forth. His wife, Mary Alice, was a real quiet, friendly woman, very pleasant. And those kids were pretty well-behaved."

"How about the cousin, Gayle?"

"Now there's another real nice person. Very bouncy and well-spoken. Marvelous with those kids. She's a pretty little bit of a thing, not even five feet tall. We understood she was a nursery-school teacher from someplace in Minnesota, and we found her good, pleasant company to be around. Matter of fact, we liked her so much we told her to consider herself a friend of the family, come down to visit us any time she liked. Since we knew her cousins lived way off there in California. And she did take us up on that invitation two times—last February, I think it was, and then again last weekend."

"You knew she was a nun?"

"Not then, when we met her. Matter of fact, we found out pretty early that Walter Russell was an ex-priest, had been for fourteen years. But it wasn't until, oh, I'd say about two weeks before we broke camp that it came out in conversation that Gayle was a nun herself." Tucker hunched forward over the table. "And I'll tell you something, Frank, I never would have suspected it. Never at all. The way she'd bounced around the beach in that skimpy bathing suit—well, of course now, she did have a pretty well-endowed figure. Nothing much she could do about that. But I did think, after I found out she was a nun, I did think that wasn't *my* idea of how a nun ought to go around dressed. Vacation or not."

"You spent a lot of time with these people, Ralph?"

"Oh, not so much. But you know how it goes. We took them for some rides in our powerboat—went for groceries once in the boat, if I recall rightly—and sat around with them some. Had sing-songs around their campfire, that kind of thing."

Sullivan was taking notes on a spiral pad as Tucker spoke. Now he looked up from under his glasses at the boy as he asked, "Gary, I guess you were up at the camp too?"

"Not much," said Gary.

"Gary and my brother Brad were home minding the shop," Tucker explained. "You understand, Frank, I'm trying to get used to this idea of retirement now, so Tess and I take some real vacations. But Gary only came up there two weekends."

"Okay," said Sullivan. "But when you were up there, Gary, you had occasion to have contact with this Gayle Flynn?"

Gary shrugged. "Well, sure, some. Mostly around the beach. We went swimming and waterskiing some. And the last weekend I was up I taught her to scuba dive."

"She was real enthusiastic about that," Ralph Tucker interjected. "She took to that scuba diving like a duck to water. And she made a point of telling me what a great teacher Gary was. I remember her saying a couple of times, 'Mr. Tucker, you have an exceptional boy there. A boy any father would be real proud of.' I recall that's just how she put it."

Just the way Tucker was talking, an unexpected question popped into Sullivan's mind. "How old, offhand, was this Gayle Flynn?"

Gary said, "I think twenty-nine, thirty. Somewhere like that."

Sullivan wrote the numbers on his pad. "And how old are you, Gary?"

"Twenty-one."

Sullivan cleared his throat, tapped the end of his ballpoint on the metal table. "Gary, I guess you understand that I have to ask this straight out, for the record. Did you at any time have sexual intercourse with this Gayle Flynn?"

Gary blushed and shook his head, like a dog coming out of water. "No. No."

Ralph Tucker pressed in closer to the metal table. "Frank, I may as well say this right now, save us all a lot of fishing around. I talked with Gary and Brad about what you said, and we figured out there was another fellow up there around our camp who may be the one you're looking for."

Now Sullivan's ballpoint was poised over the paper. "Who was that, Ralph?"

"Roy Danziger. Now, I should explain, Frank, this boy Roy used to work for me in the shop, and he turned up on his motorcycle a few days after Tess and I made camp. I never did figure out how he knew to find us up there. He sure didn't have any invitation, but he just dug in and hung around. For a little more than two weeks, I'd say. I suggested a couple of times that he move on but he's not one to take much of a hint, so he made himself right to home. He didn't leave until about five, six days before us."

"He stayed in your trailer?"

"No, no. He had a sleeping bag with him and he just bunked down in that, out by the beach."

"Out in the open?"

"That's right. I guess he considers himself some kind of rugged hippie-camper type."

"I see. How old is this Danziger?"

"About thirty." Tucker exchanged a glance with his son, who nodded. "Thirtyish, I'd say."

125

"And this Danziger had contact with Gayle Flynn?"

"I should say so. They were pretty good friends, spent quite some time together. That first weekend Gary was up, the three of them pretty much palled around together. But the rest of the time, when Gary wasn't around— Well now, I'd have to say I guess the two of them spent quite a piece of time together."

Sullivan was jotting notes again. "Ralph, would you say this Danziger had occasions when he could have sexual intercourse with Gayle Flynn?"

Tucker pulled himself more erect in the metal chair. "Well now, Frank, I have to tell you that idea is pretty shocking to me. Knocks me off my pins, so to speak. And I sure never thought anything of that sort was going on. But if you ask me did he have occasion, I would have to say yes. I guess he did."

That was the part Gary Tucker had been trying to push out of his head—her with Ziggy. Like that. Like you saw in the movies, her legs wrapped around his naked back, her making those sounds, doing those things. Doing them with Ziggy.

Annnhh, no. He didn't want to think about that.

Now the cop was asking, "Gary, did you have any knowledge of any sexual intercourse between these two persons?"

Gary made a shuddering gesture, pulling up his shoulders. "I dunno. I mean, I guess they could have. But I don't know anything about it." He paused. "I just know it wasn't me."

Now his dad was really rolling, telling the cop what a bad guy Ziggy was. How he'd given him the job in the shop because he was a Vietnam vet who used to pal around quite a lot with Brad, and how he'd been a good worker, all right, real good with his hands. But finally the Tuckers had to let him go because he was a bad moral influence in the shop— always bragging about his exploits with women, and his marijuana smoking. Even bragged about that time he came down with gonorrhea.

Geez, Ziggy wasn't really such a bad guy. And he could be real fun to be around. Gary always kind of figured his dad and Brad gave Ziggy the can mainly because they thought he might maybe lead their little boy Gary astray. Which was such a dumb idea. Gary just thought Ziggy was fun to have around.

His dad didn't know the half of it anyway—like the time Ziggy was arrested down in Texas. But that still didn't make him such a bad guy. And here was this cop writing down like crazy about the girls and the grass and that time with the clap. Gary knew that was just what he wanted to hear—his father's friend, from this nice, clean little town.

Gary was listening to them in a kind of brownout. At least they weren't coming after him, figuring this must all be his fault just because Gayle was his girl friend.

Kind of a girl friend, anyway. God, he'd never for a minute figured it could end up like this.

Now the cop was asking didn't they know Gayle Flynn was pregnant when she came down to visit last weekend. Gary could feel his father looking at him, but he just stared down at the table. His father said, "Well now, Frank, we sure noticed something must be wrong there. I said myself to Tess, 'If that was anyone else but a nun, I'd say that girl must be pregnant.' But her being a nun and all, I figured it must be a tumor, something like that. And anyway it didn't seem to be any of our business."

Gary hoped to hell they weren't going to ask him about that. He hadn't even figured it out himself, and he sure didn't want to think about it now, like this, in front of these two.

The cop let it go. Now his father was saying, "I will say, Frank, I didn't consider Roy Danziger a good influence to have around anyone who was considered a friend of the family. And up there at the lake I wondered some about

127

whether a fine person like I considered Sister Gayle to be should be spending so much time with a fellow like Roy Danziger. I did wonder some about that, Frank. But I figured, well, she's a grown woman, a teacher and all. She must know what she's doing."

The cop said, "Okay, Ralph. Do you have an address, a phone number for this guy?"

"Well now, I don't. You understand, he's kind of a drifter type, never seems to have a phone. We haven't seen hide nor hair of him since last summer—and good riddance to him, I say."

Gary Tucker finally volunteered a statement. He said, "I hear Ziggy might be back at his old job at Midwest Mutual."

There were two periodically necessary things that Meg Gavin genuinely loathed to do—scrub bathroom fixtures, and sit out a big, breaking story. Right now, as she hung around the town hall basement smoking too many cigarettes, she was consumed with jealousy for cops. Dumb fucking bastards, most of them, flat in a lot of ways besides their feet. And right now they were neck-deep into this case with all their magical official clout, asking all the questions, getting all the answers, finding out anything and everything they cared to know.

While she was left to stand around and wait, jotting compulsive notes on irrelevant details like that poster on the community bulletin board: "BETTER SAFE THAN SORRY. Learn about Fire Prevention *Today.*"

Sometimes—most often at moments like these—Meg thought she might have missed her true calling. Christ alive, she would've made one hell of a good detective.

One of the radio newsmen passed along a tip that the Ramsey County D.A. and the Cambridgeport police chief were supposed to be inside, got in through a back door. "Big fucking deal," Meg muttered to Kevin Corrigan when he drifted down the hall to bum a Virginia Slims menthol from her pack. "Come on, Kev, how can they *not* make a statement?"

"Well, they're gonna have to, sooner or later. But I think they'll stall it as long as they possibly can."

Suddenly, finally, Meg spotted someone she knew— Nick Scotti, the D.A.'s oddball chief investigator, her periodic drinking companion at the Blind Justice Bar, who was barging out the buzzered gate heading for the soft-drink machine. Meg reached him in six long strides. "Hey Nick, what's coming down?"

"Hi, Meg." Scotti dropped a quarter into the machine, punched out a Fanta Orange. "Sorry, I got nothing to say."

"I understand Mark Abrams is in there. Is he going to make a statement?"

"I dunno." Scotti popped the metal tab and dropped it into the can as he walked back to the gate. "Ask him."

Meg Gavin was still rolling questions at him when he dodged her at the gate. Scotti walked into Chief Marwick's cramped inner office, where Andy DaSilva was remarking to Abrams, Marwick and Vance about the amazing change of pace in the place since they started the interrogations of the nuns that morning.

Abrams made a slight grimace. "Yeah, well, somebody got the good word out to the press. Which cuts down our lead time on this thing. Did you get anything significant out of the sisters?"

As Abrams was talking, Scotti drained the Fanta can, crumpled it and aimed it for a wastebasket. "You got a hanky budget on this case, boss?" he asked.

DaSilva smiled slightly. "Nick and me just lost our handkerchiefs. Sister Julia borrowed mine and Sister Dorothy took Nick's."

Abrams asked dryly, "Anything else?"

"Well, there's not much you didn't hear last night." DaSilva was consulting the notes he had scribbled on his

129

yellow pad. "They pretty much agree she was especially withdrawn—'aloof,' one of them called it—in the last few months. They say the other nuns made efforts to draw her back into the group, but she pretty much stayed by herself, in her room."

Marwick tapped the desk with his pipe cleaner. "Didn't anybody wonder why that was?"

"Well, apparently that wasn't all that unusual for her," DaSilva said. "Sister Claudine said she'd known her for about twelve or fourteen years, since she was her superior at St. Basil's school. She said Sister Angela was always real good at her job but 'never divulging of herself.' Here's another quote—'I never felt I got below Angela's surface. Even living with her all those years I never felt I knew the real person.' She said Sister Angela 'would be friendly and smiling. Never surly or sour. But her conversation was all surface.' And Sister Julia said something about her smile." DaSilva was flipping the pages now, scanning his own scrawl. "Oh yeah, here it is—'When she came out of her room her external friendliness was like a mask she put on. You wouldn't know what she was really thinking.' "

Scotti prompted: "Don't forget that stuff about the car."

"Oh, yeah. Sister Julia said Sister Angela made inconsiderate, surprising demands on other people, other nuns. Like she didn't know how to drive, and sometimes she arranged for one of them to drive her someplace without consulting the other nuns. Sister Julia found that"—DaSilva consulted his notes—" 'insensitive.' "

Abrams was frowning intently, rolling his lit cigarette between his fingers. "Is that supposed to be why none of them picked up on the pregnancy?"

"You got it, boss." Nick Scotti was pacing the carpet in this small office, itching, belatedly, to get inside this case. "I'm telling you, those nuns just plain didn't *like* her. That's why nobody saw her belly. They thought she was a snob, high and mighty, hoity-toity—the *principal* of the Benedictine Kindergarten School." He said that last phrase in an arch, rising falsetto.

"Well, it's a little more complicated than that," DaSilva said mildly. "Apparently the nuns have their own kind of system for dealing with something like a medical problem. It's kind of complicated, but apparently the way it worked, different nuns in the house mentioned something to Sister Julia and Sister Claudine about Sister Angela's condition, about how they were worried about her. So Julia and Claudine both talked to a nun in the Motherhouse who's apparently Sister Angela's superior at the nursery school, Sister Mary Christopher. And Mary Christopher about three weeks ago saw Angela at a regular school business meeting and asked her permission afterward to talk to her about a personal matter."

"Asked her *permission?*" said Tim Vance.

"Yeah, apparently. And then she brought up the medical stuff. I think she said—yeah, here it is, according to Sister Claudine—'the weight you've put on is all in one place. And your walk is not the same.' And the upshot was Sister Angela promised her she would see a doctor. So Mary Christopher reported back to Sister Julia and Sister Claudine. She said they'd raised the question with Sister Angela, and that was as far as they could go."

"Yeah, kid you not," said Scotti. "That's what they said."

"My God," said Vance. "Didn't any of them talk to the nun herself?"

"I guess not. Except Mary Christopher," said DaSilva. "But then on Holy Thursday night—that's about ten days ago—Sister Angela came down for the evening Mass wearing a coat and skirt. Sister Claudine said she hadn't seen her out of pants in she didn't know how long, and she was real shocked when she saw her legs so swollen and discolored."

"Like piano legs," Scotti interjected.

"Well, she made a gesture like that. So right then she

131

asked Sister Angela directly about it, and Sister Angela said she'd turned her ankle. So Sister Claudine said—here's the quote—'This is not a turned ankle. You have to get to a doctor.' And Sister Angela said she had gone, to her mother's doctor, and he'd said she was okay. But just the way she said it, Sister Claudine didn't believe her. So she decided to speak to Sister Mary Christopher again about it. But then before she got the chance this all happened."

"Jesus H. Christ. It sounds like the Polish Army," Marwick remarked.

Tim Vance was staring blankly at Andy DaSilva. "You're telling me not one of them ever asked this woman what the hell was going on, what that big lump in her belly was?"

"I guess not, except for what I told you," DaSilva said mildly. "Apparently that's the way the nuns handle what they consider are personal problems."

Mark Abrams's expression had darkened. Now he said quietly, "So, in effect, nobody ever asked her if she was pregnant, if they could help her out. Well, I guess maybe that explains one whole hell of a lot."

"And it was *Holy Thursday,*" Nick Scotti pointed out. "She came down those convent stairs like fucking Judas Iscariot, waving her sick legs in front of those other nuns. I'm telling you, she's a fucking murderess."

Scotti had distinct liabilities in the area of tact, which he was presently demonstrating. D.A. Abrams had inherited him as an investigator from the previous political administration, and kept him on in the job because he had quickly learned that, for all his shortfalls in social nicety, Nick Scotti also had an intuitive brilliance, a pure nose for detection, that Abrams had never seen matched. But there were times when Scotti overstepped, and this was one.

Abrams snapped angrily, "Knock it off, Nick. I expect you to give this case, like any other, the total professional objectivity it requires." He consulted the scrap of paper on which he was trying to keep track of this harassing day.

"Okay, Nick, Andy—we've got the gynecologist, Dr. Talbott, coming in to give a statement around one P.M. I'd like you two to handle that."

"Fine. No problem," said DaSilva.

"The good doctor is not enthusiastic about being debriefed, so you may not get much out of him. But give it your best shot. Then I'd like you to get over to the St. Rose convent to interrogate the other nuns when they get home from their teaching jobs. That should be around three P.M." Abrams leaned back in his chair, loosened his tie. "If you get a chance to grab lunch in between you're luckier than us."

Angela wasn't expecting to see Sister Philomena coming through the door. But wasn't surprised either. After all the fuss and trouble she'd caused yesterday.

Philomena gripped her hand so hard it almost hurt, and said, "Angela, my dear. How are you feeling?"

Angela murmured that she was better, oh, much better. She was looking past Philomena at the big man in the rumpled suit who had followed her into the room, standing nervously by the door. A strange man she had never seen before. Why would Sister Philomena bring a strange man in here where he could see her right in bed, in this hospital nightgown?

"The doctors tell me the same thing," Philomena said firmly. "They're very pleased with your excellent progress, which of course we're all most gratified to hear."

The doctors. Oh, she hoped they hadn't mentioned anything to Sister Philomena about that Ward Five place. She didn't want Philomena to have to worry about anything like that, because Angela certainly wasn't going to go there.

"Sister Philomena, I'm so sorry for all the bother I made." Her voice came out more thin and tremulous than she intended. "I never meant to cause the sisters any trouble."

"I know, my dear. I know." Philomena squeezed her

133

dry, limp hand. "We're just very glad that you're coming through this so well. Now we just want you to concentrate on getting strong, getting better."

"Oh, I will. I'll be back to work very soon." She looked again at the big man by the door.

Following her glance, Philomena said, "Angela dear, I'd like you to meet Mr. Haverty. Mr. Benjamin Haverty."

The big man moved up to the foot of the bed and made an awkward sort of bow. "I'm very pleased to meet you, Sister Angela," he said in a surprisingly soft voice. Angela pulled the nightgown up tighter around her neck. "I've heard a good deal about your excellent work at Benedictine Kindergarten. I was wondering if you perhaps know my sister, Sister Mary Margaret? She's a Holy Name nun who works somewhat in the same field."

Angela shook her head, her green eyes large with alarm. "No. I don't know her," she whispered.

"Ah well, I thought perhaps you might." Haverty paused. "And I believe my niece, Susan Dougherty, has been a pupil at Benedictine Kindergarten."

Susan Dougherty. Susan Dougherty. "Oh, yes. I remember Susan. A lovely intelligent child. She wasn't in my class, but I remember her."

Haverty bobbled his head in acknowledgment of the compliment. "Thank you, Sister Angela. The family happens to share your opinion, but it's nice to hear that confirmed by an expert."

"Susan must be about—seven, now?"

"Yes, she's in second grade at St. Michael's. Doing very well, thanks to her excellent start at Benedictine."

Angela didn't understand. What was this strange man doing in her hospital room, making polite talk about a child she hardly knew? She looked at Philomena, appealing mutely for deliverance.

Philomena said firmly, "Angela dear, Mr. Haverty is an attorney. A very excellent attorney. I wanted you to meet him, because I feel he is going to be a good friend and an excellent guide to yourself and to all of us in this affair."

She flinched when she heard the word "attorney," shrank back into her pillow. "No, please."

Philomena reached out for her shoulder, squeezed it firmly. "Now, Angela, listen to me. I don't want you to concern yourself about these things right now. I want you to concentrate all your energies on your rapid recuperation."

"But I don't understand," she whispered. "Why would I need an attorney?"

That grip so strong. Voice so commanding: "Now, Angela, will you do what I ask? Will you trust my judgment in this?"

Impossible to say no. So she nodded her head, a very slight gesture.

Philomena was saying she would come back to see her very soon; now she just wanted Angela to rest. Angela kept her eyes down on the blanket. She did not want to look again at the big man.

When they left the room she curled on her left side, pulling the sheet up around her face.

Sweet Mother of God. Make them stop.

Eleven

Nick Scotti realized as he eyed the gynecologist on the other side of DaSilva's desk that in the ten years he'd been doing interrogations he'd never seen a contrast starker than this—first the whispering, sniveling nuns. Now this fuck-you doctor.

Well, fuck *him.* Fuck all those fathead doctors, all of

them figuring they were second in line to God, with shit that never stunk.

But this one here had stepped over the line. Played God right down to the hospital morgue, sending the nuns home to cart off the body, never calling in the cops. Nick Scotti knew there was a damn good obstruction-of-justice case to be made against this poker-ass doctor sitting all steamed across the desk, if anyone running this case had the guts to initiate it.

Which they did not. Scotti was nothing if not a realist, and he knew nobody on this case was going to take on the doctor. Bad enough they had to take on the nun.

Then the least they could do was peel Talbott right now in this interrogation, like a ripe banana. Scotti, for one, would be happy to volunteer for the job.

Fucking wimp Andy DaSilva, always so polite, so by-the-books. If Scotti was doing this interrogation the goddam doctor wouldn't get out of this room before he admitted he'd been a partner to an attempted cover-up of a murder that might very well have been pulled off, except the nun who committed it did such a gross job in the first place.

Unfortunately, Scotti's assignment right now wasn't interrogating. His job was to stenotype the technical medical terminology that Talbott was machine-gunning across the desk, almost like he was defying them to take it in, let alone keep up.

Dr. Keith Talbott went through the medical aspects of the treatment given to Sister Angela Flynn in the Emergency Department of Parkhurst Hospital as if he were delivering a lecture to OB-GYN residents.

He had been brought up with a strict reverence for the rules, for the system. Had never really questioned the rightness of that reverence until he finally quit the seminary. Much of that early guiding principle had been shaken, bruised, by the unpredictable turns that later came into his life.

But at bottom he still wanted to believe. Believe that the system would somehow deal mercifully and wisely with this broken woman.

The question that bedeviled him now was, how much was that wish rooted in his own cowardice? Because Keith Talbott knew that Sister Angela Flynn was hovering now on the brink of irretrievable madness. He'd seen her, felt her, hanging there. He'd given everything that was in him to help her, and it had come down to nothing. Worse than nothing.

So he'd come here to this police station, and he was cooperating. But nothing in what he saw or heard here reassured him that he had made the right decision.

Now the balding, soft-faced district attorney was saying, "Did you speak to Sister Angela after the surgery?"

"Yes."

"What did you say to her?"

"I told her we had found the problem, and asked if there was anything she wished to discuss."

"What did she answer?"

"She said no. She still didn't remember much of the day, except that she was dazed, bleeding heavily and passing clots."

"Did you find that a credible answer?"

Keith Talbott looked at the earnest little man across the desk. So it would come down to that question. And other questions like it.

That old reflex toward blind faith had tripped him one more time. He had let himself hope that the system could somehow save her. But he realized as he looked across the desk that the system was made up of little men like this one, men even more fallible than himself. Men who would not, could not, for the life of them understand.

"Yes," Keith Talbott said finally. "I found that a credible answer."

137

Around 1:30 Meg Gavin decided she had had it, *had it* with patrolling this miserable hall. She called her city editor from the pay phone and said she was going to try for some color background, anyway, over at St. Rose Convent.

She was backing distractedly out of the parking slot when she heard the crunch of metal on metal. "Damn!" She eased the Camaro forward and stepped out to find a brown BMW behind her car, with an apparently fresh dent in its right front fender.

The driver made no move to get out, so Meg walked over to his side of the car. He got out then, a tall, bony, lean-built guy in corduroys and an old tweed jacket who was for some reason smiling. Meg said with what she hoped was disarming charm, "I seem to have hit you."

He walked around and looked at his fender, still smiling. "It's completely my fault," Meg went on. "I obviously wasn't looking. But hey, I'm in a real rush to get somewhere." She fished in her blue suede shoulder bag for her wallet, pulled out a business card and scribbled her home phone number on it. "This is where you can reach me. Business or otherwise. I'm very sorry, it's obviously my fault. But I have to go. Okay with you?"

The BMW man was still looking at the dent, still smiling. "Should I say no?"

"I hope not, because my business is very pressing." Meg was acutely aware that half the cops, not to mention the prosecutors, in this city were holed up right that moment in the town hall police station. "And I promise to fix your car. Get it fixed. Okay?"

He moved very slow, very cocksure. Despite the graying temples and fuzzy black hair, he wasn't bad-looking, if you liked the type. Meg didn't. He took her business card and fished his own from the ratty tweed jacket. "That sounds fair enough. I'll get in touch with you, Meg Gavin."

She glanced at the card he handed her—Dewey Wald,

architect. "Thanks, Dewey Wald. You're a prince among men."

She ran to the Camaro and was shifting back into reverse when she noticed he was still parked behind her, fingering his kinky hair as he stared in her direction. She opened the car door and called out, "You want to try for two?"

Wald lifted his hand in a wave of acknowledgment and drove out of the way.

The four-story red-brick convent at 205 Windsor Avenue was even more startling than she expected—1930's ecclesiastical style, ugly and obtrusive as sin. It was set amid gracefully aging suburban houses with big trees in the manicured front yards, houses that *looked* expensive, but Meg figured that any piece of real estate located across the street from that treeless, lifeless parish complex had to sell for a discount on the open market. On grounds of pure aesthetics, St. Rose of Lima had to be a drag on the neighborhood property values.

The complex was laid out like a half-block football field: convent filling one end zone, stone-faced church across the other. The midfield was made up of the ugly red-brick parochial school, the ugly red-brick rectory and a huge black-topped parking lot.

She circled the convent on foot by way of the parking lot, glancing embarrassedly at the blank windows and drawn curtains. If there was one thing Meg despised about her job, it was this part of it—invading privacies, intruding on raw pain. Unfortunately, it went with the territory—mikes thrust into the faces of surviving highway victims, strobes freezing frenzies of grief. It went with the job, but that didn't mean she had to like it. Or trust it.

Still, nothing ventured, nothing gained. She rang the doorbell under the cement lintel poured into the shape of a plain cross, with the numbers 205 nailed into the brickwork above the bell.

The door was opened, narrowly, by a tall, hefty guy with heavy glasses and a skinny striped tie. He looked like the chairman of the parish mortgage committee, but Meg thought she vaguely recalled seeing him around the D.A.'s office. She said cheerfully, with firmness but no real hope, "Good afternoon. I have an appointment with the Mother Superior."

This guy had her number in one glance. Said, "Sorry, she's not available. This is private property you're standing on. If you don't immediately leave—"

Meg lifted her hand, a peacemaking gesture. "Okay, Officer, thanks. Nothing personal. You understand."

The Flynn family—Ed, his wife Annette and his soft-spoken bachelor brother Dan—spent most of the day keeping vigil in a glassed-in sunporch on the hospital's surgical ward, West Wing Three. Around 2:15 they were joined by their brother Tom and mother, Theresa, who had just flown in from Arizona.

They exchanged handshakes, stiff embraces. "Didn't expect you so soon, Tom," Ed said.

"Yeah, well. We made good connections."

"Mom, how are you doing?" Ed asked.

Theresa Flynn was a thin, worn, gray-toned woman who looked older than her sixty-four years. Her mouth worked silently for a moment before she said, "I'm all right. How is Gayle?"

"Pretty good, pretty good. The doctor's coming in to talk with us soon."

Theresa Flynn nodded and sank into a chair like a collapsing marionette, her bony hands clutching her purse. It seemed to Ed she had aged ten years in the few weeks since he had last seen her.

When Dr. Heilbron came in to confer with the brothers, Theresa Flynn got up and, moving slowly, as if in pain, went to the far end of the porch, where she would not have to partake in the conversation. Heilbron filled the men in on Sister Angela's present psychological status, and asked several questions about her customary moods, her usual behavior patterns. After one angry outburst from Ed—"You mean to tell me she doesn't remember *anything* about it?"—Dan handled most of the questions.

It was decided that Ed and Dan, the two brothers who lived in St. Paul, should talk to Sister Angela. "You understand, I don't want you to mention any baby. I don't want you to indicate any special alarm," said Heilbron.

"Right. Got it," said Dan.

"What I'd especially like to know is whether she appears normal to you. Whether her mood is something you have noted in her at other times."

"Okay, okay. Can we see her now?" asked Ed.

When Angela saw her two brothers walking in the hospital room door her face crinkled in dismay. "Oh, Dan. Ed. I told Julia not to call you until I was home and all better."

"Well, hey." Dan Flynn walked up to the bed, holding out a paper-wrapped cone of flowers. "I'm sure glad she did. I wouldn't want to miss this chance to visit." He handed the flowers to her, awkwardly, and leaned down to kiss her cheek.

"Thanks, Dan, that's very nice," she said faintly, dropping the paper cone on the blanket. "I just didn't want to have you all worried for nothing."

"Hey, what's family for, if not when you're in the hospital," said Dan.

"Absolutely," Ed agreed, moving up to dispense his stiff-necked kiss.

The nurse who was sitting by the window came up to the bed, picked up the flowers and peeled back the paper wrapping. "Oh, red roses. Aren't they beautiful, Sister?"

"Yes. Very nice."

"Now why don't I find a vase for them before they start to wilt."

"All right. Thanks."

Ed was standing very straight beside the bed, his fists jammed into his jacket pockets. Dan sat on the edge of the mattress, slapping his hands together. "So—how're you feeling?"

"Much better. I'll be home soon."

"Well now, don't rush it," said Dan. "We hear you had a pretty rough time of it."

"Oh, it wasn't so bad." Angela twisted the gold ring on her left hand. "You won't have to tell Mother about it, will you? Because I'm all right. I'll be back home by the time she gets back from Arizona."

"Oh, hey, don't worry yourself about that," said Dan. "We just want you to get on your feet again and get well."

"Did you talk to Dr. Talbott?"

"We talked to some doctor—I can't remember his name. He said you're making real good progress."

"Oh, yes, I am. You know how healthy I always am. So don't pay any attention if they tell you—" She dropped that thought, helplessly. "I'm fine, I'll be home soon."

Dan said, "Hey, we don't want to tire you out. Maybe we should go, come back tomorrow."

"No, I'm not tired." Then, weakly: "How's your job going?"

"Oh, fine, fine. A lot better than it was. Not so much overtime." Dan slapped his hands together. "So when you get out of here we can spend a lot more time together. Take in some movies, go out to dinner."

Angela smiled faintly. "That would be nice."

"Well, we'll do it. I'm just realizing, I don't see near as much of you as I'd like."

"That's right," Ed spoke up. "And we'll have you out to the house. As soon as you're up and around." He

142

paused. "Is there anything we can get you? Anything you need?"

"No thanks."

"Maybe some books? How about some books?"

"That's okay. I don't feel much like reading yet."

"Okay. But anything you think of, anything you need, you just give a holler." Ed went on in a slightly louder voice, "I'd like to think you could come to the family anytime. If you had any problems."

"Well, sure, I would. But I don't."

Dan slapped his hands together again. Funny, Angela had never noticed him doing that before. "Hey listen, Gayle, I think we better get out of here. Let you get some rest. But I'll be back to see you again real soon."

As he bent to administer the ritual kiss Angela murmured, "Thanks for coming, Dan. And for the flowers. You won't bother Mother about this, will you?"

"Hey, don't you worry. You just take care of yourself, Gayle. We all care a whole lot about you."

Ed's kiss was like a flicking of straw across her forehead. Angela thanked them again for coming, but she wasn't sorry to see them go.

Especially Ed. He seemed somehow to be angry with her.

Why would Ed be angry with her?

Dr. Heilbron was waiting for them in the sunroom at the end of the hall. As they came through the door Theresa Flynn looked up. "Mom, she's all right. She's going to be all right," said Ed.

Theresa turned her head away, looked back out through the glassed-in porch window.

When Heilbron asked how she seemed, Dan said, "Uptight."

"Not her usual mood?"

"No, for sure. She's usually very—outgoing. Kind of

143

perky, like. Now she's like—all washed out. Her eyes seem kind of glassy. The way she kept looking away—it was half like we weren't there, almost."

"Look, she's been through hell. What do you expect?" Ed asked angrily. "What do you want from us, anyway?"

Rather primly, Heilbron explained that the reason he was making these inquiries was to facilitate his judgment about her psychological status. They must appreciate that when he did not become involved in treating a patient before the patient was already in an acute stage of reaction, it was sometimes difficult to ascertain exactly which psychiatric diagnosis might apply. That was the reason he was seeking this information from them. "Yes, sure, Doctor, we understand," said Dan. "Only I don't know what to say, exactly. She's usually all—cheerful. Smiles a lot. Now she doesn't seem to want to talk."

"She seemed withdrawn to you?"

"You could say so, yes."

Ed said testily, "Considering what she's been through, what's so crazy about that?"

Heilbron ignored the remark, and asked Dan, "But she carried on a fairly normal, logical conversation?"

"She made sense, if that's what you mean."

Heilbron thanked them for their input and said they had been a considerable help. After he left the room, Tom, the Arizona brother, asked quietly, "So?"

"Jesus. I don't know," Ed muttered. He was looking across the room at the drawn, elderly woman staring out the porch window.

"Hey, give her a few days," said Dan. "She's going to pull out of this fine."

Her, maybe, Ed Flynn thought as he walked over to his mother. *But what about us?*

Julia spent most of the day in the small office off the community room, rearranging schedules, making notifications, and so forth. State Police Inspector Nevelson and several plainclothes Cambridgeport policemen stayed out in the front hall. At first Julia resented their presence as an offensive intrusion on the convent routine—not that this dreadful day could be considered routine.

But after the news reports mentioning the St. Rose convent went out over the local radio, Julia began to appreciate their usefulness. The phone rang almost constantly. The policemen answered it, and only occasionally passed along the calls to Julia. Inspector Nevelson would knock at the office door, say, "Sorry to bother you, Sister, but there's a Joseph Gurso asking for you by name. Says he's from the parish council."

Julia would frown, try to think. "Gurso? I don't know any Joseph Gurso."

"Okay, Sister. Sorry to disturb you." And he would not knock again until there was another call that sounded legitimate enough to check out.

The cars were beginning to come, too—all different kinds of cars, driving slowly in front of the convent, then circling for another look. Julia had made sure all the front curtains were drawn, but through the white net veiling the office window she could see people staring from the cars, snatching for a glimpse of something—anything—inside the convent. And once when she was walking by the window she saw Inspector Nevelson and another policeman escorting some little man with cameras around his neck across the convent lawn. They walked him so fast, each of them gripping one of his elbows, that his feet barely skimmed the ground.

So by the time DaSilva and Scotti came to interview the other nuns around 2:30 Julia realized that these men—some of them, at least—were there more as protectors than intruders. And she knew enough, now, to be grateful for that.

She suggested that the two interrogators use the small office again, and DaSilva agreed. Other policemen were still coming in and out of the house, carrying different things—boxes, bags. Julia tried to ignore them, since that was not her area of responsibility.

She spent most of the next few hours upstairs, talking to the various nuns as they came in and out of the interrogation room, reassuring them that they were doing the right thing in speaking frankly to these police investigators. Reassuring them that it was quite natural, perfectly understandable, to react emotionally to that unfamiliar experience. They must not feel, Julia told them over and over, one by one, that their behavior was in any way incorrect.

Around 5:30 she decided there was no more reason to put off what she had been trying to get to all day—a visit to Angela. Inspector Nevelson suggested that he take her down to the hospital in an unmarked police car, and he drove the black car around to the kitchen door, so none of those people out front could see Julia slip into the passenger seat.

He spoke very little on the way to the hospital, and Julia was grateful for that silence. She was beginning to see that in their own way these men were trying to be sympathetic, sensitive, to this situation.

Inspector Nevelson parked the car at a back door of the hospital—the delivery entrance, Julia supposed from the meat truck parked beside them—and guided her briskly through the back halls, into an elevator, up to the third floor, without anyone stopping to ask them questions. One more thing to be thankful for.

Julia waited in the hallway while the inspector checked with the nurses at the desk. Then he said, "It's okay, Sister." He pointed to a door just down the hall. "You can go right in."

Julia fixed her face into a smile as she tapped at the door of Room 308. When no one answered she pushed it open. Angela was lying in the bed, still very pale and wan, with one tube still running into her arm. She looked up and said faintly, "Oh, Julia."

"Angela, dear," Julia said cheerfully. Some nurse got up and left the room as she walked over to the bed. "You're looking *so* much better." Julia wasn't sure if it was right to kiss her but when she reached the bed she didn't know what else to do, so she leaned down and touched her cheek to Angela's. It felt hot and dry.

"I meant to come see you earlier," Julia said, "but I was so busy I just never got the chance." She choked up for a moment when she realized what a cruel echo those words were of what she'd told Angela just yesterday.

But Angela didn't seem to notice. "That's all right, it's nice of you to come."

She *did* look better than last night, but still so pale—pale and remote. Blanked out, almost.

"Of course I was coming. I told you I would, and anyway I wanted to see how you're doing."

"Oh, I'm much better. I'll be back to work soon."

Julia hadn't known what to expect before she got into the room. But now that she was here she was remembering the closeness, the extraordinary feeling she'd had for Angela the night—oh, was it only one night, amazing to think—before.

She reached again for that closeness, but it wasn't there. So much had happened; so many other people in the way. So Julia said, "Everybody in the house sends a big hello. They're all so concerned about you, and they want you to know they're remembering you in their prayers."

"Well, thanks. Tell them I'm fine, I'll be home soon." Angela wasn't feeling the closeness either. Julia could tell from the way she looked down at the blanket, so far away—almost like she was turned inside herself.

"I can *tell* that you're fine." The Good Lord would forgive her that one small lie. "And I'm sure you're going to be all better soon."

147

"But I promised you I'd be home today. I hate to miss so many days of school. Did they get somebody to sub for me?"

"Oh, sure, no problem. Sophia came in from St. Basil's."

Angela smiled faintly. "Oh, poor Sophie. She said last year she never wanted to see another set of Macomber rods in her whole life."

"Oh, that was last year. Now she's so sick of fourth grade, she's really tickled to get a chance to be back with the little ones for a while."

"Well, tell her I'll be back real soon."

Lord, this was hard. They'd told her all the things not to say, but they hadn't told her what *to* say. "Now, you just take your time. I think Sophie won't mind at all filling in for as long as it takes you to get all better."

Angela flicked a glance at Julia's face. "You look tired, Julie. Did the kids give you a hard day?"

Julia laughed; it came out a harsh, artificial sound. "Oh, not so bad. You know how it goes—some days are easier than others."

Angela was tracing a line with her thumbnail along the starched sheet. She was frowning, seemed to be thinking, reaching. Softly: "Julie, did you talk to the doctors?"

"No, not today. But I understand from Sister Philomena that they're very pleased with how well you're doing. Angela, is there anything you need from home? Like your hairbrush, or anything?"

"No thanks. I won't be here that long." The frown was very intent now. "Julie, did they say anything to you? About what happened yesterday?"

No, no, this was not her part. Her part was yesterday and that was already too much, too much. Julia's controls were very stretched and bruised, and she could feel them slipping again now, slipping at the one time she could not let them go. She made herself laugh again: a harsh, coughing sound. "Oh, nothing special," she said.

Before Angela could speak again, Julia patted her arm. "Listen, Angela, I'd better go now." It was up to the doctors, now, to help her if they could—it was out of Julia's hands, past her responsibility. "They're probably all waiting dinner for me. But I'll be back to see you again very soon."

When Angela looked right at her, the pain and confusion in her eyes was almost more than Julia could bear to see. Angela said, "Don't feel you have to come, Julie. I know you're awfully busy. And I'll be home soon anyway."

"Of course you will." She leaned over and kissed Angela's forehead; it didn't feel so strange this time. "But I *want* to come. Take care of yourself, Angela."

"Sure, I will."

"And I'll tell everybody you said hello."

As Julia walked dazedly to the elevator with Inspector Nevelson she realized what was missing.

Angela wasn't crying. Didn't look like she had *been* crying. All the rest of them weeping and sobbing in front of those strange men like they never had in their lives before, so guilty and tormented.

And Angela wasn't crying.

Twelve

Ralph Tucker decided they might as well have Brad and his wife, Evie, over to the house for dinner that night to talk all this out. Personally, Ralph would have preferred to keep it from the women, but Frank Sullivan had told him that probably wouldn't work out.

Brad started in as soon as he walked through the front

149

door. "So what you think about your little boy now, Tess? What you think about this mess he's got himself into?"

"Oh, that poor girl. That poor Gayle," said Tess. "I still can't believe any of this really happened."

"You better believe it, Tess," said Brad. "You got a look at that belly good as we did last weekend. What'd you think that was, a bowling ball in her pocket?"

The bald brutality of that question confused Tess; she looked helplessly at her husband. Ralph said irritatedly, "As a matter of fact, Tess and I did talk some about that. But Gayle being a nun and all, I figured it must be something else."

Brad made a snorting sound. "What's so different about a nun? Those penguins are just like anybody else, they sweat on Sundays too."

Seventeen-year-old Beverly was sitting with her legs curled under her on the brown flowered couch, her plain face uncharacteristically animated. "Gee, I sure had no idea. I mean, Gayle acted just like she always did. So bouncy and fun. When we went out shopping and she bought that blouse we had a lot of fun. I can't believe she just went home and *killed* her *baby*."

"Well, if she did that, she obviously wasn't right in the head," Ralph said. "She couldn't be, to do a thing like that. Not a nice, well-bred girl like that. Somebody who was so good with little children. You remember how she was up at the lake with her cousin's kids?"

"She was wonderful with those children," Tess said firmly. "I can't help but feel this is all some terrible mistake."

"Na, it's no mistake," said Brad. "You don't get the St. Paul cops coming after your little boy on some mistake." Brad looked at Gary, who was sitting impassively in a recliner chair, staring at the shag rug. "How about you, golden boy? Let's hear it from the peanut gallery."

Gary looked up. "Oh, I'm just thinking."

"About what?"

In fact he was thinking about the hot, sunny afternoon he'd taught Gayle Flynn how to scuba dive. She'd caught on to the fundamentals pretty quick, so he'd strapped the extra tank to her back and put some fins on her little feet and taken her down into the water.

She did so good at it that they swam pretty far out, Gary holding her hand. The sun was coming right down into the water, lighting up the weeds and rocks and fishes. Gary would point out things to her with his free hand and she'd nod, her red hair waving around her face mask. Even with all the gear she was wearing she'd looked so pretty, almost like something in a dream, floating in the green water.

When they swam back into the shallows she'd stood up and popped off the mask, spat out the mouthpiece. She was so happy, so excited. Geez, she was lit up like the goddam sun. And she'd hugged him right there in the shallows. Gary still remembered the feel of her wet arms around his neck, her big boobs squashed up against his chest.

Almost like you read about it in books. Gary just figured right then she was in love with him. He didn't know how he knew it. He just did. And it felt good.

Now Gary looked up at his uncle's face and said quietly, "Gayle. I was just wondering if she's okay."

"If she isn't it's no skin off your nose, kid. I told you when she was down here—stay out of it. Keep away from her. This mess has nothing to do with you."

"Well, even so," said Gary. "I'd still like to know how she's doing."

She had to pull back the thread. Somehow pull back the thread of that yesterday.

Why were they all acting so funny around her? Like they knew something she was supposed to know. She could tell that from the way they looked at her, talked to her.

It must be something important. That she was supposed to know.

Probably something bad. That she must have done. Or else why would they think she should know about it? And they were all telling each other, talking about it; she could tell that from the funny way they acted around her.

Then why didn't they tell her about it? Just *tell* her? But none of them did. Would. Not even that one who wanted to send her to the crazy place.

All of them acting so strange. Even Sister Philomena. And her brother Dan.

Why wouldn't Dan tell her what she was supposed to know?

Julia, too. Julia had been there last night when that purple thing came out of her. And then the doctors had asked her again about that "pregnant," asked her if she was very sure she wasn't that thing they kept saying, even though she told them no, no. So Julia must also know the bad things they were saying behind her back. Some bad thing about that "pregnant."

She was very uncomfortable thinking about that word, that word that meant a baby, so she pushed it out of her head and reached for another thought.

Body. Her body so strange, too. So strange and hurting. Feeling different all the time, violently, turbulently different. Not like her own.

Now another nurse was coming in again with another little paper cup of pills for her to take. Two big red ones and two white ones and a little green capsule this time. She swallowed them obediently, with water from the clear glass on the little table beside the bed.

When the nurse left the room she lay flat on her side, nesting her head back into the pillow, trying to find the thread where she had left it.

Body. Yes. This alien strange body.

Suddenly she could feel in her stomach the pills she had just swallowed. The two big red ones and the others. And at the same time she felt a warm, bursting wave of relief, of almost happiness.

That must be it. Why she felt so strange. Because they

had taken her body at this hospital and they were doing such strange things to it, blacking her out, pulling and pressing. Changing the messy stained pad between her legs, looking right at it and saying, "Very good, Sister." Pouring things into her down those tubes, making her drink all those pills.

So it was *their* strangeness, then. Not hers.

She could feel the warm spreading all through her now, even through the soreness, the strangeness.

Then she should not worry so much about what was happening to her here. All these things they were doing to her. When they let her go home—and they *would* let her go home, she knew the Good Lord Jesus would see to that—she would have her own body back again. So it didn't matter so much, whatever was happening to her here.

Because she would leave it all here behind her when she went home.

Over meat loaf and baked beans in the Tucker dining room, the talk still revolved around Sister Gayle. When Beverly asked her father what he thought about it, Ralph Tucker paused. He'd been turning the same question in his own mind ever since Frank Sullivan had called him out of the gym. Now he said slowly, "Well now, I'm hurt."

Brad demanded, "What you mean, *hurt?* That she stiffed you like this?"

"Well, I'm hurt she went ahead and accepted our long-standing invitation to the archery shoot last weekend. Under the circumstances. I think she should've written us a letter, said some unforeseen circumstances had come up and she couldn't make it after all. That would've been the ladylike thing to do, all things considered."

"Damn right." Brad speared himself another serving of meat loaf.

"But she didn't say till last week she was coming," said Gary. "I didn't think she was gonna make it."

"Well, she still came, didn't she?" Ralph demanded.

"And I'm hurt that she's got you mixed up in this mess, Gary. Now, I don't know as Gayle actually gave them your name, but she still got you into it."

"But that's okay, Dad. I didn't do what they said."

"Well, I know that." Tucker moved on to the more troubling part of his thought. "But on the other hand, if it should turn out that Ziggy was involved—I surely do feel some responsibility for that. Now here was this person staying at our campsite—uninvited, all right, but we still treated him like our guest. We're the ones introduced him to the Russells, as a person who knew our family. Now if it should turn out to be Ziggy was responsible—well now, that's another thing entirely."

"I'm *telling* you, it was Ziggy," said Brad. "I've seen that guy operate. Ziggy always had all the girls he wanted. And he didn't treat them so terrific. You remember that student nurse he used to date over at St. Hilda's, a nice girl, Joanie I think was her name—Ziggy saw a lot of her. We'd go over there some nights and if Joanie wasn't around Ziggy would just order a bunch of girls downstairs and he'd say—'Here, you and you, you'll do.' And they'd go out with him, too. I never saw a guy used to operate like Ziggy."

"I guess he did some operating last summer, all right," Ralph said grimly.

"He used to be a good-looking kid, too, before he put on all that fat and let his hair go all faggy like that," said Brad. "And he really knew how to live. He was making a real good salary—he was at Midwest Mutual, that time I'm thinking about—and he'd blow it all, living high. He'd buy maybe fifteen, twenty records at a time. He always had women around too, and he didn't give a damn about them. I remember once we were at a bike meet, some girl comes up to him and sez, 'I'm pregnant, and it's your kid.' You know what Ziggy sez to her?"

All eyes fixed now on Brad. Gary asked it: "What?"

"He sez, 'Tough. You lose.' Just like that—'You lose.' "

Beverly asked breathlessly, "What happened to her then?"

Shrug from Brad. "Who knows? Nothing. She just went off, and that was the end of it for Ziggy. I think he's got other kids down in Texas—I *know* for a fact he's knocked up other girls before this one. And Ziggy's the type, he just wouldn't give a damn."

Tess Tucker shot a glance at her two teen-age daughters, wishing the men would just get off this whole nasty subject of conversation. What kind of talk was this to have around a family dinner table?

Gary said wistfully, "But he's real fun to be around sometimes. Ziggy can be real fun."

Brad made that snorting noise again. "*Used* to be. Before he got into this Youth Revolution stuff, smoking dope and growing that fag hair and talking all the time about the goddam Vietnam War. You remember when he got into that acid rock and threw out his whole record collection? And that was a terrific collection he had."

"He didn't throw it out," Beverly said. "He gave it to you."

"Well, he was going to, so I took it off him. And there was some real classics there—Frank Sinatra, Mantovani, Henry Mancini. All the good stuff. You still got those records, Gary?"

"Yeah, I guess. They're pretty good."

"I tell you, he used to be a good kid. But then he changed. Went real bad. Screwing around with some nun—that wouldn't bother Ziggy none. Anyplace he could get it was all right with him."

In his slow, methodical way Ralph Tucker had been trying all day to sort out certain images in his head. One was of Gayle playing on the beach with her cousin's kids, spending almost a whole day with them building a beautiful fancy sandcastle. But another was of the table in his trailer that night when he and Tess came home from the restaurant—

an empty whiskey bottle sitting out on it, a bottle Danziger had just helped himself to without asking and left out on the table bold as brass. Tucker remembered wondering then if Danziger had been drinking it by himself.

Now he remembered shadowy ideas, concerns for Gayle, once he realized she was a nun—not that she was like any nun *he* ever knew, running all around in that tight, low-cut bathing suit. Especially when it was wet a man just couldn't help seeing just about every goosebump on that chest of hers. Built like Jane Russell practically, she was, that little girl. And those curly brown hairs at the top of her legs that stuck out of the crotch in her suit—he couldn't help noticing them one or two times, the way she'd sit with her legs right open. Not that he paid it any mind, but he couldn't help noticing.

Tucker cleared his throat and said aloud, "I did wonder some if Gayle should be spending all that time she was with Ziggy, her being a nun and all. I even said something about that to you, Tess, now, didn't I?" Tess nodded. "But I figured what the heck, she's a grown woman, a teacher—she must know the score. Know how to take care of herself."

"Well, I guess she sure didn't," said Brad. "Else where did that bowling ball come from?"

Geez, this was the part Gary Tucker hated—them talking about her and Ziggy like that. He got up abruptly from the table and carried his plate out to the kitchen, trailed by Brad's loud taunt: "What's the matter, kid? You don't like hearing the goods on your girl friend?"

Gary turned at the kitchen door and said angrily, "Hey, listen, I just liked her. I thought she was a real nice girl."

"Well, you thought wrong."

Tess murmured anxiously, "If it *was* Ziggy, you don't suppose he might have—forced her?"

Brad snorted again. "At *that* lake? Not a chance."

"Now, you can't say that, Brad," his brother said sharply. "You just don't know."

"The way those campsites up there are all packed together, around that skinny little beach? You can't throw a rock up there without somebody hearing. Let alone somebody yelling like if they were attacked—there's just no way nobody wouldn't hear 'em."

Doggedly: "Well, you still don't have the facts."

"You give *me* a fact, Ralph. Did you ever see her acting scared around Ziggy? Acting like she didn't want to see him, talk to him? Like she would've if she'd been raped?"

There was another image that had haunted Ralph Tucker's head all afternoon: the small smiles, tiny flashes, passing between Gayle and Ziggy. He'd hardly noticed them then, but he remembered them now. "No, I can't say as I did," he said slowly, reluctantly. "Not so as I can recall."

Brad's wife, Evie, opened her mouth for the first time that evening. "If you ask me I think the two of them got what they both deserved—each other."

Meg Gavin stayed late at the newspaper office, phoning compulsively around town, trying to turn up something, anything. A *name*, at least. All those parishioners at St. Rose, for instance—*some* of them must've noticed which nun it was at Sunday Mass who was growing that interesting belly.

Finally Dick McAlpine said with irritation, *"Drop* it, will you, Gavin? Even if you get a name, we can't run it without confirmation, and we're out of time for that now."

So Meg handed in a brief three-take, minimally informative article in which the two salient points—that a nun from St. Rose in her mid-thirties was brought hemorrhaging into the Parkhurst Hospital ER, and that a dead baby was later found in the convent—were left carefully disconnected. McAlpine scanned it, grunted, "Okay. Fine."

"It's not fine, it sucks. How long are you going to let Mark Abrams sit on this thing, Dick?"

"Hey, hey. Simmer down, Gavin. If they haven't made

a statement by noon tomorrow I'll do a little squeezing at Parkhurst Hospital. I've got a few favors owed over there."

"Why tomorrow? Squeeze them *now*, Dick."

McAlpine was looking atypically amused. "Well, look at this. I do believe we've stumbled on a subject that stirs Mizz Gavin out of her customary ennui." As he slash-marked her copy for typesetting he said, "Go home and get some sleep, kid. If it helps any, you can keep your radio tuned and see if the guys beat you to it."

"Piss on you, Dick. Piss all *over* you."

"Gavin, do me a great favor and go home."

Dr. Keith Talbott left Sister Angela for the last call of this harrowing day. He told himself he was doing that to allot her as much time as might be necessary.

Which was truth, but also an unconscionable lie. In fact Keith Talbott was dreading this confrontation. Bruce Heilbron said she had reacted very negatively—the most emotional response he'd gotten out of her yet—to the news of her transfer to Ward Five. Heilbron had risked telling her about it because he knew they were running out of time in being able to shield her from the legal authorities, but he was not encouraged by her response. And her interview with her two brothers had been equally unpromising.

So now it was left up to her gynecologist to see what he could salvage from it. Talbott was already fighting off a feeling of bleak, angry helplessness when he stopped by the West Wing Three nursing station at 7:45, checked the notations on Sister Angela's chart and said, "Okay. Let's get two more units of whole blood into her tonight."

The brief sensation of warmth, of relief, was gone by the time Dr. Talbott came into her room. He walked up to the bed and asked her how she was feeling, like everybody else had done—so stupid, the way they all asked the same thing. Then he asked a lot more, about any pain she was having—

"We can give you medication to relieve that, Sister, so please feel free to mention it, because I want you to be as comfortable as possible"—and about her appetite, how much sleep she was getting, and so on.

She didn't feel much like talking but she didn't have to do it anyway, since the nurse did it for her—"She hardly touched a bite of her dinner, Doctor. She's eating less than a bird."

"Well, I wasn't hungry. All that pudding . . ."

Talbott smiled. "We have you on a low-bulk diet for the moment, Sister. I realize the food isn't very appetizing, but I'd like you to eat as much as you can. You need it to rebuild your strength."

"All right."

Then he asked her to roll over on her right side and move her left knee up to her chest. The nurse lifted up the sheet and unloosened the pad she was wearing, moved it out of the way.

She stiffened, clenched her fists, waiting for the touch. But he only said, "All right, that's healing very nicely," and stepped back from the bed while the nurse put the pad and sheet back into place.

When she was lying on her back, he said in that grave, gentle voice, "I have some good news for you, Sister Angela. I think we can remove the catheter tonight. That will make you a little more mobile, a little more comfortable."

She nodded. "Yes. I'd like that."

"When you have an urge to void, you can get up and use the bathroom. Or the bedpan, if you prefer. But I'd like to have you up on your feet, moving around. Any exercise you can get will be very beneficial for you." He seemed very tall, standing beside the bed. "How are you feeling generally? Is there anything you'd like to talk to me about?"

She looked up at him. Such a kind, gentle, sad face. She said, "Yes," and flicked a glance toward the nurse who was standing near the foot of the bed.

Talbott nodded at the nurse, who turned and left the room. He pulled a chair up to the bedside and sat, looking at Angela with a feeling of suspension in time, waiting for her to speak.

At eight P.M. the various materials impounded from Sister Angela's possessions were spread out over the conference table in the Cambridgeport Police staff room. The investigators gathered around the table were the same men who had taken part in the meeting twelve hours earlier, all of them showing the effects of the long day.

Chief Marwick opened: "In case any of you haven't heard, Ben Haverty is now the attorney of record on this case. Which means it'll be a snowy day in hell before we get to interview his client. Okay, let's see what else we have to work with."

Andy DaSilva made a brief recapitulation of the interviews with Dr. Talbott and the other St. Rose nuns. Most of the nuns had confirmed the overt friendliness but recent withdrawal in Sister Angela—except Sister Sylvia, who dated the withdrawal back to about two years earlier, after Sister Angela's father died.

None of them had talked to Sister Angela about the possibility of a pregnancy, and none had knowledge of any relationship Sister Angela might have had with a man, although Sister Irma recalled her talking once about the Boston filmmaker. "And Sister Virginia said Sister Angela told her Monday night that the reason she missed her plane home last Sunday was that her friends were competing in an archery contest," said DaSilva. "She said they won some prizes, which were in the form of camping equipment. That's about it, the rest was mainly just repetition."

"Except Sister Margory using the john," prompted Nick Scotti.

"Oh, yeah." DaSilva went back to his notes. "Sister Margory said she came back to the convent Tuesday noon on her lunch hour to brush her teeth and use the toilet in another bathroom. She saw the bloody footprints on the hall rug but thought they were just water. She assumed somebody had just used the shower, or maybe the roof was leaking again in Sister Angela's room. She didn't think much about it, and didn't know anybody else was home. She heard no sounds to indicate anyone being there."

"Which must mean the baby was born before noon, and also probably dead by then too," theorized Tim Vance.

"Mmmph." Mark Abrams rubbed his hand over his chin and reached in his coat pocket for his cigarettes, his third pack of the day. "It sure sounds that way. Tim, what have you got for us?"

Vance began with the smaller details. The physicians the police had contacted—Sister Angela's own allergist, and her mother's doctor—had not seen the nun for six months at least. The seven doctors listed on the card in her purse all said they had never heard of or from her. Since they were all obstetrician-gynecologists whose names began with *a* or *b,* listed alphabetically, Vance assumed she had simply written out their names from some directory, possibly the Yellow Pages.

The pills found in her purse were diuretics she'd borrowed from Sister Montecito, apparently to try to bring down the swelling in her legs. A search warrant served at the convent had yielded bloodstained cleaning materials and an empty wrapper for support panty hose taken from a wastebasket in Sister Angela's room, but nothing else of significance. The May notation for "Week of the Child" on Sister Angela's closet calendar apparently referred to some special event planned at the kindergarten school. And the cash found in her purse seemed to have been borrowed from a locked box in her desk at the school which contained the funds collected to finance that event. The school nuns said $320 was missing from the box and unaccounted for; the cash found in her purse totaled $263.

"Okay, that's real good." Nick Scotti yawned, stretching his arms over his head. "If she beats the murder rap they can still get her for petty larceny."

D.A. Abrams threw a cutting glance of reproof at Scotti as he said, "You got anything else, Tim?"

"Nothing conclusive," said Vance. "The Boston filmmaker, Martin Downson, was sorry to hear about her fix, said she's a real nice lady but he hasn't seen her for about twenty months. The shoes found in the wastebasket with the baby, by the way, she'd apparently thrown out because her feet were so swollen lately she'd had to buy a bigger size."

"Mmmph." Abrams lit a fresh cigarette from his butt. "What's happening with the situation over in Oak Creek?"

"Okay. I've had five, six telephonic conversations with a Sergeant Frank Sullivan. I guess you talked to him once too, Mr. Abrams." Abrams nodded. "He says this Gary Tucker is flatly denying paternity, and Sergeant Sullivan tends to back him up. But I'm not sure how objective or reliable his judgment is here. Sullivan seems to be a friend of the family, keeps talking about what an upstanding moral bunch the Tuckers are, Boy Scout leaders and so forth."

"What did you get on Gary Tucker?" asked Marwick.

"Nothing too incriminating, that's for sure. He sounds about like his letters—an inarticulate, sort of immature kid who lives at home, works for his dad and so forth. Anyway, the Tuckers have come up with another possible lead, a man who was visiting the Tuckers' campsite when they met Sister Angela last summer. Name of Roy Danziger."

Angela twisted the sheet in her fingers. She knew what she meant to say, as soon as she got that woman out of the room. She meant to ask Dr. Talbott to send those nurses away, and tell Dr. Heilbron not to send her to that crazy place.

But when she spoke, what came out was, "Dr. Talbott, people are saying terrible things about me that aren't true and I'm very concerned about that. Can't you stop them?"

He waited a long moment. Then said, "What are they saying, Sister Angela?"

"That I had a baby and killed the baby and that isn't true, that can't be true, because obviously I couldn't have been pregnant."

The shock-volt seemed to move through the whole of Talbott's body. A useless question flashed into his mind— had she actually overheard that, maybe from a careless nurse, or were those her own voices she was hearing?

No matter: she had thrown him that single thread to save her with. Now maybe, just maybe . . .

Very carefully: "You're quite sure of that, Sister?"

She nodded vehemently, her expression so fierce. "Yes. I just know they are, I can tell."

"No, I mean that you could not be pregnant."

"Oh, no, I couldn't possibly. Like they keep saying."

Cautiously, so cautiously: "Well, Sister Angela, you remember you delivered a placenta. You remember Dr. Kovaleski showing it to you?"

She nodded, her face pulled into a tight knot of concentration.

"Do you know what a placenta is?"

"An afterbirth?"

"That's right."

Anxiously, intensely: "But Doctor, couldn't you have been mistaken about that? Couldn't it have been something else that *looked* like an afterbirth?"

Ah, she was coming. Coming on her own. He needed only to guide her steps, very gently, very surely.

He said quietly, "No, Sister Angela, I couldn't possibly be mistaken. There *is* nothing else that resembles a placenta."

163

Small voice: "Oh. I see."

Like a shriveling flower she settled back into her pillows, back into her thoughts. And the room was very still.

Keith Talbott watched her go deep into herself, into that private place where none of them had been able to reach her. Whether or not she could face the nightmare that was waiting for her in that place, he couldn't say. Couldn't know. But if she could go there and come back out to him, he knew there was a real hope of saving her. Bringing her through safely.

Keith Talbott had no idea how long she was lost in that place. But for every one of those moments, minutes, he was with her as fiercely as he had been with no other person in his life.

When Tim Vance finished his rundown on Roy Danziger a stunned silence hung over the conference table. "Jesus, I can't believe it's *him*," said Andy DaSilva. "I just can't imagine a nun like Sister Angela running around with a character like that."

"Well, Sullivan leans strongly toward that possibility," said Vance. "But I think we have to take into account the fact that Oak Creek is a pretty small town, and Sullivan knows the Tuckers pretty well. My guess is it wouldn't be too hard to persuade him it's anybody *but* Gary Tucker."

Mark Abrams's mind was snagged on a startling fact that had surfaced in the interrogation of the gynecologist: the fact that Sister Angela presently denied any knowledge of the pregnancy. So his original assumption that one person, at least, knew the truth about this case might not turn out to be accurate.

Fingering the packet of money found in her purse, which was sealed now inside a plastic evidence bag, Abrams said, "I think we're going to have to consider the possibility that this nun never did realize she was pregnant."

Marwick grunted as he scraped the tobacco from his

pipe bowl into an ashtray. "Jesus, Mark. I never heard of a lady into her ninth month who didn't."

"Well, we're into pretty bizarre circumstances here," Abrams said. "In the event this case ever *does* come to trial, I think we might find Ben Haverty standing up there in court saying that Sister Angela never knew what her condition was, and therefore was not responsible for any subsequent events. That's hypothetical, okay. But it sure could throw a wrench into any case we could make against her." He tapped the packet of money. "Now this 'borrowed' cash she had in her possession—okay, that's circumstantial. But I'd like to hear some ideas about what it was doing in her purse."

Marwick shrugged. "Maybe to pay for an out-of-town abortion in Milwaukee."

"Kind of late for that, wasn't it, Chief?" Vance asked dryly. "Pay for a hospital delivery would be more like it. She could've been feeling pre-labor pains, figured she was about to deliver. That could explain the trip over there—she was hoping to have the kid out of town. I'd say that money might hold up as evidence she damn well knew what was going on."

"Could be. Could be." Abrams was still looking at the money. "But it's goddam circumstantial. And if we can't prove knowledge of pregnancy we're going to have a rough time making any murder charge stick."

Tim Vance could see where Abrams was heading, with his usual elliptical reasoning. To save them all a little time at the end of this grueling day, Vance said it for him: "So if we want to nail down just how much she knew, we'd better find the daddy."

"Damn right," Abrams said grimly. "And we'd better find him fast, before Ben Haverty gets to him."

She turned her eyes down to the sheet, the white hospital sheet. So, then. It was true, what they were saying. No way out. True.

The sparklings around the dark space in her mind dropped away like vanished fireflies. True. Real. No way out.

Slowly, very gently, she stepped into the dark space that was opened up now in her mind.

Still dark. A large darkness. But now defined by traces of light. Faint traces, like moonlight on a dark cloudy night.

Trees around her, above her. Trees like quilting in the dark night.

Moving in the dark. Not afraid. She knew she was not afraid.

But not alone. Another body there with her in the trees. Moving beside her through the trees.

Then, suddenly, all changed. Body pressing against her. Touching her skin. Kissing her face.

Hair, hair on the body. Pressing, strange. Trees shifting, spinning as the body pushed her down to the damp ground.

Not safe. Nothing safe now. Hands hurting her, pulling at her clothes. Nothing safe now in that cold, thin white light.

Scrambling, thrashing. *Something hurts, hurts.* Strange panting noise in the whispering of the trees.

Something finished, done. Covering. Running. Out of the woods, back to the small room with the electric light. Safe now again in the small room.

That was the dark space, then. The lost dark space.

And they knew about it, too. That was why they had asked her all those strange questions. They meant what had happened to her in the dark space, in the trees.

She smoothed the hospital sheet across her body. In the stillness of the room on West Wing Three, she looked up at the doctor, who was watching her quietly, intensely.

Kind eyes. Good eyes. Safe eyes.

She said to those eyes, "It's not impossible that I was pregnant."

Thirteen

There it was: that single thread. She was touching him with those huge, wounded green eyes, murmuring, "It's possible I *could* have been. But I never thought I was."

Warily, confusion mixed in his relief, Talbott said, "I see. You've remembered something?"

She dropped her eyes back to the sheet. "Yes. It's not impossible. It could have happened. But I never strongly believed I *was* pregnant because I knew there would be obvious signs. I had no obvious signs."

Talbott understood then that the memory that had come back to her was of the sexual incident. But it was still something to work with, something to open up the rest of the taboos. Delicately, carefully, he told her what they had not dared to tell her before.

She heard him out with a quiet, stricken astonishment. That baby, then, the baby they had all meant with that "pregnancy" talk—that baby was real.

She couldn't remember it. But it was real. And dead, he was telling her in that quiet, gentle voice. They had found the baby, the real baby, and it was dead.

She knew she must help them as much as she could. Because they knew about things she did not, but ought to—wanted to. Like the baby. Her baby, they said.

So when he said, "I think the police will want to talk to you about this, Sister," she nodded earnestly, with that puzzled, intense frown. "Well, I'd be glad to talk to them, Dr. Talbott. But I don't think I could help them. Because I don't know anything about it. Except what I'm telling you."

He led her gently through her memories of the morning of the twenty-fifth. She spoke in short, gasped phrases, retrieving what she could as much for herself as for him. "That night. I remember I woke up that night. With a pain in my stomach. The clock said three. Ten after three. So I got up and took two Bufferin."

As she spoke, her eyes were filling, finally, belatedly, with tears. She seemed not to notice as two single drops brimmed and tracked down her cheeks. "I couldn't sleep for a while. But then I guess I did.

"Then I woke up again when the alarm went off at six forty-five. But I didn't feel so good. I still had that pain. I wanted to go in to school—I've never taken a day out sick, never. But I really didn't feel good at all. I kept having that pain." Her cheeks were now very wet. "So at seven I went next door and told Sister Julia I couldn't go to school yet, I had flu. I said I'd go in later, when I felt better."

As she wiped her nose on the back of her hand he picked up a box of tissues from the nightstand and held it out to her. "Oh, excuse me, " She said as she blew her nose. "I didn't mean to—"

"No, no, please." He was smiling. "After what you've been through, tears are quite to be expected. I'm very glad to see them, Sister Angela."

"Well, anyway. I was trying to get my mind off the pain. I lay down for a while. But it didn't seem to help. So I got up and—"

"Could you describe the pain for me? Where you were feeling it?"

"Down here." She pressed her hand against her lower abdomen. "It was kind of—like cramps. Period cramps. But quite—strong. I got up and walked around the room. I think — I remember I was reading a book. But it was hard to concentrate. And then—just before school started I was walking by the window, watching the children. And I saw Sister Margory coming back to the convent. Probably for something she forgot, that she needed for class. Margory forgets things a lot. I remember just when she was coming up to the kitchen door"—she pressed her hands flat against her cheeks, pressed her eyes shut against the thought—"I just—something just ran down my legs. A lot of liquid. Sort of like blood, pale blood."

So her water broke around nine A.M., Talbott understood.

"I cleaned it all up," she said distractedly. "But the pain kept coming, worse and worse."

"Did you think about calling someone for help?"

"No. I guess—well, maybe I did, but not— I kept thinking I'd feel better soon."

"Did you have any idea what was causing the pain?"

"No. Because I'm never sick. So I expected it to just go away, like it had started."

More statement than question: "But it didn't."

She shook her head, a shuddering motion. That still uncomprehended pain was real again on her tight, anxious face. "And when it got worse I was—I did want someone to help. But I didn't know—what to do."

"You were frightened?" he suggested gently.

"Oh, yes." Her tearful, blotchy face was pinched in an agony of concentration. "Especially when it—got worse. It was hurting so bad. And I was bleeding too. I tried to clean it up, but— And then I thought if I just took a bath, I could get clean." She stopped. Searched her thoughts with that pained, tight expression.

After a pause he prompted, softly: "So you took a bath?"

She stirred, moved her legs under the sheet. "I tried, to wash off the blood. Only I realized I couldn't, because I was just sitting in a pool of it. And then the pain—changed." Breathy, gasped words. "So bad. So bad."

"How did the pain change?" he asked, already knowing the answer.

"Down. Low. In—my hips. So bad. Pushing, making me push." She rolled her head tormentedly on the pillow, her eyes pressed shut against the image in her head. "I remem— got out of the tub. Push against the tub."

So she delivered in the bathroom.

When she said nothing more he asked quietly, "Do you recall what happened after that period of pushing?"

She shook her head, bewildered, exhausted. "No. Nothing except—so much blood. I kept trying to—clean up. But I was so weak." The words seemed wrung out of her, wrenched from her anguished snatches of memory. "I kept falling down. I think— I guess I was fainting. I wanted to get the mop. Clean up. But I kept fainting. And—*so much blood.*" She waved her hands weakly in front of her, pushing the image away. "Just, everywhere—all that blood."

Keith Talbott knew quite precisely the medical condition she was describing—the placenta retained by her resisting body, just as the infant would have been, if her body had had its way. And the blood spurting from that severed cord, as if from a cruelly opened spigot.

He was afraid now to ask about the baby. She knew now that it existed; she had not argued against what he had told her. But it was also clear to him that there was no baby present in her tortured recollections. Talbott didn't know how to handle that. Whether he dared to handle that. At least this much had come back; the rest might come later, when she was able to face it.

So he asked, "Do you recall anything else, except the blood?"

She sifted those fragmented, cloudy thoughts. "No. Except the sisters coming. To take care of me."

The talk around the conference table at the Cambridgeport Police Department went back and forth. But produced no glimmer of the escape Mark Abrams was so bleakly hoping for. So at 8:55 he slapped the table and said, "Okay. Greg, I think now that the press has gotten onto this thing there's no way we can stall an action. Have you decided what charge you're going to lay, and against whom?"

Marwick gripped his pipe in his teeth, a MacArthur gesture. "Well, Mark, I think considering the evidence, we've got no choice here but second-degree murder. Against Sister Angela Flynn." The silence around the table took into account the fact that Marwick and Abrams had spent much of that afternoon closeted together, deciding on precisely that charge. "How do you feel about that, Mark?"

Careful not to betray his personal reluctance, Abrams said, "That's about the way I see it at this point, Greg."

"Okay. Unless something changes during the night I think we should serve the arrest warrant tomorrow morning. I guess we could make some kind of press conference around the same time. To announce the arrest."

Abrams said evenly, "Okay, Greg, if that's your decision." His mind had already jumped ahead to the unresolved questions that still nagged at him. "But I'm still concerned about this business of the father. I'm concerned about the kind of information we're getting out of Milwaukee. Conflicting, unverified. Frankly, I think we've got to get to the bottom of it." He looked across the table at DaSilva. "Andy, I'd like you and Nick to get over there to Milwaukee tonight, check out these two guys. I want to know what the hell's going on down there."

"Fine by me," said DaSilva.

From Scotti: "You got it, boss."

"Okay, fine." Marwick looked nervously at Tim Vance. "Tim, I'd like you to go with Andy and Nick."

Vance made a shrug that translated as *You talk, I walk.*

In fact, Tim Vance had serious objections to that order. With so much nuts-and-bolts investigation still to be made at the scene of this major homicide, he couldn't see why in hell the chief investigator of the ranking police agency should tool off out-of-state on a fucking goose-chase after the guy who supposedly played nooky with this nun nine months earlier.

But Vance had been aware since the previous evening of the name of the game being played out on this case: Greg

Marwick, small-town P.C., was trying to hold his own against the big-city D.A. Trying to keep control of this important case. So if Mark Abrams was fixated on finding the daddy, Greg Marwick was going to be too. And if Abrams was tossing his top hounds into the chase, Marwick was going to throw Vance after them.

What the hell, all they could lose was one day, two days. Maybe not critical days. Maybe the stuff they really needed to know would still be diggable, once this fucking sidetrack was laid to rest. Maybe—and then again, maybe not.

Who cared who screwed the nun, anyway? The point was *who murdered this baby.* And Tim Vance strenuously doubted they were going to come any closer to answering that compelling question by nailing down the goddam daddy. If he was running this P.D., running this real big case, he could think of a lot of items that took higher priority.

Vance said curtly, "Whatever you say, Chief."

Abrams was asking, "That's a drive of—how many hours?"

"About six," said Vance. "If we move it along."

"Okay," said Abrams. "If you leave tonight you can get there by morning. I'd like you to check out every lead, and keep in constant touch with us back here. I want to know everything that's happening."

"Damn right," said Marwick. "If you want to take my car, Tim, that's all right with me." To Abrams he said, "It's a new Buick, maybe a little more reliable than Tim's. Anyway, a more comfortable ride."

"Thanks, Greg. That's very generous." Abrams checked his watch. "Okay, it's about nine P.M. I suggest you guys go home now, grab a few hours' sleep and leave from here around midnight."

They talked for an hour, almost an hour and a half—gently, safely. Keith Talbott was careful not to press into the

172

privacies of her precariously balanced mind. Mostly he listened, as she plucked shreds and bits of that tortuous day from her own darkened memories.

Now her talk was all of the blood—red blood, brown blood, clots. So much blood, all that terrifying blood. "I think I went down the hall, to get more towels," she said faintly. "I thought about getting a mop from downstairs. But I was—so weak. I didn't think I could walk that far. I kept— falling down."

Talbott nodded. "You were probably unconscious, Sister Angela. From the loss of blood."

A slight, shuddering motion ran through her body. "Oh. Oh. Yes. I guess." The sheet clenched in her two hands. "Because all I remember is, every time I woke up I was lying in all that blood."

She was struggling, working so hard to retrieve the memories. But they were sparse and oddly formed, like patches of fog in a dark nightscape.

Now she was hearing the sounds in the empty convent. Heat pipes banging. Children calling and chattering outside the school.

Now she remembered around noon, seeing Margory coming back to the convent. Coming into the house, walking around downstairs. She could hear her walking around. She remembered calling out to her for help. But Margory must not have heard, because she never came.

Angela was tired. So tired. She went over and over it in her head, trying to find and clutch the thoughts, but what came back mostly was that wet, ugly blood that she could see, she could feel, almost like it was real again.

But. But. Something missing. That other thing he'd told her about—wasn't there.

A baby. They said there was a baby.

Her own baby they said they knew was there, that must have come out of that dark time in the woods.

173

She knew the baby must have something to do with the pain. Must have. Why else would this doctor be asking her so much about it? But there was no baby there, in the pain.

Ah, now she could remember *that* so well. How it cut her, sliced her. Hurt her like she could never have imagined. Cutting like knives into her live body.

But—no baby. That was supposed to have come from the pain. Only the blood, all that unstoppable blood.

Why couldn't she remember that baby? That was supposed to be there.

But *he* knew. He had told her about it.

She looked at him with huge, bruised eyes, whispering, "But Dr. Talbott . . . I can't remember anything about a baby."

"That's all right, Sister Angela. That's quite all right." He reached forward and lifted her hand from the sheet, gripped it. "You've made a great deal of important progress tonight. Enough for one night. I'm very pleased with that. That was very important."

She rolled her head on the starched white pillow. "No, no. But I want to—"

"No, please. Please believe me." He squeezed her hand. "It's all right. You've done a great deal. Now I'd like you just to rest, and get your sleep."

He laid her hand on the white blanket. Moved to go. And then she remembered what she had meant to tell him —about those nurses, and that Ward Five place.

So she told him then. Maybe not like she had practiced it all afternoon, because now she was so tired and muddled. "So please, Dr. Talbott," she finished, "can't they just leave me alone? Because I'm all right. I'll be fine again as soon as you let me go home to the convent."

Keith Talbott understood very well what she was asking. For peace, for oblivion. But that was no longer any real choice for her, and he knew he must try now to keep her from burrowing deeper into that lie of refuge. Because the only real refuge available to her now, whether she knew it or not, was madness. Total madness.

After the pained journey they had unexpectedly shared, Talbott believed she might yet come to terms with the truth. Hard, yes, it was going to be wretchedly, cruelly hard. But he believed now it was possible.

So, touching her only with his eyes, he said, "Sister Angela, do you trust me?"

Softly, so softly: "Oh, yes, Dr. Talbott."

He leaned forward in the chair, resting his elbows on his knees. "Please do, Sister Angela. I want only the best for you. I want to help you in the best way I know how. I'd feel most remiss if we didn't provide you with the best care that our judgment sees indicated."

"Oh, I know that." She moved her eyes off his, up to the ceiling of that hospital room. "But I don't want—I don't want—that. What Dr. Heilbron said."

"I understand, Sister Angela. Truly, I understand. But please believe that the treatment we suggest for you is what we judge to be in your best interests. I won't let any harm come to you. Nothing will happen to you that isn't in your best interests. Can you trust me to do that for you, Sister Angela?"

She seemed to clutch for a moment to her fiercely felt objections. Then murmured, "Yes, I do, Dr. Talbott." And let go, softly, gracefully, of something tightly clenched inside her.

When he left the room a few minutes later, she had already slipped from exhaustion into sleep.

Keith Talbott walked back to the nursing station, left orders for those two units of whole blood to be administered now to Sister Angela Flynn, and the catheter to be removed when she was awake. Then he scrawled in the hospital chart, *Conversation with patient. Terminated at 9:15 P.M.*

Gary Tucker was cleaning his .22 target pistol at the kitchen table, pushing the oiled rod up and down the bore, when Sergeant Sullivan called. His mother, washing dishes at the sink, answered the wall phone, and passed it to Gary.

The conversation was brief and to the point. Gary said into the phone, "Yes, okay. Sure."

When he hung up, his father was standing in the kitchen door, watching him with that same funny look he'd had on his face that morning. Gary said, "Sergeant Sullivan says some detectives are coming over from St. Paul. He wants me to see 'em at eight thirty tomorrow morning."

"Well, that's okay. That's fine. As long as you're sure you've got nothing to hide."

"Right." Gary moved back to the table, picked up the gun. He could feel his father's eyes, hitting him with accusations.

"You sure about that, Gary?"

Shortly: "Yes, sure. Like I told you."

From the sink his mother said, "Oh, Ralph, leave the poor boy alone. It's hard enough on him like it is."

"Well, I just want to make sure we're getting the whole story here."

"Ralph!"

"Okay, okay." His father went back to the living room TV. Gary pushed the oiled rod in and out of the barrel, dodging his mother's nervous looks.

He wasn't out of this thing yet. Else why were they still coming after him?

Detectives. Real detectives. A whole bunch of them, coming here just to talk to him.

It wasn't like he'd lied to them. It was right what he'd said.

Well, pretty right. Except he didn't know what they were going to— Geez, and even his own father was acting like he

176

figured Gary did it. Must've done it. A thick lump of bad feeling—almost a scared feeling—was stuck in Gary Tucker's gut. He tried to push it away, but it kept coming back.

Oh God, he wished tomorrow was already over.

Fourteen

On her way home Meg Gavin dropped by the Blind Justice Bar, to see what loose talk she could pick up. But none of the A.D.A. regulars was around. A couple of FBI stiffs in three-piece pin-striped suits hadn't even heard about the case. So much for the mighty shades of old J. Edgar.

She drove home after two drinks and shucked her clothes as soon as she stepped into the rambling four-room apartment in the renovated Victorian house. Pulled on an old cotton caftan, switched on the stack of records on the KLH turntable, and poured herself a large, stiff mugful of vodka and Diet Pepsi in the small kitchen off the living room.

Now it was workout time, pacing the oriental carpet between the orange velvet couch and the ficus tree, trying to order her thoughts between infusions of vodka and Pepsi.

The weird thing was, she'd been pacing the same rug in the same caftan just one night earlier. Then, she'd been cranking herself up to quit, walk out, take her damn chances. Find some better outlet for her frequently rude curiosities than exploring the suburban tax rate of this rat-ass town she'd never meant to come back to anyway.

But that was then. Last night. And—

Meg was suddenly into *now*. Into this weird, mythic replay of all the medieval fantasies she'd been raised on, tiny skeletons buried in the vaulted convent cellars. Maria Monk stuff all the way.

Except that, as far as she knew, it had never actually happened before. Until yesterday. In that ugly red-brick convent across from the manicured suburban lawns in Cambridgeport, Minnesota. Happened probably, since St. Benedict's was only a diocesan order, to some girl who'd come up through the local convent-school farm system right alongside Meg Gavin.

She'd seen some bizarre human stories in her checkered career, but never one that gripped her, locked her like this one. Images, fantasies of this nun had crammed her head all day. But they were so goddam *faceless.*

Christ, if she just had the woman's name. Something, anything to go on. She needed the name, at least, before she could start to get a hold on this fantastic truth.

Ah, God knows *this* wasn't the out she'd been pacing after the night before. Because this one was no out at all.

No way she could persuade herself she didn't give a sweet shit about this odd case Dick McAlpine had tossed her before lunch. She was stuck here now, for as long as it took her to figure this thing out.

Really figure it out. Not that shit they would wind up showing on TV or printing in her miserable newspaper. She had to know it all: the *how, where, who, what, all* of it.

What wasn't quite clear yet was *why* she was going to track this thing so relentlessly.

Not that she would actually have to explain it, anyway. It would be easy enough to wrap the whole package in the red Career ribbon, justify it simply as a way to muscle herself ahead.

Obsession? Phooey. She would just be utilizing the lucky fluke of coming from the same socio-backdrop as the nun. A good reporter used whatever edge she had, with as much shamelessness as the job required.

And it was nobody's damn business but her own if her

digging should also yield a few clues to . . . unraveling herself.

That unfamiliar thought put a grimace of distaste on Meg's face. There were few things she loathed more than belly-button gazing, whining clichés about *getting it together* and *finding the real me.* She said aloud, "Fuck *that* shit," and walked to the kitchen to refill the mug of vodka.

The dreams tonight were different. Still vivid, still tortured.

But more defined. She dreamed she was in the trees, running. No darkness to hide in. Cold light all around.

Someone grabbing her, touching her. Rough hands, hands on her body. When the hands came away she could see herself, white body in the white light.

Everywhere the hands had touched her there was blood.

When the phone rang, Meg's first thought was that it was someone from the office, some late-breaking lead. So she snatched up the receiver before the second ring: "Yeah. Gavin here."

Bemused voice: "Hello there, Gavin. Wald here." Brief, baffled silence. "The man whose car you swacked this afternoon."

"Oh, yes. Sorry, I didn't connect." She shifted the phone to her other ear. "What can I do for you, Mr. Wald?"

He said he happened to be having dinner in the neighborhood, and wondered if he could drop around to exchange insurance numbers. Her first impulse was to say *Fuck off, I'll send you a postcard.* But she realized before she spoke that once this case broke she would have no time, even for postcards. And tonight, let's face it, she could use a little light entertainment. A brief diversion from this goddam pointless traffic on her rug.

So she said, "Okay, Mr. Wald, drop around. Provided you can make it in ten minutes."

179

She had already pulled the manila folder marked INSUR-ANCE BITS from her file before he rang. She said crisply at the door, "Thanks for coming, Mr. Wald, that's very considerate of you. Can I offer you a coffee, Scotch, wine, whatever?"

"Scotch would be fine, thanks." He was still wearing that goofy smile. "With ice and a little water."

She poured a skinny portion from the cheap-Scotch bottle. Said as she presented the glass, "I certainly appreci-ate you not making a fuss this afternoon."

"Not at all." He was spread out in her expensive chair, the imitation Eames. "I figured you were working on some-thing important. Do you mind me asking what it was?"

Meg flipped her hand as she sat on the orange couch. "Oh, just the usual. Nothing so interesting." She picked up the folder from the pine-barrel end table and read off her insurance data—names, numbers. When the klutz made no move to write them down, she seized the pad beside the phone and scribbled them out herself.

"Well, you seemed to me quite—lit up. I'm always inter-ested to see people who really care about their work." He hesitated. "I've read some of your stuff in the paper. You're quite good."

For some reason that *quite* rankled. She stood up and passed him the slip, saying, "I'm sure if you just call my insurance agent they'll iron it all out. Your fender, anyway, and speaking of work, I have a very heavy schedule tomor-row. So if you don't mind, Mr. Wald . . ."

He made no move to drink up and decently depart. Instead looked at her with that idiotic grin and said, "I'm sorry you're in such a rush."

She tapped a cigarette out of her pack. What the hell, the guy had actually been quite nice about this whole thing. Five minutes of the charm treatment might be well invested. She turned on one of her seventy-five-watt smiles as she said, "Well, I'm sorry to seem like I'm rushing you. I don't turn back into a pumpkin until midnight, actually." And asked

him politely, with as much enthusiasm as the situation required, about his job, where he lived, what he thought of this
town, anyway.

He had a way of thinking out answers that should have
been as automatic as "thanks" or "how d'you do" that Meg
somehow found irritating. Bad enough that his pensiveness
implied she was actually interested in the questions; worse
that it suggested Wald was fascinated with his own answers.

She was about to phrase another graceful ease-out when
he said, "I don't mean to sound abrupt, but are you by any
chance interested in making love?"

She laughed aloud as she tilted back her head, ran a
hand through her loose hair. Christ alive, she'd had to draw
one of these—on a night like this. She said, "As a matter of
fact, not in the slightest."

He bobbed his wiry head. "Well, I just thought I'd mention it. Since I happened to find the idea on my mind, and
in my experience that's usually not one-sided. It seems to
occur to both people around the same time."

She tried not to smile as she said, "Well, Mr. Wald, I
hope you'll excuse the observation that your experience
must be somewhat limited." She looked across at this guy
with the steel-brush head and the legs so skinny his knees
looked bony even in corduroys. "Because I am always quite
aware of what's on my own mind, and what's on it right now
is that you're not at all my type."

"Type." He smiled at that. "Type. Okay, what type is
that?"

"Young." She flipped a hank of hair behind her left ear,
watching with some pleasure the mild wince that came out
of him at that word. "And beautiful. Young, beautiful bodies."

"Bodies. Plural?"

"That's right, plural. And fortunately there happen to
be a few good ones around."

"Okay." He was nodding now. "And the head doesn't matter?"

"Not that much." She pulled her feet up onto the couch cushions, wrapped her arms around her shins. "Head stuff I get plenty of in my job. In the department you're discussing—which, by the way, let's be precise, because I have no taste for phony euphemisms, is fucking, not 'making love'—in that department I prefer young bodies. Young, energetic, beautiful bodies. And since that seems to leave you out, Mr. Wald, since you don't attract me in the slightest, and since I think this is one hell of a devious way to get your car fixed, and since I have a real heavy day tomorrow, Mr. Wald, I wonder if you'd mind drinking up and just clearing out."

"Fair enough, Ms. Gavin." He raised his glass, smiled at her over it. "I really don't give much of a damn about the car, you know."

Coldly: "Nor do I, Mr. Wald. Nor do I."

He lifted his other hand, palm out, a surrender gesture. Drained the glass in two quick gulps. Stood then, bowed with an awkward sort of *politesse* and said, "Thanks very much, Ms. Gavin. For your Scotch, your cooperation and your interesting thoughts."

The maroon Buick turned onto I-94, heading east, at 12:15 P.M. Tim Vance was at the wheel, Andy DaSilva beside him, Nick Scotti in the rear seat.

Scotti was staring at the back of Vance's close-cropped dirty-blond head. He understood this Tim Vance was a fucking rich boy. Fat-cat daddy back in Cambridgeport, some kind of high-class executive.

Scotti asked abruptly, "Tim, you a college boy?"

"Hunh?"

"You go to college?"

Vance smiled. "A couple of semesters. Let's put it this way, with my high school grades the only college that would have me was a little place in Kansas that needed fresh meat for their football team.''

"So you went.''

"Well, just for as long as I could take it. Which wasn't long. Dorm living in a two-bit Kansas town wasn't exactly my idea of how to go.''

Scotti was somehow pleased with that answer. "So you've got no degree.''

"Yeah, I picked one up a few years ago from Ramsey County Community College. Night-school stuff.''

"Mmmph,'' Scotti grunted. "What'd you take?''

"Police science and psychology, mostly. I took all the psych and sociology I could get my hands on.''

For Nick Scotti this was a toss-up: whether he entertained more contempt for anyone who took psychology courses, or for cops who learned their business from college lectures in police science. Yet as a C-grades high school graduate who had wandered into legal detection by way of a course in courtroom stenotyping his father had pushed him into, Scotti recognized the dollar value of a college degree. "So what're you doing in a dead-shit town like Cambridgeport?''

"I like it,'' said Vance. "I backed into police work kind of by accident, because I didn't know what the hell else I wanted to do. I liked most of it more than I expected to, but I sure didn't like where I started out.''

"Which was?'' DaSilva asked.

"A couple years on a downtown Minneapolis beat. Jesus, that was the *pits*. Every day I'd confiscate maybe a dozen guns and knives, and the next day it was the same thing all over. Jesus, I hated it. I just couldn't feel I was getting anything accomplished. It was all just fingers in the dike. And some dike—pimps, muggers, chicken hawks. The real social cream.''

If there was one thing Nick Scotti prided himself on, it was his street sense, his rich, intuitive knowledge of precisely the kind of street people rich-boy Vance had just brushed off. He grunted, "Mmmph. At least you get some action downtown. So what the hell happens out in Cambridgeport?"

Vance chuckled, tapping the wheel of the Buick. "Jesus, Nick, not a hell of a lot. And I like it that way. You get to know the people. Feel you're really providing them some kind of service. I know that's not your style, Nick. You'd be bored out of your nuts there in one week. But I like it that way."

"Mmmph." Scotti flicked off the porkpie, tossed it on the rear-window shelf. "How many homicides you get out there?"

"About one a year. Lately, anyway." Vance smiled. "Our crime rate is picking up."

"Jesus Christ." Scotti unhitched his belt. "You think the big town's too big for you? I'll tell you the truth—it's too small for me."

"Nick's idea of a good week is ten homicides and a couple of rapes," DaSilva explained mildly.

Vance shrugged. "Well, like they say in the song, different strokes for different folks."

Goddam cherries, thought Scotti. A pair of goddam cherries Abrams was sending him off to bust this case with. Well, piss on them. He'd do it all himself if he had to.

If these cherries would just keep out of his way.

As the maroon Buick crossed over the Wisconsin state line they took a straw vote on the most likely candidate for Daddy.

Andy DaSilva thought it had to be Gary Tucker. "You can tell from the letters they had a pretty strong relationship going. Some kind of relationship, anyway. A guy like this Danziger—I just can't see a nun like Sister Angela getting mixed up with him."

"Well, okay. Maybe it was a rape," said Vance. "But I think we've gotta discount at least half of what Sullivan says.

Hell, he spent most of today trying to turn up a yellow sheet on Danziger anyplace he could think of. All he came up with was a couple of traffic citations in Milwaukee. I've got a feeling this Danziger's not going to turn out to be half as much a bad guy as Sullivan wants us to think."

"So what the fuck's a yellow sheet got to do with it?" Scotti demanded.

"Okay, nothing, necessarily. But Jesus Christ, look where Sullivan's been getting his input—from the Tuckers. The worse they can make this guy sound, the quicker they get their own kid off the hook."

Fucking cherry, what do you know, Scotti thought irritatedly. "Yanh, sure. So what else is new?"

"Well, I just figure there's more to this thing than we're getting out of Sullivan," said Vance. "I still think Danziger might turn out to be the one who screwed the nun. The ages fit better, anyway—I mean, an older guy."

"Sure there's more to it. Why else are we busting our hump to get over there?" Scotti kicked off his boots, put his feet up on the car seat. *Fucking rich boy, you don't know shit.* "But Danziger still doesn't fit. A nun and a fucking doper? Nanh, I don't buy that. Even from a nun who could murder her own kid." He slid his spine flat on the seat. "I'm telling you—whatever we turn up, it ain't gonna be that."

"Annh, we're probably way off track anyway," said Vance. "Assuming we ever *do* pin down his identity, Daddy's probably gonna turn out to be the curate at St. Rose. Nobody we're after yet."

Against his will, Scotti silently agreed with the probability of that last remark. DaSilva was saying, "Maybe. But the dates fit pretty good, Tim. And she was on vacation, don't forget that. People do funny things sometimes when they're on vacation."

"You're telling me?" said Vance. "I remember a couple times on my own vacations I was lucky not to end up in jail."

Ah yeah, sure, cherry, I just fucking bet, thought Scotti. "Tell

185

you what, Tim," he said as he rolled over to sleep on the rear seat. "If it *is* one of those Milwaukee turkeys, we're gonna find it out. We're gonna find it all out for sure."

One thing about nursing the graveyard shift, ten to six A.M.—you got plenty of time to yourself. Not every special liked that, sitting alone a whole night in a gloomy room, but Norma Knudsen never minded—especially not this week, when she had a cable-stitch sweater to finish up for her granddaughter Cara's birthday.

Around two A.M. Knudsen suddenly felt another presence in the dim-lit room. She looked up and saw the patient sitting bolt upright in the bed, looking at Knudsen with a small, peculiar smile.

"Oh, mercy me!" Knudsen fluttered her hand over her heart. "Excuse me, Sister, you gave me a start. I thought you were sound asleep." She pushed her knitting into the crack of the chair arm and approached the bed.

That little smile took Knudsen by surprise. She hadn't yet seen her patient awake, but from reading the hospital chart she'd expected her to be depressed, unresponsive, withdrawn. Reluctant to talk. Yet as Knudsen pushed the *low* switch on the light-bank behind the bed the nun said brightly, "Which one are you?"

"Why, I'm Mrs. Knudsen, your night special. Is there anything you'd like, Sister? Some water, fruit juice?"

"Maybe some water, thank you." As Knudsen poured a fresh glass from the Thermos on the bedside table the patient looked across the room at the four vases lined up on the dresser. "Oh, I like the flowers."

"Yes, they're lovely, aren't they?" Knudsen handed her the glass. "You see how much your friends think of you?"

She shook her head, firmly but cheerfully. Knudsen had expected her to look—well, haggard, maybe. Certainly not so young and lively. Even pretty, almost. Knudsen asked as she automatically smoothed out the sheet, plumped the pillow, "Is there anything else you'd like, Sister? Anything I can get you?"

"No, thanks."

"Maybe a pill to help you sleep? Dr. Talbott has one ordered, if you need it."

"No, that's all right." Taking her cue from Knudsen, she handed back the glass and lay down on the pillow. But her eyes were bright, disconnected from sleep. Knudsen could tell she wanted to talk.

Frankly, Knudsen was fascinated to hear what she might have to say, this famous patient of hers who was all over the TV, but since she wasn't sure this conversation should be encouraged, she switched off the light behind the bed and said, "Well then, Sister, you just try to get your rest. And if there's anything you need I'll be right here."

She went back to the chair and took up her knitting. The bright eyes followed her from the bed. "What's that you're making?" the nun asked.

Knudsen held up the unfinished sleeve. "A sweater for my granddaughter. It's her sixteenth birthday on Sunday."

"Oh, that's very pretty. I like the color."

Knudsen nodded. "Heather blue, they call it."

"Well, she's very lucky. Your granddaughter." In one swift motion she sat up again in the bed, looked at the flowers dimly visible in the shielded light from the lamp beside Knudsen's chair. "I guess they're all blaming her, aren't they? They all think she did it."

"Did what?" Knudsen asked, still thinking of her granddaughter.

She flipped her hand, said in a strong, clear voice, "Oh, the baby, and all that. I guess they're blaming her. But they shouldn't, you know." She stared for a moment at the flowers, while Knudsen waited in anxious confusion. "They just don't understand. But it's not fair that they're all blaming her."

Dear, oh dear. Knudsen realized that this was why the

doctors had ordered her into this medically routine case, what they'd told her to watch out for: some sign of mental deterioration. What the nun was saying now, it made no sense. No sense at all. But sakes alive, she looked so calm, so collected. And Knudsen had no training in psychiatric nursing.

Pushing the needle into the yarn, she said as calmly as she could, "Why, Sister, whatever do you mean?"

She shook her head. "Never mind. You don't understand either. But I wish they would just—be nicer to her." She paused, looking with that odd liveliness around the room. "Because she really didn't do it, you know. What they think."

Knudsen kept on knitting, flicking furtive glances at the young woman sitting up in the bed. "Well now, dear, I don't think anyone isn't being nice. Don't you worry yourself one bit about that—I think everyone cares a great deal. They're very sympathetic, don't you know."

She sighed noisily, and lay back down on the pillow. "Never mind," she said in a faint, faraway voice. "I can't change it now, anyway."

Knudsen kept watching, anxiously. She was ready to go for help to the nursing station, go for medication. Anything to stop this strange flow of talk.

But the nun dropped into sleep a few minutes later. Knudsen could tell by the sound of the breathing in that silent room. She waited out the rest of her shift a little nervously, half expecting—maybe half hoping, if she was going to be honest with herself—that the patient would wake up again, still wanting to talk.

But she never did. The nun slept restlessly, but she slept. By the time the squat orange sun came up over the hospital parking lot, Knudsen had decided the incident was probably not significant. But as she went off her shift at six she added one line to the hospital chart on Sister Angela Flynn: *Two A.M. Patient had brief period of inappropriate conversation.*

Fifteen

At 6:45 on Thursday morning the alarm rang beside her convent bed. She reached to turn it off, groping in the air.

No table.

No clock.

Her eyes flew open.

Oh, yes—she was still in the hospital. The clock must have sounded in her own body, her head.

She rolled toward the wall of closets, blinking, lying very still. She didn't want that nurse who was probably sitting in that chair to know she was awake. She needed private time, time to sort all this out.

Body still strange. But not as sore as yesterday. Not as —battered. Except that, for some reason, she was crying into the mattress.

Then it came back to her. Vivid but muddled, like one of those dreams.

Talking with Dr. Talbott. The night before. Those things he told her about.

She remembered it so clearly now—his thin head outlined against the closet, that grip of his strong hands—that it must not have been a dream.

Must be real. Have happened. And if it happened, then it must be true.

Sweet Mother of God, if that was true—what Dr. Talbott had said. And it *must* be true—that and so much else—

She must have done some terrible thing. A thing so terrible they would not tell her about it.

Then why couldn't she remember it?

A thing like that—how could she *not remember it?*

Slowly, groggily, as she lay feigning sleep, Angela began to replay the tapes in her head.

· · ·

At 8:28 Gary Tucker was sitting in a folding metal chair in the small interrogation room of the Oak Creek P.D., with its ceilings and walls soundproofed with thick acoustic tile. Lined up facing him across the metal table were the three strange cops, plus Sullivan.

As Tucker nervously fingered the knee-crease in his chinos, the one who said he was a D.A., DaSilva, dragged him through the same stuff Sullivan had asked him about the day before—how he met this woman, what they did and said. Tucker's answers were brief, monosyllabic.

"Did you correspond with her after she went back home?"

"Some. She wrote me a couple of times."

"And you wrote back?"

Tucker hesitated, looking warily at DaSilva. They probably had those letters. "Yeah, I guess."

"Did you see her again?"

"Yeah. In February. My parents told her she could come visit any time." He paused. "This archery club my uncle and me belong to was having their annual dance, so she came by for that."

"She went to the dance with you?"

The kid blushed. "Yeah, kind of. I, ah, didn't have a date, so she came with us."

Holy mackerel, thought Scotti. *The kid didn't have anybody else to date, so he took a seven months' pregnant nun to the big dance.*

"What transpired on that visit?" DaSilva was asking.

"Nothing. I mean, she went shopping with my sister. We went out to dinner. That kind of stuff."

"When did you see her again?"

"Last weekend. When she came down for the annual shoot."

"Annual what?"

"The archery club tournament."

"You invited her down?"

"Yeah, I invited her when she came for the dance."

"Were you aware then she was pregnant?"

"No. She didn't say anything about it."

"You couldn't tell just by looking?"

The kid's hands were sweating. He rubbed them on his pants. "Well, Gayle said she'd put on some weight this winter. Because she wasn't getting any exercise."

"Did you at any time have sexual contact with her?"

Tucker ducked his head, pulled his chin into his shoulders. "No, no. Like I said yesterday—no."

When Angela felt the urge to urinate, she murmured to her morning-shift nurse, "I think I'd like to get up, please."

Mrs. Langton brought her a cotton bathrobe, and helped Angela step down from the bed, stand on her astonishingly rubbery legs. "That's all right, dear, everyone feels like that at first," the nurse said. "You'll be surprised how soon your strength comes back."

She helped Angela to the bathroom, stood outside as Angela closed the door.

Alone in the small white-tiled room, Angela lurched to the white toilet and sat down, pulling up the hospital robe. She looked around the room, so bright-lit the light seemed to bounce off the tile walls. And felt the rush of that recaptured sensation: *privacy. Finally alone.*

Ah, such relief. Such blessed relief. She was smiling to herself when she looked down and noticed her legs jutting out from under the hospital gown.

The shock went through her like a slow electric volt. So swollen—discolored. Those ugly yellow and purple stains.

Why would her legs look like that?

Was this what Dr. Talbott meant about her being pregnant, those bloated, ugly legs? Oh, it could be. She'd told him she had no symptoms. But that was before she'd seen these strange, frightening legs.

The stinging sensation when she urinated was another shock. All this strangeness in her body—nothing like her own. But she'd told Dr. Talbott she had no symptoms.

When she opened the bathroom door a little later, the nurse was right there, saying, "Would you like to sit by the window for a while, Sister?"

"No, thanks. Not just yet." So tired. So weak and tired.

Odd, how comforting that bed felt, as Mrs. Langton smoothed the sheets back over her body. Odd that comfort would finally come from such small things.

Ben Haverty had talked to Dr. Talbott the night before, so he knew when he knocked at the door of Room 308 that the situation he faced this morning was a little less rough than it might have been. The question now was, *how much less rough?*

The nun was sitting up in the bed, crying. Blowing her nose into a Kleenex. When she saw him she shook her head. "Oh, Mr.—"

"Haverty. Ben Haverty, Sister Angela."

"Mr. Haverty, I'm sorry to be like this. I just—"

"Quite all right, quite all right, Sister Angela. I'm sorry to be disturbing you like this. At a time like this. But I would like to speak with you."

She looked up at him from the bed, those green eyes sliding liquidly through her pain. Said politely, in her little-girl, little-nun voice, "Of course, Mr. Haverty."

He pulled up a metal-legged chair, sat spilling over it alongside her bed. "You understand that Sister Philomena has asked me to look after any legal concerns you might have."

"Yes, I understand that. But I don't know wh . . ." She stopped halfway through that questioning word, as something seemed to flash behind her eyes. She frowned, and said slowly, "Dr. Talbott told me the police want to talk to me. Is that why you're here?"

Haverty nodded. Softly: "Yes, Sister. It's something like that."

"Well, I told Dr. Talbott I'd be glad to talk to them. But I don't know what I could tell them. I don't know anything about what happened."

He shook his head. "No, no, Sister, you won't have to talk to them. I don't *want* you to talk to them. Please rest assured of that."

She was listening intently, her face pinched in an anxious frown. "All right, Mr. Haverty."

"Unfortunately there are other legal processes that we cannot avoid. Some of those will be happening this morning, Sister."

"I see."

"I'm here to look after that for you, Sister Angela. I want you please not to worry about this. I want you to concentrate all your energies on resting and getting well again."

She nodded. Seemed to be waiting for more.

He said again, "I am here to take good care of your interests, Sister."

So strange. So confusing. "All right. Thank you, Mr. Haverty."

He heaved himself up from the chair, said he would be back to see her very soon.

Such a strange, big man, that Mr. Haverty. Angela still had no idea what he was doing here. What he was telling her about. But she believed him when he said he was trying to help her.

Like that doctor, Talbott, and she *wanted* to believe them. But if it was really true, what they were telling her, how much could they help?

They had given her so few pieces. Like this was a jigsaw she must solve with those few pieces that didn't fit together.

She needed more pieces of the puzzle. But she thought she would probably have them soon. She could tell that from the way that big man talked to her.

Ben Haverty moved like a rumbling storm through the doorway of the assistant hospital director's office.

Two Cambridgeport police sergeants, Michael Leighton and Robert Paige, were waiting in the reception room with the arrest warrant for Sister Angela Flynn laid on the table in front of them. Haverty snatched it off the table, ran his eyes down the typed print. *"Murder in the second degree?"* he bellowed. "Are you out of your mind—*murder two on that poor girl upstairs?"* The two policemen watched him blankly, silently. *"Premeditation?* You're trying to tell me that poor nun who lost so much blood she was practically dead on the floor committed premeditated murder on her own child?"

"We're not telling you anything," Leighton said shortly. "We're just here to serve this warrant."

"Well, I goddam well won't stand for it. Who's responsible for this—Mark Abrams?" Haverty whirled on his heel. "Get Abrams the hell on the phone. *Right now!"*

He seized the phone on the receptionist's desk. As he was dialing the district attorney's office the hospital's A.D. tapped him on the arm, and pointed wordlessly into an inner office, where an inspector from the regional crime lab was also waiting. Haverty slammed down the phone and went in.

Inspector Vito Maggiore, who was waiting with a female chemist from his office, handed him a court order for blood specimens to be taken from Gayle Flynn, also known as Sister Angela Flynn.

Haverty slapped at the order. *"Blood specimens?"* he raged. "What the hell is this? This is insane. What are you trying to do to this girl?"

Maggiore stood and turned toward Haverty. He was a tall, beefy old ex-cop with a size twenty-three neck, one of the few law-establishment guys who could face down Ben Haverty pound for pound. "Just serving a court order, Mr. Haverty."

Haverty slapped the paper again. "This is totally without justification. As her attorney of record I order her not to obey it."

"Don't talk to me, Counselor. Talk to the judge who signed it."

"I *am* talking to you. *I won't have this girl disturbed.* Do you understand that, Inspector?"

Maggiore faced him down: "You call Judge Bloch. If he rescinds the order to me verbally by phone, I'll accept that. Otherwise I don't leave this hospital until the order is served."

Two could play at this jowl-rattling game. "Understood, Counselor?"

Gary Tucker's interrogation dragged on for about forty minutes without denting his story. The kid was getting tired, and a little testy, shorter with his answers. But the gist of them did not change.

Finally DaSilva said, "Okay, we'll have a short break." He wanted to check in by phone with Abrams, and get a better look at what Sullivan had turned up yesterday.

Vance and Sullivan followed him out of the interrogation room. As they walked down the hall toward Sullivan's office DaSilva asked, "What you think, Tim?"

Vance shrugged. "I dunno. The kid seems to be holding back, all right. But he's pretty hard to shake."

DaSilva's normally mild face was tight, angry. He said, "Well, I think he's lying through his naive teeth."

Sullivan cleared his throat. "Well now, Mr. DaSilva, I sure wouldn't want to argue with your judgment on that. But let me tell you, I've known that Gary Tucker since he was just a lad. And I've never once caught him out in a lie."

"Sergeant, let me put it this way," DaSilva said wearily.

Christ, that all-night drive had really taken it out of him. "The way he's talking and acting in that room is consistent with the behavior of a lying witness."

As they reached Sullivan's office Vance said, "Well, what the hell, give Nick some time alone with him. I've got a feeling whatever he's covering up Nick's gonna get out of him."

"Maybe," DaSilva said shortly. "We'll see. Anyway, I'd like you to get out there and try to locate this Danziger. Sergeant, you got any idea where he should start?"

"Well now, I do." Sullivan flipped open his small black leather notebook. "I've got an address here—I think it's his mother's place, in Glendale. I've already alerted the Glendale police that you'll be coming, and they've offered the loan of a squad car and an officer if you need 'em."

"Okay, Tim. Keep in touch, and see what you can turn up." DaSilva smiled grimly. "And I hope to hell you have better luck than us."

Nick Scotti watched the kid's face as the three interrogators left the room, watched his mouth curl into a small smirk of relief.

Yanh, laugh while you can, schmuck. Scotti loosened his tie and put one booted foot up on an empty chair. After two days of frustration, *inaction,* he was finally about to move in on this fucking case. The impatience that had gagged him for the last forty minutes melted into an expansive calm as he said, "Kinda rough, hunh, Tucker?"

"It's okay."

"Hey, listen, I understand this is no picnic for you. District Attorney DaSilva can be pretty tough with those questions."

"That's okay. I got nothing to hide."

The kid was wiping his hands on his pants again. Not a bad-looking kid—clean-cut, muscley, built. Scotti liked the type. "Well, it's about time you got a break. You mind if I call you Gary?" Tucker shook his head. "My name's Nick Scotti. You can call me Nick."

"Okay."

"So tell me, Gary, what kind of stuff you interested in? Besides this archery."

Warily: "Well, I do a lot of hunting. Fishing in the summers."

"Oh, yeah? You hunt with guns, or those bows and arrows?"

"Both. My uncle Brad, he got a bear once with his bow."

"Oh, yeah? How about you?"

"Oh, I got a couple of does. And smaller stuff—birds."

"What kind of birds?"

"Partridges, wild turkeys. That kind of stuff."

"Hey, I've done some hunting myself. But I gotta tell you, Gary, I wouldn't go after no bear with no bow and arrow."

Tucker smiled—his first smile of the morning. "It's not that tough. If you know what you're doing."

Scotti leaned his elbow on the metal table, pushed his fingers up through his thinning black hair. The kid was too fucking green to the game to understand the carrot part of the stick-and-carrot routine. Scotti said, "Hey, tell me about it."

Ben Haverty raged around that hospital office for the better part of an hour, shaking his dewlaps like a wild old bull, hollering at judges, A.D.A.s, anybody he could raise on the end of his phones.

When he finally accepted the arrest warrant, Leighton and Paige headed for West Wing Three to arrange for the police guard. Haverty trailed them into the elevator, snapping, "You are not to talk to her. *Do you understand?* You are not to go anywhere near this girl."

Leighton snapped back, "The guard is strictly routine in a felony arrest, Mr. Haverty. As you know."

Up at the nursing station a corporal from the Cambridgeport P.D., dressed in plainclothes, was already waiting. With Haverty glowering in the background, Paige arranged for a chair to be placed outside Room 308, and ascertained that the telephone and television had already been removed from the room. Handing the corporal a typed sheet, Paige said, "This is the list of approved visitors. Nobody else allowed in without special permission from Chief Marwick."

Haverty demanded, "Let me see that list."

Paige nodded; the corporal passed it to him. Written as an official police order, it specified that only her immediate family, her attorney of record, her private confessor, and her three direct religious superiors were to be allowed right of visitation. Paige said, "If you've got any objections, bring 'em to Chief Marwick."

Haverty handed back the list without comment. The corporal folded it, slipped it into his jacket pocket and walked toward the chair outside Room 308.

In the acoustic-tiled room of the Oak Creek P.D., Nick Scotti said, "Come on, Gary. You knew she was pregnant, right?"

The kid searched for the right words. "Well, somebody told me she was."

"Who somebody?"

"My uncle Brad."

"When was that?"

"The morning of the archery shoot. Last Sunday."

"So what'd he say?"

"Well, he got me aside and said something like, 'I'm telling you, that lady is pregnant. Get out of it, stay out of it.' Something like that."

"What did you say?"

"Nothing. I didn't say nothing."

"What did you think?"

"Well, I didn't know." The confusion showed again on Tucker's broad, blank face. "I mean, if you thought Gayle was pregnant, she sure did *look* it. I just hadn't figured anything like that because—well, she didn't act it or anything."

"How'd she act?"

Shrug from the kid. "Just like she always did. Laughing and joking and kind of—sparking around."

"Did Brad ask you if you did it?"

The broad face reddened. "Nah. He knew I didn't."

"What'd he say."

"Something like, 'I sure as hell know it wasn't you.' Something like that."

Now they were getting down to it. Scotti rubbed his left hand along the surface of the metal table. His voice was soft, confiding: "So what's the story, Gary? You like to go with boys?"

Tucker jerked upward in his chair. "What you mean— like, fag stuff?"

"Hey, listen, Gary, that's okay with me. I know a lot of guys like to go with guys. What the hell, that's not so bad. One way, the other way, there ain't so much difference." He paused, letting the silence work on the kid. *"But you gotta tell me."*

Tucker was shaking his head violently, his face a wide tomato of indignation. "Hey, I'm no fag!"

Then it was the other thing. Scotti said quietly, "Okay, Gary. Now you've been trying to feed us a line of bullshit in here this morning, and I let you run with it because I knew just what you were up to. But now we're gonna knock off this bullshit, and you're gonna level with me." Silence. The kid tossed a sullen, defiant look into Scotti's face. "You got two choices, Gary: you say it. Or I will."

More angry silence.

Christ, this was what Scotti loved about interrogations. This moment that was as good as coming in a fuck. But he kept the triumph carefully filtered from his voice as he said flatly, definitely, *"You've never been with a woman."*

The kid's eyes dropped to the table. The red face, the silence, said it all.

More softly now: "Hey, listen, Gary, there's nothing so freaky about that. You're just a kid, twenty-one, still living at home. What the hell, I'll tell you the truth, Gary—I was nineteen before I did it myself. And I come from a big city."

Pause. "Well, okay." The words came slowly out of Tucker—reluctant, relieved. "I guess I haven't. Not all the way, anyways."

"Listen, why the hell should that bother you? You got plenty time for that stuff later. Hell, a couple years from now you'll be screwing your head off."

"Sure. I know that."

Okay, so this much was out. But the come didn't feel good, didn't feel clean. The kid was still holding out. Scotti could feel it, as real as the hand-sweat the kid was surreptitiously wiping on his pants again.

Scotti tipped his chair backward, folded his hands behind his neck. He looked up at the ceiling, giving the kid that much privacy as he asked softly, "But you did get into it some with Gayle, didn't you, Gary?" Silence. "You did a little kissing, a little fooling around." Another silence. *"When was that, Gary?"*

The words came out in a blurted gasp: "Last Sunday. After the archery shoot." The kid bent forward in his chair, spilling the words like vomit. "I mean, she missed her plane and everything. She kept saying, 'Don't rush, it don't matter, I can get one tomorrow.' So I thought—I figured maybe she was asking for it."

"So?"

"So we all went out to dinner after the shoot and I had a couple drinks. Hard stuff. Mostly I just drink beer." He paused. "I guess I got pretty drunk."

"So what happened after you got drunk?"

200

The sweat was popped now in little beads on his forehead. "Well, when her and me got back to the house everybody else was already sacked out. So I got us both another drink. We were sitting around talking in the living room."

"So you fooled around some on the couch?"

Sweat coming off him now like steam. "Yeah, some. A little."

"Did you get her clothes off?"

"No, no." Fright in those blank blue eyes.

"So what happened?"

"Well, I kissed her some."

Rapid-fire now: "Kissed her how?"

"Well . . . on the mouth, like."

"Ever kissed her before?"

"Not like that." He swallowed. "And I touched her some. Her—bra."

"You get your hands inside? Feel up her breasts?"

His eyes rolled whitely. "No, I just kind of—outside. Just a little." He looked down at the table. "That's when I felt the bandages."

Ah, here it was, here was the come. Scotti asked softly, "Bandages?"

"Yeah. Like Ace bandages. Around her stomach. She had her stomach all wrapped up in Ace bandages."

Sixteen

At eleven A.M. several dozen reporters, plus four television camera crews and sets of lights, were crammed into a conference room of the Cambridgeport P.D. Meg Gavin sat in a front-row seat, frowning nervously over a messily scribbled checklist headed *BLAST-OFF!* Her gut felt tight and fluttery, almost premenstrual.

At three minutes past eleven Chief Gregory Marwick strode in the front door of the room, followed by D.A. Abrams. Marwick looked stiff and self-conscious as he stepped up to the bank of microphones set up on a table moved in from the library next door. With Abrams standing behind his right shoulder, he said nervously, "If I can have your attention, gentlemen—I have a statement I will read without comment. Copies will be available for any of you that need it."

He cleared his throat and read from the typed sheet: "In conjunction with a joint investigation with the District Attorney of Ramsey County, the Cambridgeport Police Department has today arrested Gayle Flynn, also known as Sister Angela Flynn, of 205 Windsor Avenue, Town of Cambridgeport, and charged her with the Crime of Murder in the Second Degree in violation of Section 125.25, Subdivision 1 of the Penal Law of the State of Minnesota."

Noisy scrambling from the radio newsmen as they rushed for their phones. Marwick glanced up, startled, as they jostled each other at the door. Then he read on in a flat monotone, detailing the points of the indictment: That between the hours of 7:30 A.M. and 3:15 P.M. on April 27, at the St. Rose of Lima Convent, Town of Cambridgeport, the defendant gave birth unattended to a male infant weighing approximately six and three-quarter pounds. That during the same hours and in the same location, the defendant did cause the death of the infant child by asphyxiation with article or articles of clothing. That the defendant, at approximately 3:30 P.M. on April 27, was transported to Parkhurst General Hospital, where she remained in satisfactory condition.

"A warrant of arrest, charging Sister Angela Flynn with the crime of murder, has been served on her," Marwick finished. He folded the typed sheet nervously. "As I indicated, copies are available."

The questions rattled at him like rapid artillery: "Who was the father?" "Has she made a statement?" "Will there be a trial?"

Marwick lifted his hand in a traffic-stopping gesture. "I have nothing to add to this statement."

From the front row Meg Gavin asked, "Chief, are you satisfied that the nun acted alone?"

"Sorry, no comment." The questions were still coming at him, like hard rain on a roof, as Marwick escaped through the door.

Lieutenant Tim Vance circled warily around the peeling, run-down yellow bungalow with an unsprung couch on the screened porch and the skeletons of two junked cars in the backyard.

No answer to the doorbell. While the Glendale sergeant waited in the patrol car out front, Vance rang the right-hand neighbor's bell. A thin, graying woman wearing men's slacks and an old plaid shirt said yes, Roy Danziger's mother lived next door. Except she was Pisani now—Mrs. Kathryn Pisani. She'd been divorced from Mr. Danziger oh, about fifteen years now.

No, Roy didn't live with her. She thought he was living someplace down on the beach. A lot of those kids rented houses there cheap in the off-season. Yes, she thought she'd heard something about Roy working back at Midwest Mutual again. She didn't know much about it—those Pisanis pretty much kept to themselves.

Yes, Roy came around sometimes to see his mother, mostly when he had dirty laundry to be done, but the neighbor hadn't seen him now for maybe a couple of weeks. No, she didn't know where Kathryn Pisani was now. Maybe out shopping. Or gone to the beauty parlor. She got her hair done a couple times a week.

Vance thanked the neighbor for her cooperation. She followed him out the screen door, folding her arms against the crisp April air, eyeing the sergeant in the parked squad car. "What's this all about? Has Roy got himself in some kind of trouble?"

"No, not at all," said Vance "We'd just appreciate his help with an investigation we're doing."

The woman sniffed her disbelief, her gaunt face hawkish with curiosity. "Well, it wouldn't surprise me if he was in dutch again."

"Why's that?"

"It just wouldn't. That kid's no good. He's been in trouble most all his life."

Vance thanked her again and walked back to the patrol car. With any luck now, they'd get this Danziger at work.

Frankly, that was where Tim Vance hoped to get him. Where he'd have some leverage, some authority to hold him. Vance thought he might need that. From all he'd heard, this guy was a pretty unstable, unpredictable type.

Mr. Haverty was coming into the room again, moving across the floor in a kind of tiptoe-step that was almost funny, coming from such a big man. He said in his soft, gravelly voice, "Ah, Sister Angela—there is a person here who would like to have a specimen of your blood."

Angela nodded passively. Blood in, blood out—that's all they'd been doing to her since she came to this place.

"Sister, that person is Inspector Vito Maggiore of the Ramsey County Regional Crime Lab. Do you understand that?"

Crime—what? Angela was trying very hard to understand. But no, she did not, of course she did not. That didn't seem to matter, because they went on doing these things to her anyway.

She made a small, fluttering gesture with her left hand. "It's all right. Whatever you say, Mr. Haverty."

. . .

Maggiore and the chemist from his office were waiting at the West Wing Three nursing station, with a nurse from the hospital blood bank. Ben Haverty approached them, walking directly up to Maggiore. Glaring full into Maggiore's face, he said, "Okay, you can have it. But I won't allow you into that room. I won't have you bothering that girl."

"Just one minute here, Counselor," Maggiore snapped. "Unless I am physically present in the room while the blood is being drawn, unless I witness the person this blood comes out of, I'm not leaving this floor. Is that understood?"

Part of Haverty's rage was derived from the fact that he knew Maggiore was legally correct, had him dead to the technical rights. Haverty growled, "All right. But only you. Not"—he thumbed toward the chemist—"her."

Maggiore shook his head. "My female witness comes too. That's a regulation when the blood sample comes from a female defendant."

Wrath, pure wrath in that look. Haverty hissed, *"I won't have you turn this thing into a three-ring circus."*

"All strictly regulation, Counselor. As you know."

"You are not to speak to her. You're not to disturb her in any way. Is that clearly understood?"

"No objection, Counselor."

Their eyes battled for a moment. Then Haverty turned on his heel and walked to the door of Room 308. The other three followed, the blood bank nurse pushing a small wheeled cart.

As they moved through the door Maggiore was struck by the instantaneous change in Haverty's body language. Suddenly he was soft, gentle, reassuring. "Sister Angela, this is—ah, the gentleman I told you about."

The young woman was young and pale; her downcast eyes were red-rimmed, and she clutched a Kleenex in her right hand. She looked to Maggiore like any girl might who'd been doing a good deal of crying.

He stepped up to the bed and said, "Sister Angela, do you know who I am?"

Haverty glared. The nun flicked her eyes up to Maggiore's face, looked away again. "Yes, I know," she murmured.

Maggiore stepped back. The nurse pushed the cart up to the bed and snapped a piece of tubing around the nun's left arm. She slipped a hypodermic needle into a vein, pulled back slowly on the plunger of the syringe.

The room was very still. Everyone except Sister Angela watched the two syringefuls of blood come out of her arm.

The nun herself looked out the window.

Roy Danziger came awake as the shaft of sunlight from the bedroom window moved across his eyelids. He stirred, blinked.

Clock by the bed read 11:32.

He lay there for a couple of minutes, loosening his head from that deep sleep. Then he got up, zipped on his jeans, went downstairs, and walked barefooted out across the beach.

Sand warm, shifting under his feet. Sun so bright he lifted a hand to shield his eyes as he looked out across the lake, watching a couple of early sailboats running, tipped in the wind.

A goddamn nice day.

He was feeling pretty good now, spring days like this. Not so—down as he'd been, that whole fucking miserable winter. That dragged on for like a year.

He walked down to the water's edge and waded in a little. The cold water lapping in off the lake jolted his feet, soaked the bottom of his jeans. And it felt good.

So maybe he'd come out of it. Left the worst behind.

Up from the dumps—by God, it almost felt like that, today.

Maybe this Sunday he'd get out, see some people. Do some biking with Al or something.

On his way back into the house he switched on the living room TV automatically as he passed it. He was making tea in the kitchen when the noon newscast came on.

As he was pouring the boiling water into the pot, he thought he heard the name . . . Gayle Flynn.

He slapped the kettle back on the burner and moved quickly to the archway door. Some guy talking: ". . . warrant of arrest for murder has been served on Sister Angela Flynn." Then some shit about inflation.

Danziger went back to the kitchen and finished making the tea, feeling a little—shaky.

Weird. He could have sworn he heard . . .

Gayle's name. And something about a baby, murdering a baby.

He shook his head and said aloud, "Weird."

When Dr. Bruce Heilbron dropped by Sister Angela's hospital room on his lunch hour he found that her remoteness, that peculiar lack of affect, was gone. The nun wept openly, wadding a tissue in her hands as she haltingly told him about her conversation with Dr. Talbott the night before.

But she had no fresh recollections to offer. She still insisted she had had no obvious signs to alert her to the pregnancy. "Except—my legs are very bruised. I don't know how that happened."

Heilbron kept their conversation deliberately brief. Since she seemed to be tolerating her present level of stress fairly well, he did not want to add to her confusion.

When he left the room he noted in her hospital chart, *1:15 P.M. Patient was tearful, sad-eyed. No tangible recollections of pregnancy.*

As Meg walked up the wide stone steps of the gray granite building with the gothic towers and arched windows, she felt something in herself shriveling to child-size.

The front entrance of the St. Benedict Motherhouse

was a pair of ten-foot-high wooden doors held by huge black iron hinges. Only thing missing was a moat. As Meg pushed the right-hand door open, what she sensed first was the bottomless silence of the place.

The nun at the switchboard by the entrance blinked behind plain-rimmed glasses as Meg explained the purpose of her visit. After whispered consultation through her headset, she told Meg that any press inquiries on this matter would be handled by Sister Bernadine, who was in charge of public relations for the order. Sister Bernadine could see Meg briefly now in her office, in Room 118. She pointed: "Down that hall, please. Turn left, fourth door on the right."

As Meg walked down the long, gloomy hall, over parquet waxed to such a gloss that the light from the adjoining rooms glowed in oblong patterns on the wood, she felt herself moving backward.

Remembering her first feast day in the ninth grade at Holy Name, a convent that was the cloned image of this one. Remembering the starched white uniforms and the crisp white feast day veils moving, gliding in precisely choreographed lines.

Ranks, ranks. Always those silent, graceful ranks. Genuflecting in long lines to the snap of the Mistress General's wooden clapper; curtseying in long rows to the Reverend Mother.

And then the unearthly beauty of the singing in chapel as the ranks of nuns glided fluidly to the communion rail, long black habits skimming the floor, gauze veils floating over their downturned faces. All of it so goddamned eerily *perfect*. Meg could still remember the thrill that had gone through her when she'd realized she was *part of it*, that first Feast of the Immaculate Conception.

But that was before she wised up to their game. And fought back against the implanted "innocence" of those white veils with a long litany of acts that were variously classified as "disobedience," "insubordination," and once—Meg remembered *that* one very well—"sinful pride."

It had ended in a kind of truce. On her graduation day she copped all the top academic prizes, and minded not at all that the hoopla went mostly to the girls recognized for their "spiritual achievements"—the goody-girls of the Sodality and the Altar Society. With her parents waiting outside in the car, Meg had taken a moment to stop in the communal john and stuff all her convent battle gear—veils, uniforms, missals—into a conveniently large trash can.

Now Sister Bernadine was waiting like a trapped mouse behind the gold-lettered door of Room 118, a little wisp of a nun probably in her mid-fifties, dressed in a blue double-knit suit. Meg introduced herself and said, "I'm truly sorry to have to trouble you like this, Sister Bernadine. I know this must be a very difficult time for you all."

"Thank you, Megan." Bernadine looked about as pale as the papers she was twisting in her hands. "I understand that you have your job to do."

"Exactly. I'm very glad you understand it that way, Sister. I know the press must seem to you right now like a most unwelcome intruder into your grief. But we *do* have a job to do, now that this unfortunate incident has become a matter of the public record. And the sooner we can get it done and out of the way, the sooner you'll be rid of us." Basic PR lesson number one, which she devoutly hoped Bernadine was enough of a pro at her job to recognize.

A faint, twisted smile. "Well, I'm afraid I can't be much help to you, Megan. Mr. Haverty has told us that the best course to follow, the course he as our legal adviser recommends, is to make no comment at all."

Okay, so it would be the tough sledding route. She'd *known*, of course, that it couldn't be any other. Meg folded her hands demurely on her lap as she said, "Of course, Sister. I quite understand. But the brief biographical facts about Sister Angela—I'd much prefer to get them directly from you, so I'll know that they're accurate. I'm afraid you're going to find out very quickly as this incident becomes more widely publicized just how atrociously inaccurate so much of what the press puts out can be. Myself, I very much hope not to contribute to any of that confusion."

Bernadine was quiet for a moment as she mulled the unwelcome logic in Meg's suggestion. So Meg pressed on, probably too soon, saying that she was a Holy Name girl herself—she'd always wanted to go to Benedictine, actually, because of its superior academic reputation, but since her mother was a Holy Name girl, family tradition had won out.

Too much, that. Bernadine gave her a crisp nod that Meg translated as *That and a buck will get you a Big Mac for lunch.* Over the next fifteen minutes Meg managed to extract from her that Sister Angela had entered the order sixteen years ago. That since September of the previous year she had served as the director—in effect, the principal—of the Benedictine Kindergarten School. That she was a native of St. Paul, and had been a teacher for fourteen years.

Meg asked, "Did she get her teaching degree here at St. Benedict's College?"

The pinch on those thin lips was more than symbolic. "I'm sorry, Megan," the nun said in her wispy, correct voice. "On Mr. Haverty's advice I cannot give any information on Sister Angela's background or education."

Meg got that response five more times over the next ten minutes. Bernadine had given her precisely the information that Sister Philomena and the General Council had decided would be given to representatives of the press—nothing more, nothing less. The order's brief acknowledgment that Sister Angela Flynn was indeed a part of their religious community.

Finally Meg said, "Sure, I understand. Quite all right, Sister." She pushed her notebook into her blue suede purse and stood up to go. "I'd like you to know I really do appreciate your seeing me at all."

Bernadine got up from behind the desk to see Meg out the office door. As they shook hands Meg said, "Thanks again for your help, Sister Bernadine. I understand the difficulty all of you must be having with this thing."

A slight but grateful smile. "Thank you, Megan. I'm sorry I couldn't be more helpful."

Meg made a brief, dismissing gesture. "Quite all right. By the way, I've been told her parents are still living in St. Paul."

That feint caught Bernadine off guard. She shook her head, frowning thoughtfully. "No, Mr. Flynn died some years ago. I think her mother, Theresa, lives with one of her sons." Then she caught herself, glared accusingly at Meg.

Meg had a particularly blank smile that she held in reserve for moments like these. She was using it as she said, "Well, thanks again. I really would like to extend my deepest condolences to you all."

Bernadine clicked her teeth sharply, a nonverbal reprimand to the presumption implicit in that offer of sympathy. Nodding curtly, she snapped, "Can you find your way out?"

As Meg started down the long, polished hall she could feel the nun's eyes on her back. Hear the echoes clicked in the long, silent hall by the heels of her blue suede boots.

Back again. This time as the enemy.

A mortal enemy, like those ones they'd spent years teaching her to recognize and shun.

She realized this was probably the last time she'd be let back into this place. Where it had all begun.

They'd allowed her one visit, a *pro forma* to inform them on the shape and nature of the enemy. But if Bernadine had read her at all correctly—and Meg thought she probably had; nuns were good at that, in their own way—*they* now knew there was no way Meg Gavin would be steered off the Angela Flynn story with those thin official droppings.

At least she was carrying off four nuggets more than Bernadine had meant to give her: Angela's father was dead.

Her mother's name was Theresa. There were brothers, at least. And Theresa lived with one.

Okay, Meg would settle for that. And find the rest somewhere else.

The enemy.

She'd never meant to be that. But if that was what it would come down to, so be it.

She'd meant to take her time heading for the fortress door. Savor this surrealistic stroll down memory lane, for whatever it was worth.

But as she reached the main corridor and saw the tall doors looming dimly at the end of that long, waxy hall, the clicks of her blue suede boots came more and more quickly.

As they waited in a hospital staff room for Gary Tucker's blood specimen to be drawn, Andy DaSilva and Nick Scotti passed time by reading Gayle Flynn's letters—letters Gary himself had eagerly volunteered as evidence, "provided you send 'em back when you're finished. I'd kinda like to keep them."

As love letters went, they weren't much—"I've been awfully busy at school, but not too busy to think a lot about the fun we had together up at the lake. . . ." "It was really terrific to see you last weekend and I had a great time, especially at the dance . . ."

What should have been a routine twenty-minute operation had already stretched into a three-hour battle with hospital red tape. As Scotti wandered down the hall to look for food, DaSilva checked his watch again: *1:25 already!*

To help kill the time, he asked Gary Tucker why he'd never mentioned anything to Gayle about her pregnancy on the previous weekend.

"Well, I did, sort of," said Tucker.

It never failed to amaze DaSilva—how many times you had to ask some questions before you got the right answer. "When was that?"

"Monday morning, when I drove her to the airport."

"What did you say to her?"

"I said I was real concerned about her weight gain and asked her if she'd seen a doctor."

"And?" DaSilva prompted.

"She said she hadn't. I told her it might be something serious and she shouldn't fool around with it. I kinda pushed her—asked her what doctor she was going to see. She said she guessed her mother's doctor. I made her promise she'd call him as soon as she got back."

"Did you use the word 'pregnant'?" Tucker shook his head. "Why not?"

Tucker knitted his stubby fingers together. "Well, I didn't *know*. I only thought so. And geez, a nun like Sister Gayle—I just didn't want to talk about something like that."

"So that's how you left it?"

Tucker hesitated. "Well, I asked if I could buy her plane ticket back home." He paused. "See, that's something my father always likes to do for any priests or nuns who come to visit."

"What did she say to that?"

"She said thanks, that would be fine. So I bought it and put her on the plane."

Nice kid, thought DaSilva. *He reminds the pregnant lady she's a nun, and sends her home with her two hundred and sixty-three hot bucks in her purse.*

As the big man came back into the room, moving his large bulk delicately over the floor, she said anxiously, "Oh, Mr. Haverty. What's happening to me?"

He nodded to the nurse, who slipped from the room. He sat on the chair beside the bed and looked at her, his face drooping in sad folds.

Silence. Then, softly: "Sister Angela, how are you feeling?"

She slapped the bedcovers. "Very—confused, Mr. Haverty. I want to know what's happening to me."

"Well, as I told you earlier, certain legal processes have been entered into."

She rolled her head anxiously back and forth on the pillow. "Please, please. I *want to know.*"

Gently: "Sister Angela, at the moment you are considered under arrest."

"Arrest?" The word went into her like a stab from their knives. She pulled the sheet up around the neck of her hospital nightgown. "What do you mean, arrest?"

"Please don't let this alarm you. This is only a legal technicality, and I am convinced that the situation will soon be resolved satisfactorily, in your favor."

Bewildered, so bewildered, clutching at the sheet: "But why would they arrest me?"

"You understand that your child was found dead."

Child. Dead. "Yes, Dr. Talbott told me that."

"The circumstances of the death were—suspicious." He rubbed one palm of the knee of his suit. "That is why the police have placed you under arrest. For, ah, second-degree murder."

Her body arched upward on the pillow. "Oh, my God. Oh, Mr. Haverty, I don't understand."

"That is only a technical phrase, I assure you. I beg you not to concern yourself unduly about it."

"Murder." She made herself say it aloud. "Oh my God, Mr. Haverty, what does that mean?"

He leaned forward toward her. "That means that the police are looking for an explanation of how the child died. All right, we will give them that explanation. And then this will all be finished for you as a legal technicality. Because I assure you, that is all this arrest represents. A technicality which we will dispose of, in due time."

She knew he was trying to reassure her. But there was no comfort to be squeezed from what he was saying, none at all. She asked tremulously, "But how *did* the child die, Mr.

Haverty? No one has told me and I want to—I want to know."

He shook his big head. "Please, Sister Angela, I don't want you to concern yourself with that just now. We have plenty of time ahead of us to deal with that. When you are feeling stronger. Right now I only want you to know that the situation is under control, that we are looking after your best interests."

She was turning that word "arrest" with some bewilderment in her mind. "Do you mean— Am I going to jail?"

A firm headshake. "No, no. You will stay here in the hospital, for as long as your doctors advise. And in a short time there will be an arraignment, and we will arrange for bail. Then you'll be free to resume your normal life, pending the court proceedings."

Your normal life. Her green eyes pierced him like skewers. "But right now—you say I'm arrested. What does that mean?"

"Very little, Sister Angela. Except—they would prefer that you not leave your hospital room."

Angela turned her head restlessly on the pillow. So. This was the jail, then. But it had been that for her all along. Ever since they put her in this place.

"And they would prefer that you not make any phone calls. Otherwise, I assure you, you will be living the normal hospital routine. You can have visitors, do as you like."

Do as you like—oh, they said things like that to her, and then they said *she* was the crazy one. She reached again for that thought stuck like a fishhook in her troubled mind: "Mr. Haverty, I would like to know what happened to—the baby."

He looked at her—such dark, sad eyes—and said, "Sister Angela, I have taken you into my care. Do you understand that?"

She nodded.

"I personally feel the charges made against you are a great miscarriage of justice, and I intend to fight them every step of the way. I think we have an excellent, very strong case." His big face so serious, sad. "There will be processes to go through. But we will take them step by step, and I will be with you. I mean to see you safely through this difficult time. Will you trust me to do that, Sister Angela?"

Oh, why did they always ask that? That act of faith.

But he had asked it. And wearily, exhaustedly, she gave it: "Yes, Mr. Haverty. I do."

Those unbidden tears were starting again now. The big man said almost plaintively, "Please, Sister Angela, try not to distress yourself unduly. And quite soon all this unpleasantness will be past."

Meg Gavin was driving back to the newspaper office, pushing the speed limit, mentally listing all the things she must do *right now,* when the all-news station coming over the car radio did the quarter-hour spot on the nun.

Meg thumbed up the volume as Chief Marwick's deep, resonant voice filled the car: "Let me put it this way, Jim. At this point in time the identity of the father is unknown, but my office will attempt to locate him."

She braked for a red light without reacting. Then immediately switched on her directional blinkers.

As she steered into a right turn, heading back to the Cambridgeport P.D., she was devoutly hoping the rest of them hadn't heard what she heard over that radio: *yes, we found something, and we're going after him.*

The *father.* Of course. What *else* did everyone want to know except who fucked the nun?

Maybe she'd left letters. Photos, diaries. Women so often kept those. Maybe nuns did too.

Or phone calls. Long-distance calls showing up on the convent phone bill. Since it happened in the summer, when she might've been out of town.

Whatever—she must've left some trail. Because what Meg had heard that cop say over the radio was *we found it.*

Seventeen

When Meg Gavin needed to, she could project such a stillness, a calmness, that she became virtually invisible to those around her. She was exercising that asset as she stood by the lighted case of athletic trophies in the hall of the Cambridgeport Police Station, watching the comings and goings through the buzzered gate.

Activity level lower than yesterday, but still abnormally high. She noted especially who was *not* present. That Chief of Detectives, Vance, for instance. Come to think of it, he also hadn't been there at the morning press conference.

Nick Scotti was also nowhere in evidence. Nick had been in and out plenty yesterday, always with Andy DaSilva, who happened to be one of Meg's favorite A.D.A.s.

Meg drifted to the pay phone down the hall, dialed DaSilva's office. The secretary said he was out of town.

Back to the trophy case. Ten minutes later Chief Marwick walked into the staff room behind the gate, reading from a sheaf of papers in his hands. Distractedly, he asked the cop on the switchboard, "Tim called in lately from Wisconsin?"

"Not since one thirty, Chief."

Nobody noticed the brown-haired girl who was smiling luminously at the PeeWee Hockey League trophy for 1973–74.

Angela never had an easy time talking to her mother. But this was the most difficult conversation either of them could recall. Moats of silence surrounded their discussions of Theresa's trip to Arizona, Daniel's print-shop job and Aunt Iris's pottery classes.

Theresa Flynn picked the moment a nurse was coming

into the room with another assortment of pills to ask, "So. What happened to you?"

Angela swallowed the pills and waited for the nurse to leave before she said simply, "I don't know, Mother."

In her reconnoiter of the Cambridgeport town hall the day before, Meg Gavin had noted a door by the basement entrance that was marked "Private." On the hunch that this was the rear entrance to Marwick's private office, she tried a knock. A muffled male voice called: "Yeah, come in."

Bingo. Marwick was sitting behind a cluttered desk in the small wood-paneled room. He was a tall, bluff, attractive man in his late forties with a full head of wavy black hair and a modest paunch under his striped suit jacket. Looked to Meg like an ex-jock. She turned on her hundred-fifty-watt smile as she said, "Hey, Chief, sorry to trouble you. Meg Gavin from the *Eagle-Bulletin.* I know you've got a real heavy work load right now, but I sure would appreciate two minutes of your time."

"Sorry, Meg," Marwick smiled back at her. "I have to tell all you press people the same thing—I haven't anything more to say than what I said this morning."

"Oh, sure, I understand. Actually, all I wanted was to check out a heavy tip that came drifting our way. Mind if I sit?" She cocked her head toward the vinyl-upholstered chair next to his desk.

"Not if this won't take longer than two minutes." He flexed his arms to break the tension in his shoulders.

"Cigarette break?" Meg stretched her pack of Virginia Slims across the table. "You look like you could use one, Chief."

"That I could, Meg." He pulled out a cigarette, lit up hers with a gold lighter. "I don't mind telling you, this has been a couple days I wouldn't care to go through again soon."

"Well, you're doing a great job of a very tough assignment. I'm hearing that all over town."

"Thanks, Meg. I think we're doing a pretty damn good job of it myself. But it's good to hear that confirmed." He smiled again, a male-to-female smile. "Now what's this big tip you're sitting on?"

She had already decided to shoot the wad. "Well, I understand that Tim Vance, Andy DaSilva, and Nick Scotti are over in Wisconsin right now, checking out the identity of the father."

Almost instantly, that smile retracted into a look of wary astonishment. *Score one.* Marwick inhaled from the cigarette, blew the smoke like a screen across the desk. Cautiously: "That so? Where'd you hear that, Meg?"

"Hey, Chief, you know I'm not at liberty to say. But our source was pretty good."

Nervous, real nervous: "Well now, you understand I'm not commenting one way or the other. But I'd like to know why you think we'd be looking in Wisconsin."

This one was a pure intuitive leap. "Well, Chief, I guess I can say that much—our information was that you were led to the guy's identity by correspondence found in Sister Angela's possession."

His eyes darted off hers, flitted over to the paneled wall. *Score two.* "Well now, I don't know where you got this thing, Meg. But you understand that I can't comment one way or another."

Ah, she had him now. Deftly, with instructional charm, she reeled out her customary rap: that they were going to run this anyway, because their source was very reliable, but they wanted to check it first with Marwick's office. Maybe steer him a little of the credit for this big break in the case.

His smile had an edge of sheepishness to it now. He fingered some papers on his desk, then blurted, "Where'd you get this thing, Meg? Out of the D.A.'s office?"

"Ah, come on, Chief. Give *me* a break. The point is, we'd just as soon tip the credit to your office, if you're willing to confirm it."

"Well, you understand I can't give you any specifics."

"No, sure."

"But on the general points, I'd say your source is pretty good."

She tipped her cigarette ash demurely into the ashtray, "Like I told you, Chief. Are you expecting to lay any charges in Wisconsin?"

"No, I wouldn't say so. We haven't got any admission of paternity yet anyway."

Lord alive, she could kill for moments like this. She asked with a confiding smile, "But you're expecting one, Chief?"

His face looked quite handsome when he grinned. "Let's put it this way, Meg, we're working on it. And we've got our fingers crossed."

Before this amicable conversation was terminated, Marwick had dropped a few more pieces of news: that Ben Haverty and the doctors were prohibiting the police from interrogating the nun. (No surprise there.) That according to the doctors Sister Angela was still denying having given birth. (*That* one was pure gold.) And that the putative father was someone Sister Angela had apparently met on a vacation trip last summer. (Meg had already guessed that much, but in this business a guess was worth about three cigarette butts.) Now she was beginning to stitch it together. "If the nun is denying the birth—hey, I can see how that guy over in Wisconsin could be a very big link in the case."

Marwick nodded emphatically. "That's about how we see it, Meg. One of the things we're after here is evidence that would show that Sister Angela had knowledge that she was pregnant."

She shook her head, smiling. "Boy, Chief. This is sure one hell of an interesting case."

"Couldn't give you any argument on that, Meg. Speaking of which, I've got a pack of work to get to here. So if you're about done . . ."

"Yes, sure." She stood up and flipped her purse strap over her shoulder. "A thousand thanks, Chief. Mind if I check back with you later, see how your guys did over in Wisconsin?"

"Not if you can catch me. I'm a pretty hard man to catch these days."

A double entendre that was probably unintended. But she noted it anyway as she smiled, "Okay, later. Been real nice talking to you, Chief."

All afternoon Roy Danziger kept thinking about that item on the TV news. Weird—like a snatch of a dream. Made no sense. But he couldn't forget it.

He smoked one more joint as he drove his black camper pickup downtown to make the four P.M. shift. One way to get through their dumbfuck job. Tonight, especially, he would just as soon not feel much.

He parked in the underground parking lot of Midwest Mutual and took the elevator to level C. He punched the time clock and was changing into his uniform in the engineering department locker room when somebody tapped him on the shoulder. "O'Rourke in Security wants to see you. Room 2407."

"Oh, yeah? About what?"

"Dunno. He just wants to see you as soon as you get in."

Roy hesitated. Then pulled the shirt and sweater back over his head. As soon as, the man said. Whatever game was waiting for him upstairs, he preferred to play it in his own clothes. Not in their dumbfuck blue uniform.

He'd never been up to this swanky executive floor, twenty-four. Except once to fix a broken air-conditioning duct when the stiffs who fucked off all day here behind the big desks had gone home to their fancy split-levels.

221

Even the hallways said money. Soft carpet, fancy plants, walnut doors with brass numbers. The kind of guys who worked up here, they still wished Richard Nixon was king of the U.S.A.

He pushed open the walnut door of 2407. Shit, the spread inside was big as a house. Slick. Leather couches, marble tables. Fucking Nixon-lovers.

He caught the look the skinny blonde at the front desk threw him, and tossed it right back. Fucking hair-sprayed bitch. He said, "Roy Danziger. I'm supposed to see Chief O'Rourke."

She hit a button on her phone, mumbled something into it, and looked up at him with a pussy-sucking smile. "Chief O'Rourke will see you now. In there." She pointed with a bloody-looking fingernail.

Big, sharp office. More carpets, more plants. The guy behind the big desk didn't fit with the rest of it. Looked like an ex-cop kicked too many times in the face. The guy said, "Roy Danziger?"

"Yeah." He shifted his feet on the carpet. "They told me downstairs you wanta see me."

"That's right. I'm Mel O'Rourke, the chief of security here. Reason I called you is there's somebody here wants to talk to you." The guy got up from his chair and opened up a door on the side wall. Big room inside. Beefy guy sitting behind a long table put down some magazine and walked up to the door.

"Danziger, this is Lieutenant Tim Vance of the Cambridgeport, Minnesota, Police Department. He's got a few questions he'd like to ask you."

The guy put out his hand; Roy shook it. "Nice to see you, Danziger." Jock type, short hair and bad skin, maybe mid-thirties. Hair already going. White shirt, skinny cheap tie.

The house dick said, "If you gentlemen want to talk privately, you can use this conference room."

"Okay, thanks a lot," the cop said.

He followed the cop into the room. Long polished table sitting on a shit-brown carpet. The cop walked back to the end of the table. Roy took a chair halfway down, up close to the wall.

The cop lit up a cigarette. The ashtray in front of him was already spilling over with butts. When the guy crossed his legs a gun in an ankle holster flashed above his black socks.

What the hell was this?

The cop said, "Danziger, I guess you're wondering why you're here."

He nodded.

The cop cleared his throat. "Some of us are down here from the St. Paul area investigating a possible homicide involving Sister Angela Flynn. You probably know her as Gayle Flynn."

Roy nodded again, trying to keep his head blank.

The guy went on talking about a child, a male child, about some Sister Angela Flynn allegedly killing the infant. "We're interviewing a number of persons in this area who knew her. We understand you met her last summer."

"Yeah, I guess. Maybe."

"Like I say, we've got quite a few people down here to interview. All strictly routine, you understand. I'd just as soon not get into it until the other investigators get here. So we don't have to go over the same territory twice."

"Okay by me," Roy said flatly.

He knew all this must make sense somehow. He was just afraid to figure out how.

The guy with the gun on his ankle was talking now about baseball, about the Milwaukee team.

Shit, if he could just get back to the pickup, get to the rolled joints he had in the glove compartment. This one was going to be a rough go to get through straight. He'd had a nice buzz when he punched in, but he was stone-cold straight sitting at this big table, trying not to think.

223

Not to think why the hell he was sitting here in this weird fucking unreal place.

It was already 4:15 by the time they got the two tubes of blood extracted from Gary Tucker. Andy DaSilva knew that Tim Vance was probably holding Danziger at the Midwest Mutual Building by now, after he'd reported for evening shift. DaSilva also knew that whatever answers they'd been sent here to find weren't in this Tucker kid, who'd spent most of the day talking about shark-fishing and moose-hunting with Nick Scotti. DaSilva had probably heard more talk about dead animals in the last few hours than he'd ever wanted to listen to—and none of it had diddley-squat to do with finding out who may have fathered the nun's baby.

Yet when they dropped Gary off at the building-supply store where he worked with his father and uncle, the temptation to hear whatever new information might be dug out here was irresistible. DaSilva and Scotti sat in the father's small cubicle office, with the elder Tucker behind the desk and Gary and Brad standing in the doorway.

DaSilva said, "We'd just appreciate hearing your impression of Sister Gayle. Anything you might've discussed with her or noticed about her."

Most of what Ralph Tucker had to say was repetition. But some details, at least, were fresh.

He remembered how she had sometimes drunk wine down on the beach. Along with the others, sure, but she had certainly drunk her share. DaSilva traded a glance with Scotti as he asked, "Did she do an exceptional amount of drinking?"

Tucker pushed his thumbs together, looking thoughtfully at them. "No, I shouldn't say exceptional. Except there were times— Well now, I remember one afternoon she was down at the beach with her cousin's kids, fully dressed, and she just jumped in swimming. In all her clothes. And then she didn't go change, she just sat around with her clothes sticking to her wet all over her body." He swallowed. "Now, I'd say that's the kind of thing you might do if you'd had a little too much wine."

When DaSilva asked about her visit the previous weekend, the three Tucker men exchanged glances. Brad spoke up first: "Hey, I'm probably the wrong one to ask, because I hardly knew the lady. But *none* of my family knows her, actually. And I'd say she had one hell of a nerve turning up with her big belly on our doorstep last weekend."

DaSilva asked, "How do you feel about that, Mr. Tucker?"

Ralph stirred in the desk chair, rubbed a fist over his chin. "Well now, Mr. DaSilva, I'd have to say I was hurt. Hurt that she went ahead and accepted our long-standing invitation and got my boy involved in a sordid thing like this."

Andy DaSilva decided to allow himself a brief editorial comment. "Mr. Tucker, it's our impression that she came over here looking for help. She had to know she'd just about run out of time, and she had a good deal of money in her possession, possibly to pay for a hospital bill. She was pretty active that weekend, I understand."

Ralph Tucker looked at Brad, who blurted, "God, yes. Out there at the archery range she was hopping all around, keeping the scores. She—"

Gary interrupted: "You remember she fell off the back of the Scout? When you did a fast-brake?"

"Yeah. And after we finished the shooting, it was raining and everything, and you two went running in the woods."

Brief silence in the cubicle. DaSilva broke it with, "Well, I have to think maybe she was hoping to bring on her labor while she was visiting down here. She may have hoped that if she had the baby here, you people might have helped her with her problem."

Nick Scotti stirred his bulk against the cubicle wall. He

225

said flatly, "You people are a family. I think she was looking for a family to help her."

A stunned expression came over Ralph Tucker's face. "Well now, of course we would have. If we'd had any idea what was happening here, of course we would have helped that little lady. I told my wife when we first met her, 'Now there's a fine, likable young person.' And we'd told her to consider our home like her own, come down anytime she liked." He was twisting his tightly knotted hands. "And if it had worked out that way, if she'd had that baby down here at our house, of course we would've helped her. Done anything we could."

DaSilva said, "Well, I think she knew that. But her timing was a little off."

He tossed out a few more routine questions that drew predictably negative answers—no, Gayle Flynn had not asked them for the name of a gynecologist; no, Gayle Flynn had not asked to borrow money from them. Then he asked, "Did she try to get in touch with Roy Danziger, to your knowledge?"

As his father was saying no, not at all, Gary spoke up unexpectedly from the cubicle door: "Yeah, come to think of it, she did."

All eyes on Gary. His father said sharply, "You never told me that."

Gary shifted his weight. "Well, I never remembered. It's just when she was down in February, she asked me if I'd seen Ziggy, if I knew where he was. I told her I didn't."

From DaSilva: "And she didn't ask again?"

"Nope."

"Did you in fact know where to find him?"

"Yeah, probably. But I figured—what did she need with him?"

Okay, so finally Tim Vance had the guy sitting there. And something told him this was the one they were after.

He couldn't tell why he felt that. There was nothing in the looks of the guy to connect him to Sister Angela Flynn. In fact, when the guy first walked in, Vance had been more than a little stunned.

For starters he was fat. Stringy blond hair, five o'clock shadow. And the clothes—

He wasn't clean. Okay, so the guy was just turning up for a dirty eight-hour shift. But still—those greasy jeans, the sweater with elbow holes so big the dirty shirt-sleeves stuck right out—*this guy* had made it with a clean little St. Rose nun?

Yet there was something tense and real about him that made that Tucker kid look like a paper doll. Something tougher, more acute. Tim Vance couldn't quite read it right. But Andy probably would.

If not Andy, Nick for sure. Nick would read this guy like a bus ad—if Vance could just hold him here till they came.

Every cop instinct in him said *This is it—don't blow it.* The end of their string. If it wasn't this guy, the whole trip was fucking mush.

So Tim Vance worked hard to keep the guy there and distracted, knowing Danziger could get up and walk out, take a powder anytime he wanted to. He kept telling himself *Hold on, this is the guy.*

Yet all the time he was making small talk about baseball and football and motorcycles, anything to keep the guy from bolting, Vance was thinking, *Not* him. *This can't be the guy she actually fucked.*

The weird cop with the short socks and the ankle gun seemed to be some kind of jock nut. Kept talking about scores, teams, crap like that. Roy listened with half his head, answered when he had to.

With the other half he was tried to figure out what the hell he was doing here. The whole thing didn't figure, didn't add up.

He was almost afraid for the cop to stop talking. The crazier he talked—now he was into RBI's, ERA's, baseball statistics—the easier it got not to take in what was happening.

The cop was lighting up another Camel now, talking about bike racing. Normally, Roy couldn't tolerate anybody smoking cigarettes around him—the stuff irritated spots he had on his lungs. A doctor told him once he shouldn't expose his lungs to that shit. And here was this cop chain-smoking stuff like those French cigarettes, no filter or anything, raw like cigars, you could tell it even in the smoke—

And Roy couldn't raise a peep. Couldn't tell that cop to stop blowing that crud in his face. All he could do was hold himself down in the chair and breathe as shallow as he could.

He knew he had to keep real cool now. He knew that from other run-ins he'd had with cops—*cool,* that was what worked.

But those other jams—none of them was as heavy as this one. Shit.

He kept telling himself whatever it was they wanted, they had the wrong guy. He hadn't done what they thought.

But he knew he was in trouble. Maybe big trouble. It felt like that for sure, for damn sure.

And he still didn't know what he was doing in this fucking weird room.

When DaSilva and Scotti finally swept into the Midwest Mutual conference room at 5:15, trailed by Sullivan and O'Rourke, Andy DaSilva was about at the end of his rope. No sleep, no lunch, *hours* of wading through idiotic hospital red tape—what the hell kind of dog-ass assignment was this?

All right, now they finally had this Danziger. Now the job was to get what they needed out of him—*fast.* For once in his life, DaSilva was in a get-tough mood.

Nick Scotti took in the suspect in one glance: Slumped body. Sulky, defiant face. Some unwashed hippie, forty pounds overweight, not counting the dirty blond hair hanging down past his shoulders. *A doper for sure,* Scotti knew instinctively. *A loser and a doper.*

He walked up to rich-boy Vance, who was stubbing out another butt. He snapped, "You get any lunch?"

Vance glanced up, startled. "Yeah."

"What'd you get?"

"A hot dog and a Coke."

Scotti grunted and stalked to the chair at the other end of the table. Fucking cherry—Vance'd had the whole day to fart around, piss all to do, and all he'd had was a hot dog for lunch. Fucking dork didn't even have the smarts to eat on the job when he could.

Right about then, Nick Scotti figured he'd never in his goddam life been so hungry.

Roy Danziger tried not to react as the fucking door opened and five guys walked into the room. One of them, a big guy with a Fu Manchu brush, seemed pissed off about food. What the hell was this?

A skinny little bald guy sat in the chair opposite. "Okay, I assume you're Roy Danziger?"

He nodded, one sharp jerk. The guy whipped through a speech introducing himself and the rest with their fat-ass titles. Ran off some stuff about voluntary cooperation and collecting all the facts relevant to their investigation. Then he looked right at Roy and said, "I assume you know why you're here."

He moved his legs under the table. Said loudly, "Nah. Matter of fact, I got no idea."

Both new cops looked at the first guy—real pissed-off looks. The short one said, "Jesus, Tim. Didn't you *tell* him?"

The cop flipped his hand. "Sure I did. He just didn't take it in. Run it past him one more time, Andy."

The little guy turned back to him and snapped, "You're here because we're investigating the death of a child born two nights ago to Sister Angela Flynn—you probably know her as Gayle Flynn—and we have information that leads us to believe you're the father of that child and we want to know exactly to what extent you're involved in this possible homicide, that's why."

The word "father" went into him like a bullet. For a long moment he stared blankly at the little guy, showing no reaction at all.

Then, with his face pulling, grimacing against the reaction, he began to cry.

Eighteen

Roy was mortified by the tears. In front of these guys, of all people. He pulled a handkerchief from the back pocket of his jeans, coughed into it and asked, "What're you talking about, man?"

The cop was staring across the table. "Well, it appears that the baby was killed. We haven't completed our investigation yet, but at the moment it appears that Gayle Flynn may have done it, and she was charged this morning with second-degree murder. We're down here in Milwaukee to find out how persons like yourself who knew her may have been involved."

Roy bent forward from the waist. Muttered almost to himself. "My God, I can't believe she actually killed the kid."

"Nothing's been proven yet," the cop said. "We're still in an open investigation."

Roy looked up at him and asked, "What are my rights?"

He barely listened to the answer. "You are not presently under any suspicion. We're just asking you to cooperate voluntarily with our investigation." *Father. Oh, shit, what did that mean*—father? "You have a right to have a lawyer present during this interrogation if you want one, but I'd like to emphasize that you're not the subject of the investigation. We don't see you as the target of any charges the agencies we represent might lay." *Okay, so he'd known all along that's probably what it was. It had to be. But what did that mean*—father?

Now he was back under control. "Okay. That's okay. Listen, how is she? Where is she now?"

"In the hospital."

"Is she okay? Is there anything I could do for her?"

"I don't think so."

"Well, Jesus. Does she want to see me? Is there any way I could help her out?"

"You can help her by cooperating with us. We're trying to put this case together, and we need to know more about the circumstances, about her frame of mind. We understand you met her last August."

"Yeah, I guess so."

"Did you during that period of time have sexual intercourse with her?"

Roy looked out at that wall of faces. Pulled into his chair, pulled away from the question. "Hey, some things are personal, private. I don't want to talk about that."

DaSilva was very tired. This had been a too-long, exhausting day. He got up from his chair and paced the carpet in front of Danziger, looking mostly at the Japanese barkcloth walls as he tried to formulate a chain of questions.

Danziger gave them his age (thirty), marital status (single) and address (159 Fox Point Road) without resistance. He said he had met Gayle Flynn when he was between jobs and took off camping for a while in August. He'd heard that his friends, the Tuckers, were also camping up in Menominee, and he'd happened to find their trailer his second day up there.

DaSilva asked, "Did they introduce you to Gayle Flynn?"

Danziger shrugged, a heaving motion of his big shoulders. "Look, the way it was, she was staying in the trailer next door. I could tell just by looking over there she didn't belong with that family either. She looked like a nice girl, pretty, really built—I mean, it was a natural. The two families were getting together some anyway. So Gayle and me, we just started talking."

"What else did you do with her?"

"Went swimming. Goofed around talking on the beach. Sat around the campfire at night. Like that."

"At what point did you have sexual intercourse with her?"

Danziger moved his legs, only his legs, under the table. "Hey, man, that question's out of line."

Nick Scotti felt a mounting, choking rage. First that fucker Vance burns up the whole day without even telling this turkey Danziger what he's doing here—what the hell did Vance think they were all doing down here, playing kissy-face?

And now Andy's brain was stuck in park. He wasn't linking his questions, wasn't pushing them in any direction. Jesus, he wasn't even maintaining eye contact with his fucking subject. Three times Scotti watched him let this fat guy shuck off the key question, louder and cockier every time. It was *Danziger* who was eyeballing Andy, for Chrissake. And with a fucking doper like this, every time you let him slip past he got that much harder to nail.

If somebody didn't do something quick they were going to be here till fucking midnight. With no dinner.

All of a sudden the cop with the Fu Manchu stood up at the far end of the table. He shucked his jacket and hitched his belt around so Roy would see the big butt of some gun stuck above his pants.

He walked down the table and sat opposite. Said in a quiet, conversational voice, "They call you Roy?"

"Yeah. Sometimes."

"You got a nickname?"

"Ziggy. They call me Ziggy."

"I'm Nick Scotti. You can call me Nick." The cop leaned over the table toward him. Face all black mustache, little beady black eyes. Real soft: "Hey, Roy, you know what's coming down here?"

He shrugged.

BAM! Scotti's fist hit the table. Moving so fast Roy hardly saw the blur. Loud now: *"You're shitting around with an assistant district attorney from the state of Minnesota, Roy, that's what you're doing.* Now I want you to get this straight, Roy, because it's real important to you. You're not accused yet of any crime. But if you lie now to this district attorney you're gonna be guilty of perjury. Now perjury's a real serious rap, Roy, so you better start talking straight to us." Voice was low, drilling. "We're only interested in what happened up in Menominee as it relates to our homicide. What we want to know is did you screw her, did you fuck her? We don't care if it was rape—that's Wisconsin jurisdiction, that's nothing to do with us. All we want to know but we want to know it *right now* is *are you the father of this baby?"*

He looked away from those hot, dark eyes, coming at him from across the table. Looked down at the dark polished wood.

It was all so long ago. But yes, he did remember, how could he forget, those times of snatched, uneasy coupling.

He said slowly, "Well, yeah, I could be. I guess I could be. I mean, we did have sex."

The face across the table pressed in closer. Now the questions came real fast: "How many times?"

"I don't know." He clutched, shuffled his rusty memories. "Six times, I guess. Maybe five. Something like that."

Face so close he saw the tooth gaps, the spined mustache hairs. "Where was that, Roy?"

"On the beach, I guess." Trying to pull it from his blanked, foggy head. "Mostly on the beach."

"Mostly. Where else?"

"Well, one night she sneaked out to my sleeping bag. But she didn't stay the whole night. It was mostly on the beach."

"Was she having sex with anybody else?"

"Nah. Not up there, anyways." Danziger took a deep, steadying breath. "I guess if she had a baby, it probably was mine."

The small cop sat down beside the other one. Said, "Did she tell you she was pregnant?"

"Who, Gayle? Nah, I never heard from her after that summer."

"No phone calls, no letters?"

"I told you, I didn't hear zip."

"You didn't give her money, help her in any way?"

"I just told you, I never heard from her."

"Where were you on April twenty-fifth?"

He blinked, considering. "What day was that?"

"Tuesday. Last Tuesday."

"I was here, working." He jerked his thumb toward the Midwest security chief. "Ask them, it's on the work sheets."

The Fu Manchu cop asked, "Did you know she was a nun when you had sex with her?"

He hunched his shoulders protectively. "Nah, not then. I mean, who would think a thing like that? I thought she was a teacher. Here was this nice-looking girl, really built, always laughing and smiling and joking around—who'd think a thing like that?"

"How'd you find out?"

"I guess her cousin's husband dropped it to Ralph Tucker. Jesus, he was as surprised as me. Then I asked Gayle about it and she said yeah, it was true, but it shouldn't make any difference. I mean, she still wanted to do it. But anyway I didn't hear that until after my second conquest."

Murder.

Such a strange word. They couldn't mean her. She was a good person. People who did murders were—not good people. Strange people, other people. Dark, other strangers.

She was sure of so few things now. Except that—she was a good person. A good person could not do that thing that they said.

That *need to know* was growing in her like a consuming pain. She had to know what she could possibly have done so terrible, unspeakable, that they were arresting her and sending her off to some crazy ward without even telling her why.

Now she was beginning to put it together—why she had no TV or radio in the room. Why no one would give her a newspaper. When she asked for one, the afternoon-shift nurse said nervously, "Well, Sister, I think you'd better talk to Dr. Heilbron about that."

A few minutes later she said calmly, "If I just had a television to watch, I think that would help me to relax."

"Now you just tell that to the doctors, dear."

So. The TV was part of it, too.

At Danziger's peculiar use of the word "conquest," the feeling in the conference room froze. *Jesus, this guy's right out of* Playboy *magazine,* Tim Vance thought with some dismay.

Scotti asked, "What d'you mean, 'she still wanted to do it'?"

Danziger shrugged. "Well, like make out. When I heard she was a nun, I thought maybe we shouldn't be doing it. I don't know—a nun. Hey, I'm no Catholic, but it didn't seem right. But she said no, it was okay."

From Scotti: "So you did it again?"

"Yeah, a couple times. Maybe three or four."

DaSilva looked up from the pad where he was scribbling notes. "Were the others at the camp aware of your sexual relationship with her?"

235

Danziger shifted uneasily in the chair. "Hey. What you think?"

Scotti snapped, "We don't think. We're asking."

"Listen, I was staying with my friends. She was staying with her cousin—they were close, like sisters. All real straight, family types. I mean listen, Gayle was a single girl, didn't have no regular boyfriend. I knew that right off. Girls like that—they get what they can on the side. But you don't make a big thing out of it. It was just between the two of us. Like—an understanding. Put it this way—I knew where she was coming from. The rest of them didn't."

DaSilva looked at the unkempt, overweight young man sitting across the table. He sensed the veracity in what Danziger was saying, but still found it hard to believe. Now he asked, "Are you saying she wasn't at all—reluctant to have sex with you?"

Danziger mulled that question. "Well, it's—funny you'd say that. Sometimes, when we were really into it, she'd say, 'No, no, I can't do this.' Like—flashes."

"What did you make of that?"

Bristling: "Hey, I didn't push her. If she didn't want it, that was okay with me." He paused. "But it only lasted a few seconds. Just—a flash like. Then she got right back into it. Like that—other thing never happened."

Scotti repeated DaSilva's question: "What did you make of that?"

Another shrug. "Lots of girls are like that. They start hearing their mothers say no-no or something, I guess. But that's somebody else talking. It isn't them. Girls, they want it as much as we do. Sometimes more."

As Dr. Keith Talbott walked off the elevator onto West Wing Three he was thinking about Bruce Heilbron. Sister Angela and Bruce Heilbron.

Right now he was wishing he knew the man better. Wishing he could feel reassured that Heilbron really understood what they were up against here.

All the classical neuroses, psychoses—he guessed Heilbron knew his stuff on that. But there was a special difficulty with pregnant women after they'd delivered—two, three days after the delivery. A peculiar, tenacious depression that seemed to have some root in the violent hormonal changes their bodies were going through. So delicate. He wondered how much Heilbron understood about that.

Not to mention the grieving, the mourning, they went through if they lost the child. No matter what the circumstances of the death were, or how near it came to term. That acute, agonized mourning—they all went through that.

But for Sister Angela Flynn, all these normal factors were multiplied. Keith Talbott knew he could only begin to conceive of the hell she was going through right now. As he pulled her hospital chart from the metal rack, he hoped, not for the first time that day, that Bruce Heilbron knew what the hell he was doing here.

The figures on the chart were all within normal range; her physical recovery, at least, was proceeding as predicted.

Her psychological state was something else. Propped on the pillows in Room 308, she was tearful, distraught. After answering a few routine questions about her physical state she burst out, "Dr. Talbott, I'd like to know more about—what happened. Nobody will tell me, nobody will talk to me."

He hesitated. It was all so precariously balanced. "What won't they tell you, Sister Angela?"

"I want to know more about—the—baby. I want to know what happened to it."

Talbott hesitated again. It was hard, so damned hard to look into that crumpled, tormented face and not tell her what she was begging him to know. But if her lawyer and her psychiatrist had decided between them that she should be told no more for the present, it was not Keith Talbott's place to intervene.

His purview was her physical recovery, strictly her physical recovery. And he could certainly see the basis for their concern. Despite all the powerful tranquilizers she was taking, she was still experiencing an extreme agitation.

No part of the information she was begging to know could be calculated to allay that agitation. Her own brain was shielding her from that information, that she knew better than anyone else. Heilbron and her attorney were, in effect, concurring with that judgment of her own brain.

Personally, Keith Talbott thought it was probably more stressful, more anxiety-producing for her *not* to know than to know. The plain facts, even facts as agonizing as these, would probably be easier for her to handle than her frantic imaginings.

But he was not about to risk tipping her from the silk-thin grip she presently had on this reality. Last night she had come to a certain truth herself; Talbott had simply helped her to deliver that out of her, like a good obstetrician.

Now she wanted more. Wanted what *he* knew. But it was not Keith Talbott's place to give that. Not his place to tinker with the delicate balance those others were trying to maintain in her.

Looking down at the floor now, he mumbled ritual assurances to please trust those who were caring for her to do what was, in their judgment, in her best interests. To please not burden herself now with unnecessary concerns.

A small, defeated whisper: "All right, Dr. Talbott."

"Are you getting some exercise? Walking around the room?"

"Well, I'm trying. I'll do more tomorrow."

"Very good. And perhaps one of the nurses could give you a shampoo."

She ran her hand self-consciously through her stringy red-gold hair. "Oh, I'd like that."

Talbott stood and gave her one of his odd, awkward bows. "One thing I've learned in my practice as a gynecologist, Sister," he said gravely. "Women tend to care a great deal about their hair."

When he left the room she tried to fight off the panicked, choked feeling in her chest. *No, no.* She must stay very calm. She must concentrate all those feelings on finding someone who would tell her what she had to know.

From the end of the conference table Tim Vance watched the unfolding interrogation with a certain astonishment. He still wasn't sure exactly what Nick Scotti had done to break this Danziger. But one minute the guy was sullen, resistant. Almost *condescending,* for Chrissake. And the next he was peeled open like a ripe tangerine, spilling answers. Tim Vance had watched it happen, right in front of him. And he still wasn't sure how Nick had done it.

Now Andy DaSilva was saying something typically polite, telling Danziger he'd like him to understand that nobody there was prying gratuitously into his private life; they only wanted to know what bore directly on their investigation into Gayle Flynn's frame of mind.

Nick Scotti pushed his elbows forward across the polished table, fat elbows with the shirt-sleeves rolled up over them. "Hey, Roy," he said quietly, "was that her first time?"

Danziger shook his head, a vigorous, water-shedding gesture. "No, man. No way."

A taunt laid into the question: "How d'you know that, Roy?"

Danziger pulled himself up in the chair. "Hey, I could tell. I sure could tell that. She was kind of inexperienced like, but it wasn't her first time." He ran his eyes over the faces of those men around the shiny table. "I mean, you can tell. She knew—the moves. She knew all the moves."

Scotti lifted his hand, his open palm expressing an almost contemptuous doubt. "Come on, Roy. How you gonna tell that?"

239

Hotly: "Hey, man. It sure wasn't *my* first time. I been with a lot of women. I know about women. When it comes to sex I damn well know what they're thinking."

"Oh, yeah?" Distinct taunt. "How many women you been with, Roy? Say ten, twenty? Two hundred?"

Danziger hitched up his shoulders. "Well, maybe something like that. A lot, anyway. Hey, I don't keep score. But I know how they are in—when you're having sex, like."

Soft, insinuating: "You think she liked it, Roy?"

"Yeah. As a matter of fact, she did."

"How d'you know that?"

Defiantly: "Well, she kept coming back for more, didn't she?"

DaSilva asked: "There was no force involved in the sex?"

Angrily: "Hey, don't try to lay that on me, man. I'm telling you, she wanted it. Listen, when we were starting to get into it, sure I guess I brought her around. Warmed her up for it. You know—like, I made my moves. But then she got right into it. I'm telling you, she was up for it as much as me."

From Scotti: "And then you dumped her, Roy?"

"Nah. It wasn't like that." Danziger moved around on the chair. "Like—that first time, when we went back to the trailers, I kissed her good-night on the cheek. Everything was cool. And it stayed cool. When I had to go 'cause I had a job interview in town, I knew she was leaving two days later anyways. I kissed her good-bye, gave her my address, said I'd be real glad to hear from her. Hey, we left it nice."

From DaSilva: "But you say you never heard from her again?"

"Not a peep, man. Until today."

Scotti slapped the table hard with his right hand. "You sure it was five or six times, Roy?"

"Yeah, sure. At least."

They ran him once again through how he met her, how

their friendship developed. How that friendship became a sexual connection. Danziger made a faint motion with his shoulders. "Hey, what do you want? She was right there, a pretty girl, real built. She was hanging loose, kinda bored, nothing else to do at night. And she wanted it. Hell, I knew she wanted it."

"How'd you know that, Roy?"

Danziger shifted uncomfortably on the chair. "Jesus Christ, you just *know* it. I mean, girls got a way of letting you know they got the same idea you got. They just go at it a little different."

Now they were getting into contraceptive devices. Danziger said no, he hadn't used no rubbers, if that's what they meant. He didn't know if she'd used anything. These days he figured girls just took care of that stuff. No, he hadn't thought to ask her.

That question seemed to jolt him back to a realization of what he was doing here, in this strange room. He bent forward in the chair, holding his forehead in his left hand. "Jesus, I can't believe she did—what you're saying she did. Killed her kid. Hey, she loved little kids. That's the main thing I remember about her."

DaSilva asked, "She told you that, specifically?"

"Well, not right out like that. But when we talked—we talked a lot up there, she was about the only one I *could* talk to—she mostly talked about her job. How much she liked teaching little kids. She really liked that a lot. And you're telling me—" Danziger's shoulders pulled together as the idea came at him again, like a smashing hammer.

Scotti said quickly, "What'd *you* talk about with her?"

He dropped the hand from his forehead and looked blankly at the north wall of the room. "Well, I was looking for a job. That was a lot on my mind. And my girl friend— I'd broken up with my girl friend maybe two, three months before. I guess that was on my mind too."

241

"You discussed this girl friend with Gayle Flynn?"

"Yeah, I told her about it."

"What'd she say?"

"Well, mostly she listened. Said maybe it was better in the long run we broke up—the kinda thing most people say."

Scotti asked quietly, "How much marijuana do you use, Roy?"

Danziger shifted his weight. "Well, some." He looked at the beady little black eyes. "I smoke once in a while."

Flatly: "You smoke a lot."

"Well, quite a lot."

"You take LSD, mescaline, heroin?"

"No smack, no. I used to drop a little acid. A couple years ago. Mostly I just smoke."

"Was she smoking up there with you?"

"Nah, she wasn't into that. But we drank some." Danziger paused. "Gayle could really belt them back, boy—straight, no mixers."

"Would you say she was under the influence when she had the sex?"

"Hey, no. She was pretty weird that way. She'd take maybe five, six hits and not even bat an eyelash. I'll tell you the truth—I think she could hold it better than me."

They grilled Roy Danziger for about a half hour more, without much result. When they came back over the same points his answers were always consistent. To the point. No evasions now. Every one of the five men listening around the table was persuaded that Roy Danziger was telling substantially the truth.

Finally Andy DaSilva said, "Okay. Are you willing to make a voluntary statement, and submit to a blood test and polygraph to ascertain the veracity of your statement?"

Danziger pulled himself upward in his chair. "Sure. I guess. I got nothing to hide."

As DaSilva rattled through a restatement of Danziger's legal rights in this instance, which he was agreeing voluntarily to waive, Danziger brushed the words away. "That's okay. I got it."

"Okay. Then Mr. Scotti will take your statement."

As Scotti reached for DaSilva's pad to draft the doper's statement, Vance and DaSilva made quick moves toward the phones in the outer office. Both those fucking cherries hoped they'd be the first to reach home with the good word. Fucking glory boys all the way.

When the cop with the Fu Manchu read back his version of what was said in this weird, fancy room, Roy hardly recognized it: "That a relationship developed also at this time between Gayle Flynn and Roy Danziger who is also known as Ziggy. That during this period of time in August both Danziger and Gayle Flynn did engage in sexual intercourse. . . ."

That sure didn't seem like the way it had been. But he didn't know how else to put it. So he said, "I guess that's about right."

"Okay." The cop led him to the outer office, spun some papers into a typewriter and banged out the words from his pad. "Now!" He shoved a paper in front of Roy. "Read this through. If that's what you said, sign it and we'll get the hell out of here." He slapped his belt. "And get ourselves some dinner."

As they waited in a staff room of the Emergency Department of the University of Wisconsin Medical Center, Roy felt his thawing anxieties build. He said to the Italian cop, "What're they going to do to me?"

"Just take out some of your blood. Don't worry, a tough guy like you won't miss it."

"How do they do it—with needles?"

"Sure. What you think—teeth in the throat?"

Roy blurted, because he had to tell someone, "I hate needles."

The cop yawned, "Hey, anybody else want a sandwich?" When he got no answer he left the room.

Roy pushed the needles out of his mind, and started to think about the baby.

Death. Then life. Life and death touching him was what they'd told him about back in that weird room.

Death and life all at once. And one more thing—trouble. Maybe big, ugly trouble.

Too much. Too much all in one whack.

He thought for a moment about the word "baby," which meant so little to him, except flickered images—small things wrapped in blankets, crying. Floppy little things drinking from bottles, messing their pants.

His baby. His. Dead.

Vance and DaSilva, were sitting together at one end of the tacky hospital room when Danziger walked up to them blowing his nose in one dirty hankerchief, and said, "What do you mean, she killed the baby? How did she kill it? Can't you tell me some more about what happened? I mean, what did she *do?*"

DaSilva looked up at him, surprised. Wary. Danziger blew his nose again. "You're telling me she killed it—I mean, what did she do?" DaSilva was just looking up. Vance was looking down at his hands. "Okay, I know that it's dead. But what makes them think she did it?"

DaSilva realized in one glance that Danziger was finally absorbing the news. The guy was starting to come apart on them. And they hadn't finished with him yet.

DaSilva said, "I can't really tell you, Roy. I wasn't in on that part of the investigation. I don't have any information on it."

"What you mean, you don't have any information? You're the cops, aren't you?"

"Sort of. But that wasn't my assignment."

"But they must know. They sent you down here, didn't they? I can't believe she could actually, flat-out— Couldn't it be some mistake?"

Tim Vance picked it up: "We don't know the whole story, Roy. They're still making tests. They haven't come up with any firm conclusions yet."

Danziger made a kind of whistling, keening noise through his teeth. He said softly, almost to himself, "I can't believe she actually killed my baby."

Vance made a mental note that this was the first time in the course of this interrogation that Danziger had put those two words together—*my baby.*

At 7:56, four minutes before the *Eagle-Bulletin* press run closed for the night, Meg Gavin yanked a last sheet from her typewriter, ran across the city room, and slapped an untidy heap of pages onto Dick McAlpine's desk. "Done!"

With one eye on the wall clock he skimmed the article, his pencil slashing it automatically with markings for the typesetter. As he read it he grunted: "So they got the daddy."

"Damn right." She sat on the edge of his desk, folding her arms over her chest. "And nobody's got it but us."

Another grunt. He peered up at her over the rims of his glasses. "You sure Mark Abrams confirmed it?"

"Him and Marwick both, plus my source." She smiled to herself, savoring the brief glow of the moment. She didn't need Dick McAlpine to tell her this was a great job. There wasn't another reporter on the paper who could have gotten it. Christ, but this moment felt good.

McAlpine stood abruptly and walked to the layout desk, conferred briefly over the remake of page one that this story would require. When he came back to his desk he dropped into the chair, took off his glasses and rubbed at the bridge of his nose. "Okay, Meg, you're a good girl. That's a nice little yarn."

She grinned sarcastically. "Dear old Dick. So famous for the graceful understatement."

"Well, you still leave a lot of questions open. Did the guy know she was pregnant? Is he married or what? Why didn't he help the lady out of her jam?"

McAlpine had a way of doing that: grinding the fine edge off any high moment. She shook her head. "Jesus Christ, you're an ungrateful bastard, Dick. It happens I asked them all that, and they declined to say. But if you'd heard how pissed off Mark Abrams was to have to confirm this thing, you'd realize what a nice little nugget I've mined for you, you miserable fucker."

McAlpine favored her with one of his rare, dry smiles. "Well, I told you it was a nice yarn. You wouldn't care to mention, strictly *entre nous,* who your source was?"

"Not a chance, Dick." She stood up. "But I'll tell you this much—he and/or she is damn well-situated in this case. I think if I play my cards right, I may get a lot more leaks. I've got to guarantee them anonymity, but this could turn into a regular old spigot if I work the pump handle right."

Finally a young doctor showed up, with a nurse from the hospital blood bank. He asked cheerfully, "Okay, who gets it?"

Nick Scotti jerked his thumb at Danziger. Danziger blanched and looked away as they stuck the needle in his left arm. Whole operation took two, maybe three minutes.

Scotti locked the two polyurethane-cushioned tubes into the trunk of the maroon Buick, alongside the other ones taken from Gary Tucker. As they drove Danziger back to the Midwest Mutual Building DaSilva and Vance invited him to join them for dinner. *Off whose per diem?* Scotti was thinking. *Not mine, fucking cherries.*

Danziger declined the invitation anyway. He was quiet and withdrawn, seemed to be lost in his own thoughts. When they let him off at his black camper in the parking lot, Chief O'Rourke told him he could have the rest of the night off. "I'll cover for you. And by the way, Danziger, all this will be strictly confidential. I'll tell 'em you were just cooperating with an investigation of the St. Paul police."

"Okay, thanks." Danziger stumbled as he got out of the car, he was that anxious to get away.

"How about you, Chief?" Vance asked. "We sure would be glad for your company at the chow table."

"Don't mind if I do. What're you boys in the mood for —steak sound right?"

"You got it," said Scotti. "Thick and rare. And the biggest in town."

Roy drove the camper out of the underground garage, drove for three blocks until he was sure nobody was following. Then he pulled over to the curb, got one of the joints out of the glove compartment and lit it up with a shaking match.

He smoked it down sitting there, letting the blotting-out come. Kept another handy as he put the truck back into gear, and lit up after four blocks.

His head was just starting to settle down. Jesus Christ. He still wasn't sure what had happened back there. Except that none of it was good.

He was trying to get Gayle into focus in his head. But it hadn't happened yet. All he could remember was a big smile, lots of laughing and some red slacks.

What he couldn't figure out was—why she hadn't come to him. Told him what was happening, what was coming down. Shit, he would've helped her if he could.

Maybe even would've married her.

She was a nice girl. He remembered that good enough. Kind of a sweet young kid. Nothing he didn't really like about her, except maybe that weird nun stuff.

Maybe they could've made something out of it. It wasn't

anything he would've gone for except for the kid. She just wasn't that high on his list. Shit, he hardly knew her.

But he liked her. He would've wanted to help her. A baby—that wasn't so bad. It happened that way to a couple of his friends. Sometimes it worked out, sometimes it didn't. There wasn't much way of knowing beforehand.

What she did instead— Nah, he still couldn't believe it.

He was crying again as he drove out to the Fox Point beach house, but now he could let it run. He still wasn't sure what all this meant. Except that, apparently, he'd had a kid, and Gayle Flynn killed it.

What did that mean, she'd killed his kid?

He was trying to think who he could talk to about this. Jesus.

In his whole life he'd never felt so alone.

Nineteen

Almost as soon as they settled into the padded red leather banquettes around a table at the Red Lion Inn, Andy DaSilva fell asleep. Tim Vance said as the waitress brought their first round of drinks, "So what worked out with the Tucker kid, Nick? Fill me in."

As Scotti told him, Vance felt a rising gorge of anger. "Jesus Christ. You mean when the kid realized this woman was pregnant, his first response was to make a *sexual pass?* A sexual pass at this pregnant nun who's supposed to be his friend? My God, what kind of a guy *is* he?"

"Anh, lay off him. He's a good kid." Scotti downed his drink and signaled for another. "He's just scared of girls is all."

"Scared of *her?* Jesus, Nick, you tell me what's more

helpless than a nine months' pregnant nun. And she came
down here looking for *help*, Nick, you know that. She could
hardly walk by then, she had to be in terrific pain. And she
dragged herself onto that plane last weekend because she
was that desperate to find somebody to help her out. And
now you're saying *that's* what she got instead—her own boyfriend assaulting her on a couch?"

"Ah, simmer down. All he did was cop a little feel. Don't
make no federal case out of it."

Vance glared. *"A little feel,* hunh? I'm telling you, Nick,
what he did to her, in the condition she was in—it's worse
than a rape."

Nick Scotti never held his liquor well; now, in his exhaustion, drinking on an empty stomach, his mood shifted
rapidly to a truculent belligerence. "And why in hell
shouldn't he be scared of her? She's a fucking murderess."
As their redolent platters of steak arrived, Andy DaSilva
stirred himself awake. "And that other one, the daddy, is a
fucking doper."

DaSilva smiled apologetically toward Mel O'Rourke.
"Nick has a certain sensitivity to the subject of marijuana,
Chief."

But Vance was rankling, unwilling to defuse Scotti's
attack with polite table talk. "Fuck you, Nick. Where the hell
do you get off, calling this a murder?"

"What the Christ do you think it was, a suicide?" Scotti
demanded. "You think that little baby got himself born all
by himself, stuffed those panties down his own throat and
jumped into that wastebasket behind the bookcase? Hey,
turkey, I got an uncle in Brooklyn has a bridge he'd like to
sell you."

"Hey, I'm not saying she didn't do it. Probably. But I'd
have to know one hell of a lot more about the circumstances
involved here before I went around calling it a murder."

"Oh, yeah? Then how come that's what your boss had
her arrested for?"

"Listen, my personal opinion is that she got charged too

high. Manslaughter, maybe—that fits it better. But *premeditated murder?* How about her mental state, all that bleeding she was doing? You're telling me she could premeditate what she did in *that* condition?"

"Damn right." Scotti forked a large chunk of steak into his mouth and spoke through it. "And somebody's gotta stand up now for that kid. That fucking nun snuffed him in cold blood, before he ever had a chance. And I hope to hell she hangs for it."

"That simple, hunh?" Vance's face was red with an anger he rarely allowed himself to feel. "You want to know why you think that, Nick? Because you're a goddam Catholic yourself. Always ready to pop off with those goddam easy Catholic answers. But real life's a lot more complicated than that, Nick boy."

Fucking WASP rich boy, what did he know? Scotti signaled the waitress for another drink. "Piss on you, Vance. I'm telling you, she's a fucking murderess."

When Norma Knudsen showed up for her ten P.M. shift she stopped at the nursing station to check the chart on Sister Angela. The duty nurse remarked, "She ought to sleep okay tonight. She's worn herself out crying all day."

"Well, the poor girl," Knudsen said.

The man sitting on a chair outside Room 308—sakes alive, that must be her police guard—nodded to Knudsen as she approached the door. Coming out of the room the afternoon special murmured, "Phew. You'd better get some more pills into her or you'll be up and down all night."

The nun was leaning back against the raised head of the bed, her anxious face drawn and tight as a fiddle string. When she saw Knudsen she sat upright, wary, alert.

"Well now, hello there, Sister Angela," Knudsen said cheerfully. The poor girl looked so much *older,* so much more haggard than she had the night before. "I thought you might be asleep by now."

"No, I'm not sleepy." She looked at the closed door of the room. "Which one are you?"

"Why, I'm your night nurse, Mrs. Knudsen. Don't you remember—we talked some last night."

"Oh." She turned to the bedside table, pulled a fresh tissue from the box. Blew her nose, shaking her head. "I'm sorry, I don't remember."

"Well, that's understandable enough, it was awfully late. Is there anything I can do for you now, anything you'd like?"

"Yes." She looked again at the closed door. "Mrs. Knudsen, do you have a newspaper?"

That she wasn't expecting. Reluctantly, Knudsen said, "Well now, I don't know about that. Did you ask Dr. Talbott?"

The poor girl looked right at her, with those miserable puffed eyes. "Oh, please, Mrs. Knudsen. They won't let me have a TV, they won't tell me what's happening." Looked at her like a poor whipped dog. "But I really *need to know.* I want to know what—happened."

Knudsen hesitated. The doctors who were in charge of this case should know what was best for Sister Angela Flynn; it wasn't Knudsen's place to go against them. But the poor girl was saying, "And none of them will tell me. Please, can't you help me?"

Now Knudsen knew who the nun reminded her of—her daughter Dora. How Dora had looked, so beaten and pushed-down, made old before her time in those years her miserable good-for-nothing husband was running around on her all over town, and everybody knew about it but Dora. And they all kept trying to spare her from knowing—God help her, even her own mother did. It wasn't until Dora finally got out of that farce of a marriage that Knudsen realized her worst misery had been *not knowing* what she was up against. Just not knowing.

Now this poor girl, in her terrible fix. Last night she

hadn't seemed quite right in the head, but tonight she seemed to Knudsen to be making perfect sense. Oh, sure, those doctors probably thought they were doing right in keeping all this from her. Those muck-amighty doctors always thought they were doing right—when they prescribed without explaining, when they lied to terminal patients. But looking at this poor girl who reminded her so much of her battered, defeated daughter, Knudsen couldn't for the life of her believe any newspaper could make her suffer any more than she was suffering right now.

If that was any daughter of her own, begging her from that hospital bed, Knudsen would feel the girl had a *right* to know. And the fact was, the evening paper she had picked up from the machine outside the *Eagle-Bulletin* office on her way over to the hospital was tucked right now into her knitting bag.

Knudsen said again, "Shouldn't you ask the doctors?"

The nun made a fluttering, helpless gesture with her hands. "Oh, please. I was counting on you to help me."

Knudsen reached into her knitting bag. "Well now, Sister, you won't tell on me, will you? Because I could get in a whole peck of trouble for this."

"Oh, no. I promise." She took the newspaper from Knudsen's hand. "Oh, thank you."

Knudsen settled in the chair by the window, trying to knit, trying not to watch the young woman in the bed. If she went funny, psychiatric on her again like she did last night, Knudsen knew this time she would have only herself to blame. But she pushed away her own alarmed doubts with the firm thought, *Norma Knudsen, you did the right thing.*

So that was how she learned about it. About the baby being found upside down in a green straw wastebasket. *That must be the one beside her desk.* A six-and-three-quarter-pound male baby. *Almost seven pounds. A real baby, then.*

The basket found behind a bookcase in her convent

252

room. *BEHIND the bookcase? But how would it get there?* Found by two nuns sent back from the hospital by the doctors to look for the baby. *Julia. They must mean Julia. But who else? Only Julia was there.*

The part about the second-degree murder charge she already knew. And the part about the afterbirth, her delivering the afterbirth at the hospital—she knew that, too. *But how strange to read about it here, where everyone could see. About that ugly purple thing like a monster fished up from the sea.*

The hardest part to read about was the white panties found stuffed in the baby's mouth. And the pink shortie nightgown tied around his neck. *Which must be hers. Could have been hers. That pink gown she'd been wearing that morning when she was walking by the windows. But how could it possibly get around the baby's neck?*

And the autopsy they'd performed. *Autopsy. Cutting up. Cutting her baby up.* And the Medical Examiner's verdict: death by asphyxia.

Asphyxia. She put the paper down, looked over at the closet doors. Asphyxia meant choking, didn't it?

So that was what they all thought she had done: choked her baby to death. With the white panties and the pink nightgown.

There was a kind of peacefulness in the terrible pain she was feeling now all through her sore body. Now it made sense, why none of them would tell her. Because they truly believed she must have done that thing. Must have, because no one else was there.

She knew she must not blame them for thinking that. She herself didn't understand what had happened, and she was the one who was there.

She looked back at the newspaper, at that quote from the Medical Examiner that the infant had "met the two criteria for life: it was born alive, and it breathed air before it was asphyxiated by gagging with an article of clothing."

She turned those words in her mind: "born alive." And

253

"breathed air." This was where it all got so confusing to her. Because she could not, could *not* imagine how she could possibly forget seeing something like her own baby, *born alive.*

Yet at the same time she also knew, as fiercely as she'd known anything in her life, that she *could not have done that thing they said in the newspaper.* That terrible thing. To her own baby.

At least now she knew what she was fighting. She must make them understand, somehow, that she could never have done a thing like that. Never, *never.* She knew it was quite reasonable that they must *think* she had done it—it was her room, her basket, her nightie, after all. So she would not blame them, *must* not blame them. She must just pray for the strength and wisdom to make them see, somehow, that she *could not have done that thing.*

With the help of Lord Jesus and his Blessed Mother, she must make them understand.

She knew that a lot of what was there in the newspaper must be true, must really have happened. Why else would it be there, in the newspaper?

But part of it, at least, she knew was *not* true—that part about a murder. She *knew* that was not true. About that she had no doubt, no confusion. And if *that* was not true, it was hard to know how much of the rest she must believe was true, had really happened.

What Angela wanted most of all was to know *what was true here.* What made it so confusing was that she couldn't remember, exactly, what had happened.

But if she *had* done that, what they said—oh, surely she would remember.

But she didn't remember *any* of it, not the basket, or any of that other. So it was hard to say why she was so *sure* it couldn't be true about that murder when she couldn't remember even the green basket. Yet about that murder part of it she felt a terrible calm and sureness—she still didn't know what, exactly, had happened. But she knew it was not, *could not be,* what they said.

She lay quietly for a while, thinking, staring at the closet doors, before she picked up the newspaper and read it through again. It didn't hurt so much, this time.

But then she noticed the other article. That said that three detectives had gone to Wisconsin to find the baby's father. And they had found him.

Her first reaction was confusion—even a little panic. *Roy, they must mean that Roy.*

She tried to imagine three detectives sitting there with that Roy, asking him about everything that had happened.

But after a moment that feeling of pained peacefulness came back to her. Because if that Roy talked to them, he must have told them about that dark time in the woods. He was a good person, really, Roy was; he must have told them about that time.

And then they would know, those detectives, that Angela was not to blame for all those bad things they said had happened.

The noisy argument was carried from the restaurant into the maroon Buick, with Vance insisting, "Where's the intent? Can you show me one fucking proof of intent?" and Scotti bellowing, "She's a fucking murderess, and you're a goddam asshole. Let me out of this car!"

The third time he said that, Vance slammed on the brakes and leaned across Scotti to push open the passenger door. "Done. Get your ass out."

Fortunately, Scotti's gun had been locked with Vance's in the car trunk before they went into the restaurant. Scotti stumbled from the car, lurching along the sidewalk as Vance drove down the street. In the back seat Andy DaSilva yawned with fatigue. "Jesus. I don't know who's the bigger clown, Tim, you or Nick."

"Ah, I'm just cooling him off. Getting a little oxygen

into his Sicilian bloodstream." Vance drove for two blocks before he turned around at a gas station and headed back.

Scotti was gratifyingly subdued when he climbed back into the car. They drove in silence to the Holiday Inn twelve blocks away.

Since Scotti was charged with custody of the blood samples, he got his own room. The desk clerk provided a plastic garbage bag; Scotti filled it with ice from the hall machine, tossed it into the bathroom sink and nested the vials of blood among the cubes.

Vance and DaSilva were already sacked out in the room across the hall when Scotti appeared in the door, saying, "How about it? Who's for a couple of drinks?"

DaSilva groaned. "Jesus, Nick. Have a little mercy, will you?"

Chief Mel O'Rourke, who was still hanging around this bunch because he hadn't had such a good time in the five years since he'd retired from the Milwaukee detective force, said, "What the hell, Nick. Can't have you drinking alone in a strange town." Scotti and O'Rourke went down to the hotel bar and traded war stories until the bar closed at two A.M.

Around midnight she asked the nurse if they could give her something to help her sleep. Mrs. Knudsen brought her a white pill. "This should do it nicely, dear," she said as she handed her the glass of water. "Just you relax and let it work."

Oh, she wanted it to work. To take her someplace out past dreaming.

It wasn't so much that she was afraid of being awake, of thinking about that *murder,* and the boy-child upside down in the green wastebasket.

It was more that she was afraid of the dreams.

Rolling the maroon Buick westward along I-94 in the early morning light, with Scotti sacked out on the backseat and DaSilva napping in the front, Tim Vance finally had time to think.

The first thing on his mind was an acknowledgment that he'd been dead wrong in his objections to coming along on this "goose chase." Vance realized now that up until yesterday morning they'd known zip about what was coming down with this case. But now it was blown wide open, with a large store of facts, incidents, observations—almost all of them shockers.

He turned the scattered revelations of the past day slowly, methodically in his head, looking for some kind of shape to them, feeling for the place where they fit. He knew he had no flash to his method, like what Nick Scotti had. But it was the only way he knew how to work.

The gently rolling farmland they were moving through was exceptionally beautiful in the delicate, thin-gold light of dawn, but Tim Vance barely noticed it. He was ticking off a mental checklist of every fact he had heard about Angela Flynn since he was yanked out of his basement den on Tuesday night. And suddenly he realized that his thoughts were taking a peculiar, unexpected shape.

It was as if two different persons were sitting there in his head. Alike, but also very different.

One was Sister Angela Flynn, the good little nun. Who never stepped out of line, always put others first. Who focused always on other people's needs, never her own.

And the other was Gayle Flynn—a girlish, seductive woman who laughed and romped and drank wine on the beach in her low-cut bathing suit. Who seemed to be coming on to men, in a tentative, almost adolescent way.

One question that had nagged at Vance all along—*what was a thirty-three-year-old nun doing fooling around with a naive kid like Gary Tucker*—suddenly came a little more clear.

If you just thought of *Gayle* . . . now that was a different story.

For sure, Gayle had come on to Gary. Which probably explained the savage pass he'd made at her last weekend—

he'd been too shy, too sexually insecure, to handle the message she'd probably been sending out to him, up there at the lake. But once he realized she *had* done it, with somebody else, he'd moved in to claim what she had one way or another been inviting him all along to take.

That other guy, that Roy Danziger, he'd been old and experienced enough to decode the message Gayle Flynn was sending out. And he'd acted on it.

The jagged pieces were suddenly fitting together in Vance's head. The confusing part, always, had been Sister Angela. But if you just fixed on Gayle Flynn . . .

Vance felt a strange excitement, almost a chill, as he moved the pieces back and forth in his head. The idea was farfetched as hell, but it did seem to fit. The more he thought about it, the more it seemed to fit.

Everything he'd heard about Sister Angela Flynn said duty, caution, diligence. Even without meeting her, he knew she was a real good little nun. Even allowing for the vacation syndrome Andy DaSilva had talked about—which Vance knew from his own experience was too damn powerful to discount—it was hard to imagine Sister Angela Flynn tripping down the beach five, six times with that Roy Danziger.

Even once.

But Gayle Flynn now, the girl who'd helped Roy kill off the whiskey bottle in the Tuckers' trailer, the girl who'd said, 'No, no, it's all right' when Roy found out she was a nun—that was something else.

Andy DaSilva was stirring sleepily on the seat beside him. "You okay, Tim? Want me to drive?"

"Nah, that's fine. I'm doing great," said Vance.

DaSilva sank back into his catnap, leaving Vance alone to play with his fantastic, farfetched idea.

What she'd meant was *it's all right for Gayle Flynn.* Not for Sister Angela.

And that last weekend—it was *Gayle Flynn* who'd flown

over to visit there in Milwaukee. It was all there in what that Tucker kid had been saying, if they'd only heard him right. Maybe it was Sister Angela who got herself on the plane, but it was *Gayle Flynn* who'd climbed off it—bouncing around, laughing, shopping, hanging out with his kid sister. Gayle Flynn who was running with Gary through the woods in the rain after that archery shoot.

Except that this time Gayle had come to visit in the exhausted, bloated, nine months' pregnant body of Sister Angela Flynn.

Tim Vance knew the idea that had come to him was too far out to share with anyone else on the case. Jesus, they'd say he was as psycho as the nun. This kind of thinking—it wasn't his job anyway. His job was just to put together whatever facts might be relevant to a criminal prosecution of the nun.

This idea that hung on his mind like a waking-dream fantasy, it was no fact. More a strange perception that made some faint sense of the strange facts of this case that made no sense otherwise.

Okay, enough, stop: Tim Vance knew what his job was here. His cop's job. And he would do it the best way he knew how.

But that other part of him, that always wanted to know the *why,* was still clutching to his strange idea.

Because the more he turned it around in his head, the more persuaded he became that the giggling, flirtatious girl they'd heard these Milwaukee guys describe was not the same person who told Sister Julia, "I'll take a taxi to work later, when I'm feeling a little better."

Twenty

When she came awake at 6:45 on Friday morning, sliding down that quick, reflexive chute into consciousness, the first thought that came back from that refuge of sleep was her pregnancy.

Now she remembered. Of course. How strange that she could have forgotten.

Now she remembered those wakings in her convent room. Lying on her side, cushioning her belly against the mattress, hoping each morning it was all some terrible mistake.

But then the baby would wake too. Stirring, punching at her. Reminding her that he was there.

And then she would get out of bed, knowing it was *not* some mistake, it was there and real but also so oddly unreal, and she would plunge into her busy day.

Some of it was still fuzzy, strange. But most of it she seemed to remember in that sudden sluice of knowledge.

So strange that she could have forgotten. Because she knew now what that strange soreness of her body had come out of. For so long it had been there—that swelling, that pain. She had fixed her life around it, never admitting to anyone else it was there, because— Well, because.

But when she was alone in her room, propping up her legs to keep down that swelling, private and alone, of course she'd known he was there.

Now, lying quiet in that hospital room so the nurse would not come fussing, she was remembering how it began. The missed periods, first. She didn't notice them at first. She'd even been pleased when they hadn't come, those strange, messy times, those pointless bloody stains that were so hard to get out of her clothes.

But then she was waiting, counting. Marking the calendar on her closet door with tiny pencil strokes.

She'd been so sure it would come again, that messy bleeding that she'd never really liked to see before but now hoped for, prayed for, even. She'd been so *sure.*

And then that day in the classroom when she was bending over the fingerpainting table and she'd suddenly felt that moving inside her. She remembered thinking that first time it must be some mistake. Indigestion, something. But then it happened again and kept happening, stronger, and then she knew, she knew it must be true.

When she'd told Dr. Talbott she had no symptoms, she just hadn't remembered that part. She'd never meant to lie to him. But she really just hadn't remembered—but how *could* she forget that, all those times he'd moved in her, when she was eating dinner in the St. Rose dining room, when she was working on her lesson plans, even once when she was playing croquet on the lawn behind Ed's house, when she went for a family Sunday dinner.

Now it was all back in her mind, like a flood from some distant place. Times like—the baths. How she'd come to hate, tried to avoid, taking those baths. Because every time she went down into that warm water he would kick, punch against her—as if he liked the feeling of the bathwater.

How she tried not to look at that swollen body she mostly kept hidden behind the bulky sweater Robin Evans had given her, or that shirt she'd borrowed from Dan. How she'd wanted, needed, to *be alone.* The relief she felt each night when she could close the door of her own room.

Except she was never, especially in those last months, alone. He was always reminding her with those brutal, unpredictable thrusts into her body, into her own self, that he was there.

She remembered lying on the floor of her room, the door locked, trying to do her school work with her legs elevated on the bed. That was supposed to bring down the

261

swelling in her legs that she knew, from those books from the convent library, was caused by water retention.

Those pills she'd gotten from Margory were supposed to bring down that swelling too. But they didn't, not enough. He was always in there, with those moves that were so strange.

Not a real baby, with a face and a head and arms—just something she knew was in there, punching apart her serene, satisfied life.

But she didn't—hate him. She never hated him the way they must have thought, if they said she did those things to him.

So much was fuzzy still. But *that* she knew very well. Even when she hadn't known he was a real baby, she never had hated him.

She must explain that to Dr. Talbott, and the rest of them. She'd tell him she'd been wrong—that of course she remembered being pregnant. Remembered that baby being in there, but more important—*she had never meant to harm him.* She'd known he must have somehow come out of that dark time in the woods and yes, it was true she had not really wanted him to be there, but she had never wished *harm* to him. Ever.

Oh, *that* was the soreness, the strangeness. That had been with her, she remembered now, for such a long time.

He had come out of that strangeness, then. And she understood that now, understood it very well. She couldn't remember him in any real way, but she did understand that.

But she also understood that other thing: *she never meant to harm him.*

So they were still wrong about that. She knew that they were somehow wrong about that. But what frightened her most as she lay very still in that hospital bed, trying not to alert the nurse, was that powerful question pressing at her.

Because if she had been wrong about having no symptoms, maybe she could have also been wrong about the rest of it. And that possibility frightened her very much, but it did not really shake her firm hold on that sureness.

What they said—*murder*. A murder.

It was so hard, so confusing to lie here and realize that all those terrible, private times between her and the thing in there, that baby, those times she recalled so vividly now, had somehow been blanked from her mind. So if she had been wrong about that, about what she had said to Dr. Talbott, could she possibly be wrong about—

No.

No!

All that time he was never real to her, in that way. A baby like they had talked about him in that newspaper.

But they said she *had* seen his face. And she had—

No. *No.*

There was still no face in all the rememberings she had of him now.

And if she had never meant him any harm in those terrible, frightened times when she locked the door of her room and propped her legs up on the mattress to bring down the swelling enough to get her through another painful, exhausting day in the school, how could she ever have . . . done to him what they said?

When Ben Haverty sat down to his fried egg with three strips of bacon and picked up his morning edition of the *Eagle-Bulletin,* his eyes went immediately to the two articles on Sister Angela that began on the front page.

Splot! The newspaper smashed against the wall of the breakfast nook of his kitchen. Sudden silence in the room. Marie Haverty said sharply from the stove, "What's *that?*"

He glared into the faces of the three children who were wall-eyeing him from across the table. "Nothing. I'm sorry. Forget it. That's— Nothing that matters. I'm sorry, I'm just in a bad mood this morning. Forget it, kids."

The father. They had the father already.

263

. . .

When the phone rang at 8:10 in the St. Rose convent hallway, Sister Margory answered it.

A woman's voice said, "So don't you all feel so high and mighty now, all you fucking nuns lifting up your short skirts for those fucking priests to get into. I see you, don't think I don't—"

Margory slammed down the receiver, trembling as much from shock as from anger. For Margory—for most of them—this was the worst part of the whole nightmare, the unimaginable worst.

She found Julia in the kitchen. "Julia, how soon will the phone company put in that unlisted number?"

Julia searched her face. Patted her arm. "Another of those calls?" Margory nodded. "Well, forget it. They promised to change it today. Before the weekend. It will probably be in before we get back from school."

Roy Danziger came out of a heavy sleep to focus on the wall beside his bed. Cracked yellow wall with the lake breakers rolling in the window beside it.

His first thought was that he'd just got so flat-out stoned he dreamed the whole thing up. But as the thing shaped itself rapidly out of the grogginess in his head he knew it was there. Real. Really happened.

He lay there staring at the yellow wall, letting the words roll images into his head: *Gayle*.

Murder.

Baby.

Killed.

Annnnnhh, no.

He rolled over in the sheet-churned bed, reaching for the rolled joint on the chair.

Shit. This was going to be a rough day.

He lit up, inhaling deeply, trying to float back out.

The whole thing so heavy. A real bummer, all the way.

. . .

They parked the maroon Buick in Chief Marwick's special slot in the Cambridgeport town parking lot. The reporters were on them almost as soon as they lurched out of the car: "You found the father?" "Did he make any statement?" "Hey, Nick, how did she get knocked up?"

Saying, "No comment. Let us through please. No comment," they pushed their way through the microphones and cameras, carrying a sudden, astonishing sense of their own importance here.

The big lights came on as they moved down the narrow hall of the town hall basement. Nick Scotti thought, *Shit, I gotta watch tonight.* He'd never yet seen himself on TV.

Abrams and Marwick were waiting for them in Marwick's small office. Andy DaSilva ran through the gist of their interviews, in more detail than he'd managed to convey over the telephone. They listened, grunted, asked a few questions. Finally Abrams said, "Okay, men. Good job well done. I think you touched all the major bases. I don't mind telling you now I never expected that trip to be as fruitful as it turned out. And I want to thank you all for a first-rate, excellent job."

"Right, right," Marwick agreed. "First-rate."

Tim Vance said, "Well, I guess we got lucky."

Luck, shit, you fucking cherry, Scotti was thinking.

Gregory Marwick was running his mind on Sister Angela, feeling an uncurling sensation of disgust. This delicate, holy little nun they'd been hearing about for three days, the one everybody involved with this case had seemed so anxious to protect—she'd sat there on a couch in Milwaukee less than a week before and let that Tucker kid paw her up, feel up her private parts. What the hell kind of nun would do that?

"And the daddy turns out to be the fucking doper," Scotti was saying. "Who the Christ would've expected that?"

. . .

265

Ben Haverty looked across his disordered desk at the anxious, resisting couple and said, "Please understand my purpose in asking you to come here, asking you these difficult questions. I want to give Sister Angela the best defense possible. When I understood from Edwin that you were in town visiting the family, I thought perhaps you might be able to help me in preparing that defense."

Walter Russell's body was hunched tensely forward on the edge of his chair. "I understand that, Mr. Haverty."

His wife, Mary Alice, a thin, fragile woman with tightly clenched hands, murmured, "Of course we want to do anything we can to help."

"Well, yes, of course. That's the point here." Haverty shifted his bulk in the desk chair. "And you must understand that the present circumstances are—rather difficult."

Russell repeated flatly, "Whatever we can do—"

"Well, I understand that Sister Angela was visiting with your family last August." Mary Alice nodded mutely. I'm sure you understand why I have to ask—was she particularly close to any men during that period?"

The Russells exchanged silent, frozen glances. Walter said, "Well, certainly there were some men around the camp that Gayle was friendly with. Like all of us were." Angrily: "In the normal, friendly way of camping. If you mean to suggest—"

Haverty pushed that away with a gesture of his hand. "Please, please. I mean to suggest nothing, Mr. Russell. I would simply like to hear—whatever you might care to tell me. For my general enlightenment."

There was no evident relaxation in the tension of the Russells' bodies. Walter said, "Well, what I'd like to say to you very plainly, Mr. Haverty, is that me and my wife never believed for one moment that Gayle had a—boyfriend, in the sense you mean it. In any way that would lead to—this thing. Never for one minute. Gayle isn't that sort of girl. No sir, not a bit of it."

"Thank you." Haverty was nodding his head. "That's

helpful. I—ah, understand from the newspaper that the district attorney may have located a man who admits to paternity in this case. Do you by any chance know the identity of this man?"

More muted, shared glances. Angrier, louder now, from Walter: "Well now, I'll tell you the truth, we can't figure that at all. Unless it was— Now, there was a kind of strange fellow hanging around the campsite next to ours. Kind of a worldly fellow. I understand his moral character was not the highest. Now if he took advantage of Gayle's innocence and— Well, I don't know about that. This whole thing comes smack out of the blue on us, you might say, Mr. Haverty. And Gayle's family seems to think— Well now, all I can tell you is we don't know anything about it."

"I understand," Haverty murmured. "Then it is your impression that this man *might* have been the father, but you were not aware of any—causative incident?"

Mary Alice Russell shuddered visibly and looked away from Haverty. Walter said loudly, angrily, "That's dead right, Mr. Haverty. We're way out in left field on this thing. I don't mind telling you that we've been over it and over it between us, ever since we heard, examined our consciences about it. And I have to tell you flatly, I don't see anywhere we went wrong. I don't see any way in heck we could be considered responsible for this thing."

"I understand. I know it's a most difficult period for you all, and I'd like to extend my sincere sympathies."

"Well, thank you."

Haverty looked at the thin, pretty woman who seemed to bear so little family resemblance to Angela Flynn. "Mrs. Russell, is there anything you'd care to add?"

She looked right at him then, and Haverty saw that the resemblance was in the eyes—haunted like Angela's, full of uncomprehended pain. She said in a high, faint voice, "No, Mr. Haverty. What my husband told you—that's all we know. All we can say."

Ben Haverty saw them courteously out of the office,

down into the elevator. Then he walked back to his desk and threw himself into the worn leather chair.

So. They saw no rape, those people she was living in such close quarters with.

But if Ben Haverty had learned one thing from twenty-four years of defending accused criminals, it was not to trust the testimony of third parties.

He might call them into court if that suited his intricate purposes, put them on the stand to tell their righteous, persuasive tale. But what Ben Haverty was after here was the truth of this case, and he knew that he had not found it in that anxious, unforgiving pair. The truth he must have would only come from Sister Angela Flynn—in its own, *her* own good, healed time.

Dr. Heilbron came in around lunchtime and asked if she had any new recollections.

"Yes, I did." She twisted a portion of the sheet.

"What were they, Sister?"

"Well, I remembered—" *Yes, you must say. So they will know you are not crazy, you remember.* "I remembered being pregnant."

"I see." He pushed himself up, sitting straighter in the chair. "What, specifically, Sister, did you recall?"

"Just—I remember I was pregnant. That I knew about —the baby." She dropped the sheet and pressed it smoothly against her body.

"I see. How did you know that, Sister?"

"First, because I missed my periods. And then later I felt it—moving inside me. I remember all that very well now."

"I see." He was nodding very solemnly now, dropping his head up and down. "And did you then consult a doctor?"

Oh, she'd known they would come at her with questions like that. Of course they would come at her with that. And how could she make them understand? Because she *must* make them understand. She said, "No," and gripped the sheet again. "Because I knew what a terr—what grief and sorrow this would bring to my family and my religious community, and I wanted to spare them that as long as I could, so I did not—no, I didn't tell anyone." Now, when she most wanted not to, she was crying again, sobs from deep in her, from that place where she could not stop them. *"But I knew."*

He ducked his head into his neck. "I see. But, Sister, did you make any specific plans to deal with this pregnancy?"

"Oh, yes. Yes, I did."

Silence. "What plans, Sister Angela?"

She was not sure what the question meant. But knew what her answer should be. "I planned—that he should never come to harm."

"I mean, did you plan to have your child adopted? Or were you perhaps considering terminating the pregnancy with an abortion? I mean—I would like to know what options you were considering, Sister Angela."

Oh, how could she make this man see, make him understand? She was trying to push down the sobs, so she could talk clearly, when he interrupted: "I know these were very difficult decisions for you to make, Sister Angela. But I'd like to know what was on your mind."

She knew this was the man who was trying to put her in the crazy ward, so she wanted it to come out right. In a way he would understand. "Well, I thought about a—but I don't approve of—abortion. I think it's like a—"

No. Not that word. She retreated. "No, I couldn't have an abortion. That would have been wrong." So hard to talk through those tears. "I wanted very much—to do the right thing."

"I understand. But did you, perhaps, consider adoption?"

She shook her head, pressing the tissues to her eyes as if they could staunch the flow. "Oh, yes, I thought of that. But to do that I would have had to leave my religious com-

269

munity. I—didn't want—I wanted to keep him. To raise him as—my own child. But as long as I could. . . ."

He patted calmingly on her arm. "I think I understand. That choice would of course have been very painful for you to make. So you wanted to delay it as long as you could."

She nodded into the tissues as she blew her nose. "Yes. I wanted to keep on working, to keep—as long as I could. I wasn't expecting it to come until May tenth. I thought then I could do—what I—"

"I understand how difficult that confrontation would be for you to make, Sister."

She pulled in her breath, tried to pull herself together. In front of this man who wanted to put her in the crazy ward. "But I never— I only wanted him to be all right. I never, ever meant to *harm* him."

"I see. Was there anyone you confided in, to help you make these decisions?"

She shook her head fiercely, the tissue pressed to her mouth. "Oh, no. I knew—how hard they—what a terrible shock that would be. I wanted to spare them from knowing for as long as I— But I never meant to harm him. In any way."

Now he was patting her arm again, telling her that that was very good, excellent progress, and now he wanted her to rest. Like they always said when they were ready to go.

She summoned everything that was in her for one last effort: "Dr. Heilbron, that Ward Five you told me about— I don't want to go there."

He was saying please, please, she should not tax herself now, that they could make that decision together, when the time was right.

"But I'm not— Oh, Dr. Heilbron, please don't send me to that place." She was trying to tell him again that she would be all right, she would be fine if he would only just let her go home to the convent. But he stood up, cutting off her words. Said they would talk again soon.

· · ·

At 2:45 Roy Danziger came by his mother's house with a load of laundry to be done. As he came through the kitchen door she looked up from the enamel table where she was playing solitaire and stubbed out the cigarette she was smoking. "Well, well. Look what we got here," she said as she fanned the smoke away from her.

"Hey, Ma. How you doing?"

"*I'm* okay. What's this with you? I understand the cops are after you."

He froze in the act of lifting the bag of laundry to the top of the washer. "Hunh?"

She stood up and walked to the stove, turned on the burner under the water kettle. "I asked you, why are the cops after you?"

"Where'd you hear that?"

"They were around here looking for you yesterday, that's where. Nosy Grotowski next door filled me all in on it. And don't think she didn't like that plenty. What've they got you for, selling your funny cigarettes?"

Roy hesitated. He guessed maybe he'd come over here to talk about it. But not this, not like this. "Hey, come on, it wasn't anything. Just a bad lead they were working on."

She sniffed her doubt.

"Hey, really. I talked to them at work. It was just about some other guy they're after."

"So why were they nosing around here looking for you?"

"They just thought I knew where to find him. Hey, it's got nothing to do with me, Ma."

"Hmmph." She poured the boiling water into a teapot. "Did they want *him* for that dope you're always smoking?"

"I dunno. They didn't say."

"So did you tell them where to find him?"

"Nanh. I don't know where he is now. Hey, let's change the subject. How's everything with you?

271

"I'm not complaining." She poured out a mug of tea for him. "So what else is it, besides you want me to wash your dirty clothes? You want to borrow some money? Because you already owe me that twenty-five."

"Come on, Ma, what is this? Did I ask you for money?"

"Well, I never knew you when you didn't need it."

"Hey, come on. Forget it."

He stayed for a half hour, talking about something. Afterward, he couldn't remember what.

When he left she said, "Okay. Come around more often, stranger, okay?" And pushed a five-dollar bill into his shirt pocket.

Twenty-one

When Dick McAlpine agreed to a personality profile on Sister Angela Flynn, Meg Gavin quickly tossed every source she had to work with. Unfortunately, since the Church lid was still nailed tight on this story, that came down mainly to her sister Babs, who had a friend whose children went to Benedictine Kindergarten, and the 1961 St. Benedict's Academy yearbook. Meg reasoned that most of Angela's classmates would be married now, going under different names—but *their* parents, at least, should still know where to find their daughters.

She skipped over the names like Reilly and O'Brien—two columns of Reillys in the St. Paul–Minneapolis phone book, two and a half of O'Briens—and concentrated on the more unusual ethnics. Her dialing finger was already fairly numb by the time Mrs. George Carpozzi said why, yes, that *was* her daughter Janine. Janine Vitale now. Oh, wasn't it a terrible thing that happened to that poor sister. She didn't know if Janine would want to talk about it, but anyway her phone number was 792-4468.

Janine Vitale said oh goodness, of course she remembered Sister Angela. Very well. "But I wouldn't want you to quote me—use my name or anything."

"No, sure, that's fine," said Meg. "I'm just interested in your general impression of what she was like. Maybe a few anecdotes, if you could remember them."

"Well, Sister Angela—she was Gayle Flynn then, of course—was just a sweet, lovely girl. A perfect lady. I'm just completely *shocked* about this murder charge against her. I just can't *believe* it's true."

When Meg asked if she could be any more specific, Janine said well, that was kind of hard. Actually she'd been in Gayle's class for three years at Blessed Sacrament before they both went to St. Benedict's, so she'd known her for seven years all together. And Gayle was always a good student, always at the top of her class. She also participated in quite a few school activities—Janine remembered they were both in the Sewing Circle and the Camera Club. Gayle also belonged to all the religious clubs, like the Mission Crusade and the Sodality, Janine seemed to remember. Mainly, she just knew Gayle as a lovely, lovely person.

"You don't recall anything more personal—any incidents, particulars?"

"Well, of course we all knew all along that Gayle was probably going to enter. She never made any secret about that. And she was really such a *pious* girl. You might even say on the holy side. I remember one day, for instance, when she was carrying some holy water home from school, and some big, tough girls pushed her into some bushes. I remember that Gayle was more worried about spilling the holy water than she was about what might happen to her."

273

When Janine Vitale hung up the kitchen telephone, Linda Boylan looked up from the coffee she was drinking at Janine's table and said dryly, "Boy, I can hardly believe the crap I just heard. 'Sweet, lovely'—my God, what bilge. You *know* you couldn't stand her, Jan. You *never* could, and neither could I—that pious little prune, always the nuns' pet. Such a prissy little *pill* she was."

"Sure I liked her. We were pretty good friends in the ninth and tenth grades."

"Oh, come *off* it—I remember how you'd keep us all in hysterics describing how Gayle would probably act if she ever went out on a date with a boy."

"Well, we all *knew* she was going to be a nun anyway."

"Oh, yeah. Some nun she turned out to be. 'Miss Goody Two-Shoes.' I guess you don't happen to remember who started calling her that?"

"Oh, come on. We *all* called her that."

"Yeah, but it was you who started it, Jan. I remember that even if you don't. Like that cute little story you came up with about the time those fat-lipped niggers from Morningside Avenue roughed her up in the bushes—I seem to remember you getting quite a few laughs around school about her spilling the holy water—'Oh, good for Gayle, she's finally committed a real sin.' "

Janine Vitale was not pleased with the drift of this conversation. Now Linda was saying, "You couldn't *wait* to get me yesterday with the big news that the mystery nun was little Miss Goody Two-Shoes. All this 'sweet, lovely' crap you just ran out on the phone—listen, if she wanted to be a nun, she should've *been* one."

There was a prim snap of irritation in Janine Vitale's voice as she said, "Well, I *do* sympathize with her, Linda. And right now I bet Gayle Flynn could use a few old friends."

The woman who let her in the door of the handsome suburban house turned out to be one of those skinny, energetic young Jewish women that Meg admired so much. Lena Schwartz led her automatically, distractedly, into the kitchen and offered her a coffee. Meg said, "Thanks, I'd love one," and sat at the large, round Formica table in the smartly decorated kitchen.

Lena said as she poured from the pot on the Mr. Coffee machine, "Oh, Meg, I still have the feeling I shouldn't be talking to you. That I'm being disloyal or something."

Meg smiled disarmingly. "Hey please, Lena. Like I told you, this doesn't count. It's off the record, like it never happened, I promise you that."

"Well, I hope so. Because we got a letter from the school, or the order anyway, asking us please not to talk to any of the press." Lena looked into her cup, drowned it with milk from the pitcher. "The letter also gave us a number to call if we wanted to talk about it. My Wendy's still in the school, and Peter just finished Benedictine last year— Well anyway, I called the number. And the nun said—she sounded very cautious, very careful—that they had of course noticed Sister Angela's medical condition and they'd offered her help but she refused it." Lena pushed a folded fist up against her chin. "Do you mind if I tell you, just to start, how I heard about this thing?"

"I wish you would."

"Well, I was here in the kitchen, keeping busy with some damn thing or other. I mean, I knew the nun's name was probably going to come out that day, but I didn't know when. And suddenly Wendy, my four-year-old who's in Sister Angela's afternoon class at Benedictine—she'd been watching Captain Kangaroo on the sunporch and she ran into the kitchen, all lit up, and said the man was talking about Sister Angela on the TV. Sister Angela and her *baby*. And Wendy said"—Lena folded her arms across her sweater—"'Mommy, I didn't know Sister Angela had a *baby*.' As if this was some wonderful, marvelous thing we'd kept from her—you understand, Wendy's very entranced with babies at her age."

Meg knew well enough when to say nothing. She sipped quietly at her coffee.

"We'd all noticed it, of course—all the other mothers at the school." She pulled a Kleenex from her sweater pocket, blew her nose. "We knew even before they announced it, that the nun would probably be Sister Angela. We all saw her every day. So there was no way we could pretend we hadn't noticed." She blew her nose again.

Meg asked, "But what could *you* do?"

"Well, of course that's what we're all asking ourselves now." Lena stuffed the Kleenex back into her sweater pocket. "We're all mothers—we've *been* pregnant. We ought to've known what it was we were seeing. So it's very hard for us now, and most of us are saying naturally we would've helped, done anything we could—she could've taken a leave of absence and we'd have arranged a discreet adoption—but why didn't she *come to us and tell us?*"

Quietly, very quietly: "I guess that's not an unreasonable question."

Lena Schwartz got up from the table with a quick, spinning movement. Walked over to the sink, leaned against it, and talked about what she had heard from the other mothers. How one of them had been helping in the class one day and had actually seen the baby *kick.* But she still hadn't said anything to Sister Angela. And how Lena herself had gone to a parent-teacher meeting about three weeks ago at Benedictine, and on the way driving home, her husband Art had said right out of the blue, "If I've ever seen a pregnant woman, that's it."

Silence. Meg prompted softly, "So?"

"So I said, 'Oh, you dirty old man.' God help me, Meg, that's what I said." Lena was rocking now against the sink. "I actually said that. So of course we didn't discuss it again, until all this happened."

Quietly: "Hey, I can very easily understand how all that could happen."

"Understand!" Lena Schwartz reached into a cabinet, spilled some cookies onto a plate. Moved to the round kitchen table and slapped the cookie plate onto the table. "Listen, the whole reason I agreed to see you, I just wanted to tell you this—Angela Flynn is just a remarkable teacher. I try to be one of those modern together mothers but I don't mind telling you that my son Peter was quite a mess until he got into Sister Angela's class. She had a way of combining discipline with enough stimulation—I still don't know how she did it. I was *thrilled* when Wendy got put in her class last year."

"That's nice to know."

"She has an almost uncanny way of bringing the very best out of those kids. I'm their mother, God love them—I love them too. But I couldn't give them what Sister Angela did, somehow pulling the best parts out of them. It's just that wonderful, gifted way she has about her. And the main reason I agreed to see you was that I wanted to make sure you understood how special she is in that way—whatever else has happened to her."

"And *is* happening," Meg said quietly.

"Oh, yes, that especially." Lena Schwartz was pacing around the kitchen, her hands jammed into her sweater pockets. "And the question all us mothers have to answer, that I hope you'll be very confidential about, Meg, is *how much was our fault?*" Pacing, pacing. "I mean, *we* should have known. We even *did* know. But we still didn't help this woman.

"Look, in my case, I'm Jewish. I figured what do I know about nuns, they must have their own way of dealing with these things. But now I find out even the Catholic mothers felt the same thing."

Meg shook her head, pushing a strand of brown hair behind her ear. "Look, Lena, forgive me for sticking my two cents into something that's absolutely none of my business, but I can't help thinking— Look, there's such a load of guilt already being shoveled back and forth on this case. . . ."

Lena smiled faintly. "Well, it's true that she didn't really *let* us help her. She was always so cheerful, so damned *normal.* Except there she was with that big stomach that looked so much like a— But there was something about the way she was that was so—private. As if she was saying, 'Just don't ask, stay away.' "

"Well, see." Meg was nodding. "That's what I mean, I guess."

Lena said almost to herself, "She was such a dedicated, able teacher—I've never seen anybody tuned to little kids the way she was. So I guess we all thought—" She made a convulsive movement with her shoulders. "Well, I guess we all thought she could deal with *that,* too. Like she did with our kids. And that's what we have to live with now. Because who had a better chance to help her, really, than we did? But we didn't, any of us, *make* ourselves help. Ask any of us—our children never had a more marvelous, gifted teacher. And *not one of us reached out to help her.*"

At 4:30 the duty nurse on West Wing Three phoned Dr. Keith Talbott to suggest he might drop in earlier than usual on Sister Angela Flynn. Talbott came at 5:05 and found his patient weeping uncontrollably, pleading that she be allowed to go home, that she not be sent to "that psycho place."

Talbott offered her the old arguments: that although this might seem to her to be a harsh move, it was what her physicians felt to be in her best interests. "I myself would feel quite alarmed about sending you home now, in view of the—pressured circumstances you're likely to be exposed to there."

There was anguish and bewilderment but no new comprehension in the old arguments she threw back at him—the plea to go back to her old life, back to the convent, where she would be safe again. He cut the discussion short after several minutes and stopped at the nursing station to phone Bruce Heilbron.

"Bruce, I'm a little concerned about how badly she's taking the news of this transfer. If you have no objection, I'd like to have Fred Salter check in on her. Get his input in the case."

Short hesitation on the other end of the wire. "Of course, if you think so, Keith. If you think that's necessary."

"I'm damned if I know what *is* necessary here, Bruce. This is such a damned peculiar case. But since Fred's the senior psychiatrist on staff—I thought maybe an older man, a man with all Fred's experience, could calm her down some."

Testily: "Whatever you think best, Keith, I'll go along with."

When Meg read over her notes for the Sister Angela profile she muttered, "Jesus Christ, what eyewash." There was still no feel of a real woman in anything they said.

That stuff she was hearing out on the street, of course, especially from the women—that was something else. "Unnatural" was about the kindest description they were laying on her. But the *Eagle-Bulletin* was not in business to pass along street wisdom of that nature.

What Lena Schwartz had said, at least, was real. More than she could say for Janine ex-Carpozzi. But since "lovely, lovely person" had slightly more snap to it than "marvelous, marvelous teacher," Meg quoted Janine in her lead, and the headline writer liked it well enough that he slugged the story, "Nun 'Sweet, Lovely,' Shocked Friends Recall."

. . .

When Norma Knudsen came on duty at ten P.M. she sailed past the police guard carrying the evening and morning newspapers in her bag of knitting. Sister Angela was waiting for her, sitting up in bed. The poor girl still looked weepy, but she brightened when she saw Knudsen. "Oh, hello, Mrs. Knudsen. Did you—"

Knudsen smiled, and slipped the newspapers out of her bag. "Now, you remember, Sister, this is just our little secret."

"Yes, sure. You're a real friend, Mrs. Knudsen."

She skimmed through the day's articles. Then she looked up from the paper and said, "Mrs. Knudsen, is there a phone someplace around here I could use? Maybe a pay phone?"

Knudsen was smiling as she nodded her head. In thirty-five years of nursing she'd never broken as many rules as she was doing on this case. But everything the poor girl wanted seemed so innocent. Just having something to *do* besides lie there and cry seemed to make her feel better.

Knudsen had no idea whom she wanted to phone. Maybe her family—maybe the baby's father. Now what business was it of the police if the poor girl just wanted to do that?

Or what business of Norma Knudsen's?

She said, "Well now, Sister, don't tell anyone I told you. But I guess it's no secret that there's a pay phone down the hall, by the elevators."

Angela put on a hospital bathrobe.

The chair outside her door was empty. She supposed the guard was that black woman standing inside the nursing station, laughing with the nurses.

She found the phone with no difficulty, dropped the dime she had borrrowed from Mrs. Knudsen into the slot and dialed the number of her friends, the Hogans.

Margaret answered. "Oh, Angela dear, we're so *glad* to hear from you. We tried to come down and visit but they wouldn't let us in."

"I know. There's an approved list of visitors. But I got the flowers you sent, and they're beautiful, Margaret."

"Oh, Angela dear, I wish they were more. I mean, I wish they were *us*. We'd like so much to see you, dear."

"Thanks, Margaret. They said pretty soon I'll be able to have all the visitors I want, and I'd certainly like to see you then."

"Oh, of course we'll come. As soon as we can." Brief silence. "How *are* you, dear?"

"I'm okay. Much better. They're talking about moving me to another ward, but I'll let you know when you can come see me." She hesitated. "I really *want* to see you, Margaret. I really miss—just having you to talk to."

"Oh, it's so good to talk to you now. How are you really, how are you feeling?"

"Much better, thanks."

"Well, you *sound* fine. You sound very good. Oh, Ron is signaling me—he sends a big hello. A big hug, he says."

"Tell him a big hello back." Angela heard some commotion behind her. She turned to see that woman deputy from the nursing station running toward her.

"I will. Oh, Angela, we were all so sorry to hear—I mean, I wish we could have *helped* you, dear. We care so much for you, we would have done anything at all to help. Why didn't you just tell us?"

As the woman got quite close, making signals that clearly meant *hang up,* Angela said dryly, "Why didn't you ask?"

Twenty-two

The smiling, middle-aged man who came through the door at 8:30 on Saturday morning introduced himself as Dr. Fred Salter, the senior psychiatrist on the hospital staff.

Her hands moved protectively over her chest. "Oh, please. Not another psychiatrist."

He laughed. "You know, I think I might feel that way too, if I was in your shoes, Sister Angela. But the truth is we're not such a bad lot."

"I didn't say 'bad,' " she said petulantly. "I just want to be left alone."

He nodded. "A reasonable enough request. Well, let me explain why I'm pestering you. Dr. Talbott asked me to drop by and explain a little about why we're asking you to stay on with us for a while."

"In that crazy ward," she burst out. "That place Dr. Heilbron wants to send me to."

He lifted his hand. "Oh, please, not a 'crazy ward.' It's just Ward Five, as we call it. An ugly name for a rather attractive place. It's just another part of this rather large and efficient hospital—but since the regular ward is presently undergoing renovations, it's located for the time being at another hospital." His voice was very warm, very reassuring. "Now, the main reason we'd like you to stay on with us is for our own selfish convenience. So we can drop by more easily to see you, chat with you, keep tabs on the excellent progress you're making."

Bitterly: "If I'm making so much progress, why are you sending me to that place?"

He *tttched* gently, shaking his head, with a small smile. "Now, Angela—you don't mind if I call you Angela?" She shook her head. "Angela, I'd like you to think of yourself as a kind of accident victim. Who is temporarily on the mend, but will soon be fit as a fiddle again. Now, some of your healing is physical, like your stitches. And *that* part is almost done. But your mind also has a little healing to do. And we can't leave you here on the surgical ward to do that, because we have other patients who need the bed much more than you do."

She smiled faintly as she looked out the window, on that view of roofs, air vents and grated skylights that by now she knew almost as well as the view of the black-topped parking lot out her bedroom window at St. Rose. She had no more fight left in her against what he was saying since that painful visit from Mr. Haverty the night before. When he had made her understand that the alternative to the hospital was not St. Rose, anyway—it was jail. At least until that "arraignment," whatever that was, happened.

At first she'd found it hard to believe that the police would actually mean to do that to her, but Mr. Haverty said unfortunately, they would. Because of the technicality in the law that they were presently involved in, as he had already explained to her, they would be obliged by law to do that— take her to that jail.

At least she knew the doctors, knew they did not *mean* to be cruel. So it must be better to trust them and go where they said than it was to let herself be delivered up to those strange police.

This friendly new doctor perched himself at the foot of her bed and talked with her for about an hour, asking the now-familiar questions about her work, her family, her interests. Asked what she liked to read and watch on television, how she liked to spend her spare time.

When he asked about her general health she said, "Oh, I'm a very healthy person. I've never really been sick at all, except for a couple of allergies that I have. That's one reason I find all this"—she waved at the hospital room—"so upsetting."

283

"Of course. If you *didn't* find it upsetting I'd be quite alarmed about you." Her laugh came easily. "But now that we've talked, I'm not alarmed in the least, Angela. I find you a sound, basically healthy person who would like very much to be well again."

Now, *now* was the time to say it. She looked down at the sheet and blurted the one fear that was pushing the other ones out of her head: "But if you say I'm healthy and you still put me in that crazy ward, when I *know* I'm not crazy and you say I'm not, too—how can I be sure you'll let me out again?"

He shook his head vigorously. "You can be sure because I'm promising you that right now, Angela. Now I don't want you to feel anyone is pulling a fast move on you, spiriting you off to some strange place and throwing away the key, because it isn't anything *like* that, Angela, I promise you."

Oh, she wanted to believe him. And almost did. But— but—

Always there was that "but," stuck somewhere in her frightened, uneasy mind. That fear that if they put her away in that strange place, like they had put her in this hospital, against her own will, she might never find her way back.

A little tremulously, she asked, "But how long will you keep me there?"

"Now I can't tell you that *exactly* yet, Angela, you understand. But I can promise you now, just on the basis of our talk, since I can see now for myself what genuinely good progress you're making in your healing—I can promise you it will probably not be longer than, say, two or three weeks. We would like to keep you with us for that period because we would like at this point to have fairly frequent talks with you, and your being there handy for us on Ward Five will facilitate that for us." Such a warm, low, grave voice. "But I would expect that within a few weeks we won't have to have those talks with so much frequency, and then you'll be free to go home again."

Ah, *that* was it. What she needed to hear before they made her leave this now-safe room. She was crying again now, just a little, but this time she was crying at least from a relief that almost felt a little like—a happiness.

She smiled at him through the tears. "All right. Thank you, Dr. Salter."

He reached forward and tapped her knee, echoing the smile back. "And you *believe* me, young lady, don't you?"

Almost, she did. Enough, at least, for her to say honestly, "Yes. I do."

Lieutenant Tim Vance came in early to work on Saturday morning so he could have some time to himself to sift through the pileup of reports on Sister Angela that had accumulated on his desk.

Career, educational background pretty much what he expected. A couple years teaching with Head Start in the inner city. A few years summer post-grad training in preschool theory at Seton Hall University, New Jersey.

Family background also pretty routine, except for one entry: Early home addresses 47 Holmes Road, Roseville, and later 375 Springs Street, St. Paul—the address of her aunt, Mrs. Iris McManus, a divorced woman who then worked part time as a secretary at a neighborhood insurance office. The aunt's only child, Mary Alice, now age forty, was the same Mrs. Walter Russell whom Angela had visited at the Wisconsin campsite the previous August.

Vance checked back on the dates and addresses on her educational record. Gayle Flynn had moved to her aunt's house in the fifth grade, and apparently remained there through high school.

There was one other interesting item, concerning Sister Pamela Donegan, who had been Sister Angela's superior at the kindergarten school when she started teaching there in 1971. Sister Pamela was considered to be Sister Angela's best friend at the St. Rose convent, where they both lived.

Notations about Sister Pamela—"She was said to dress more like a model than a nun." "Apparently a dominant personality who appeared to dominate Sister Angela."

In the summer of '77—the same summer Angela became pregnant—Pamela left the convent to marry a former professor of hers, and Angela was assigned to take over her job as general director of the Benedictine Kindergarten School.

Vance also paused briefly over one notation on the report from Jackson, the functional subliterate of the department: "First evadence of any mental abbaration on the part of Sr. Angela was her father died & she persisted in talking abt. him as alive also writing him letters after he has died. Variaus persons talk to St. Angela abt. this, tell her her father is dead, she should not wright him letters."

Vance pushed the reports into a manila folder and took them to Chief Marwick's office, to brief him on the present status of the investigation. As he walked down the hall, one item from the reports stuck tenaciously in Vance's mind: at age eleven Gayle Flynn was sent clear across town to live with a divorced aunt. Her parents didn't separate, the rest of the kids apparently stayed home, but Gayle was sent away to live with a divorced aunt.

Marwick was sitting at his desk. He grunted a greeting and heard out Vance's recap of the reports. When Vance got to the part about the aunt, he looked up from the papers and paused. "You make anything out of that one, Chief?"

"Maybe." Their eyes locked briefly over the desk. Then Marwick tapped his pipe against the large glass ashtray, scraped at the bowl. "How about you?"

Vance shrugged. "Well, shipping an eleven-year-old girl out of an Irish Catholic family like that—that's pretty unusual. Until I heard a better reason, I guess I'd have to suspect maybe some kind of sexual hanky-panky might've been going on."

"Could be," Marwick said flatly. "Or could be something else. Anyway, it's no business of ours." He stuck the unlit pipe back into his mouth. "You getting any feedback out of the D.A.'s office?"

"Well, they're still steamed about the press leak. They think it might've come out of here."

"Bullshit," Marwick said firmly through his pipe. "It was *their* leak, period." He stretched back in his chair, his hands folded behind his neck. "So what else have you got?"

When the morning special went off duty at two P.M. another did not come, because Angela was scheduled to check out very soon. After the nurse left, when the room seemed so oddly—empty, somehow, she went into the bathroom and changed into the street clothes that Julia had brought her in a suitcase, the yellow turtleneck and the brown corduroy jumper.

Once she was dressed it didn't seem right to go back to the bed. So she was sitting in the padded chair by the window, looking out on the roofs next door and saying a mental rosary, when someone knocked.

When she said, "Come in," Mrs. Knudsen peeked around the opening door. "Sister? Now don't you get up. But would you mind having a visitor?"

"Oh, Mrs. Knudsen! No, please come in."

Mrs. Knudsen looked rather fat and lumpy in a red pant suit. Angela smiled at the thought of how odd they must both look to each other, out of "uniform." As Mrs. Knudsen pulled a straight-backed chair up to the window, she was saying, "Now don't you look nice, Sister, all dressed up like that. Yellow's such a pretty color on you, with your fair hair."

Angela smiled again, and thanked her. Mrs. Knudsen was saying she'd had some business to do downstairs and had just taken that chance to drop in to say good-bye because she knew Angela was leaving so soon. Angela thought she had probably made a special trip to come in just because she knew Angela was probably sitting alone after the morning special left at two, but she didn't mind that. It was kind of this nurse to come, really. And Angela was surprisingly glad to see her. So she said, "Thank you for coming, Mrs. Knudsen. That's very good of you."

"Well, I thought you might like to have the afternoon paper." Mrs. Knudsen whipped it out of her knitting bag. "Should I just tuck it in your suitcase, Sister?"

"Oh, yes, thanks. Would you?"

When Mrs. Knudsen came back to her chair she reached back into the knitting bag. "And I wanted to show you my granddaughter's sweater. I finished it up last night."

Angela murmured her admiration as she fingered the blue knit ribbing. The nurse said, "I waited to wrap it because I thought you might like to see it first."

"Oh, yes, I do. It's beautiful. Really, your granddaughter's very lucky."

"Well, I just hope it fits her right. You never know for sure, but I *think* it's a perfect fit."

"That's nice," said Angela. "When I used to make my own clothes, after we stopped wearing the habit, they never fitted quite right."

Then Mr. Haverty was there, to take her away. Mrs. Knudsen said something about how much all of them on the ward would miss her, and wished her the very best of luck with everything. Angela nodded, because she didn't quite trust herself to speak.

As they left the room some thin, tall woman followed them. When she stepped into the elevator right behind Mr. Haverty, Angela realized that must be the police guard. She flicked a sidewise glance at the woman—sharp nose, harsh makeup, green trench coat—who was looking fixedly at the elevator buttons.

In the humming silence of the elevator Mr. Haverty cleared his throat. But none of them spoke.

.   .   .

The first thing that startled Angela as they drove up to the front entrance of the Ramsey County Community Hospital were the gargoyles—strange, twisted creatures leering down from the parapets and eavespouts of the rambling red brick building. A lilac tree in full bloom bent gracefully over the carved stone entrance, with its stained glass side windows. "It looks almost like a church," she remarked to Haverty as the sheriff's deputy climbed out of the backseat and opened the passenger door for her.

"Actually, Angela, it's a fine old period piece of the thirties," Haverty said as he led her up the steps, carrying her suitcase in one hand, gripping her elbow with the other. "I suppose they'll tear it down one of these days and put up an ugly new box instead."

Ben Haverty's mind was not fixed on modern architecture. Mainly, he was grimly hoping that no one here would see fit to mention to Angela Flynn that one wing of this old building happened to house the Ramsey County Morgue, where the body of Baby Boy Flynn was still stored on one of the slabs.

The hospital lobby, with its stone arches and stained glass windows, also looked like a church. But as they walked beyond it, into the hall with pipes hanging from the ceiling and dingy tan paint peeling from the walls, Angela was overwhelmed with a feeling of dismay.

Old men in wheelchairs sat around the hall—balding old men in baggy, wrinkled hospital clothes, with glazed, imbecilic faces, some of them drooling. "Now, Angela, don't let this upset you," Haverty said nervously as he steered her toward the admitting office. "This part of the hospital happens to deal with chronic invalids. But that has nothing to do with Ward Five, where you'll be staying."

At the admitting office they seemed to be expecting her. A woman took them almost immediately down a long hall to an elevator.

The four rode in silence to the fourth floor. Angela

stepped off the elevator into a kind of cage—blank walls on both sides, a locked door with a painted iron grillwork ahead.

The admitting officer rang a bell; a nurse in a white uniform stepped up to the door from the other side and unlocked it with a key hanging from a large ring of keys on her belt.

They stepped inside, and the heavy metal door clanged shut on them. *Trapped. Trapped.*

Angela turned in panic to Haverty. The nurse with the keys was saying ". . . very good to have you with us, Sister Angela. Now you just follow me and we'll get you settled in your room."

Angela looked at Haverty in mute appeal.

Ben Haverty felt those green eyes go into him like grappling hooks. She seemed so incredibly small and delicate, standing beside him. He handed the suitcase to the deputy as he said, "Angela, I know I'm leaving you in good hands. I'll be back to see you again tomorrow."

She reached out toward him. Maybe just to shake his hand, but Ben Haverty was afraid to touch that soft, trembling skin. Afraid if he touched it he could never leave her in this place.

He turned on his heel. The nurse unlocked the metal door; Haverty and the admitting officer walked out of it. The door clanged shut on them.

Through the open grillwork Haverty could hear the nurse saying, "We have a lovely room for you with a view of the south gardens, Sister. Right this way."

The thing was, Gary Tucker just didn't get much chance to meet girls. At work he was mostly in the stockrooms or out with the carpentry crews. The stuff he liked to do in his free time, like hunting and fishing—you didn't run into too many single girls doing that.

He wasn't in any rush to settle down with a girl anyway. His uncle Brad, for instance—Brad didn't get married till he was thirty. Brad always said there was a whole lot he wanted to do before he put on the old ball and chain. Even after he bought that big house down right on the water in Oak Creek, four bedrooms and a private dock, he still spent most of his free time out in the bush with his buddies. And then one day a girl came into the shop that Brad remembered from high school—Evie Campbellton. They started going out, and six months later they got married—just like that.

Gary had that thought kind of in the back of his head when he asked to work the front counter on Saturday afternoon. Then, bang—around 2:30 a girl came in. A short girl with a good figure, pretty stacked. Red hair. A quiet type, she looked. Shy.

Gary helped her figure out what kind of bookshelves she needed to buy. Got her name and address when he made out the bill—Nancy Baroni, 1300 Parkview—one of those big high rises where a lot of single girls lived. He checked out her left hand: no ring.

When the sawed boards came up from the back room Gary helped her carry them out to the car. Nice little orange Datsun, pretty new. Gary said, "That's a nice car you got. Had it long?"

"Just three months. Yes, I love it. It handles so easy."

"They're real good on mileage."

"And real good for getting into little parking places." She laughed.

"I drive a four-wheel Scout myself," said Gary. "Because I do a lot of hunting and fishing."

The girl said, "Oh," and got into the car. Gary closed the door for her before he could think what else to say. Then she rolled down the window and said, "Hey, thanks for all the help with the shelves."

He gave it a last shot: "Hey, Nancy, what're you doing tonight?"

She blinked, surprised. "Excuse me?"

"You wanta take in a movie?"

She looked down at the steering wheel. She wasn't real pretty, but he liked her well enough. "Well, I don't know. I don't know who you are."

"I'm Gary Tucker. My father and my uncle and me own this business here."

"Oh." She threw him a tentative, sort of scared smile. "Well, I don't know. I have some papers to correct."

"I can bring my drill along, put up those shelves for you. I'll come by at seven thirty, okay?"

"Well, I guess that would be okay. But could you make it eight thirty? I really *do* have to correct those papers."

"Sure thing, Nancy. See you later." She nodded, and drove off.

So. It wasn't so hard, after all.

At 3:20 Meg Gavin chanced a swing by the Medical Examiner's office. Normally she checked in with routine phone calls—"Hey, Dr. Rhoades, you got anything perking over there?" But with the tight lid still operative on this case, she was leaving nothing to chance that might be better accomplished with a quick application of the personal touch.

The morgue rooms in the east wing of the Ramsey County Community Hospital were virtually deserted on that Saturday afternoon, but through the open door of his inner office she spotted Kenneth Rhoades sitting over paperwork. She rapped lightly on the doorframe. "Hey, Dr. Rhoades. You got time for a quick break?"

He looked up, grinning. "Well, Meg. They got you working weekends now?"

"Not they—*him*. Your presently most famous resident corpse. Anything new in that direction, Doctor?"

"Matter of fact, Meg, we just finished up our tests on Baby Boy Flynn this afternoon. We're ready now to release the body."

"Hey, how's that for timing. You got any idea what the arrangements will be?"

"Well, I spoke a little earlier to the nun's family and to the representatives of the Catholic diocese. I understand her brother Daniel Flynn is going to arrange for a private funeral and cremation some time early next week."

"Is her family going to foot the bill?"

"As far as I know, Meg, the Sisters of St. Benedict have agreed to pay all the costs. But her family is handling the arrangements."

"Hmm. An interesting protocol."

Rhoades shrugged. "Well, it's hardly routine, but neither is anything else about this case. I gather that's just the way they've worked it out between them."

Rhoades chatted for about ten minutes with the Gavin girl before he said, "Well, I hate to cut short this pleasant conversation, Meg, but I've got an appointment to get to."

She walked him to his car, thanking him for the fresh input. "If anything new turns up, will you let me know, Doc?"

"You just keep in touch, Meg. We've got no secrets in this office."

At the corner stoplight he watched in his rearview mirror as her car peeled right, heading downtown. Then he stopped at the Black Watch Bar two blocks down for a quick one on his way home.

That one drink quickly became two. As Rhoades twirled the glass slowly on the varnished wood bar he could almost sense the frowning presence of his wife, his secretary and his psychiatrist, hear their echoed suggestion that he didn't really need that drink. They were watching him now like a bunch of she-hawks, watching for signs of the old trouble that had sent him to the sanitarium, worried about the pressure this nun case was putting on him.

Well, piss on them. Rhoades said loudly, "One more over here, Jim."

Rhoades was remembering that day in med school when he'd told his old pathology professor, Wallace Murdoch, that he'd decided on the specialty of forensic pathology. Sitting in his fusty old office, flanked with all those dusty bottles of pills and specimens, Murdoch had talked to him for a couple of hours that day about the "killing business" that pathology could be. About how many medical men involved in it came apart, cracked up, suicided—so many more of them, for some reason, than homicide detectives. Rhoades had listened respectfully, as always, but he remembered thinking that day, *Not me, old man. For sure that's not me.*

But these past few years, rough years, he'd often found himself thinking about that talk.

He smiled a little grimly to himself at the idea that his own precarious but substantial balance could be toppled by Baby Boy Flynn.

The problem, God knows, wasn't that handsome, wretched Flynn infant, snuffed out in the act of struggling into life—it was the seventeen-year accumulation of bodies, that massed army of mute, inarticulate corpses.

The problem was death, and the terrible, now tormenting fascination it held for Kenneth Rhoades.

He'd promised himself he would leave after the third drink. Instead he heard himself saying, "Jim, hit me again."

Dr. Heilbron was right about that much, at least—this hospital room wasn't so different from the other. It *looked* a little small and shabby, with its cracked blue walls and the blond wood furniture with dark brown cigarette stains around its edges, but Angela wasn't used to fancy living anyway. It was nice not to have those special nurses hovering around her. And the view out this window was so much nicer than roofs or blacktop—rolling green lawns and blooming fruit trees. She sat by the window for the rest of that afternoon, soothing her eyes with that green view.

The guards were still out there, she supposed, but now again she didn't have to see them. So she finally had that one precious thing back, at least—privacy. Real privacy.

She was already missing Mrs. Knudsen, already worrying about how she could keep track of what was happening to her without Mrs. Knudsen to bring her the newspapers. But when the nurse came in with her supper tray and Angela asked casually if she could see the Sunday morning paper, the nurse said, "Why, sure, Sister. It isn't up yet, but I'll ask Mrs. Fowler to bring it in for you when she comes for the evening shift."

She waited until the nurse left the room before she let her face relax into a slight, tentative smile.

Meg Gavin pushed the last of her veal Marsala around her plate. "Anyway, that's how I found out about them finding the father. And I shouldn't have told you and I swear, Dewey Wald, if you blow my cover on this—"

"Hey, Meg." He smiled, holding up his hands. "Please don't alarm your rather attractive head about *that.*"

"Well, I don't know. I just know I talked too much. As usual." She reached into her purse for a cigarette. "An occupational hazard, I'm afraid. I never could figure out why the CIA hired all those reporters—we're so congenitally willing to talk."

"It's okay to talk to me," said Wald. "Don't you know that yet?"

Halfway through the recital of her Life Story As Told to a New Man script, she still wasn't sure what she was doing out with this Wald. She'd come home in a high, horny mood, deciding to drop a call to one of her on-tap lovers. Maybe Benny, or Will. Benny-the-carpenter or Will-the-part-time-bartender—she tended to think of them as attached more to jobs than to surnames. But then Wald had called just as she got in the door, saying he happened to be eating in the neighborhood again, asking her to join him—and here she was.

She said abruptly, "Enough about me, Wald. Let's hear a few chapters from *your* life story."

He smiled, pleased with that suggestion. "Fair enough. Where do you want me to start?"

She snapped, "Well, why don't you just tell me how *you* feel about fucking a nun?"

She regretted the question as soon as it was out of her mouth—*smart-ass, always the smart-ass.* But Wald was looking thoughtfully into his wineglass as he said, "If you want to know the truth, I don't think I'd care for it."

"What, Everyman's fantasy? Fucking a *nun?*"

Another bent smile. "Well, I can see how there might be a certain novelty attraction. Forbidden fruit and all that. But I think I got that part of our mythology out of my system when the U.S. Army had the good grace to station me in Japan." He went on talking about the hold that Japanese women had on some Western men—how some of those men, after they'd been in the country for six or seven years, could never leave again. They were too hooked on that diet of happy little sexual slaves.

Meg frowned. "Excuse my density, but I don't quite see what that's got to do with—"

"I don't know much about nuns, sexually or otherwise, but it's always seemed to me that psychologically they're coming from that kind of space. I've always thought of them somewhat like Japanese women—totally obliging, totally accommodating. Total—servitors."

Meg was stunned, frozen, by the accuracy of that startling perception. "That's an interesting idea, Wald."

Cheerful grimace. "Oh, probably not. But I stuck it in here anyway, because it seemed to fit. Basically, when you boil it all down, I think men deal with two kinds of women. There are the ones who are there mainly to serve the man, without investing too much of themselves. They take their cues, basically shape themselves according to what *he* wants them to be." He took a drink from his wineglass. "And then there's the other kind."

Meg was looking with wary surprise at Wald's sharp-angled face. "Which is?"

He shrugged. "The—challengers, I guess. They want what *they* want too. They want to be partners—in fact, they insist on that. They want their fair share, and they won't kiss ass unless they get their own back too." He grinned a little shyly across the table. "Now don't get me wrong, Ms. Gavin—I don't mean there's anything *wrong* with a guy who goes in for the Japanese thing. Or gets off fucking a nun. Hey, we all take it where we can find it. But if you're asking about me—"

"Yeah. That was the question."

Smiling, he ducked and shook his head. "Oh God, Meg, who knows? I mean—the point is, what's out there, anyway? I don't know, maybe men and women never can put it together. Maybe a man never does get to that place where he can really believe himself when he thinks he knows what that woman is thinking. What she's feeling. But unless they're in this thing together, I think it's probably not worth too much more than a warm, comfortable shit." He grimaced. "God, that sounds preachy. All I mean is it's probably a lot less boring to try for that than to settle for one who gets off washing out your socks."

As they approached the darkened Fox Point beach house Eddie Staszic said, "Hey, he's not home."

Al Packer said, "Nah, let's give it a try."

When they had got up on the front deck they could hear the radio and TV both going in the blacked-out living room. Packer kicked at the loose screen door and called loudly, "Hey, Ziggy, you in there?"

A minute later Danziger opened the door. Of all the

297

strange guys on the Midwest Mutual maintenance crew, Staszic figured this was the weirdest. He held out a six-pack of Schlitz. "Hey, Zig. We were just driving around, picked up a sixer. You got any weed on you?"

"A little." Danziger stepped back from the door, switched on a lamp.

"Jesus, man, you sitting in the dark?"

"I was just watching some TV."

"Well, hey, if this is a bad time . . ."

"No, no. Come on in." Staszic and Packer sat on the couch. Danziger took the chair in front of the TV. Staszic passed him a can of beer. Danziger popped the tab and dropped it into the can.

"So what's happening, anyway?"

"Nothing much." Danziger took a rolled joint from the antique silver container by his elbow. He lit it up, inhaled sharply and passed it to Packer.

"Jesus, I don't know how you stick out a winter down here," said Staszic. "That cold wind on the beach—it would give me the creeps."

"I like it," said Danziger.

"Hey, wait another month," said Packer. "Wait'll we crank up the old volleyball games, get out that old Frisbee. This beach is someplace else then." He passed the joint to Staszic.

"Maybe so," Staszic said between inhalations. "But if I was gonna live on a beach, man, I'd make it Florida. Not this goddam Eskimo climate. Give me the brown skins and bikinis, man."

Danziger said, "Too much sun gives you cancer."

"Well, we all gotta go, one way or another. Me, I'd like to go in Coppertone country, man."

"So move down there," said Danziger.

"I been thinking about that. If I could just get laid off, man, shuttle those unemployment checks down to the sun—"

"Big talk," said Packer. "Always the big talker, Staszic."

Danziger drained his can and crumpled it; Staszic passed him another. Staszic had the impression Danziger was already plowed to the gills on booze or smoke or whatever. *Sitting down here in the wind and the dark,* thought Staszic. *Jesus, this was one weird guy.*

In the kitchenette of her apartment Meg poured a long splash of Diet Pepsi over the ice and water in a large mug. When the mug was full she set the bottle back on the counter and buttoned, absentmindedly, the silk shirt she had plucked from the chair as she came out of the room.

Oh God, she wanted not to have to go back to that bedroom. Wanted not to have to play out the rest of this scene, right now, tonight, when she was feeling so oddly unready for it.

She should never have fucked him. Not now, not like this. She knew even before she did it that she shouldn't have fucked him, knew it *so well.* But the knowing wasn't enough. In the end she went with the habit.

So hard to say no, once she let her mind play on that old curiosity about what that body would feel like, moving naked against hers in the bed. How it would smell, how it would taste. And once she let herself think that, it was so easy, so irresistibly easy, just to slide into it, to find out.

Except that she had never meant to do it with this Wald. Hadn't even known the itch was there, to guard against. And then he had said that amazing thing about nuns, that odd, true thing, and then kept on talking and while she was sitting there, listening, not even knowing it was there to be guarded against, she was—opened.

And she'd known that. She'd also known all along that the reason she was bringing him back here from the restaurant, tucking his thin arm against hers as they went striding down the street, laughing, was to kill it. Knew that was the sure way to do it, and it was so easy to slip into it, into that warm, familiar place—

299

Nuzzling as they came in the door. Sitting spilled against him on the soft velvet couch, her leg swung up over his. The joint passed back and forth. The electric connections of their fingers, dancing to the music from the KLH. The sharp, moist sealing of their mouths as they moved their bodies to fit against each other in that long, astonishing first kiss.

Ah, God, she loved the heat, discovery, mind-blotting, of those first connections.

Once again she'd let herself go quickly, fiercely, down into the fucking.

All right, the drink was poured. The deed was done. Now for the next act, the not-so-nice one.

She picked up the mug and headed back down the narrow hall.

In the spilled light from the hallway she could see him lying naked on the unmade bed, propped into the blue pillows. His sharply planed face looking so serious. Even sad. She slipped onto her side of the queen-sized bed and murmured, "Thirsty, pal?"

"Thanks." He took the mug, drank, then coughed. "My God. What's that?"

"Water and Diet Pepsi. Very good for the digestion." As he set the mug on the bedside table she moved her body into a contact fit with his, laying her right hand softly over the bristled hairs of his chest.

Silence. She broke it, softly, with, "Hey. How're you doing, friend?"

"Okay." He pushed his arm across the pillows, pulled her body gently into the crook of his elbow. His fingers rubbed softly at the silk on her right shoulder. "Gavin, why'd you put on that shirt?"

"Oh, that." She flexed her body closer to his. "That's my congenital weakness for cold air."

He didn't speak. Looked out through the bedroom

door, his face so sad in that soft, diffused light. She tweaked at his chest hairs. "Hey, stranger. Speak. A nickel for your thoughts."

He covered her hand with his, stroking her skin. "Ah, thoughts. I've got a thundering herd of them right now."

"Okay. Start with one."

Silence. "You feel so soft, so good."

"Thank you. Or rather, thank Vaseline Intensive Care."

After a long pause he cocked his head around to look at her face. "Hey, Gavin, I'd like to ask you something. But I don't want you to take it the wrong way. Make anything out of it I don't mean."

Ah, no way was this one going to be fun. She moved her leg away from his as she said abruptly, "So, ask."

"I'm just wondering, why did you—rush it so? Push it so hard?"

In one rapid motion she sat up cross-legged on the bed, disconnecting a second time from his body. "Oh, boy, what's this? Couch time following the bed?"

"Hardly. It's more an affectionate,"—he took her hand —"friendly question."

"And the next one is, 'Did you really *come*? I didn't feel you really come.'"

He chuckled. "Nah. I swear. Maybe a couple of years ago, but I swear not now."

The sadness she'd been feeling in the kitchen was energizing anger now. She said very coldly, "Well, the friendly answer to your original friendly question, which you'll probably wish very soon you hadn't asked, is that you don't really turn me on, Wald. I told you that right from the first. You're not the type of man I like to fuck, that I get wet for. You're not—"

He squeezed her hand, nodding, looking toward the light, as if to say *okay, all right, skip that part.* "So when I decided to go to bed with you I knew all I'd get out of it was a nice, quick jack-off. Like I would from any capable male

301

body. And since I knew that's all that was there for me, I took it—rather—efficiently. And if you don't like hearing that, Wald, if that bruises your almighty male pride, I'm sorry but you asked."

He was smiling into the hall light now, running the fingers of his free hand through his steel-wool hair. "Ah, Gavin, Gavin. You're going to be a battle, all right, I can see that. A battle all the way."

She was trying to think what to say to ease him gracefully *out* when he suddenly turned toward her and pulled her down into his arms, a gesture made so swiftly and so strongly that her head spilled awkwardly against his chest. He stroked at the brown hair fallen over his shoulder. "Listen, Gavin, I know that, tactically speaking, we probably shouldn't have jumped into the sack tonight. But we did anyway, and it's okay. A beginning, at least."

With a *swoosh* of her long hair she pushed herself irritatedly off his chest. Sat very sharply upright, the silk shirt spilling onto her crossed legs. "Listen, Wald, I'm working tomorrow. Would you mind terribly much just taking yourself home and letting me get a good night's—"

His smile interrupted. He said softly, smiling at her, "Hey, Ms. Gavin. *Aloha.*"

"Oh, nice choice of words. Practically Japanese. You know an interesting thing, by the way, about that word, Mr. Wald? It means good-bye as much as hello. Speaking of which . . ."

He reached up to touch her swinging hair. Made a *sssshhhing* sound. "It's okay. I'm going. Relax, little Meg."

She jerked the sheet over her lap. "I'm not little. And I'll be quite relaxed, into rapid sleep in fact, as soon as you get your ass out of here."

"Okay, Gavin. Okay." He swung his legs off the bed, began groping for his clothes. "Done. I'm on my way."

She lay flat on the bed and turned toward the wall. They didn't speak in the few minutes it took him to dress.

Then he came around to sit on her side of the bed. Stroked her head, softly, sadly. *"Alors. Aloha,* Meg Gavin."

"Eh bien. Just pull the door tight when you leave, will you, Wald?"

At the bedroom door he turned and said, "By the way, that word also means 'welcome.' Check your dictionary, Gavin."

Twenty-three

As Dan Flynn knocked at the door of his sister's hospital room at 10:30 on Sunday morning he was trying to wipe the look of alarmed confusion from his face. She was sitting over by the window, wearing a green plaid skirt and loose green sweater. She did not echo back the smile Dan gave her as he said heartily, "Hey, Gayle, you're looking great. It's real good to see you up and looking so good again."

Coldly: "Hello, Dan. Thank you for coming."

"Well, sure I came. As soon as the nurse called and said you wanted to see me." He crossed the room, leaned down and kissed her cheek. "I was planning to come anyway, see how you're doing in your new digs." He glanced awkwardly around him at the room as he sat in the chair across from hers. "Hey, it's not bad. Kind of—cozy. You like it okay?"

"Yes, it's okay. It doesn't matter—I won't be here long anyway. What I wanted to see you about was *this.* " She picked up the *Eagle-Bulletin* that was tucked against the arm of her chair and tossed it into his lap.

"Oh, that." Dan glanced confusedly at the article on the

303

front page. He hadn't realized they were letting her read the papers. "I—ah, saw it already."

Her voice quivering with anger, she said, "Dan, why didn't you ask me about—the funeral?"

He blinked. "Well, gosh. I'm sorry, I just didn't— I thought you wouldn't want to be bothered about that stuff."

There was a look on her face—an anger, almost a fury —that he hadn't seen there in a real long time. Years, even. "I don't approve of cremation, Dan. I thought you knew that. I never have."

"Oh. Well, gosh—no, I didn't know that."

"Well, I don't. I want to have him buried."

He laid the paper facedown on the table between them. "Okay, fine. No problem. We'll have him buried, then." He swallowed. This visit was going to be even tougher than he was braced for. "Actually, I think your lawyer, that Mr. Haverty, wants us to wait a while, until he gets more tests done. But when they're finished with that, we'll have him buried. Whatever you want, Gayle."

When Dan walked back into the apartment his mother pulled her chenille bathrobe tight against her neck as she asked, "How's Gayle?"

"Oh, she's real good, real good, Mom. She looks just fine, and she says she's feeling lots better." Since Dan had no intention of telling his mother why Gayle had asked to see him, he swiftly changed the subject: "Hey, I thought you'd be dressed by now. We're due out at Ed's in about an hour. You'd better get a move on, Mom."

Wanly: "Oh, I don't know. Why don't you just go by yourself."

Theresa Flynn had barely left the apartment since her return on Wednesday afternoon. When she stopped once at the corner grocery to pick up a quart of milk the clerk had said that she was very sorry to hear about Mrs. Flynn's troubles. So Theresa refused to go out again, even to daily Mass.

So hurtful, so unbearable—*that everybody knew.*

At least she could keep her grief private, here in the apartment. When Dan was out she did not answer the phone; and when he was home, she still refused to talk to anyone.

Dan had teased, cajoled her into at least agreeing to go to Ed and Annette's for Sunday dinner. He'd promised that none of them would talk about this business, and they could all go to evening Mass.

Now he was smiling, saying, "Come on, Mom. You promised us."

"Oh, all right." Theresa went to her bedroom and put on her gray wool dress. She was standing at the living room mirror, pinning on her black hat, when someone knocked at the apartment door.

Dan opened it. A tall, brown-haired girl said, "Daniel Flynn?" He nodded slightly. "Hey, I'm sorry to bother you on a Sunday, but I'm Meg Gavin from the *Eagle-Bulletin.*" She looked past Dan, looked right at Theresa, who was standing, frozen, at the living room mirror. "I was wondering if I could perhaps talk to you and your mother. Just for a few minutes."

Theresa fled to her bedroom as Dan pushed the door almost shut. He hissed angrily through the crack, *"Please leave us alone.* We've got nothing to say to any of you people."

Theresa Flynn did not go to Sunday dinner at Ed's that day. Did not, in fact, leave the apartment for another three weeks.

At 2:30, when Sister Julia went down to the laundry room in the St. Rose convent basement to iron a skirt, she found Margory pushing a load of clothes into the dryer.

They talked for a few minutes, about nothing in particular. Then Margory asked if Julia knew anything about the story that was going around, that Angela had been—attacked.

Julia slapped the iron back on its heel. "I don't have the

vaguest *idea,* and I don't think anyone else does either," she snapped. "And frankly I'm *surprised* at you, Margory, for passing along such a nasty, vicious, unwarranted piece of *gossip.*"

Meg Gavin took the chance she might find Chief Marwick in his office, catching up on the week's heavy work load. And sure enough, there he was, smiling up at her across the cluttered desk, apparently welcoming the interruption.

"Hey, Chief. I just thought I'd check in with the horse's mouth, you'll excuse the expression. You got anything new for us?"

"Not too much, Meg." He leaned back in his chair and lit up his pipe, blowing drifts of smoke across the desk. "How're *you* doing on the case?"

Meg slipped a slow smile across the desk. "Pretty good, thanks, Chief. But I wouldn't mind doing better."

He grinned, showing the teeth clamped over his pipe. Then: "You know she checked out of Parkhurst yesterday?"

"God *damn,* I didn't. Where is she now?"

"Well, I guess it's no state secret." He scratched behind his right ear. "I guess there's no good reason it shouldn't go into the public record. They've moved her to Ramsey County Community Hospital."

"Ramsey *Community?*" Her expression shifted to spontaneous dismay. "My God, that *snake pit?* They put her in that snake pit? For God's sake, why?"

"Well, apparently that's where Parkhurst puts its psychiatric patients. They've moved her to a psychiatric ward."

Slowly, thoughtfully: "Well, okay, that figures. Sure, I guess that figures. But why Ramsey *Community?* I was just over there yesterday seeing Dr. Rhoades. My God, that whole *building* is like a morgue. It's just the bodies in one part are already dead."

Marwick was taking a certain satisfaction in finding himself the first to pass along that bit of news. He smiled as he shifted the pipe in his mouth. "Well, I dunno. You'll have to ask her doctors about that, Meg." He stretched his arms, folded his hands behind his head. "I guess I can tell you that Tim Vance isn't any too happy about that move. He wants to get her in here for fingerprinting and ID. Vance wasn't too pleased when we found out they already had her moved before we heard about the transfer."

Meg reached again for that slow, soft smile. Oh, this was going to be good. Real good. "What, Chief, you mean you're going to bring her in here to the P.D.? For mug shots and everything?"

Marwick shrugged. "That's required police procedure in any felony arrest, Meg."

"Boy, oh boy. You certainly have one hell of an interesting job these days, Chief."

He grunted, pleased. Leaned forward to tap his pipe into the ashtray. "Unfortunately, Meg. And believe you me, it's nothing that I want to have. This past week I've been wishing I was the police chief of, say, Roseville. Or Paxton. Just about anyplace but Cambridgeport."

"Oh, come *on*, Chief. You really mean to sit there and tell me you're willing to pass up your one good shot at getting famous?"

"Come on yourself. Where'd you come up with a half-cocked idea like that?"

She held up two fingers in her Boy Scout gesture. "Hey, swear. Before this thing is over you're gonna be seeing yourself in the movie. Chief Gregory Marwick, played by—hey, how's about Burt Reynolds?" He accepted the implied outrageous ego-stroke with a grin. Scratched the stem of his pipe quizzically along his nose. "Now, don't you sit there and tell me you wouldn't get off on that, Chief. Because frankly I wouldn't believe a word of it."

He shifted in his chair. Different, confidential tone of voice: "No, come on, be serious, Meg. You really think anything that big's going to come of this thing?"

Emphatic nod. "I damn well *bet* it will, Chief. Hey, this is an amazing case. Something fairly new under the sun, which is pretty hard to come by these days. Hell, yes, I think it will probably wind up on the silver screen." Silk, silk in that smile. "With you one of the leading characters."

Ah, she had him now. Had him as good as if he was in her queen-sized bed.

Men like this one, she knew them so well. Especially the good-looking middle-aged ones. Good lookers with un-banked fires, who felt themselves about twenty years younger than their aging, fattening wives.

Meg loved to sit across from men like this and stroke them with smiles, stroke them with applause. All's fair, all's fair. It didn't always work. But never hurt to try. And this time, *this* time—

Now he was saying, "Nah, I don't think so, Meg. This is just a local case. Maybe a little more interesting than most. But I can't see it getting—that big." But he *could* see it, of course. At least he was beginning to let himself see it.

Meg did not have to invent the pleasure in her voice when she said, "Oh, take my word for it, Chief. Before this thing is over I'm going to be bragging around town that I actually know you."

Angela sat straight upright in the chair by the window, clicking her fingernails on the armrests as she said angrily, "Mr. Haverty, I don't know why I wasn't consulted about this. Why you're doing all these things behind my back."

Now it was Haverty's turn to be bewildered. "Well, Angela, I can assure you no one intended to do anything secretive, behind your back. We simply felt you might not, with so much else to concern yourself with right now, wish to be directly involved in this sort of—arrangement."

"Well, you're quite wrong. I do." The green eyes were hard and cold now, sharply focused. "I want to know every-thing that's happening to me. And incidentally, Mr. Haverty,

I don't know why you were all trying to keep the newspapers away from me. I read them anyway, and they were— I *wanted* to see them."

Haverty nodded. He'd made a point of dropping in this Sunday afternoon because he was concerned about Angela's fragility, her ability to adjust to this quite threatening environment. But there was no fragility evident in the small woman glaring at him across the round blond-wood table. He said with some confusion, "Well, very good. I'm glad to see you feeling so—positive about your situation, Angela."

"I saw Dan this morning. I told him I don't approve of cremation—I never have. I don't want that to happen, Mr. Haverty."

"Very good," he repeated. "Whatever your wishes are, Angela, of course they will be respected."

"Well, I still think somebody should have asked me about it first. Before it got into the newspapers and everything."

He nodded apologetically. "Well, now that we know your feelings about this, Angela, of course you will be consulted. On all the various steps of the processes ahead of us."

Coldly: "All right. Thank you." After a moment she said, "Dan said you'd ordered the funeral to be postponed, until you had some tests made. What *kind* of tests, Mr. Haverty?"

"Ah—routine pathological. We would like to have the pathologist who may eventually be called to testify on your behalf do his own investigation. Of the—ah, routine pathology."

"I see. How long will that take?"

"Oh, not very long. That depends mostly on Dr. Von Bargen's work schedule. But I shouldn't expect that it will be longer than, say, perhaps a week."

She nodded tensely. "All right. I want to have him buried as soon as possible."

309

Gently: "Very good. I assure you, Angela, your wishes in all this will be respected." Since she seemed ready now to handle it, he went on speaking, quietly sketching the broad outlines of what she could expect from the arraignment, which would probably take place in the next week.

She listened, concentrating tensely, tapping her fingernails against the chair arms. The few questions she asked were sharp and to the point. He finished up: "You understand, Angela, that when there was some concern initially for your physical condition, that it not be unduly aggravated, we had no wish to burden you with unnecessary concerns. But now that you're recovering so well, I promise we'll keep you fully informed." Then his face folded into one of his rare, extraordinary smiles. "Okay, Angela?"

A little of the tension went out of her as she echoed the smile back. "Okay, Mr. Haverty."

As Ben Haverty took the elevator down he was still astonished by the overnight change in her. Damnedest thing he'd seen yet on this case. Remarkable—and damned encouraging, the way she was taking hold.

Meg Gavin's face was radiant as she strode up to the city editor's desk. "Richard, you lucky beast, I have some goodies for you. *Good* goodies."

McAlpine looked up and grunted, unimpressed. "Did you get up in time to cover the Sunday Mass at St. Rose?"

"Yes, damn your hide. The supreme sacrifice, I might add." She flipped open her notebook. "Nothing to write home about. Monseigneur McCloskey took the ecclesiastical escape hatch and skipped the sermon altogether. I jotted down whatever seemed to fit from the liturgy of the day, but it's mostly genuine claptrap—'We find forgiveness when we turn to God. As an example of our forgiveness we forgive those we find it difficult to forgive.' Et cetera, et cetera. He did mention once 'our sorrow of the past week,' and he said something about 'preaching penance for the forgiveness of sins.' " Meg lowered the notebook. "Dick, dear old Dick, you're not going to make me make a piece out of *that?*"

He lurched backward in his desk chair, fiddling with a pen. "Didn't you pick up any personal reactions?"

"Oh, sure. Lady in a brown feathered hat said of course their hearts are bleeding, and furthermore they've had police, reporters and so on hanging around all week. Quote, 'It's been a dreadful, dreadful time for us all.' Lady in a blue coat with a rabbit collar called Sister Angela, quote, 'the sweetest, cutest little thing.' Said they were all so very sorry about the whole thing."

"Did you talk to the priest?"

"McCloskey? Yeah, I got him in the sacristy afterward. The poor guy's almost embarrassing to talk to—he still keeps breaking down and blowing his honker. Says the congregation is obviously grief-stricken, still struggling to come to grips with this thing. He thinks they're all trying to understand, without convicting, italics on that convicting, poor Sister Angela in their own minds." She looked up from the notebook. "Which, just between us, is so much cowplops. Damn straight they've already made their minds up."

"Mmmph."

"McCloskey said there's been a great outpouring of sympathy and concern. Here's a nice little quote—'It's made us all more aware that everyone is human.' That's it, zip." She slapped the notebook. "Hey, how about it? Can we pass on the Sunday Mass?"

"Nah, write it up. A couple takes at least. What else have you got?"

"Well, I tracked down her mother and her brother, in their apartment, but they didn't want to talk." Meg made an unconscious grimace. "I think we should let that end of it alone. The *big* news is"—she flipped a page of the notebook—"I saw my confidential informant again, who is now saying some very interesting stuff. First, the doctors had Sister Angela moved yesterday to the psycho ward at Ramsey County Community Hospital." She shook her head. "Boy, I'm still trying to figure *that* one out. If you were trying to *drive* someone crazy that's the place you'd send them to."

McAlpine asked abruptly, "You confirm that with the hospital?"

"Not yet, but I guess they will. Now that they've got her safely moved and locked up. A psycho ward—hey, they came up with just the right ploy to stash her out of reach of the police. Not to mention us. I do believe I see Ben Haverty's fine hand in that one."

Curtly: "Okay, if you can get that officially confirmed we'll run it. Next item."

"Well, the Cambridgeport police are pissed off that they still haven't gotten her over to the P.D. for mug shots and fingerprints. That one I kind of like. Can you imagine what the *National Enquirer* would pay for a pic like that? Anyway, moving right along, the *big* one is—" McAlpine was wearing a tight, uncomfortable expression that escaped Meg's notice as she threw her head back, ran one hand exultantly through her hair. "God, Dick, you're not gonna *believe* this one. Jesus, it's too good to be true." She looked him squarely in the face, grinning triumphantly. "Guess where Sister Angela Flynn went visiting *last weekend.* Just give a guess."

McAlpine played nervously with his pen, saying nothing. Meg slapped her thigh exuberantly. *"Wisconsin,* for God's sake. She went to the *same town in Wisconsin* where they located the daddy. Got back here just one day before the baby was born. Jesus, Dick, isn't that *mind-blowing?"*

McAlpine tapped the pen against his knee. "You got an official confirmation on that?"

"Sure, it's official. My source is plenty official. This is *real good stuff,* Dick."

Flatly: "We need a name to confirm it."

Meg stared. "What the hell do you mean by *that?"*

"Just what I said."

"Well, hey. My source certainly can't go for us using his name. Of *course* I had to guarantee him anonymity, Dick. Listen, this stuff comes from right inside the investigation."

McAlpine tossed the pen on his desk. "Then we can't use it." He did not look at Meg.

"We can't—What the hell are you *saying*, Dick?"

Angrily: "Look, there's been a front-office directive come down on this thing. No more *unattributed information* will be printed on this story." He crossed his arms over his chest. "The front office thinks we've already printed too much loose stuff on this case, too much unnecessary, inappropriate detail."

"Dick! Fuck, Dick, you've got to be kidding."

"Not only am I not kidding, but I go along with the thinking behind that directive. You've just gone so overboard on this assignment that you've lost your perspective, kid."

"Pers*pec*tive, oh boy." Now she was stalking in a furious oblong in front of the desk. "You want to know where *that* little perspective comes from, Dick? Straight out of the goddam Catholic bishop's palace. Bishop picks up the phone, has a little chin-wag with his good friend the publisher. And lo and behold, ticketty-boo, the *Eagle-Bulletin* prints no more embarrassing articles about what happens to be, *happens* to be, Dick, and you damn well *know* it, the most important story that's come out of this fucking dull town in the last ten years."

The acute discomfort McAlpine was taking from this conversation was somewhat derived from the fact that he personally felt almost as strongly as Meg Gavin did about the fundamental issues involved here. But he knew after his own brief, stormy session in the front office that this was one order it would do no good to fight. So he was killing the best piece of reporting Meg Gavin had yet done—an astonishing piece of work; he still had no idea how she'd pulled it off.

313

He said flatly, "Overboard, kid. You've just gone a little overboard on this one."

She yanked with both hands at her hair. "Oh God, I feel like I'm going *crazy*. I bring you in a thing like this, a fucking *pipeline* into this case, and my city editor sits there on his fucking asshole and says I'm *overboard*, and by the way, he isn't going to use it."

McAlpine spun toward his typewriter, his usual signal for termination of conversation. "I'll overlook that last remark on the grounds that you're a little overinvolved emotionally, Gavin. Now go write up what you've got the attribution for."

Bitterly: "Boy oh boy. Just like that, hunh?"

"Don't push it, Gavin. Now please get out of here and let me do some work."

At 8:25 P.M., on instructions phoned in by Medical Examiner Rhoades, the morgue attendant on duty moved the body of Baby Boy Flynn, with the accompanying wastebasket, from Compartment 7 of the refrigeration unit to Compartment 2. Within fifteen minutes the body tissues were frozen solid at zero degrees Fahrenheit.

Twenty-four

Those St. Paul cops told him to get a lawyer, so Roy Danziger got one. Figured he needed a real good one, so he asked around a little, awkwardly, without explanation, until some guy he knew from work put him onto a Monroe Dickson.

At 9:30 on Monday morning he was sitting in Dickson's

office, eyeballing the guy across the desk. Young, big-nosed. Sharp dresser. Looked smart.

And bored, real bored. Said in a drawling voice, "Okay, Mr. Danziger, what seems to be the problem here?"

That's when he froze up. Jesus, he hadn't realized how hard it would be, talking about this. Having to, like, spell it all out.

He got out the first part, about the detectives showing up from St. Paul to question him about this possible homicide. Then Dickson took it over, getting the rest out of him with questions. Guy didn't look so fucking bored now. But that didn't make it any easier to get out.

Finally Dickson said he didn't see how he had much to worry about—his alibi was good, he'd had no contact with the woman since last summer. Roy nodded: "Yeah, but they want to come back, put me on a lie detector."

When Dickson asked if there was anything he wanted to conceal, he shook his head. "Nah. I told them everything pretty straight, like it was."

"Well, in that case, I can't see where we have any problems here. If you like I'll phone the district attorney myself, set up an appointment. I'll tell them you're available, and fully willing to cooperate."

"Okay." Roy hadn't meant to mention that other thing that was bothering him. But he heard himself blurting it out: "What I wanta know is—are they gonna want me to testify, like? Stand up in court, get into all this stuff, right out in public?"

Dickson shrugged. "I'd say it's probably too early to tell, Mr. Danziger. That will depend on how the case shapes up. I would certainly think"—dryly, eyeing him across the desk—"that various parties to the case would prefer to keep you out of it, if they can."

"Because I—" He shuddered, a heaving motion of his shoulders. "Hey, there's just no way I could do that. No *way*, man."

． ． ．

In a slightly rancorous session with Meg Gavin on Monday morning, Dick McAlpine finally agreed to her writing a backgrounder on religious celibacy, and how the issue affected present-day nuns. "But I want it quick, Gavin," he warned. "This story's dying quicker than a chicken with no head."

At her desk Meg shuffled through a stack of spiral notebooks tossed into the lower drawer, looking for the one she'd used in covering a two-day conference on the role of women in the Church fifteen months earlier. Belatedly, during furious traffic on her oriental rug the previous evening, she'd remembered the ex-nun contacts she made there, the names and phone numbers she had scribbled inside the back cover of her notebook.

Ah, this was the one. A green Sterling TopSpeed.

Dumb, gutless bastard Dick McAlpine, she'd get him yet. She was smiling again as she reached for the phone.

The first was Jeanette Netzer, a forty-two-year-old ex-Holy Namer out four years, married now to a widowed engineer with four kids. Jeanette was still teaching philosophy and ethics at a nearby community college. A thin, fairly gorgeous woman with a warmth and compassion that came through on a clear track.

She talked quite candidly about the sexual problems she'd seen in the convent—that *need* for love so many nuns had, and the dangers of "falling in love," even slipping into an affair. Jeanette knew quite a few nuns who had done that, but only one who stayed in the convent after her affair was over. You really *couldn't* have both, Jeanette said with her understanding smile: "That's just the way it is, like it or not. You have to understand, Meg—especially once the nuns stopped wearing their habits and went out working in the world and all that, the only thing that made them overtly different from other women was *that*—sex. Or rather, the

316

choice to live *without* sex. It became the *main* difference, the thing that still makes them special. So you just have to accept that condition of celibacy if you want that particular kind of religious life, that kind of commitment, because you just aren't a nun without it."

Meg grinned. "Well, that's a damned regrettable, unnecessary and probably unhealthy fact, if you ask me."

Jeanette laughed. "Oh, I can see how it would seem that way to a liberated girl like you, Meg. But it's not so hard, really—you just get in the *habit* of it, if you'll excuse a lousy pun. I know a lot of priests and nuns who live very busy, happy, *satisfying* lives."

Jeanette was pretty good at helping Meg put together some understanding of what realistic options were open to Angela Flynn once she became pregnant, and how she must have perceived them—or failed to perceive them. "She would have had to go to her superiors for help, of course," Jeanette said. "I'm sure they *would* have helped her, arranged a discreet delivery and so forth. I can't *imagine* them not helping her, in a very compassionate and understanding way. But I *can* imagine Angela being afraid to go to them— afraid of being thrown out on the street. I can imagine her believing she'd never recover from the shame and disgrace. But how awful to think of her going through that pregnancy and that terrifying delivery all alone—in all that pain and *blood,* and her probably quite ignorant."

A new question suddenly occurred to Meg: if Angela Flynn had come clean with her superiors and agreed to give her child up for adoption, would she have been allowed to stay on in the order?

Jeanette shook her head: "I doubt that, Meg. But they would have arranged for her to leave with all the support and counseling she needed."

"Hey, no fair, Jeanette. You know damn well they wouldn't throw out a *priest* who got himself in the same fix."

Jeanette agreed, with a rueful smile.

"So, assuming that Angela Flynn really did *want* to stay a nun—because otherwise why wouldn't she have left before it came down to what it did—the option she probably should've gone for was abortion."

Jeanette shook her head, a quick, vigorous reflex. "No, no, Meg. That wouldn't have been any different from what she ended up doing."

"Oh, come on, Jeanette. There's a slight but rather significant difference between declining to lend your body to the development of a speck of protoplasm and snuffing the breath out of a living, crying baby. Even you've got to admit that."

"Not at all, Meg." Still that firm, serene headshake. "They're both murders—violent, painful, arbitrary deaths."

Colleen Grabe, a thirty-year-old ex-Bennie who had been out for eighteen months and was working as a state social worker, was clearly upset by Meg's implied suggestion that the rule of religious celibacy was in some way responsible for the unfortunate tragedy of Angela Flynn. She admitted there were always a few individuals like Angela who couldn't handle that—pressure. Well, they should simply choose another way of life. It was easy enough to get out of the vows these days.

But to suggest that there was something *wrong* with the Church, something *crippling* in the idea of celibacy—that's what Colleen found so offensive, so unjustified. Meg probably didn't realize this, but nuns these days knew a great deal about sex. Six years ago, when the St. Paul diocese had implemented sex education into the parochial-school curriculum, all the diocesan nuns had undergone a very *intensive* training in sexuality—all aspects of it, V.D., intercourse, masturbation, everything. The nuns around St. Paul knew as much about that subject as lay persons—probably more, in fact. So it wasn't from any *ignorance* that they still chose to live a celibate life.

"Well, that's a real interesting point," said Meg. "I didn't know that, actually. But—"

"One more thing—all the sensational press coverage of this case. Like it was World War Three or something. A lot of Catholics resent that very much, Meg, all that sensationalism people like you are using to sell your newspapers."

"Listen, Colleen, I'm not about to defend the press coverage of this case—which by the way I think has been quite restrained, tactful and accurate—because that's not what I'm here for."

"And that's what I'd like to know—what *are* you doing here? Except getting more material for another attack on the Catholic Church?"

"You want it straight, Colleen? Okay, but I hope I don't disappoint you. I'm just trying to—understand a little better."

"Oh, really, Meg?" Colleen's face was flushed with anger. "Well, excuse me for thinking that you're just trying to sell more newspapers. Because if you really think you're going to understand anything better by blowing up this one unfortunate case into an attack on the Catholic Church and everything it stands for—well, let me say I think you've got a pretty funny idea of what real understanding is."

"Okay, that does it, Tucker." The young detective unsnapped the rubber coils from around Gary Tucker's chest, peeled the blood-pressure cuff from his right bicep. He walked back behind the desk and sat in the chair that was slightly higher than Tucker's. "You got anything else you want to add?"

"No, I guess not."

That's all there was to it? He'd flown all the way over here to St. Paul to take this polygraph test, and they'd taken him into this dark, slick little room, wired him all up to that machine in the aluminum suitcase. Then, *bang*—it was all over. When he'd thought it was still just starting.

319

Nick Scotti was waiting for him in the hall outside. "Okay, what you say, kid?" Scotti asked heartily. "You think you passed?"

Tucker hid his vague feeling of disappointment behind a cocky smile. "Yeah, I guess so."

Scotti had already picked up the *zero* signal that Peter Juhl, the polygraph operator, had tossed him over Tucker's head. "Yanh, you guessed right." He put his arm on Tucker's shoulder, turned him in the direction of the doors that led from the Ramsey County Sheriff's Department to the Hall of Justice. "Okay, what you wanta do now?"

"Well, I'd like to go see Gayle. If they'll let me."

"Okay, tell you what. I got some things I got to do, so why don't you make yourself to home in my office, see if you can fix that up with the hospital."

Nick Scotti knew this was a long, long shot. But the reason they had flown Gary Tucker up to take the polygraph in St. Paul was that the kid was anxious to visit his friend Gayle Flynn, if he could get in to see her. D.A. Abrams was more than willing to add Tucker's name to the list of approved visitors, since anything the nun told the kid relating to the alleged crime would be admissible evidence in a court case. And the kid was playing along, still somehow persuaded by Nick Scotti's suggestion that by helping them out he was also helping her.

When they reached his office Scotti handed the kid a paper with the names and phone numbers of the hospital and the doctors scrawled on it. "What the hell, see if they'll let you in. I know you'd really like to see her, kid."

Tucker was beginning to feel good, feel important again. "Well, yeah, I would," he said solemnly. "I'd like to make sure she's, like, okay."

When Scotti got back to the office an hour later the kid was still sitting at the desk, doodling designs for speedboats. "No luck, hunh?" Scotti asked.

"Nah. Boy, it took me a long time to get through. But

then her doctor said he's sorry but she's still too sick to have any visitors yet. He said he'd tell her I was up here asking for her, anyway."

Doctor, fuck. It was wily old Ben Haverty who wasn't about to let this kid within confessing distance of his little nun. "Well, tough luck, Gary. At least you tried. Tell you what, I'll stake you to a little lunch before you catch your plane."

Sitting over a pair of burgers in the Blind Justice Bar, Scotti asked, "So how's everything going?"

"Pretty good. My uncle Brad got his boat in the water last weekend, so we been doing a little fishing. Lake bass and pickerel."

"Hey, real good. You ever take Sister Gayle out fishing with you?"

"Once, last summer. Up in Menominee." Tucker paused, looked down into his beer stein. "She was supposed to come down to our place this spring, do some off Brad's boat. But I guess now . . ."

"Yanh, I guess. So how's everything else? Like your love life, for instance?"

The kid brightened perceptibly. Dropped a sly grin. "Hey, it's pretty good."

"You getting any?"

"I'm doing okay."

Scotti read two things in that last exchange: one, that the Tucker kid was telling Nick he'd finally gotten laid.

And two, that the kid was probably lying.

She realized she was feeling better when Dr. Heilbron came by for their daily session and she didn't feel upset when she saw him. They even smiled a little about the extreme anxiety she had experienced concerning her transfer here. "You can see now for yourself, it's just a hospital room like any other," Heilbron pointed out a little smugly.

"Yes, I understand that now." And if they hadn't lied to her about that, maybe they weren't lying about the rest—that she would be well again, home again, soon.

Today he wanted to talk more about her family, her brothers. She said she guessed she'd always felt closest to Dan—he was just two years younger than her, and as kids they were quite alike. Both of them great readers, and collectors—stamps, matchbooks, postcards, all that sort of thing.

"And your other brothers—what were your feelings toward them?"

She smiled. "Just—ordinary, I guess. They were older than me, and they always seemed to be off somewhere doing their own projects. Ed had a big paper route, and Tom did a lot of odd jobs around the neighborhood. They just weren't around as much as Dan."

"I see. Which parent would you say you were closest to, Sister, your mother or your father?"

"Oh, my father, I think. I was the only girl, you know, so I guess I was kind of his favorite. My mother is a very good person, but I never felt as close to her as I did to my father."

"I see. Were you a smart little girl?"

"You mean, in school?" He nodded. "Yes, I guess. I always got straight A's."

"Were your parents proud of that?"

The smile now was small and private. "Oh, yes. My father especially. He used to call me his 'brainchild.' But that was just to make me feel good—my brother Ed always got straight A's too."

"Tell me more about your father."

Softly: "Oh, he was a wonderful man. So kind, such a— and he was a wonderful father. I used to look forward so to Sundays, because I knew I'd see him then."

He blinked, startled. "You only saw him on Sundays, Sister?"

"Oh, that was later, after fifth grade. When I was living with my Aunt Iris, and going to Blessed Sacrament school.

We all used to go to my house every week for Sunday dinners, so I always saw my father then."

When the doctor asked her why she was living with her aunt, there was something in his tone of voice—as if suggesting that this arrangement was something strange, something to be defended—that made her feel quite irritated with him again. "Well, it was just so I could go to Blessed Sacrament School, in my Aunt Iris's parish. That was a much better school than ours, and I already told you I was a good student. Always straight A's. So my parents decided I should go to the better school, even if that meant living away from home. Because I saw them every week anyway."

Now he wanted to know what the difference was between the two schools. She shrugged. "Well, you probably don't know anything about Roseville. But out there where we lived hardly any of the kids went on to college. They just went to work in gas stations or supermarkets, things like that. And my parents knew I'd probably be something like a teacher, so they wanted me to get a really good education, and they couldn't afford to send me to a boarding school. My father always worked hard, but he didn't make much money. He was just a hardware salesman."

"Do you think he was disappointed in that?"

"Disappointed how?"

"With his job, with his life. With not making more money."

She said proudly, "My father wasn't the kind of person who cared about making a lot of money. He was just a good man and a good father. He never wanted a lot of *money.*"

"Not a lot, perhaps. But enough to keep you living at home, keep you in a good school."

There were times when she hated having to talk this way to this doctor. "My father was a good man who did the very best he could," she said fiercely, flatly. "I don't think you can ask anybody to do more than that."

. . .

As Meg Gavin drove to her third interview she felt her-self sinking into a tenacious depression. Goddam Catholics —she hated talking to them. The lingo, the shorthand, was still familiar. But sooner or later, even in a conversation that seemed to be unfolding with sweet reason, she ran smack into one of their fucking damned unreasonable brick walls.

As she looked for the house numbers on the street of shabby little semidetacheds where the third ex-nun, Carolyn Hearne, lived, she was weighing a quick impulse to dump the whole story and just drive off. But Carolyn was already out on the porch of number 38, waving a welcome. Meg parked her car and bit the bullet.

Carolyn reintroduced herself as Cal. Another ex-Ben-nie, age thirty-three, eight years in, eight years out, married now to ex-priest Matthew Hearne. Three kids, age two, four and five.

She led Meg into a living room furnished with Goodwill rejects and sat on an overstuffed couch with a green flowered elasticized slipcover. Said yes, she knew Angela Flynn slightly from the time she was in the order—not very well.

Suddenly she pitched her head back on the couch and dug one hand into the long blond hair pinned up on her head. "Meg, you're going to have to ask me all the questions, get me started. Because I just don't know where to begin."

"Well, how about—why don't you just tell me, Cal, what you make of all this."

She was staring across the room at the ceiling molding. "What do I think. Oh, boy. Where to begin." She paused, dropped her hand heavily to her lap. "I just think the Church is so *crazy* on the whole subject of sex, so absolutely *demented*, and when I think what they've put that poor Angela Flynn through with their craziness, what they've *done* to that woman—well, my God, what would *anyone* think?"

Ah, yes. *Yes.* No depression now. Meg slipped her note-book from her purse. "Well, actually not everybody has the same opinion about the case. But I'm certainly anxious to hear yours, Cal."

"*Opinion.* I don't even know if you could call it that, it's just such an overwhelming— Listen, the night the first news came over the TV I was in the kitchen serving the kids dinner. And I heard it, sort of, but I thought I must not've heard it right. So I ran into the living room and said, 'Matt, did you hear that?' And he said yes. And I said something terribly stupid like, 'My goodness, I don't know what this world is coming to. Here someone broke into a convent and stabbed a nun, and then they left behind a dead *baby.* Whatever is the world coming to?' So Matt said he didn't think I had it quite right. And then of course I realized. What they'd really been saying all along on the TV. And the worst part was it *made perfect sense to me. I knew* that would happen, have to happen, something like that, sooner or later. I mean, considering all the craziness they expect nuns to live with, it *made perfect sense.*"

Ah, yes.

Meg went through half a pack of cigarettes as Cal Hearne talked on for an hour, more than an hour. Talked about the lesbian crushes so many nuns fell into when their sexual feelings were finally aroused—"and I was one of them. Oh God, I thought I must be the worst kind of pervert, and I kept *praying* for it to— Really, I didn't even know what sexual arousal was, except that every time this one particular nun walked into the room I felt strange all over. I didn't realize then, of course, that the feelings just come out lesbian because the only people you're *around* are women. Like it works in prisons. I didn't realize that this was really quite *natural* in those unnatural circumstances. And I didn't know that it also happened to a lot of other nuns. I just thought *I* was the strange, sinful exception, the sexual pervert, the *lesbian.* My God, even the *word* made my skin crawl. But there was nobody I could talk this out with, nobody who could give me some counseling. Not about a problem like *that.* But

325

finally I just couldn't bear it any longer, I had to tell somebody. So I picked a good friend, a nun I'd known since
before we were in the novitiate together. She's out now too,
and she's still a good friend. We've talked about this since,
now that we understand it better, and she's very— But back
in those days, of course, she was just as ignorant, as brain-
washed, as I was. So when I finally blurted out my terrible
confession, crying just from the *shame* of it, she gave me the
only advice we had to offer for something like this. You know
what that was, Meg?"

She smiled faintly. "I'm afraid to ask."

"She said, 'Well, Dolores'—that was my religious name
then, Sister Dolores—'you must find a way to control yourself.' Just that—'you must *control* yourself.' Here I couldn't
eat, couldn't sleep, seemed to be on the edge of just cracking
up, and my best friend told me, 'You must learn to control
yourself.' Because that's all we'd ever been taught, you
know, us poor dumb pious little *children* who went right into
the convent when we graduated from parochial school because it was such a dramatic, serious, exciting thing to do.
Such a *good* thing. And everything in the convent training
system—boy, let's get into that training system in a minute,
I mean the Marines could take *lessons* from the nuns in basic
training—just fortified that ignorance. Deny yourself, hum-
ble yourself. Offer it up, serve the Lord. My God, when I
think what was done to us, all in the name of goodness and
mercy, you understand—honestly, sometimes I think I can
just never ever really forgive them for what they did to us
with that—self-defeating—craziness in the name of God."

Meg Gavin felt as if someone had just kicked open the
door to a locked, secret room. She'd sensed what was in
there. She'd *known* it, more or less. But never actually seen
it until Cal Hearne kicked open that locked door.

Cal talked for quite a while about the novitiate training,
about the contemptuous rages and humiliations meted out
as "training" in the proper method of peeling potatoes or

scrubbing floors. She talked about the brutal disconnections made from natural families, with nuns forbidden to kiss or hug their parents, to have "physical contact" on the rare Sunday visits.

She told Meg about the psychosomatic illnesses so many nuns were prey to, but concentrated on her own—the headaches and abdominal pains that intensified in the two years prior to her leaving the convent. And about the swift brutality of that final leaving, when none of the nuns who lived in the house with her was available to help her load her possessions into the borrowed station wagon.

"That leaving—oh, Meg, I should have done it at least two years earlier. And when I finally got the courage to make that brutal break, I expected to be so *relieved.* But my God, when I finally did it, it turned out to be the hardest thing I ever had to do." She shook her head as she said, "Oh, Meg, I know I'm not talking much about Angela Flynn, and I don't know if all this is any help to you—"

"Oh, yes. It sure is, Cal."

"Well, I hope so." Cal was wiping her hand on her forehead, pushing strands of hair up from her damp face. "The thing is, when you called I knew I couldn't tell you anything important about Angela Flynn. But I've been *wanting* to talk to some reporter, to get some of this dumb, barbaric stuff—just—out. Because ever since this thing happened to Angela, I've been just going crazy with needing to talk to somebody besides Matt about it. To get some of this stuff out. Because it's all so damned useless. Such a human *waste.*"

Meg didn't need to be told that. What she was getting now from Cal Hearne was pure, unprotected flow—no "Don't quote me on this," "Please don't use my name."

Now Cal was talking about the first tentative stirrings of her relationship with her husband Matt. "I mean, *I'd* already left the convent, but he was still the pastor out in Granton. And when we finally went to bed, about nine months after we should have, *needed* to, we did it in his pastoral bed out in St. Mark's." They laughed together. "Well, physically it was just such an enormous *relief.* Such a—release. We didn't do it very well, but finally we'd done it. But I still felt so guilty that I shopped around to five churches for someone to confess it to. Five, by actual count. Because I felt that—unforgivable. Matt didn't even know that, until I told him the other night when we were talking about Angela Flynn. And he was quite amazed to hear I'd taken it so hard."

Meg smiled. "Well, I can see that. The pastoral bed and all."

"Oh, yeah, but that was just the excuse. Lord, I am unworthy, and all that. The main thing was I had finally broken this terrific *taboo.* When you said on the phone you wanted to talk about religious celibacy and how it might be related to this thing with Angela Flynn—I mean, that *is* what you're writing about, isn't it, Meg?"

"Yeah. More or less. But I really do appreciate—everything you're saying."

"Well, why I really wanted to talk to you—" Cal thrust a hand again into her hair, dislodging a large hairpin from her loose topknot. "But I can't help asking you—where is that baby's *father,* anyway? Why isn't *he* here now, helping Angela through all this pain?"

Meg shook her head. "Nobody knows that, Cal. But apparently he isn't available."

"Okay. Well, forget that. Except that *somebody's* got to help her now, because I have some small idea of what she must be going through. Look, that main point is, of course celibacy has *everything* to do with it. I think that's practically the whole story. That's it, right there."

"I think I follow you, Cal. But how, exactly?"

Fiercely: "Because everything that's causing so much trouble in the Catholic Church today, birth control and abortion and clerical celibacy, even the ordination of women, all of it, really—it comes down to *sex.* That's the one part of the human fact that the Catholic Church just can't handle. They never could, and they still can't. And that's what creates—all this—pain."

"Oh, yes," Meg said softly.

Cal pressed a hand against her stomach. "Ever since this happened to Angela, I've been feeling physically—sick. Almost throwing up, almost like I was pregnant again. I can hardly stand it, Meg. When I think about her having to deliver that baby alone . . ." She shook her head, close to tears.

"Well, don't. I mean, that's done, Cal. And the point is, what happens now?"

She was nodding. "Yes, that's what I want to know. I guess it's crazy, but I wrote a letter to Angela's lawyer, that Haverty man. I don't suppose I'll ever get the nerve to send it and it probably wouldn't do any good if I did—but anyway, I wanted to tell him he had the *wrong client* on trial here. I think his defense should be that the *Catholic Church* is guilty for what happened here, not that poor, pathetic Angela Flynn. After all those years of immersion in that medieval idiocy, all the years of conditioning they pounded into her with their nun training, Angela Flynn *just should not be considered responsible* for whatever she might have done."

Meg smiled again. "Well, knowing Ben Haverty, I don't think he'd be too crazy about your suggestion. But mail it anyway, Cal. He probably needs to hear it."

Cal tossed up her hands. "Well, I just wanted to tell him that, as a person who spent eight years under the same system Angela Flynn lived under, I'd be glad to testify in court about that, if he thought it would be useful to her defense. Oh, Meg, I'm sure that sounds very *silly*, written down. I think probably it's much more useful just sitting here with you, talking about it."

"Well, I do appreciate you doing that. And I want to promise you, Cal, I'll be very discreet about any quotes I use. I'm not about to—blow your cover."

329

She flipped her hands again, exhaustedly. "Oh, I never thought you would, Meg. Look, the main reason I wanted to see you now, I'd like you to realize—but I have some friends who consider me completely bonkers on this subject. Good friends, all of them ex-nuns, and we get together in a kind of CR group every week—Well anyway, I know most of them think I put far too much emphasis on sex. And maybe they're right, maybe they're right. But what I just wanted to make sure you understand is *what is the big sin here?*"

"Sure, Cal, I know it." She grinned. "Of course. That's why I wanted to see you."

"It's not the *murder,* not for most Catholics—do you understand that, Meg?"

Meg was nodding, smiling. "Yeah, Cal. I sure do."

"Oh, I hope so." Cal pushed her fingers agitatedly into her spilling hair. "The point is they could understand the murder. Even condone it, cover it up. Not even *notice* it. The big sin they're all so excited about, all those real good Catholics, the one they'll never forgive Angela Flynn for, is *that a nun had sex.*"

Twenty-five

When Roy Danziger called his lawyer's office from the pay phone at the grocery store, Dickson's secretary told him the polygraph appointment had been set for two days later, 11:30 A.M. Thursday, at the Glendale Police Department. She said Mr. Dickson wanted to know if Danziger would like him to be present at the interview.

"Yeah, I guess I would."

"Mr. Dickson said to tell you he could fit that into his schedule, but you understand there will be a charge for his time."

He felt a sudden flash of anger as he said, "That's okay, I can pay. Tell him to come."

Roy wasn't feeling much anger these days. He wasn't feeling much of anything. Mostly, he just wanted to be left alone.

He kept thinking about Gayle, wondering if she wanted to see him. He didn't even know where they had her, where to get in touch with her. The cops said last week she was in the hospital, but she must've got out by now. He kept thinking maybe she wanted to talk to him. Hell, the two of them —they had a stake in this thing, nobody else did. That was supposed to be their baby, wasn't it?

He still didn't know what he thought about the baby. If he could see Gayle, he wouldn't talk to her about anything like that. He wasn't going to ask her why she did it. Not even why she hadn't got in touch with him.

He just wanted to—talk to her. See if she was okay.

He knew this thing must be real rough for her to get through. A girl like her, especially. She must be having a real hard time just—getting through it.

Well, he just wanted her to know it was okay. Maybe she'd want to talk about it. That was up to her, strictly up to her. If she wanted to talk, there were maybe things she could say to him that she couldn't say to anybody else—

Especially he wanted her to know he didn't hold it against her. The baby—well, that was rough, but it was behind her. Behind them. He wanted her to know it was okay.

Whatever she wanted to say, he could handle it. He knew it wouldn't be easy, but he still wanted to see her. Wanted to help her through this thing.

When you came right down to it, this thing was mainly between the two of them. Now there were all these other guys in the act—cops, lawyers, D.A.s, all of them. But still

331

there was something special there just between him and Gayle. Something nobody else had any business in.

He kept trying to remember her face, her moves. It was all kind of rusty, half gone from his head. But the girl he *did* remember, she was a good kid. Somebody he liked, could talk to.

If he could just see her now, maybe she would tell him it was okay too. It was hard not having anybody to talk to.

He wouldn't ask her anything about the baby. He'd just say hey, how are you, you're looking pretty good—that kind of stuff. Then she could take it from there.

He did *want* to know. How it had happened. But he wouldn't press her any about that. He'd just say hey, don't worry your head, we'll get through this okay.

If she wanted to talk about it some later on, that would be okay, too. He wondered if she was still living with those nuns out there. Jesus, she sure couldn't talk to them.

Or her cousin, that Russell bitch. Or her cousin's tight-ass husband. People like that. He hoped she had somebody else around she could talk to. He guessed she probably didn't, or she wouldn't have got herself in such a mess on this thing.

God, he wished he could talk to her. Just talk, just be together, quiet like. They could just start with that. And see where it went.

No matter how many of those other turkeys tried to get into the act, the real thing there was just between her and him. Maybe they could work something out, even now.

The hardest thing was to be stuck in this goddam thing with nobody to talk to.

Behind the closed door of her room, Angela picked up the daily rhythms of Ward Five. In some ways hospitals were as predictable in their routines as convents were, she began to understand now. But here on Ward Five, at least, she was not required to be a part of that routine. The other patients had to keep their room doors open all day; they ate together, had group therapy sessions together.

But she was excused from all that. As a "special patient." She ate on trays in her room, filled her days pretty much as she liked.

And she was pleased with that arrangement. She had no wish to mix with the "real" psychiatric patients she was coming to know through the closed door—the querulous middle-aged woman who lived across the hall, or the old man in the room next to hers, who sometimes screamed in the night, or sang odd snatches of song.

Dr. Heilbron came by to see her once a day, and sometimes Dr. Salter came too. She came to enjoy her sessions with them, as a break in the anxious monotony. She remembered now what they reminded her of—the "self-criticism" sessions of her novitiate years, when the young nuns gathered with the Mistress of Novices to publicly acknowledge their faults and failings, and discuss the ways in which they could best improve themselves.

Mr. Haverty came by on Tuesday night, too, to tell her the arraignment had been set for Thursday noon, in the hospital ward. "Now I want you to know exactly what to expect, Angela. The judge will come here, with an assistant district attorney and a court stenographer. They will explain the technical charge to you. It will not be necessary at this point for you to enter a plea."

She made a startled motion. "But I would *like* to, Mr. Haverty." Drilling green eyes turned on him. "I want to plead not guilty."

"Ah, yes, I understand that." Haverty nodded his shaggy head. "But that will come at a later time—if at all. You understand, Angela, this arraignment is a purely technical proceeding that has no bearing on the outcome of your case. Except that after the legal formalities have been observed, you will be rid of the police guard and the other restrictions that are—presently operative."

Vigorous shake of her head. "But I would *like* to plead not guilty, Mr. Haverty. So they would understand—how I feel about this."

"Well, in due time, Angela, we will certainly do that." He looked down at his hands, pushed his fingertips carefully together. "Speaking of which, Angela— Now, please understand that I have no wish to push you unduly. To inquire into any sensitive areas you might feel you have difficulty talking about. But for the purposes of building your case, it would be most helpful to me if you felt up to discussing the—ah, circumstances of the child's conception."

Sudden silence in the room. He broke it with, "Please understand, Angela, that anything you might wish to say here would be held in the strictest confidence. It will go no further than this room. But if this is too difficult for you, if you'd prefer to leave it till a later—"

"No, that's okay. I understand, Mr. Haverty." She took a Kleenex from her skirt pocket and held it tightly as she said, "The man in question was someone I met when I was visiting my cousin and her family up in the Menominee peninsula last August. He was the guest of a family staying in the next camp." Her voice was high-pitched and firm, yet also curiously remote. "I was introduced to this man, and he was present at numerous family gatherings. He was well-spoken and respectful on those occasions. I thought he was a good person, a person I could trust. It never occurred to me that he could be in any way—dangerous."

Haverty stared fixedly at his hands as she told him about the man asking her one night, she believed it was the tenth of August, to take a walk with him, "because he wanted to talk to me about some personal problem he was having. I went along without thinking twice—which I realize in retrospect was probably quite foolish."

Her voice was shaking a little as she told him about the sudden . . . romantic change in the mood of their conversation. About the . . . things he did to her, in those dark woods.

334

"I didn't know exactly what . . . was happening. And I was too frightened to cry out for help." She wiped her cheeks with the Kleenex. "Afterward he said . . . said he was sorry. That he didn't know why . . . he had done that. And he let me go back to the camp."

The lawyer hunched forward in his chair, staring at his knotted fingers. "Angela, I understand all this is most painful for you to recall. Most painful. But I must ask—did you tell anyone of this attack?"

She shook her head. "No. No one."

"Not even your cousin?"

There was a slightly chiding edge to her voice as she said, "You understand, Mr. Haverty, I was very frightened. I didn't understand what happened, but I felt very— ashamed. I didn't think anyone else would—understand."

"Of course, of course. Very natural. Angela, this man— was he related to the family in question?"

"No. He used to work for Mr. Tucker once. I understand he was fired."

"Do you happen to know why?"

"I think because Mr. Tucker did not consider him a good moral influence, a good person to be around his sons."

"I see. Angela, do you happen to know his name?"

"Oh, yes." She spoke it softly, like a malediction: "Roy Danziger."

Her hospital days may have seemed drearily routine to Angela, but there was nothing routine about the interest that her presence there stirred in various quarters. On Tuesday afternoon, for instance, a thin, reasonably well-dressed young man claiming to be a victim of amnesia turned up in the Parkhurst Hospital Emergency Department, asking to be admitted to the psychiatric ward. When the hospital personnel searched his clothes for some clue to his identity, they found the name and phone number of a *National Enquirer* editor tucked under the leather lining of his right shoe.

Meg Gavin picked up that bizarre item through a routine phone call to a woman she was presently cultivating in the hospital's PR department, and included it in her daily update on the case because new hard news was so difficult to come by.

The Cambridgeport police investigation of Angela Flynn was also winding down, as fresh cases moved ahead in the order of priority. Lieutenant Tim Vance had not personally conducted any of the interviews with the nun's friends, family or professional contacts, but on Tuesday night when he was over in the neighboring suburb of Plunkett shopping for a pair of resistors for his basement sound system the names of Margaret and Ron Hogan flashed into his head. The Hogans lived in Plunkett, and they were said to be among Angela Flynn's closest friends. Since none of his men had managed yet to contact them, Vance decided to do that one interview himself.

Margaret Hogan answered the door—a fat, serious woman with soft eyes and a nervous mouth. She led Vance to the winterized sunporch where her husband Ron was watching TV. Vance explained that his office was carrying out the investigation of Sister Angela Flynn in conjunction with the district attorney's office, and they were talking to some of the nun's friends in an effort to help them put together a better understanding of what kind of person she was, what motivations may have been operative in this case.

The Hogans exchanged troubled glances. Margaret said firmly, "She is a *very good friend,* and I wouldn't feel at all comfortable—Ron, what do you think?"

Hogan shook his head and said he was sorry to seem uncooperative, but they had no wish to talk to any policeman about this matter.

Vance thanked them anyway, and said he understood their feelings in that regard. He dug one of his business cards out of his wallet. "Please understand, there isn't any *persecution* of Sister Angela involved here. But we have to put together as fair and accurate a case as we can, and to do that right it helps to get a little steer from her friends about where she might have been coming from." He paused. "Our investigation is just about concluded, and the evidence accumulated so far points to certain conclusions. I don't know if they're the right ones, but they're the best we've been able to come up with so far. That's what I was hoping you folks could help me with—to get a better fix on this thing."

More glances exchanged. Hogan cleared his throat and said, "Well, she's mainly *your* friend, Margaret."

Margaret shook her head, a sharp, definite movement. "I'm sorry, Lieutenant, but I have nothing to say to you."

"That's okay. I know it isn't easy for a good friend." Vance passed his card across the coffee table. "If you should happen to change your minds, I'd sure appreciate a call."

On his regular visit on the Wednesday lunch hour Dr. Heilbron asked her how she felt about the arraignment scheduled for the next day. "All right," she said.

"What I mean is, Sister, do you have any anxieties about that process, any uneasy feelings you would like to talk about right now?"

"Oh, no." She was shaking her head with a firm, serene smile. "Because Mr. Haverty explained it all to me and told me I didn't have to be concerned about it. I believe everything Mr. Haverty tells me, because I know he is a good person, very intelligent and well—qualified, who is trying his best to help me. The same way I feel about you and Dr. Salter. When you tell me I don't have to worry about being —kept—in this hospital." *This beastly, unnatural place.* "Because you've promised me I can go home soon. So why should I be afraid?"

The doctor chuckled, pleased with that answer. She always felt a little proud of herself when she came up with an answer that pleased him like that. *An A-plus mark,* it almost seemed. "Well, that's very good. I'm very gratified that you see it that way, Sister."

Firmly, serenely: "Oh, yes, I do."

He said in that case, perhaps they could talk a little more about her earlier experiences. He seemed especially to like talking about her early years in the convent—because that was a little exotic to him, she supposed. He'd already told her that she was the first patient he'd had who was a nun.

This time he was asking about how she got that name, Sister Angela.

"Oh, that was given to us when we finished our postulancy. When the rest of the congregation accepted us in as nuns, and gave us our new names in religion. As a kind of symbol of our acceptance into the order, into that different way of life." She paused. "The name meant—that we were someone else now. Whoever we were before we came in, now we were first of all a *nun.* "

"I see. Why were you called Angela?"

She shrugged. "I don't know, exactly. They picked them partly by—see, if a religious name was already being used in the order, they usually wouldn't give you that one. Because it made it too confusing to have two nuns with the same name."

"And when you came along, there was no other Sister Angela?"

"No. I think the other one had died about ten years earlier."

"What did you think of that name?"

Another shrug. "I liked it. But that didn't matter, really. I would have taken whatever they gave me."

"How did you feel when they first started to call you Sister Angela?"

Small smile. "I felt—comfortable, I guess. I liked being called Sister Angela."

"Did you like that more than Gayle?"

"Oh, not especially. I didn't think about it that way. The *name* never mattered, you know. It was just the idea behind it—that I was really a nun, now. I just really wasn't Gayle Flynn anymore—I was Sister Angela, a nun, and that was someone—different."

"Did you feel they were talking about you, when they first began calling you Sister Angela?"

Another smile. "Oh, yes. Right from the first, I liked being Angela. So when we had the choice, that's what I picked."

He perked up in his chair. "What choice was that, Sister?"

"Oh, about 1968, when all the changes started. The congregation decided every nun should have the option of taking back her family name or keeping her religious one. They just gave us that choice, around the time we stopped wearing the old habits."

"Hmmm. And you chose to keep Angela?"

"Yes, I did. Because I liked it better."

"What did most of your friends do? The other sisters?"

"Oh, most of them took their own names back."

"How many did, would you say?"

"Oh, I don't know. Just most of the younger ones. The old nuns mostly kept their religious names. It didn't matter, really, either way—the choice was left up to you."

"Why didn't you decide to be Gayle again? If most of your friends were taking their own names back?"

She shrugged again, a little irritatedly. He had a way of asking questions, sometimes, that made them sound almost like *accusations*. "No special reason. I just liked Angela. I just liked—the sound of it. When people called me Sister Angela."

"I see. And being Gayle again just didn't interest you?"

"Oh, Gayle was all right. I mean, my family still calls me that. I guess they always do that, call you by what they knew you as a child. But I still felt, except with my family, more like *Sister Angela* than I felt like Gayle."

"But what was the difference? Between Angela and Gayle?"

She hesitated, considering. "I don't think there was any difference. I just liked being Angela better."

"Why did you like that better?"

"Because Gayle was—that was all right, but that wasn't me. That was what I *used* to be. Angela meant something different."

"Different how?"

"Angela was—me, now. Angela was happier."

"Why was Angela happier?"

She was frowning with concentration now. "Because—because she was a nun."

"But a nun is also a person, with all the problems and complexities that implies, isn't she, Sister?"

Sharp, impatient motion of her head. "Oh, yes, of course. But a nun is dedicated to something much bigger than herself. And there's a great deal of *satisfaction* in that kind of commitment, Doctor."

He nodded. "Satisfying—yes, I can see that. But it's also very safe, isn't it, Sister?"

Reluctantly: "Yes, maybe. I guess that, too."

"Wasn't Gayle safe?"

Now she was getting quite angry with him. "Well, yes, of course. That wasn't the *point.*" Before he could ask another of his irritating questions she said, "The point is, it's just a very different kind of life. When you become a nun, you're someone special. You belong to something very special."

"What do you belong to, Sister?"

"A community. Of religious persons, where everyone is committed to the same ideal."

"What ideal is that, Sister?"

She wished this man would leave now, leave her alone

to walk around the room and get back to her own thoughts. She said flatly, "Just—serving God. Helping other people. Leading a spiritual life that helps other people but also gets you closer to your religious ideals. The reason that life is *special* is because it gives you so many chances to do good things for other people, to make their lives a little better."

"But didn't Gayle do good things for people too?"

She made an irritated gesture with her hand. "Really, I don't know why you're making such a big *thing* out of just a name. Of course Gayle was a good person. But she just— I mean, Gayle was me *before I grew up*. Before I got a chance to make my vocation real. Become the person I always wanted to be. Now if you don't mind I'd like to talk about something else."

After Dr. Heilbron left, she tried to read one of the historical paperbacks that Dan had brought her. But it was hard to keep her mind on the words. Outside her window the sun disappeared behind a dark, lowering sky. Minutes later a violent spring storm broke.

She got up from her chair and pressed her hands against the windowpane. Rain was streaming, flowing in rivulets down the glass. Then the wind shifted, driving the drops directly toward the pane.

Almost like that time in the Tuckers' speedboat, up at the lake, when they went waterskiing. She moved her face closer to the pane, watching the water smash and splatter on the glass, almost like something alive. Like the spray had hit the windshield of that speedboat, when the Tuckers' son pushed up the throttle and made it go very fast, the boat roaring with noise as it crashed, shuddering, through the lake waves. That boy smiling at her as she tried to smile back, tried not to show she was afraid. . . .

Knock. Knock at the door.

She looked bewilderedly around her. She was sitting up

341

cross-legged on the hospital bed, leaning against the headboard, her pleated skirt pulled up over her thighs.

She straightened her legs and smoothed down the skirt. When the knock came again, sharply, she called out, "Yes, come in."

A nurse bringing her supper tray. "Creamed turkey tonight, Sister," she said cheerfully as she crossed the room.

"Oh, very good." She got off the bed, and walked with her usual tight, prim movements to the table by the window where she took her meals.

"Is there anything else you'd like, Sister?"

"No, thank you." She unfolded the paper napkin, smoothed it over her lap. *Just leave me alone. Get out and leave me alone.*

When the woman left the room she pushed away the tray.

Supper already? But it was too early. Too—

It was . . . as if she had lost time. Lost two, maybe three hours.

Twenty-six

Roy Danziger arrived at the Glendale Police Station at 11:28, accompanied by his lawyer, Monroe Dickson.

Investigator Nick Scotti and Investigator Peter Juhl, the Ramsey County Sheriff's Department polygraph expert, were already waiting in the police staff room.

Scott noted that the doper's clothes—frayed jeans, shirt, and sweater—were cleaner than last week. And the guy had shaved, even shampooed his shoulder-length hair. But the biggest change was his attitude. That sulky self-protectiveness was gone. His first anxious words to Scotti were, "Hey, how's Gayle doing? What's happening to her?"

"She's still in the hospital, and she's under arrest for murder," said Scotti. "Apart from that, I hear she's doing pretty good."

Danziger paled. "Jesus. Isn't there something I could do to help her out? Does she want to see me, or anything?"

"I doubt it," Scotti said dryly.

"Well, if she wanted to—would it help if I went up there, tried to see her?"

"Nah, I don't think so, Roy."

Peter Juhl was talking to Danziger's lawyer, explaining the purpose of the polygraph examination—"to nail down any relevant facts or circumstances relating to this conception, pregnancy and birth. Your client isn't charged with anything. We just want him to fill in the background of this case."

"We understand that," said Dickson, "and I don't think Roy has any hesitation about cooperating as fully as he can."

"Okay, then let's get started." Juhl led Danziger down the hall to the chief's office, a small, cluttered room where Juhl had already set up his Stoelting polygraph equipment. "Sit there," Juhl ordered, pointing to a chair placed parallel to the front of the desk.

He waited until Danziger was seated before he settled himself in the taller chair. "I'm Investigator Peter Juhl of the Criminal Investigation Division of the Ramsey County Sheriff's Department, and as you know, we're here to ascertain the veracity of certain statements you have given to the police regarding your relationship with Sister Angela Flynn." Danziger was nodding blankly. "We'll start with the data on yourself."

He asked Danziger's full name, aliases or nicknames, address, age, date and place of birth, jotting the answers on a Xeroxed form. "Education?"

"I did two years' college in Texas."

"Major?"

"Well, I was mostly taking art."

"Height?"

"Six one."

"Weight?"

"Two twenty, maybe two twenty-five." *More like two forty,* Juhl estimated, but he wrote down the figure Danziger gave him.

"Color of hair?" Juhl glanced up from the sheet.

"Blond."

"Color of eyes?"

"Brown."

"Marital status?"

"Ah—single."

"Not divorced? You've never been married?"

"No."

"Any dependents?"

"Nah."

"Occupation?"

"Well, mostly—like, construction work, I guess."

"Military service?"

"I was in the Army about three years."

"Rank on discharge?"

"E-three."

"Type of discharge?"

"Honorable."

"Present employment?"

"Midwest Mutual insurance. I'm a maintenance engineer."

"Previous employment?"

"I've worked a bunch of places, not very long. Mostly I been with Midwest Mutual."

"Okay." Juhl flipped the paper over on his desk. "Now, you understand we are here to verify your knowledge concerning Sister Angela Flynn."

"Yeah, sure."

Juhl was noting the slumped posture, the passive, defeated attitude. "Let's take it from the beginning, Roy. Under what circumstances did you meet her?"

"Well, I was out of work, kind of down. So I went camping on my bike up in Menominee and Gayle was staying in the next campsite. I looked over there, saw this girl, and I kind of wondered about her. I mean, I could tell just from looking she didn't belong with the family in that trailer. She was an outsider, like me. Then later that day the friends I was staying with got together with that family and somebody introduced me to Gayle."

Gayle? Peter Juhl was puzzled by the switch in names. But it was evident that, for whatever reasons, Danziger was referring to Sister Angela as Gayle. Juhl was too good a polygraph operator to interrupt the flow of the interview by asking Danziger for an explanation. Instead he flipped a switch in his own mind and said, "What was the gist of your first conversation with Gayle?"

A.D.A. Andrew DaSilva was feeling unexpectedly shaken as he sat beside Judge Samuel Aaron around the six-foot-long wooden table in the conference room of Ward Five. The dreariness, the decrepitude of this hospital had been his first shock. But nothing he saw in the halls jolted him as much as the locked door of the psychiatric unit, clanging shut behind them.

A few minutes later a group of people filed into the conference room. The pale young woman walking beside Ben Haverty was tiny, almost doll-like. She sat in the chair Haverty indicated, at the foot of the table.

Another man and woman took chairs against the wall, beside a uniformed nurse. DaSilva figured them for Sister Angela's brother, and maybe another nun from the order. But when the stenographer asked for the identification of all persons present, for the court record, the man turned out to be Vincent Andretti, a young lawyer from Ben Haverty's office, and the woman a sheriff's deputy.

Sister Angela kept her eyes firmly fixed on the tabletop, her hands folded in her lap. DaSilva had heard people describe her as very young, very pretty.

Pretty, yes, she was that. And very short, very petite. But the face was too haggard to be called young. Maybe two weeks ago she'd looked young. But not anymore.

Judge Aaron was talking, explaining for purposes of the court record why the arraignment was being held in the hospital. Then he nodded to DaSilva.

Feeling extraordinarily nervous, DaSilva cleared his throat and said, "Sister Angela Flynn, also known as Gayle Marie Flynn, you are hereby charged with murder in the second degree in violation of Section 125.25, Subdivision 1 of the Penal Law of the State of Minnesota, whereas you did cause the death of an infant child known as Baby Boy Flynn by asphyxiation with an article or articles of clothing. Do you understand the charge made against you?"

Sister Angela lifted her head and looked at DaSilva. He felt the voltage coming out of those green eyes as she said softly, firmly, "Yes. I understand."

At first Danziger was hesitant, reluctant to talk about the time he spent with Gayle Flynn and her family. But as he got into it, most of what he said meshed with what Scotti had filled Juhl in on during their plane trip to Milwaukee.

D.A. Abrams had dispatched Juhl to this polygraph examination with a laundry list of areas he wanted better information about. Abrams wanted to know, for instance, how much Roy Danziger knew about Gayle Flynn's attitudes toward marriage and children. Also toward death. How much Danziger knew about any prior sexual contacts she might have had. What the actual number of her sexual contacts with Danziger had been. And—"I think this one's a central area of concern, Pete"—which one had initiated the sexual contacts between her and Danziger.

The more routine items on Abrams's laundry list—any gynecologists Danziger may have referred the nun to, or money he may have given her when he became aware of her pregnancy—were eliminated by Danziger's firm insistence that he had had no contact with the nun, verbal or otherwise, since he left the lake last August.

"So how did you find out she was pregnant?"

"Just—when those cops got me at work last week." Danziger paused, hunching his shoulders protectively. "Jesus, I still can't believe she actually killed her baby. I guess she must've, but hey, that's real hard to believe."

"How do you know she did it?"

"Well, the detectives told me. Last week."

"What else do you know about that?"

"Nothing. Just what they told me."

"Nobody else talked to you about it?"

"Nah. Nobody else knows." He paused. "I saw some about it on the TV, in the papers. But mainly I just know what the detectives said."

"Do you admit you're the father of that baby?"

Again the hunched shoulders. "Well, I guess I must be. If you're down here now."

"How do you mean that, Roy?"

Numbly: "Well, they took my blood, didn't they? So if you're back here now, I guess I must be the father."

Danziger was equally blank about questions relating to Gayle Flynn's interests, her attitudes. "Well, mostly I just remember her talking about how much she liked little kids. That was her job, teaching little kids someplace around Minneapolis. She really liked little kids and she knew a hell of a lot about them."

"What about her frame of mind? Do you know if she was under any special pressures, any mental strains last summer?"

Danziger considered the question. "Well, Gayle had a big promotion on her job. She was going to be running the school where she taught. Now you mention it, I think she was kind of uptight about that."

"Under what circumstances did she tell you that?"

"On the beach, mostly, I guess. We talked some most every day. And then when her cousin's family was sacked out for the night, we started taking walks by ourselves on the beach."

Juhl asked, "Was that when you felt an attraction, a sexual connection, beginning to build between you?"

Danziger's expression was blank, puzzled. "Well, I guess so. Sure."

It was clear to Juhl that the subject did not relate to questions implying a subtle, intricate nature to his relationship with this woman. So he automatically blanked any inquiries suggestive of that from his line of questioning.

She kept her eyes on the tabletop. Pale varnished wood with two sets of initials scratched into it, *D.B.* and *R.S.* The judge was talking on and on, about her right to have an attorney of her choice present at every step of the judicial proceedings against her and so on and so on.

She didn't seem to be required to answer, so she didn't look at him. Mr. Haverty kept saying, from his chair beside her, "My client is agreeable to that," or, "Your Honor, my client is aware of that."

The *strangeness* was what frightened her most. Just the whole idea of having to be here in this place while they did this thing to her. They didn't look like cruel men, the judge or that district attorney. In fact they looked quite kindly. But still—they were doing this thing to her.

She wanted to tell them she was *not guilty.* But Mr. Haverty only talked about other things, like the bail money. The district attorney asked for ten thousand dollars, but Mr. Haverty objected. So the judge said, "All right, bail will be set in the amount of five thousand. Is there any problem with that, Mr. Haverty?"

"No, thank you, Your Honor. No problem."

Five thousand dollars, which Dan and Ed were going to have to borrow from a bank. Five thousand dollars to keep her from running away.

It was all so strange, so ridiculous. All she *wanted* to do was go home to the convent and be left alone. But these people here seemed to think they needed the money to keep her from running away.

That showed how little they knew about her. How little they understood. Even in the late months of that pregnancy she remembered now, even in those times she was choking with worry and fear about what she should do, she'd never really thought about running away.

And if she hadn't done it then, why in merciful heaven would she do it now?

The polygraph detective was a young guy with a real quiet voice. He asked questions like he knew already what the answers would be. Like he knew them better than Roy, and he wanted Roy to find them out.

Damn if that wasn't how it felt. So much of what happened those few weeks in the summer he couldn't remember so good. If he'd known it was going to be so important maybe he would've remembered it better. The big things—that they'd been together a lot, that they had sex—he had those right. But the small stuff, the details—what they'd said, what they'd felt—Roy hadn't been able to pull a lot of that out of his head.

Now this guy with his quiet questions was starting to pull it back for him. The guy was asking now, "When did you get into having sex?"

He tried to figure it out. "I guess it was about the third night we went for a walk on the beach. We were just walking along, talking, like, and all of a sudden she took my hand."

"What did you do then?"

"Nothing. We just kept on walking." He stared at the opposite wall. "Then every once in a while we'd stop to talk, turn toward each other—you know. Like you do when you're holding hands." Pause. "Then one of those times we stopped she just leaned forward and—she kissed me."

"How did you react to that?"

Shrug. "Well, I liked it. It was nice. So I—kissed her back."

"What happened then?"

Funny, how it was all coming back now, finally. "Well, we kept on walking, and then we sat down to talk by a big pile of rocks. We talked for a while, and then we—I guess we wound up—having sex."

"Whose idea was that?"

He hesitated for several long moments, replaying the incident in his head. The idea that was coming to him now, no way did he want to think it. But when the guy put it that way, yeah, it did make him think. Of those tangled, awkward moves. Tangled, awkward bodies. Made him—remember.

Reluctantly, a little bewilderedly, he said, "Well, Jesus. It must've been *her.*" He pulled up his shoulders. "Hey, don't get me wrong, I got nothing against it. It was okay with me. Hey, I like it whenever I can get it. But—I just wasn't thinking about sex that time I was up at the lake. I mean, I just didn't have the idea nowhere in my head."

"So what happened then?"

Long, thick pause.

Ah, *now* he was remembering that quick, almost frantic fucking. The cries, almost like smothered screams that came out of her—yes, he did remember that.

And then that awkward fumbling for the clothes. Yes, now he remembered that. And him wanting, *wishing* he could know what she was thinking when she was back in her pants, her body rolled up against his on that rocky, uncomfortable beach.

She seemed to be shaking, kind of. But it might've been —him.

That one thing, he never did figure it out, then or now —*what she was really thinking.*

In that polygraph room he said blankly, flatly, "Well, we stayed there for about a half hour. Maybe a little more."

"What happened then?"

"We walked back to the camp, and I kissed her good-night on the cheek. She went to her cousins' trailer and I went to bed in my bag."

"When was the next occasion you had sexual contact, Roy?"

Pause. "Well, we took another walk the next night, and we did it again. Then I found out from something somebody said—I guess it was her cousin's husband—that Gayle was a nun."

"You didn't know that before?"

"Nah. How would I? I mean here's this nice-looking little girl, really built, and she's kind of larking around, laughing a lot, having fun—I mean, who would think *that?*"

"What was your reaction to that, Roy?"

He shrugged. "Well, first off I didn't believe it. Flat didn't believe it. But then Gayle said yeah, it was true. She was kind of pissed off at her cousin's husband for letting that out, but she didn't say it wasn't true." He stirred on the chair. "So I told her I didn't think we should be having sex. It didn't seem—like, right. But she said no, no, it was okay. So we did it again that night."

"On the beach?"

"Yeah. Then she told me she'd got her period, so we'd have to lay off for a while."

The cop was scribbling something on the back of some paper. "What did you think about that, Roy?"

Shrug. "Hey, I didn't care, one way or another. I just told you, man, I didn't go up there for sex. I mean, I had a lot of other things on my mind. Sex, no sex—any way was all right with me. Mainly, I just wanted to get my head straight."

"So that was the end of your sexual contact?"

"Nah." He hunched forward in his chair. "I mean, it could've been, for all I cared. Sex on all those rocks and sand —hey, that's not my idea of real terrific." He paused. "But then after three days she kind of threw me some signals, let me know it was okay again. So we took another walk on the beach."

"One more time?"

"Two. Maybe three. I can't remember exactly. I think one night she just came out to my bag, where I was sleeping. Anyway, then I had to get back to the city for a job interview. I knew she was moving out two days later. I told her I was real sorry I had to go so soon. I gave her my address, told her I'd really like to hear from her."

"What did she say?"

"She said thanks, she'd keep in touch. 'Real nice to meet you, Ziggy'—that kind of thing."

"When did you next hear from her?"

"I told you, I never did, man. Not till those detectives came around last week."

"Not even a Christmas card?"

"Nah. I told you, zip."

"Did that surprise you, Roy?"

"Well, yeah, it did. A little. We seemed to get along pretty good. I thought maybe she'd keep in touch."

"Did you think about her much?"

"Oh, once in a while. It was no big deal, but I did think about her. And I was kind of surprised when I didn't hear from her. But I figured—you know, that's the way it goes."

"Just a summer fling on the beach?"

"Something like that."

"She didn't ask you for money? Or to get her a doctor?"

"I'm telling you, man, I didn't hear zip from her." He

paused. "And I'm real surprised about that now, seeing how things turned out. I just—can't figure that."

"But you're convinced you're the father of her baby?"

Shoulders up again. "Well, I guess I must be. I mean, if you guys say so, I guess I am."

"To the best of your knowledge did she have sexual contact with any other man?"

"You mean up at the lake, last summer?" The cop said yes, that's what he meant. "Nah, I don't think so."

"What was her attitude to the sex?"

"Well, she was kind of a novice. Kind of inexperienced, like. But it wasn't her first time, I'm sure about that. I mean, you can tell. So I knew it wasn't her first time. But I don't think she'd done it much."

"Did she talk to you about that—how she felt about the sex?"

"No, not much. She didn't want to talk about that. It was just—like, body language. I mean, she was telling me in a lot of ways she wanted it. *When* she wanted it, even." Hesitation. "I remember one night we were sitting around the campfire with her cousins and somebody was playing a radio and she got up and danced in these red pants she was always wearing. Danced away from the others, like just for me." He paused, delving, recapturing the images of that campfire— Gayle weaving, spinning with her eyes half-closed, face turned toward the dark woods, her red slacks gyrating slowly near his face. He shook his head as he said, "I sure figured I knew what she was saying with that dance."

"But she never suggested the sex verbally?"

He hesitated. "Let's put it this way, she was more action than talk."

"Did she talk about any sex she'd had with other men?"

"Not much. I mean, no, she didn't. But she kind of hinted about some guy she'd met the summer before, from back East. I figured for sure she'd gotten some with him."

353

"Did she ever talk to you about how she felt about marriage and children?"

That question took him by surprise. "Kids—sure, I told you. She really loved little kids. Marriage—" He hesitated. "That's funny. I remember one day early on when I was talking about this girl I used to live with, and Gayle and me got talking about how we felt about getting married. I figured *she* would be all for it. I mean, most girls like that, single girls, they're always engineering to get married. But Gayle kind of tossed her head"—he imitated the gesture—"and laughed. She said, 'Oh, I got a whole lot of things I want to do first, before I settle down and get married.' Kind of like a college girl might say— you know?"

"Yeah. I know."

"Then later on, when I found out she was a nun, I figured she was kidding. I mean, nuns kind of think they *are* married, don't they?"

"So I hear."

Juhl stood up, walked to the other side of the desk and said, "Roll up your right sleeve, please."

Danziger did as he was told. Juhl wrapped the blood-pressure cuff around the fat bicep. "Lift your arms." Danziger raised his arms; Juhl snapped the pneumo springs in place across his chest. "Lay your left hand flat on the desk." Danziger put down his hand. Juhl slipped the metal plates that measure galvanic skin response under his first and third fingers, attached them to the fingers with black Velcro straps.

Juhl went back to his own chair. "Have you ever taken a polygraph before?"

Danziger hesitated. What the hell, he knew the machine wasn't going yet. "No."

"The only uncomfortable part of the test will come from the pressure on that cuff." Sitting behind the desk, Juhl pumped up the cuff and adjusted the machine for a median reading on the graph. "Answer the questions with a simple yes or no answer."

Meg Gavin was already waiting there when Andy DaSilva got back to his second-floor office in the Hall of Justice. "Hey, Meg," he said as he came into the cubicle, pulling off his coat. "How you doing?"

"Hey, *Andy*. What happened at the hospital?"

He went through a brief recap of the routine proceeding —the persons present, and the amount of bail set. Meg was staring at him as he finished. "*Damn,* Andy. That's all?"

"Just about, I guess."

"Shit, you're the first one I've talked to who's actually *seen* her. What did she look like, what did she *say?*"

"Well, after I read off the charge and asked her if she understood it she said, 'Yes, I understand.' I'm sorry, Meg, but that's all she said. By the way, I liked that piece you did on religious celibacy."

She grimaced. "Thanks, Andy. Let's say you liked the half of it my fucking craven editors were willing to print."

"Well, I just thought it was a pretty interesting insight into what the nuns are up against these days."

"What *she* was up against, anyway." She crossed her legs restlessly. "Jesus, Andy, what else did you see? Here you actually got in there, vaulted over the Great China Wall— you've got to at least tell me what she was *like.*"

DaSilva considered for a moment. "Well, she's real small. Much smaller than I expected."

"Small, okay. What else?"

"Hey, Meg, I don't know what I can say. She was just— real small. And quiet."

"Didn't she say anything, except what you said?" DaSilva shook his head. "During the whole thing?"

"Yes, that's all. Listen, the whole thing took maybe ten minutes."

"Oh God." She thumped a fist on her forehead. "What was she wearing, at least? Did you notice *that?*"

"Some kind of orangish shirt. A turtleneck, maybe. And a brown jumper kind of thing."

"Jesus, Andy. That's all you noticed?"

"Yeah. That, except—she seemed pretty strong. Pretty together. A lot stronger than I expected, in a situation like that."

"Okay. Who's putting up the bail?"

"Her family, I think. You'd better check with Ben Haverty on that."

"Oh my God, Andy. *That's* all you've got to give me, the first one who actually saw her face to face?"

DaSilva considered for a moment. "Well, she looked older than I thought. Older than I expected."

"Was she worried, upset, crying, screaming, *what?*"

"No, she was pretty quiet. Intense and quiet, I'd say." DaSilva paused. "Considering what she's accused of doing, I'd say she looked very—sane."

Juhl asked, "Are you planning to lie to me during this test?"

Danziger said, "No."

Juhl watched the red ink marks flow across the rolling graph paper, as he scribbled his shorthand version of his questions and observations at the bottom of the paper. "Is your name Roy Danziger?"

"Yes."

"Have you told the police the entire truth in this matter?"

"Yes."

"Have you seen Gayle since August 1977?"

"No."

"Do you drink coffee?"

"Yes."

"Have you had any communication at all with Gayle since August 1977?"

"No."

"Did Gayle tell you she was pregnant?"

"No."

"Do you believe you're the father of Gayle's baby?"

"Yes."

"Are you thirty years old?"

"Yes."

"To your knowledge did Gayle have sex with anyone else during the period when you knew her?"

"No."

The red lines flowed smooth and even. "Are you withholding any information on this case?"

Danziger said, "No," and sighed. Juhl scribbled an *S* on the bottom of the graph paper to account for the irregularities in the respiration measurement.

"Do you wear glasses?"

"No."

"Have you had conversations with anyone else regarding Gayle's pregnancy?"

"No."

"Did Gayle contact you for help at any time?"

"No."

"Are you attempting to protect anyone in this investigation?"

Danziger paused, then said, "What do you mean, 'protect'?"

Juhl scribbled *TT* at the bottom of the chart, to indicate *subject talking.* He said, "Just answer yes or no."

Pause. "No."

Juhl decided to take a break, and released the air pressure on the cuff. After more than a minute on the machine most subjects experienced a painful, distracting tingling in their right hand from the pressure on their arm veins. Juhl said, "Roy, you gave me a significant reaction to that last question."

"Well, what did you mean?" Danziger asked. "I mean,

I'd protect her if I could. If I had the chance. Hey, listen, I still want to help her if I can."

"Even now?"

"Yeah, sure. I feel real bad that this whole thing happened. I guess some of it must've been my fault. But now she's left taking all the guff herself. Sure, I'd protect her even now if I could."

"Okay, Roy, I can understand that. But please answer with a straight yes or no." Juhl reinstated the pressure on the cuff. "Have you told me the complete truth so far since we've been talking?"

"Yes."

"Are you making up any part of your story?"

"No."

"Did you give any money to Gayle for the baby?"

"No."

"Are you a citizen of the United States?"

"Yes."

"Have you deliberately tried to lie to me on this test?"

"No."

The red lines were all smooth, the reactions consistent. "Have you ever had sexual intercourse with Gayle?"

"Yes."

"On more than one occasion?"

"Yes."

"Have you attempted to communicate with her since August 1977?"

"No."

"Did you know she was pregnant prior to the police talking to you?"

"No."

"Have you told me the complete truth in this interview?"

"Yes."

The red lines told the story: smooth, cadenced, rhythmic. Juhl released the pressure on the arm cuff and stepped around the desk to detach the sensors from Danziger's body.

Danziger sat still in the chair, his shoulders slumped forward. Most polygraph subjects asked at this point in the interrogation, anxiously, "How'd I do?" Even the innocent ones.

But Roy Danziger sat passively, waiting for whatever else was coming.

Peter Juhl had finished the job the D.A. had assigned him to do. Now he was into the part of polygraph work that interested him the most—getting into the heads, finding out what made them tick. What really went on in there. Fuck the criminal part—this was what caught Peter Juhl.

He asked in his steady, barely audible voice, "How do you feel about this thing, Roy?"

"What, you mean everything that's happened?"

"Yeah."

Danziger spoke slowly. "Well, I wish she'd told me. I wish she'd let me know. I would've done whatever I could to help her—money, whatever. I guess I even would've married her, if that's what she wanted. But the way it turned out—shit, sure I feel bad about that."

Quietly: "How do you feel about your life, Roy?"

Danziger stirred in the chair. "You want the truth?"

"Yeah."

Bleakly, flatly: "Well, not much. Hey, I'm looking for something to get into, but I haven't found it yet. What the hell, I'm thirty years old, I'm getting along. But I haven't figured out yet what I want to do with my life."

"What about the art you studied in college?"

"Well, I liked that, but that was like fooling around. You can't make a living at that unless you're real good. The best. I was never that good."

Juhl was never sure exactly what the process was, but he knew when that *click,* that fix was there, inside his head. And

359

he knew the next question should be *when did you.* Not *did you ever.*

He asked quietly, "When's the last time you tried to kill yourself, Roy?"

Danziger's head swiveled toward his, so quickly that Juhl could still see the reaction in his pupils. He asked with genuine fear in his voice, *"How'd you know that?"*

Juhl shrugged. "That's just how I read you, Roy."

Danziger looked back to the wall in front of him. Flatly: "Well, I tried it about three months ago." Tense pause. "I don't know, I just felt washed out. I just didn't want to—Anyway I got a gun and I put it to my head. But I couldn't pull the trigger. I figured I must need help, so I went to see some psychiatrist."

"Was he any help?"

"Not much. It just didn't seem to be—going anywhere. So I stopped seeing him. Then last week these detectives come in, they unload this thing on me—shit."

Juhl said with some urgency, "Roy, I hope you're going to try again to get some professional help. Somebody to help you deal with this thing."

Danziger lifted his hand, limply. "Hey, forget it. I already got an appointment. I mean, I know this thing is too much for me to handle."

"Have you got any friends? Anybody you can talk to about this?"

"Nah. I got friends, sure. But I don't want to— Nah, I'm not talking to them."

They conversed for a while longer, but Danziger was wary now, afraid of the fearsome knowledge Juhl had somehow pried from his head. Juhl decided there was nothing more to be gained from the interview. He said, "Roy, I'd like to urge you again to go for professional help. A thing like this is too much for any man to cope with by himself."

"Yeah, I know that." Danziger nodded slowly, heavily. "I sure do know that."

"That about terminates our interview. Is there anything you'd like to ask me?"

"Yeah." Danziger got up slowly from the chair, turned around to face Juhl at the desk. Hesitantly, he asked, "Was it a boy or a girl?"

Twenty-seven

With the arraignment finally over she could concentrate on her main job, which was remembering.

For hours every day she played and replayed the tapes in her head, struggling to retrieve her memories from the dark space. Especially she tried to remember that last day in the convent.

But most of what happened on that April 25 was still lost somewhere in the tormented fogbanks of her head. She went over and over it in her mind: waking at three A.M. Taking the two Bufferin. Telling Julia she was sick, she couldn't go in yet to school. Walking by the window, trying to read, when the pale blood suddenly ran down her legs. And so on, and so on.

Then always, when she got to that part in the bathroom, climbing out of the tub, the tape fuzzed and darkened, like a browned-out film. All that came back then were snatches, flashes: the blood-soaked towels. The dizzy pitching into blackness. Lying on the floor in the blood and the clots.

Dr. Salter and Dr. Heilbron both urged her not to try so hard, to let it come back naturally, in its own good time. But she rejected that advice with anguished shakes of her head. She *had* to know, *had* to find what was lost in that dark space. And who could tell her, except herself? Because she was the only one there.

And if the child really was there with her, like they said he was, *why couldn't she remember him?* How *could* she forget that, her own baby, his own real face?

The crying jags still came and went, not as often as before. Dr. Salter said that it was good for her to let her feelings out in that way, that she should not fight the tears. But she still didn't like to do it when those doctors were there. Regardless of what they told her, she was afraid they might consider those unpredictable crying jags some reason why she should be kept here longer, in their crazy ward.

On their visits the doctors spent most of the time asking her about her earlier years. So strange—funny, almost. So many of those things she hadn't had time to think about for years. But now it was like her job assignment, her luxurious, nostalgic job assignment—recalling those Christmas trips to Grandma Moriarty's house in Indiana. The piano lessons she took with Mrs. Finsler. The nature walks she took with Daddy in the woods around Culver Creek.

Explaining to these non-Catholic doctors about what it was like to wear the habit or keep the Rule of Silence or make a seven-day retreat. Explaining the reasons behind the order's rules, that sometimes seemed on their face a little silly, like never walking in twos, or writing and receiving only two letters a month.

Usually the doctors would wind up the session asking how she felt about all this. She knew by now that they meant two things by that question—how she felt about *that,* those things recalled from her earlier life. And how she felt about *this,* what was presently happening to her.

About the past she never seemed to have very strong feelings, one way or another. About the present—"Well, I don't know," she said slowly to Dr. Salter on Friday afternoon. "I mean, that's what I'm finding out now, isn't it? How I feel about it."

"Yes, that's a good way to put it, Angela."

"Of course it's very—terrible. What happened. To the child, I mean, not to me—everyone's really being quite kind to me. But I still can't see how it could have happened, like they said it did. I can't—think I could possibly have done—that. So I'm—very confused."

Dr. Salter was nodding, looking quiet and wise. "That's all quite reasonable, Angela. A very reasonable way for you to be feeling right now."

"But it seems to me I should—understand more. I try to remember, I try almost all the time to remember. But it's all very—muddy. Muddled. In my head."

He reached forward and patted her hand. Solemnly, so gently and seriously: "Now listen to me, Angela. I don't want you to press yourself. I don't want you to *work* on this. Everything will come back to you in its own right time, Angela, when you yourself are ready for it. I don't want you to push yourself now. You'll get there yourself when you're ready for it."

Crying again. Oh, she wished she could get through just one of these sessions without crying. "But I *feel* ready now. I want to *know.*"

"Trust your own mind, Angela. Trust *yourself.* It will come back to you when you're ready."

The doctors didn't come over the weekend. And that made it a long two days to get through, with so few people coming into this blue-walled room to break her sometimes so anxious rush of thoughts, rush of remembering.

She knew that the police guard was gone now. So she could have called people, friends who wanted to come to visit with her. Like Margaret Hogan. Oh, she wanted so much to see Margaret, to feel her fat, warm crushing hug again.

But not here. Not in this place. She didn't want any of her friends to think she could possibly belong in this dreadful place, with those drooling old men in the halls. Not even a good old friend like Margaret.

Soon she would be out. Soon she would be home again.

She could see Margaret then. But not here, not in this crazy ward where they had put her away for safekeeping.

So she was quite surprised when someone knocked at the door of her room at 5:15 on Saturday afternoon. The nurse who opened it said, "Someone special to see you, Sister."

Dr. Keith Talbott was standing in the door, looking tall, shy and awkward, making one of his funny bows. She got up from her chair by the window to greet him, her face bright with surprise, beaming. "Oh, Dr. Talbott! Please do come in."

The nurse offered to bring them coffee. "Oh, that would be nice," Angela said. When the nurse left, she clapped her hands together. "I'm so glad to *see* you, Dr. Talbott."

"Well, thank you, Sister Angela. I'm very pleased to see *you.*" He sat on the edge of the plastic-upholstered chair, his elbows on his knees. "I wanted to come by and check on you, and this is the first chance I've had. How are you feeling, generally?"

"Oh, I feel fine. Very good. I'm almost my own self again."

He asked some technical questions about her bowel movements, her vaginal discharge, and so forth. She answered them briefly, succinctly. "Well, I seem to have done my work very satisfactorily," he said. "I don't think you'll have much further need of my services, Sister, until it's time for your six-week checkup."

She nodded: "Yes, thank you, Dr. Talbott. But it's still very nice of you to come by."

Her *mood* was the first thing that struck Keith Talbott— her oddly manic, upbeat mood. He realized that Heilbron

364

might still have her on medication that would account for it
—Thorazine or Stelazine, maybe. But that didn't jibe with
the intensity of focus she was also projecting.

Keith Talbott hadn't known what to expect when he
came to see her in this place. But it certainly wasn't this—
very energetic good cheer.

When the coffee came they both relaxed a little, and
talked for about half an hour. Mostly about Talbott's family,
and his life outside the hospital. A little shyly, he finally
found the chance to tell her that he himself had spent six
years as a Holy Cross seminarian.

The nun reacted to that news with great interest. Even
a certain conspiratorial relief. She smiled toward him as she
said, "You know, Dr. Talbott, those other doctors, like Dr.
Heilbron and Dr. Salter—they aren't Catholic, of course. So
when they're asking me about Catholic things, like the
novitiate and all that—I mean, I know they're *trying*. But of
course they can't really understand."

Talbott returned the smile. "I think I know just what
you mean, Sister Angela."

She asked how he had felt about leaving, and Talbott
said he thought those years in the seminary had given him
many valuable things. Things he would always—appreciate
having had. But finally he'd felt it was necessary for him to
leave, to seek a satisfying life outside the priesthood.

She was nodding very earnestly. "Oh, I can understand
that very well, Dr. Talbott."

"Can you, Sister?"

"Of course. Like my friend Pam, Sister Pamela—she
was very happy as a nun for thirteen years. But then she
left, and she got married last year. Pam thought maybe I
wouldn't understand that, but I did. And I was very glad
for her."

"Glad how?" Talbott asked, sipping at his coffee.

"Well, that she'd found—something else. Another way
to use all the love and commitment she had for people. You
don't *have* to be a nun or a priest to use the gifts God gave

you for helping other people, of course. And I was very glad for Pam that she'd found another way to make her life—valuable again."

Talbott nodded. The words made sense. But something in the way she said them—so intense, so damned doggedly *charitable*—made him a little uncomfortable.

"Like *you,* Dr. Talbott," she was saying. "Think of all the people you help as a doctor. Think how you helped *me.* "

Wry smile. "Well, thank you, Sister Angela. I did try."

"Oh, and you succeeded. You were a great help to me in a very difficult time, Dr. Talbott." She stirred the cooled coffee in her cup. "But of course, it's different for me."

"Different how, Sister?"

"I mean, different from you and Pam. I can certainly understand how some people might find a better way of fulfilling themselves outside the religious life. A very good, valuable way." She paused. "But it's not like that with me."

"How so, Sister?" Talbott drank again from his cup. Swill, dishwater, they passed off for coffee in this place.

"I mean, I never wanted to be anything but a nun." Small, fixed smile on her serene face. "I'm very happy being a nun. That Dr. Heilbron keeps asking me why I wanted to be a nun, and I think he still doesn't understand it. Even though I've told him quite a few times." She was staring, smiling at the cracked blue wall of this room. "I mean, I don't think he understands about vocation. How you *know* when you have found your vocation. I think I was one of the lucky ones, because I found mine very early."

Quietly: "When was that, Sister?"

She stirred, smiling. Pleased that she had such a precise answer to give this doctor. "Well, I still do remember. It was in a sixth-grade history class, when Sister Mary Theophane was talking about what a lot of different kinds of lives people could lead. Some of them very good. But she said the most *perfect,* the most difficult and challenging, was the religious life. Because that was the one where you could never be satisfied until you had made yourself as perfect as God intended you to be. And when she said that, for me it was like"—she gestured vaguely with her left hand—"a strong light had suddenly come on in the classroom. Because I *knew* then, I just *knew* what my real vocation was."

Quietly, very quietly: "Which was the one you followed, Sister?"

"Oh, yes." Luminous smile turned on him. "It wasn't that I had to decide it, like I tried to explain to Dr. Heilbron—it was already decided for me. And it didn't turn out to be as hard for me as it was for some of the girls I went in the novitiate with, because it fitted me so well. The *rules* never really bothered me like it did some of them. I've been very happy being a nun, a teaching nun. I found what I wanted, and it's all I ever really wanted to be. And I feel very blessed in that, Dr. Talbott."

He felt a little choked as he said, "Well, that's very nice for you, Sister."

She was directing a full, charitable glow on him now. "But that doesn't mean I don't understand how it can be for other people. Like Pam, or you, for instance, Dr. Talbott. I think *your* real vocation is probably to be a doctor, to help people like you helped me. And I do thank you for everything you did for me, and I hope you get a lot of real satisfaction from your work. Because it's such a *worthwhile* way to live, doing good for people the way you do. You certainly don't have to be a *priest* to do that, Dr. Talbott. But I'm very glad to realize now that you—understand what that kind of vocation is."

Talbott ducked his head in one of his awkward bows. He knew what she was saying was intended to be flattering, confiding. Reassuring.

He'd like to read it that way himself. Easier, so much easier that way.

But he didn't. Couldn't. This convent life she was rhapsodizing on—that had to be finished now, for her. Keith

Talbott couldn't imagine that any order of nuns, no matter how "liberated," would keep her on after all the exposure that had happened in this case. With more to come, surely. That brutal, shriveling exposure.

But that idea did not seem to have occurred yet to Sister Angela Flynn. If it had occurred, what she was telling him now was that she rejected it out of hand.

I'm very happy being a nun. Keith Talbott might have believed that from this woman if he'd met her professionally a year, two years ago. But now—

God, he hoped Bruce Heilbron knew what the hell he was doing with this case.

Meg Gavin was running late all day Saturday. When Dewey Wald rang her doorbell at 8:30 she was just climbing out of the tub. She pulled on a clean pair of panties and her long purple silk bathrobe and went to answer the door.

He leaned forward to kiss her as it came open. "Hey, kid. How're you doing?"

"Hey yourself, Wald. Running late is what I'm doing. It's been that kind of day. Fix yourself a drink while I finish my magic transformation."

As she turned away he grabbed her hand and said softly, "Wait up." He squeezed the hand as she tilted her face to look at his. "Where's the rush? We've got, if I remember right, the whole night ahead of us. Now why don't you just sit those busy bones down and have a drink *with* me?"

She smiled, a little sheepishly. "Well—now that you mention it, Wald, the rush is all in my head."

"Exactly." He cupped his long, thin hands around her cheeks, pressing her hair softly against her skin. "And it's a nice long warm Saturday night when the lilacs happen to be in bloom, and that's no damn time for rushing."

"Hmmm." She leaned her forearms against his chest, grinning. "You had something else in mind, Wald?"

"Yeah. Quite a few, in fact."

Swaying in his loose hold. "Care to name 'em?"

"Sure. How about, for starters, we just—float."

She was laughing as she pushed away from that awkward embrace. "Okay, fast talker. You just convinced me." And went into the kitchen to fix them both a drink.

He was sprawled out waiting for her on the couch, smiling. She handed him the glass as she sat beside him. "Okay, Wald, here's to you." Their glasses clinked. "Here's mud in your eye."

He nodded, sipping. "And mud in both yours, Ms. Gavin." He laid his hand on the silk robe covering her knee. "So what kept you so busy on a Saturday? You still chasing down that nun thing?"

She smiled, shaking her head. "As a matter of fact, no. I *do* work on other stories sometimes, you know. Sister Angela isn't quite a full-time job yet."

"Well, she just about *seems* to be that, for you."

She tilted her head to look quizzically at him, grinning. "What is this, *jealous?* Wald, you don't mean to tell me you're jealous of that poor damned twit nun?"

He echoed back the grin. "Nah. It's just— Listen, I'm interested to know why you're so wrapped up in that case." He laced the fingers of his right hand into hers. "You know, when I first met you, I thought you must be pretty religious yourself, to care so much about that story. But now I don't think that's it. Your head's very—clear of those cobwebs, those Churchy hobgoblins. So I just wondered—what's it to you, anyway, Gavin?"

She shook her head in mock despair. "Oh boy, Wald, you disappoint me. I thought you were sharp enough in the bean department to've figured that already. You being a kinky-haired Jew and all." She slapped his knee. "Okay, then listen good, Wald, because I'm only running this out once. First, it's a real big, real good news story. Reason enough to put in a little overtime. But second, a bigger second, it's one that really grabs me—a living dip into vats of tribal magic.

Mystery. Real *evil,* even. Putative evil. Anyway, real *sin,* for sure. All the good stuff I was raised on but never hoped I'd live long enough to see this close up."

He cocked his head to look at their twined hands. "Interesting."

"Fucking right it is. I mean, what do those poor damned dim WASPs know from mythic nuttiness like this?" She ran her free hand loosely through her hair. "Look, the point is, Wald, I figure all I really got out of that wonderfully kinky Catholic total immersion they did on me as a nice unsuspecting little kid was that—gift. For recognizing the power of that kind of magic, whatever. So, at least they left me with a real good ear for mumbo-jumbo. Which happens to be exactly what this case is all about."

He was grinning again, dancing his fingertips slowly on the back of her hand to the rich sounds of Roberta Flack coming from the KLH. "See, Gavin? I knew there must be some reason I went for you besides your terrific legs."

She swung her right leg up through the opening of the purple robe, stretched it into the glowing orangish living room light. "Well, sure. I would hope." Moved it, angled it in the warm glow. "But the legs aren't bad, Wald. I have to admit."

He waited, squeezing her hand.

She could feel something like a big clock spring loosening in her chest as she slowly turned toward him. Slid toward him in that silken robe, locking her right foot to the back of his calf, sliding her left hand into the crack of his arm. Moving her mouth, very slowly, very alively, up to his.

As she flexed her body against his with that long kiss . . . touch . . . connection, he pulled her like one half of an X across him. The response that volted through her was so strong it mimicked an orgasm. She stirred, shook her head. "Oh boy."

He gripped her hand, sharply. "Oh, yes. Oh boy, Gavin."

She rested there for some moments, panting, collecting herself. Then: "Boyo." She pushed herself up off his body. Stood up and pulled the robe tightly around her. "Mmmph. Yeah."

She took their glasses into the kitchen for a refill. Was still pouring, recapping, when he came into the light of that small room wearing only his loose blue shorts, his penis already thrusting through the fly.

He came up behind her, pushed his lean body against hers, murmured into her ear, "Definitely not just the legs."

She turned slowly to face him with small cries of resistance. Then she was pressed to his body, pressed through the open front of the silk robe to those sharp, hungry bones, that sharp, hungry penis.

He moved her against the tiled back wall of her small kitchen. She bent her hips forward, opened her legs and took his penis gently between her thighs. Danced it softly, strongly between the silk skin of her thighs. And came for the first time.

"Mmm*mmph.*" She shook herself loose from his embrace, pushed him away. Moved to the counter where their drinks were already poured.

But he kept the connection volted, through one sharp fingernail moving on her back, moving through the padded silk robe.

She put her hands on the counter and pushed against them, arching her back in a dance with his finger. Moaned, "Jesus, Wald. What *else* was it you had in mind for tonight?"

The nail dug; the knuckles danced on her spinebones. "Italian food," he said very flatly, very deliberately. "To go with the lilac season. A pearl of a restaurant under stairs that I bet not even you know about, Gavin."

"Ah, very nice." She dropped her head over the counter, pushing her spinebones forcefully into his knuckled fist. "Magic food, I devoutly hope you are saying. Now, what particular magic food did you have in mind for me?"

"Scungilli," he said strongly. "The best scungilli you could find for a thousand miles."

"Ah, so. Octopus, is that?"

"The best."

"That's it. Just—boiled tentacles?"

"Also fettucini. The best in, say, thirteen hundred miles."

"I'll have *that*, then, please, Wald. If you don't mind."

"Not one bit."

"Because I don't . . . really"—rocking in his arms now, their foreheads against each other, swaying in his loose hold —"believe in octopi, Wald."

He laughed from deep in his chest. Said happily, unmistakably happily, "Is it you, Gavin? Or is it us?"

She shook her head, pressing it roughly against his forehead. "It's *us,* dummy. Jesus, don't you even know that? In some weird way I don't want to think about right now it's— obviously us."

"Okay, then." He moved his body away from hers, picked up his glass from the counter as he shoved his right fingers into the hair at the back of her neck. Moving her very slowly ahead of him, toward the living room, he said as they walked, "Do you *know* how great this is gonna be, Gavin?"

She did not want to answer him. Only moved, murmuring, turning her neck slowly against his hand.

When they reached the living room he said, "Take the robe off, Gavin."

"Oh, yes. Oh, about time."

He slipped the robe off her shoulders, then flipped it out over the oriental carpet. Said as it settled lightly on the rug, "Lie down."

"What?"

"Lie down on your gorgeous tummy."

Laughing, she did as she was ordered. And then his strong feet were moving over her body in a hard massage. "Ahhhhh, God." Slowly, so slowly, as she melted to that hard, knowing touch: "Damn you, Wald. Damn your . . . oriental magic fingers."

"Shiatsu, thank you, ma'am. A little souvenir of Occupied Japan."

"Annhh, God. Those clever little Japs."

He kept pressing surely, knowingly, into her. Sometimes fingers, hands. Sometimes feet. Or toes. When she knew for sure she was too loose to move he ordered her to turn over.

And she did it, floating in hot, light, salty water.

He lay beside her on the robe, his body held away from hers, touching his blunt fingers to her face.

Soft, so soft. Those featherings of touch.

From her ear to her cheek.

Cheek to her neck. Adam's apple. Across her collarbone. Tracing so slowly, so softly, those blunt fingers. When they reached her nipple she came again.

She could feel the swelling of her flexed body, the expansion in the warm light. As if she was—bursting to the light. Bursting from those breasts, so tight and full, full of the feeling.

Ah, God, *how she wanted to fuck this man.*

She turned her face toward him and spread her arms, spread her legs. God, how strange, those panties still on her. She rubbed the back of her hand softly across the prickly hairs of his chest. "Come on, please. Please, Wald. *Fuck me.*"

"Not yet." His toes moved over the sculpturing of her ankle. Bones connecting through skin.

She moaned, "Aannnnhhhh, no fair. I want you inside me. I want to *fuck* you."

"Later." The toes still moving, still connecting. "Later, Gavin."

"Anh, no fair." She rolled her head on the purple robe. "Sexist no fair."

"Sure it's fair." He rolled his body up near against hers, reached with both hands for her head. Held it as he murmured tensely, "Sure it's okay. Because it feels like that for me too, Gavin. I'm coming *with* you, you know, I'm in there with you all the way."

Faintly: "Oh God. That's nice to hear, Wald."

"Not nice. True. Because—don't you *know?*—if we were really fucking it couldn't feel any better than this, Gavin."

She turned her head away from him and smiled dizzily, out of focus, at the living room wall. "Oh God, I feel like—scungilli."

He was laughing a little, quietly, as his fingers moved from her face, lightly, to her ribs. From her ribs to between her legs. "Annhh, no, not again. Such a goddam controlling bastard you are. I want you *inside,* I want you *in* me, Wald."

"You think that's what I'm doing, Gavin? Controlling?"

"Annhhh, sure it is. Come on, come *inside* me, bastard."

Moving very quickly, strongly, he flexed his body flat against hers on the purple robe, rolled their hips together, his face over hers. She murmured into his ear, "Whether you know it or not. Sure, that's what you're doing. Come on, Wald, come on, dear man, come *in* me."

"Maybe that's right, Gavin. Because I think I've been wondering since I met you—who's in charge here?"

She lifted her yielding hands to stroke his sharp-hollowed cheeks. "Jesus, you must know—you. Right now it's you." Moaned as she slipped her arms over his shoulders, rolling him back into the music, "Oh God, come in me, *come inside me.*"

His body still resisting—bony, strong. "Okay. Pretty soon. Pretty soon I'm gonna fuck you, Gavin. For a good, long, sweet time. And it's gonna be like nothing we ever did before. You know that, Gavin, don't you?"

Annnnhh, God.

So many years, so many struggles it had taken her to get to this place. To this place where she could cup one soft hand over the sharp cheek of this good, knowing man and say very softly, "Oh, yeah, Wald. Yeah. I do know."

．　．　．

From her bed she was watching the moon make parallelograms of pale luminescence on her walls.

She wanted to be fresh, alert, tomorrow, so she could work at her best. But it was hard to get very tired in this little room where the hours, the days, were measured mainly by sunlight and meal trays.

She had thought she would sleep well after that pleasant, unexpected visit from Dr. Talbott. Especially when she heard out what he had clearly come there to tell her—that he *understood.* Because now she knew that at least *he* would understand. That good, kind doctor of hers.

Except—there was something she remembered from his pale eyes that made her feel cold. Abandoned, almost cold.

Now the old tape starting again in her head. She hadn't wanted—but it was in there, running again.

She waited it out tensely. Hoping that the weird moonlight would make a difference, make it come out differently. But it stopped where it always had before, in that same place.

The tub.

The clots. The muddled thoughts of—mops.

She twisted her head to look at the luminous dial of the windup clock on the bedside table: *1:15. Already 1:15!*

She rolled firmly away from the moon-pouring windows, pulling the sheet up around her face. *Enough. Enough, Lord Jesus. Now let me sleep.*

She tried very hard to let go of the tightness, of the wary liveness she could feel still all over her body. Since that doctor had come by, so unexpectedly, with his strange confession.

But even as she tried, she could feel the tape beginning to roll again in her head.

375

Twenty-eight

After a Sunday breakfast of bagels, lox and ome-
lets—just about the only family tradition Mark Abrams still
managed to make time for in his life—he went to his small
study off the TV room, pulled the Angela Flynn file from his
briefcase and began to outline on a yellow pad the case that
would be presented to the May grand jury.

The approach he had already decided on was to pull
every available witness into the grand jury hearing—cops,
nuns, doctors. Even the hospital chaplain. Especially—if she
would only agree to testify—Sister Angela herself.

Abrams was enough of a political realist to recognize
that his own best shot at salvaging a political future from this
quagmire of a case was to avoid the open prosecution of a
trial. For her sake, for his. For the other nuns—for the whole
town, everyone involved in this tragic, idiotic case.

And now they could end it quickly, cleanly, with a no bill
from the May grand jury. That might prompt a brief stir in
the press, a few angry charges of cover-up. Some accusations
that the D.A.'s office might not have prosecuted this case as
vigorously as it might have. Abrams figured he could live
those down easily enough.

Especially if they gave it the full shot. Laid out every
shred of evidence they had, for the twenty-three odd-lot
citizens serving on the May grand jury.

Abrams was being very careful not to let anyone on his
own staff know how anxious he was to have the case termi-
nate here. How *hungry* he was to get that no bill. He did not
want his private emotions, private hopes, to have any bearing on the diligent presentation other men would be making
of this case.

But in fact, he fiercely hoped the Jewish D.A. would
never have to prosecute this damned Catholic mess.

At 11:40 he called Ben Haverty at home. "Apologies for the intrusion, Ben. I'm doing a little workup on the nun case, and thought you might be burning a little weekend oil yourself."

Haverty grunted. In fact his Angela Flynn file was already spread out over the dining room table.

"Ben, I guess you know that the grand jury hearings on the case are set to open on May fifteenth. We'll be presenting the state's side of it, of course. But I'd like it clearly understood that any witnesses, technical or otherwise, that your side might want to present would be welcomed."

Haverty grunted again. "So understood, Mark."

"That includes, of course, the nun herself." Abrams was rubbing one hand nervously over the back of his head. "Just between us, Ben, I'd like to make the observation that this case is particularly—ah, delicate. I'd like to say that I personally believe a statement from her, an appearance by her, might be particularly helpful. Both from her own viewpoint, in—um, experiencing something approximating a trial process, and from the viewpoint of the grand jury. So they can get some picture of the—ah, broad scope of the case."

"Appreciate your concern, Mark. We're considering all options, and we'll keep your office informed."

When Haverty hung up the phone he had one new piece of information to add to the convoluted structure forming inside his head. So Mark Abrams wasn't hot to prosecute, after all.

Interesting, thought Ben Haverty.

At noon on Monday Roy Danziger was sitting in a sparsely furnished office in downtown Milwaukee. The girl social worker sitting on the other side of the desk said, "You understand, Mr. Danziger, this is only a screening interview, to help us decide on which form of therapy might be most helpful to you."

"Well, yeah. I just wanted to talk to somebody."

She ran through his biographical data, jotting it down on some sheet in front of her. Like that polygraph cop had done. Then she said, "All right, Mr. Danziger. Could you just tell me in your own words why you came to see us?"

"Well, I got a lot of problems. I figured I could use some help with them."

"I see." She was sort of a fat girl, very serious. Fiddled a lot with her glasses. "Would you like to tell me about those problems?"

"Well, I haven't been feeling so good lately. I been— kind of depressed. Then just lately I found out some girl had my baby, and the baby died. That was—kind of rough. I figured I needed some help with that one."

Heavy nod. "How old was the baby?"

"Oh, just born. It died when it was born."

"Were you living with this girl?"

"No, no. It was just somebody I knew. Earlier. I didn't even know she was pregnant. Until I heard about—that the baby died."

"I see. Then you had no sustained relationship with this woman?"

"Nah. She was just somebody I met last summer. Somebody I liked, but—she lives someplace else. So I didn't see her after the summer."

Fiddling with the glasses: "Mr. Danziger, what gave you the idea that the child was yours?"

Roy hesitated. All that stuff about the cops, about that fucking nightmare in the Midwest office—he didn't want to get into that now, with a fucking bitch like this. So he said simply, "Well, somebody told me. Somebody that knew for sure."

"*Somebody?* The woman didn't tell you herself?"

He shook his head. "Nah. I haven't—like, seen her since last summer."

"I see. Did you try to get in touch with her?"

"Well, I wanted to. Especially after I heard what happened. But I don't know where she is."

"I see." When she nodded, her chin sort of wobbled. "And did *she* know where to contact you?"

"I guess. I gave her my mother's address, told her I'd like to hear from her anytime."

"Well then, if she didn't contact you herself, I think we'd have to assume she didn't *want* to."

Roy couldn't argue that, exactly. He didn't like to think about it a whole lot anyway—why she hadn't let him know.

What he really wanted to talk about with this bitch was the baby. He wanted to figure out how he—felt about it. He knew he *wished* it was still alive, but—well, he knew that much for sure, it wasn't. So he guessed what he wanted now was somebody to help him figure out how to accept the fact, the *way* that it was dead.

But the bitch didn't seem interested in talking any more about that. Now she was getting into relationships—"ties," she called them. Asking how he felt about his parents, his older sister, his girl friends. She seemed real interested in the girl he'd lived with last year, and how he felt about her walking out on him. Then she asked about his "moods," and how he felt about his job.

It felt like he was just starting to get into it when she flicked a look at her watch. "I'm sorry to say, Mr. Danziger, our time is up."

"That's okay. I just— Look, I went to see some psychiatrist earlier this year, when I was feeling down. But he didn't seem to help much, so I quit going. But now I—I figure I'd like to try again."

The girl hunched forward, important-like, across the desk. "Mr. Danziger, you understand that this has been a very brief preliminary interview, to give us some idea of the area of your problems. Of course we'll get a much more clear picture in your subsequent therapy sessions. But just on the basis of what we've covered so far, I would definitely urge

379

that you *do* continue in therapy. I think you might find it very helpful."

She was tapping the sheet of paper where she'd been writing stuff down as he talked. "And I think the important area we might concentrate on first is this anxiety you feel about your inability to sustain permanent relationships."

Ben Haverty had mixed feelings about whether or not his client should elect to testify to the grand jury. His assistant, Vince Andretti, was for it without reservation: "Hell, Ben, it's a natural. I can't believe any grand jury would look this girl in the face and vote to indict. I just can't *believe* it, Ben."

Haverty wasn't so sure about that. Wasn't sure how Angela might react to that bizarre, unfamiliar experience. But his own reservations quickly became irrelevant when he went to the hospital to tell her the hearings had been scheduled, and pass along the D.A.'s offer to have her testify.

She said immediately, "Of course. I want to do that, Mr. Haverty."

He nodded, tugging at the knee of his baggy trousers. "Well now, Angela, I can understand your feelings in that regard. And I must say that my legal assistant, Mr. Andretti, feels there might be considerable advantage to the idea of your testifying. But there are also some—disadvantages that we must consider carefully, Angela."

She was frowning, genuinely puzzled. "But I'm *not guilty*, Mr. Haverty. I have nothing to hide."

"Of course. But I think you should understand, Angela, that once you agree to testify you will be required to answer any and all questions they might put to you. Unfortunately, due to the present structure of the grand jury system, your attorneys cannot be present during this testimony. I'm afraid you'd be on your own in there, Angela."

She stilled herself, and tried for a moment to imagine what that would be like—alone in some strange room, answering those strange questions. Little fingers of fear began to move in her chest. But she repeated firmly, "That's all right, Mr. Haverty. I have nothing to hide."

Small, sharp nods. "Naturally. I understand that, Angela. But you should understand there are areas they might get into—personal areas. Questions about yourself, your private life." She had a way of looking intently at Haverty whenever he talked to her. He usually looked back at her, feeling the power of those green eyes. But now he found himself up on his feet, pacing, looking at the faded striped curtains on the hospital room windows as he said, "Angela, they will almost certainly inquire into the circumstances of this conception."

"I understand, Mr. Haverty." Cold. Cold feeling in her body. "Of course I—don't like that. That idea. Of people—prying into things like that." She paused. "But I am *not guilty,* and I must make those people understand that. So if that is what I must do to—yes, Mr. Haverty, I *want* to testify."

So Ben Haverty surrendered, yielded his doubts. And spent the rest of his visit rehearsing her for the crucifying experience she was electing to undergo.

On Tuesday afternoon Lieutenant Tim Vance took two suspected car boosters down to the Ramsey County Sheriff's Office to undergo a polygraph examination, an operation which he knew from irritated experience would translate into at least three hours of red tape. After he delivered over the suspects Vance sat down by the coffee machine and slipped a *North Dallas Forty* paperback from his trench-coat pocket.

A half hour later the polygraph guy, Peter Juhl, came by to pour himself a coffee. "Hey, Tim," Juhl said. "I understand you're one of the guys who had the daddy of the nun's baby." Noncommittal gesture from Vance. "Interesting guy, isn't he?"

Vance glanced up, startled. "What, you saw him?"

"Sure. I had him on the machine last Thursday."

Vance felt suddenly snapped awake. "Oh, yeah? I hadn't heard that. So how'd it come out?"

Juhl shrugged, sipped from his polyurethane cup. "Poor fucking schmuck. He never knew what hit him."

"Well, that figures. I mean the guy comes into work one day and the next thing he knows there's a roomful of cops coming down on him about the homicide of his baby. A baby he didn't know anything about. That's got to be kind of rough to take."

"No, I mean what hit him back on the beach."

"Come again?"

"When that horny little lady took that poor fucker by the hand and led him down the beach."

From the blank expression on Vance's face Juhl could tell the guy didn't know what the hell he was talking about. Briefly, with a small, private satisfaction, Juhl ran out a recap of the sexual events at Menominee as Danziger recalled them now—of his hapless, unexpected, even reluctant seduction by the nun.

"Well, I'll be damned," Vance said blankly. "The way he talked about girls in that interrogation room, bragging and blowing, I had him figured for a real macho. A biker-type macho."

"Yeah, well. When I get 'em alone, on the machine, I usually get a better fix on 'em." Juhl shrugged. "What the hell, it's basically the same old story—she was fucking Dad-dy-O."

The shock of *that* one went right to Vance's feet. "Hunh? How you figure that, Pete?"

"Ah, that was an easy shot. Nine out of ten screwed-up girls, that's what you've got operating there. You ever hear how Charlie Manson got all those whacked-out little girls so stuck on him?" Vance shook his head. "He got 'em talking about their fathers, all the fighting they did with their fathers. Then when they got to the ceremonial initiation fuck he told 'em, 'Close your eyes and pretend I'm Daddy.' "

Vance felt a resistance even as he laughed aloud. "Hey, come on, Pete. Where do you fit Charlie Manson with Angela Flynn?"

"Okay, nowhere, probably. *Gayle* Flynn, the biker called her, by the way. But I gather from what Nick Scotti said that Flynn's father was kind of a passive loser-type like this Danziger."

Slowly: "Well, maybe. Yeah, that's possible, maybe."

Juhl shrugged again. "Okay, then, there's your basic setup. Look, they're probably both nice enough guys—in fact I liked Danziger pretty well, felt damn sorry for the poor schmuck. But basically both guys seem to be the same personality type. Sweet, passive losers. And if you want my two bits on this, for what they're worth, I think that's just what the lady was after."

Vance was slapping the *North Dallas Forty* paperback thoughtfully on his lap. "Boy, Pete. That's pretty heavy shrink stuff you're getting into there."

"Nah. Not so much." Juhl aimed his empty cup at a trash basket, lobbed it in. "The main thing I'm saying is, I think that little lady had something pretty definite on her mind. And she had it there way before she led that poor sucker Danziger down the sand."

On Wednesday evening the phone rang in the kitchen of the Tucker home in Oak Creek just as Gary was getting himself a cold beer. He slapped the fridge door closed and picked up the phone.

"Yeah, hello." He tucked the receiver into his shoulder, popped the top off the beer.

A faint, girlish voice: "Gary, is that you?"

"Yeah. Is this—Gayle?"

She started almost immediately to cry. "Oh, Gary, I'm so sorry for all the trouble I've got you into. I'm so sorry they had to get you involved in this thing. You've been such a good friend to me and I—"

"Hey, Gayle, that's okay. Look, please don't cry."

"Are you okay?"

"Sure, sure, of course I'm okay. What about *you*? I'm awful worried about you."

"Oh, I'm much better." But she didn't sound better— her voice was weak, wavering, blotted with sobs.

"Well, look, that's the important thing, that you get better. Are they taking good care of you?"

"Yes. I'm still in the hospital, but I think I'll be getting out soon."

"I tried to come see you, but they wouldn't let you have any visitors. Maybe I could come up when you're out of the hospital, if you want."

"You don't have to do that. I just wanted to tell you— I'm so sorry for everything I did to you." More tears, more choked sounds.

"Hey, hey. Please don't cry. I'm fine, really—it wasn't anything. I just wish I could help you out—at least get you to stop crying."

She made a sound halfway between a laugh and a sob. "I'll be fine. Don't worry about me."

"Okay, then, I won't. On one condition—that you stop worrying about *me.*"

When Dr. Heilbron came by for his regular visit on Thursday he started off, as usual, by asking if she had any new recollections. She finally had one to offer, with a small, shy smile: "Well, yes, I did. A little one, anyway." And told him about that list of obstetricians she'd written out last February, to have handy when her time came. How she'd carried that list everywhere with her, in her purse.

"Well, very good, Sister." Dr. Heilbron looked—disappointed. "That's very good."

"Well, what I mean is—you see, I *was* making plans for

—him. I knew when the time came it might be hard to think straight, to know just what to do. So I kept that list with me, so I'd know just who to call." She looked up at him anxiously, under fluttering eyelashes. "Dr. Heilbron, doesn't that *show* that I—never meant to harm him?"

"Of course, Sister, I understand that." He paused. "What were you planning, exactly, to do with that list?"

"Well, I thought when my labor started, I could—call a doctor, and ask someone to drive me to a hospital. Or take a taxi. When I knew I needed to, that's what I was planning to do."

"Mmm, yes." His voice flat, offering no congratulations. "Well, very good, Sister."

They spent most of the rest of the session talking about religious celibacy, and whether or not Angela found it difficult to live that kind of life. She told him no, not particularly. It wasn't *sex,* anyway, that nuns missed—it was more other things, like not having a family of your own.

She tried to explain to him about the special grace that helped people in the religious life to live without things like that. Irritatedly: "Maybe you think that's just *fiction,* Dr. Heilbron. Religious fiction."

"No, no. I wouldn't say that, Sister. But of course sex *is* an integral part of our human makeup. It's a part of all our lives, in one way or another."

She was angrily shaking her head. "No, it's not, not in —that way, that you mean it. It's very different for people who are committed to the religious life. And it's not so *unnatural,* you know. It isn't as if you have to decide *every day* that's the way you want to live. You just *do* live like that because there's something much more important you want to do. All this *fuss* people make about sex these days—in the movies, on television, everywhere. They act like it's the most important thing in life. But I don't believe that it is."

When Dr. Heilbron was leaving he said he had to go out of town, so he would not see her again until next week. She nodded, glad to see him go. This doctor who never quite understood.

A few hours later she was sitting in the chair by the window, hugging her arms against her body, replaying her tapes.

This time she was remembering mostly the sounds—the children's voices in the school yard, the kitchen door banging shut behind Margory. Car noises in the street. Heat pipes banging in the empty convent.

Water running in the tub. Splashing sounds as she stepped into the water.

Trying to wash away the blood. Realizing she couldn't, because she was sitting in a pool of it. A ragged whimpering sound coming from somewhere. The pain, so bad now, suddenly changing, harder, sharper. Then—

Pain changed. *Deep,* deep in her hips. Making her push, *push.*

Like a bright sun bursting from behind a large, dark cloud, she suddenly remembered. She got up from the chair and walked around her hospital room, nodding excitedly, her hands pressed against her chest.

In the tub. Realizing that the baby was going to be born. Climbing out of the tub, shaking, whimpering. Shaking, so cold.

Kneeling on the pink bath mat, shuddering, gripping the side of the tub, pushing against it, the pain like a hot sword slicing her alive, and—

In a sudden silence the baby coming out of her body onto the pink mat. Moving, arms and legs moving. Red, wet baby on the pink mat.

She so faint, so cold.

Baby wet, red. Unfolding from the wetness, lurching, moving.

Danger.

Feeling of danger, terrible danger. To her and the baby.

Picking up the baby, in the pink mat. Moving down the

hall, walls lurching. Carrying the whole mat in her arms. Holding it close against her body to keep it safe.

Carrying it off the hall carpet into her room. And—

Nothing. Dark space. Nothing.

She must have fainted as she came across that threshold. And—the baby, that she was carrying. She must have dropped her baby when she fainted.

The rest so ragged still. So faint in her head.

Mostly she remembered waking up so many times on the bloody floor. Calling once for help from the nun who came into the house.

Thinking of cleaning up. Mops. Phones. Blood. Pails.

Weak now. So weak now.

Still fainting, pitching in and out of that blackness. Praying, whimpering for someone to help.

But—no baby.

Gone. That baby, her baby gone.

Only clots, towels, blood. No more baby.

The new tape was halting, indistinct. Mostly—Julia. And those men in white who carried her out.

No baby.

But he *was* there, had been there, her own baby. She remembered him now. Not his—face.

But himself. Red. Small. Waving his arms and legs.

Oh, finally she *had* remembered him. Her real, live baby, that she had brought back from that dark, tormented space.

In the five days until Dr. Heilbron's next visit, she played the new tape over and over in her head.

Finally she had something to tell those uncomprehending doctors who kept asking. So now, maybe, they would let her go home from this place.

Twenty-nine

Mark Abrams had assigned Andrew DaSilva to stick with the case through the presentation to the grand jury. DaSilva's preparation was almost complete on Saturday afternoon, two days before the hearing opened, when he took a brief break from his bedroom desk to play a little one-on-one basketball in his driveway and broke his right arm in three places.

Abrams went to the hospital as soon as the doctors would permit a visit, which was Sunday morning. He brought along Max Bloom, another young A.D.A. attached to his office. DaSilva, still groggy from the anesthetic and painkillers, was lying in the bed with his arm spread out on a pillow in a clumsy plastered butterfly arrangement.

"Jesus, Andy, you don't fool around," said Abrams. "How are you feeling?"

"I'm okay. Listen, Mark, I'm sorry as hell about this. I still don't know what happened. Freddy and I were just playing a little ball, and all of a sudden—"

Abrams held up his hand. "Hey, Andy. It could happen to anybody. No apologies in order."

"Yeah, but the timing." DaSilva scratched at his shoulder above the cast. "Can you postpone the grand jury? Because I should be out of here soon, and I've got the case pretty well together."

"I think what we'll do is let Max run with it," said Abrams. "He's kept up on it pretty well. I think Max can take it over without much trouble."

"Hey, I appreciate you giving me this shot at the limelight, Andy," Bloom interjected.

DaSilva wanted to know what he could do to help and Abrams said nothing; Marian had already given them his notes, and they could take it from there. "You just take it easy and take care of that broken wing, Andy."

DaSilva was still apologizing when Abrams got up to go. ". . . sorry as hell about this, Mark. Falling in my own driveway—it's the damnedest thing."

"Ah, well," Abrams said dryly, "that fits right in with the damnedest case."

He and Bloom drove directly from the hospital to Abrams's office, where they ran through a final map-out of the grand jury presentation—the extensive witness list, order of appearance, issuance of subpoenas, and so forth. When Bloom asked if they were going to subpoena the baby's father Abrams said, "I don't see any need for that, Max. We'll save that shot for the trial, if it comes down to that."

"But if she testifies herself, we may need him to rebut her story. What if she runs out a defense like rape, something like that?"

Then with any luck at all we'll get a no bill out of that damned grand jury, Abrams was thinking grimly. But he kept his face flat, impassive as he said, "We don't rebut her, Max. Not this time around."

Dr. Heilbron had taken off a long weekend to bring his mother back from Florida for the summer. He was not back at work again until Tuesday, May sixteenth, which also happened to be the day Sister Angela was scheduled to be discharged from the hospital. So Heilbron made a point of dropping by to see her briefly on that first busy morning back at work.

When he walked into her room she was beaming at him, like a child guarding a surprise. She waited impatiently through his usual questions about how she was feeling till he got to the one about any new recollections. Then she leaned forward in her chair, her hands clenched on her lap.

"Oh, Dr. Heilbron, I remembered the baby being born.

While you were gone over the weekend. I remembered being in the bathtub and realizing it was happening, so I stepped out of the tub and kneeled down on the mat and I —delivered him. Except I didn't know then it was a him."

The nun was talking excitedly, animatedly. Heilbron listened with the same excitement, his head nodding rapidly up and down.

She told him about seeing it move, waving its arms and legs on the mat, and realizing she—they—were in danger because she felt so weak and picking up the baby in the mat and carrying him down the hall, holding it close against her body to protect him, and then falling down into blackness as she came into her room.

She paused; the spark went out of her face. "And then?" Heilbron prompted.

"I—fainted, I guess. Then I don't remember any more. Except what I remembered before about all the blood and that bothering me so, to be lying in all that blood. But I don't —remember the baby being there then. I don't remember— seeing him again. Or even knowing that—he was there, somewhere."

"Well now, that's very good, Sister." Heilbron leaned forward and patted her clasped hands. "That's really very good. That's a big step forward you just made."

"But don't remember—harming him. I can't remember anything about that. And something else that bothers me— I don't remember hearing him cry. He *must* have, but I—I remember—wondering about that—*why didn't he cry?*"

"Never mind. That's very good, what you've already done, Sister. That's a very big stride forward for us."

Angela suddenly felt exhausted, tired to her very bones. She said faintly, "Dr. Heilbron, can I still go home today?"

"I don't see why not. I think your recovery has been excellent, Sister, and in my judgment you are ready now to take on your normal life again. I think you're quite prepared for that."

She nodded. It seemed too much effort to speak.

"Of course, as I've already explained, I'll continue to see you on a regular basis, Sister. I'll be there to render support in all the stages of your recovery ahead of us. We will be making that journey together, Sister."

Small, exhausted voice: "Thank you."

"And I want you to feel free to call me at any time you like, anytime you feel the need to, Sister. I'll give you my private unlisted telephone numbers so you can get in contact with me anytime you feel the need."

He said that last as if he was giving her something special, something valuable. So she repeated obediently, "Thank you. I appreciate very much everything you've done for me, Dr. Heilbron."

Except that she never went home at all.

She didn't accept that, *never.* She could not understand why they would not let her go back where she belonged, back to the St. Rose convent, even after Sister Philomena had explained it very firmly, very carefully to her: "Our judgment is that it would be better for all concerned, Angela, if you went now to a more secluded, private environment, where you will not be troubled with—unfortunate attention. From people like reporters, or prying strangers. We are all very anxious to avoid that, of course, Angela."

"Of course. But I wouldn't talk to them anyway, Sister Philomena. Of course I wouldn't talk to them."

Firm nod. "Naturally, Angela. But we would still like to avoid putting you in that situation. And you'll be kept very busy at Our Lady of Pompeii Convent. We have quite a list of projects we'd like you to do for us. But you will be able to work on them alone, in privacy. Away from any unwarranted intrusions."

"But my job at Benedictine Kindergarten—now that I'm well again, I want to get back to my job, to my teaching."

The headshake very brisk, very definite. "Now, Angela,

you must understand that until this legal situation is resolved it would not serve the best interests of anyone involved, yourself included, to have you put in such an exposed public position. I'm sure you can understand that very well. And I think you'll find the sisters at Our Lady of Pompeii to be quite a remarkable religious community. I think you will grow spiritually from the experience of joining that community, Angela."

So. They were going to hide her away again, then. Like they did here, on Ward Five.

She barely knew the two nuns who came to take her from Ward Five that afternoon, Sister Francesca Sutton and Sister Ruth Trzaska. Ruth carried her suitcase as they walked out through the locked iron door, into the elevator, out through those awful depressing halls past those old men in wheelchairs still, out through the gothic lobby with the stained glass windows into a warm spring day, with the lilac tree by the door still in bloom.

The car they walked to was not the St. Rose Ford Angela usually rode in, but a strange green Toyota. Francesca opened the passenger door for Angela, then got behind the wheel herself. Ruth and the suitcase went into the backseat. "We're all very happy that you're coming to be with us, Angela," Francesca said as she started up the engine.

"Thank you. That's very nice," said Angela.

"I hope you like movies," Francesca said cheerfully, "because I'm a regular freak for them myself, and I love the idea of having somebody to go with me."

"Yes, I like movies."

"Thank goodness. We're going to get along fine," said Francesca.

So instead of the green-lined green streets and pretty white houses that made up the world outside the St. Rose convent, she was driven to an inner-city section of downtown St. Paul that looked like a World War II bombsite. In the midst of a wasteland of razed blocks, flattened rubble and bricks, a few new public housing projects towered. And dwarfed in the shadow of those concrete towers, huddled like lonely, tenacious anachronisms, she saw Our Lady of Pompeii's church, rectory and convent.

The paint on the yellow stucco church was peeling, flaked away in cancerous patches. The wood siding of the small convent next door was sealed under cheap gray asphalt siding.

Like a relic from a time left behind, she thought as the green Toyota pulled into the convent driveway. *A rotting relic from a forgotten time.*

And this was where they had sent her to heal. To heal and remember.

Sister Julia decided she should be the one who packed Angela's belongings into the trunk and the cardboard cartons—only three, as it turned out. Julia did not want any of the other St. Rose sisters to have to share that stressful, unpleasant task.

It took her several nights to finish the sorting, laundering and packing. She tried to do that unfamiliar job without invading the boundaries of Angela's privacy. But there were still times when she felt she was poking into a locked closet, sorting, judging pieces of Angela's life that under normal circumstances she had no right to see.

In a private session of spiritual counseling, Sister Philomena had urged Julia to be kind to herself, to give herself time, not to judge her own lapses of responsibility too quickly. She was doing that anyway, of course—accepting, *embracing* the blame that was due her, suffering the full, searing weight of her remorse and guilt.

Why she hadn't come to check on Angela that noon as she'd promised—*that* Julia understood and accepted the full responsibility for. It was because she'd been luxuriating in the private indulgence of obsessive concern for *herself.* That Julia understood only too well.

What she still had much more trouble with was why she

hadn't seen that pregnancy, right there before her eyes—so many other sisters so concerned about it and consulting her about it. So many of them that Julia had finally taken the matter up with Angela's superior at the school, Mary Christopher. And then relayed back to Claudine that report that Mary Christopher had given her: *that they could do no more.*

But still Julia had not seen, not *recognized* that pregnancy. Right before her own eyes, so obvious every day. That thing so alien, so unconceived of in their kind of religious life. That thing she *never would have expected* to see, ever, that thing that was simply no part of her thoughts—

Now should she—*why should she*—feel guilty for *that?*

Truly, Julia found it very difficult to believe she should. Not for *that, that* part of it.

But part of the turmoil she was still experiencing came from the small voice in her own mind that kept insisting, *Oh yes, yes, Julia, you should have.*

It was easier to think this through when she was here at the convent, here in this environment where her own comprehensions of this question would be understood by the other nuns. Perceived as—true, and within their shared commitment, reasonable and correct.

But *those men* would never understand it. Those men who interrogated her, sat her down in those chairs and attacked her with those cruel, pointed questions.

She had seen it there on all their faces, those men, their —disbelief. Their conviction that she *could not,* truly, have *not* seen it, that baby right in front of her so obviously every day.

And she remembered very well those other thoughts so clear in their faces, those assaultive personal thoughts—*a young girl as pretty as you are, Sister Julia—why are you hiding yourself away in a place like this? A pretty girl like you, Sister Julia?*

Oh, Julia knew what they meant by those thoughts written on their faces so clearly, on all those strange men's faces. Something about *sex.*

And that was what she found it so difficult to forgive

Angela for. Exposing them all like she did, so rawly, so openly, to the contemptuous uncomprehension of those polite, hard men. Forcing them to make that uncomprehended defense of their own chosen way of life to those men who saw them all—oh, Julia read it very well on their faces—as *freaks.* Virginal paper dolls, puppets. Some kind of idiotic, less-than-female *freaks.*

As if a life of religious commitment, of service, was nothing better than some neurotic, frightened retreat from the real world. *Their* real world.

God help her, but Julia still felt very angry with Angela for doing that to them—to all of them, all her sisters. She tried to temper her anger by reminding herself of the terrible pain Angela must have gone through, the terrible, lonely agony she must have endured—that crucifixion, almost, it must have been for her.

But still the anger was there, even as Julia felt the ragged edges of her own commitment healing, becoming more strong from this bitter trial, more *sure.*

She guessed maybe that was what she was looking for, in the back of her still troubled mind, as she sorted and packed up the scattered pieces of Angela's life: some way to *help her forgive Angela for doing that to them.*

Some of Angela's things were still missing, of course. Taken by those policemen. The purse, and all that.

The rest left so untidily behind that closed door—papers tossed all around her desk, clothes hurled about in her drawers. Like a last reminder of that—invasion.

Julia realized as she worked that she was hoping to find something in all this jumble that would help her to—understand. Because even now this whole thing was still so inexplicable. Not how that pregnancy might have happened—Julia simply did not let herself think about *that,* and she refused to listen to the rumors, speculations, that Margory was still spreading around the convent. That part was simply *no business* of Julia's.

No, what she was looking for here was some clue to

how Angela could have led such a deceptive, contradictory life. *Pretending* that everything was fine, everything was normal. Pretending to be a good, dedicated nun. When all the while . . .

Yet the accumulated remnants of her life all seemed so —ordinary. Family letters, and birthday cards drawn by nieces and nephews. Rosaries, missals, books of spiritual exercises. Simple, serviceable clothes—not very many of them. Family photographs, scrapbooks, clippings of her brothers' wedding announcements.

Then Julia found, facedown in the bottom bureau drawer, a framed, hand-scripted copy of the vows Angela had written for her final profession: *I will live simply in poorness of being to be more free to respond to the needs You show me, Lord God. I will live celibately, choosing this way to be a loving member of the community of my sisters and of Your Church.* And at the bottom of the page: *I will live my life depending on You, because without Your voice and Your strength, I cannot answer You in men.*

For a moment she was genuinely moved. But that brief emotion was followed by her realization that if Angela had kept those vows hung in a more visible place, if she had read them more often and *kept* to those promises, then all this agony . . .

Julia shook off that thought with a brisk, shuddering motion, and laid the glass frame facedown in the opened trunk.

The appointment at Dr. Salter's office was quite early, at 9:15 A.M. Sister Francesca drove her over for it in the green Toyota, chatting very easily, very glibly, as she drove. Angela was grateful for that, since she could murmur easy answers back at Francesca as she seized, *drank in,* what she saw outside the car.

Ordinary streets. Shops, cars parked at red lights. People walking, carrying shopping bags. Bits of trash, pieces of newspaper swirling and dancing in the high wind. It seemed like years since she had passed through ordinary streets like these.

Now the Toyota was moved down Westlake Road, a wide, tree-feathered boulevard. For one quick, suspicious she wondered if Francesca could possibly be taking her to the St. Benedict Motherhouse, a few miles down this road. But then the car pulled into a parking lot beside a sharply angled modern building set amid tall, soft trees.

The two nuns walked inside together, found Dr. Salter's office. When Angela gave her name to the woman behind the desk, the woman said, "Oh, yes, Sister! The doctor is expecting you. Come right in, please."

She was feeling very cheerful, very strong, as she greeted that nice Dr. Salter and sat in the chair he gestured her toward, a padded beige chair by a high, wide window that looked out on a banked sea of pine trees. She felt genuinely glad to see this warm, gnomelike little doctor. And very happy that she finally had some real news to give him—watching his face in anxious, side-slipped glances as she told him about her remembering, finally, the birth of the baby.

When she got to the part about carrying the mat, that *baby,* back into her room she faltered.

Dr. Salter said quickly, "But Angela, that's very good! That you've brought that back."

She could feel the sobs knotting deep in her belly as she got out, *"But I can't remember anything else.* The baby—any more. I've tried—so hard—but I can't rem-remember anything else."

Urgently, from behind the desk: "That's all right, Angela. Don't push yourself. That's very important, what you've brought back, Angela."

She turned her face out toward that wall of green as she felt the heavings, convulsions, come out of her belly. *"But—I—must have—been the one. Because I was—the only one there."*

He got up from behind his desk, walked to put his two

hands firmly on her moving, heaving shoulders. "Listen to me, Angela. Be easy, be gentle on yourself."

Terrible flashing of sights, possible sights on that leafy green wall. "But I've got to understand—what I—did. If I was the one who—*must have.*" The wringings torn from her almost like that other time. "But if I never meant to—harm him before he was—born—*how could I harm him after?*"

He pressed calmingly on her shoulders. "Angela, you don't have to think about that now. This is enough. This is very good. What you've recalled."

No way to stem it now. Blurted, wrenched out of her between those agonized heavings: *"But I must have. But how could I—"* Torn, torn from her: *"It's all so confusing. Because I was the only one there."*

The grand jury hearing, carefully monitored by D.A. Mark Abrams, was proceeding along predictable lines: the St. Rose nuns testifying mainly to that flood of post-factum blood, which could be interpreted as much in favor of the defense as of the prosecution. The state's gynecological expert witness countering the nun's gynecological expert witness. The state's pathological expert witness countering the nun's pathological expert witness.

All of it so far inconclusive, Abrams's legal nose told him. Hers versus theirs, just about a fair draw.

Except that the nun herself, according to Ben Haverty, was electing to testify. Which would probably tip the balance, one way or the other.

Realist that he was, Mark Abrams found it hard to believe that an appearance before the grand jury of Sister Angela Flynn could tip the balance anywhere *except* toward a no bill. His mind was already moving ahead to the next potential problem: how to supply a reasonable explanation of that no bill to the aroused, strongly opinionated general public of the county, given the utter secrecy in which the grand jury proceedings must by law be sealed.

Sitting at his desk at 8:15 Sunday night, weighing his notes and schedules for the grand jury proceeding, Abrams suddenly moved to a decision. He lifted the phone and dialed the home number of Meg Gavin.

No answer. He phoned around town a little, and located her in the Blind Justice Bar.

She said warily into the phone, "Mark? What's happening?"

"Oh, nothing much, Meg. But I'd like to see you in my office, if you've got the time."

"Sure, Mark, you've got it."

She showed up in the office doorway seven minutes later, her face alive with questions.

Abrams smiled. "Hey, Meg, thanks for coming by. Sit yourself down, make yourself comfortable." She sat without speaking, reaching for a cigarette, looking toward him for explanation.

Abrams hesitated. He was wishing he could feel more sure, more *reassured* that he was making the right move, the right choice here. But all he sensed ahead of him, as usual, was that live minefield.

"Meg, we have an expert witness in the Angela Flynn case, an eminent psychiatrist, flying in tomorrow to examine her and testify before the grand jury." He paused. "I thought you might be interested in knowing that."

"Well, sure, Mark," she said, puzzled. "Who is he?"

"Dr. Neil Bellamy, the director of the Copley Psychiatric Institute of Scarsdale, New York."

Her rattrap mind did one of its instant retrievals. "Jesus, Mark. Isn't that the place where they shipped Joan Kennedy to dry out?"

Nettled, irritated by that question, Abrams snapped, "I don't know anything about that, Meg. I just know Dr. Bellamy came highly recommended by professional sources for whom I have the highest respect."

Another name was floating up: Truman Capote. They'd

treated *that* wierdo at Copley, too. But she had enough sense to keep that recollection to herself as she smiled across the desk. "Real good, Mark. So where do I fit in?"

Abrams shrugged. Said carefully, "Meg, I have no idea what input Dr. Bellamy is going to give to this case. Maybe it will be helpful to the prosecution, maybe to the defense." He hesitated. "We here in this office just want to lay the chips out fairly, Meg. Whatever way they fall. Whatever way. And to that end—" He broke off, in a brief freezing of his resolve.

She supplied softly, unbelievingly, "You want me to interview him."

Abrams stirred nervously behind his desk. "As a matter of fact, Meg, I think that might be helpful. So that the community at large would have some idea of how dispassionately and professionally this tremendously tragic case is being pursued on the official levels. As the dictates of justice require."

Meg knew she was hearing rightly. But still she could hardly believe it. That Mark Abrams was offering her the fat, ripe plum of a *private interview* with the psychiatrist whose very identification, under normal circumstances, she would be hard put to pry out of this office.

She could think of only one explanation for this extraordinary offer, and she knew instinctively it was the right one: Mark Abrams was expecting a no bill. Had probably been praying for one all along, and now *expected* it.

And was now gnawing his gut with worry about how to explain that no bill in politically reasonable terms to all those little citizens out there—so many of them presently enraged, irate about this case—who'd voted him into his job. So just in case, *just in case,* Mark Abrams was willing to risk slipping the chains of legal confidentiality enough to let Meg Gavin tell them all how hard this Jewish D.A. had worked to *do right* by this damned treacherous case.

Rubbing nervously at the back of his head, Abrams said

uncomfortably, "Meg, I think it might be helpful to the general public if they had a little more understanding of the—ah, various elements that go into a grand jury presentation like this. Especially in a case with such, um, clearly indicated psychiatric aspects as this one."

Poor schmuck Abrams. Stuck with this brutally thankless case. Meg had always liked, admired the guy. But never liked him more than now, as she smiled warmly, generously, across the desk and said, "Good enough, Mark. Understood. Just let me know when, and of course I'll make myself free."

At 9:45 A.M. the next morning Meg Gavin was led into the small office down the corridor from Mark Abrams's office where Dr. Neil Bellamy was already waiting, riffling through papers stacked alongside his Mark Cross attaché case.

Bellamy turned out to be a tall, silver-haired shrink with a professionally concerned expression veneered onto his very handsome face. Overnight, Meg had checked the file on him, discovered he'd also gotten himself invited into the Jack Ruby case as an eminent professionally disinterested expert witness. And wound up writing four articles about it. *Starfucker,* she had instantly decided. *Ambulance-chasing star-fucker.*

And now the handsome silver-haired star-fucker was sitting on the other side of a desk in the D.A.'s office, hers for the plucking.

Meg started off by asking what he made of the Sister Angela case so far. Bellamy said cautiously, "Well, it's certainly a complex set of behaviors that allegedly occurred."

Since she knew she would only have about ten minutes with him, she went straight to the point: "Dr. Bellamy, I hope you'll forgive any lese majesty implied in this question, because I certainly do acknowledge that you're tops in your field—but how can you possibly unravel that complex set of behaviors you just alluded to in what I understand is a court-ordered two-hour interview with the defendant, chaperoned by her lawyers?"

401

Bellamy stroked at his well-tailored dark tweed suit, obviously displeased by the question. "Of course, that's not an optimum situation for diagnosis, Miss Gavin. But a great deal can be determined even within that limited framework. I'll also have access to all her medical records. But more importantly, I'll try to reconstruct her state of mind on the day of the alleged murder by observing how she reacts in the interview."

Eyebrows up. "How so, Dr. Bellamy?"

Slight shrug. "The interview is a form of stress, Miss Gavin. From how she reacts to that stress, I will be able to project backward in time to how she reacted at an earlier time. I'll also try to assess her social awareness, and determine whether she had any physical problems that could affect her mental processes."

Stress of an interview, bullroyalshit. Bellamy was being subjected to that same stress *right now,* wasn't he? And Meg considered herself a damn good, intuitive interviewer. But she was getting no bright bolts of insight from *his* stress, if indeed this cool star-fucker was feeling any.

She murmured, "Well, of course, Doctor, in her case there was a very particular physical problem—the problem of a term pregnancy."

That crack Bellamy did not care for at all. He crossed his tweedy legs as he said frostily, "There are a great many levels of expert evaluation here that a layman like yourself —excuse me, a lay*person*—might not comprehend. Since they are quite—specialized. In any case, after interviewing Sister Angela Flynn and reviewing her complete medical records, I will describe her state of mind as accurately as I can to the grand jury. Then it is up to the jurors to make the adjudication of whether or not she was legally sane."

Mark Abrams intruded his tall body into the office door. "Excuse me, Dr. Bellamy. Meg. I'm afraid that's about all the time we've got to give you."

As Meg went out the back entrance of the Hall of Justice

building, crossed the wide alley to the *Eagle-Bulletin*'s rear door and flashed her employee badge to the guard on the door, she was focusing very clearly on a thought that had nagged at her since this damned case began.

The realization that it was *all quite crazy*. Not just what the nun had done, but what they were doing to her now—measuring, quantifying, qualifying her with their own weird yardsticks. Yardsticks like *legally sane*. And *medically sound*.

Meg had been troubled all along by the realization that this enormously intricate, enormously mysterious case was being played out by men like her own good drinking buddies Nick Scotti and Andy DaSilva. Who meant well enough, did well enough in their own areas of competence—

But the competence was *so limited*. Much too limited, she had suspected all along, to unravel the huge, powerful mystery of *this case*.

And now this pretty, silver-haired shrink, who would decide from a two-hour interview what was going on in the tormented head of that nun, and testify expertly to it.

Meg didn't *blame* them, couldn't blame them, any of them. That was how the system worked, after all. And this Dr. Bellamy, at least, was probably one hell of a lot more innately intelligent than most of the rest of them.

But Meg could also not shake the cold, unhappy conviction, as she punched the elevator button for the third floor, that there was not a single person involved in this case who had the vaguest goddam idea what it was all about.

You included, kid, she reminded herself grimly. *You, especially, included.*

Mr. Haverty pulled out the chair where Angela was supposed to sit. He introduced that new psychiatrist, such a cold, authoritative-looking man.

Angela nodded curtly. Some strange woman was sitting a little back from the table, taking down everything that was said on a strange black machine.

403

Angela did not like that strange woman being here in Mr. Haverty's office, listening, taking down everything she said. But she knew the real threat in this room was that white-haired doctor gazing at her across the table, fingering a yellow lined pad.

He asked Angela for her understanding of why she was there. She said coldly, "Because Mr. Haverty told me I had to be. Because it was ordered by the court."

"Ah, yes. But could you perhaps tell me something about the problem that brought you here?"

She answered strongly: "They think I harmed my child. Did something to cause his death."

The doctor nodded, jotting notes on his pad. "Sister, what is your understanding of that accusation made against you?"

Angela felt a fierce swelling in her chest. *That,* at least, she knew how to answer: "I don't believe that it's right. That I could possibly have done what they said I did."

"All right. Sister, have you ever been in trouble with the law before?"

She stiffened. Didn't this man *know* she was a nun? What kind of question was *that* to ask a nun? Sharply: "No, never."

The strange doctor took her all through the events of April 25. She told him everything she could remember. So many, many times she'd been through it already. But she still tried to tell it very precisely, to make everything she said absolutely true. Because if she only got it *right enough* then maybe they would finally understand, and leave her in peace.

The doctor seemed especially interested in how she felt about all the blood. She said faintly, "I was—frightened. I tried to clean it up but I couldn't. And there was no one to help me . . . I remember lying on the floor with the clots and blood all on me, around me, and I knew I was maybe dying and I felt very—frightened."

Now he was asking her for the meanings of proverbs— a stitch in time, don't cross your bridges, don't put your eggs. She tried not to let the anger, the *indignation* she was feeling show as she interpreted them all quite correctly. They had forced her to come to this place, forced her to sit down in front of these strangers, answer all their questions —and then they asked *things like that.* In order to decide, according to what Mr. Haverty had explained to her, whether or not *she* was crazy in the head.

"Sister Angela, if you found a stamped addressed envelope in the street, what would you do with it?"

She glared. "You mean—a letter that had already been sent?"

"Not necessarily."

Hotly: "Well, I suppose I'd mail it."

The questions kept coming, coming—did she ever feel blue, feel depressed for no particular reason. Had she ever experienced a great disappointment. Had she ever suffered a memory loss, or been told things she didn't remember having done.

No. *No, no, no* to this hostile man. "Except—I don't remember what happened to my child."

Did she ever hear voices in her head that told her to do things?

"You mean like religious visions? No, I don't have visions."

She knew from all those hours spent with the other doctors that he would surely ask her about her childhood and, sure enough, there it came, slipped into the questions as if by accident: Did she remember much about her childhood? What was her home life, what were her mother and father like? What could she tell him about her brothers?

"Sister, do you think your parents liked you?"

"Yes, of course. They—loved me."

"Was your mother a warm, loving person?"

Hesitation very slight, like a skipped heartbeat. "Yes, she was. She still is." Pause. "She's a very *good* person."

"What about your father? Was he a warm, loving man?"

"Oh, yes."

"Which parent were you closest to?"

That question again, that seemed to her so unfair. She said reluctantly, "Well, maybe a little more, my father. But I loved both my parents." She glanced toward the window. "They were both very good persons."

Now he was asking her about her appetite and her sleep habits. About her bowel movements and her menstrual periods. In front of Mr. Haverty and Mr. Andretti, even that strange woman with the black machine, he was asking if she had recently become constipated.

"No," she snapped. She was never so thankful for anything in her life as when Mr. Haverty looked at his watch and said loudly, "Dr. Bellamy, your two hours are up."

D.A. Mark Abrams slipped into his empty chair at the grand jury table just as Dr. Neil Bellamy was running down the last of his considerable professional credentials.

The notes Abrams jotted on the pad in front of him had two thrusts: Bellamy's diagnosis was hysterical neurosis, dissociative type. Also organic brain syndrome resulting from the severe blood loss suffered by the subject in the course of undergoing an experience that caused her severe, intolerable psychological strain.

A.D.A. Max Bloom up on his feet, pacing, asked: "Dr. Bellamy, is it your opinion that Sister Angela was legally sane at the time she committed these alleged acts?"

Bellamy said firmly, in his deep, resonant voice, "My opinion is no, she was not. She did not possess the necessary mental capability to be responsible for her acts."

The warm, suffusing glow that Mark Abrams experienced on hearing those words precluded further note-taking, precluded even sharp attention to the polite mopping-up of testimony that followed. *Their own man* had said it—their own *objectively selected psychiatric expert*.

As the session terminated and the various persons present in the room drifted toward the door, Bloom muttered to Abrams, "Jesus Christ, whose witness was *he?*"

"Mmmph."

"My God, if I was Ben Haverty, I'd turn around and hire that guy to testify for her defense at the trial."

IF it comes to that. Which, please God, it will not, Mark Abrams was thinking.

Aloud he said, "Well, that's the way the law game goes, Max. You play it as honestly as you can, and some you win, some you lose."

Except that this one, maybe, just maybe, Mark Abrams had not lost.

Thirty

She'd been over it so many times, mostly in Mr. Haverty's office, once in the shabby little parlor of Our Lady of Pompeii Convent. Sometimes Mr. Andretti had sat in on the rehearsals—to help her understand how it would be, telling her story in front of strangers.

And they'd asked her so many questions—hard questions, some of them. Mr. Haverty had said it was quite all right for her to express her feelings, even to cry a little, if she felt moved to that. But she had shaken her head, pleased about *that* much, at least—that the tears finally seemed finished, dried up, after that last painful session in Dr. Salter's office. She told Mr. Haverty with a steady, calm smile, "No, that's all right. I'm not *afraid* of this testifying, Mr. Haverty. I feel quite ready to do it."

But as Mr. Haverty drove her into the huge, dark parking lot under the Hall of Justice on May twenty-fourth, she realized that nothing he could have told her could have prepared her for this.

The parking space by the glass-walled elevator bank seemed to have been prearranged; a blue-uniformed court attendant was there to open the car door for her. She hesitated just for a moment, then forced herself to step from the car.

Mr. Haverty led her to the glass-walled elevators; Mr. Andretti followed behind. As Mr. Haverty punched the second-floor button she tried to calm the panicked flutterings in her stomach, tried to freeze her face in a look of serenity. *Help me, help me, Lord Jesus. Help me to make them understand.*

Up on the second floor another attendant opened a locked door, and Mr. Haverty led her briskly down a long stone-surfaced corridor to an office with MAX BLOOM in white letters above the door.

A dark-haired young man with glasses and long sideburns, sitting behind the desk, jumped to his feet as they came through the doorway. "Ben. Vince. Come in, please."

Introductions were made. She shook Mr. Bloom's hand, looking into his pale, bespectacled face as she said firmly, "I'm glad to meet you, Mr. Bloom."

A moment later two more men came into the small office—District Attorney Mark Abrams and Assistant District Attorney Andrew DaSilva. The short, balding one she remembered from the arraignment at the hospital. She nodded toward the cast on his arm. "I'm sorry about your accident, Mr. DaSilva."

"Well, thank you, Sister Angela."

Since there weren't enough chairs in the office, most of these big men stood up against the wall as Mr. Bloom explained to her about the grand jury setup, like Mr. Haverty had already done so many times. She nodded. "Yes, thank you, I understand about that, Mr. Bloom."

"The main thing is—we'd just like you to tell your story in your own way, Sister. This isn't really an adversary procedure. We aren't going to be asking you any questions to trip you up, catch you off guard. Really, we're just there to help you tell your own story."

"Thank you," she said.

The men were glancing at each other now. Mr. Abrams said, "Any questions, Ben?"

"I don't think so, Mark."

Now they were walking briskly down the hall again, into a small wood-paneled room. The brass plaque on the door read GRAND JURY. Mr. Haverty squeezed her elbow nervously. "We have to leave you here, Angela. But we'll be waiting right outside."

"Thank you, Mr. Haverty." She followed the district attorneys into a high-ceilinged room that reminded her, except for its dark wood-paneled walls, of the surgical theaters she had seen on television. The twenty-three grand jurors sat in three tiered rows above the red-carpeted floor. Along one wall there were tables for the lawyers from the district attorney's office. Off at the far end of the room, on a small raised platform, was a large wooden chair upholstered in red leather. Mr. Abrams motioned her toward it.

The people in the tiered rows were all looking at her with sharp, hungry, curious faces. She tried not to look back at them as she sat and folded her hands in her lap, breathing very deliberately, very steadily. *Help me, Sweet Jesus. Make me strong.*

Mr. Bloom stood up. "The State calls as its next witness Sister Angela Flynn."

A man in a blue uniform stepped up to the witness chair, holding out a red book, and said rapidly to her, "Put your right hand on the Bible and repeat after me: I swear to tell the truth, the whole truth and nothing but the truth, so help me God."

She did as she was told. Then Mr. Bloom said, "Sister Angela, would you give us your full name and address for the court record."

Mr. Haverty had said it was all right to give the St. Rose address, because that was still her real home. So she said, "Sister Angela Flynn, 207 Windsor Avenue, Cambridgeport."

"Are you also known as Gayle Marie Flynn?"

"Yes, I am." Her voice sounded, to her, very steady, which surprised and pleased her.

"All right, Sister Angela, would you please tell the jury in your own words what transpired on the day of April twenty-fifth."

She cleared her throat. "Yes, Mr. Bloom, I'd be glad to."

All those gaps in her memory of the events of that day —Mark Abrams wasn't surprised to note those, after the testimony of her psychiatrists. What startled him much more was her manner, her whole presentation. She sat up in the witness chair in a pinafore-type pale blue dress and white sweater, so short-legged that her feet dangled a few inches off the carpet, addressing the jury in a flat, high-pitched voice. Primly, precisely. Almost as if lecturing them on pre-school education.

Not, Abrams conceded glumly to himself, what he was hoping for. Not what, given the brutal circumstances of the case, would work with this grand jury.

But they still had an hour, two hours to go. She could still save it. Save herself, save *him.*

If she just *unbent* a little. Showed a little appropriate—emotion. Not this cold, unreasonable calm.

It wouldn't take much for her to save herself. Abrams had sensed the sympathy for her building in the jurors during the past few days' testimony, especially from the psychiatrists.

But she had to do *her part,* now. Had to yield a little. Give them some glimpse of the anguish, the remorse any normal woman would be feeling in circumstances like this.

Instead of this cold singsong lecture.

. . .

Now Mr. Bloom was asking her about the circumstances of the conception. She gripped her hands together on her lap as she told them about that dark time
in the woods, just as she'd rehearsed it so many times in
Mr. Haverty's office.

The few questions Mr. Bloom asked were the same ones
Mr. Haverty had told her she should expect—had she told
anyone else of this attack. *Why* hadn't she told them, had she
seen a doctor, and so on. She answered them very earnestly,
very steadily.

Now surely they must see what a mistake they had made
in forcing her to come to defend herself in this strange,
intimidating place. Now surely they must understand that
she was *not guilty* of what they said.

Max Bloom had expected that eerie, powerful calm she
had exhibited back in his office—God, every *man* in that
room seemed more nervous, more anxious, than her—to
dissolve once she got up on the stand.

But it did not. And as Bloom watched her composed,
occasionally smiling expression, listened to that curiously
flat, high, emotionless voice, he was feeling a whipsawing of
reaction.

Part of it was empathy, pure empathy for the pathetic
little nun perched on that red chair, forced to bare herself
in this intimate way, describe that sexual act to all these
strangers, these strange *men.* Bloom realized that kind of
testimony was rough, terribly rough for any woman to go
through. But for a nun like her it must be pure hell.

Yet another part of his reaction was dismay, unbelieving
dismay. Christ, hadn't Ben Haverty coached her *at all?* That
passive, paralyzed act of sex she described experiencing—
that wouldn't even constitute a rape under Minnesota laws,
which required "some degree of active resistance."

But more important—where was the regret, the cha-
grin, where was the appropriate sense of *guilt?* Here was a

woman whose newborn child had died in a particularly brutal manner, apparently by her own hand, and where the hell was the appropriate *remorse?*

Instead she was sitting up there like a brave little Christian soldier, talking so earnestly, so seriously, without emotion. Max Bloom thought frantically, *Come on, Sister Angela,* give. *You've got to* give *'em something.*

His own part of the interrogation finished, Bloom shuffled through the questions that members of the grand jury had written out for him to ask her. Most of them came from the middle-aged female jurors, all of them mothers themselves.

He discarded a few of the most clearly prurient, such as, "Did she have a climax?" Fucking female buzzards perched up there in those chairs, feeding on this woman's private agony—the nun's sexual response was in no way germane to this case. But he did ask, "Sister Angela, did you have sexual intercourse with this man on more than one occasion?"

She shook her head firmly. "Oh, no."

In the anteroom outside the hearing chamber Vince Andretti paced and chain-smoked cigarettes. Ben Haverty sat quietly, miserably squeezed into one of their little theater chairs. The silence he could feel coming at him through that closed walnut door was deafening.

Ben Haverty had done his damnedest to prepare her for what was going on right now behind that closed door. And been less than pleased with his results. On the matter of her testimony she had been quite—intractable. Reciting the story always in the same way, *her* way.

Haverty would have preferred to rearrange, script it a little differently. *Stage* it a little differently. When it came to female witnesses—in particular, female witnesses in a sex-oriented case—he knew that the truth was not nearly as good an armor as three wet handkerchiefs.

So there was that small worry in there chewing on

his anxious mind—that wish that she'd been a little more coachable, a little more pliable. Yet at bottom Ben Haverty was able to sweep away his own doubts by remembering Vince Andretti's first strong, spontaneous reaction: *that surely no grand jury could look this poor girl in the face and vote to indict.*

When the grand jurors began to ask their own questions, she tried to look very intently into the face of whichever one was speaking. But with so many faces turned toward her it was hard sometimes to find the questioner.

Until the women started. Seven or eight of them, sitting clumped together on the chairs nearest to her. And something on their faces—some sameness about the look on those women's faces, so bitter, *angry* almost—made her feel quite . . . frightened. The men's faces all looked different, some of them kind, some stern, some embarrassed, even apologetic.

But the women's faces all looked the same. All—frightening.

Now one woman was asking if she had ever had sexual contact *with a man*—she sensed the stress on that word "man"—before. She snapped back the question with a single firm word: "No."

Had she had any communication with this man since the incident she described?

"No."

Hadn't she realized this man probably had sex on his mind when she agreed to take that walk with him in the woods?

"No."

Hadn't she realized she was pregnant, known she was going to have the baby?

"Yes."

Well, then, why hadn't she done anything to protect that

baby's welfare—seen a doctor, been under proper medical care?

"Well, I've always been a very healthy person. And I hoped and prayed my child would be the same."

Had she had sexual contact with any other man since that incident last summer?

"No."

Had she considered having sex again with that man who took her into the woods?

"No."

Max Bloom was thinking frantically, *Now, NOW! It's not too late!*

She was handling those assaultive questions from the women like she'd been properly coached—batting them back with a single word. But when that one juror asked about her baby, about her concern for his welfare—*now, now's the time, Angela!*

If only she would hesitate, choke up a little. Blow her nose, crank up a few tears. Even crocodile tears—even that would do it.

But she had to *give them something*, some sign of the emotion a grieving mother would for her dead infant feel. Tears, sniffles. Anything. Just some *feeling* for her dead child.

Now, now. Cry a little, it's not too late, Max Bloom was urging desperately in his telegraphed thoughts.

But Angela did not bend, did not flicker. And now she was fending increasingly pointed questions about the sex. Bloom knew pretty soon someone would ask that one about her "climax"—those women were getting bolder, hungrier for blood. Blood that had no appropriate place in this grand jury hearing.

Bloom stood up and cut them off with, "Thank you, Sister Angela. Is there any final statement you'd like to make?"

Even now she could save it, retrieve it. If only she *would.*

· · ·

She said, "Yes, thank you, Mr. Bloom."

These thoughts she'd gone over and over in her mind, preparing to say, were most of the reason she had insisted on coming here, subjected herself to this excruciating ordeal.

Now she said calmly, "I regret most sincerely everything that has happened. I regret the great pain I have brought to my religious community, my family and my friends. I never intended for any of this to happen, and I would have spared them all the shame and anguish that has come to them if I could have. Most especially I never meant to harm . . . my child. Whatever this court decides on, whatever—punishment to me, it could not be any worse than the punishment I am already suffering from my own thoughts. I am already a prisoner, in my own mind. I keep trying to remember, to think if I could possibly have harmed the child that I only wanted to have and keep safe with me and protect.

"I understand that whatever happens here in this courtroom is your decision to make. But I would like to say that I am already a prisoner of my own thoughts, and I cannot suffer more from anything you could do to me here than I am already suffering from knowing that I might somehow have caused to happen to my child what I stand here accused of doing."

Mr. Bloom said faintly, "Thank you, Sister Angela. We appreciate your cooperation in coming to testify before this hearing today."

She nodded. The rest of them seemed to be waiting. So she stepped down from the witness stand and walked calmly toward the door as those men at the table stood, almost as if at attention.

A man in a blue uniform opened the door to the anteroom where Mr. Haverty and Mr. Andretti were waiting for her.

Mr. Haverty took her elbow without speaking, and

415

steered her out of the anteroom. As they stepped into the hall someone to the left of them shouted, *"There she is! Get her, get her!"* In one confused glance she saw a mass of people behind a row of policemen just down the hall, holding up huge, blinding lights, pointing at her with big black cameras.

Mr. Haverty turned her sharply in the opposite direction. As they walked very quickly down the long, empty hall she could still hear shouting behind her. But ahead of her was a long, silent, empty hall.

After the nun left the grand jury room Max Bloom did something he had never in nine years of courtroom experience done before: he cried. As he lifted his glasses, swiping furtively at his eyes, he noticed that some of the men in the grand jury were also blowing their noses, wiping their cheeks.

Mark Abrams also looked, for him, unusually emotional. Only Andy DaSilva seemed unmoved.

The three district attorneys left the chamber, pushing their way wordlessly through the noisy pack of reporters. As they moved back inside a cordon of guards and turned a corner into the relative tranquillity of a nearby empty corridor, Max Bloom blurted, "Mark, you've got to get me off this case."

"Hold it, Max."

They walked without further words to Abrams's office. Abrams slammed the door behind them, and in the abrupt silence, dropped into his desk chair and looked up at Bloom.

Bloom was already pacing, edging on tears again. "Mark, I mean it. I'm telling you, you've got to take me off this case. If I have to stick with it I'd rather do her defense."

Abrams said quietly, "Jesus Christ."

"And I'd give her one hell of a defense. Better than she got in there. Christ, Mark, what are we *doing* prosecuting a thing like this? What the hell are we doing here, making a case against that poor goddam little nun?"

Abrams stroked the back of his head. He was wearing the peculiar fixed smile he generally wore when he was working to hide his own feelings. "Appreciate your input, Max," he said dryly. "Andy? What have you got to offer to this discussion?"

DaSilva was leaning against a bookcase, cradling his arm cast, his face impassive. He said, "I think you Jewish guys are too involved."

Even Bloom smiled at that one, as he said, "Andy, you fucking spic Catholic."

"No, I mean it," said DaSilva. "I was brought up all my life around nuns. They don't have the same kind of—mystification for me that they seem to have for you Jewish guys."

Abrams said dryly, "Well, Max, I think we've heard from the R.C. contingent."

"Fuck you, Andy," Bloom said heatedly. "I don't know what kind of private beef you're running out here. But I'm telling you, that little woman back there has no business being tortured like this in a court of law. A case like this— it's just nothing we've got any *right* to be dragging out in public like this. There's *no good* gonna come from dragging a tragic thing like this all through the courts."

Sharply, from DaSilva: "Jesus, Max. Talk about *overreacting*. You *know* she was lying up there on the stand. One act of sex—a rape, at that. You *know* she was lying. I do, anyway. And she did it about fifteen, twenty times up there, flat-out, without even blinking."

Abrams murmured to Bloom, "I gather Andy was not moved by the good nun's testimony."

"That last part of it, yes, that moved me," corrected DaSilva. "Mainly because she made me realize what havoc and pain this has caused to so many other people. What a hell of a wrench she'd thrown into the whole system. But her —no, I don't feel any special pity for her. Just because she's a nun."

Bloom was still pacing frenetically around the spacious

417

corner office. "I don't care what you say, Andy, I hope to hell she gets no-billed." He paused, looked at Abrams, who was sitting impassively behind his desk. "You want to hear something crazy, Mark? I'm married to a Catholic, and Andy isn't. But he says *I'm* the one who's prejudiced. Jesus, what a crazy case this is. What a fucking can of worms. Well, all I want from it is to *get out* of it."

"Done, Max," Abrams said flatly. "But I appreciate the valuable contribution you made to it. You did a good job in there, Max." He turned to DaSilva. "Andy, thanks for the input. Now get your ass home and get that elbow healed."

.

When they were safely back in his five-year-old Buick Ben Haverty asked, "Angela, how did it go?"

She waved her hand. Said faintly, wearily, "Oh, I don't know. All right, I guess."

Without speaking again, Haverty drove her quickly one block down the street to a parking lot and escorted her briskly up to his office.

They sat around his disordered desk, Angela perched on the chair Vince Andretti pulled over for her. Both men were looking at her with bright, pointed, expectant faces. Haverty said, "Now, Angela. Could you tell us from the beginning what was said?"

Angela detailed those two hours in the grand jury room as truthfully as she could recall them. The two men sat very still, listening. Sometimes one or the other would interject with a question, but mostly they let her tell it.

When she finished Haverty said, "Well, thank you, Angela. I think that went quite well." Stirring in his chair, he looked at Andretti. "Vince? What you think?"

"I think yes," said Andretti.

Haverty spun his chair toward Angela. "Angela, we have taken the liberty of drafting a statement. We've discussed this with Sister Philomena, and she agrees that the general gist of this communication is something that would be desirable to make at this time."

Andretti handed Angela a few typed sheets of paper, corrected with inked-in deletions or additions. Feeling their eyes on her, she skimmed the text, sensed the graceful phrases.

She handed the sheets back. "That sounds fine to me, Mr. Haverty."

"Thank you, Angela. If there are any changes or additions you'd like to make—"

"No, no. Whatever you think best, Mr. Haverty."

Haverty heaved himself forward in the chair, leaned his elbows on the desk. "All right, Angela. Now, the purpose of this statement is—this could be the termination of the legal case against you. If the grand jury brings in the no bill that we expect. And we as your attorneys, along with Sister Philomena, felt that some final public statement on the case would be appropriate at that time."

The image of those women's faces suddenly flickered alive in Angela's mind. What she had sensed from them was a feeling, not a fact. Nothing she could tell Mr. Haverty or Mr. Andretti about.

But she had those faces vividly in her mind as she asked, "But what if the grand jury doesn't bring in a no bill?"

Ben Haverty smiled gently, wearily at her. "Then, Angela, we will deal with the new situation that will present itself," he said softly. "Like I told you, Angela—one step at a time. One step at a time."

After Meg Gavin filed her daily update on the grand jury proceedings she felt too keyed-up to go home. So she stopped by the Blind Justice Bar, where she found Peter Juhl, the Sheriff's polygraph guy, leering admiringly into the drooping cleavage of a badly dressed legal secretary.

Juhl spun his barstool away from that pursuit as he spotted Meg. "Hey, Gavin. How're you doing on this nun case?"

"Not as good as I'd like." She signaled for her customary vodka and Diet Pepsi. "Except I finally *saw* her today, at the grand jury hearing. Jesus, was *that* weird."

"Weird how?"

Meg shrugged. "She's right out of Central Casting. Real pretty, and *tiny*. Like a little doll, almost. And she walks like that, like kind of a tight little windup doll." She jerked her stiffened arms, imitating Angela's moves.

"Mm. Interesting," said Juhl.

"She looked so goddam *helpless*, Pete. So goddam bewildered, with the TV crews all bellowing at her. And the *clothes*—my God, I wonder if Ben Haverty bought that dress just for this one shot. A little pale-blue dress with embroidery on the front and a sash tied down the back. If I remember right, I drew the line on dresses like that when I was ten years old."

"Yanh, well, it's gonna take more than clothes to get her out of this one, Meg."

"Oh, yeah, sure. Don't I know. But Jesus, just the *look* of her, Pete—how the hell is any jury going to indict a pretty, helpless-looking little nun like that?"

Juhl was brooding, spinning his half-empty glass on the polished wood bar. Then, quietly: "You think she would've done this if that kid hadn't been a boy, Meg?"

She hunched her shoulders over the bar, considering. "Well, I don't know. That's a pretty interesting question, actually. Maybe seeing that real little pecker right there in the convent—"

"Frequently erected in the stress of birth."

"Well, okay. Maybe seeing that—*shit*, Pete, *I* don't know. But that's a real interesting question."

"Okay then, try this one: you know how she did this thing, Gavin?"

She moved restlessly on the barstool. "Sure. Like Rhoades said, with the panties."

"No, I mean *how*. She didn't just tap that stuff politely into that kid's mouth, you know. Hey, I've seen some of the reports. In order to get that much knit material into a mouth that small she had to go *unnnhh—unnnhh—unnnhh!"* Juhl gestured emphatically, lifting his right elbow, smashing his right fist repeatedly down into his opened left hand. "She really *packed it in there,* man, I'm telling you."

"Oh God." Meg closed her eyes against that graphic vision, dropped her head on her arms, folded on the bar.

Quietly: "You know, some deaths are almost peaceful, Meg. Drowning, for instance. Or a bullet, if it gets you just right. But suffocation—that's one of the worst. Because the body *fights* it so. *Has* to fight it. Even a newborn kid, who probably started out sucking in those panties because that's just about the strongest instinct he has in him, except for breathing—sucking."

Meg moaned. "Pete, I don't want to hear this."

"For sure that's what he did, Meg—*suck 'em in.* But then he'd be *fighting.* For air, breath, life. No choice—the body's gotta fight, hang on for every second it can, in that kind of death. Even a newborn. Maybe especially a newborn."

"Don't, Pete. I don't want to *hear* this."

"So he probably fought her like hell, with everything that was in him. And she had to hold him down while she *packed it in there.* She probably had him in her lap, and she had to watch that struggle, *feel* that struggle. Because he wouldn't go easy, not that way. Even a newborn. She'd have to hold him down until he finally stopped fighting." He let that sink in, watching her face. "But it took a long time, Gavin."

Meg was making a slight moaning sound, rolling her head on her folded arms.

"And all that's still in her somewhere, Gavin. Every fucking incredible second of it. You know the word to describe that kind of act, Meg? *Rage.* That lady acted in a white heat of rage. Rage for that kid, probably rage for her whole goddam life."

421

"Mmmph." She raised her head, wiped one hand over her mouth.

"You're wasting your pity if you're dumping it on her, Gavin. How about some pity for that nice little kid, who all things considered probably had more right to live than she did. And you know what would've happened to that kid, if it hadn't been for the medical accident of her hemorrhaging like that?" She shook her head numbly, side to side. "That kid would've been down in the dumpster, Gavin. Tossed into a plastic bag and thrown out with the rest of the garbage, I'm telling you. And by the time the other nuns came home from school the mess would've been mostly cleaned up. Your helpless little Sister Angela would've said 'No, no, don't call a doctor. I'm all right, I'll be in class again tomorrow.' And she probably would've been. And nobody would've known any better. Least of all the guys who buried that kid in a rotting city dump."

Meg Gavin had not heard too much of what Peter Juhl had said since her mind had snagged on one word, which she repeated now, slowly, *"Rage.* I never thought of it that way."

"Damn fucking right it was. Premeditated rage, at that. Listen, Gavin, I think she'd meant to get rid of that kid, whatever way she could, since the first time she noticed she wasn't bleeding into her panties on schedule. And I hope they throw the goddam book at her. But that soft-touch judge they put on her case, Mr. Suspended Sentence—you know what his nickname is around the office?"

Meg smiled faintly. "What?"

"Jingles."

"Why Jingles?"

"I dunno. But it's no compliment, let me tell you. So with him on the case, she's probably gonna walk. Little blue dress or no. But I'm telling you right now, Gavin, if it wasn't for that accident of her hemorrhaging, because she was too goddam dumb to massage her belly to get that placenta out, you wouldn't be here picking my brains about this tonight.

And that baby with the mouthful of panties would be pushing up compost in the city dump."

Meg pressed one hand on her hip, arching her spine on that barstool. God, she was tired, bone-weary now, finally. "You know the most interesting thing you just said, Juhl? That thing about the rage. Sure, you're dead right about that. And this was a woman who probably hadn't let herself feel rage in her whole goddam good little nun life. And d'you realize how much rage people have *in* them, these days? Women especially?"

Juhl climbed abruptly off his stool, signaling for another drink. "Oh, shit, now we're into *that*. The goddam Women's Lib tundra."

"Fuck you, Pete. Fuck you through the eyeballs, in fact. I still appreciate that little nugget of insight you had to offer."

"So that's what you're gonna do with this case, Gavin? Make it over into some kind of goddam Women's Lib flag-waver?"

She laughed aloud, shaking her head. "Jesus Christ. Talk about a both-hands-quickly-to-the-athletic-cup reaction. I'm surprised and rather gratified to find you're so goddam sensitive to the issue, Juhl."

"Fuck you, Gavin. I'm telling you, she *meant* to kill him. She meant all along to kill him, any way she could."

"Shut up and *listen* for a minute, Pete. What I'm *thanking* you for, if you'd just stop running your damn mouth long enough to hear it, is making me see how that could have happened. Because I hadn't figured that, actually. I hadn't realized that about the *rage.*"

Juhl snorted as he lifted, tilted his drink. "Just do me one big favor, Gavin." He drained half the glass, slapped it back to the bar. "Just don't let me hear you say one more goddam time, *'That poor little nun.'*"

Thirty-one

In some ways the hardest part of the grand jury ordeal was waiting out the vote. Mr. Haverty had explained to her that the jurors would not begin their deliberations on the various cases they had heard in the course of that month until the end of May; the decisions on those cases would be made public a few days later. "Say, seven or eight days from now, Angela," he had told her on the afternoon she testified. "You think you can wait that long?"

She smiled as she said, "Of course, Mr. Haverty." *Of course.* The waiting would be a small price to pay, if only it would bring, finally, an end to this strange torment they were doing to her.

She tried to put those eight days to good use. She went to daily Mass and Communion, praying for courage and calmness, for strength. Offering up the pain of this ordeal to the Lord Jesus as a proof of her love, a signal of her faith.

On the second day her trunk and boxes were delivered to Pompeii from the St. Rose convent, so she was able to spend a good deal of time unpacking and settling into the small third-floor room that looked out on a wide, flat expanse of brick-strewn rubble.

So strange, to see all the pieces of her life neatly folded and packed up by someone else. Her final vows, for instance, facedown on the top of her trunk. She felt very—moved as she read through them. Felt stronger, felt calmed. Yes, *that* was the purpose of this whole so protracted time of trial— some purpose of *His,* that He would make clear to her in His own right time.

She decided to hang the wood frame on the nail already there on her room door, so she would see those vows, be reminded of them every day.

Some of the clothes that were worn out or didn't fit her anymore she set aside for the poor box. Folded in among her summer clothes she found a pair of slacks. Red slacks. They looked like they would still fit, but she decided with a quick pinch of her mouth that she had never really liked those slacks. Red was a color she never wore, anyway. She put them at the bottom of the pile for the poor box.

There were two items from the trunk that she took with her to her next appointment with Dr. Heilbron, three days later, on Monday afternoon. As she pushed them across the desk she murmured, "You said you wanted to see these."

He picked up the 1961 Benedictine Academy yearbook. "Oh, yes. Very interesting, Sister."

"I marked the pages where it mentions me."

He paused over her senior photograph, the same one the newspapers had recently run of her—an earnest, sweet-faced girl with pale bangs tweaked in a comma-shaped curl across her forehead. "Mm-hmm. Very pretty." Then he flipped to the Sewing Circle page, where a group of girls in white blouses and school-uniform jumpers sat in studiedly casual arrangement around a plump black-habited nun. "Oh, yes, there you are again. With glasses this time. Ah— was that the habit *you* wore too, Sister, when you entered the convent?"

"Oh, yes."

"It looks quite—uncomfortable. Starchy around the face."

"Oh, not so much. You hardly noticed that, once you got used to it."

Now he was on the Home Economics page, reading aloud: *"What could please a young Christian man more, as he carried his bride across the threshold of their new life together, than knowing that their love will endure because she can cook and she can sew."* He peered over his eyeglasses at her, smiling: "That sounds rather—old-fashioned, today, don't you think, Sister?"

425

She shrugged. "Maybe a little, now. But that was just the way everybody thought, back then."

When he got to the section on the Senior Prom—conga lines of flat-topped crew cuts and bouffant organdy skirts—he asked, "Did you also go to the prom, Sister?"

"Yes, with a friend of my brother Ed's. But I didn't usually go out on dates. It didn't seem right to me, because I already knew I was going to enter."

The doctor set aside the yearbook, and picked up a small booklet with "1964 Daily Reminder" printed on its flower-strewn cover. The entries made up a kind of diary. "Do you mind if I read some of this aloud, Sister?"

She said a little nervously, a little reluctantly, "Not if you want to."

He cleared his throat and started off with: *"You really need to love the children you teach. Our Lord wasn't annoyed with the Apostles. He loved them."* He smiled at her over his glasses. "I gather the children were giving you a difficult time that day, Sister. Because you wrote underneath that, *FORBEAR-ANCE: overlooking faults and offenses."*

"Well, that was just to remind me. Of what my job was really about."

"When you're humiliated, frustrated, overcome, say thank you. *It's the only way to keep pride from getting a hold on us."* He paused. "Is pride such a bad thing, Sister?"

"False pride, yes. I was trying to work then on the virtue of humility." She was beginning to feel quite uncomfortable, wishing she hadn't brought in that notebook that was written so long ago.

"Ours is an unnatural life. We love everyone we meet, rather than naturally limiting our love to a few. And it takes a great deal of strength to love and accept everyone."

"Well, that was just a quote I remembered from an older nun, someone who helped me quite a lot in my junio-rate year."

He was turning pages randomly, pausing when something caught his eye. *"When you have a critical thought, just don't say it. Or it may eventually become a habit that reaches into our realms of thought. Even if I don't* feel *sympathetic, antipathy* isn't expressed. *It's so HARMFUL."* Looking up at her: "Would you agree with that thought today, Sister?"

A little confused now, unsure of what her answer should be. "Well, the substance of the idea I agree with, I guess. I might put it a little differently now, but I still try very hard not to be critical of other people."

The doctor was about to set the booklet aside when he noticed an entry for Holy Saturday: *"It's here again—so lonely, so empty, weary. There must be more."* Raising his eyebrows quizzically, he looked to her for explanation.

Oh, she hadn't realized *that* was in the book. Definitely she should not have brought it in here. Smiling to cover her embarrassment, she said, "Goodness, that certainly doesn't sound like me. I must have been in a very bad mood that day, because that certainly wasn't how I usually felt." She hesitated. "I told you, I've been very happy being a nun. It's a very satisfying life for me."

Soothingly: "Well, Sister, perhaps you were having a little more difficulty adjusting to it back in 1964. But are you telling me that you never *do* feel 'lonely, empty, weary'?"

"Not *never*. I suppose everyone feels that at one time or another, don't they?" He was nodding, smiling his approval. The right answer, then. She wasn't always sure which was the right answer. "But I'm not lonely very much of the time. I have so many things to do that are—more important than myself, my own moods. So when I *do* feel a little blue sometimes, it doesn't really bother me, because I know it isn't anything that will last."

His head was bouncing owlishly up and down. "That's a very mature, constructive attitude, Sister. I think you're making excellent progress."

So for the next week's session she brought along the 1970 notebook in which she had analyzed various tasks—like learning to skate, or relate more generously to her fellow teachers—under the headings of *Situation, Approach, Process* and *Evaluation.* Dr. Heilbron was so interested in that notebook that they spent the next two sessions going over it in some detail.

The May grand jury went into closed session to deliberate on Monday morning. All told, they had twenty-seven cases to deliberate; Angela Flynn's was the last of them.

At 9:05 on Friday morning, June 2, a bailiff brought the results of the grand jury's deliberations to D.A. Mark Abrams's office.

The entry concerning Angela Flynn seemed to spring up at Abrams from the page. He grimaced, stroking the back of his neck. *Okay, that was it, then. Fuck it. Some you win, some you lose.*

He pressed the intercom switch and told his secretary to get Ben Haverty on the phone.

"Ben? I'm afraid the news isn't good."

"How bad is it?"

"First-degree manslaughter."

Haverty made an explosive, inarticulated sound.

"The indictment takes note of her 'extreme emotional disturbance,' Ben. I assume that was their grounds for bumping down the charge."

"Goddamned outrageous! *Manslaughter one* on that poor girl?"

Abrams said evenly, "We'll need her down here for the arraignment as soon as you can manage it. I think the quicker you can make it, Ben, the less buildup we may get from the press."

"Okay, I'll get back to you."

"One more thing—I know you've been objecting to having her printed and mugged. I've gone along with that as long as I could, Ben, but it's going to have to be done this afternoon."

"I'll get back to you," Haverty repeated.

．　．　．

She knew the call might be coming that morning. Mr. Haverty had told her to expect that much, so she stayed by the phone in the parlor, doing her paperwork. Fran was also staying home that day, hovering somewhere in the dining room, tactfully out of sight. Angela didn't ask why Fran was there, didn't have to: Fran was the one who drove the car.

When the call came at 9:25 she answered it herself. Mr. Haverty said, "I'm sorry, Angela, the news isn't what we'd hoped for."

"What is it, Mr. Haverty?"

"The grand jury is, ah, charging you with first-degree manslaughter."

Manslaughter. Another strange new word that sent a chill through the whole of her tired body. *Slaughter.*

How could they possibly think that was what she had done?

Mr. Haverty was still talking. "Now, Angela, I know we weren't expecting this. But I'd like you to consider it just a temporary setback on the road to your ultimate vindication. As I told you all along, these things are sometimes unpredictable. But we'll deal with each step as it comes up, and eventually we'll get to the end of it."

"I understand," she said.

"So all this present development means is that this will take us a little longer than we had hoped. That's all this setback means, I promise you."

Slaughter.

This time they had to go into the Hall of Justice through the front door and the public elevators. Mr. Haverty and Mr. Andretti walked protectively at her sides, and she kept her eyes down on the stone floor, so she would not have to look at the strange people who were staring at her.

The elevator doors opened on the second floor on a scene of milling pandemonium. Suddenly strong lights were turned on her, blinding her. She kept her eyes fixed on the floor, *sensing* rather than seeing the mass of bodies as Mr. Haverty steered her quickly through the crowd.

Inside the courtroom there was sudden quiet. They showed her to a chair behind a long wooden table. She sat and fixed her eyes on the brass letters IN GOD WE TRUST nailed to the high wood-paneled bench in front of her. *Help me, help me, Lord Jesus.*

A court attendant called out, "All rise, please. Court is in session, Judge Samuel Aaron presiding." Wearing a black robe now, the little judge who had come to her hospital arraignment came through the front door of the room and climbed the three steps to the bench. The lawyers sat again after the judge settled in his chair, so she did, too.

The judge nodded to Mr. DaSilva, sitting at the other end of the long wooden table next to theirs. Mr. DaSilva stood and read out a long legal-sounding text. She heard very little of it, except that peculiar beginning: "In the matter of the People of the State of Minnesota versus Gayle Flynn, also known as Sister Angela Flynn . . ."

Now Mr. Haverty was whispering, "Angela, stand up."

She stood. The judge looked down at her and said, "Gayle Flynn, how do you plead to this indictment?"

Angela said, "Not guilty." She meant to say it loudly, firmly, but her voice came out sounding quite small.

There was some talk about bail, and the judge said the five thousand could stand. When the judge stood and stepped down from the bench, she felt the stir in the large room behind her as those people back there rose to their feet.

Behind her she heard someone ordering in a loud voice, "Clear the courtroom, please. Clear the courtroom," heard the rustle of bodies moving out of the room. Mr. Haverty pulled back her chair. "Sit down, please, Angela. Sit down and relax."

She tried to do as she was told. Mr. Haverty turned

toward her now, his big, pouchy face trying to smile through his concern. Softly: "So, Angela. That wasn't so bad, was it?"

She shook her head, not trusting herself to speak.

Two people came up to the table—a dark, Spanish-looking woman in a blue uniform, and a fat, glowering man. When Angela looked up at them Mr. Haverty said, "Now, Angela, these two marshals are here to escort us to the Sheriff's Department for fingerprinting. Like I explained to you. I'll go down there with you, and I'll be right outside. It won't take long. And Mr. Andretti will stay behind here to read the statement we prepared." He paused. "How are you, Angela? Are you feeling all right?"

She was wrapping herself in the silence, the peaceful stillness of that room behind her. "Yes, thank you, Mr. Haverty," she said quietly. "I'm fine."

"You can rest here for a few moments if you'd like, Angela."

"No, I'm ready."

As they walked out of the courtroom the heat, light, noise, press, struck her body like the blast of a hot shower. Mr. Haverty walked slightly in front of her, pushing a wave into the crowd. People were shouting questions at them. This time she saw the huge black cameras pressing close to her face.

Mr. Haverty was saying, "No comment, no comment. Let us through, please." She blinked. She hadn't known those lights would be so sharp, so cruel.

Now they were in the elevator again, Mr. Haverty and the two marshals and some strange man who kept staring at her. No one spoke. Angela looked straight ahead at the ribbed brass doors until they opened again, and Mr. Haverty steered her briskly toward a glass door and out across a concrete plaza, up to another glass door with RAMSEY COUNTY SHERIFF'S DEPARTMENT in gold letters above it.

No one spoke until they reached a locked wire-mesh gate on the bottom floor. Mr. Haverty said nervously, "Now,

431

Angela, I'll be waiting right outside. This isn't going to take long."

Like that time he delivered her to that terrifying Ward Five. She looked at him, mutely appealing. Mr. Haverty tried to smile. "Five minutes at the most, Angela."

The dark-skinned woman took her by the elbow and said, "Please come with me, Sister."

The policeman behind the wire gate unlocked it, swung it open, and Angela stepped through.

It was just like she'd seen it so many times in TV movies. The policeman told her to relax, please; then he rolled her fingers one by one across an inked pad and moved them across to a printed sheet and rolled them onto the squares marked out on the sheet.

When all the squares were filled in he handed her a jar of cold cream and a couple of Kleenexes and said, "Clean off your hands, please."

She tried to get the black stuff off as quickly as she could. But smears of it were still clinging to her fingers when he said, "Step over here, please."

She kept wiping at her hands as she walked to the cubicle where they had a small camera fixed to a tripod on a table. The white wall facing the lens was marking off in feet and inches.

The policeman was pushing white letters and numbers into slotted grooves on a black plastic rectangle. She read "FLYNN, SR ANGELA," and at the bottom in smaller white letters "Ramsey Co Sheriff Dept." There were quite a few numbers too, but she recognized only the date, "6/2/78."

The policeman lifted the black rectangle and hooked it around her neck with a thin chain. "Stand back against the wall, please."

She tried to look calm and composed as the flash went off. The policeman stepped forward, turned her body in a quarter-circle and said, "Please hold the plate facing front with your right hand."

She did as she was told. The flash went off again.

The policeman unhooked the thing from around her neck. "All right. Sign here, please." She signed the form in her rounded, even signature. "All right, thank you, Sister," the policeman said. "You're free to go."

Free? Such strange words these people used. First *slaughter.* And now *free.*

She followed the dark-skinned woman back to the locked wire gate.

As DaSilva walked into Mark Abrams's corner office Abrams said, "So, Andy. How'd it go?"

"Okay, I guess. There's a hell of a lot of press people out there." *Tell me something I don't already know,* Abrams was thinking wearily. "And Vince Andretti's in the hall, reading some kind of statement to the reporters."

Abrams stiffened warily in his chair. "What the hell is that?"

"I dunno. He's reading it off for the TV cameras."

Two minutes later Meg Gavin stuck her head in the office door. "Mark? Got a minute?"

"For you, Meg, always."

She said as she walked into the room, "I figured you might like to make some response to Andretti's statement."

"Matter of fact, Meg, I haven't seen it yet. You got a copy?"

She resisted saying *For you, Mark, always* as she passed the Xeroxed sheet across his desk.

With DaSilva looking over his shoulder, Abrams read through the extraordinary pretrial statement that had been hastily updated that morning by Ben Haverty. In eighteen years of practicing law, Abrams had never seen anything quite like it.

433

The charge of the felony indictment was "emphatically denied. Incident and prior to the delivery of the infant, Sister Angela sustained a massive, severe loss of blood, resulting in a loss of consciousness and awareness. This will be established by medical and psychiatric proof, which confirms that Sister Angela never possessed any intent to harm the child."

All right, Abrams was willing to give them that much. They'd lost their case in the grand jury; now they were playing it in the press. Ethically debatable, from the viewpoint of the law, but maybe understandable in the heated emotional climate of this case.

But in the next paragraph Haverty deemed it "appropriate at this time to dispel some of the misstatements in the media, as well as rumors, suspicions and conjectures relating to the conception in this matter. All of the facts surrounding this enormous tragedy will be disclosed at the trial. The uncontroverted evidence will show that no past or present member of any religious community was involved in the conception. In addition, the evidence will show that Sister Angela never met or communicated with the individual prior or subsequent to the incident which occurred in August of 1977. The facts will further demonstrate that the event was not the result of any romantic relationship."

Translation: *rape.* Abrams had let them run out that wishful fantasy unrebutted in the grand jury because—all right, face it: mainly because if they had managed to sell that to the grand jury Mark Abrams might have been let off the hook of having to prosecute this treacherous trial.

But *this,* now—this was too much. In the rush of anger Abrams was trying hard not to reveal, he was already bitterly regretting his decision to let them play their game out unchallenged up to this point.

But now at least, now, *here,* it would *stop.*

Abrams quickly scanned the rest of the statement, mostly flowery acknowledgment of the "hundreds upon hundreds of expressions of compassionate understanding and support" Sister Angela had received, for which her attorneys wished to express "sincere appreciation" on her behalf.

As he handed back the Xeroxed sheet, Meg Gavin noted that both his ears were bright red. Odd. She'd never seen red ears on that cool, pale district attorney.

"Well, Meg," Abrams said evenly, "I would have to say that this office disagrees with substantial portions of that statement."

"Care to specify which ones, Mark?"

"Let's leave it at 'substantial portions.'" He got up from his desk and began to pace his office—something else Meg had never seen.

"Mark, for the record—I asked Andretti if the statement was meant to imply rape, and he said, 'The statement speaks for itself.'"

Which, of course, very craftily, somewhat brilliantly, it did not. Abrams smiled. A grim, choked smile. "No further comment, Meg."

"Okay. Let me at least ask, have you decided who's going to prosecute this case?"

Abrams nodded toward DaSilva. "Sure, Meg. This case will be in the very capable hands of Andrew DaSilva."

DaSilva took that news with a grateful nod. "Thanks, Mark."

When Gavin left the office Abrams felt himself coming into the grip of a genuine rage—a rage he hadn't felt since he'd been thrown into this crucifying job. Oddly enough, it helped him to throttle his own emotional reactions when he heard the normally mild-mannered Andy DaSilva saying heatedly, indignantly, "Jesus Christ, Mark, they're still trying to run this thing out as a *rape*. First in the grand jury, now in the press. I don't know exactly what constitutes unethical legal performance in a thing like this, but—what the hell is Ben Haverty trying to get away with here?"

435

Abrams said, and realized as he said it that it was probably true, "Well, maybe Ben believes it himself."

Nick Scotti suddenly came bursting through the office door, waving another Xerox. "Mark? *You seen this thing?*"

"Yep." Abrams sat heavily behind his desk. "I saw it."

"They're trying to sell this case as a fucking *rape*. They're yelling rape all over the news. Jesus, can you believe the balls of that?"

Abrams felt a cold, sure calm coming over him as he stroked absently at the back of his head. Quietly: "They're staking out a defense for their client, Nick. Which is their legal privilege."

"A fucking *lie* like that? That son-of-a-bitch liar Ben Haverty—are you gonna let him get *away* with it, Mark?"

Quietly, very quietly: "Not a chance, Nick." He pressed the intercom switch, told his secretary to get Ben Haverty on the phone. As he waited for the call to go through he said distractedly, "Andy, stay on tap this afternoon, will you?"

They waited in a tense silence. Then: "Ben? I'd like to see you up here in my office. At your earliest possible convenience."

By the time Ben Haverty and Vince Andretti got to Abrams's office at 4:15 that afternoon most of Abrams's reactive anger had run its course. But it flared again as he saw Haverty's looming, stubborn bulk filling his office door.

He leaned forward, pressed the intercom switch and asked his secretary to summon DaSilva to his office. "If you have no objection, Ben, I'd like to have Andy DaSilva sit in on this meeting."

"No objection."

As Haverty and Andretti settled into chairs Abrams smiled coldly at them. "Well, Ben. Vince. I see the battle lines are being drawn."

"If you want to put it that way, Mark," Haverty said.

"Well, Ben, it looks that way to me. And I thought we should get a few things clearly understood right up front." Abrams was speaking now with his usual calm. "You understand, this office does not of course wish to interfere in any way with whatever defense you choose to make for your client. That goes without saying. However, I must in all candor say I was somewhat surprised by the tenor and content of certain portions of your pretrial statement."

Haverty said, "We stand by that statement, Mark."

"I'm sure you do, Ben. *Up to this point.*"

As DaSilva slipped into the office he nodded at Ben Haverty. "Ben, how you doing?"

"Okay, Andy. You?"

They looked back toward the desk as Mark Abrams said deliberately, correctly, "Of course, Ben, it's also your privilege to make use of the press in any way you feel might be useful to your case. But this statement you released—" Abrams tapped the Xerox copy lying on his desk. "Ben, I think you should be made aware that this office has in its possession certain information which constitutes a direct contradiction to certain allegations—perhaps they should more properly be termed 'suggestions'—in your statement."

Haverty sat slumped in heavy silence, elbows dug into his knees. Abrams continued, "Particularly on this matter of the paternity—Ben, have you spoken to the man in question?"

Haverty didn't answer. Didn't have to.

"Well, gentlemen," Abrams said softly, "I'd strongly suggest that you talk to the alleged father. If you talk to the father, as this office has, I think you'll learn that there were five or six separate instances of sexual intercourse involved here."

Haverty lurched backward in the chair as if he had been slugged. Andretti looked down at his knotted hands. Abrams continued in his quiet, calm voice, "This information has been verified by a thoroughly satisfactory polygraph examination."

Haverty jerked upward out of his chair like a huge, string-yanked puppet. Pacing in front of the desk, he growled, "Inadmissible evidence."

"Oh, quite. But we also have a collaborative body of evidence to support it, if you choose to make this an element in your defense."

Haverty pacing, saying nothing. Quietly, from Abrams: "You're not gonna get far with five or six rapes, Ben."

Suddenly, astonishingly, Haverty was crying. He pulled a handkerchief from his pocket and blew his nose into it. Mumbled through it, *"I don't believe it, Mark.* I don't goddam believe it."

Astounding. Mark Abrams had expected to see a lot of startling things on this case, but tough, battle-scarred Ben Haverty breaking down in his office was not one of them. Now a fresh worry was laid into the back of Abrams's already troubled mind: if Ben Haverty, that superior old courtroom veteran, was *that* involved, that emotionally transfixed by this case, how good a defense was the nun going to get out of him?

Abrams said quietly, compassionately, "I'm sorry to have to tell you this, Ben, but he checked out on the polygraph. Five or six incidents—most of them at her instigation."

That last bomb blast drew a visible reaction from both Haverty and Andretti. Haverty shook his head, a violent, forceful movement, as he pushed the handkerchief back into his hip pocket. *"I don't goddam believe it."*

"Ben, I strongly urge that you contact the father. This office would be very willing to put you in touch with him." No response from Haverty, who was still pacing, his large, expressive face pulling, reacting. "Because if you insist on pursuing that line of defense that you ran out in the statement today, we're going to have to go down that avenue with you. And very frankly, between the four of us in this office, I don't think that's anything either party to this case would like to have happen."

Silence in the room. Abrams looked at DaSilva. "Andy, you have anything to say here?"

DaSilva cleared his throat. "Just—Ben, I did believe him. And I think Mark's on the right track. I think you guys ought to talk to him."

"Okay." Abrams slapped the desk. "Then it's up to you, Ben. Ball's in your court. But I'd like to say one thing right now. Ben, I certainly hope you're going to consider the possibility of a plea bargain on this case." Haverty turned toward the desk, eyeing Abrams with a glowering expression. "I don't mind telling you right now, this office would certainly be willing to consider one. We're certainly not anxious to pursue any unnecessary public prosecution of this unfortunate woman." He paused, then said quietly: "From what I saw in that grand jury room—I'm not sure how well she could hold up against the extraordinary ordeal that a public trial of that nature would constitute. With all the press attention it would draw."

Haverty pulled himself upright, rallied for one last shot: "There was no mention of rape in that statement, Mark."

"I noticed that," Abrams said coldly. He picked up the Xerox copy. "I notice you said, 'not the result of a romantic relationship.' Very smooth work, Ben. Nimble footwork. *But it's not gonna wash.* I think five or six separate incidents of sex might reasonably be construed by any jury to constitute a romantic involvement."

Haverty winced again at those numbers.

"Listen to me," Abrams said urgently, "I understand the pressures on you in this case. We've experienced a few pressures of our own in this office. That business of your stating the father wasn't a priest—I can understand why you felt the need to get that into the record, Ben. And that much this office would not dispute." Abrams flicked a fingernail against the Xerox copy. "But the *rest of it*—listen, Ben, this office intends to play completely square with you on this case. Keep you informed of every witness, every piece of evidence we plan to present. All cards on the table, and let them fall where they will. There'll be no sandbagging out of this office—particularly not on this case."

In the compelling silence Haverty turned back toward the desk. Abrams slapped his hand lightly over the Xerox sheet. "This thing you say here in this press release, that 'all the facts surrounding this enormous tragedy will be disclosed at the trial'—okay, Ben, that one was your serve. And if you persist in pursuing that line of defense, that the evidence this office has turned up would indicate was not, shall we say, a valid description of the circumstances of this conception, we will certainly put that putative father on the stand."

Slaughter.

She ran that new word over and over her mind in the long hours when she was trying to get to sleep that night.

Slaughter. In some ways it was worse than *murder.*

Like Herod's *slaughter of the innocents,* when he killed all those Jewish boy babies, trying to kill the baby Jesus.

She'd gone down there and testified to those grand jury people, told all those intimate, terribly private things to those strangers, answered those frightening questions, because she was so sure that once she *explained* to them what had happened, then *surely* they would understand the terrible mistake they were making. And leave her in peace again.

Now they came back at her, instead, with that charge of *slaughter.*

She kept thinking of those words from the evening newspaper: *twenty-five years.* They said if she was convicted of this charge they had brought against her, she might serve twenty-five years in jail.

The number was so enormous it had no real meaning, except—her whole life.

She rolled over in the narrow bed, pulling her knees up to her chest. *Lord, help me. Help me to bear the pain, without doubting You. Help me to accept this trial You sent with a generous, loving, believing heart.*

It might be, could be, that those strange people out there who were doing these things to her never would understand the truth.

Lord, help me to be strong. Help me to forgive *them for what they do.*

When Tim Vance read about Sister Angela's indictment in the morning newspaper, laid up against that peculiar two-column verbatim statement from her lawyers strongly implying a rape, he was consumed with a gnawing, irresistible curiosity. Since he was now fairly officially out of the case, he made it a point to make a little business in the Ramsey County Hall of Justice that week.

The second time he drifted casually past Andy DaSilva's desk Andy was sitting there, his right arm all in plaster.

"Jesus, Andy!" Vance exclaimed. "What the hell happened to you?"

"Would you believe, a basketball game in my own driveway? How the hell are you anyway, Tim?"

"Right now, curious. Real curious, Andy. All this stuff implying rape that the nun's lawyers are running out in the papers—what the hell's going on with that?"

"Well, I guess you got it right enough, Tim. I guess that's just about what they're trying out."

"Well, Jesus Christ. Is that what *she* ran out in the grand jury?"

DaSilva ran his eyes nervously around the walls of his office cubicle. The grand jury proceedings were privileged, secret under pain of jail sentence for divulgence. But Tim Vance felt like family to DaSilva, after what they'd shared on that amazing, unexpected trip to Milwaukee. And from the look on Vance's face right now, DaSilva knew he was hungry, *needing* to know.

DaSilva said abruptly, "Hey, come with me." And led him to an empty conference room down the hall.

DaSilva closed the door behind them and sat down on one of the chairs, cradling the cast on his cross-legged lap. In the sudden intimacy of that large, empty room, Vance was looking toward him with naked expectation. DaSilva said slowly, "Look, Tim, you understand I'm not supposed to talk about this. But—"

"Sure, sure, understood. Sealed lips, Andy. But I just—would really like to know."

"Well, she didn't testify to *rape,* exactly. But it was one real passive sex act in the woods, that she said she wasn't expecting and didn't really understand when it was happening."

As DaSilva recounted her testimony of that single, vague, sparsely recalled act in the woods, Vance was staring at him, dumbfounded. "Well, Jesus Christ," he muttered.

"Oh, yeah. But the grand jury didn't buy it anyway, I guess. We didn't rebut her statement but I think maybe if they'd believed it, she might've gotten herself off with a no bill."

Vance muttered, "Jesus, Andy. That's goddam fascinating."

"What, fascinating? *You* know she was lying, Tim. Lying through all her little nun teeth. But it didn't wash anyway, so now it's gonna come down to a trial. And I hope Ben Haverty doesn't try his hypothetical rape case in that, because if he does I'm gonna have to take him apart."

"What, you've got the case?" DaSilva nodded. Vance said slowly, "Well, hey, that's terrific, Andy. That's a real big case you've got there."

DaSilva grimaced. "Big, yes. Easy or clean, no."

"Well, hey, you've got the truth on your side, Andy."

Another grimace. "Yeah, sure. Tell that to Judge Aaron."

"Did you talk to Pete Juhl about the polygraph?"

"Not talk, but yeah, I heard the results."

"Well, I happened to talk to Pete, and the main thing that struck him was—how the whole thing of having the sex was her idea. Not his at all. Pete was real specific about that, Andy."

DaSilva shrugged, his normally mild face tight with expression. "Yeah, that's what I gather. That's one reason I was so—unmoved by her grand jury testimony. I mean, there she was, sitting up there so sweet and appealing, telling us her little story about being taken advantage of in the woods. A real touching little story, Tim. Except that *not one word of if happened to be true.*"

When he left DaSilva and moved toward the Hall of Justice elevators, Vance was charged with a very private excitement.

Now he had a fix on how *both* the women involved in this case had experienced that sex—Gayle Flynn, and Sister Angela.

Gayle Flynn tugging that guy Roy by the hand down the rocky, sandy beach. Insisting, *"No, no, it's all right."*

And Sister Angela—violated innocently, even unknowingly, by that unnamed man in the dark woods.

No way was that the same woman. *No way.* Tim Vance knew as surely as he was punching that real, actual elevator button. One of them loose, laughing. Urging, pressing, coming on. The other tight, frozen—supposedly paralyzed with fright by what had *been done* to her.

Every detail, every nuance different. Every *feel* of it different.

An odd thought suddenly poked into Tim Vance's head: he wondered if Sister Angela Flynn would pass a polygraph exam about her memories of that sex. If they could only get her on the machine, Vance thought she probably would.

And *Gayle Flynn,* if they got *her* on a polygraph, would she pass it too? Probably—yes. If they could just get her to tell *her own* truth.

Vance couldn't agree with Andy DaSilva that Sister Angela was obviously lying. Nothing he'd heard, read about that little nun squared with the view that she could cheerfully, smilingly, lie her way through a crucifying experience like that grand jury testimony had to be for her. Vance thought it much more likely that she *believed* what she had testified to. He was willing to believe that for Sister Angela that probably *was* the truth of this case.

He wondered how often Gayle Flynn was around, in these high-pressured days. Suspected she wasn't there too often, and then only in flashes—probably only when Sister Angela felt confronted, overwhelmed by the intolerable pressure of her guilt.

When she had to somehow *express* that guilt—*then,* always, it would be Gayle Flynn talking. Because the one thing Tim Vance already understood very well about Sister Angela was that she was *not guilty.*

As he moved off the elevator he caught himself, chided himself one more time, like he had so often lately: who was *he,* small-town cop with four night-school psych courses to his credit, to be pop-shrinking this obviously heavy, obviously exceptional case?

Yet that old conviction bounced back at him as he pushed through the glass door into the open space of that plaza: he *knew he was right.* Even if none of the rest of them saw it, her well-trained shrinks, those brainy D.A.s—

It wasn't that strange, sad little nun who had tripped that guy Danziger down the beach. Probably wasn't even her who'd killed the baby.

The trouble with this whole goddam case was that they *probably had the wrong woman on trial here.* But Tim Vance didn't expect he could persuade anybody else of that.

Even if he tried, which he already knew he wouldn't. His part of it was already done, delivering the raw material of the Cambridgeport Police Department's investigation of Sister Angela Flynn. It was up to her shrinks, her lawyers, all those people trained so much better than him, to help her now.

Let *them* find the guilty one, that Gayle Flynn. And save *her,* too, if they goddam could.

Thirty-two

Ben Haverty recognized the irony even as he was glaring across the glass-topped table in the conference room of attorney Monroe Dickson's Milwaukee office. Like some bizarre closing of a circle in his own career.

For eighteen years now he had poured out his energies defending losers, misfits in the system like that one slouched across the table. As often as not they lied to him as well as the court, and wound up stiffing him for his fee. That never bothered Ben Haverty much. His payoff wasn't money anyway. Or even winning the cases. What kept Haverty going, fueled his nervous drives, was a satisfaction so quaint and private that he rarely admitted it even to himself.

Mainly, Ben Haverty just liked helping out where help was needed most, which happened to be at the bottom of society's barrel—the place this Roy Danziger came out of.

With one dismayed glance Haverty knew the mind-fix, the alibis, even the life history. The body language so predictably sullen, sulking, withheld; the studiedly inappropriate dress, in effect a uniform of his type. Under normal circumstances Haverty would have met this Danziger as one

445

more hapless criminal defendant, proffering inadequate explanations of his arrest for burglary or narcotics or whatever, which Ben Haverty would have to try to make stick in a court of law.

But this time it was Angela Flynn who was his client, Angela Flynn's fragile salvation that was trusted to his care. And Ben Haverty understood quite well that this unkempt loser, this sociopath Danziger, had it in his power to effectively jeopardize her life.

The answers to his questions about Danziger's employment, education, background, Haverty predicted fairly accurately before they came sullenly across the table. He asked how Danziger became acquainted with Angela Flynn, how that acquaintanceship developed, and the answers squared fairly well with Angela's own recollections.

Then they moved, inevitably, into the area of sex. The questions became sharper, more pointed; the answers more reluctant.

"You admit you had carnal knowledge of Sister Angela?"

"I had sex with Gayle. Yeah."

"Under what circumstances?"

"We were walking on the beach. We stopped to talk."

"On the beach? Not in the woods?"

"Woods? No."

"Was there any force involved?"

"What, force? You mean, like, rape?"

Glaring nod. "No, it wasn't no rape."

"How many times did you have sexual contact?"

"Like I told the cops, about five. Maybe six."

Haverty could feel the heat, the pressure building under his shirt collar. He asked coldly, "Under what circumstances?"

"On the beach, at night. After the others were sacked out."

"Always on the beach?"

"Yeah, when we went for walks. Maybe one night she sneaked out to my sleeping bag, but she didn't stay the whole night."

The tension building in Haverty, like a winding clock spring. But his voice coldly controlled: "You are saying you never had sex in the woods?"

"Nah. I don't know where you got this woods. It was all, like, around the beach."

"Were you drinking on those occasions?"

"Sometimes. Sometimes we were both drinking."

"Drunk to excess?"

"Nah, I wouldn't say so."

"Were you using narcotics?"

Pause. Shifting movement of the eyes. "What you mean, narcotics?"

"*Narcotics.* I assume you know what narcotics are, Danziger."

Pause. "Well, I smoked a little grass up there. Not a whole lot."

"Do you mean to suggest she also smoked narcotics?"

"Gayle? Nah, she wasn't into that."

"And you're telling me you never forced your sexual attentions on her."

"Nah. I never pushed her."

"You're telling me you had five or six incidents of sex with a nun without forcing yourself on her?"

"Well, I didn't know then she was a nun. Not at first." Danziger pulled in a steadying breath. "Then when I found out, I thought maybe we shouldn't be doing it. It didn't seem —like, right. But she said no, it was okay."

Haverty's tight controls were beginning to slip. *"She said it was okay?"*

Shrug. "Yeah. So we did it again a couple times, when, like, she let me know she wanted to."

Long, stricken silence. Then: "You mean to sit there and tell me, Danziger, that a fine, sensitive, educated, intelligent woman like that *was initiating sex with you?"* Louder now: *"You expect me to believe that, Danziger?"*

Impassive shrug. "I don't care what you believe. I'm just telling you what happened."

At this point Danziger's attorney leaned forward and interrupted nervously, "Mr. Haverty, I think I should point out that my client has volunteered full cooperation in this inquiry, both with the authorities and with yourself. He's under no obligation, of course, to speak with you, but he's cooperating voluntarily."

Haverty had swelled in his chair like an aroused puff adder. "Cooperation? *You call this cooperation?* You telling me that an innocent, defenseless nun who's now facing a murder charge as a direct result of your actions told you the kind of behavior you describe was *okay?"* Flatly: "I think you're a liar, Danziger."

Danziger blinked against that word. Stirred in his seat as he said softly, "Hey, I'm real sorry about what happened to her. I'd help her now, if I could."

"You'd help her?"

"Sure. But I don't know—nobody's told me how I could."

Seething, rumbling in his chair. *"I'll tell you how,* Danziger. You can stop fabricating these pathetic stories to protect your own hide. You can stop trying to destroy the character and reputation of a good woman who never meant any harm to you, and you can *tell me what really happened."*

Roy Danziger hesitated. Then, very softly: "Hey, I know what you want to hear. But that wasn't the way it was."

Their eyes locked, grappled briefly over the glass-topped table; Danziger's were the first to drop away.

"You're a chronic unemployable, Danziger. An admitted narcotics user. You probably have a criminal record. Why in hell should I believe anything you say?"

Danziger answered loosely, helplessly. "Hey, okay,

don't. It's no skin off my nose, man. You're asking me, so I'm telling you—that's how it was."

"She hasn't suffered enough? She hasn't already suffered enough from you, Danziger, that you can't back off these pathetic alibis?" Danziger made no response. "How big was that beach where you say you had sex five or six times, Danziger?" No response. "How many yards—say, five hundred? Five thousand? You're saying you had sexual congress five times on that beach and *nobody saw it, nobody heard it?"*

Shrug.

"Didn't that surprise you, Danziger, that nobody else heard it?"

"Well, at night they were mostly inside their trailers."

"Nobody was outside?"

"Nah, I guess." He hesitated. "There were lots of mosquitoes up there."

There was a moment of terrible silence in the conference room. Then Ben Haverty said again, flatly, "You're a goddamned liar, Danziger."

Danziger looked at the blank cream-painted wall in front of him.

"She said it was okay? I'd like to get you and your goddamned mosquitoes under oath on a witness stand, Danziger. I think you're a deadbeat hippie liar who is trying to destroy a beautiful, innocent young girl who never did any harm to you. I think you're raping her all over again with what you're doing to her now, Danziger, and before you're finished you—" He broke off abruptly, as his voice veered out of control.

Brief silence. "I know what you want me to say," Danziger muttered. "And I'd say it now if I thought it would really help her. But—that's not how it happened."

Haverty said flatly, "You're a liar, Danziger. And I hope to hell I get a chance to prove that on a witness stand."

. . .

Later that afternoon, when Dr. Kenneth Rhoades was in a particularly peckish mood, Meg Gavin called to find out if anything new was coming down in the M.E.'s office. "Old's more like it, Meg," Rhoades snapped into the phone. "That Baby Boy Flynn body has been around here for five weeks now, and I think that's goddam long enough. Just out of simple decency, I'd like to see that baby have a proper burial."

Meg grabbed for the notebook in her blue purse. "Hey, Doc, I thought that was done weeks ago."

Rhoades said they had kept the body frozen for the purpose of further pathological testing, at the request of Ben Haverty. "And I complied out of courtesy. I certainly don't want this office to be accused of disposing of any relevant evidence, but in my view the freezing of the tissues and the considerable length of time since the death would probably defeat the accuracy of any tests they might still want to do now."

"Well, Jesus Christ." Meg was scribbling with unanticipated urgency. "Why d'you think they let it go this long?"

"I can't answer that, Meg. Speaking in generalities, I'd have to say that the only reason we usually keep a body this long is because nobody claims it."

Angela Flynn went out to dinner that night with her brother Dan. She picked up a morning newspaper on the way home. When she got back to the convent and read the unexpected item about her baby, she called Mr. Haverty at home. His wife said he was out of town at the moment, but she would certainly have him get in touch with Sister Angela the next day.

At 11:45 the next morning Ben Haverty was pacing again in Mark Abrams's corner office, wiping his sweating hands on his handkerchief as he said, "Mark, I'd like to have some idea of what kind of deal you're willing to make."

Quietly, from Abrams: "You saw him, Ben?"

Haverty's quivering reaction to that question showed on his face. "Goddam liar."

"Ben, he did pass a satisfactory polygraph. Like I told you, he tested out on—"

Haverty silenced the D.A. with one angry thrust of his hand. *"God, I've seen them all my life.* Lying pathological bastards trying to save their own miserable skins. They'll say one time, five, six times—two hundred times. It's no difference to them. He'd say two, three hundred times, if he thought he could get anything out of it."

Now those bizarre tears again, that so disquieted Abrams to see.

"Christ, I'd like to take him apart. I'd like to get that fucking pathological liar on a witness stand and tear him and his pathetic story to pieces."

Abrams reacted with alarm. "Well now, Ben, I certainly hope you're going to think twice before you pursue that route. And I think we could avoid this whole trial if you're willing to plead to, say, criminally negligent manslaughter. And take a very brief suspended sentence."

Haverty shook his head slowly, exhaustedly. "I don't think she'll go for it. I don't think she's willing to plead guilty to anything."

"Hey, Ben, we've got to have *some* kind of guilty plea to go with. After the charge the grand jury brought in, criminally negligent is as low as we can go."

Haverty's face tightened. He said again, quietly, savagely: "That goddamned liar."

That afternoon Angela Flynn was shown into Haverty's private office by Andretti.

As soon as she was seated she burst out, "Mr. Haverty, I don't understand how you could leave the baby there in that—place. I told you I wanted him buried as soon as possible."

Ben Haverty was thinking infuriatedly, *Damn Rhoades. And damn that Meg Gavin. Where the hell did they get off, publicizing that kind of information?*

Aloud he said calmly, reassuringly, "Now, Angela, I explained to you that our own pathologist, Dr. Von Bargen, still has certain tests to conduct. Unfortunately, his schedule has been very crowded. But he's promised to get to them as soon as he can."

Quivering, frowning, edging on tears: "But it said in the paper it was already too late for tests. I just want this to be *finished.* I want him out of that place. Why can't you just *bury* him, Mr. Haverty?"

He shifted in his chair, leaned toward her. "Angela, I promise you we'll do that as soon as we possibly can." He paused. "You have my promise on that. All right, Angela?"

She turned the green eyes on him, gave him the faint smile his tone of voice was demanding. "All right. Thank you, Mr. Haverty. But—*soon,* please."

He asked how things were going for her at Our Lady of Pompeii Convent, listening distractedly to her brief, polite answers.

Then, looking away from the green eyes: "Angela, I must tell you that I have had an interview with this Roy Danziger person." He lowered his voice: "Angela, I must tell you that this person is claiming that there were five or six separate incidents of, ah, contact in this case."

She blinked, genuinely bewildered. "What do you mean, Mr. Haverty?"

He explained, unhappily, a little more specifically. She still seemed bewildered. "Well, he's wrong. I don't know why he said that, but he's quite wrong."

Haverty was up on his feet now, standing with his hands jammed in his rear pockets near the office window. She could see the doubt written on his unhappy face. She turned to the younger lawyer sitting beside her and said intensely, *"You believe me, don't you, Mr. Andretti?"*

452

He nodded mutely, blankly. She turned the green eyes back across the desk. "I don't know why that Roy person said those things, Mr. Haverty. I thought he was a basically good person, even though— I never thought he would *lie* about this. But that still doesn't change what happened. *No matter what he is saying now.*"

Haverty nodded. "But you must understand, Angela, this puts a slightly, ah, different complexion on your case. Now we have, as I told you, a very strong defense based only on the medical evidence. A very strong case, from many aspects."

"*Well, then,*" she said softly, firmly.

Haverty's face twitched back toward the window; he leaned heavily against its frame. "But, Angela, as you could see from the grand jury experience, these legal processes are not always predictable in their outcome." He paused. "Angela, I think I must tell you now that the district attorney has offered us an opportunity to avoid the ordeal of an open trial in this case. He would be willing to let a judge dispose of the case out of court, so to speak, provided you would agree to—plead guilty to a lesser charge."

Her body went very stiff in the chair. He was trying to explain to her about something called *criminally negligent manslaughter,* explain what it would mean, but she barely listened. Only repeated several times, "*But Mr. Haverty, I'm not guilty.*"

He kept saying he understood her feelings in that regard, but she shook her head angrily: *obviously he didn't understand at all.*

She let him go on talking, explaining for as long as he wanted. So many cruel, bewildering things still happening to her, and now even *her own lawyer* coming at her with that strange story that Roy person had made up.

When he finally seemed finished, she said quietly, intensely, "What that Roy told you—*that wasn't what happened, Mr. Haverty.*" That worn-out tape of the dark woods still so vivid in her mind. "It was—the way I told you. I remember it very well, everything that happened. And it was just like I told you before." Softly, persistently: *"You believe me, don't you, Mr. Haverty?"*

As she pulled him into those huge, pained green eyes, there were still nagging shadows in his mind, unanswered questions that had torn into him like barbed hooks since that first meeting in Abrams's office.

But his heart was ripped open, captured, delivered. *"Yes, Angela. Yes. I believe you."*

The daily routine at Our Lady of Pompeii turned out to be almost like the hospitals: measured, predictable. She fitted quite easily into the new grid of time.

After some initial embarrassment about having her there at the convent, most of the other nuns simply went about their business, leaving her fairly much alone. The ones she felt most curious about were the three who taught at the parish day-care preschool run out of the little house next door. She saw and heard the children coming in and out every day, so she was always being reminded in that way of her job at Benedictine Kindergarten.

She would have liked to spend a little more time with those three, but none of the Pompeii nuns seemed to want to talk much to her—except Francesca.

Wary at first, she soon moved into a comfortable closeness with Fran. She knew she was probably Fran's *assignment*, knew Fran had probably been told to keep a fairly close eye on her. And although that idea seemed very strange to her, she did not really resist it.

Especially after that first time Fran dragged her off to the movies. In the darkened theater she was suddenly caught up in an unexpected sensation of—comfort. Darkness, safeness.

She groped behind Fran to a seat, and sank into the worn maroon velour chair. Fran was whispering happily,

"Rex Reed said this one was awful, which is probably a pretty good recommendation for it."

Angela barely heard her. She was staring, moving forward somewhere into the flickering images of that huge screen, into the safe and dark silence behind it.

At 4:10 on the afternoon of June 18, two men, one of them dressed as a priest, rang the bell at the front entrance of the O'Dwyer Funeral Home, a large white clapboard house fronted with a tall, flat neon-lit cement wall, located on Hinchley Street in downtown St. Paul, diagonally across the street from a McDonald's restaurant.

Raymond O'Dwyer came in from the back rooms and opened the door himself. He said to the younger man, "Ah, Mr. Flynn?"

Dan Flynn nodded. O'Dwyer extended his hand as he said solemnly, "Good to meet you, Mr. Flynn. I'm pleased to be able to be of service to you."

Flynn introduced Father George Cooney. "A friend of the family. We've asked Father Cooney to—ah, say a few prayers at the grave." As O'Dwyer murmured through his ritual of professional welcome Flynn interrupted with, "Is everything ready?"

"Yes, indeed. I thought perhaps to avoid attracting attention—if you have no objection, I could transport the body in my station wagon."

Flynn said, "Fine, whatever you think best. Let's just—get going."

At the building's rear entrance O'Dwyer loaded the small white polyurethane casket into the back of the green station wagon he'd used to make the pickup at the county morgue about six hours earlier. Wished all his jobs were as easy as this one. Since the body wasn't quite thawed and there was to be no viewing anyway, O'Dwyer simply left it in the same condition it came in from the morgue. They did a very neat job of stitching on those county autopsies, anyway.

455

O'Dwyer thumbed down the volume on the station wagon radio as he drove out from behind the house and signaled the two men in the gray Chevy to follow him to the Holy Ghost Cemetery, nine miles out Route 127.

The grave was already opened, in the children's section of the bleak, treeless cemetery. O'Dwyer lifted the small plastic casket out of the back of the station wagon and carried it over to the planking laid over the grave.

Father Cooney slipped a purple stole around his neck and read from his missal: " 'May the angels lead thee into Paradise; at thy coming may the martyrs receive thee, and bring thee into the holy city, Jerusalem. May the choir of angels receive thee, and with Lazarus, once a beggar, mayest thou have eternal rest.' "

O'Dwyer and Flynn said in unison, "Amen."

The priest began the Our Father, which the others said along with him. As Cooney reached the phrase, ". . . and lead us not into temptation," he sprinkled the casket with holy water from a silver shaker.

" 'But deliver us from evil.' "

" 'From the gate of hell.' "

" 'Deliver his soul, O Lord.' "

" 'Eternal rest grant unto him, O Lord.' "

" 'And let perpetual light shine upon him.' "

On June 19 a baby sparrow was blown out of a nest near the Fox Point beach house that Roy was renting in the off-season. He found it when he went out on the deck that morning to check the weather over the lake.

He pushed the bird carefully into a bowl and carried it into his kitchen. The bird's bulging eyes were still closed, its feathers spiny, wet-looking twigs. It squawked weakly through its always open beak.

He built a kind of nest in a dishtowel wadded into the bowl. At the beach house next door he asked if he could use the phone to call a veterinarian friend of his. "I just found a bird blown out of his nest," he explained to the neighbor as he waited out a busy signal.

"Oh, my," she said. "Is it very small?"

"Yeah, pretty."

"They usually can't make it on their own. Isn't there some way you could put it back in its nest?"

"Nah, I don't think so," he said. "I don't know where he came from. Have you got some tweezers I could borrow? I thought I'd feed him some bread and milk."

"I think they need insects," said the neighbor. "I don't think they can digest milk."

"Well, I'm gonna see," he said.

Talk about odd birds, the neighbor thought as she busied herself in the kitchen, watching him in side glances as he talked to the vet. They'd been living near him on the beach all winter, and this was the first time she could remember talking to him.

He came back two more times that morning to phone the vet. Then the neighbor didn't see him again for three days.

When she ran into him in the parking lot behind the houses she said, "Hey, how's the bird?"

"Oh, him," Roy said flatly. "He died."

Thirty-three

The summer passed slowly and warmly, almost like any other.

Most days Angela worked on the preschool projects that Sister Philomena had devised as her special assignment. With most of the seven other Pompeii nuns periodically away on vacations and study trips she sometimes had the convent almost to herself to work in.

Every Tuesday morning someone—usually Fran—drove her to Dr. Heilbron's office at the Parkhurst Mental Health Center. She worried a little about how much those weekly appointments must be costing the order, but otherwise she did not object to them now. She and Dr. Heilbron usually talked about interesting, constructive things, and he continued to be very pleased with her progress. So she came to look on these visits as a pleasant break in the routine, something to look forward to a little every week.

Every Thursday afternoon the nuns living at St. Rose Convent also came in to the Parkhurst Mental Health Center, for their weekly group-therapy sessions with Erica Reagan, a particularly tactful and discreet social worker in her mid-thirties who happened herself to be an ex-Holy Name nun. The purpose of this group, as Sister Philomena had explained it to those eleven nuns on an evening visit to St. Rose, was to give them some professional help in thinking through the recent pressures and changes in their lives. To help them break through the isolation this tragedy had suddenly thrust them into.

At first some of the St. Rose nuns strongly resented being forced to come here, to bare themselves one more time in this unfamiliar way. But most of them soon came to look forward to what amounted to a weekly hour-long community bull session.

After the first few awkward, halting sessions, they rarely talked about Angela and *that business*. What usually came to mind were much more general concerns.

Julia was surprised, for instance, to find herself talking a good deal about money—about the powerful hold it seemed to have on so many people outside the convent, and how much she herself resented and distrusted those values.

Margory talked a good deal about cleanliness. She

still remembered how hard it was as a child growing up in a messy houseful of six children to keep herself clean and neat.

Sometimes they talked about their families, parents, nieces and nephews. Some mentioned the struggles they felt in their teaching careers. Roxanne complained a good deal about feeling tired, feeling unappreciated. Mary Luke went on for quite a while one day about how "weird" she felt in conferences with the parents of difficult children from her class when the parents "treat me as if I must have all the answers, of course. Because I'm a *nun.*"

When they talked about the ideals of religious life, religious community, and how they felt about all the recent changes in the conceptualization of those ideals, Julia noticed that the discussion usually bogged down fairly quickly in mundane details. Like housekeeping schedules, or use of the cars. When Julia complained one afternoon that she couldn't really see what laundry charts had to do with a fully realized spiritual life, the social worker said that laundry charts maybe weren't so irrelevant after all, as long as talking about them helped the nuns to open up a communication, an exchange of ideas about how each of them felt about these things.

The next week they spent almost the whole session talking about how hard it was to dress in "civilian" clothes on an allowance of thirty dollars a month.

Early in July Sister Philomena Levesque convened a special meeting of the General Council of the Sisters of St. Benedict to review and discuss the question of whether Angela Flynn should remain in their congregation, at least for the time being.

The nuns had already dealt with the huge volume of mail they received after the news about Angela became public knowledge. Much of it was obscene, odious hate mail, instantly discarded. Some of the appropriate letters of condolence were forwarded to Angela; others the sisters responded to themselves.

Philomena was particularly touched by the offers of help, financial or otherwise, that came from several dozen religious orders scattered around the country. Two orders in particular had offered to take Angela Flynn into their own ranks as a nun, "at any time she and the sisters of your congregation might deem that move appropriate," as one Mother Superior put it.

Philomena mentioned those two offers as she opened the discussion. After a brief silence Mary Christopher murmured, "Well, I can't imagine that she could possibly *want* to stay in any order. Or *expect* to."

Philomena said that on the advice of Angela's attorney and physicians, no one from within the community had yet inquired into Angela's own views in that regard. "We will, of course, continue to give her total support, financial and otherwise, through the period of the legal ramifications." Philomena could not yet bring herself to use the words *public trial*. "But since that now appears quite likely to be a rather protracted process, I thought it appropriate that we might discuss some means of arriving at a consensus of opinion as to the views of the community as a whole concerning this unfortunate matter."

The community-wide vote she was nudging them toward was a calculated risk on Philomena's part. A majority vote of *no,* she already realized, would place her in a quite untenable position *vis-à-vis* the larger community of the town. But she had decided to risk it, on the assumption that, actually given the chance to *vote to expel* their suffering sister, most of the St. Benedict nuns would be roused to a sense of Christian charity and compassion that would make their own suffering a little easier to endure.

Then, perhaps, the dangerous resentments, the flaring angers Philomena had sensed so often around her when the subject of Angela Flynn came up could be allayed, made manageable. At least until that public trial was terminated.

Yet her suggestion of a vote provoked quite an animated dispute around the council table. Claudine—who knew Angela better than any of the others—offered the observation that a "yes" vote might work adversely in this instance, in that it might encourage Angela to believe she would be welcome to *stay on* in the congregation after the trial. As the nuns reacted visibly to that suggestion, Claudine added, "Angela is a very—closed, private person. It's hard for me to predict how she might react to this situation."

Bernadine nodded in emphatic agreement. "Surely—of course, Sister Philomena, I agree that we should *at this point* continue to give Angela every necessary support. As I believe we already have. But if this vote could possibly be construed as an *invitation to Angela* to continue on as if nothing had— Well, I can't see at this point why we should initiate any move of that nature."

Dissenting views vented, Philomena made a brief, moving speech about the shared responsibility, shared *commitment to mutual dedication,* that made up the heart of a religious community. In the end they went along, as she had known they would, agreeing to the arrangements for a secret ballot of the 723 nuns.

When the final tally was tabulated two weeks later, Philomena was shocked by the closeness of it: 457 nuns voted that Angela Flynn should be permitted to remain as a member of their congregation, 266 voted that she should not.

More anger, more resistance, than Philomena had expected to find expressed there. But enough support, at least, to see them through the barbarity of that public trial with a semblance of their willed community support intact.

For Meg Gavin this was like served time. Waiting, pure waiting.

461

She knew she probably would've dumped this town by now, been long gone, if it hadn't been for that one case—and maybe for Dewey Wald.

She saw him three or four times a week. Weekends, especially, they spent together, usually at her apartment—fucking for long, slow, wondrous hours, sometimes stoned, often to opera. Meg never had been much of a fan of opera, but she learned to love it *that* way at least, in those long, warm hours.

She knew every inch of the topography of his body, like a treasured, much-used map. The odd strings of black hair that grew out of his left ear. The surgery scar—souvenir of high school football—on his left knee. The flat, very pink nails that covered his very calloused toes. The poked-in dimples on both of his ass cheeks. The delicate joint of skin where his ass reshaped into the base of his balls. That he loved to have licked, wetly stroked.

In some ways she knew that thin, kinetic body better than she'd known any body before—better, almost, than her own, because the images of his were stamped so deep in her mind. Not a beautiful man, but beautiful, somehow, to her.

When she touched that body now, there was no judgment in the touch. She loved it, loved *him* in some way she had never let herself feel before.

She understood that this was only a pause she was taking with him, a loving pause that felt almost suspended in time. She did not look too closely at it, because she knew that for now, for *her,* it was right. Later—well, that would be another time, in a different space.

Near the end of July, Wald went to Houston for a week-long architectural conference. Meg sent him off with cheerful hopes that he would finally get it on with that knockout lady architect friend of his from Seattle. On the second night he was gone, she decided what the hell, and dropped a call to Benny the Carpenter.

Almost pathetically grateful to hear from her, Benny

loped to her apartment within twenty minutes, bringing several joints of amazingly excellent dope.

Meg was quite delighted to see him there again in her living room, this outrageously beautiful face, this beautiful body moving so fluidly as he leaped up to change records or posture his anger against his dumb-fuck boss. She was willing to forgive him almost anything, even his boringness, his stupidity, because he was *so goddamned beautiful.* Now he was complaining about his apartment being ripped off, his eight-hundred-dollar retail stereo snatched. The one he bought hot for two eighty.

She tried not to smile as she said, "Hey, what the hell, Benny. It's a dangerous world we live in."

He whipped out and lighted up the second of his splendid joints. Said as he passed it to her, kneeling over her on the couch, "Hey, Meg-o, it's real good to see you again. I really kinda missed you a lot."

God, she loved the idea of making love to a body as beautiful as that. And once they were tumbling naked, laughing, in the queen-sized bed, she retrieved the forgotten language of his body, tuned to it effortlessly, easily.

And loved that wild, amazing terrain she moved very quickly into. Words had never worked well between her and Benny, but the bodies always had.

And still did. Later as she watched him sleeping, his mouth hanging open, his arm flung back on the pillow, she felt a little surprised—and more than a little pleased—to realize that she could still pleasure herself so thoroughly with a body that was not Wald's.

For the next few days she toyed on and off with the idea of dropping a call to Will the Bartender. To sample a little more of her reclaimed bachelor prerogative.

But in the end she used the spare time to catch up on her bills and backed-up correspondence. Then it was Sunday, and Dewey Wald was standing in her apartment doorway, grinning crookedly, his arms spread wide in welcome.

463

She moved happily into them. "Hey, Gavin," as he wrapped her in that so familiar enfolding. "You miss me?"

She murmured, "Actually, Wald, I almost did." And moved easily, willingly back into *his* skin, *his* specialness.

Angela's days were quite dull, quite lonely and routine.

But her evenings now were very busy, as her friends rallied around with invitations—to family dinners, buffet suppers, cocktail parties. Most of them from parents connected to Benedictine Kindergarten; a few from old classmates from her school years.

She felt quite nervous about those first invitations, and declined several times. Finally accepted the fourth—from Lena and Arthur Schwartz—with feelings of disquiet, even trepidation.

Yet it turned out to be a very pleasant, reassuring evening. The two other couples there also had children at Benedictine Kindergarten. And they all treated her—as if she was someone valuable. Someone prized. So many people—even some of her own family—seemed quite uncomfortable to be around her these days. Like those nuns at Our Lady of Pompeii. They just didn't—act like themselves when she was around.

But sitting at the Schwartzs' glass-topped dinner table, that first night, she could feel the warmth flowing toward her from all around the table. Some of her own anxious defensiveness melted as she took that warmth inside her. These people, at least, then—*they understood.*

After that, she accepted as many evening invitations as she could fit into her schedule. Some evenings went better than others. But every time some husband came to pick her up at the Pompeii convent, Angela set off with the same thought firmly, warmly, fixed in her mind: maybe these people at least, these friends, *understood that she was not guilty.*

.   .   .

At the buffet dinner at Janine Vitale's house, Margaret Hogan watched Angela very sharply as she held court in center stage, tossing back five or six drinks with no apparent effect.

What troubled Margaret most was her extraordinary bouncy *cheerfulness.* So brittle and plastic, almost unreal. And the attentions Angela permitted, even seemed to encourage from Janine Vitale—the hugs, the pats, the fawning smiles and laughs.

Margaret remembered Janine very well from their high school years as a bitter, fiercely self-promoting girl—and a ringleader in the periodic persecutions that were launched against little Gayle Flynn. Surely *Angela* must remember that too. Surely she must recognize that this woman had never been her friend—and was surely not one now, as she displayed Angela like some kind of parlor trick to that circle of gibbering, valueless people who hung so brightly on her animated conversation. As if she was some kind of a *star.*

Yet Angela seemed not to mind at all. Seemed, in fact, to *bask* in their empty attentions.

Silence in the car as the Hogans drove home. Ron broke it finally with, "So? What do you think?"

Margaret said flatly, reluctantly, "Well, I saw it, but I'm still not sure I believe it."

He waited, saying nothing.

"Oh, Ron, that isn't the Angela we know. What's *happened* to her? I wouldn't even *know* her there tonight, all arm in arm with that incredible ass-kissing bitch Janine Vitale."

Ron Hogan showed no reaction to those amazing, vulgar words he had almost never heard his wife utter.

"And Angela didn't even seem to *mind* it, Ron. All that bizarre fawning and ass-kissing. She even seemed to *like* it. Ron, I swear I don't recognize her at all."

"Well, maybe that's her way of trying to deal with everything that's happened to her. It can't be easy for her, Peg."

"Oh, I know that. My God, I know that. But bouncing around like that, like some giggling little actress on a stage —my God, Ron, I swear I wouldn't even *know* her."

Soothingly, from Ron: "Well, give her some time to get back on her feet. Just give her a little time, Peg."

Typical, so typical of Ron, to think that any problem could be fixed with a little time. "Ron, that policeman who came by to see us—do we still have his card?"

"I guess. Someplace in the den."

Margaret cradled her neck exhaustedly on the passenger seat. "Well, I'm calling him tomorrow."

Once Lieutenant Vance was actually *there,* sitting in that flowered chair on their sunporch looking expectantly across the room at the Hogans, Margaret suddenly no idea at all of what she should say. But since Ron was obviously leaving it up to her, she did the speaking—hesitantly at first, then increasingly rapidly as she tried to put into words all the things that were bothering her so much lately about Angela. Like that fierce *cheerfulness* that seemed, under the circumstances, almost a little—unnatural. And her strange behavior at these parties people were throwing in her honor. Almost as if she *enjoyed* being fawned over by all those people, some of them hardly more than strangers. Angela, who had always been so totally self-effacing. One of the most genuinely selfless, devoted women Margaret had ever known. "But now —it's almost like she's just a *shell* of that person I used to know so well."

Margaret Hogan talked for about an hour. And most of her troubled, disjointed impressions fanned a mounting excitement in Tim Vance. This was the first chance he'd had to hear an unedited flow of information about Angela Flynn —the *before* and *after* Angela Flynn. And so much of what Margaret was blurting out seemed to fit almost eerily into the only keyhole Vance could see into this case.

God, he wished he could let his hair down with these

Hogans, lay the whole idea right out for them—these caring, concerned people who knew Angela well enough to tell him *whether or not it was true.*

Margaret was asking, almost pleading for that now as she said, "Oh, Lieutenant, the main reason I wanted to talk to you— Look, I know you people must know a good deal about what's going on here. She's such an old, dear friend of mine, and I feel so helpless, right now, to help her. I thought—maybe if you could help me to just—*understand* it a little."

Vance's hesitation was very brief. The good cop in him recognized that if he shared this crazy idea of his, he would also be delivering over the makings of one hell of a good defense against a manslaughter-one charge.

Just about ironclad. And that was not Tim Vance's job right now to deliver that kind of ammunition over to the other side. *Not his job.*

For now and through the trial, Vance had to play this one for his own team. So he said evenly, "Mrs. Hogan, it happens I do have some ideas. And I know you're real genuinely concerned for Sister Angela's welfare, so maybe sometime I'd like to share them with you. I think maybe you *could* be—helpful to her." He paused. "But I hope you'll understand why I can't do that until this case is legally terminated."

She wasn't happy with that answer. Argued against it in her polite, halting way, her fat, motherly face creased with the pain of her concern.

Vance promised to come back and talk to her again once the trial was over. She finally accepted that, reluctantly, and saw him to the front door. Turned before she opened it and asked anxiously, "But can't you just— What *can* we do to help her, Lieutenant?"

Vance put as much encouragement as he could muster into the smile he offered her. "Just what you're doing, Mrs. Hogan. Be a real good friend."

467

．   ．   ．

A week later Tim and Alison Vance were invited to a poolside barbecue at some neighbors, the Martinos.

It was turning out to be a pretty good party until Vance got stuck with his plate of ribs and chicken on one end of a redwood bench shared by a neighborhood bitch who liked to corner him at parties and complain about Cambridge-port's crime rate.

Tonight she was running on the nun case. "Such a *shocking* thing. You know I'm no Catholic, Tim, but I certainly was shocked about that. So what's happening to that investigation?"

"Well, we're giving it our best shot, Bella. Great chicken, isn't this?"

"It could use more soy sauce." She leaned conspiratorially toward him. "I couldn't believe it, Tim, when she was the *only one* you people indicted. I couldn't believe they were actually getting away with it."

"What 'they' is that, Bella?"

"Well, those other nuns, I suppose. The ones who helped her do it. You don't mean to tell me you really think she did all that *by herself,* Tim? Delivered her own baby and cut the cord and killed it and hid it and all that, *all by herself?"*

"Well, that's one theory, Bella. But I guess you're entitled to another."

"Well, I can tell you this much, Tim—that woman didn't do all that by herself. That's just plain *not possible.* You ask any woman who's had a baby, Tim—she had to have some-one else in on it, somebody helping her."

"Well, Bella, if you figure out who that was, you be sure to let us know. Hey, excuse me, I'm going to go get me more of that good chicken." Jesus *Christ,* what a boring, ugly woman.

Yet something from that conversation hovered, itched at Tim's mind. An hour later as he was jawing with Len Martino at poolside, it finally hit him.

Abruptly, he excused himself, and moved out to the end of the lawn, almost beyond reach of the lights and the noise.

One woman didn't do that herself. She had to have help.

His own strong conviction, on that dizzying first night, which he'd dropped later as an unworkable loose end when the evidence piled in a different direction. Now Bella Smithers had brought it back to him, and with a pounding rush of adrenaline, Vance realized what he'd been sensing there all along: *two women* did *kill this baby.* Sister Angela—and Gayle Flynn.

Vance felt an eerie kind of shiver move over his skin as that instinctive perception finally took shape as a realization in his mind. Ah, sure, it took *the two of them* to do it.

Alone, neither one was a killer. Both seemed to be well-intentioned, basically harmless little ladies, each one kind of likable in her own way. No malice, no violence, evident in either one.

But when Sister Angela was actually confronting the long-denied reality of that howling baby, confronting the terrible moment of discovery that she'd struggled for so long to avoid—maybe *Angela and Gayle had fused together* in an explosive, murderous psychic collision. . . .

That could be what the inexplicable energy came out of —*Angela and Gayle acting together,* acting as one in a huge, violent moment of psychic fusing. Fusing like an H-bomb, releasing that devouring energy that made the impossible real.

Now there was a new question to skitter at the edges of his mind: in the unlikely event this case did come down to a public trial, could Angela endure *that* excruciating pressure without flipping out one more time into Gayle?

Or would the *two of them* fuse again in the glare of that courtroom?

Thirty-four

For Meg Gavin there was a feeling of odd nervousness about the summer, a sense of something missing.

It helped to be so tied up in this thing with Dewey. He talked every so often about them moving in together, but she resisted that idea with very little self-debate—especially after the four straight days he spent at her apartment when his was being painted. "Fucking klutz," she murmured from the circle of his arms the morning she was sending him disgruntedly back home. "I really *do* love you, you know. Just because I don't want your underwear in my gooddam drawers—hey, come on. What matters, anyway?"

He was swaying her back and forth in a slow-moving embrace. "Okay. Message received, Gavin. I just think—listen, there's even better levels we could get to if we shared more time together. More give-and-take, day-to-day shit."

She was laughing, prodding at his thin ribs as she pulled away from the embrace. "Point well taken, Wald. My shitting I handle quite well by myself, thank you. It's that other good stuff I like having you around for, sweetiepie."

On the last day of July, she picked up a message to call some editor at *WomansWorld* magazine in New York. *Fucking bra-burners,* she was already thinking as she dialed the operator to make the call collect. Whatever they wanted from her, the pay better be damn good.

The editor thanked her for calling back and said they'd just been going through a file of clips on the Sister Angela Flynn case and noticed all the good reporting she'd been doing on it. They wondered if she'd like to write a fifteen-hundred- to two-thousand-word piece for them.

Her hesitation was not so much a pause as an exploding of possibilities in her head. It never occurred to her to ask how much they paid as she slapped her desk and said, "Okay, sure. You got it."

So she plunged once more. This time determined to flip every goddam stone she could lay her hands on.

She started with the official sources. The editor of the Catholic diocesan weekly newspaper, a mild, likable little Milquetoast in his mid-fifties, said regretfully that he'd *wanted* to cover that case, was in fact bothered a lot in his journalistic conscience that his paper wasn't doing it, but he still felt the case was a personal tragedy, not a religious one. Too technical for their limited resources to handle—and unnecessary, since it was being reported so well in the daily press. He pulled the back files for his paper's only comment on the case, a cryptic editorial printed in the first week of May: *"TIME TO PRAY. Regarding the recent tragedy in our diocese, things we must not do—moralize, generally judge. Rather three things we must do—pray. Pray. And pray. For all concerned."*

The secretary to Bishop Paul Roche, Father Joseph Brenner, said graciously that the bishop still had no comment to offer on this matter, and was referring all inquiries to the sisters of St. Benedict.

Sister Bernadine, the order's PR mouthpiece, said wispily that she was very sorry, Megan, but the order, following the instructions of Mr. Haverty in this matter, would have no further public comment to make on the case at this time.

Fucking hypocritical stiffs, the lot of them. Meg had known before starting her re-digging, of course, that the official Church position on this case was still going to be the ostrich stance, head firmly tucked in the sand, ass waving in the cold wind. But it still pissed her off to hear it.

Late Friday afternoon she dropped in for the usual week's end happy hour at the Blind Justice Bar. Crowd thinner than usual in the summers, but she did catch Mark Abrams briefly to alert him to her new assignment. Abrams grimaced wearily when she asked if he had any new imputs to make. "Well, you might mention the callousness certain of the news media reporters have demonstrated to this very sensitive case at the press conferences."

"Oh, Mark, has it been *that* bad a week?"

At the end of the bar Nick Scotti was propped, his pork-pie turned sideways on his head, his black-haired belly hanging out through his unbuttoned shirt. "Hey, Nick." Meg smiled. "I see you're feeling a touch of the grape tonight."

She kept hoping if she got Nick deep enough in his cups some night he might spill something about the father of the nun's baby—some kernel to conjure on. A *crumb,* even. But when she tried a delicate feint now, Scotti leaned both elbows on the bar and mashed the porkpie down over his face. Muttered indistinctly through the hat: "You want to know what nuns do for sex in this town, Meg?"

"Hunh?"

He straightened up, readjusted the hat. "I said, you want to know what nuns do for sex in this town?"

Smile. "Damn straight I do."

"Well, a lot of them get their birth-control pills from an old gynecologist at St. Michael's Hospital who's so senile he's not real sure what he's doing. They get the pills real easy from him, no questions asked."

She shook her head admiringly. "Jesus, Nick, that's good stuff. Where'd you get that?"

"And then sometimes they cruise the singles bars. Always in pairs. One of them's allowed to get drunk, and the other stays sober enough to drive. So if she wants to get rid of the guy she's picking up she can just say she has to drive her roommate home."

She was laughing now. "Oh, come on, Nick."

"What, you think I'm kidding?" He glared at her, his small black eyes drunkenly irate. "Hey, I don't kid around with this stuff. But they stay away from guys in black socks and black Bostonian shoes. You know why?"

Meg had to work a little on that one. "That's gotta be —because he could be a priest, right?"

Scotti glowered appreciatively. "You know something, Meg? You're pretty goddam sharp."

Rippling laugh. "Oh, Jesus, Nick. That stuff's so good I almost hope it's true."

He reached under his opened shirt to scratch his back. "Okay, so don't believe it if you don't want. I'm telling you, that's how they work it."

"So how'd *you* find out?"

Shrug. "I hung around the right bars, asked the right questions. Hey, I'm a fucking good detective, Meg."

"Damn straight you are, Nick. *The best.*" She grinned. "Well, hell, I guess it could work that way. Now that they're coming out of the cloister closet, so to speak."

Scotti's face twisted in a grimace as he leaned both hands against the bar. "Jesus, those people—they used to stand for something."

"Well, hell, Nick, they're human too. What d'you want from them, anyway?"

Scotti was shaking his head, drunkenly irate. "Nah, they're not *supposed to be* 'human too.' Those people took a vow. They're supposed to be something special. What the hell is this now—it's *okay* if they fuck off, run around like those cunts down on Central Avenue?"

Meg watched, slightly astonished, as he rocked his grieving body against the bar, muttering, "That's the whole fucking trouble these days. Nobody cares, nobody holds up standards. And that Angela Flynn is a fucking murderess."

He jammed the porkpie down around his nose, an almost anguished gesture. "I got standards too. My job's like theirs, twenty-four hours a day. The night this case came down I was out drunk and Mark Abrams couldn't get ahold of me. And that was *my fault,* Meg—I was wrong, I let the standards down. But those fucking priests and nuns, now— they don't even care. They got no respect, no commitment.

They think it's okay if they're out fucking around the town like some twenty-year-old steno. Well, it's not okay with me. They're letting me down. They're letting everything down. They're fucking cheats, and I hate them for it."

Meg was watching him with a sudden thoughtfulness. "Jesus, Nick, I'm just realizing—you think like them. You still buy the rules, the absolutes. You think almost like *one of them.*"

"Ah, fuck 'em," Scotti growled, yanking off the tie that was still hanging loosely around his neck. "I just hope that fucking murderess fries like she fried that little kid."

On her first office visit in August Dr. Heilbron decided that she was making such excellent progress that they could cut her sessions down to one every two weeks. To celebrate that good news Fran dragged her out to see *All the President's Men* when it came back to town on neighborhood re-runs.

Fran loved the movie, watching the screen raptly, prodding Angela's arm at various high points. But Angela felt strangely disturbed by that film. The way those reporters trapped and hounded the President, destroyed all his defenses, pinned off his escapes—watching that made her feel very uncomfortable, almost anxious.

Look what they can do.

She knew the reporters were out there somewhere, waiting for *her*, too. Ready to hunt her, like they did that President. And as she watched them corner him, bring him down, a choking clot of tension built in her chest.

When they stopped afterward to have a few drinks in a small neighborhood bar Fran was burbling her enthusiasm. "Oh, Angela, wasn't that terrific! I love that Robert Redford in anything he does, but this one was such a terrific *story.*"

She said distantly, "I guess. I don't really care much about politics."

Fran was saying she would have loved to be a reporter —"If I hadn't gone in the convent, I think that's just what

I'd like to've done. Not just for the fun—I mean, look at how much *good* they can do."

Dryly: "You'd probably be quite good at that, Fran."

"Oh, I don't know. I'd like to think so, but I don't know if I'd have the nerve. The way they just *found it all out,* that Deep Throat and everything—boy, that was really something."

The next morning, working in her room, she ran out of graph paper. Since no one else seemed to be in the house, she decided to walk to the stationery store six blocks away. It was a sparkling, sunny day, a good day for a walk, anyway.

The little shop was a kind of catchall storefront that sold candy, newspapers and cigarettes as well as writing supplies. The clerk was a tall, smiling black boy, his dark skin stretched like live elastic over his quick-moving face bones. He said he guessed they had that kind of paper someplace, he'd have to look. He pushed a ladder down the narrow aisle and climbed up it to search for the paper.

She stood below the ladder, watching the seams of his tight jeans move as he shuffled the boxes on the upper shelves.

Then he was smiling down at her, teeth very white in his dark face, reaching down some papers in his left hand. "This what you want, lady?"

"Yes, fine. That will do fine."

As he bounced off the ladder into that narrow aisle he misstepped, and his tall, thin body lurched against her. He looked down at her, laughing, as he balanced himself against her arm and said, " 'Scuse me, momma."

She followed him back to the front counter. A little laboriously, he filled out the sales slip she had asked for. Then spread his hands wide on the counter and leaned toward her, smiling again. Big white teeth, wide smiling brown lips. "Anything else you want, little momma?"

475

She blinked into the sudden, sharp sunlight.

She was walking down some strange street, carrying a paper bag. Her eyes darted in panic to the shabby tenement buildings around her, recognizing none of them. Three black children ran past her on the sidewalk, shouting random obscenities. Strange people lounged on the steps of the buildings, staring at her. *Oh, Jesus Mary and Joseph help me. Help*—

Ah, *there* it was. Through an empty lot she could see the green steeple of Our Lady of Pompeii Church thrusting above that ravaged cityscape, a few blocks to the north. *Safety.* Home, safety.

She tried to push away those small quivers of panic as she walked rapidly, purposefully home. Back in the refuge of her own room she made herself sit at the desk and take the graph paper out of the paper bag.

The bag still heavy; other things were in it. She looked into it and found a wide red pen marker. A Milky Way bar. And a packet of—it seemed to be cheap skin decals, mostly birds and flowers, in garish, ugly colors.

What . . .

She rolled the bag up very tightly, and threw it out in the bathroom wastebasket down the hall.

Meg Gavin kept tossing sources, any she could lay hands on.

Janine Vitale and Lena Schwartz both said they were sorry, but since they were seeing Angela socially now they couldn't talk to Meg. Cal Hearne provided a diverting afternoon reminiscing about things like the young St. Bennie nun, a classmate of Cal's, whose mental breakdown went unnoticed until the afternoon she walked out of her convent room stark naked and announced she was going downtown to the movies. Interesting stuff, but not much to do with Angela Flynn.

She called Father Dennis Jacques, the young priest who ran the diocesan Human Resources Division and was one of the key members of Bishop Paul Roche's left-wing brain trust. A little reluctantly, Jacques agreed to give her thirty minutes—"but no more than that, Meg"—in his book-strewn office in the ramshackle downtown house where the HRD was headquartered.

A real good looker this one was, nice build and fabulous cheekbones, wearing an open plaid shirt over his Roman collar. Oh, this one could park his black Bostonians under her bed any night he wanted.

He talked with rueful candor about the "unfortunate psychiatric condition in Angela Flynn that unfortunately no one noticed until it was too late," and said he thought a lot of local priests and nuns "were taking a real lesson from that about the need for a community to be a little more aggressive, a little more *forceful* in their caring for one another."

When Meg asked almost idly if the Angela Flynn case was having much influence on what she understood was a pretty lively ongoing debate within the Church on the subject of religious celibacy, Jacques looked genuinely startled. "No, of course not. Why should it?"

"Hey, Father, I should think that's pretty obvious. As a, shall we say, unavoidably striking example of the kind of problem that the denial of sex constitutes in a celibate life."

Vigorous headshake. "Not at all, Meg. I see that dialogue as concerned with the need for commitment and community support, with the responsibilities of family. And within that context Sister Angela's case is not relevant at all. It's a tragedy that happened—not a mainstream event."

Meg lifted one protesting finger. "Hey, wait up a minute, Father. The question I asked was about *sex*. That powerful, discrete human function of *sex*. Not family, commitment and that nice stuff."

The momentary reaction—distress? embarrassment?—on Jacques's face slid quickly into an expression of almost smug satisfaction. He smiled patronizingly across his littered desk. "Well, Meg, I guess that's where our viewpoints differ. The way I see it, you can't separate love from sex."

In her exhaustive rounds of telephoning, Meg even called her family's old parish priest, Father Jim Leonard, who promptly invited her around for dinner. Leonard was a nice old guy, bluff and hearty, and so obviously grateful for company around his lonely dinner table that Meg stayed off the subject of Angela Flynn until he raised it himself, when the housekeeper was serving their coffee and dessert.

When she told him about the magazine assignment he said, "Well, I just hope you're not trying to pin this whole mess on the Catholic Church."

Meg laughed. "Hey, Father, if you've got a better candidate—"

"Sure I do. It was that Flynn family," he said firmly. And astonished her with the revelation that he'd known that family for years, when he was the pastor of St. Paul's out in Roseville. "The fact is, Meg, that family never dealt with any real problems in the whole time I knew them. You take Angela's father, for instance. Now Francis Flynn was a good enough man in his own way. He tried, at least. But that man was a serious alcoholic for years. Always taking the pledge, but he was still drunk three nights a week, had trouble holding down jobs, that sort of thing."

"Wow, Father. I didn't know that."

"And that family *never faced up to it,* Meg. Just wasn't in them to do it, I guess. That's why Angela was sent off to be raised by some cousin she calls her aunt—to get her out of that situation, away from that alcoholic father. That's where that poor little woman learned this business of not facing up to cold facts, just avoiding them for as long as you could— from her own family."

Meg cleared her throat and said that sure was interesting. But she still didn't see how that explained eleven nuns living right in the convent with Angela and not seeing that pregnancy right under their noses.

"Well now, I don't know about that. But you listen to me now, Meg. Nuns these days have just as many choices open to them as any other women. And God knows they're *exercising* them, running all around town doing Lord knows what in those short skirts and little cars. There's been a whole lot of changes since you left this Church behind, Meg girl. So don't you go writing it off like you did back in convent school."

She laughed at the accuracy of his aim. "Okay. I'm listening, Father. Kid you not, I'm listening. But hey—I still don't see how you can let the whole Church off the hook on this one, Father."

Leonard was shaking his head, a strong, masculine gesture. "What happened here was Angela Flynn's own problem, Meg. That she didn't *see* the choices that were wide open all around her. And if you want to figure that one out, you go back to that Flynn family. That shipped a little girl out of her own home rather than deal realistically with the father's problem." When she started to interrupt he held up his hand. "If you're bound and determined to find a culprit here, it shouldn't be the Catholic Church. It's *that family* that taught Angela right from the first how to think."

The "lost times," the blackouts, didn't seem to be happening now as often as before, so she tried to feel grateful for that. She realized they must somehow be part of her healing, like the remembering. Or that discharge that had come for quite a while into those pads.

But she'd thought by now they would surely *stop.* Because she felt so healthy otherwise.

She knew from the start of them that those lost times were something *no one else must know about. No one.* She was trying so hard to work out this new life they had pushed her into, and most of it was going quite well. Most of the time

479

she was quite pleased with it, almost happy. She was working very hard, seeing lots of friends. People were really being quite *nice* to her.

But if they knew about those times like the day she went to buy paper at the store, they might decide again she must be crazy. Might send her back to that Ward Five. And she had struggled so hard, suffered so much to *get herself out of that place.*

She *could not* go back there. *Could not.* Because this time she might not be strong enough to get herself out again.

When Dr. Heilbron asked her in their sessions about what she was experiencing these days, she tried very hard to be honest. Except—she said nothing about those blackouts.

She told herself it didn't matter, really, if she just didn't mention those times. Because she talked quite sincerely about all the rest.

Dr. Heilbron kept congratulating her on how well she was adjusting, and she felt so good most of the time that she knew it was true, she was getting better.

She thought probably they would stop happening quite soon, those blanked-out times. But what frightened her most was that she never knew when they were going to come.

When they came when she was alone in her room, she knew nothing so terrible could have happened. But that day at the store—oh, that was—scary. And what if one of them happened when she was with someone she knew?

Like Dr. Heilbron. Or the Pompeii nuns.

"Now, Angela, you have to admit—we've ordered you up a *perfect* day," Margaret Hogan beamed. She was sitting with her in the cockpit of the Hogans' powerboat as they took a day-cruise down the upper Mississippi with Ron and three of the Hogan children.

"Oh, yes. It's really perfect, Margaret." She was looking out over the sun-drenched water, watching the small daggers of light twinkle all across the river.

When they moored in a little cove downriver, Angela joined in a noisy cannonball contest with the three kids off the upper deck, trying to see who could make the biggest splash, until Margaret called them out of the water to eat.

After lunch Ron took the children off in the dinghy to look for snails. Angela wanted to go with them, but Margaret said firmly, "Oh, please stay and keep me company, dear. It's been so long since we had a good talk."

So they carried two air mattresses to the upper deck and stretched out in the sun. Margaret said, "So, Angela. How are things going for you?"

"Oh, very well." She talked very brightly, very animatedly, about the research projects she was doing, planning those preschool programs for Sister Philomena.

Finally Margaret murmured, "Well, that's all very interesting. And the doctor, dear? Are you still seeing that nice Dr. Heilbron?"

Angela smiled. "Oh, yes. But only every two weeks now, because he says I'm making such good progress." Proudly: "He thinks pretty soon I'll only need to see him once a month. He's not Catholic, you know, but very intelligent— Phi Beta Kappa from the University of Michigan."

"Well, I hope he's a great help to you, dear." Margaret Hogan wasn't sure just how to put this next thing she wanted to say, but knew this was the time to do it. "I hope he's more help to you than your friends have been. It still bothers me so much—how badly we all let you down." As Angela murmured a demurral Margaret held up one hand: "No, please, let me speak. I've been thinking so often lately about what a great friend *you've* been to *me,* all these years. Like that time I was pregnant with Danny and having all those problems, so worried I was going to lose him. I must've called you three times a day. And you were always so understanding, so patient and generous with your support."

Angela smiled. "And look at Danny now—such a strong, healthy boy."

"Yes, that's the whole point. That's why I'm so sad and disappointed with myself for failing *you* so badly, dear. Not being there for you the one time when *you* really needed help. I'll never get over feeling bad about that, Angela."

With one quick, athletic movement she suddenly flipped over on the mat and sat up. For a moment she sat in silence, hugging her knees. Then: "It's true. They were all rotten friends." Her voice high-pitched and girlish, yet oddly forceful. "They could have helped but they didn't. They just didn't really care."

Breathless from the unexpected savagery of the attack that she knew she herself had invited, Margaret propped herself on her elbows. "Oh, Angela dear, that's true. That's so terribly true. And I want you to know how mortally sorry I am for that."

She wrapped her arms around her knees, leaned her face down into her arms. Muttered, almost inaudible: "They all let her down. Every one of them."

Bewilderedly: "What did you say, dear?"

She lifted her head, ran one hand through her short curls. "Oh, it doesn't matter. It's just that it's so unfair. That nobody even really *tried* to help. And now they're all saying, 'It's all Angela's fault, all of it.' And that's just not *fair.*"

What she said was true enough to make Margaret Hogan feel physically ill. But she was almost as troubled by the *way* Angela said it—so flip, so *harsh.* So—peculiar. Not like her at all.

She tilted her face toward the sun, twining a strand of red-gold hair around one finger. "Well, it doesn't matter anyway," she said almost dreamily. "They're all such dummies. They don't understand anything anyway."

"Like a sick child," Margaret kept repeating agitatedly to her husband when they were lying in bed that night. "Like a pathetic, confused sick child."

Thirty-five

One constant note ran through Meg's digging: the one thing everyone *wanted to know* (or had their own wild conjectures about) was who the daddy was.

Most people figured he was probably a priest. One woman neighbor of Meg's, a pillar of the local Right to Life organization, thought it was more likely "some guy she picked up running around town, the way all those damn nuns seem to these days"—and "in *this* case" the "right, decent" thing for Angela Flynn to have done was "to get herself an abortion."

One of the local radio newsmen told Meg he "had it on real good authority" that the guy was a one-night stand Angela met at a carnival when she was on vacation. Others suggested a few too many drinks, and maybe a moonlit boat ride. The *Eagle-Bulletin*'s regular court reporter suggested "rape—maybe even rape by a friend."

The most bizarre theory came from one of the mothers at the school, who blamed it all on Angela's former boss, Sister Pamela. (Her reasoning was that Angela was very dependent on the attractive, charismatic Pam, and when forced to fill Pam's shoes after she left the convent to marry, Angela had reacted to that crisis by "having an affair or something, I suppose.") But the most prevalent rumor around town was that the father was Angela Flynn's own cousin's husband, who "took advantage of her" when she was visiting their family in Milwaukee.

The one thing Meg was sure of was that all of them were dead wrong. Yet of the three men who knew the right answer to that tantalizing question, Scotti and DaSilva were clearly not about to talk.

Meg made it a point to drop back to the Cambridgeport

P.D. In her chatty debrief of the various cops who had been involved in the case, the one she was really gunning for was Tim Vance.

The dispatcher caught Vance coming out of the Records Room. "Hey, Lieutenant, there's some lady waiting in your office. Says she wants to see you."

"Oh, yeah? Who is it?"

"Gavin somebody, from the *Eagle-Bulletin.* I think she wants to talk about the nun case."

Vance's senses went on instant alert. He realized this was the bird who'd probably pried that confidential stuff on the baby's father out of Chief Marwick. Marwick still insisted she'd gotten it from the D.A.'s office. But Vance knew the chief wasn't always too cautious with his words around a sexy bitch like that Gavin.

As he strode down the hall to confront her, he was already locking up his mouth.

When Vance finally showed up in the Detective Division, he seemed to be in a remote, slightly nettled mood. Meg followed him into his small office, saying, "Hey, Lieutenant, you got two minutes to spare a working girl?"

No smile in that wary, preoccupied look he tossed at her. "Okay, I guess. But not much more than two."

She threw him a two hundred watter anyway, as she slipped into the armchair at the far end of his desk, crossing her stockinged legs. "What I'd like now, Tim—you mind if I call you Tim?" He shook his head. "Well, I'd like just your general impressions about the case, the investigations. No state secrets, Tim, I swear." She grinned prettily.

A little grudgingly: "Well, this was one hell of a strange case from word one. It's just the setting, police detectives interviewing nuns. In a situation like a murder investigation, it's usually tough for the survivors to sit down and talk about it. But because those women are all so highly trained in dealing firsthand with other people's personal and moral problems, they turned out to be a lot more helpful than I expected."

"Helpful how, Tim?"

Vance shrugged. "Well, they were all pretty much in control of their emotions, more able to *cope* than the average person. On a case like this in a normal family situation, we usually run into a lot more panic."

As she asked the usual run of questions—had the other nuns *really* not noticed the pregnancy, what kind of impression of Sister Angela did the police investigation turn up— she recrossed her legs and flicked at the red linen blend skirt spilled over her knees. Not a bad looker, actually, this Vance, in an ex-football-jock kind of way. She liked those bull shoulders, the tense energy in his face.

Suddenly he interrupted one of her questions with, "So what is it you're really after, Meg?"

Smiling shrug: "Just about anything I can get, I guess, Tim."

"And what're you willing to trade for it?" Flat, steady, unsmiling gaze. "Say, an invitation home to your bed?"

No way was she braced for *that* one. In her off-balanced confusion she smiled nervously as she reached for her cigarettes. "Well, hey, Tim, that wasn't exactly what I had in mind. Not yet, anyway. I mean, we kind of just met, didn't we?" Her nervous laugh rattled like a tin cup against his cold, unsmiling stare. She tried to counter the blush—that dismayed, infuriating blush—that was flooding her face. "Hey, I'm not saying that isn't kind of an interesting idea, Tim. Now that you mention it. But no, that wasn't exactly what I was asking."

"Okay, then let's leave the bedroom eyes out of this interview and stick to the facts of the case." She was still off balance, trying to figure what advantage she might yet pull from this unexpected turn in the conversation, when he said flatly, "Sex trade-offs work real good in quite a few professions. But the last I heard, journalism wasn't one of them."

The rest of the interview was very brief, very correct and very cold. Worth, Meg estimated as she strode furiously to her parked car, about two shovelfuls of warm cowshit.

One last thing she *did* want was to witness an autopsy. Preferably of a newborn. Figured she might get a feel, a handle from that that she couldn't get any other way.

The M.E., Dr. Rhoades, said he wished he could help Meg out, but right now that was out of the question. So she dropped a call to Hank Fullerton, the chief pathologist at Carlisle General, whom she'd run into at several parties. Good-looking guy, mid-forties, liked to laugh. A gun nut, she seemed to recall.

Fullerton said well, hey, he'd see what he could do. Infants were pretty hard to come by unless it was a stillbirth or a crib death, something where the parents were anxious to pin down the cause. Meg said she'd take whatever she could get, because she was right about on deadline. Fullerton said a Saturday morning would be best, because there'd be fewer people around to ask questions; if he had anything on tap he'd let her know.

"Thanks, Hank. You're a prince." When he laughed she amended that: "Anyway, a real handy guy to know."

When they walked into the hospital morgue room the next Saturday at 9:15 the corpse was already there on the table, green napkin-type cloths laid discreetly over the face and genitals. Body that of a huge, fat, old—judging from the massive wrinkles covering the skin—black woman. *With one mastectomy,* Meg was thinking as she circled the table warily, stoically. Then she saw that the missing breast was simply slung over the left shoulder.

Fullerton said any time she felt sick she should go out in the hall—"I don't want you throwing up in here."

Meg said with a bravado she did not really feel: "Hey, didn't I tell you? I'm a doctor's daughter. This kind of stuff's duck soup for a medical kid."

The first few moments were the worst. But she managed to lose some of her squeamishness in the powerful curiosity that was stirred in her as he extracted the different organs and glands, explaining them, dissecting them. By the end of the ninety-minute autopsy she was almost fascinated by the process.

As they left the room Fullerton smiled, patted her shoulder appreciatively. "Well, Meg, I'll give you this much. You were a good girl, back there."

She managed to echo the smile back. "Is it considered rude to say I told you so, Hank?"

"Nah, not from a girl as cute as you. Tell you what, since you've been so good I'll stake you to lunch. And then if you want you can help me with the abortions."

"The what?"

"Never mind. I'll show you later."

After lunch in the hospital cafeteria, Fullerton took her to a gleaming, bright-lit lab. As they walked in, Meg noticed several dozen lidded paper cups lined up on two trays on the counter. She pointed: "What're those, Hank?"

"The stockingettes. Never mind, you'll see soon enough." Fullerton bustled for a few minutes, assembling materials. Then he pulled two stools up to the counter, perched on one and pointed to the tray by her left hand. "Okay, Meg. Hand me one of those cups."

Peeling the lid off that first one, he used the forceps held in his left hand to lift out a dripping cotton mesh bag, which he dropped into a low glass dish. With the bag steadied in his forceps, he slashed open the mesh with the scissors in his right hand and spilled the pulpy reddish contents into the dish. "See, Meg, Saturday morning's when they do the weekly vacuum abortions in the GYN clinic here. So the

487

on-duty pathologist for that day has to do the pathological workup on them every Saturday afternoon."

Faintly: "What workup?" She still had no idea what was going on here until the forceps fishing in that bloody spilled mass lifted out, incredibly, a very tiny, very pink leg.

A perfect miniature leg with knee, foot, even toes.

She fought the nausea tugging at her lunch as Fullerton dropped the leg into a small round plastic container and snapped a lid on it. "See, Meg, we have to verify and examine fetal parts and placental material. Fetal parts to confirm there actually was a pregnancy, placental material to check for choriocarcinoma, a rare but virulent form of cancer that would show up already in the placenta."

She swallowed. The autopsy, at least, she had been braced against. But she had no defense prepared for the horror of that small pink leg. She made herself say, "Well, hey. That's very interesting, actually."

More than interesting. She realized even as she spoke that this appalling wonderment Fullerton had tossed her way was also painfully relevant to the case of Angela Flynn.

Now his forceps were lifting something that looked like a tiny, limp, raggedly shaped red sponge. "Okay, that's placenta." He dropped it into another container, slapped on a lid, dropped a label on the lid and flipped both containers onto a tray beside his right elbow. He gestured with the forceps: "Okay, pass me the next one."

She soon saw the pattern to it: the heaviest cups, the ones leaking slightly around the edges, contained the largest, most developed fetal parts. Which were technically the most interesting.

The labels on the paper cups lined up beside her left elbow—so weirdly like coffee takeouts—gave up only two pieces of information, besides the date and the case number: name and age of the mother. Meg scanned the labels, found a wide variety of ethnics. Quite a few Catholics—Italians, Poles. Ages ranged from fourteen to forty-three.

She realized instinctively that this process would be easier for her to handle if she could sink her mind in the observation of its details. Her outward calm was apparently convincing enough to prompt a startling offer from Fullerton: "Say, if you want to help speed this up, I'll give you your own set of forceps."

She blinked. "Sure. Okay. Sure, I'd like to help."

Since the body parts were easier to identify, he let Meg search for those while he concentrated on the fragments of placenta. She told herself it was really no different from that pickled frog she'd dissected in high school biology as she fixed her mind with detached, scientific curiosity on the revelations of each new stockingette.

Quite soon the nausea yielded to fascination. Sometimes she found arms, hands. Sometimes heads that were almost intact, the embryo-eyes bulging in the soft skulls like fish eggs.

A few times she found legs in pairs. Tiny legs still attached across the hips, with—"Look, isn't that a penis?"

Fullerton peered closer. "No, that's undifferentiated phallus. Too early yet to tell the sex." But three cups later, triumphantly: "Ah, see! Now this one's male. That's a penis forming there."

Meg looked very closely, but couldn't see any difference from the other.

When half of the thirty-two cups were done, Fullerton declared a break, and slapped the kettle on the lab stove to brew them some instant coffee. Meg sat hunched on her stool, saying slowly as he poured the water out of the whistling kettle, "So, Hank. Say if Sister Angela had gone for an abortion in this town, this is where she would've wound up?"

Fullerton nodded. "Sure, probably. Most of the first trimester abortions get done here. Private patients, Planned Parenthood referrals—most of 'em come through here."

"So, let's say she just came in, using a phony name. What would've happened then?"

"Well, she would've had to come in to the clinic that week, so they could verify that she actually *was* pregnant, and for how long. If it was first trimester, they would've given her an appointment for Friday night, when the doctor on call would've inserted a sliver of laminaria, a highly absorptive material that's actually a Japanese seaweed, into her cervix.

"By the time she got back for her appointment the next morning—they schedule 'em for every fifteen minutes, because the whole operation is pretty routine—her cervix would've been sufficiently dilated for the vacuuming to take place with no additional preparation except a local anesthetic."

Meg nodded, fascinated. "Is that—painful? The overnight seaweed?"

Fullerton shrugged. "Depends on the individual. Some women come in swearing it was worse than labor, and some say they hardly noticed it."

She mused, digesting this totally unanticipated blast of insight. "So. It could've been—finished, for her, then. As easy as that. Bingo—no more Baby Boy Flynn."

"Well, it's easy enough on the women. A very simple, clean procedure, usually with very few complications. But it's not so easy on the medical personnel." Flatly, unexpectedly, he said, "Most of the doctors hate this part of the job."

"*Hate?* My God, Hank, why?"

Fullerton shrugged, moving on his stool as he said almost embarrassedly, "Look, you understand I'm no Catholic, Meg. I've got no theological argument with abortion. I think most of those women"—he gestured toward the cups —"probably made a right, intelligent choice in terms of managing their own lives. But, as a doctor—look, you're trained to save life. Preserve it. This thing here—it just goes against the grain. It's different if you're doing it for a private patient and you know her, know her problems. Then you can do it knowing it's the best choice for her to make. Knowing you're helping *her.* But these anonymous ones who come through the clinic, where just about all you know about them is their case number . . ."

Meg asked softly, "But aren't you helping *them* too, in the same way?"

Fullerton shrugged, trying to push down the emotion that was showing on his face. "Oh, sure. Theoretically. But all you *know* is—what you're doing to that fetus."

Coffee break over, they went back to work.

Now she was refining the search of her probing forceps, finding organs as well as limbs. She lifted them from the mass quite expertly now, those fascinating miniature body parts: "Hank, what's that?"

A liver, he would say. Or an eye. Or—"Hey!" His forceps nudged an interesting miniature that hers had just delivered into the plastic container. "Fascinating. That's the *heart.*" He turned that rounded shape of fetal flesh. "Remember that heart this morning from the autopsy? See, there's the chambers—hey, I usually don't take this much time over—but that's definitely *a heart.* Very interesting," Hank Fullerton said.

She went out that night to a party with Wald, and got very, very drunk. At two A.M., when he was half-carrying her up the stairs to her apartment, she mumbled, "You know what, Wald? You're kinda nice."

The next morning she decided her record hangover was not a sufficient alibi, and forced herself to drive to Our Lady of Pompeii Church for the eleven A.M. Mass. She understood from Nick Scotti that Angela Flynn was being stashed at that convent. Meg wasn't expecting to run into her, but she still wanted to check out the feeling, the physical setup of the place.

She realized as she drove down Germain Street—saw that bombed-out urban moonscape, with the church looming so huge and decrepit in the middle of that rubble-paved flatness—that this trip outweighed any hangover.

The church must once, very long ago, have been quite a splendid place, before the ceiling frescoes lost their war with the roof leaks. But now there was a dark, hushed sadness about the place that for some reason reminded Meg of an aging, painted Southern beauty, languishing amid old laces and satins on her invalid bed.

With the numbers of the faithful so severely reduced, the Masses were celebrated now in the "chapel," a rear corner of the large church partitioned off with cheap prefinished plywood paneling. At least there was some life, some cheerfulness, in the chapel—fluorescent lights behind the dropped paneled ceiling, thick blue-and-tweed shag carpet underfoot, folding metal chairs arranged around a flat tabletype altar.

The parishioners drifting in the doors were mostly blacks and Hispanics, with a sprinkling of elderly white women. One middle-aged woman with cropped brown hair, wearing a navy turtleneck and navy corduroy skirt, Meg recognized instantly as a nun. She was thinking with a rush of surprise, almost alarm, *My God, maybe* she's *coming too,* when suddenly Angela Flynn was standing in the chapel door.

Still so small, so damn pretty and small. But now her face was tanned and happy, almost—radiant. She bounced across the chapel to greet the young priest and fell into animated conversation.

Torn between eavesdropping and minding her own goddam business—God, she had never meant to *trap* this poor woman, especially not at a Mass, where Angela belonged much more than she did—Meg managed to overhear talk of some outing, some trip to the beach. She couldn't catch the details. But also couldn't miss the unexpected message Angela's whole presence was sending out —a powerful, slightly eerie cheerfulness. A fervent, almost forced *gaiety.*

Now Angela was crossing the room, sitting on the metal

chair directly in front of her. Meg wondered for one panicked moment if Angela could possibly have recognized her, but decided she could not. Until the trial, anyway.

As she watched Angela chatting brightly with the black woman sitting to her right, Meg could not resist the strong impression that *something was wrong here.* Okay, it was months since the baby's birth. No reason Angela should still be playing Grieving Mother. But still, but still—

Since that Sunday turned out to be the feast day of St. Anne, the mother of the Blessed Virgin, the young priest chose to preach a sermon about mothers. As he talked piously, cheerily, about how we owe all things to our loving mothers, how it is only through our dear mothers that we come to Christ, Meg took those words into her like slashing knives. As if she was hearing them *as Angela must hear them.*

But the perky young woman sitting in front of her showed no reaction at all. Tilted her tanned head interestedly, nodding agreement with those pious thoughts. As if *none of this, of course, had anything at all to do with her.*

When they came to the communal kiss of peace, Angela turned to the child on her left, the woman on her right. Then she paused, hesitated. *God, maybe she recognized me after all. Maybe she knows who I am.*

Suddenly Angela turned around, stretching her soft hand toward Meg. As their palms touched, Meg felt herself somehow pulled forward into that determinedly smiling face, into those amazingly powerful green eyes. "Peace be to you," Angela murmured over the handshake.

"Oh, yes. And peace to *you,* Angela," Meg murmured back at her.

A warning stab of fear shot through Angela as she let go of that strange hand and turned back to the Mass.

Who was that girl she had never seen before, that girl who *knew her name?*

493

· · ·

She went home and phoned Dick McAlpine. Said she was sick, very sick, and she'd be back to work when she was feeling better. Say, three or four days.

McAlpine said get off it—she wanted the time off to work on that goddam magazine piece, and she couldn't have it. She said as a matter of fact she seemed to have a virulently contagious case of V.D., but she thought the shots would probably fix it in four days or so. He said fuck *that*—she showed up tomorrow or she was fired.

She said hey, could she count on that? He was still bitching when she hung up the phone.

For the next three days she sank into a space measured only by energies, mental energies. Lost track of time, except that some was sunlit and some was not, as she paced, wrote, drank, wrote, smoked dope, wrote. Propped open on her desk she had a British forensic pathology textbook lent to her by Fullerton, opened to a photograph of a male infant with a handkerchief crammed into his mouth that could have been Baby Boy Flynn.

On Wednesday afternoon it was finally finished. She read it straight through with a rush of exhilaration, realizing she had never written anything half so good. It was as if all these years she'd been calling herself a writer were only a dress rehearsal for this moment when she finally *was* one.

She took a long, hot, sudsy bath. Changed into clean clothes and decided to call Dewey. She was tired, sure, but not too tired to treat herself to a little well-earned delectation.

But as she walked back toward the living room phone she decided to treat herself first to one more reading of the piece. Curled up on the cushioned sun-drenched window seat by her desk, she turned the typed sheets one more time on her lap.

When she finished, she looked for a minute at the neat

stack of pages. Then slapped them, scattered them on the polished dark wood floor.

Damn. God damn.

She didn't have it, after all.

Thirty-six

In September the first day back at school turned out to be painfully hard for Angela in a way she had not expected, was not braced against.

Suddenly the Pompeii convent was filled with that purposeful energy, that anticipatory hum that came with leaving off vacation and cranking up the new school year. For so long this had always been one of her favorite days. And when she heard the children's voices outside her room, children coming with their parents to enroll at the day-care center next door, she felt almost unbearably lonely.

That back-to-school rush, exhilaration, that she remembered so well—for the first time in fifteen years *she had no part in it.* That hectic, optimistic resettling of the classrooms, the bright expectation on the faces of those new children—*there was no place in it for her.*

Angela had dutifully accepted this transfer to Pompeii as some kind of temporary assignment. But now, with the whole new year beginning outside her window, outside her room, she was terrified to realize that this—*outsideness* might not be temporary at all.

She was still not back where she belonged—at Benedictine Kindergarten. She was still, even with the new year beginning, not back at the only place she wanted to be. *Belonged* to be.

And *would* she ever, now, again? Even after this horrendous trial was finally over?

As she sat at her desk trying to work she was telling herself that *soon, soon* this so difficult ordeal would be over. Finished. And then she would be back where she belonged.

This terrible waiting was supposed to be only a kind of frozen time, that would soon be over, finished for her. She was trying very hard to believe that as she sat at her desk working on a curriculum for those programs for Sister Philomena that she was not even sure anyone ever intended to read, let alone use.

Yet all she could feel was the silence, the echoing emptiness of that convent, like a premonitory chill. Did they possibly mean to *leave her here,* in this empty, lonely coldness?

When the day-care children came out to play during the morning recess, she heard their voices, their live laughing, as if she were standing among them, tossing a big red plastic ball, or pushing them patiently on the swings. Yet out the open window in front of her desk, she saw only the brick-strewn rubble of the razed lots across the street.

One child crying now. A skinned knee, probably. So many Band-Aids she had peeled onto skinned knees. So many times she had "kissed to make it all better" in a trade-off for their tears.

Suddenly she was up from the desk, pacing the small room, her tensed, unhappy body trembling as if from some resisted pain. As she walked toward the window she heard a strange voice something like her own saying, *They aren't being fair to you. You know they're not being fair. Why can't you admit that, Angela?*

As she reached the desk she turned, facing the door where her vows were hanging below a small wooden crucifix. She heard herself say aloud, "They *mean* to be fair. They're trying to do what they think is right. I mustn't blame them for that."

496

Turn toward the window. *They want to be rid of you, you know. They're praying to be rid of you. They hate you for what they think you've done.*

Turn toward the door. Trembling all through her body. "Hate? Why would they hate me?"

Oh, come on. Sometimes you make me sick, you're such a ninny. Do you know what they're doing today at Benedictine?

Turn. Whisper: "They're opening the school. They're sitting down together for lunch, talking about the summer."

Talking about you, probably. And they're glad you're not back. Sophie especially. Now she has your job, and she means to keep it. She doesn't want you back there, ever.

Pain through her body like a quivering bolt. "But Sophie's such a bad teacher. She never really liked the school, and she never liked the children."

She hates them, always did. Almost as much as she hates you, you ninny. Why can't you hate her back?

Whispering, trembling: "I don't hate anybody."

No, I know you don't, you dummy. You just simper and smile and let them do these things to you. Sometimes I can't stand that about you—that you're so stupid that way.

She stopped in the center of the room, pressing her shaking fingers against her eyes. "Oh, leave me alone! Stop this. Leave me alone."

But you don't belong with these people. Why can't you see that? They don't like you anymore. They don't really even want to help you. They hate you. They don't care about you like I do.

Wrenching cry: "Go away, go away! Just leave me alone!"

Suddenly, mercifully, the voice was gone. She looked dazedly around the room.

Dizzy, racked. Exhausted.

She lay down on the bed and pulled the spread up around her chilled body. Rest, just a few minutes' rest. She would be all right again with a few minutes' rest.

.   .   .

497

Knock at the door. Fran's voice: "Angela? Come on down for lunch."

When Angela didn't answer right away, Fran pushed the door open. "Hey, what's the matter? Are you okay?"

"Yes, sure." She got up quickly from the bed and smoothed out the spread, repairing the rumpled evidence of her body. "I just had a little headache, so I lay down to rest a bit."

Fran looked closely at her. "Well, you still don't look very good. Would you like a pill? I've got some Excedrin Plus."

"No, no, I'm fine." She smoothed her hair, her hands still trembling. "I just fell asleep and had a bad dream."

In October Roy Danziger ran his motorcycle into a United Parcel delivery truck. When the driver jumped out of the cab and ran to the rear, he found Roy unconscious on the shoulder of the road, his cycle mashed under the truck's rear wheel.

He was already in the hospital when he recovered consciousness. Some doctor was asking, "Roy? How do you feel, Roy?"

"My shoulder. Oh Christ, my arm."

"Okay, take it easy. It's going to hurt you a little for a while, but you're a real lucky man."

The mild brain concussion lasted only a few days, but it was worth a few bucks in disability insurance. The torn muscles and ligaments in his shoulder would take much longer to heal. His other injuries were incidental, mainly contact burns from the asphalt paving. His bike was a total loss.

When he was discharged from the hospital after four days, he was still facing a long recuperation. Since there was some doubt as to which party had caused the accident, the insurance money flowed freely: Workmen's Compensation, disability layoff, unemployment. Totaled up, it came to approximately $275 a week.

"Jesus, Zig, you lucky bastard," his friend Al Packer said. "Did you do it on purpose?"

Roy asked blankly, "Why would I do that?"

In November Meg and Dewey went to a party that Meg expected to be quite dull, since it was thrown by one of Dewey's button-down architect friends. For a while it followed her expectations, despite some rather good joints being passed around. She sat on the carpet leaning against Dewey's legs, pretty much tuning out until a shy-looking girl with frizzy black hair sitting across the glass coffee table from her said, "Meg, was that your article on Angela Flynn that I saw in *Womans World?*"

She nodded, inhaling from a joint. "Guilty, I'm afraid."

The girl said hesitantly, "I was almost going to call you after it came out, but I didn't have the nerve. Anyway, I wanted to tell you I thought it was an awfully good piece."

"Well, thanks. It's nice to hear somebody's actually out there reading that crap."

Still hesitating. Then: "I think you captured Angela really quite well. But some of that stuff, like about Sister Pam —well, I just wondered where you got that."

She blinked across the table. "What, you know her?"

Nod. "I'm Robin Evans. I taught for four years in Angela's classroom at Benedictine."

Meg beamed. "Well, son of a bitch. Excuse me, but— oh, Robin, *am I glad to meet you.*"

Dewey stirred his legs impatiently. "Oh, boy, here we go. Brace yourself, folks. We're about to get a whole evening of the ever-fascinating little nun."

Meg stood in one swift motion, stretching a hand down to pull Robin Evans up from the floor. Firmly: "Come on, Robin. We've got to have ourselves a little talk."

They huddled together on the carpeted stair, talking almost immediately with the fluency, the verbal shorthand, of old friends. Robin's hesitations dropped away as she explained that she'd been abroad when it happened, on a year's sabbatical in Geneva with her psychiatrist husband Ned. And when a mutual friend called with the news—"Oh, Meg, I just literally couldn't believe it." Her arms folded over her stomach in response to that remembered pain. "Not *Angela,* anyway. Any of the rest of those Benedictine nuns, maybe, because some of them are really quite whacky. But *Angela* always seemed to me the most sane, the most stable of the lot."

She looked away from Meg as she added, "She'd *seemed* that, anyway. But when we had her to dinner after we got back from Europe last summer, I realized maybe I'd never really understood her at all. Or else she'd—changed so much I hardly recognized her."

When Meg asked what she meant, Robin said confusedly that she wasn't even sure. In some ways Angela was more her old self than ever—"so lively and animated, like she was on some kind of high. But when I tried very delicately to get her to talk about what happened, because I just couldn't stand to sit there *pretending it hadn't happened,* she put me off very neatly. Said her lawyers didn't want her to say anything about that. But I had the feeling she'd say the same thing even without the lawyers. I mean, I knew she really *just didn't want to talk about it."* She hesitated. "And I realized then if she'd been the same way the year before, when she was pregnant—well, maybe if I'd been around then, I would've just stood back and let it happen, like all the rest of them did. Because Angela just *wouldn't admit* anything had gone wrong."

Now Robin was cushioning her chin in her hands, musing about what Meg had implied in her article about Angela being quite dependent on Pam. *"Dependent?* I don't know, Meg—but you could be right. You could be right. I've even wondered if maybe Pam *was* the one who got her involved in this sex stuff in the first place. And then when she left, poor Angela was just too damn naive to handle it without getting herself knocked up."

Meg felt another huge chunk of the mystery coming clear in her head as Robin described the bizarre teasing about "boyfriends" that went on at the staff lunches at Benedictine. "And the nuns *loved* to be teased that way by the lay teachers, Meg. I never understood why, but they really seemed to get off on it. It was just part of the whole"— helpless shrug—"craziness that went on with those nuns. Some of them drank a lot at parties, and a few of them spent *every weekend* out visiting friends, away from the convent. I'm not Catholic myself, but before I went to work there I always thought nuns had a real tight community life among themselves, that made up for what was missing in the rest of their lives. But *those* nuns, anyway, my God—*Angela Flynn* was really the only one in the whole school who lived and acted like I thought a nun would. Which is one reason I was so— incredulous that *she* would turn out to be the one that really flipped."

Meg prompted: "But what about Pam?"

Slowly, thoughtfully: "Well, Pam's really quite terrific, in her own way. I liked her a lot, actually. And you're certainly right about her being a very strong personality. And very beautiful, and very sexy. Really a knockout, and she certainly knew it. I wouldn't be surprised to hear *Pam* was having affairs when she was still in the convent. She *told* me she was on the Pill—to 'regulate her periods,' she said. And Pam loved to brag about picking guys up on airplanes when she flew anywhere. She'd really flirt, lead them on outrageously, and then when the plane was landing she'd drop on them that she was a nun."

Musing, thoughtful: "The thing is, if Pam *was* having an affair, she'd handle it right. It wouldn't be *Pam* who got herself accidentally pregnant—or if she did, she'd know just what to do about it."

"You mean—abortion?"

Shrug. "Sure. I think Pam could talk herself into that one without too much trouble. But naive little Angela, such

501

a good nun—of course it would've been very different for her."

Now Robin was reminiscing about that time Pam took a vacation trip to Spain, and the teachers all chipped in for a good-bye present, that Angela actually bought for them— ". . . a very *skimpy* backless yellow halter dress. Put it this way, Meg—*I'd've* been too embarrassed to wear it. But *they* all seemed to think it was just the perfect choice."

And one weekend before Pam left the convent, when Pam and Angela went off to a singles resort, checking in under their "maiden" names: "I remember them laughing, even *boasting* about what a great time they had dancing with the men, having a 'real ball'—not telling anybody they were nuns, of course."

"Wow. That's fascinating stuff, Robin."

"So maybe you're right, about Pam. Maybe it *was* her who got Angela started in this business of coming on to men, and then after Pam left, it turned out to be more than Angela could handle by herself. Maybe Pam's really the key to it, and if she'd only been around last year she could have, *would have* made Angela handle the pregnancy. I still don't know, Meg. I mean, the sex, that could happen to anybody. But this whole—bizarre rest of it—I still don't understand that *at all.*"

They started to talk about the inexplicability of the act of which Angela stood accused, and Meg mentioned what she'd read about maternal infanticide in Fullerton's forensic pathology book—that it was almost invariably committed directly after the birth, and usually in circumstances of self-delivery.

Robin was crying a little now, shaking her head as she stared at the geometric-patterned wallpaper at the foot of the stairs. "Oh God, Meg, I can still hardly bear to think about that. Such an incredible, *primitive* thing. When I think of Angela . . ." She shook her head, unable to speak.

Meg said urgently, "Well, listen, Robin, I'm really glad

to hear she has good friends like you two. Ned being a psychiatrist and you such a close old friend—you two might really make a difference for her."

Robin wiped her cheeks with her thumb as she said sadly, exhaustedly, "Oh, Meg, I don't see how. I wish we could but—I really find it very *hard* to be around her now, when she's just not—acknowledging what happened." She hesitated. "And I don't think she wants to be around *us,* either. I gather from the kind of friends she's still seeing a lot of that she spends most of her time with people who—just buy her line. Buy into that craziness, that everything is *just fine.* But I just can't *do* that, Meg."

Meg said okay, she could see that. But surely Ned, such a well-trained therapist—surely Ned could point her toward some kind of . . .

Robin shaking her head again, with that contagious sadness. "Oh God. Ned thinks what happened here was so *enormous,* so psychically *devastating,* he wouldn't begin to know who could treat her adequately. Except maybe somebody like R. D. Laing, who'd let her lie in one room for six months, acting it all out— Ned can't imagine what other kind of treatment might be effective. And she *is* very functional now. She's pouring a tremendous amount of energy into her defense mechanisms, but *her defenses are working,* they're keeping her going. So Ned says he wouldn't even conceive of trying to tinker with that. At least until she gets through this trial."

Urgently, from Meg: "But *then,* Robin. *Then,* for sure, you could—help her, as friends."

Robin was staring blankly at that patterned wall, as if there were answers coded somewhere on it. "Oh, I don't know, Meg. I don't know. It's just so—unfathomable. So goddam terrifyingly *unfathomable.* "

"But if *you* can't help her, you good friends who really care and really understand—then who will?"

Robin pressed a hand against her stomach. Blurted, "Excuse me, Meg," and ran to the upstairs john.

Meg went back to the living room. When Robin came downstairs she and Ned left soon after. Meg embraced her at the front door: "Hey, Robin. Thanks so much. Let's keep in touch, okay?"

Robin nodded, not speaking.

Driving back to her apartment Dewey said dryly,"Nice party, didn't you think."

"Yes, sure. Top drawer."

He threw her a sharp, reproving glance. "Well, it *was* a good party, Gavin. Until you had to run off for your little *tête-à-tête.*"

She said nothing.

"You know, I think I've been pretty patient with this mania of yours, Meg. But I've got to tell you, it's starting to get to me."

Coldly, very coldly: "Oh, is that so?"

"I wish you'd admit it, Meg—you're fucking *obsessed.* And she just isn't worth it—what you're putting into this, what you're letting this *do to us.*" When Meg said nothing he pressed on: "You're fucking *obsessed* with her. Whether you recognize it or not. And I'd sure like some idea of when the hell you think you're going to get this thing out of your system."

She stared at his sharp-edged profile, anger putting a quivering force in her voice as she said, "Jesus Christ. You *are* jealous, Wald. It's fucking crazy, but you're *jealous* of that woman."

"Not of *her.* Of what you're letting this do to your head. I'm waiting for you to move past this fucking irrational obsession with all that bullshit left over from your childhood. To get past that so you and me can get on with what really matters. Which happens to be what's *happening with us.*"

She snapped the car radio on, at a loud volume. "Shut up, Wald," she said over the blast of music. "Just shut up while I'm still talking to you."

Over the Christmas vacation Tim and Alison Vance were invited to Vail, Colorado, by an old school friend of Tim's, now a real estate developer in Santa Barbara. The other couple shoehorned into that amazingly overpriced two-bedroom condo turned out to be a San Francisco psychiatrist and his ex-social-worker wife.

Since Vance and the shrink, George Hirshman, turned out to be the only good skiers in the bunch, they drifted off to do it together—into the lift lines by 8:15 A.M., scouting the tougher slopes where the lines were a little shorter.

The second morning they were out, Vance thought unexpectedly of Angela Flynn. What the hell, this guy was a shrink. Enough removed from the case to confide in.

As they waited in the next lift line Vance said, "Hey, George, I'd like to ask your advice about a case I was involved in back in St. Paul. You know I'm no expert in your department, but I think maybe it was a case of multiple personality."

Hirshman smiled condescendingly. "Said who?"

"Well, nobody. But I just have this hunch—maybe that's what it is."

"Well, Tim, I've got to tell you those cases are very rare. Very exceptional. Big on TV and in paperback books, maybe, but very rarely seen in clinical practice."

"Hey, sure. I know that. But I still don't know what else would explain it."

Hirshman pulled a cigarette from the pocket of his parka. What the hell, these lift lines were long, dull waiting. And Hirshman was actually rather interested to hear what the psychiatric fantasies of a small-town cop might be. He said with as little condescension as he could muster, "Well, why don't you tell me about it, Tim."

Halfway through Vance's halting recapitulation of the case Hirshman interrupted: "Is there any chance this woman was sexually molested as a child?"

505

Vance glanced sharply at him. "Well, actually—why'd you ask that?"

Hirshman shrugged as he explained that in a large majority of the cases of hysterical neurosis in women that Freud had treated, it turned out this was reported as a common denominator. So Vance told him about Angela—*Gayle* Flynn, rather—being sent out of her home at age eleven to live with that divorced aunt. And about the mental problems that first surfaced with her bizarre, sporadic denials of her father's death.

Hirshman nodded, his expression now very absorbed: "So she went out looking to find him."

As Vance ran out every pertinent shred of evidence he had available to him, the lift lines unexpectedly became more interesting to both men than the skiing. Finally he said, "Okay, George. You tell *me*. What's happening here?"

Hirshman stabbed thoughtfully with his right ski pole at the packed snow. "Well, just on the basis of what you've said —this is a top-of-the-head opinion, you understand, Tim— there are about five diagnoses that might apply. But I have to admit the one you've arrived at is probably the most likely."

Vance was experiencing a huge, almost disbelieving wash of relief. "Well, Jesus. What does that mean?"

Hirshman shrugged. "In itself, it has no meaning. It all depends on how the patient is perceived, how she's treated medically."

"Well, I guess that's what I mean—I hear she's being treated by some young psychiatrist. But how would he—like, isn't this grounds to get the whole trial thrown out?"

"Sure, maybe. If he picked up on her condition—and could prove his diagnosis. But I think it's more likely that he's unaware of it himself." He interrupted Vance's question with, "Look, in most of these MP cases the patient—the core personality—has no *consciousness* of what's going on. That's one of the reasons it's extremely difficult for the consulting psychiatrist to pick up on the diagnosis, unless the other personalities actually evidence themselves in the course of a therapy session. Which they generally don't."

"Yeah, I can see that," Vance mused. "He might not see it unless he'd heard, for instance, about the contradictory versions of the sex."

Hirshman nodded. "That's right. And put it together with the other parts of the clinical picture, in much the same way you yourself did."

"But he probably had no access to that information. Except if her attorney passed it along—which I doubt he did. Knowing Ben Haverty, for sure he probably didn't."

"Okay. Then I would have to presume that her psychiatrist is quite unaware of her condition. You have to understand, Tim—he's treating *Sister Angela.* And *Sister Angela* probably has little to no understanding of what's going on here."

"But those times she flips out, becomes Gayle—she must *know* something's wrong. Like if she can't account for that time."

Hirshman shrugged. "Well, even if the core personality becomes aware of the problem, they tend to conceal that 'amnesia' as part of their very strong defensive system. Sometimes these patients simply decide that time is discontinuous—that blackouts are normal, that everyone has them."

Vance looked out bleakly over the glittering, postcard-pretty ski mountain. Such a bizarre setting for this grim conversation.

He was almost afraid to ask his next question, the one about suicide.

The St. Rose nuns had meant to ask Angela over to dinner some night during the holiday season, but for one reason or another the date was put off until January 3.

She was in quite a state of excitement by that Monday

afternoon. And when Julia came to pick her up in the familiar old "Kindergarten School car," the blue Chevette, it felt almost like she *was* going "home again," finally.

At first the conversation in the car went a little stiffly. When she asked how everything was going back at St. Rose, Julia said, "Oh, pretty much the usual. You know." There was an awkward silence. "We've been meaning to have you over for quite a while, Angela, but something always seemed to come up."

"Sure, I know how it is. But I'm very— I think quite a lot about all of you, Julia. I keep wondering how everybody's doing." So for most of the rest of the drive, Julia brought her up to date on Margory's Spanish course, and Dorothy's Braille classes, and Julia's work on the Women in the Church task force.

Dorothy was standing by the stove as she came in the kitchen door and gave her a quick, spontaneous hug: "Oh, Angela. It's so *good* to have you back again."

So she was feeling quite welcome as she walked into the community room. As the other nuns straggled into that room that still looked so familiar—except for a new orange chair and a bigger TV—she greeted them warmly, almost a little effusively. She realized they might be feeling a little shy and awkward, seeing her again after all that time, and she wanted to put them at their ease. She was really very happy to be back here, even just on a visit. And she wanted them to understand that she didn't *blame* them in any way for all the painful things that had happened to her since the last time she was sitting around this room.

As the different sisters drifted in, she kept chatting very animatedly about the preschool programs she was working on, and the news from Benedictine that she'd picked up from the school parents she was still seeing sometimes.

She wasn't sure just when the chilling began, but suddenly the feeling in the room was very silent, very cold. She tried to keep talking into that silence, but now the words were halting, a little uncertain.

Finally she stopped. In the thick silence she reached for the pillow on the maroon velour couch, pulled it across her lap.

Margory spoke first: "Angela, I wonder if you have any idea, any idea at all, what you've done to the people in this house." With a controlled fury in her cold voice: "How you've *made them suffer.*"

She clutched the pillow. When no one else spoke she said softly, "Yes, Margory, I think I do."

The dinner was served mercifully soon after. She tried to eat but wasn't feeling hungry. The halting conversation around the long refectory table was very polite, very correct. Very—difficult for them all.

She had planned to spend the evening, but as soon as the meal was finished she told Julia she was very sorry, but she had to go home early to finish up some work.

On the long drive back to Our Lady of Pompeii, they didn't speak much. Angela was pinching her lips together, swallowing frequently, trying not to think. Not yet, not until she was in her room, by herself.

When they were parked on the street outside the convent, Julia clutched the wheel and bent her head toward it as she said softly, "Angela, I'm very disappointed about tonight. And I know you are too."

She nodded, saying nothing.

Gripping the wheel. "Angela, I've been wanting so much to tell you— Look, when that—happened to you, back in April—I've been wanting to tell you that I was—in the middle of quite a serious spiritual crisis then. Which was why I wasn't—able to help you like I should have. And I'll never forgive myself for that, Angela. Never."

Quietly: "That's all right, Julie. You don't have to explain."

"No, but I—want to, Angela." Looking down at the car dashboard. So hard to say these things that she had never shared with anyone before. "I failed you very badly, Angela. I was just too—wrapped up in my own—doubts to even *see* that you needed help. And I don't *excuse* myself for that, not ever. But what I really wanted you to know— Somehow, through everything that's happened, I've come to a so much stronger feeling of my vocation. Come to really feel it, *understand* it. And I wanted you to know how—grateful I am to you, Angela, for—giving me that chance."

Softly, opened again: "Oh, Julie. I'm very happy for you, for that."

Julia twisted away from the wheel, facing her now: "And a lot of it was *because of you,* Angela. I'm very glad to finally have the chance to tell you this."

She reached out and patted Julia's arm. "Well, I'm really happy to hear that, Julie. And thanks for sharing it."

Julia looked back to the car wheel. "And that's why I really wish so specially for you, Angela, that you'll be very happy in whatever life you choose. After all this—legal business is finished."

Whatever life? She understood quite easily the rest of what Julia was saying. But not that "whatever."

She said softly, serenely, "I think I know just what you mean, Julie. About how it takes—something like this kind of trial of our faith to make us understand what our real vocation is." She paused, then said strongly: "And I feel that too, Julie. That—affirmation. So it hasn't been for nothing. Because we both came out of this with a real blessing of faith."

The last disappointment of this bitterly disappointing night was the blank, uncomprehending look on Julia's face as Angela said good night, and climbed out of the car.

In January a cleaners' delivery boy making a stop in Cambridgeport noticed a car running behind the closed garage door of the house across the street. He ran over, pulled the door open and saw a man slumped over the wheel.

Coughing violently from the fumes, he switched off the motor and dragged the man out of the garage.

The man in the car was big, and dead weight, about two hundred pounds; the delivery kid weighed only 129, but he managed to drag the guy by his armpits onto a snowbank down the driveway. Guy's eyes were open, glassy, unseeing. The kid shouted, *"Hey, mister, you okay?"*

No response. But the guy seemed to be breathing still.

The kid sprinted for the telephone across the street.

Since the police were called in on the resuscitation, there was no way the attempted suicide of the county medical examiner, Dr. Kenneth Rhoades, could be kept out of the newspaper. Meg Gavin caught up with his wife later that day at Carlisle General, where Rhoades had been admitted to the Psychiatric Unit after treatment in the Emergency Department. Apologizing for disturbing her at a time like this, Meg asked how the doctor was doing.

"Much better, thank you, Meg." Shelley Rhoades had a brave, tremulous smile pasted to her thin face. "He wants the public to know that he had been ill, but he will get better. We don't know yet how long that will take, but he will recover."

This goddam bloodsucking job, Meg was thinking as she asked if Mrs. Rhoades knew how it happened.

Shelley Rhoades shook her head. "I'm sure it was an accident, Meg. He said he was planning to drive in to work when he had this spell of dizziness. He got very confused, and then—well, I think it was just an unfortunate accident."

But she did speak quite frankly about the personal pressures Rhoades had experienced lately—a son recovering from pneumonia, a good friend dying of cancer, two medical colleagues who recently committed suicide. "And all that added to the stress of his own particular mental disease, Meg. Our knowledge of depression is kind of like looking at

Mars—you can see the surface, but you can't know what's underneath."

When Andy DaSilva heard about the suicide attempt he asked Mark Abrams, "So what's this going to do to our case?"

Abrams grimaced wearily. "Nothing good, that's for sure."

"Is he going to be able to testify?"

Abrams allowed himself one brief moment of sarcasm. "Not if he can't do it from a padded cell."

DaSilva wanted to know if that would hurt their case. "It could," Abrams conceded reluctantly, rubbing at the back of his head. "Which probably means, the way our luck has been running on this thing, that it certainly will."

Thirty-seven

In January the opening date of the trial—which Angela knew was her last chance to make them understand—was set for Wednesday, the fourteenth of February.

As the preparations of both prosecution and defense went into double time, Andretti researched the legal precedents, Haverty concentrated on the medical and psychiatric. The one break in their concentration Haverty allowed was their rehearsals with Sister Angela, held three times a week in his office.

With the transcript of her grand-jury testimony spread out on his desk, Haverty took her back through it, over and over. Until the memories she had struggled so hard to retrieve gradually began to fuzz.

"Angela, when you say you saw the child's limbs move —couldn't that have occurred *when you were carrying him down the hall?*"

"I don't think— I think I saw that in the bathroom, when he was lying on the mat."

"You *think.* But couldn't you have been wrong about that, Angela? You were very confused, you'd lost so much blood. Couldn't that have occurred when you were carrying him down the hall?"

Yes, maybe it *could* have. She never, ever meant to lie. Not even now. But when he said it that way—

And Mr. Haverty knew what was best for her—he was the legal expert, after all. So if Mr. Haverty thought that was the way it might have been—yes, maybe it *could have.*

That first shift in her story, that part about the limbs, troubled her a little. But as the weeks passed and they went over and over her story, she felt the rest of her hesitations drop away.

When Mr. Haverty told her, for instance, that it would be quite all right to say she didn't recall those incriminating conversations she'd had with the doctors that first night in the hospital, because after all she was much too debilitated by shock and blood loss to recall anything like that *in its entirety,* she nodded, absorbing that notion into herself as the new version of her own truth.

And every time she told it back to him again, like that, it became a little more real.

So real that, finally, she almost believed it herself.

The main thing—*the only thing*—that mattered was making them all finally understand the truth about this case: that she was *not guilty.*

Two days before the trial, Meg Gavin got an alert that Ben Haverty had asked to present motions in the Sister Angela case before Judge Samuel Aaron. When she got up

513

to the courtroom four minutes later Kevin Corrigan was already outside it, with a three-man camera crew. *"Damn, Kev. You think they're copping a plea?"*

Corrigan shrugged. "Sure looks like it."

"Damn, son of a bitch." Those ten months of waiting put a bitter edge to her voice. "We waited all this time for a *cop-out?"*

Corrigan was smiling. "Come on, Meg. Did you really think you'd ever see this thing come to trial? Open court for the 'poor little nun'?"

"Damn right I did."

Corrigan tapped his notebook on her arm. "Tell you what, if it's a washout I'll buy the first five rounds of drinks."

But when Ben Haverty turned up fifteen minutes later, he only moved to waive his client's right to a trial by jury of her peers.

Judge Aaron went through a ritual protest that in the light of this development perhaps he should disqualify himself, since he had already had access to certain of the grand jury minutes. But when Haverty and DaSilva both expressed gracefully worded hopes that he would preside over the bench trial, Aaron finally agreed: "All right then, gentlemen. See you on the fourteenth."

After that development, Meg retired to the Blind Justice for a quick pretrial celebration with Corrigan.

The relief was still running in her as the bartender slid their drinks down the polished bar. "Ah, shit, Kev. That was a close one. God, I've been *expecting* a bench trial for so long I forgot Ben had to move for one. Damn straight he's not going to throw *this* one to twelve good little citizens."

Corrigan smiled. "How'd you like Aaron's maidenly reluctance to take the limelight all to himself?"

"Oh, yeah." They grinned as they clinked a toast to that. "Can't you just see Sam Aaron giving *this* one away? Christ, he'd·sooner cut off his putting fingers."

There was no more refuge now.

The lawyers were leading her once again into that towering Hall of Justice, into that crucible of lights, bodies. She tried to fix her mind in a kind of prayer as she moved through the noise, the press.

But felt only that huge, cold fear.

The tumult followed them all the way to the courtroom door. As they slipped through into the silence, Mr. Haverty said, "There, Angela. That wasn't so bad, was it?"

She shook her head, trying to smile as she wrapped herself in the peace, calm, of that vast, empty room.

Shaking almost imperceptibly, she sat where Mr. Haverty indicated, at the end of a long table in front of a low wooden gate.

Then he was talking in a low, private voice to Mr. Andretti. So she folded her hands in her lap, staring at the gold letters on the high desk in front of her, IN GOD WE TRUST.

Behind her she could hear the room filling up.

She knew the trial would not begin until that judge came through the front door. But he seemed to be taking a long time.

Dan tapped her shoulder from the seats behind, murmuring something encouraging. She turned her head just enough to smile at him. She knew lots of people back there were friends. Family. But she still didn't want to see them. Not now, not yet.

Part of her wanted this thing they were going to do to her now here never to begin.

But another part of her felt urgently *yes,* now! *Yes, begin. The beginning of the end.*

Out in the courtroom corridor, Sister Philomena moved unobtrusively among the assembled nuns, ministering, reassuring with her stolid, powerful presence. Most seemed a little nervous, unsettled by the threatening strangeness of this place. But they were keeping themselves well in hold.

She had meant for now to leave Angela to her lawyers, concentrate on the other sisters. But once they were settled into their seats in the courtroom and the trial opening still seemed so long delayed, Philomena decided otherwise.

She got up and walked down the aisle to Angela's chair. Bending down, smiling, she said in a low voice, "Angela my dear. How are you feeling?"

The green eyes blinking up at her were clouded, blanked. But the round little face seemed quite controlled. "Oh, Sister Philomena! I feel fine, thank you."

Philomena said that of course all the sisters were praying for her, and quite a few of them had come here to be with her today, to show their support. As Angela murmured her thanks for that, Philomena reached out and gripped her shoulder. "And I want you to know, Angela, that I'll be here with you every day of the trial. I want you to know you can count on that."

She nodded. Seemed—eased. "Oh, thank you, Sister Philomena. It's very . . . helpful to know that."

From her front-row seat in the press section at the left of the courtroom, Meg Gavin was seizing, raking in odd fragments of observation from the standing-room-only crowd.

Bizarre. Fucking bizarre. Like no trial she'd ever covered before, or probably ever would again.

For starters there were the St. Bennie nuns—maybe twenty-five, thirty of them, clumped in the seats off the right-hand aisle, dressed in a weird assortment of civvies that provided about as much disguise as a Groucho Marx mustache.

In the wider middle section the first two rows were reserved for Angela's family and close friends.

What struck Meg most about the people in those two

rows was how uncannily those women resembled the nuns, with their tight, frozen bodies, dowdy clothes, short haircuts. Except they wore small diamond solitaires instead of gold crosses.

And the men, with their pale, blank faces and skinny bad ties—for the life of her, Meg could have sworn they were all ex-seminarians.

Up front, beyond the wooden barrier, the casting yet more bizarre—the natty, well-built little district attorney roughly half the size of Haverty in his extraordinary baggy suit, which resembled oversized Doctor Dentons. Andretti between them like a neat three-piece gray buffer, his short, kinky hair greased into place.

And then the defendant. The allegedly murderous little nun, marooned at the end of those long tables.

Still looking so pretty. And *tiny.* So incredibly fragile. Dressed in a good-girl brown corduroy jumper and blue turtleneck. Her face fixed in a look of cheerful, undaunted, even untouched *calm.*

And here at 10:18 came the last star player—the folksy little Jewish judge, bounding through the front door as the court attendant bellowed, *"All rise. Court is in session, the Honorable Judge Samuel G. Aaron presiding."*

Bizarre or not, it was finally beginning.

From a wooden lectern, Mr. DaSilva read out in a high, nervous voice, "The People move consideration in the case of the People of the State of Minnesota versus Gayle M. Flynn, also known as Sister Angela Flynn."

She could see him if she turned slightly sideways. Which she tried not to do as he said that "the facts will speak for themselves in this case. And the State will prove beyond any reasonable doubt that the defendant on or about April twenty-fifth did act with intent to cause the death of an infant known as Baby Boy Flynn, acting under the influence of extreme emotional disturbance."

Holding her face very still, she looked straight ahead at

the dark wall over the head of that fat woman sitting below the judge. Now the district attorney was saying that she had been "left alone in the convent that fateful morning of April twenty-fifth because she was suffering from severe abdominal cramps. And during that day, we can only make an approximation of the time, but probably around twelve noon was born a full term baby boy. Around twelve noon Sister Margory Montecito returned to the convent from the St. Rose school, and as she came across the walkway Sister Angela must have seen her from the window of her room. Must have heard her come into the convent.

"And after nine months of pregnancy, after nine months of continually hiding this pregnancy, dodging questions, lying to other nuns about going to the doctor, now seeing this baby alive before her, hearing the baby cry and hearing those footsteps of the nun, under extreme emotional disturbance Sister Angela *thrust a pair of panties down this baby's throat as far as she could.*"

Words into her like blades of pain. Shock, gasping in the room behind her, Mr. Haverty jumping up: *"Objection! These are unproved remarks. Hypothetical, with no basis in fact."*

She blinked toward the wall, still taking that thing he had said inside her body.

So, that was it.

What she had wanted most to know all this time. What things they would be doing to her here in this strange room.

It was starting now with those words, *"thrust down his throat as far as she could . . ."*

Ah, but she *had not* broken. Had not cried, had not broken.

If she must suffer this *to make them understand,* she could do it.

She twisted her head a little, lifting her chin, still looking at the dark wall. Now the district attorney was talking about her wrapping the baby in a pink nightgown and "discarding it in a wastebasket."

And how "the evidence will show that she began to bleed profusely after the delivery, because she allowed the birth to occur with her alone."

And her "wishing, attempting to clean up the evidence, until she collapsed on the floor of her own room, where she was found, and an ambulance was called under Sister Angela's protests to take her to the hospital."

More angry objection from Mr. Haverty. She leaned forward a little in her chair, waiting, wanting only to hear what the little man would say next.

"And under persistent questioning from her physicians at Parkhurst Hospital, Sister Angela constantly and consistently denied the birth of any child. She repeatedly denied the birth until she could do it no more, after she passed a placenta, which is proof positive of a birth."

Ahhh.

Then all those brutal, private . . . things . . . they had done to her would be talked about here too. Where anyone who wanted could listen. Nuns, Dan.

Anyone.

Now Mr. Haverty was speaking his words, like a healing balm. "This accused has pleaded not guilty before this court, admittedly a difficult ordeal for someone in her position, because she wants to demonstrate her innocence to all concerned."

Yes. Oh, yes, Lord Jesus.

Louder, commanding: *"There is no direct evidence involving any kind of harmful act by Sister Angela.* The proof will show that at relevant times not only an acute blood loss but other acute physiological factors at the time these events occurred which deprived the accused of any rational control, caused a mental defect that made her irresponsible for her actions."

Mental—defect?

519

Oh, yes. That "court language" he had warned her about.

Because she knew what Mr. Haverty was saying now for her, *explaining* to all of them now for her, was only that one true thing she had come here to tell them, to make them understand.

The first witness was a State Police inspector. Talking mostly about the photographs he had taken that Mr. DaSilva kept pulling from a pile and showing to him: "Bloodstains in the shape of a footprint on the convent hall rug." That was People's Exhibit number six. Or People's Exhibit number fifteen, "the stripped-down mattress of Sister Angela's bed, showing red stains on it." Or People's Exhibit number thirty-two, "photograph of the deceased baby, taken at the Medical Examiner's office on Wilcox Road."

Mr. Haverty demanding to see each picture. Looking at it, frowning. Sometimes showing it to Mr. Andretti, whispering about it, holding it tilted away from her eyes.

So unimaginable, what Mr. Haverty was seeing now looking at those pictures. Especially those ones of—her real baby.

"I enter into the record People's Exhibit number forty-four." Mr. DaSilva passed it to the policeman. "Can you identify this?"

Loudly: "That is a photograph of a stainless-steel pail three-quarters full of water showing the infant's lungs floating on top."

So. *This,* too, then.

She clenched her hands tightly in her lap, as the two lawyers arguing about the bloodstains on those two lungs floating in that pail of water, the judge asking the court stenographer to read back one part of the testimony.

Cutting the lungs *out of her child.* Somehow never thinking of them doing that.

But of course they must have cut him into many little pieces. And he was so small to begin with.

All so they could prove she had killed him *like she meant to.*

Oh, Lord Jesus Christ, this would be hard. So much harder than she was braced against.

Yet surely—not too hard to bear. If she only could *believe in Him enough.*

When the judge called the lunch recess she steeled herself for another march through those lights. But Mr. Haverty leaned over as the room was emptying behind her and said that since the jury room was not being used in this case, he had arranged with the judge for her to lunch privately there, with her family and her sisters.

Outside the courtroom Meg approached an elegantly bearded, tweedy stranger who had been sitting in the press section. "Hey, excuse me. Do you mind me asking who you are?"

"Not at all." He flicked a three-colored business card toward her: Sherman Wellington, associate editor of the *National Enquirer,* heading up the four-man team in town to cover the trial.

"Oh Christ. I might've known. Are *you* the only outside press?"

"I believe there's a girl here from the Chicago *Tribune,*" Wellington volunteered helpfully. "Nice little town you have here. But a trifle *cold,* don't you know."

"Cold to *you,* anyway. Damn, I wish— But I guess I knew you guys would have to turn up. It's such a natural for you."

"Not really. I doubt we'll run it."

"Oh, come on. *Four guys covering?* A nice little lip-smacker like this one?"

"No, really. We cover three or four stories for every one that runs, you know." Wellington wrinkled his aquiline nose. "And this one's really too *sordid* for us."

. . .

521

When the rest of the people went inside the courtroom for the afternoon session, Sister Julia sat very upright on a leather-covered bench outside the door, with Dorothy and Roxanne murmuring conversation as she waited to be called in.

Back at the convent, the nuns had discussed a little what they should wear for this testifying. Julia had decided on her orange miniskirt and green plaid jacket.

After about forty-five minutes, a gray-haired uniformed man pushed open the courtroom door and said, "Okay, Sister Julia. You're up now."

"Oh, good luck, Julie," Dorothy murmured. Julia stood up and walked through the door and down the far aisle the man pointed her toward, feeling every eye in the room watching her.

Up on the witness stand, she tried not to look at all those people as she swore the oath on a Bible another uniformed man pushed toward her.

DaSilva said, "Please identify yourself by name and address for the court record."

"Sister Julia O'Gorman, 205 Windsor Avenue, Cambridgeport."

"Do you know Sister Angela Flynn?"

"I do."

"How long have you known her?"

"I have known Angela since I came to the St. Rose convent four years ago."

"Could you identify her now, for the court record?"

Julia bit her bottom lip as she looked across the room to where Angela was sitting at the end of the long brown table. She said faintly, "Angela is next to Mr. Haverty."

Prodded by the district attorney's questions, Julia said she taught second grade at the St. Rose of Lima parochial school and was local coordinator of the parish convent.

DaSilva scratched at the rim of his bald spot. "Is that similar to what I knew in the past as a Mother Superior?"

"Yes, it is."

Was it part of her duties to talk to the sisters about personal problems? "Yes."

Did she discuss personal matters with any of the sisters in 1977, 1978? "Yes, some."

Prior to April 1978, did she ever discuss personal problems with Sister Angela? Julia was already saying, "No," when Haverty jumped to his feet: "Objection! No relevancy."

The judge leaned down toward Julia, cautioning, "Don't answer before there's a ruling." After some argument between the lawyers that Julia had trouble following, the district attorney rephrased his question: "Subsequent to August 1977, did you have occasion to observe the physical appearance of Sister Angela?"

"Yes, as with any other sister in the house."

"Did you make any observation of her physical condition changing?"

"Objection!"

"Sustained."

"Did you observe that she had gained weight?"

"Objection!"

"Overruled."

Julia swallowed hard. "Yes, I thought she had gained weight at that time."

"Gained weight where?"

"Around the waist."

Then he pulled the whole terrible story out of her with his questions. Like Angela coming to Julia's room around seven A.M., saying she could not go in to school because she had intestinal cramps.

And Julia coming home from the school around 3:10, finding Angela: "I think I knocked on her bedroom door.

But there was no answer. When I opened the door she was lying on the floor, in quite a bit of blood. . . . I was concerned about Angela on the floor. I—"

"Objection! Mental process."

"Sustained." The judge leaned toward her again, more impatiently this time. "The fact that you were concerned is a mental process. Just testify to what you saw and heard, Sister."

It was all so confusing, so painful and confusing. Trying to speak very correctly, give them what they were demanding from her here, Julia told about her telling Angela she would go with her to the hospital, and Angela asking her to please close the door to her room and leave it alone.

About Angela twisting her head around in the ambulance, asking if Julia was there. And then the man giving her oxygen.

And Julia seeing her sometime later in the emergency room of Parkhurst Hospital. And Julia asking her when she had her last menstrual period, and Angela saying two months ago, and maybe that's why she was bleeding like that.

And then when Julia was in the room again later, Angela delivering that thing the doctors told them shortly after was the placenta.

And the doctors sending her and Sister Dorothy home to look for the baby. And them finding it, behind that kitty-corner bookcase in Angela's room.

The district attorney walked back to a wheeled chrome carrier, similar to a shopping cart. He reached into a red plastic bag and pulled out a green straw bloodstained wastebasket.

Waving it before the nun, he asked, "Is this the container you found the child in?"

She murmured, "It could be. I think I've seen that in Angela's room." She paused, swallowed. "But I thought it was larger than that."

Angela pressed two fingers tight over her quivering mouth. She knew Julia *had to* say those things, was forced by law to come in here and say them. So she had been ready for Julia's testimony.

But not that basket.

Pulled out so unexpectedly. Those stains she knew were *his blood.*

Quickly reaching into her purse for a Kleenex, she blotted it to her cheeks.

Julia kept on talking in that faint voice about taking the baby back to the hospital and all that.

Now she could feel the two kinds of pain they were doing to her here.

The hurtful things she *didn't know yet,* like those lungs floating in the pail.

The hurtful things she *knew already,* like that green basket waved so unexpectedly in front of Julia's face.

Outside the courtroom, while the rest of the crowd was slowly dispersing, the TV camera crews were still milling, posting sentries at every possible exit the nun could use. "Look for the flying V-wedge," one of the cameramen warned.

Suddenly, from the locked glass-windowed door at the end of the corridor, a lighting man bellowed, *"Shit! There she goes!"* Frantic sprinting for a useless shot through the wire-ribbed glass as Angela Flynn, flanked by her two lawyers, disappeared briskly down the locked hallway of the judicial offices.

On their way to the trial the next morning, Mr. Haverty told Angela a little nervously that he had good news: due to the unusual nature of the case, he had obtained permission for her to use a private courtroom elevator. For as long as the trial continued. So she need not be so—ah, harassed by the press.

So she had that to feel pleased about as they drove his car into the basement entrance of the Hall of Justice. Some man in a blue uniform seemed to be waiting for them, over by that single elevator to the left of the others. When he saw them coming he turned a key in a slot and the elevator door came open.

As Angela walked into the car she caught a look from that man that was—cold. Almost angry. Angela didn't understand that look.

Only felt as Mr. Haverty pushed the *2* button such a *blessed relief,* that those cruel lights and cameras, those loud crushing bodies, would not be waiting for them when the elevator doors came open again.

It felt easier today, too, that she knew now what to expect in there.

And she had the pills Dr. Heilbron had given her in her purse. He had said she could take an extra one anytime she felt the need. Which she understood as some kind of test of her.

She hoped, with the help of Lord Jesus, that she would not need that extra pill. But she was *determined* not to cry again, like she had yesterday. Those few tears, that they had all been back there watching for, that happened when Mr. DaSilva had pulled out that wastebasket. That they all *made such a thing about* in the newspapers. Even talked about on the TV.

Now Angela *understood* that those reporters were back there always in this big room. Watching her every move.

Wanting, waiting, for her to . . . break.

Today the witnesses were all St. Rose nuns—Dorothy, Mary Luke, Margory and Roxanne. Talking mostly about the blood, and how long it took them all to clean it up.

She tried to keep reminding herself that Mr. Haverty *wanted* her sisters to give this testimony, wanted all that in the record, so the rest of them would know how much she had bled. Because that would help her case, all of it.

Still it was hard to listen to. Her own sisters, telling all about her swollen belly and that sea of blood and all.

Now Luke was talking about the clots on the bedroom floor, saying, "Some I could scrape up with my fingernail. But others were darker, dried."

Mr. DaSilva asked what she thought a clot was.

"Clots are like a massy substance, a concentration of blood . . . I don't feel qualified to answer more specifically."

Now he walked back to that strange silvery cart. Reached into a brown box and pulling out Angela's knee-length pink nylon bathrobe that was now mostly brick-red.

Holding it up so it wouldn't drag on the floor, he said it was People's Exhibit fifty-five A.

He pushed that thing forward toward Mary Luke, almost touching her knees with it: "Sister, can you point out to me anything you would call a clot on this robe?"

Angela could hardly hear Luke's voice. "Yes . . . the darker spots."

"Can you indicate one?"

Angela could feel that loathing, that shrinking, in Luke as she touched the robe with one fingernail. "Right here."

"Let the record show that the witness indicated a circular dried bloodstain approximately three inches in diameter, darker in color than the bloodstained surrounding material."

It almost made it a little harder to bear, somehow— knowing that she *never needed to be sitting here at all.* Mr. Haverty arguing so strongly for her to agree to that "lesser plea." So they could "avoid this trial."

Ah, now she knew what he meant.

But she could only have done that by letting them say she was guilty of that thing. Which was *not the truth.*

No matter how strange and confusing they made it for her in this place. No matter how many reasons they would give for why she *must be* guilty. She knew that much with a terrible strong cold sureness—she *must not let them say that thing.*

Surely *He* could not mean for her to agree with them. To say that was how it happened.

No, never. *He* would not ask that.

So . . . He must be asking *this* from her, then.

Because the only other reason she could see to agree to what those men wanted her to say would be to . . . spare herself.

Spare *her,* dear Lord, from this pain.

Oh, yes, there were times when she was sitting so still in that chair when she almost wished she *had said yes.* But only—flickers. Not even thoughts.

Mostly taking the pain into herself as lovingly, as believingly, as she could. Giving what *He was asking.*

So in that way at least it was really not so . . . impossible . . . at all.

Today she was seeing more than yesterday, too.

Seeing snatches of faces in the big, packed room behind her. Some of them familiar. Like Margaret Hogan, throwing a quick, excited smile.

Then, as she walked into the jury room, she noticed a tall girl standing right behind the little wooden fence. Brown-haired girl looking so strongly, sharply, at her.

A girl that Angela knew from somewhere.

Ten minutes later, as she was eating a tuna sandwich that Aunt Iris had brought in her bag, Angela remembered.

At that Mass. Sitting right behind her, at Our Lady of Pompeii. That strange girl who knew her name.

She asked Mr. Haverty as soon as he came back from his lunch who that tall brown-haired girl was, and he said it was probably Meg Gavin, the *Eagle-Bulletin* reporter.

That thought made her feel quite strange as she walked

back into the courtroom for the afternoon session. looking down at her feet so she would not have to see that girl again.

So one of *them* had found her, after all. And—gone away again. Left her—in peace.

She could remember so well everything Meg Gavin had written about her. Even in that women's magazine. Never feeling, really, that Meg Gavin was trying to *hurt* her.

But even so, quite—strange to know the reporter sitting back there watching her now was that strange girl from that Mass.

Due note was taken in the local media about the extraordinary privileges being extended to this defendant—use of the jury room as her private suite, use of the locked judges' elevator, and the locked rear hallways leading to the courtroom. None of the long-timers working the Hall of Justice could recall similar kid-glove treatment being given to *any* criminal defendant.

Meg Gavin agreed in principle with the grousing, the rude objections to those privileges voiced around the press section.

But still, but still—

She could not help but feel that if there was some simple way to mitigate the extraordinary hell Angela Flynn was enduring here, maybe it ought to be done.

The press section kept a running score on the courtroom game. Nuns' testimony somewhat incriminating, but also helpful to the defense: two for one, prosecution. Hospital chaplain, ambulance driver, toxicologist, all washouts— zip to zip. Odd-lot M.D.s, like the radiologist and the GYN resident, pretty effective for the prosecution, say three to one.

The FBI special agent, who identified infant hemoglobin on the nun's bloody robe and the paper towels used to clean the bathroom floor but otherwise couldn't

529

go so far as to swear under oath that this infant and this female adult were related, scored one thin point for the prosecution.

Then DaSilva recalled State Police Inspector Nevelson to the stand to testify about the clothing he had seen Medical Examiner Rhoades remove from the infant's body at the autopsy, and Meg realized with no great surprise that DaSilva's case was falling apart.

Nevelson hadn't even got out his first sentence about seeing Rhoades remove a nightgown and a pair of panties from the baby's throat before Haverty was bouncing up: "Objection! Hearsay."

DaSilva argued in his quiet, mild voice, "The witness says he observed this with his own eyes."

When the judge said he would allow it, DaSilva walked back to the cart and picked up a white object. "I introduce into evidence People's Exhibit number fifty-five B." He handed the object to Nevelson. "Can you identify this?"

"Yes, sir. Those are the panties that were stuffed down the baby's throat."

Roared: *"Objection!"*

"Sustained."

Nevelson coughed nervously. "That I saw withdrawn from the baby's throat and oral cavity. Approximately five to six inches of this material."

When it was Haverty's turn for cross-examination, he picked up some papers and walked close to the witness chair, glaring at Nevelson. "Did Dr. Rhoades use any instruments to look back into that baby's mouth?"

"No, sir."

Haverty waved his copy of the autopsy report. "I want due note taken that the man who made the observations in this report is apparently not being called as a witness. Yet Dr. Rhoades said"—Haverty peered down at the paper—" 'Around the neck are a pair of blood-tinged white panties which also extend into the infant's mouth extending all the way back to the nasopharynx.' " Haverty slammed his hand down on the wooden railing. *"He's the man who saw it!* Is there anywhere it says in this autopsy report that those panties were in the throat?"

"No, sir."

Angela was swallowing repeatedly as Haverty snatched up the panties, held them spread out in front of the witness. Those wide, stretched, soiled panties splotted with blood-stains. "I show you exhibit fifty-five B—is it marked *in any way* to indicate how much material was around the baby's throat, how much in the mouth and how much in the baby's pharynx?"

"No, sir."

"No marking at all? No distance measured?"

"From what I myself observed, I estimate a matter of inches." Nevelson held up his hands, six inches apart. "The distance between my thumbs."

Haverty twirled, flipped the panties in the air. "The circumference of this garment is approximately thirty-two inches. Approximately nine inches from the waist to leg portion." Glowering at Nevelson: "Did Dr. Rhoades *measure the distance to the pharynx?"*

"I don't recall."

"Read the report," Haverty snapped.

Nevelson bent his head over the autopsy report, turning its pages. Then: "No, sir."

"Yet you never took a photograph of the panties *as presented in the throat cut open?"*

Angela's mouth working as Nevelson said, "No, sir, I didn't do that."

Meg Gavin nudged Kevin Corrigan and scribbled on her pad, *WHERE ARE YOU NOW, KEN RHOADES . . .*

Corrigan smiled as he nodded his head.

.   .   .

The waits, really, were the hardest part. Before that judge came out to begin it again. Such long waits, sometimes.

Mr. Haverty and Mr. Andretti talked to her, trying to relax her, when they could. But they were mostly busy with their papers.

If the wait became very long, usually someone like Dan or Sister Philomena or Aunt Iris would come up and chat, to help her pass the time. Angela especially liked to have Dan be the one. Dan who could make her laugh so easily, with just a few words. Even laugh here, in this place.

Dan came every day.

Angela didn't really mind that Mother wasn't coming to the trial. The courtroom would be too much for Mother to take. Ed came quite often, when he could get time off work. But Dan—

Oh, bless him. She couldn't imagine how she could possibly have gotten through this trial without him.

He made a game of it as much as he could, picking her up most mornings at the Pompeii convent, often using different cars to throw those reporters off. Once he even came in his boss's red pickup truck.

Before the trial began, Dan spent quite a bit of time figuring out all the different entrances to the Hall of Justice, the different places they could park. The tricky part was just getting to the locked elevator before these photographers caught them.

A few days it was very close. One morning she and Dan were walking toward their elevator, across the big underground parking lot, when someone yelled behind them. She flipped a glance over her shoulder and saw four men, one of them bouncing a big black camera on his shoulder, running, shouting, toward them.

Dan grabbed her hand and pulled her across the blacktop as fast as she could run. As the elevator door slid closed on them she could see those men still coming, so close now.

. . .

So often in the courtroom Mr. Haverty was up on his feet, shouting that loud, *"Objection!"* Snarling it, almost.

It made her feel almost—safe when she saw that fierce way he attacked them, *defending her.* She'd never known Mr. Haverty could be so powerful, so authoritative. *Frightening,* almost, the way he came at those witnesses.

Those were the parts of the trial, really, that she liked best. When she could watch Mr. Haverty fighting so fiercely to—defend her.

She listened very carefully to all the testimony. Because she knew what they were explaining to her in that strange, ceremonial way was *why they had brought her to this place.* Why they thought she deserved to be put away in one of their jails for twenty-five years.

So as she listened to what they said, she kept trying to sort out *what could harm her most.*

Like that Dr. Kovaleski telling them how, when he'd showed her that ugly purplish thing in the silver bowl and told her it was a placenta, she'd said she didn't know anything about it. She knew she must somehow find a way to explain those things before she could make these strange people understand that she could never, ever have done what they accused her of. That *slaughter.*

When she asked Mr. Haverty later about the parts of the testimony that sounded so harmful, asked him what that meant for their case, he always answered reassuringly. But she could tell by the look in his turned-away eyes that he was worrying about those same things too.

On the fifth day of the trial, it was Dr. Talbott's turn in the witness chair.

He perched there with his long legs folded awkwardly. When DaSilva asked him to identify the defendant in the courtroom, Talbott glanced at her and said flatly, precisely, "That is Sister Angela seated at the end of that table."

He gave his professional credentials in the same definite, toneless voice. Then, with little prompting from DaSilva, he began to describe the normal process of a human birth. Told it in elaborate yet extraordinarily clear detail, as if lecturing on the process.

With pauses to consult the bulky hospital record he was holding, he described his observations of and the treatment rendered to Sister Angela Flynn in the Emergency Department of Parkhurst Hospital the previous April 25. The level, clinical tone of his voice did not change even when he described things like the insertion of the bladder catheter, "which was very difficult to do because Sister Angela was very reluctant. She refused to spread her legs apart. To have access to the urethral opening of a female you need to have the legs of the woman spread wide apart. In this case, with four medical personnel attempting to accomplish that, it was still—very difficult. It took several minutes to do it."

Now he was talking about her spontaneous delivery of a placenta at approximately 7:15 P.M. Reporting on his conversation at approximately 7:25 with the other nuns, in the hospital chaplain's office. Detailing the surgery he performed, commencing at 7:48, on Sister Angela. Describing how he collected the bundle containing the infant's body—"it was cold and still, obviously dead"—from the chaplain's office. And his visual examination of the body in the hospital morgue, after which he called the medical examiner's office as required by law, at approximately 8:50 P.M.

Under questioning from DaSilva, he reported very precisely his conversation with Sister Angela, initiated by her in her hospital room the subsequent evening at approximately 7:45 P.M., when she had said to him, "People are saying bad things about me. Can't you stop them?"

And her seeming to accept, finally, the meaning of that placenta she had spontaneously delivered: "She stated that she knew there was a chance she was pregnant, but she never really believed that because there were no obvious signs. She

534

did not find it impossible to believe she had delivered a baby, but when I stated that was what had happened she had no conscious recollection. She asked and was told by me that the child had been found, that it was not alive."

In the same flat monotone, Talbott testified to all the significant details of what Sister Angela had told him that night of her historic memory of the events of April 25—her description of her pain as severe lower abdominal cramps, changing later, when she was in the bathtub, into "a bearing-down pressure pain."

To her recollection of severe bleeding following that incident of bearing down: "When I told her I understood why she had been bleeding, that it was due to the incomplete separation of the placenta, she agreed with me. She accepted that as an explanation."

Talbott shifted the bulky hospital record to his other knee. "We had conversations every day of her hospitalization, although not as extensive. Nothing changed in her recollection of the historic events. The only history of bleeding she told to me had obviously come after this period of pushing, although she still had no recollection of any baby."

In his cross of the gynecologist, Ben Haverty attacked with an almost contemptuous savagery. Their sharply pointed discussion of various medical disorders of pregnancy and childbirth—pre-eclampsia, toxemia, fetal anoxia, placenta previa and abruptio—was too technical for most of those listening in the courtroom to grasp. But what they *could* understand clearly was Keith Talbott's precise, clinical assertion that he saw no evidence to support a medical diagnosis of any of those conditions when he treated Sister Angela Flynn.

On his recall of what Sister Angela herself had related to him concerning her own recall of what she had experienced that day, Talbott was equally unshakable.

Haverty pressed, bullied, trying to extract an admission that the child *could have been* born dead, demanding loudly if it was "not possible for an infant to ingest air before it is totally expelled from the mother's body?"

Quietly, from Talbott: "After the delivery of the head, the baby often starts making motions to breath. But in a first delivery, due to the tightness of the birth canal, there usually isn't a cry. The baby is not able to expand its lungs because of the pressure of the vagina on the thorax."

"But when the baby is expelled from the vagina, could not that sudden release of pressure have the effect of sucking air into the lungs and stomach as an involuntary muscular response?"

Firmly, precisely, Talbott answered: "If the baby is alive, probably yes. But if the baby was dead my answer would be *no.*"

When they broke for lunch at the end of Talbott's testimony at 12:43, the box score in the press section was five to one, prosecution.

Meg Gavin managed with a little adroit maneuvering to share an elevator down with Ben Haverty and Keith Talbott. She seized that irresistible opportunity to say, "Hey, Dr. Talbott, very nice job. I have to tell you, the reporters have elected you the best witness so far."

Talbott stared stonily at the ribbed brass elevator doors, his face set in a slightly twisted expression. Ben Haverty grunted aloud, a startled, almost amused sound.

They rode the rest of the way to the ground floor in silence, and scattered energetically as they came off the car.

Every day Meg was sucking in huge quantities of information to be fitted into the puzzle that was building in her head.

There was still no shape to the picture as a whole. But the information, the raw material of those jigsaw pieces, was coming now in torrents. Most of it fascinating past her most stoned imaginings.

She got the habit of meeting Kevin Corrigan for drinks, after he'd done his six o'clock news and she had turned in her day's update. She needed someone to unwind with, someone to help her digest whatever new astonishments had come at them that day.

Like that bizarre older woman with the wild-eyed expression who wore her gray hair always in that ratty ponytail. Who sat every day in the front row of seats behind Angela, wearing the same brown striped wool poncho and green flowered double-knit slacks.

Since she made such an ostentatious show of support for Angela in the breaks, the other reporters assumed she must be Angela's mother. But Meg, remembering that frail, elderly woman pinning her hat on in Dan Flynn's apartment that Sunday afternoon, realized this was probably the "aunt" who had raised Angela after her own family sent her out of their home.

Some of it she and Corrigan could laugh over. Like Ben Haverty *whirling* on that tweedy little *National Enquirer* buzzard when the guy nailed him that one day in the hall, spitting, *"Don't speak to me! Don't come anywhere near me!"*

But mostly they just sifted pieces. Those astonishing fragments.

Like *those two nuns* being sent home to the convent from the hospital to find that baby.

Or that first memory Angela had so tortuously brought back for the gynecologist, before she even remembered any baby—some *memory of that sex.*

Or that question DaSilva had flipped so unexpectedly at Sister Julia—about Angela spending the weekend before the birth *visiting friends in Wisconsin.* "Shit, Kev, that *had* to be Andy laying a base for him calling Daddy to testify. I mean, why else would he've stuck that in there?"

"Yeah. Well, I guess we'll see soon enough."

537

. . .

The Ramsey County D.A.'s office had notified Milwaukee attorney Monroe Dickson that they had a subpoena on tap for his client Roy Danziger, and expected Danziger to keep himself available in the event his testimony was required at the Angela Flynn trial.

When Danziger showed up at the office to hear that news from Dickson he shook his head blankly, stubbornly. "Hey, man, I already told you. There's no *way* I'm gonna, like, get into this stuff right in public. In the newspapers and everything." He paused in a thick, unhappy silence. *"No way, man."*

Dickson talked quietly, reassuringly, about how good the odds were that Roy would *not* be called. Very good odds, that Dickson would fix theoretically at, say, seventy-five, eighty percent.

But in the event it *did* go the other way, he wanted to stress to Roy right now how important it was that he keep himself available. In all fairness Dickson had to warn him that that St. Paul D.A. might possibly have him arrested if he tried to duck the subpoena.

Danziger was sitting with slumped shoulders, his arms limp in his lap, as if he wasn't listening. Dickson said with some urgency, "Roy, I think we can pretty much count on the fact that that probably is not going to happen. I think we can pretty much count on it working out that way, Roy."

For a minute Danziger made no response. Then he shook his head heavily and stood up.

"So, Roy? You'll keep in touch?"

Danziger looked blankly at the office wall. "Yeah. Okay."

Fat fucking deal. Roy just stayed stoned and tried not to think much about it.

Mostly, he tried to keep thinking about that boat he'd

538

bought about a month earlier with eighteen hundred bucks of the insurance money he'd been saving up. A twenty-two footer, two bunks in the cabin. Motor job.

It needed some work, but he figured when he got it fixed up he could take it out the Seaway down to, say, South America. Pick up a load of weed or cocaine in someplace like Colombia. One round trip like that and you could live off it maybe five, ten years. Live real good.

He couldn't work much on the boat in this weather, but he'd bought two books he was reading a lot at home. One on celestial navigation, the other on cruising around the Caribbean.

It felt pretty good to have something like that to get into, finally. And when guys like Al Packer and Eddie Staszic dropped around, now he had something to talk about.

Roy talked up his plans then, really got into them. Worked out some pretty firm figures on how many bucks you could probably walk away with from a deal like that. The way those guys reacted—cranked up, real excited, almost—made Roy feel pretty good.

One Monday night Al got so worked up he said shit, he might sign on for that trip himself. As a crew, like, for Ziggy. Shit, yes, *he'd do it.*

Now Al really wanted to see the boat, so the next morning Roy drove him over to the yard where it was beached for the winter.

As the camper moved down the twisted road to the shore Roy felt a sudden spurt of misgiving. Reluctance to let even Packer in on this private thing.

He said, "Hey, don't expect too much, like. I mean, it needs a lot of work."

"Yeah, sure, the old elbow grease. That's okay, I got plenty of that."

When they parked and stepped out of the camper, walked up to that hull that was tilted, so—lonely, like, in a patch of frozen dried weeds, neither one of them spoke.

539

Packer climbed up to the cockpit and stared around him with a kind of surprised smile.

Suddenly Roy was seeing what Packer saw: the missing deck planks. The little cabin with the broken hatch door. The weird bright spotty colors from four or five peeling layers of paint.

"Jesus, Zig, you kiddin' me?" Packer looked down at him with a wide, disbelieving smile. Almost a laugh. *"Colombia,* man? You want to sail this thing down to *Colombia?"* Looking down at the deck. "Hey, Zig, take my word for it— you'd get there faster if you just floated an old bathtub out in the lake and blew a few holes in it with a shotgun. I mean, shit, that'd be safer than *this* thing, man."

Roy pushed his hands into the pockets of his jeans jacket, looked out over the heavy gray horizon of that lake, over that gray, unwelcoming water. Said vehemently, bitterly, *"Fuck you, Packer."*

On Thursday morning, February 22, Dr. Henry Fullerton, chief pathologist at Carlisle General Hospital and deputy county medical examiner, drew the thankless job of testifying in the place of Dr. Kenneth Rhoades.

Under prodding from DaSilva, Fullerton did a crisp, expert job of describing the autopsy and laboratory findings on Baby Boy Flynn. His diagnosis concurred with that of Dr. Rhoades: "In my opinion the cause of death in this case was asphyxia produced by gagging, the presence of the panties in the further accessible portions of the airway constituting sufficient obstruction to produce the death of an infant otherwise normally developed."

When Ben Haverty rose for his cross-examination, he went for the kill.

In most of the current county trials in which evidence from the medical examiner's office was pertinent, there was a tacit gentleman's agreement that neither party to the case would take undue advantage of Rhoades's inability to testify, given the delicate nature of his breakdown. But Andy DaSilva realized even as Ben Haverty was still moving up to the lectern that no gentleman's agreement would be operative in this case.

Fullerton handled the assault very smoothly, very professionally. But Haverty attacked without even a *pro forma* show of respect, hammering again and again at the point that Fullerton *had not even witnessed this autopsy.*

That *no dissection of the throat* had been performed to confirm the position of the panties.

When Fullerton said in response to repeated jabs that in his opinion the presence of the panties in the throat was another indication of the child being born alive, since he could think of no conceivable reason for panties or any other foreign object to be placed there otherwise, Haverty seemed to swell with grim satisfaction.

"You can think of no conceivable reason? What are we dealing with here—medical facts or *your private suppositions unsupported by access to the evidence?"*

When they broke for lunch twenty brutal minutes into Haverty's cross Meg moved up to the wooden barrier, behind Andy DaSilva. He was standing at his table, leaning over papers spread out on its dark polished surface as she tapped his shoulder. "Hey, Andy. Bad luck, about Rhoades."

"Yeah, well," he said shortly. "I think we're doing okay without him." He pushed the spread papers into manila folders, gathered them under his arm, and turned to face her. "Anyway, Meg, I hope you're going to stick around this afternoon. I think you'll find it pretty interesting."

She blinked. "What, Andy? You got something coming up?"

"Well, you might say so, Meg." He paused. "It's a mystery witness."

Normally Andy DaSilva didn't go in for grandstand plays like this one. Wasn't his style.

But after the mauling he'd taken that morning, he could not resist drawing a small, private comfort from the way Meg was staring at him now, her eyes big as plates. She murmured, "Mystery witness? My God, Andy, *is it Daddy?*"

DaSilva allowed himself a brief smile that gave nothing away. Shook his head as he said, "Sorry, Meg, I can't say. But I think it might be worth you sticking around for."

He'd never seen a look on Meg's face like the one she was throwing at him now. "Oh, Andy, *I've gotta know.* Andy, are you calling the daddy?"

The smile that gave away nothing broadened a little. "Like I said, Meg. A mystery witness."

Thirty-eight

Waiting in line to retrieve her coat from the second-floor cloakroom, Meg dropped the word on the mystery witness to the UPI guy standing next to her.

As she came off the elevators from lunch she could see that news humming like a live wire through the reporters gathered near the courtroom door.

Other clumps of people—nuns, family, friends—seemed to be watching the reporters. Wary, worried. As if they sensed *something was up* and thought those reporters knew what it was.

Meg pushed into the press circle, anxiously asking, "Okay, who's got it?"

Nobody, it turned out. Lid was on tight, nobody leaking this one.

Meg kept insisting, "Come on, shit. Who else *could* it be except Daddy?"

Corrigan grinned. "You want a rough count, Meg?"

"Fuck you, Kev. I'm betting it's him."

"What you mean is you'd kill to *make it* him."

As Meg stalked away from the circle, she caught the eyes of Dan Flynn, who was standing eight feet away, trying to eavesdrop.

And then noticed Tim Vance, standing by himself, leaning up against the courtroom doorframe with his hands in his pants pockets. Vance, who'd been there almost every day of the trial. Trying to look casual, hanging around as if he belonged.

Which he did not, as Nick Scotti had rudely pointed out to Meg one night in the Blind Justice—"That fucking Cambridgeport dork, he's *got no business* in that courtroom." But Meg understood well enough why Vance was there.

Because he couldn't stay away from it.

With or without this assignment to cover, *she'd*'ve been there the same way.

Meg hadn't spoken much to Vance at the trial. She still rankled slightly from that interview last summer. But now, realizing that Vance actually *knew who Daddy was,* she walked up to him, smiling.

"Hey, Tim. You hear this stuff going around about a mystery witness?"

Tight, private grin. "Hi, Meg. Yep, I heard."

No clues on that pock-cheeked jock face. "Do you happen by any chance, Tim, to know who it is?"

"Maybe. And then again, maybe not." He flicked a baiting glance at her. "Anyway, I'll tell you this much—you're gonna be real surprised."

Hating herself for asking, but asking anyway: "Come on, Tim—did you talk to Andy?"

"Come on yourself, Meg. You know I'm not gonna tell you."

God, she hated to be jerked around like this. "Okay, just this one thing, Tim—is it the daddy?"

He was laughing now, that miserable son of a bitch.

As the court attendant unlocked the door to start the afternoon session, she snapped, "Okay, play it your own way, Tim. In case you're interested to know, I don't think you talked to Andy at all. And I think you don't know fuck all about who this witness is going to be."

The accuracy of that last shot finally drew a response. "Okay, Meg, I'll tell you this much at least—it's not gonna be Daddy. You want to know how I know?"

"Yeah, I guess."

She wasn't sure what she expected to hear. But certainly not that flat, astonishing, "Because Daddy doesn't have the goddam busfare to get here."

Back in the courtroom, she raked the crowd for clues to the witness.

The only new face was a pretty, skinny young woman sitting in the "family" section behind DaSilva's chair, who kept fiddling with a pleated stack of stenotype notes held on her lap.

A *court reporter?*

Meg muttered to Corrigan, "Shit, Kev, it can't be her." He shrugged, lifted one hand, palm up.

All the while Hank Fullerton was running out the end of his ragged second-hand pathology testimony, Meg watched that girl holding the steno notes, whose mounting nervousness was a strong argument for *her being that witness.* But Meg couldn't, wouldn't believe it.

What the hell mystery could there possibly be in a court reporter?

Yet when Fullerton finally stepped down and DaSilva said, "The State calls as its next witness Danielle Devers," sure enough, that skinny girl stepped up to the chair.

DaSilva established for the court record that Danielle
Devers was the court stenographer assigned to the grand
jury testimony of Ramsey County on May 26, 1978. Stipu-
lated also for the record that Angela Flynn as a defendant
testifying to the grand jury on her own behalf to facts pertinent to this case had automatically waived her right to privacy in that testimony.

Suddenly, eerily, Angela Flynn's own words, thoughts,
were finally coming aloud in the courtroom, read rapidly in
the high-pitched voice of the district attorney with refer-
ence to page and line from the grand jury transcript:
"About November, I became aware of the fact that I was
pregnant through weight gain and because I no longer had
my menstrual periods . . ." Confirmed by Devers as she
shuffled the folded pages on her lap, looking for those
quick references.

When Judge Aaron recessed for the day after this witness stepped down at 4:27, some two dozen reporters, moving as one body, rushed through the wooden barrier gate
toward Jack Poletti, the court reporter covering the trial
from his enclosed desk below the judge's bench. *"Hey, Jack,
let's have that back . . .* come on, Jack. Slower this time."

Poletti cracked his knuckles as he looked around him,
grinning. When Andy DaSilva shrugged and said he guessed
that would be okay, Poletti flipped back through his own
narrow folds of notes. "Okay, guys. But you'll owe me one."

Now Angela Flynn's words back again, this time in the
loud, rough-edged voice of Jack Poletti: " 'I planned right
from the very first sign of awareness of my pregnancy to have
the child and to keep—to keep him, to deliver him in a
hospital. I worried very much during the last months about
not getting medical help, except that I hoped and prayed he
would be healthy. I didn't think that out of the whole origin
of the problem that the Lord would let me down.' "

Standing at the back edge of the pack, Meg suddenly
sensed a presence behind her. Her pen still moving, she

545

glanced over her shoulder. Angela Flynn was sitting huddled at the end of the table, looking unbearably small and alone, staring bleakly at the wall in front of her.

A radio man was protesting: "Hey, Jack, not so fast. Back up some."

Poletti scratched at his nose. "What didn't you get?"

"Take it from that last question."

"Okay. 'Question: Had you heard any sound at all of the baby, do you have any recollections of any sounds? Answer: No, I recall—I recalled the fact that his arms moved. But I didn't hear him—I didn't hear him cry, and I can remember being disturbed about that, but in a muddled way or a muddled fashion, because of my—you know, because of my weakness. But I remember, you know, thinking that, you know—why doesn't he cry?' "

"Shit, Kev, you know why *that* was. Why she can't remember that," Meg brooded morosely three hours later at the Blind Justice Bar. "It's because that's *why she killed him.*"

"Yep, I guess. To shut up that crying."

Softly: "Oh, yeah. Shut him up with those panties." Twirling the glass slowly on the dark polished wood. "Sure. God. No wonder she can't remember *that.*"

The next morning, February 25, DaSilva opened with, "Your Honor, the People rest at this time."

Ben Haverty launched the defense portion of the trial with a wordy, predictable motion to have the case dismissed at this point for lack of evidence. When the judge said, "The court will reserve decision on your motion, Mr. Haverty. You can proceed," Haverty called as the first salvo of his defense Sister Angela's own psychiatrist, Dr. Bruce Heilbron.

The bottom line on Heilbron's extensively detailed testimony was his diagnosis of hysterical neurosis, dissociative type, "a mental disorder caused by guilt feelings that makes people perform abnormal acts out of their control." Also organic brain syndrome caused by the loss of thirty-five to forty percent of her body's blood volume, "which makes a person unable to cope with the usual stresses in life."

Heilbron stated that in his opinion Sister Angela "was both neurotic and psychotic on April twenty-fifth, and could not have formed an intent to kill her child. She also wouldn't have known if her actions were wrong or could have resulted in the baby's death." In his view, she had no conscious control of her actions "in her weakened condition, with her guilty feelings about being pregnant, being a nun and finally coming to the moment of delivery at which all events had a massive, almost explosive impact on her."

He explained away the patently untrue statements relating to her pregnancy that Sister Angela had made during her first twenty-eight hours in the hospital as "further evidence of her dissociated state. She later described her state of mind at that time, her difficulties in remembering those events, as 'not feeling like myself.'"

Heilbron consulted his notes with a small, self-important flourish. "She had a sense that her thoughts, verbalizations, were, quote, 'coming from me but they weren't coming from me. I didn't feel like I was in my same body. Almost like I didn't have control over myself. And the weakness scared me.' Unquote." He looked up from his notes. "As you can see, her thoughts and feelings were not following in a rational pattern."

Yet he testified that Sister Angela "is not psychotic today. The hysterical neurosis persisting until she recalled her child's birth a few days prior to her discharge also is not existing today."

Heilbron said that in his opinion she was sufficiently recovered from those previous conditions that he had been seeing her for therapy only once a month, "until the recent period, when we increased the frequency of our sessions to help her cope with the stress of this trial."

547

· · ·

One reason Tim Vance had been hanging around the trial, apart from his own unresistible curiosity, was his urge to talk to Andy DaSilva.

He'd held off doing that while DaSilva was still laying out the State's side of the case, because he could see DaSilva was a real mess of nerves. But once that part of it was done, Vance made it a point to grab him for a quick lunch at the Blind Justice.

DaSilva's head was still so deep in the thing he couldn't talk about anything else, musing over his sandwich and draft beer, "I don't know what you think, Tim, but I thought the FBI guy's testimony was pretty helpful. I wasn't expecting that, actually, about the infant hemoglobin."

Vance ignored his turkey sandwich as he leaned forward on his elbows, letting the guy talk. Hanging on everything he was saying.

Suddenly he burst out, "Hey, Andy, there's a crazy idea I'd like to bounce off you. That maybe could explain a lot of what happened."

He watched DaSilva's face sharply as he ran out his idea about the two personalities. No reaction except slight wrinklings of the nose, slight shakes of the head.

Finally, politely, "Yeah, well. That's a real interesting idea, Tim."

"Hey, Andy, I'm not saying that's the whole story. I'm not even sure yet that's really what's going on here. But look how it fits—like that sex stuff, Andy." He lurched back in his chair. "Look, there's probably only two explanations for those two real different versions of the sex, Andy. Either that's two different women having two kinds of sex. Or else Sister Angela's lying flat-out." Still no expression on DaSilva's face. "I mean, that's the only way I can figure it, Andy."

DaSilva rubbed the heel of his hand over his chin, considering. "Well, okay. I guess that's a fair enough way to see

it, if you want to. But I'll tell you how it looks to me, Tim
—I think she's been lying right from the start. Right from
that first night in the hospital—not to mention all through
her pregnancy." He jabbed the air with his forefinger.
"Right up to that grand jury testimony. Yeah, sure—I think
she's been lying here from word one."

"Okay. But, Andy—what if they *weren't* lies? To *Sister
Angela?*"

Stubborn headshake. "Nah, Tim. I don't say you
might not even be right. But to me the whole way she
testified in that grand jury was consistent with a pathological criminal personality. Adjusting any reality into an
alibi against their own guilt. I've come up against quite a
few of those guys the last few years, Tim. And to me everything she says, the whole way she *acts,* fits with that
type of criminal personality."

Urgently, from Vance: "But, Andy, what if that's the way
she *really sees it?*"

Another headshake. "Nope. I just can't go along with
that, Tim. Now you take that boyfriend, for instance, that
Danziger—Ben Haverty's still holding out that the guy raped
her. But I've interrogated quite a few rapists. Confessed
ones. And I couldn't see anything in that Danziger that
squares with the way a real rapist talks. Or thinks."

"Sure, Andy. *I* know the guy's no raper."

"But *her.* Sister Angela." DaSilva bit from his pastrami
sandwich and said with his mouth still full, "I've gotta tell
you, Tim, the whole way she presented herself in that grand
jury was consistent with a classic criminal personality. Lying
to protect themselves any time they see an opening."

Well, okay. Shit. At least he'd got the idea out.

But Vance felt no lessening of his somewhat pained
urgency. "Jesus Christ, Andy. A *classic criminal*—her?"

DaSilva smiled faintly. "Okay. I guess maybe that
sounds kind of like a reach, Tim. But that's just how I see
her."

"All right. Fair enough. Jesus, Andy, *I* can't say you're wrong. Sure, you're probably right. You know one hell of a lot more about this than I do. But just *consider* that other idea —that maybe it never was Sister Angela who did that screwing on the beach." He could see the idea playing, teasing on DaSilva's face as he blurted too soon, "Maybe not even her who . . . killed the baby."

DaSilva's face snapped closed like a switched-off electric light. Remote, polite again: "Well, like I said, it's a real interesting idea, Tim. But I don't buy it." He paused. "You want to know why?"

Vance nodded.

"Because it gives her an excuse."

"Hey, not an *excuse,* Andy. How about something more like—an explanation."

DaSilva's face was set in its usual mild calm as he turned his attention back to his sandwich. "Nope, I can't buy that. You're gonna see it yourself, Tim, if Ben Haverty puts her up on the stand. Like he'll probably have to do after we introduced that grand jury testimony. You just watch what she says then. How she lies her way through the whole thing. You just wait, Tim. Unless I'm real wrong, what you're gonna see up there will be perjured testimony top to bottom."

Annnhhh, God.

At least he'd gotten the idea out. Put it across.

All he could do. Leave it alone, leave it alone.

He gave it one last shot: "But it wouldn't be lies if she really *believes that,* Andy. If that's how it . . . was for *her.*"

DaSilva's face fixed, hard now. "Nope. That still sounds too much like an excuse."

Finally, reluctantly, Meg had given up on Daddy.

She realized by now that if Andy DaSilva hadn't called him, there was no way Ben Haverty would do it. Not the way

Ben was shaping *this* trial up, with his good, innocent little nun all surrounded by her suffering sisters in Christ.

So Meg let go of Daddy. And waited now, with a painfully sharp anticipation, for Mommy.

She knew she could never get hold of this, fit all the pieces together, until she had *Angela* in that chair. Talking right to Meg, explaining all this *for herself.* Face to face, finally.

God. She couldn't believe they meant to get through this whole trial *without Angela Flynn testifying.* Yet every time Ben Haverty called another of his dry little M.D.s to the stand, her fierce hold on that idea loosened a little.

On Tuesday morning, March 1, Dr. Ernesto Gomez, an internal medicine specialist hired by the defense to testify to the effects on the human body of hypogalemic shock, blew his own argument out of the water when he admitted under DaSilva's cross that a woman suffering from that condition could not lift her head off the floor, much less walk around a room. Box score on Gomez: two to one, prosecution.

Meg flexed her stiff shoulders as she muttered to Corrigan, *"Shit, when do we run out of M.D.s?"* Corrigan grinned as he scribbled on his notepad, "Check with AMA."

Almost idly, Meg watched Ben Haverty bend over the table, conferring with Andretti and the nun. Then he nodded, straightened up, turned around.

Said in a low voice, "Sister Angela, please take the stand."

When Mr. Haverty leaned over the table and asked her that one last time if she was ready, she nodded sharply *yes.*

Yes. Let it be *now.*

Standing, walking to that chair two steps up at the far end. *Help me, help me, Lord Jesus.*

Sitting on the chair. Hands folded tight in her lap. Toes brushing the carpet.

Touching the black Bible, repeating the oath from that man in the blue uniform. Hands refolding on her lap. *Oh Jesus Mary and Joseph let this be* enough.

Mr. Haverty standing quite close, behind the wooden lectern. Talking quietly, reminding her that she had waived her right as a defendant not to testify without in any way prejudicing any of her rights and so on.

"Yes, Mr. Haverty. Yes, I understand."

Almost like that grand jury again. But this room so much bigger, so many people staring at her, listening.

Trying not to see them. Looking calmly, strongly, at Mr. Haverty.

Answering to his questions that she was Sister Angela Flynn. Also known as Gayle Flynn.

That she was thirty-four years old, born November 20, 1944. That she weighed about ninety-eight pounds and was four feet eleven inches tall. That prior to November or December, 1978, she had generally weighed between 100 and 105 pounds. That her profession was teaching.

Mr. DaSilva half-standing, signaling: "Your Honor, I can't quite hear this witness."

Red-cheeked judge leaning toward her, smiling: "Sister, try to keep from hollering."

Explaining a little louder that she had become a member of the Congregation of the Sisters of St. Benedict in 1961, at seventeen years of age, straight out of high school. Listing her college degrees and the teaching jobs she had held up until last April, specializing in preschool-age children.

"Sister, in 1977 what was your general state of health?"

"I was very healthy. In fact I didn't miss any days from school. I had almost excellent health, except for an allergy to trees, grasses, animals and a few other things."

"In late 1977 did you become aware of the possibility that you might be pregnant?"

Nodding: "Yes, Mr. Haverty, about November. Around this time I began to gain weight, more weight than was usually true—about five pounds. And also my menstrual periods stopped. Certainly by January I became more certain, because of the movements of the child within me."

"Did you then formulate an idea when this pregnancy might bring result?"

Even after so many times in his office, so hard to say now. "Yes, Mr. Haverty. According to my calculations, about May tenth."

"And did you then make plans?"

Hesitating. Smiling. Answer gone from her head.

"Yes. I made an immediate decision to keep it. To have the child and to keep it. I would have him in a hospital in St. Paul."

Mr. Haverty looking, urging, saying nothing. She smiled again, even giggled.

Answer gone, gone from her head.

Mr. Haverty prompting: "Did you make any other plans? Further to how this would occur?"

"Oh, yes. I did think about how I would go to the hospital as soon as I had any signs of the delivery of my child. But I told nobody about it."

"Why did you tell no one?"

Smooth, sure again now: "Because I wanted to spare my family and friends and my religious community from the agony and suffering I knew they would undergo."

Now talking about the events of April 25, that so familiar story she could tell now almost like a Hail Mary. That was the whole reason she had come here, to *tell them all that story.* Knowing this was the telling that would count.

First waking suddenly at three A.M. with "a very intense and very constant pain in the upper part of my abdomen. It seemed to be under my chest, between the breast and the top of the stomach, between the rib cage. A constant pain— it wasn't intermittent at all."

"What did you do then?"

"Well, I thought I probably had some kind of intestinal flu or bug. I didn't think it had anything to do with the delivery of the child, because I was expecting to feel contractions."

Hard, so hard, all of them watching, listening. But she *must tell it now.* To make them understand.

Tell them what she recalled of that morning. Walking by the window around nine A.M., trying to read, trying to take her mind off that "intense, constant pain in the upper part of my abdomen." And seeing Sister Margory leaving the school coming toward the house, "when almost simultaneously my water broke, and there flowed a pinkish flow of blood. I think I fell at that point, as it seemed to me all of a sudden began a very heavy flow of blood, dark red in color."

"Did you ever notice bright red blood?"

Hands clenched in her lap. "No, I could best describe it first as a pinkish color. Then it seemed to be—very suddenly, to my mind—darkish red. To the best of my recollection, sometime shortly thereafter I began to notice clots of blood all around me. Maybe that large." Circling her thumb and first finger. "About me and right under. There were many. I can't tell you the exact measure."

Meg realizing even as she was frantically scribbling that the tape she was hearing now from Angela Flynn was edited.

Spliced. Hours missing—from pink liquid to dark red blood to clots. Hours, hours missing.

Remembering going to the supply room to get some towels to mop up the blood.

"Then it was much more than a normal menstrual flow?"

"Oh, yes, much more. It took at least two towels to soak it up."

Then later going several times down the hall to the bathroom. Remembering after maybe her third trip seeing Sister Margory coming into the house, "and I thought I cried loudly for help. I kept thinking she didn't hear, because otherwise she would have come, but I felt I was yelling. And then I went to take a bath, to try to wash off all the blood that seemed to me to be all over my body. I stepped into a bathtub, and realized a few minutes later it was impossible to wash off because I was in a pool of it. At the same time —I can't tell you the exact time—I suddenly felt a change in the pain, which became very low. About here." She touched her fingers to her hip.

"Low in the stomach," Mr. Haverty asked, "where the legs meet the body?"

"Yes. A very different pain, that I can best describe as a very sharp, bearing-down pressure pain. I became aware that I was about to deliver the child. I stepped out of the tub onto a pink bathmat. And I just knelt down on the bathmat and delivered the child."

She told how she had carried him very carefully, close to her body, down the hall. "And it surprised me to find my child didn't cry. And also as I was carrying him I noticed a slight arm movement."

"Did you observe anything else?"

"No, Mr. Haverty. No, I heard no sounds at all. I never heard the infant cry."

Now she was recalling all those times of "lost consciousness, I suppose. Because . . . I remember periods I can only describe as nothingness, and then semiconsciousness about cleaning up the blood and getting help. And then I recall hearing the children's voices, which I thought meant the end of the school day, when the sisters would be coming back to the convent to bring help."

"Do you recall anything about the infant between the time you brought him through the door and fell, and when you heard those sounds?"

555

Soft, earnest: "No, Mr. Haverty, I don't."

"Do you remember severing the umbilical cord?"

"No, I don't."

"Do you recall ever seeing the child again?"

"No, I don't."

Then remembering Sister Julia coming into the room, "and someone screaming, and Sister Julia saying she should have come over at noon, and myself trying to convey to her some understanding that it wasn't her fault. I recall someone calling the ambulance and I asking her to wait for a few minutes to help me clean up, and someone saying something like, 'There's no time.'

"I recall the ambulance attendant putting me in a sitting position. And feeling I was about to topple over."

Mr. Haverty was about to ask another question when the judge interrupted: "All right, it's twelve-twenty-five. This court will be in recess until two P.M."

Meg felt numbed as she walked out of the courtroom with her arms folded over her chest. Hurting, numbed.

For so long she'd been conjuring this moment, imagining just this—sweet-faced, soft-voiced little nun perched in that chair up there, talking, telling her own story.

Imagined just like this. But—

Never realizing somehow how rough it would be to listen to.

She so eerie calm. Polite. Even *cheerful,* in her gray-flannel vest and skirt, with the big gold cross around her neck where everyone could see it. Smiling, even *giggling* once. Reciting her down-pat little story.

That was almost unbearable to have to listen to.

And Meg realized as she crossed the lobby that those others were feeling it too. For the first time, walking among them, she felt moved by what was coming out of them.

Even those nuns—cold bitches who up to now gave off

nothing but wary, loathing looks—right now she could feel even those nuns bleeding.

Three of them stood in front of her in the cloakroom line. Suddenly, impulsively, Meg touched the shoulder of the plain, hawk-nosed one closest to her. "Hey, excuse me, Sister. I'd just like to say—how sorry I am for all of you."

The nun blinked, startled. Meg blurted, "Gee, this is hard even for just *us* to sit through. But you guys . . . and her . . . well, I just wanted to say I'm very sorry."

The nun hesitated uncertainly for a moment. Then smiled—a warm, unguarded smile. "Well, thank you."

Ice broken for once, they spent the rest of their wait in the cloakroom line talking about movies.

Nick Scotti caught up with Andy DaSilva as he was pulling his coat out of the metal locker in his cubicle office. "Fuck, Andy, *give it to her* now," Scotti urged. "Pin her down, rip her apart."

DaSilva grimaced. "Yeah, well. We'll see, Nick."

"Jesus Christ, you can *hear* how she's lying in there. You gotta *call her on it,* Andy." Scotti's small black eyes pinpointed with urgency: "You can't let her *get away with it.*"

DaSilva shrugged on his beige raincoat as he said wearily, "Okay, Nick. We'll see."

When Meg finally retrieved her coat she realized she had no appetite for lunch. She decided to settle for a can of Diet Pepsi from the courtroom cafeteria.

Turning the corner of the long stone hallway on the third floor, she saw the man sitting slumped on a bench outside the cafeteria door, elbows on his knees, head slung between his shoulders.

She could hardly believe it *was him* until she came right up to the bench. Stood beside it and said quietly, "Hey, Ben."

557

Ben Haverty looked up at her. Eyes not quite focused as he said, "Mmmpph. Meg."

She walked past him and sat on the other end of the bench, coat pulled tight around her. "Rough morning, Ben."

He was leaning over his knotted, moving hands, staring at the corridor wall.

Suddenly: *"Oh my God."* Shaking his head exhaustedly. "You don't know how rough this case has been, Meg. My God, the *hours* we put into it."

"Well, it shows, Ben."

He was muttering almost to himself. "Twelve hours a day for weeks. Months, even. But you can't ever learn enough. You just can't ever learn enough."

Meg said nothing.

A minute later Haverty suddenly stood up, blinking, then lurched away without looking at her.

She bought her can of Diet Pepsi and rechecked her coat on the second floor.

When the press guys came drifting together outside the courtroom, she told them—with an odd reluctance, as if betraying some confidence—about her run-in with Haverty.

"What, *Ben?*" Kevin Corrigan laughed. "Come on, Meg."

"Yeah, swear. That's what he said."

The improbability of *Ben Haverty* baring himself in that way to a reporter ran so strong that they only believed it because Meg had said it.

The AP man slapped his notebook on his trouser leg. "Well, that's it, then, Ben's fuckin' flipped out. I've been suspecting that for a while, watching how he's working in there. But that tips it."

Angela waited in her own chair until the judge came out. Then, after Mr. Haverty nodded to her, she walked back to the high padded chair.

Pointed by Mr. Haverty's question, she said, "I remember being taken out of my room. But I have no recollection of being put in the ambulance. Then I recall asking the ambulance attendant if I was dying. He said they were giving me all the medical help that was possible.

"Then I remember finding myself in the emergency unit —I don't know how I got there. I know I was surrounded by a number of doctors, all asking me questions. I have vague recollections of them asking me about a pregnancy, and words coming out of my mouth but I didn't have any conscious control over them. It was like the words were coming from another person."

"Do you recall speaking after your surgery to Dr. Heilbron, the psychiatrist?"

"Well, I recall some doctor asking me to do a whole list of subtractions. I remember telling him how difficult a task that was, but I tried to do it." Hesitating. "And he asked me other specific questions, like who was buried in Grant's Tomb. But I don't recall any about a pregnancy or delivery of a child. And I did not recall anything about the delivery of the child until I believe about two weeks later, when I was still in the hospital, in Ward Five."

"Have you any recollection about what happened to the child?"

"No, I haven't."

"Did you have any intention formed to harm or kill the child?"

Smiling again. "No, Mr. Haverty, I didn't."

"Did you take any action to hurt, harm or kill the infant?"

"No, I did not."

"Did you voluntarily testify before the grand jury?"

"Yes, and I told them all I could remember."

"Did you voluntarily waive your right to privacy concerning all doctors' and medical records?"

"Yes, I did."

Mr. Haverty ducked his head, murmuring, "All right. Thank you, Sister Angela."

Now that little district attorney, the one who must mean to *hurt her if he could,* came up to the lectern and pulled her back through the whole story. But this time she had to explain all those hard things.

"You thought you were pregnant in November or December, 1977?"

"Yes, Mr. DaSilva, that is correct. And by January I was sure."

"Why?"

"Because I continued to gain weight and have no periods. And I felt movement in December. I felt movement very frequently thereafter."

"When you first realized that, did you prepare yourself for any type of delivery?"

"Yes. I was aware through reading and past conversations with other women who had had children what steps were necessary. And I read several books on prenatal care. I had them in my bookcase at the school and in my room at the convent, I believe. I planned to deliver the baby in a hospital in St. Paul."

He asked her how she'd planned to get there.

"Well, whenever the contractions started, depending on the situation I was in at the time, I planned to ask someone to drive me or go by taxi. But if I'd known there was any danger to me or my child, I would certainly have done something right away.

Frowning: "How would you have become aware of that danger?"

"Well, if there had been pain or anything."

"If you had severe pain or bleeding you would have known you or the child was in danger?"

"Yes."

Reminded of Sister Mary Christopher Leahy's testimony that Angela had promised to see a doctor, she said,

"Well, yes, Sister said something about me gaining weight, the possibility of a tumor. I might have said if I knew anything was seriously wrong I would go to a doctor, but I don't recall any promise in the sense of 'go immediately.' "

"Do you recall telling Sister Claudine Schneider on Holy Thursday evening that you *had gone,* that you had seen your mother's doctor?"

She shook her head. "Yes, but—I said I would see my mother's doctor if anything was seriously wrong. I knew I would have to consult an obstetrician or a gynecologist in May, but I had not done so up to the point of the tragedy in April."

"I show you People's Exhibit number forty-seven, a list of doctors' names and telephone numbers."

She looked at the small file card. "Yes, that was written by me around February."

"Did you ever call any of those phone numbers?"

"No, I didn't."

When he asked about her waking at three A.M. with severe cramps, she lifted her hand slightly. "No, I wouldn't call these cramps—just an intense, constant pain in the upper part of my abdomen."

He read from page 407, line six, of the transcript of her grand jury testimony: " 'I woke around three o'clock with severe cramps under my chest. Just very heavy cramps which never diminished in intensity.' "

She twisted the gold wedding ring on her left hand. "Well, I recall hearing the doctor say from this stand that I had spoken to him of low abdominal cramps, but to the best of my recollection when I woke again around seven that morning the pain was still very constant, very high in the abdomen."

"Did you think then you should get to the hospital? That there might be complications with the child?"

"No, because they weren't contractions. So I just didn't think it was time for the delivery of the child."

But she herself, he pointed out, had just testified that she intended to go for help *if she felt pain.*

"Yes, Mr. DaSilva, that's true. But this pain we're talking about I thought just an unusual one, in the sense that I rarely feel sick. I had never had this pain before, but I did not understand it to be what was meant by contractions."

"Did you ever talk to anyone about what it feels like to experience the contractions of childbirth?"

"Yes, in the past. I had been in groups of women talking about them—but what I was feeling that morning wasn't intermittent at all."

"Contractions to you were intermittent pain?"

"Yes."

Now he was quoting her own words from her earlier testimony: "When you say your 'water broke' around nine A.M., wouldn't that indicate to you the process of birth was beginning?"

"Yes, but then the blood began to flow and I fell down and so many other things were happening. I was too frightened by all the blood—that's what I was focusing on. I remember thinking about cleaning it up and going to phone for help but my thoughts were very fuzzy, very muddled kinds of thoughts that didn't seem to get accomplished into action. Because the bleeding started *immediately* after—first pinkish color, then dark red."

"But your plan was, as soon as you knew the baby was going to be born, to go to a hospital and have him delivered. And when your water broke you knew that was the beginning of the birth process?"

She countered sharply: "Yes, but you have to take into consideration what was also taking place in my mind because of the loss of blood. I can't separate one from the other. And I never stopped bleeding all day."

He asked if she did not walk two, possibly three times

to the supply room at the far end of the hall to get fresh towels.

"I don't know. Maybe I got them all at the same time. But it might have been different times."

"But you never went to the phone in the room directly across from yours to call for help?"

"No, I never phoned that I know of. I know the list of obstetricians was probably right on my desk or in my purse, but I don't recall thinking about that then."

"Were you bleeding in the supply room?"

"I imagine so. I was dripping everywhere I walked. But at that time I didn't know there were footprints."

"Did you hear Sister Margory leave the house at noon?"

"I don't recall. I remember thinking when I was calling out she must not have heard or she would have come to my room and helped me."

Now he reminded her of that time she was in the tub.

"Well, I intended to but never actually took a bath. I remember just being surrounded by a pool of blood, the water still running. And then realizing what I was feeling now was a pressure pain." She gripped her hands tightly. "At that moment I knew I was about to deliver the child."

He asked how she knew what that pain meant.

"I just knew that was what came before the delivery of the child, from books and from conversations in the past, not specifically about my pregnancy."

"So you knew right from wrong when you stepped from the tub to deliver the child?"

"Objection!"

"Overruled."

"Yes. But the bleeding also continued thereafter. I know some doctors say I delivered around noon, but I have no awareness of time in that moment at all."

"Do you recall how long the delivery process took?"

"No, I have no awareness. I recall the baby only in a vague kind of way, that I saw the whole form of the baby."

563

"Do you recall seeing the umbilical cord?"

"Not specifically, more than anything else. Just the whole form of the baby."

"Did you try to clean the baby with toilet tissue, or clean yourself?"

"No, not that I recall. The baby was on the bathmat. I remember carrying him to my bedroom. And I remember going over the threshold and falling."

"Why were you so interested in cleaning up?"

"I don't know. I only know that was one of my thoughts."

"I will read from your grand jury testimony, page four fifty-two, line eleven: 'Question: Do you know what made you so interested in cleaning up? Answer: Well, I presume one of the reasons was embarrassment. I didn't want the sisters to see me in that condition because I knew exactly what their reaction would be. And when they came, it was exactly what I thought.'"

Puzzled, wondering why he was making such a thing of that *embarrassment.* When what they were doing to her now was so far past that.

She said dryly, "Looking back, I don't recall having that thought about embarrassment. But since I said that on May twenty-sixth, that would have been a fresher memory." She hesitated. "I felt it was dangerous for me to stay in the bathroom because I felt extremely weak and knew I was going to fall down."

"So you knew right from wrong at that moment?"

"Objection!"

The judge murmured, "Well, right from wrong has many meanings here. Make your questions more specific, Mr. DaSilva."

When the lawyers finished their argument, she continued, "I knew it was dangerous to stay in the bathroom so I picked the baby up in the pink bathmat and walked down the hall and I remember being disturbed because my baby didn't cry—also also seeing some movement of the arms. I don't recall specifically calling for help. I remember that was very much in my thoughts but somehow I wasn't able to accomplish it."

"You saw *some* movement of the arm. But Dr. Heilbron has testified that you told him you recalled seeing *several limb movements.*"

She shrugged slightly. Saying nothing.

Now he was making her explain why she denied any pregnancy to the doctors. "Well, I remember they were asking me questions about that, and I remember going through some kind of verbal response, as if the answers weren't coming from myself. I don't recall denying it, but I might have in the condition I was in."

"Do you recall telling Dr. Talbott that you did not bleed profusely until after that incident of pushing in the bathtub?"

"No, I don't recall telling that to Dr. Talbott. The only thing I specifically recall was signing some form before my surgery that mentioned a hysterectomy. I recall that in a muddled way."

He shuffled through his papers and handed her a Xeroxed page: "Is that your signature?"

She stared at that huge, scrawled, not even legible name. "Well, the signature doesn't look like mine. But it must be."

"Do you recall asking Dr. Talbott if he couldn't be wrong about the placenta, if there wasn't something else that looked like that?"

"No. I remember someone saying here that I said that. But I don't recall making the statement."

Abruptly, DaSilva asked for a short break. He moved back to his table, stood over it, paging through his files.

Now he saw the opening, the gap, in their tight, expert fencing.

If he could just figure out a way to nudge her through it.

Keeping her face very still as she watched the little man look through those papers, frowning, so distracted. Silence so heavy. Menacing.

Dear Jesus, what could he be looking for?

Clock on the back wall fixed at 4:18. So late, so close to recess.

Now. Now. Sweet Lord just let it finish NOW.

He carried some papers back to the lectern.

"Do you recall the doctors saying to you that you had passed a placenta?"

"To the best of my recollection, no."

"Did you know what a placenta was?"

"Yes. I knew." She swallowed. "It's an afterbirth. I knew that from the reading I did."

He scratched his black hair, stared at his papers for a long moment. "Did you know anything about that conversation with the doctors prior to your testifying in the grand jury?"

Sucking in a small breath, sensing the trap. *Careful. Very careful.*

"No, Mr. DaSilva. The first I knew about that conversation was when Mr. Haverty told me the doctors had testified to that in the minutes he got of the grand jury testimony. Prior to that date on which I testified, I also did not recall anything about the conversation I had with Dr. Talbott on the twenty-sixth. I only know I had one because I heard Dr. Talbott testifying here in the courtroom. I don't at this moment recall any conversation with Dr. Talbott at that time, *no.*" She smiled tremulously. "I do recall conversations with him about my child, yes. But I don't recall any specific date or time."

He thumbed through his papers for another long, still moment. Seemed to be weighing, considering.

Then he ducked his head and he said, "The People have no further questions for this witness, Your Honor."

Now Mr. Haverty moved again to the lectern, asking to see a copy of the hospital record. He turned Xeroxed pages, the silence heavy in the room.

Then: "On your admission to the hospital you were asked to sign a receipt for your clothing. Do you have any recollection of that?"

She hesitated, so unsure. This thing never talked about in his office. "No, Mr. Haverty, I have no recollection of that. I may have signed it, but I have no recollection."

He waved the pages with a kind of flourish, saying loudly, "Let the record show that on the second to last page of her medical records there is a signed acknowledgment that this patient was unable to sign a receipt for her clothing due to reasons of shock."

Finally, gently. "Thank you, Sister Angela. You may step down."

From where he was standing, leaning with his arms crossed on the back wall, Tim Vance managed to be the first one out of the courtroom. He headed straight for the elevators, his face set in a fixed, blank expression.

Okay, now he knew.

Nick Scotti's face was reddened, tightly focused, as he caught DaSilva coming into the judicial hallway. *"Fuck, Andy! Why didn't you take her apart?"*

DaSilva grimaced. "Hey, Nick, a case like this one— even if I'd done that it might have backfired anyway. Worked up sympathy for her or something." He shrugged. "I mean, shit, Nick, *you* know this is a real strange case."

Scotti balled his right fist, thrust it into the air. "Jesus fucking Christ, Andy. You *let her get away with it.*"

. . .

As Meg sat at her desk at the *Eagle-Bulletin,* sorting enough fact from her confusion to bang out two front-page pieces on the day's testimony, she kept seeing that face. Looking so earnestly right toward her, saying those amazing things.

Such a sweet, composed face, cheeks as pink as her turtleneck. Just about the only one in that whole dreary nun-parade who could look pretty with no makeup.

Speaking so politely, *helpfully.* As if she was doing her best to help them tidy up this messy little thing here, this trial.

With that bizarre, totally unanticipated *smile.* Even that giggle, that came when she couldn't fish her line from the script quick enough.

Chiding Andy in one part of his cross, primly, like a schoolmarm: "But you have to take into consideration, Mr. DaSilva . . ."

Even through that jaunty little Christian face you got plenty of her pain. Yet Meg realized now that none of it seemed connected to . . . what she'd done to *that baby.*

Anh sure, *that's* what was missing there today. Pain, yes. But . . . *no grief.*

No feel of repentance. Even regret. For that horrendous thing she had done to that kid.

As if she would please like them all to just understand that she had nothing to do with that unfortunate "tragedy," as she'd called it once.

As Meg typed for deadline almost on automatic pilot, two perceptions, both unwelcome, were firming out of the still-numbed confusion of her head.

One was that the good little nun had lied consistently up there on the stand today. All that "I don't recall . . ." of every damning conversation with her doctors.

All that "to the best of my recollection at that point in

time . . ." A vintage Nixon performance, delivered in that earnest, appealing, nunny little way of hers.

The other perception yet more startling, unexpected.

The realization that it probably *never would* make any sense.

Not now. After hearing it finally right . . . from *her*.

Thirty-nine

For Meg the rest of the trial started out like over-kill.

Next morning's opening witness was the defense pathologist, pretty-boy Dr. Allen Von Bargen, who justified the $5,000-*per-diem* fee he was stiffing the nuns for by testifying under oath that in the case of Baby Boy Flynn the cause of death was "compatible" with natural causes.

His examination of the lungs revealed them to be "poorly expanded, a deep purplish red—beet-like, containing little to no air." The "spread-apart air spaces" in the lung sections he examined microscopically could be explained by, for example, "the administration of vigorous but unskilled attempts at resuscitation."

Yet the bottom line on DaSilva's extensive cross was: "Isn't it possible after your entire review of this case that this baby could have died of asphyxia by gagging after being born alive?"

Reluctant but graceful: "That is possible."

"Isn't it true you don't have an opinion based on reasonable medical certainty of the cause of death here?"

"That is correct, sir."

. . .

569

Next witness was rebuttal, prosecution shrink to counter Heilbron's testimony. Dr. Marvin Mandelbaum, a nervous, expensively dressed University of Chicago import, confirmed the previous finding of organic brain syndrome. "But in my opinion she did not suffer it to a degree that would cause significant impairment of function. She carried out certain activities during that period in logical, directed, purposeful fashion, indicating a certain cognitive level. She knew where she was, that she was giving birth. The fact that she is able to account for most of her activities up until she was taken to the Emergency Department indicates to me that her organic brain syndrome was not of that degree that I would not find her culpable."

Glancing at his notes from his examination of her on March 2, Mandelbaum "observed gross inconsistencies in her statements that I felt warranted more investigation before I could confirm further aspects of this diagnosis. But as you know, I have only been allowed one two-hour examination of this defendant."

When Haverty stood to begin his cross, he leaned down and said something to Andretti. Andretti left the courtroom as Haverty moved to the lectern to demolish this psychiatrist.

Haverty's merciless strategy of impugning the prosecution's medical witnesses by contempt, calculated disrespect, finally paid off. Ten minutes into this cross Mandelbaum was flustered, squirming in the witness chair. "If you wouldn't *put words in my mouth . . .*"

Impaled on his own confused defense of his professional methodology—"My opinion *at that time* was that what I heard merited further investigation. My practice is to have a thorough investigation." Mandelbaum repeated in a high, rising voice, "But I have been precluded from an adequate examination of this defendant to form an opinion."

Softly, triumphantly: "Then your present position is

that you do not know the proper diagnosis as of that date of April twenty-fifth?"

Mandelbaum snapped, "That's right."

Ben Haverty was smiling when he said at the conclusion of Mandelbaum's testimony, "Your Honor, we'd like to request a thirty-minute recess to await the appearance of a rebuttal witness."

The short, stocky man in his late fifties who puffed through the wooden barrier gates identified himself on the stand as Dr. Fred Salter, senior psychiatrist of Parkhurst General Hospital. Asked if he could identify the witness as being present in the courtroom, he said, "Of course. That's Angela sitting down by Mr. Andretti," and flashed a warm smile to her, waggling his fingers in a wave.

Led by Haverty's questions, Salter testified to his first interview with the defendant, on April 29 in her hospital room, "when she said, 'I have no memory of a baby, but Dr. Talbott and Dr. Heilbron told me about it.' When I asked her to speculate about all that had happened she said, 'Other than tell you the same story, there's nothing else I can see.' She wept considerably at that first confrontation. And she said, 'I can't imagine putting a baby in a wastebasket. I have heard of babies being left, but I cannot imagine doing that either. I'm thirty-three years old and I am not naive.'"

In Salter's opinion, a twofold diagnosis seemed appropriate—a hysterical dissociated state and other acute psychotic brain syndrome associated with the loss of blood, "which together by geometric progression would compound a gross disturbance in her mental function, making her quite unable to deal with reality."

"After delivery did Sister Angela possess the capacity to form an intent to kill such an infant?"

"No."

"Did she possess the capacity to know or appreciate that

any such acts that may have been done by her at that time would be wrong?"

"No, because you need intact cerebral function for that. Her growing hysteria, related to her guilt as a nun for for harboring this information within her, would be almost sufficient to preclude that. When you add the physical exsanguination, it is impossible for me to imagine that Sister Angela could have had a capacity to know and appreciate the wrong nature of any acts."

Now Salter was reading from the notes of his last interview with the nun, at his office the previous May 15. And suddenly the grief, remorse, that had been missing from Angela Flynn's own testimony came flooding into the room: "She told me, 'I know it matters if I'm convicted but I've already imprisoned myself in my mind and heart. Because I can't escape from my thoughts and I want to know if I harmed my child and I know I must have because I was the only one there.' She was weeping convulsively as she said, 'I know I must have harmed him and I don't know how I could have. If I didn't plan to harm him before he was born, why would I harm him after? It's all so confusing because I was the only one there.' "

Meg did not speak to anyone as she moved out of the courtroom with one thought crowding her mind: *Enough, enough, just* let her go, *stop doing this thing to her.*

The next morning Ben Haverty opened with his summation speech. A commanding presence even in his baggy suit, he rolled one more time through his scattershot defense: "The prosecution must prove in this case beyond a reasonable doubt that this infant known as Baby Boy Flynn was born alive and totally expelled from the mother, with an independently operating circulatory system, before he met death at the hands of criminal intent. Yet as far as I'm concerned we have seen no real proof here of when the child was born, no *real proof whatsoever* of when this child died. Not one witness in this courtroom has established a *time of death* in this case, much less a cause. And no witness has offered any conclusive proof that this defendant, Sister Angela, possessed at that time the requisite physical or psychological capability to have performed the acts of which she is accused."

He worked exhaustively over the testimony of most of the thirty-eight witnesses, jabbing open as many holes as he could.

Then he went for the heartstrings: "And who is this defendant, this accused? A girl who *since the age of seventeen has devoted her whole life to little children.* I don't know what this court or this county expects of this girl, who has found herself in this most difficult human circumstance. What more can she do than she has already done, testifying twice under oath to everything she can recall, in order to *demonstrate her innocence in this case?*

"Yes, there may be some inconsistencies in her story, easily explained by her distressed mental state and acute blood loss. But I cannot conceive of any circumstances in which this girl would intentionally harm her own infant, on the same tragic afternoon when another small child reached for the convent doorbell to ask her for a tutoring lesson.

"I cannot conceive that this girl could kill. I say with all the fervor I can amass that this case lies completely limp. Certainly Mr. Andretti and I have welcomed the opportunity to serve this woman in her hour of need. We have tried to do the best we could for her and for the community of the Sisters of St. Benedict, who have come into this courtroom and testified for the prosecution even as they at the same time drew a circle of the greatest support around their member."

Quietly, very quietly now: "Your Honor, the prosecution *has not proven* a criminal act or a criminal intent on the

573

part of this girl. Now your verdict can vouchsafe the hope that beats in the heart of all people that in a court of law truth, justice and impartiality still reign. Your verdict should be *not guilty*. And if it is, who wins?" A heavy pause. "The truth—and the people of the State of Minnesota."

From the press section Meg could see that Vince Andretti—cool, slick Andretti—was crying.

Angela seemed to be crying a little too. Lifting a shining face to Haverty as he sat back down at the table and reached out his big arm to hug her.

Yet Meg felt surprisingly cold, dry-eyed.

She'd expected when she got into court that morning to be swept away, captured by the impassioned logic of Ben's last pitch. Granted, much of the testimony laid out had gone against the nun. But enough gaps, enough "reasonable doubts" had been punched into the tissue of evidence—at least on insanity grounds—that Meg had expected, finally, to *yield* to Ben's argument.

Yet—hearing it—she had not.

Even now, watching him pat the nun's shoulder comfortingly, Meg realized that the feeling Ben had tweaked from her was too—thin.

Irish, stagey. Almost cheap.

Like that overblown bit about the little girl reaching for the convent doorbell—cheap shot, overdone.

. And if *that* was Ben Haverty's best pitch for acquittal here—that "girl who devoted her whole life to children," closed inside the circle of her loving, supporting sisters. . . .

Surprised, reluctant, Meg finally let herself consider the idea that Angela Flynn *might not deserve* to walk away from this case.

Andy DaSilva walked up to the lectern to deliver his summation.

He seemed less nervous than usual as he said in an almost conversational tone that after listening for the last hour to Mr. Haverty, he thought this court would agree that this particular defendant had received probably one of the most striking and well-prepared defenses they'd seen in a courtroom.

For quite a while the previous evening he had sat at his desk, "pondering how to start this summation of the most draining, most medically and legally loaded cases I ever worked on. And after looking through all the exhibits, I picked up People's Exhibit number thirty-two, this photograph of this infant."

He waved it toward the judge. "This particular picture is the entire case before you, Your Honor. And it cries out to you as a judge and a human being, cries out for common sense and for justice in this case. It tells better than anything said in this courtroom what really happened in that convent on April twenty-fifth.

"What we got here was not just a defense, but a series of defenses. The accused says well, yes, I was pregnant, and delivered the baby in that convent bathroom. But that baby was dead before I ever carried him to my room. And if you don't believe that, I don't remember anything about killing that baby with the panties, or putting him in the wastebasket. And I don't remember denial after denial of that pregnancy —and anyway, it was 'as if someone else was speaking from my mouth.' "

He reviewed the psychiatric testimony alleging hysterical neurosis and organic brain syndrome, "which interestingly enough she now no longer suffers from. But acting *with extreme emotional disturbance* is exactly what she's charged with here. And if she is cured of those mental defects, why does she now remember so many things *except the events surrounding the death of this infant?* It's amnesia, all right—amnesia by convenience. Now that she has to explain her actions, now she begins to remember massive blood loss *before* the birth,

575

and no crying from the baby. But nothing concerning the death, because she has no way to explain it. What we have here is a well-rehearsed ten-month-old fabrication, supported by psychiatric testimony."

DaSilva conceded the facts of her profuse bleeding and periods of lost consciousness. "But common sense will tell you those occurred *after* the death. Otherwise why wasn't that baby found lying next to her on the floor, still attached to the umbilical cord?"

He detailed one by one the inconsistencies in *her own sworn testimony,* the many points where it conflicted with testimony by such objective witnesses as her physicians and the other nuns.

"But Mr. Haverty says proof is lacking in this case. Yet we *do have* one witness to a live birth—Sister Angela herself, who told us in the grand jury room *that the baby's arms moved.*

"Your Honor, you yourself have children. Can you remember the first time you saw those infants after birth—remember those jerky arm movements? Use your own experience to realize *that's exactly what Sister Angela saw.*

"And I say to you that this baby *did* cry—right after he was born, just around noontime. Until he was silenced by those panties when this defendant shortly thereafter heard the heavy convent door closing, heard footsteps coming up the stairs, possibly to discover her."

DaSilva shifted his papers and said quietly to that hushed courtroom, "This is a tragedy we deal with here, the entire situation a tragedy in our community. But the death of this newborn infant is equally deserving of compassion. In the issue of the criminal responsibility of this particular defendant, a society must be supported by the law. And no one can be allowed to take the law into their own hands—decide when another person shall die.

"Sister Angela Flynn stands guilty of breaking our law, and another law not written into the penal code, to be obeyed by all men—*thou shalt not kill.*" He pulled out that photograph again, held it up to the bench. "Look at this picture while you're deciding this verdict, Your Honor. Because that says the truth of this case better than I ever could. And this picture demands a verdict of . . . *guilty.*"

Judge Samuel Aaron glanced around the courtroom, cleared his throat. Said he would like to compliment the outstanding professional presentation of this case that had been made by the attorneys—"in particular Mr. DaSilva, who has performed far beyond your young years. It's been an outstanding job, and I want the record to reflect that."

He was fiddling with the gavel in his hands. "This court appreciates the effort you all put into the gentlemanly manner in which you presented this case. I now order that all the exhibits be removed to my chambers. You may be sure that all the criteria you expressed in your excellent summations will be observed as I arrive at this verdict."

BANG! "This court is in recess pending a verdict in this case."

Forty

Al Packer felt real bad about that thing with Ziggy and the boat. He knew Zig was feeling down enough these days.

So on Thursday night, Al dragged Eddie Staszic and his girl friend around to Zig's house to play some poker. And he talked those two college girls next door, Trish and Dianne, into the game by promising them some real good dope.

The night started pretty good, plenty of six-packs on ice and the cards falling good. Zig even seemed to be coming out of his funk a little, talking it up to the good-looker from next door, that Trish O'Loughlin, the skinny live-wire one. Talking about astrology and stuff.

Trish was kind of a chain-smoker but she knew Ziggy couldn't stand to have anybody smoking cigarettes around him so she really backed off that tonight. Really, like, trying hard. She just doubled up on the joints.

Zig was looking pretty loose, almost like he was having a good time. More like his old self than Al had seen him in quite a while.

When Zig won a big hand around 9:30, he asked if anybody maybe wanted some tea or coffee or some wine. He had a bottle he could open. Trish said yeah, she could go for some of Ziggy's high-class tea. So they took a break in the game while Zig went out in the kitchen to boil some water.

While they were waiting around, Trish leaned back from her chair and picked up a copy of the *Glendale Herald* lying beside Ziggy's regular chair. A real ball of fucking fire this one was—always moving, always talking, laughing.

Real good-looker too, dark curly hair with lots of freckles.

Al was wondering if she put the same kind of juice in her fucking as she read off the headlines from the paper: "Ooh la la, folks, big news tonight. The President has hit a *new* low in the polls." Flicking the paper back as she tossed a honking kind of laugh at Al: "How's that grab you, Packer?" Her face always moving, like an electric motor. Al wouldn't mind getting his hands on some of that.

She looked back to the paper, cackling, "Run the flag up for that one, folks. Ah, yes, and the Parks and Playgrounds Department has run prematurely out of bucks. Maybe a little skimming of the till there, folks. And let's see, a three-car accident at Semple and Aspenwood. No serious injuries except to the cars, nineteen hundred bucks' worth. Oooh yeah, here's my favorite—the nun who snuffed her little baby, oh, *yes."* She puckered, whistled over the paper toward Al, "Whoooo-*ee.* That one I love. So *sor*did."

"Oh, yeah," the other one, her roommate, was laughing, "I keep wondering what those nuns from my old high school think about *that* one."

"Oooh la, yes. Now let's see, Councilman Kelleher denies again the dirty rumors that he has some financial interest in the site picked for—"

All of a sudden Zig was standing in the archway door, looking—real mad. Face puffy, red-hot. He choked out, *"Bitch. Fucking bitch. You don't know what the fuck you're talking about."*

Nobody spoke.

Zig was still standing there, staring with that red face, when Trish tossed the paper back on the floor like it had bugs on it. She looked hard at her roommate as she said real loud, "Well, excuse *me.*"

Zig disappeared back to the kitchen. Al was trying to look real cool as he lit up a fresh joint and passed it around, trying to make small talk about what good smoke this stuff was.

The smoke, maybe. But the mood was shot for sure.

When the kettle started whistling a couple minutes later and just kept on whistling, Al walked back to the kitchen.

No Zig.

Meg was so beat when she got home that she didn't notice her apartment lights were on until she pushed open the door.

Dewey was lying with his bare feet up on the couch, grinning as he lowered the magazine in front of his face. "Hey, Gavin. Welcome home from the wars."

She waited to answer until she'd hung her coat up in the front closet. She had no wish to reveal the small, private flick of irritation she'd felt on seeing him there, uninvited, on her couch.

As she walked into the living room she said lightly, "Hey, sweetiepie, you weren't on the menu for tonight." She leaned over the couch to plant a perfunctory kiss on his forehead, then sank into the Eames chair, unzipping her suede boots. "To what do I owe the pleasure?"

"To Feldman not making it back from Chicago." He got up from the couch and pulled the boots from her feet, dropped them beside the chair. "So how're you doing? How'd it go today?"

"Okay, I guess. Recessed until verdict. Maybe eleven tomorrow, Aaron's secretary says."

"Okay, you stay put, and I'll fix you a drink."

He asked from the kitchen how the day's session had gone. She said tiredly, "Pretty interesting, actually. Andy DaSilva came up with the best fucking summation I've heard in a courtroom. So damn simple and *reasonable* it was almost brilliant."

That flick of irritation still there. That wish that he had left her alone tonight, to sort the pieces through in privacy. "I don't know, Andy's logic was just so goddam—*seamless*, he's kind of making me rethink the case."

As he brought in her glass mug she said, "Ah, thanks, Dew. Just what I need." She took a long drink and leaned her head back into the soft black leather, eyes closed, fingers rubbing on her lids.

"Rethink it how?"

"Well, I just can't see what grounds Aaron's got left now for letting her off. Except maybe insanity."

Dewey sitting back down on the couch, rattling the cubes in his glass. "So. It's zero hour, then."

"Yep. Finally."

"Well, that's damn good news to me." He paused. "I've been waiting a long time for this, Meg."

"What 'this' is that, Wald?"

"For this to be *finished for you.* For you to finally get yourself *free* of this damn mess."

God, she had never meant for him to be here now, tonight. No. Never. But—all right, let it come. Let it.

She looked across at him. "Just out of curiosity, Wald, what do you think the verdict's going to be?"

He smiled. "You really want to hear it?"

"Yeah. As a matter of fact, I do."

His face animated, pleased. "Well, I think it's going to be not guilty. I think the judge is going to come out and make a nice, graceful little speech about how he feels this poor woman has already suffered enough and so on. And he'll commend her back to the care of her sisters in religion. Which is what should've happened to this case ten months ago."

Quietly, very quietly: "Just that? Just like that?"

"Sure, Meg." He slouched back into the couch cushions. "I've been telling you that for months, if you'd just had the ears to hear it. This case should never have been tried in a public court in the first place. They should've just let those Church people handle it themselves, in their own ways. Like they've been doing for thousands of years."

A slight defiance on his face now as he watched, anxiously, her silence, stillness. "You see if I'm not right tomorrow, Meg. That judge is just very graciously going to find her not guilty and send her back where she belongs. Where she *belonged all along.*"

She sprang out of the chair, propelled by energizing fury. *"With them, Wald?"* Her stockinged feet moved swiftly over the patterned rug. "With those fucking lunatic nuns who drove her, *kept her* crazy in the first place? You think he should just *deliver her back to them?"*

"Sure. Because—and I wish you could just goddam *face this,* Meg—that's obviously where she belonged all along. Where she's chosen to, apparently *wants* to be. With her own kind of people."

Her head suddenly bursting with images from those trial days—those clumps of bleak, drab, short-haired women with the strangely blank faces. Moving always in pairs or flocks. Like—birds with clipped wings.

Furiously: *"But they're the ones who drove her crazy in the first place.* And now you say fine, very good—just send her *back to them?"*

"Listen, Meg," he said quietly, urgently. "You know how long I've been waiting for you to just get yourself past this thing. This crazy historical guilt trip of yours that's got *nothing to do with* your real life. Okay, I know you didn't go out looking for it, it came along by accident. But even so— that's *not you,* Meg. But if you can't finally get your head straight on this now, if you're still gonna hang in with this thing and *can't let it go,* you're gonna kill the one thing that really matters." He slapped the couch cushion. "Which happens to be what's happening *with us."*

Oh God, she wished he had not pushed himself uninvited into this night when she could feel those pieces finally shifting, moving in her head. Ready to drop.

Annnhh yes, it was finally coming now. Even with him arguing, pushing against them, she could feel the pieces moving together.

"Back to *them? Damn,* Wald, *that's* where you'd send her? On that straight greased trip back to *hell?"*

She was moving quickly on the rug, clutching one hand at the back of her neck. "Listen, Wald, there's a hell of a lot going on here I still don't understand. I admit that. A whole lot. But I sure do know what *that* would mean, that thing you just wished on her now—it would be sending her *back into a craziness she'll never get out of."*

She broke into the protest coming out of him with, "Because *I do know she's crazy.* I don't care how many fucking shrinks they dragged in there to say she's as sane now as you or me. I *know* somehow she's crazy."

"God*dam* it, Gavin—will you listen to yourself? Just sit down and *listen* to yourself? This thing's *finishing* now, Meg. It's *over.* And if you can't just let it go—"

"Okay, hold it a minute." She dropped her hand from her neck and blinked toward the hallway light. "I've got to piss."

As she came back into the room, snapping her panty hose back into place under her pleated skirt, she said abruptly, "You keep saying I *identify* with this nun somehow, Wald. But I don't. Never did. That poor, pinched little-girl nun—no, I never did. Don't. But that *craziness* of hers—yeah, Wald, I do know something about that."

Now that it was almost over, the pieces were falling into place. "Sure, that's what I identify with. Something in that craziness. You keep saying I'm on some kind of sick historical trip—okay, maybe I am, a little. So fucking what. Because I can see some of that craziness in me, too. All that amazing shit they dumped into us as kids, all that Vatican voodoo— sure some of it sticks. Has to. Even after you *know* it's all lunacy. Sure, some sticks."

Suddenly flashing in her mind a long dim-lighted frieze of horizontal bodies. Naked male bodies stirring in postcoital languor. One low-pitched voice murmuring in admiring surprise, *Jesus Christ, Gavin, you fuck like a man.*

Blinking against that vision, she walked slowly on the carpet, arms shivering over her ribs as she said almost to herself: "Oh yeah. That's where it fits. Someplace in that— craziness about sex."

He sprang up from the couch and bounded toward her, pulled her forcefully into his arms. Angrily: *"Come on, god-damit, Meg.* What the hell is this—your bad little girl routine we've got to go all through again?"

She pushed herself out of his hold. Moved away, arms still hugged to her sides, muttering, "Dammit, Wald. Why are you so afraid to—just *let me see it?"*

Loud, defiant: "See what, Meg?"

She turned her back to him, shaking her bent head.

He seized her arm and drew her roughly over to the

583

couch, pulled her down beside him, his face fixed in that tight, shaky smile that meant he could do without this conversation. She let her body be pulled along, moved. And listened with the same pliancy to his argument. Because she *wanted,* oh God she did want so to believe it.

"*Listen to me, Meg.*" He gripped both her hands. "I realize you're just running out the ass end of a trial that's been very rough on you. Goddam rough, all of it. What you're reacting to now tonight, that's just your own pain and exhaustion." His hands as they held her were trembling. "That's *all it is,* Meg. And I don't want to see you"—one shaky hand brushing over her hair—"go any deeper tonight into that goddam historical guilt trip of yours, Meg. That I *do not want to see.* Because now's the time we can shake off all that shit. Move clear of that crap and start thinking about *us.* "

That dear face. So tight, anxiously frowning now as he stroked at her face, tugged at her hair.

Shadows of all those strange faceless men still moving in her mind. Those strange beds where she fucked out so many fierce, clean one-night stands.

"*You* listen, Wald. Stop fighting me. Just let me go with it a little. *See* it a little. I know you *hate* talking about this but dammit, there's some kind of—craziness in all those years of cold-fucking I did that I can't just—wish away."

He burst out: "Christ, Meg, we've already been through this and *through this*—this 'beautiful young bodies you prefer to fuck' routine. But that was finished for us a long time ago, Meg. It's got nothing to do with what's happening now with us—happening *right now,* dammit."

Even acknowledging his pain, she was angered, irritated by it. "Nothing to do with *you,* Wald, right, you've got that right," she snapped. "It's got to do with *me.* Whether you like it or not. And I'm just realizing now—it wasn't for that *nun's* sake I've hung in so long with this story. It was a hell of a lot more selfish than that."

He pulled her swiftly, sharply, down across his chest, pressing her awkwardly folded body against him, his arms moving restlessly over her back. "Ah, Gavin, Gavin. Always the battle, all the way."

Now he was rocking, cradling her, almost as if comforting a child. Murmuring concernedly, "Look, Meg, I know you were very hurt, somewhere back there. And I know how rough all that was on you. All those dry loveless years you put in. You didn't even believe in love anymore, almost, when we met—I knew that right off, that you were *afraid* of that, Meg. So you'd talked yourself into thinking you didn't want that fit with somebody anyway. Because you didn't believe it could happen to you."

His knee bone rolled sharply over her hip as he murmured insistently, "And that's what you're *still running away from now,* Meg. What you've been running from all those years. Real loving. A real fit."

She was shifting, trying to move her body, but he held her tight in his arms until he had finished what he had to say: "And what you're just so goddam *dumb* not to see is that it happened to us anyway, Meg. For a long time now. And now those feelings can really—open up. We can get down into the *guts* of it, Meg, if you'll just drop that old pain behind you. Because you can't take it with you, where we can get to now. If you'll just *let yourself go there,* let it happen, Meg."

The awkward folding he was pressing her into had become almost painful.

She pushed her body up from his chest, loose from that urgent, loving embrace, and looked almost wistfully into his dear troubled face.

So. Not possible then.

She guessed she'd known it for a while now. Known but resisted that knowing.

Because she *wanted so* to believe everything he was promising her so fiercely, so lovingly.

585

Had promised her all along. That the answer was—him.

Annhh God, she wished he had not picked this argument tonight of all nights. When she was so sunk in the still raw, bewildering pain of that trial.

Because she knew what he was promising her was that she could *have all that, right now,* if she just—walked away from the mad little nun. From that flickered glimpse of *her own madness,* somewhere in the nun.

Yes yes true, he did love her. But what he loved was the her he had made her into. Not what was happening to her now.

That he had seen coming, she realized in a splattering of surprise, so much sooner than she did. Seen *all along,* right from the first. She recognized in a sluice of astonishment that it wasn't the nun Wald had been jealous of, all along. It was this—rest of it. What he'd sensed would *come at her from* the nun, like this, tonight. Sensed all along.

Annnhhh God she could not understand why he was pushing this at her *now, tonight.* Pushing this—choice on her.

Because it was almost unbearable to her to think of doing without that dear thin wrinkled body, her lover, her friend.

Those so amazing places he brought her to with their fucking. That fitting together that was always so different, so good.

No no, they *should not* be having this argument tonight. They should hold the words for now.

Later, so much time later for those painful, clarifying words.

Not tonight.

As if gesturing a truce, she reached a shaky hand to rub his nipples. Their private signal for inviting to fuck.

He caught her hand, rubbed it against his chest. Looked strongly toward her, the smile wide and real now. Even—triumphant.

Trying to keep the rush, burn of satisfaction from his voice: "Ahh, Meg, good, good." Gripping, twitching her hand. "You'll see it yourself, love. As soon as you just let that shit go."

She read with astonishment the victory coming out of his body.

Annnnhhhh God he had done it—finished the argument.

Force-read a *choice* in that move she meant only to signal a truce.

She felt a terrible quiet beauty in this moment.

Past words, then. She knew that now.

But . . . so hard to let go without even *wishing, thinking* to, of that dear thin kinetic body, those sweet real promises.

Her eyes flicked downward, away from that face. She looked sideways at the patterned rug, looking for an out as she let her rushing, whirling thoughts settle like snow in a wind.

So hard to think of *letting go* of this without even knowing—why she should. So impossible to choose. That forced cold leap.

But then he pulled her back, too soon, with an insistent tug at her hand: *"Aaahh yes, yes, Meg. You'll see, love. It's all going to start for us now."*

So. Done.

Words finished now. Time later for regrets.

She reached to touch, embrace that dear familiar treasured body.

And let herself tenderly, caringly, lovingly, fuck him good-bye.

After dinner Judge Samuel Aaron went to his study "to work."

He spread out the papers from his briefcase on his desk. And tilted his head to look at them through the bottom lens of his bifocals, shuffling the papers, clearing his throat in the silence of that small room.

In the strange glow from the green glass desklight, his face looked haggard, exhausted. Old. He would sit here and look at the stuff because that was what was expected of him right now. To deliberate, to keep on deliberating.

God, he wished this thing was already over.

Angela slept very little that night, in spite of the two pills she finally took.

Curled on her side in the narrow bed, she stared, blinked at the light patterns on the opposite wall, trying to let go of that tightness all through her body.

Trying to let go of the fluttering thoughts.

The streetlight falling diagonally across the opposite wall made the Y-shaped crack look almost like a winter tree growing out of the dresser top. A thin frost-killed tree.

She was not really *afraid* about tomorrow. She knew *He* would make her strong. As strong as she needed to be.

And she did not begrudge Him any of what He had asked of her, any *any* of it but . . .

Oh dear loving Lord couldn't this now be enough?

The next morning the press began collecting early, around 10:20, in the anteroom of the D.A.'s block of offices.

Meg tallied the late votes among the regulars: eight for criminally negligent manslaughter with suspended sentence, five for not guilty by reason of insanity. But when Meg argued, "Yeah, but do you realize an insanity verdict carries mandatory commitment to a mental hospital? And how the hell's sentencing her to a psycho ward any different from sending her to jail?" most of them shrugged agreement.

The NBC radio guy said, "Okay, that's it, then. She'll walk on a not guilty."

"Just *walk?*" Meg protested, her own vehemence startling to her. "Fuck, Chip, how can she just *walk* after Andy's goddam brilliant summation? I wasn't sure how I felt myself, until I heard that. But now I just can't see where Aaron's got any room left for a straight acquittal."

Yet the two who voted right off for exactly that were Kevin Corrigan and the UPI guy—the only two in the pack who knew their ass backwards, Meg realized with some dismay.

When she pushed, argued against their vote, Corrigan smacked away her protest with, *"Come on yourself,* Meg. This one was a fix all the way from April twenty-five." He smiled at her, shaking his head. "Fuck, Meg. Where *are* you, anyway? Because if you really think anything that went on in that courtroom had *zip* to do with this verdict you're a whole goddam lot more naive than I've taken you for."

"Anh, Kev, but not after yesterday. Not after the way Andy cut him off at the pass in there yesterday. Aaron's just got no *grounds* left now for a straight acquit, Kev."

The UPI guy was shuffling carbons of the three leads he had typed and left ready to go out on the wire. He pulled the one reporting a flat acquittal to the top of the stack as he smiled wryly, asking, "You want ten to one on that one, Meg?"

Forced one more time into that hell of lights, shouts, bodies.

Crowd so dense it seemed to have no edge. Pressing, choking her almost.

Her eyes on Mr. Haverty's big shoulder, following him through those bodies. So hard to breathe, to see.

Help me help me Lord Jesus.

In the merciful silence of the courtroom Mr. Haverty helped her take off her coat. He folded it over his arm, smiling so anxiously. "Almost finished, Angela. Almost there."

She nodded mutely and sat in her chair.

Stared at the brass letters, trying to pray. Trying to feel *Thy will, not mine.*

589

But all that came was that rush, broken flutter—*oh now surely please Sweet Lord*—now.

Just let it end.

From her front-row seat Meg watched the mood of the packed courtroom build to a buzzing high.

Faces sharp, expectant. Already emotional. Pitch mounting as they waited—11:15 already, typical of that dilatory fucker Aaron. Six tough-guy sheriff's marshals trying to patrol the aisles, hold it down with glares and scowls. The buzz conversational level, rising fast, when the court attendant bellowed at 11:18: "ALL RISE, COURT IS IN SESSION, JUDGE SAMUEL G. AARON PRESIDING."

Aaron bounded, almost skipped, up to the bench. Dropped in his seat and leaned forward, his red face very—strange. Tensed, choked. Almost—expectant.

Almost—Jesus Christ, almost like *he* was the defendant.

He grabbed up his gavel, nodding down to the fat female clerk, who read out, "To the charge of first-degree manslaughter in the case of the People of the State of Minnesota versus Gayle M. Flynn, also known as Sister Angela Flynn, how find you?"

He said loudly: "NOT GUILTY."

The terrible calm Angela had wrapped herself in exploded outward with those words, exploded on the shouts, wails, screams, coming from behind her.

She lifted into a huge fierce peace.

Finally, finally shouted right out loud to all of them—*NOT GUILTY.*

Bang! Bang! "No demonstrations! No demonstrations in this courtroom!"

"To the charge of second-degree manslaughter in the case of the People of the State of Minnesota versus Gayle M. Flynn, also known as Sister Angela Flynn, how find you?"

"NOT GUILTY."

Cries again, not so loud this time, gavel pounding still.

She lifted her face toward that man, lifted to hear it again, that so long delayed benediction . . .

"To the charge of criminally negligent manslaughter in the case of the People of the State of Minnesota versus Gayle M. Flynn, also known as Sister Angela Flynn, how find you?"

"NOT GUILTY."

Bang! "This court is in recess."

Suddenly he was gone through that door. Cries, wails, surging all around her now, Mr. Haverty hugging her in his big arms: *"Congratulations, Angela!"* Hands from behind grabbing, clutching her. Dan shouting, "We made it! We made it!"

Her thoughts whirling, spinning upward like a prayer of thanksgiving toward that benediction still showering on her —*Not guilty, he said.*

The damn thing was over almost before it started.

One second Aaron was blinking down from the bench, looking as guilty as a kid who'd peed his pants, and the next it was—over.

Meg was still totally blank, unreacting as the marshals snapped into their riot-cop roles, bellowing threateningly, "SILENCE! NO DEMONSTRATIONS! CLEAR THIS ROOM IMMEDIATELY!"

She leaned forward over the barrier to get a look at the nun. Angela was standing by her chair, maybe still crying a little. Her face lifting out of that circle of people crowding around her was shining, almost—illuminated.

Then some thug marshal—Jesus Christ, where did they *find* these guys—was pushing Meg rudely down the aisle. She wasn't surprised by the noisy ventings still going on in the courtroom—nuns blowing their noses, women hugging, screeching at each other.

591

But the scene out in the wide hallway was—amazing.

Pandemonium. The only word for it. Milling, billowing pandemonium like no verdict play-out she'd seen before this.

The women mostly crying, touching, clutching each other. Even some of the nuns. Men shaking hands, slapping backs. A few coughing into their handkerchiefs.

And, standing there, Meg *acquiesced* to that emotion. Let herself feel it with them.

Annhhh sure, maybe that was the right verdict. The *only* verdict. Yielding to the swirling emotion in that hall, impossible to think that *was not* the right verdict.

Standing by Meg, some woman there every day of the trial, fat face blotched now with tears, threw her arms around one of the nuns: "Oh, I *knew* she didn't do it. I knew all along she didn't do it."

The raw feel of it was so close, so contagious, that Meg reached out to pat her heaving back. Yet realized even as she touched that damp-patched blouse what the woman was really saying: *I knew all along she never had that sex.*

Now a flying V-wedge of bodies was sweeping out of the courtroom. Lights and lenses bobbing, scrambling to pin Angela moving in the center of it. Mikes, questions, poking at her from all sides.

Ben Haverty said as they advanced slowly through the crush, "We're very grateful, we're not surprised. No other comment. Let us through, please."

As that bizarre parade surged slowly past her, Meg got one good look at the nun.

She was shaking her head, mouthing the word "no" to some guy with his mike stuck in her face.

She looked like—a young girl, her pink, shining face lifted, smiling, in a dazed radiation of—deliverance.

Judge Aaron stopped in his chambers only long enough to shuck his black robe and order his secretary to return all exhibits in this case to the custody of Andrew DaSilva. His wife had parked the car, by prearrangement, in the underground lot by the judicial elevator.

He let her do the driving to the airport, where they were booked on the 12:55 flight to Florida. The fatigue he was finally letting himself feel went right to his bones. But another unfamiliar sensation was laid in there with it—fear.

Sam Aaron did not consider himself a brave man. Never even thought of himself that way.

For so long this case had seemed like a lucky shot for him, a plum. But he knew *that* much now, at least—there was no luck for him here. Maybe later, depending on how it worked out. But for right now, for a while at least, Sam Aaron had a pretty good idea of the size of the storm he had unwittingly pulled over his head.

He leaned his neck exhaustedly against the headrest. "Well, okay, it's over. And I think I did the right thing, Naomi. I feel pretty good about that part of it."

"All right. I'm just glad it's over, Sam."

He was finally letting himself feel the warnings of that gathering storm as he said bleakly, almost plaintively, "I just couldn't live with myself if I hadn't given her that verdict, Naomi."

Meg was so absorbed by those strange doings in the hall that she missed the start of the impromptu press conference Abrams and Andy DaSilva threw in the D.A.'s office.

As she slipped belatedly through the door of the big paneled room where the stuffed blue marlin shared wall space with the kiddie pics, DaSilva was saying, "No, I haven't talked to the judge yet, and I don't plan to. I think it's improper to ask him to explain his decision. We don't question or criticize a jury's verdict, and most times they render them without making their formal findings a factor." He was smiling slightly, a little blankly, as he added, "It might have been helpful if he *had* explained it, but His Honor chose to do it the other way."

Some guy asked Abrams when he had to run for office again, and Abrams said with politely veiled sarcasm, "The juxtaposition of these questions leaves something to be desired." Yet Meg already knew the consensus in that office was that Abrams would not suffer politically from this case —that the public rage for that unexplained verdict would fall on Sam Aaron.

When a radio man asked about the possibility of an appeal, Abrams said firmly, "The Constitution of the United States prohibits any further action by this office. She's been acquitted, and she's free."

Asked for his personal reactions, DaSilva shook his head. "I don't know exactly what my feelings are at this point. But I wouldn't say either shock or disappointment. Sure, I put in a great deal of preparation, and it's a little hard coming down from that intensity. But we take the verdict philosophically because that's our job."

"So what's next, Andy?"

Wide, tired smile. "Well, I think I'll take a couple of days off next week and get reacquainted with my family."

Now Abrams was gracefully declining to comment on the press coverage of the case, or the defendant's use of the judges' elevator: "I think that question would be more appropriately addressed to Judge Aaron."

Mark Abrams was always at his best in moments like these—eloquently, compassionately official: "I thought right from the outset that this case was one of enormous tragedy for this community—certainly not one we looked forward to pursuing. But once it was presented to the grand jury we were obligated under the law to prosecute, to go forward. And I think we discharged our duty. The job Andy did on this case has been a great credit to this office and to the community."

Pressed for his own opinion, Abrams shook his head.

"I never criticize a verdict. And I think the reporting on this case has been sufficiently detailed to allow the community to make up its own mind. It would appear there's a lot of sympathy out there for this defendant—also some ill will. But by and large I suspect the citizens of this county are a warm and generous people. And I would hope they will now look at the whole case, and put it in perspective."

His desk phone rang an interruption. Heartily: "Well, congratulations, Ben. You were your usual self, magnificent. Conducted yourself with all the excellence and fairness we expected."

Abrams winked at Meg. "Yes, right. Even in your Doctor Dentons." He paused. "Okay. Well, I'm glad you called —on to the next case. What have you got for us next, Ben?"

After the deadline-pressed reporters left the office, the mood relaxed into an easy, give-and-take bull session. When Meg asked if he thought Ken Rhoades's inability to testify had lost the case for them, Abrams loosened his tie, undid the top button on his shirt. "Nah, I wouldn't say so, Meg. Let's say all the chips just fell where they fell. And I see no point in Monday morning quarterbacking now."

Another phone call. As Abrams listened he sat up sharply, jotting notes. Then: "Okay. Don't move the body until we get there. We want this crime scene left intact until we finish our own investigation."

A slight, unrepressed grin broke over Abram's face as he hung up the phone and said dryly, "Well, gentlemen, we're back in business. There's a young man over on Mott Street who's apparently managed to hang himself on the stair railings. In a standing position."

As the questions burst at him, he cut them off with: "Don't know yet, but we'll find out soon enough."

He stood, tightening the knot of his tie, issuing swift, authoritative orders: "Andy, you pass on this one. You've done enough for one day. Nick, I'd like you to go over there with me. Get Max Bloom in here. And we'll go have a look at this thing."

Nick Scotti leaned over to mutter to Meg, *"A hanging,* huh? I guarantee you, this is gonna be the one Mark throws up at."

The Friday Happy Hour at the Blind Justice started early. When Meg got there at 5:10, DaSilva, Abrams and Bloom were already standing together at the crowded bar.

With her eyes on Abrams, she asked Bloom, "So, Max. Did Mark throw up at the hanging?"

The three men laughed. Bloom said, "Real close. But no cigar."

DaSilva still looked slightly dazed. When she asked how he felt, he smiled ruefully. "Gosh, Meg. I still don't know. Ask me later when I'm drunk enough to've figured it out."

Bloom insisted, "Hey, there's no way you can say you lost that one, Andy. Any other judge, and you would've had that one for sure."

"Well, I guess maybe." DaSilva laughed softly. "Yeah, sure. Shit. I guess I knew how it was going to come down yesterday when Aaron threw me all those flowers from the bench. For that 'performance so far beyond your young years.'"

Abrams laid his arm across DaSilva's shoulder. "Now you listen to me, Andy." The alcohol was finally loosening the muscles of his sad, tired face. "There's no way you should ever feel you *lost* that case. You did one hell of a job in there, gave it everything we had." He patted that shoulder. "And gave it goddam well, Andy. An absolutely first-rate job, that I want you to know right now was keenly noted and much appreciated."

"Well, thanks, Mark."

Abruptly, Abrams dropped his hand. "Look, we all knew going in what this case was. And we gave it everything we had to." He shrugged, then muttered, "I don't guess it matters much if none of us is too surprised at how it came down."

Meg's head was finally, after so long, *coming clear,* as she said slowly, bitterly, "Oh, yeah. That about says it, Mark. I guess we knew all along how this one would wind up. And it wasn't ever gonna be with a win for you, Andy."

DaSilva smiled. "Well, shit, Meg. I guess that should make me feel a little better."

The pieces tumbling, dropping so sharply now. "Oh, damn right. And d'you know what we saw happening in there today, guys? We saw little Sam Aaron handle this case just like Angela *handled that pregnancy.*

"Pretend it *wasn't there.* Sure, fuck, yes—he just sat up there and wiped it all away like it had never happened with two words: *not guilty.* Let's skip the 'by reason of insanity,' folks. And let's skip any explanation. Let's just flush it down now with those two little words, folks, and clean this thing up in time to get home for lunch."

The three men were stirring, moving slightly against the assault of her words.

Abrams flashed a grin that he wiped from his face with one quick motion as he said quietly, forcefully, "Well, *you* said that, Meg. Not me."

Hotly: "And it's goddam right, too, Mark. You *know* that. Her lawyers got up there and said she's certainly not guilty and her shrinks got up and said she's certainly no crazier than you or me. And that damn toad of a judge just went along with them. Said yep, that's right. Ignored the whole *fact of it.* And *goddam,* can you tell me how that's any different from the whole way Angela dealt with that poor kid?"

Silence. No argument offered.

DaSilva said quietly, "Well, yeah, Meg. I guess maybe I wasn't really surprised by the verdict. But I sure thought he'd give some kind of explanation. Not insanity, necessarily. But—something."

597

"Oh, boy, and you know why he didn't, Andy. Because he hasn't got one to offer. Not one that would stand up, that he'd dare put into words. It's just like you said about *her* in that really terrific summation—he didn't explain it because he *couldn't explain it.*"

Abrams allowed himself a careful smile. "Well, Meg, I think I should point out, as I'm sure you already know —Judge Aaron acted entirely within his judicial rights in this case. There was nothing improper in that verdict, Meg."

"Im*prop*— Oh, perish the thought, Mark." Cold fury running through her now as she felt the startling rightness of what she was saying. "I understand Aaron had the bald legal right to do it. But it's not gonna finish there, you know. You guys may be shut up now, but the press sure isn't. And in the interests of throwing a little public light on the question, I've got a feature on Aaron running in the paper tomorrow that's not gonna please the good judge one small bit. And Chet Henderson's drafting an editorial that's gonna take the skin off his little toad feet."

Smiles, small, pleasured motions of reaction from the D.A.s as Bloom said, "Well, I sure guess that's your privilege, Meg."

The overworked bartender finally slid a vodka and Tab toward Meg. She picked up the glass. "And the damnedest part of it is I think he probably did it for noble, milk-of-mercy reasons. Sure. He probably thinks he *did right* by the poor suffering little nun."

She drank deeply, the sureness, the clarity running in her like the booze. "But you know what he actually did? That easy-way-out political hack judge? He just sent her *back into her own madness.* Without even tossing her a line.

"He bought into her own craziness. And sent her back to those nuns who *made her that way* in the first place."

Andy DaSilva was finally stirred to protest. "Nah, Meg, I can't buy that part. I told you that first time I saw her, and

I haven't seen anything yet to contradict it—I think when you come right down to it Angela Flynn is really pretty sane."

The Tucker family business was winding up the workday around six P.M. when the office phone rang. Brad answered it: "Yeah. How you doing, Jim."

He leaned one elbow on the counter as he listened, looking toward his nephew Gary, a broad, flat grin breaking over his face. "Yanh, well, I guess you got it right, Jim. I guess that sure looked like her, all right."

Brad glanced away from the question on Gary's face. "Yeah. I guess." Silence. "Well, that was when the kid was still single and running around. Now he's just about hooked he's quieting down some." Silence. "Yep. June, I guess. They haven't set the date yet." Silence. "Okay, Jim, you take care."

Brad hung up the phone and walked, still smiling, to the refrigerator behind the stockroom door. He pulled out two cans of beer and tossed one across the room to Gary. Said as he snapped the tab and dropped it into the can, "You know who that was, kid?"

"Nanh."

"Jim Harrison. He was watching the TV news, said that nun in the murder case over there in St. Paul sure looked one hell of a lot like that Gayle Flynn you took to the archery club dance last year."

Gary was staring blankly at his uncle, not sure yet what he should think.

Brad grinned broadly as he raised his beer can in a mock toast. "What the hell, kid. King for a day. Live it up while you can."

Roy Danziger heard the news in a radio bulletin around noon. But couldn't take it in.

He stayed around the house that afternoon, smoking

some but trying to keep his head straight, until the TV news came on at six.

He figured if he could just *see* Gayle, see her face, like, he might still be able to figure it out.

He was hunched anxiously in front of the set when that flash of her came on just after six. One flash of her pushed around in a big crowd of people.

Then she moved forward and her face filled practically the whole screen, light full on it. Face lifted, like she was gulping for air.

Smiling. Lit up inside, too.

Kind of stunned. But—happy.

For so long now he hadn't been able to bring back that face, her face. But there it was now, just like he finally remembered it—

Young. Kind of sweet-looking.

Smiling, blinking like into that summer sun at the beach.

When the face was gone from the screen he snapped off the TV. Reached over for the silver can, pulled out a fat rolled joint.

Every instant of that flash across the screen still in his head, burned there, alive. Coming through him again as he lit up the joint.

He'd thought if he could only—*see* her, he might know —what to think. Make of all this.

He guessed he didn't hate her. Didn't even want to.

But shit it was hard not to know—why all this happened.

He'd thought it might make more sense to him if he could just *see her face* like it was live, moving, right up close. Like he remembered it . . .

But it still didn't.

The celebration party at Margaret and Ron Hogan's house felt like a real feast day, a jubilation. So special, prized, each moment of it—all her good friends like Lena and Janine here to celebrate it with her. Good friends who'd come almost every day to the trial.

And all her family was there too, Dan and Aunt Iris, and Ed and Annette and some of their children. Even her cousin Mary Alice and her husband, who'd come all the way from California to be here with her, to share this wonderful moment.

Her whole family except Mother.

Angela almost wished Mother had been feeling well enough to come to the party. She thought that maybe might have helped Mother feel a little better about everything, just seeing the *real joy* all these good people had for what that judge had said to them all—

That *not guilty.*

She stood mostly by the blue wing chair by the front window, and they all came up to her as they came in, hugging her, kissing her, saying over and over *so happy for you, Angela . . . but of course I knew all along . . . Oh, Gayle dear, such* wonderful *news, such a wonderful day . . .*

She knew they were really all saying the same thing— that they were happy for her because they were sharing her great joy, her blessed moment.

When they asked if she felt very tired, she shook her head, smiling strongly, "Oh, no. I feel very good."

Oh, so good. Feeling the words still all through her, that *not guilty.*

Time later to be tired. To let sleep take her away from this so golden moment that filled her, buoyed her, carried her up on that joyful so long waited for wave of . . . expiation.

Not guilty, he said.

Now Sister Philomena was coming in, with Mary Christopher and Bernadine. Angela smiled brightly as she walked quickly to greet them: "Oh, Sister Philomena! All of you. Thank you so much for coming."

Bernadine and Mary Christopher hugged her stiffly and murmured something pleased.

Philomena was just folding Angela in her large embrace when Ron Hogan came up to take the drink orders, and tell the nuns that a buffet supper was laid out in the dining room if they'd like a bite.

Philomena loosened her hug as she said, "Thank you, Mr. Hogan. We already ate." She was still gripping Angela's hand as she looked down at her: "Angela, you know all the sisters of the order are very pleased and thankful to God for this verdict."

"Oh, yes, Sister Philomena. And I've been so grateful for all their prayers and support. Yours especially, Sister Philomena." Angela lifted her face, beaming. "You were really such a great help and support to me."

Bernadine cleared her throat and said something about wasn't it nice of Mr. and Mrs. Hogan to invite everyone to their home. Angela was saying, "Oh, yes. They're such wonderful friends," when Philomena interrupted suddenly: "Angela, I'd like to speak privately to you."

Glancing around the crowded room, she pulled on Angela's hand, pulled her away from the other nuns. There were quite a few people standing around the dining room table, too, but Philomena found an empty pantry off the kitchen.

In that small room, just the two of them there, she put Angela's hand between both of hers.

And said in her quiet, powerful voice, "Now, Angela, I know this has been a most difficult time for you. Most difficult. But now it's over. Finished. Behind you. And the Good Lord gave us the verdict we were all hoping for."

Angela murmured, "Oh, yes, thanks be to God."

"Now I want you to take a good, long rest." Squeezing on her hand. "To get all your strength back. I want you to take all the time you need." The force of her strong, focused calm flowing into Angela. "And when the time is right, when you are fully recovered, you and I will sit down and consider together, thoughtfully and prayerfully, whatever decisions you make about your future."

Angela shook her head. "Oh, but I don't really need

any more time off, Sister Philomena. I've had so much already." That grip so strong, hurting almost. "I really feel very good, very strong. I think I'm ready now to go back to work."

Philomena let go of her hand. Looked over her head, out the pantry window, as she said slowly, "Angela, my dear, I understand this has been a very arduous ordeal for you. For you more than anyone. Certainly one it will take you some time—time and prayerful consideration—to recover from. I believe you *need time* for that, Angela. The decisions you make now for yourself will have great importance for your whole future. And I don't want you to rush precipitately into them."

Again she shook her head. "But Sister Philomena, I just want to get back to my job. To Benedictine." Slight, hurt puzzlement now on that lifted face. "I know already that's all I want to do. And you said I could, once this legal business was finished."

Philomena reached for the heavy gold cross around her neck. That strange expression on her face looked almost like —anger. But Angela knew it must be something else, because there was no reason to be angry today, when that judge had finally *told them all* that she was *not guilty.*

So she said, "I know all this took longer than anybody expected, and I'm really very sorry about all that delay, Sister Philomena. But now that the judge finished it I just want to get back to—my own life."

For a long strange minute Philomena did not move, did not speak. Then she looked down, smiling almost— coldly. "We'll see. We'll see. All in the Lord's own good time."

She reached out and laid her hand on the top of Angela's head. "We must all pray very much for His own wise guidance, Angela. But for now I want you only to rest, and give yourself His good time."

.   .   .

By the time Meg worked her way down the bar to him, Nick Scotti had already shed his shirt and tie and was wearing his coat jacket backwards.

She patted his hairy back. "Hey, Nick. You're stripping early tonight."

He lurched sideways, glaring at her. Baleful. "Hey yourself. Fucking hypocrite."

Hesitation. "Fucking what?"

"Hey, I saw you up there today, Meg." He twisted toward her. "*Crying* for the poor little nun out in the hall. What're you doing, trying to kiss ass with those nuns?"

Soft, surprised: "Hey, no. I wasn't *crying.* But yeah, I choked up some." She lifted her hand from his back. "Hey, you caught that?"

"Sure." He glared ahead of him at her image in the mirror across the bar. "I catch fuckin' everything."

She was looking down, rubbing the top rim of her glass. "Well, sure I was moved. Jesus, Nick, how could anybody *not* be, after watching what she went through in there?"

"Ah, great. So you think she got the fucking *right verdict?"*

She turned toward the bar and said slowly, "Not *right.* But maybe—only." She looked at his twisted, grimacing face reflected in the smoky glass. "Yeah, sure, Nick. Maybe that was the only verdict they ever *could* give her in there."

Scotti made a loud, unarticulated sound.

"Hey, Nick, what good would it do to put her in jail? Or a psycho hospital—even if she *belongs* there, which I happen to think she probably does. I mean, what could they do for her in those places, Nick? Goddam zip. Whatever's gone wrong in that little lady they couldn't begin to *touch* in there. So yeah, maybe Aaron did right to just—let her go."

Scotti shook his head rapidly, his features squeezed, drunkenly contorted. "Christ. You fuckin' disappoint me, Meg."

She leaned forward on her elbows, saying earnestly to

the glass, "Listen, Nick. Maybe it's as simple as what so many people were already saying—she's suffered enough, just let her go. Maybe you can't make her suffer any more than she did just having to *sit through* all that in there."

Scotti lurched away from the mirror, leaning on his elbow to look squarely into her face. Slowly, shaping his words with drunken care, he said, "Okay, great. So you're happy with the verdict, Meg. And *she's* happy with it." His face wavered closer to hers. "And those fucking nuns are all real fucking happy. Yanh, sure. They finally got the Church back off the hook. And her two fucking lawyers are probably buying drinks all over town. *Got her clean off.* So everybody's nice and happy."

He looked down at the bar and reached uncertainly for his glass as he said loudly, *"You think any one of those fuckers're remembering that baby tonight? That nice little baby she smashed the life out of with those dirty pants?"*

"Oh, Nick, *I'm* remembering him." She rubbed at the smooth worn wood on the curve of the bar. "But I'm also remembering that thing Ben made such a thing of at the trial —that *she* doesn't remember it. What she actually *did to* that kid."

Scotti made a loud honking noise. "You kiddin' me, Meg? You actually think for one fucking second she wasn't lying, lying, fucking perjuring herself ten times a fucking minute up on that stand? Just to get her nun ass off the hook?"

She patted his bare back: "Okay, calm down, Nick. Come on, simmer down." She hesitated, considering. "Sure, I think she perjured herself a lot up there. But not about *that* part of it—I honest to God think she means it when she says she doesn't remember that part."

As he muttered *annh, fucking cherry,* she continued, "Because I think if she *did* remember it she couldn't've sat through that trial, Nick. I think she just would've come totally apart in there if she'd actually realized, be-

605

lieved, *felt* that's what she did. If she'd actually *remembered doing that.*"

He drank aggressively from his glass. "Fuck, Meg. I tell you, I'm real disappointed in you."

She stared at that strange sight of his hairy back, draped in the tweed folds of his lapels, as she said slowly, "Because that's the worst part about what they did to her up there today, Nick. Not just Aaron—the whole lot of them. They just gave their blessings to her madness—said thanks very much, Sister, I guess that about winds it up now. All cleaned up now—and by the way, you're as sane as him or me. They just—sent her right back into it, Nick. With that memory of *what she actually did* rolling like a loose cannon in her head."

So clear now, finally. "All of them *pretending like her*, telling themselves everything's fine, hunky-dory now. All wrapped up. But it isn't. And it won't be, until she"—quivering, resisting that last—"remembers what she actually did. And then, I guess, she—"

Ah yes. Yes.

"Kills herself."

Scotti ignored her now, standing straight, looking over the noisy crowd, slamming his fist thunderously on the bar, bellowing, *"HEY!*

"TENN-SHUN! QUIET!"

He lifted his glass high. *"Okay. Let's hear it now for BABY BOY FLYNN!"*

The Hogans' party wound down quite quickly. One by one, the guests came up to Angela to say good-bye, giving her their good wishes one last time, squeezing her in those nervous quick hugs—*so happy for you, Angela dear.*

She still floated, buoyed. Glowing still in those sweet words, those warm thoughts.

When the crowd was quite thin around 9:30, Fran murmured to her, "Your friend Margaret looks like she might go to sleep right on the couch. Do you think we should think about heading back to Pompeii?"

Angela said oh yes, sure. So they left a few minutes later, in a flurry of good-bye hugs and congratulations.

When they were in the green Toyota, driving downtown, Fran said, "I hope I didn't yank you away too early, Angela."

"That's okay." She looked serenely out the side window of the car. "I didn't mind leaving."

"It was a terrific party, actually. And I'm not feeling tired yet myself. D'you want to just stop off somewhere, have a nightcap?"

That was one of Fran's favorite things. Angela smiled. "Sure, fine. If you want to, Fran."

Fran picked a small, dark storefront tavern with a German-sounding name in neon on the glass. About a half-dozen men, older looking men were sitting at the bar, watching the hockey game on the TV.

Fran pointed to the room in the rear, asking the bartender, "Is it okay if we sit back there?"

"Yeah. Sure, ladies."

They walked past the men and slid into the padded red seats of a booth in the room behind. Fran leaned forward across the table, giggling, pulling off her coat. "Angela, you don't suppose any of those men *recognized* you?"

The bartender came up to their table, wiping his hands on his dirty big white apron, looking distractedly at the back wall as he said, "What you want, ladies?"

Fran ordered a bottle of Bud. Angela ordered a double Scotch straight up.

As the man moved away, Angela said calmly, "No, I'm sure they didn't recognize me, Fran. I think they only watch sports anyway, in places like this."

"Well, even if they didn't—there's quite a *famous person* in here tonight."

Even before the man came back with their drinks they were reliving, sharing, this so blessed day.

Fran told her, for instance, that when the judge spoke out the verdict even Sister Philomena had cried a little. Like almost all the nuns. And at the terrific party at the Hogans', Dan had made a real point of telling Fran how "damn proud" he was of his sister.

Angela drank it all in, so thirsty for all of it still.

They decided to leave for home after one more round.

As they walked back past the bar, their faces were very serious, contained. But most of those men hardly glanced away from the TV. No one said anything except the bartender, who called out, "Good night, ladies. Come back anytime."

That remark seemed so oddly funny that they laughed about it all the way back downtown to Pompeii. As the car turned into the driveway, they hushed themselves. And stepped out into the cold, starlit night. So sharply, peacefully silent.

As Fran unlocked the kitchen door, they could see through the hall that the convent was stilled, darkened except for one sentinel lamp in the front parlor window.

Fran glanced at her watch. "It's almost eleven. Do you want to watch the TV news again?"

Angela nodded, and they tiptoed into the dim-lit front parlor.

Fran moved the color TV set on the wheeled cart away from the wall. As they pulled chairs close to it she switched it on, whispering: "What channel do you want?"

"I don't care."

She flipped to Channel 7, CBS. With the volume turned very low they watched the end of some comedy show and a string of commercials for banks and deodorants.

Now, as the news came on, some man in a bright blue suit was talking about *her verdict*. Still talking when the image was suddenly Angela, moving through those bobbing heads.

This time she noticed the sharp-nosed profile just behind her own face on the screen. *"Look,* Fran! That's *you."*

Fran reached out and clutched her arm as they watched. Such a close, special, shared moment.

The Blind Justice crowd was finally thinning around eleven when Meg noticed Tim Vance sitting alone in the back. A little hesitantly she approached his table. "Hey, Tim. You like the verdict?"

He glanced up, startled. "Oh, hi, Meg. Yeah. C'mon." He kicked out one of the chairs. "Sit yourself down."

"Thanks, I think I will." She sat. Warily: "So, Tim, what you think?" His flat, pocked face was twisting now in booze-loosened grimaces. "You want a refill? 'Cause I'm buying."

"Well, sure." Vance tilted back his chair, hands shoved in his pants pockets, shoulders hunched. "In that case I'll have three Amarettos straight up."

It took Meg three minutes to catch the eye of Suzy the waitress and pass the orders along. Then she leaned forward on both elbows, smiled full in his face, a little nervous, and asked, "So. What'd you make of all this, Tim? Now that it's safe to say it. Game called by verdict, so to speak."

"Well, Meg, I'll tell you. . . ." He frowned, blinking at the tablecloth. Then, abruptly: "Nah, I don't know what I think. Yet."

"Okay, then, let's try on that oldie but goodie, justice triumphs one more time over sweet reason. How does that one grab you, Tim?"

He grinned. "Well, sure. I'll go along with that one." He yanked one hand from his pocket and pulled distractedly at a loose thread in the tablecloth. "But that still doesn't— *explain* it, you know."

She gave him a long glance. And said softly, "Oh, yeah, Tim. *I* know that. For sure." She paused. "Here they laid out that whole damn incredible trial in there, all that amazing detail, and they somehow managed never once to say one thing about the whole fucking *point* of it— My God, Tim, *why did she do it?*"

Vance lurched his head forward, nodding. "Yep. That's one question, at least."

He'd been sitting here by himself most of this night, trying to get drunk enough not to care. But it felt a little better now just to get it out, talk about it with somebody.

He stirred, cleared his throat. "I can think of a couple others too. Pretty good ones. But you got it right anyway, Meg—game's called now. *Finis. Kaput.*" He swigged from his drink with a sharp, uncertain motion. "So I guess the questions don't matter anyway. If they ever did."

She was holding one hand to her throat, looking searchingly at him as she said quietly, "Nah, Tim. Unh-uh. Game's not called yet. Because I'm not gonna let them get away with it. *Bury* it like that." She shivered, seemed almost surprised at what she was saying. "I'm gonna go after this thing, Tim —yeah, sure. I'm gonna fucking beat their game."

"Oh, yanh, sure."

"Hey, I mean it. Swear, Tim. Because if I let those fucking miserable cowards get away with that, just send her back so defenseless into that convent loonybin—as if *none of it ever really happened,* and everything's all fine again now—"

"Okay, fair enough. That's damn straight what they're doing—"

"She's just gonna wind up killing herself, Tim. Sooner or later. But anyway as soon as she remembers what she actually did."

His body jerked slightly in his chair. For a moment he did not answer her.

The waitress interrupted with the fresh drinks. He arranged his three glasses neatly along a line in the checkered cloth as he said, "Well, okay. I wouldn't swear that's a real impossibility, Meg."

"Sure. *You* know how good the odds are on that, Tim. Once she comes down from this huge high of the trial. That's at least been something to keep her going. But now she hasn't got that holding her up anymore, God help me, Tim, all I can see is her *crashing*. Coming apart like a cracked dam." She shook her head, her face pulled in a tight, concentrated frown. "And what really gets me most is how, with this whole incredible show they laid on, nobody really *helped* that poor fucking nun. And now they're ready to just *send her back in there*. With their official blessings."

He picked up one of his three glasses. "Okay. No argument so far, Meg."

"*If I let them get away with it*. Which I'm goddam not going to do." Her voice was now very flat, definite. "Hey, I know you guys can't do any more with it now. *But I can*. The goddam Constitution even says I can." She paused. "Swear, Tim. I'm gonna shed some light on that good story."

Ahh, maybe not lost. Not lost yet. His face pulled into something resembling a smile as he said, "Well, okay. As a matter of fact, Meg, I wish you luck."

She was reading intently every flick, every move, on that pocked face now.

"*Straight,* Tim? You really do?"

"Yeah. Straight, Meg." He lifted a glass to eye level and squinted through the dark liquid. "I happen to think that's not such a bad idea."

There was a certain calm in knowing, understanding finally what she must do.

She fixed on this pained man across the table who seemed to be drawing her into some place she had not foreseen. "Okay, thanks, Tim. I appreciate that. And if you by any chance want to help out, you can give me a little confidential steer to Daddy."

He set down the glass and rolled his head forward loosely, blinking at the tablecloth. Weighing that proposition.

"Because you *know* that's where I'm gonna start, Tim. With that guy who happened to be so weirdly absent from

611

that trial we just went through of the good little nun all flanked by her virginal sisters in religion. That amazing little Virgin Birth show they did so nicely in that courtroom."

She reached out and touched her finger to his wrist. Softly: "Yeah, sure, Tim. I'm gonna start with that *fucking.*"

Silence. "Okay, Meg. I will say—I think you're starting in the right place."

"Terrific. So if you want to help out a little, thanks, much appreciated. If not, no hard feelings." She paused. "Because I'm *gonna find him anyway,* Tim. You *know* I'm gonna find him."

He swiped a hand over his chin. "Oh, yeah. I guess you probably will." The sadness was heavy on his face. "But it won't be through me. Never. There's no way I'd ever help you find that guy." Tilting his head to look squarely at her. "You want to know why?"

She nodded, her face very tight.

"Because I *couldn't do that to him.* Knowing what that poor fucker's already been up against—" He jabbed a finger toward her. "Maybe you feel you've got some kind of god-dam Constitutional right to do that to him, Meg. And I don't know, maybe you do, maybe you should. But all I know for sure is you'd just bring more trouble to a guy who's already had a goddam lot more of it than he can handle. And I just wouldn't ever do that to him, Meg."

More startling fragments of that daddy dropped so unexpectedly.

She understood suddenly that the *father's pain* here matched the mother's.

The nod she gave him now was a response to that, a withdrawal of her probe: "Okay, Tim. Understood. Fair enough. But you know I'm gonna find him, Tim."

He stared at the wall by his chair, at the cheap red velvet wallpaper, as he tried to weigh the dangerous idea rolling now in his head.

Rolling so irresistibly. *Game called.* Pass the ball.

Still he held back, trying drunkenly to sort out the dangers. Just in case. Just in case.

But it slipped from him anyway: "Well, if you really do go after it, at least you should look for the right things. I mean—at least ask the right questions. Like, did they maybe have the wrong woman on trial here all along. Maybe."

Her mouth hung open as she took those bizarre words into her.

The idea he had tossed at her was utterly incredible: *the wrong woman?*

Someone *else* killed that baby? The chief cop was telling her this after that whole trial was finished?

The wrong woman and they still put that crucified nun through *that trial* for it?

She worked, pulled at those words, until one possibility moved quickly ahead of the others.

One possibility that she shivered against as she looked up to his face, whispering, *"Oh God. You mean there's two of them?"*

Ahhhh.

His head lurched gratefully up and down. "Hey. You're real quick, Meg."

"Two persons? My God, Tim, you mean she's *two persons?"*

Ahhhh so good to finally hear that from someone else. To let it go.

He eased back more loosely into his chair, moving one finger in the air. *"Maybe* two, Meg. Maybe. Or then again maybe not." He reached for a full glass. "Like I said, Meg. That's just an—interesting possibility. That you maybe oughta think about before you go out looking."

She was shaking her head, her mouth still open. *"Two of them.* Christ. I never even—came close."

613

He shrugged. "Two at least. *Maybe.* Or maybe there's more. But—two anyway."

The idea was still sifting into her, through the resisting grids of her astonishment. She murmured, only half-persuaded: "And one of them's Sister Angela?"

He nodded firmly, drunkenly. "Yanh, sure. Sister Angela Flynn. The little nun. You already know *her* pretty good, Meg."

"Yes. Yes."

"The respectable principal of that real high-class little kindergarten. Perfect work slate. No record of stepping out of line."

"Oh, yeah. The *real good* little nun."

"Yep. Age thirty-four, by the way. Yah, sure, you know her."

He hooked one arm over the back of his chair, looking in the direction of the bar. "But let's suppose just for the hell of it there's another one involved too. Now, let's say that's Gayle Flynn. A nice kid. Bouncy, friendly. Kind of sexy. Age, say, seventeen or eighteen."

She whispered, "Oh, Jesus. *Before she entered.*"

He reached again for a glass. "Now understand, Meg. This Gayle is a nice, likable kid. But let's put it this way. She—looks real good in a low-cut bathing suit."

Starting now like a small blaze of coldness in the center of her gut. She shivered against it as she asked, "Annhh God, Tim. You mean it *wasn't Angela who did that fucking?*"

He blinked, surprised. "Bingo. Right the first time. Hey, Meg, you're a pretty fast draw."

His head wavered drunkenly over the tablecloth. "Maybe, anyway. Or maybe this is all bullshit. That's what Andy thinks, anyway." He paused, belched. " 'Scuse me. Anyway, assuming for the hell of it that maybe is the case" —he waved one warning finger—"then maybe, just *maybe,* it —wasn't Angela who killed the kid either."

Her astonishment exhaled like breath: *"Annhh. That* was Gayle too?"

Shrug. "Maybe. Or something like both of them, fused together like. Or even—I did talk to one pretty good shrink who said that could've been how it happened, the two of them kind of exploding together when she actually saw that kid. Or he said maybe it was a *third* one nobody knows about yet. Something like that."

That possibility was flowing through her now like the coldness of her gut. She hugged her arms against her. "So —*Sister Angela* was right all along. That *she* didn't do it."

He nodded bleakly. "Yeah. Maybe. Except—she probably doesn't know *why* she didn't do it."

He made a shrugging motion, as if to shake off the infinite complexities of that idea. "Or maybe that's all crap, and it happened just like Andy said it did. Shit, *I* don't know. But—that'd be a pretty interesting thing to know for sure. If you could—find it out."

She leaned forward across the table, pulling him into her eyes as she said, *"Tim, tell me about Gayle."*

He didn't know what to say, exactly. Because he didn't want to get into that stuff about the sex with Gavin.

And when you came right down to it that was just about all he knew for sure about Gayle.

He rolled the question back to her: "Well, like I said, Meg. She's a real nice kid. Bouncy. Cheerful, like. Fairly— pushy. Like she's trying it all out."

"Trying *men* out?"

Neutral, lopsided grin. "Nah. Life, mostly." He hesitated, still grinning. "Like scuba diving."

"Ah, *come on,* Tim. Was Gayle coming on to men?"

Grudgingly: "Well, maybe—a little."

"Coming on strong?"

What the hell, he'd already said a shitload more than he should have. And who was he covering for, anyway?

615

He let himself mutter reluctantly, "Okay, yes. I guess you could say Gayle Flynn was coming on pretty strong to men."

That hard cold all through her now as she asked softly, already knowing, "Tim, was it *Gayle* who pushed that fucking? Pushed that sex?"

The look he threw at her was startled, almost stunned. "Hunh? Where'd you get that?"

She flicked her hand. "Never mind. Just—*was it?*"

He looked blankly at the red velvet wall, that last resistance loosening: "Well, yeah. As a matter of fact, you could say she was calling the shots. That was pretty much Gayle's show there all the way." His broad face was still wrenched by the confusion of these possibilities. "But that's not how *Sister Angela* remembers it, see."

Ah Yes. *Yes.*

Very softly now: "How does Angela remember it?"

He moved uncomfortably. "Well—I still can't tell you exactly, Meg. Except it was like—one act of rape, kind of, maybe. In a whole different place."

She pulled her arms protectively over her ribs as she saw, *understood* it finally.

Gayle Flynn she knew already. So much better than she knew that pathetic perky little nun.

Gayle Flynn known like her own skin, her own self.

Annnhhhh, there it was, the missing piece—yes yes *Meg knew her,* that Gayle Flynn.

Gayle the flip side of that murderous repression, the dark side of that sunny little nun. The matched side of the coin.

So eerily familiar already to her, that flipped coin. That had been waiting for her in this all along. Annhhh, *there it was,* fallen, that last piece. In there all along.

Yes yes Meg knew her well, that Gayle Flynn.

.   .   .

Now he was talking, babbling almost, about what his shrink friend had told him—how *Gayle* would know all about *Angela,* see.

But Angela wouldn't know about Gayle. Or any of the rest of them, if there were others too.

Because they *existed,* see—at least Gayle seemed to—mostly just to take up the slack from the guilt Angela couldn't handle. Couldn't even let herself feel. Because it was—just more than she could handle.

Like that guilt about the killing. But as long as those others were there to feel it *for her,* see, Angela didn't have to.

The talking seemed to relieve Vance, make him feel better. But everything he was saying went into Meg like cold knives.

She shivered, holding herself, "Oh God. Like Angela was all along just . . . a hostage to *Gayle's baby.*"

He nodded, with a rolling motion of his head. "Yanh, well. Something like that."

Now that earlier fear was pressing back on her, pushing out all those other rushing thoughts: "But, Tim—if Angela finds out about Gayle, if she realizes what the two of them did together, what else can she do except—kill herself?"

Staring urgently, pleadingly, at his face. "Or Angela will kill Gayle. Or some third one does it to them both. But my God, Tim—how the hell else can this thing *possibly end?*"

He smiled happily for the first time that night. Christ, it felt good to finally have something tolerable to say.

He waved toward her, pointing: "Ah no, not necessarily, Meg. You'll be glad to hear. Because my shrink friend says if we *are* right about this, if there's at least two of them, then suicide is probably a pretty remote possibility."

He interrupted the question coming out of her with, "Because if we're right about that, see, *Gayle will protect her.*

Because that's why Angela invented her in the first place, see
—to keep her safe."

He belched gracefully against the back of his hand.
"Anyway. Something like that."

She clutched at that thing he was saying. That thin
armor against these terrifying possibilities.

Yet couldn't, even *wanting so to,* believe it.

Now he was muttering about how those others, see,
would be almost like guardian angels to Angela. If they were
just real.

Because that's why she'd made them in the first place—
just to *protect her.* From those pressures or whatever it was
she couldn't handle any other way.

So as long as she just kept them there and functional
they'd *go on* protecting her. Step in whenever she really
needed them. And somehow keep her—safe.

She whispered, *"God, Tim. What a beautiful idea."*

He stretched, crossed his legs with a quick, jerking motion. "Yeah, isn't it." He turned his sorrowing face to her.
"It really is. They might keep her alive and kicking to a ripe
old nun age, even. Outlive you or me for sure, Meg." His
look so clouded, pained. "If they just—are real."

She leaned forward over the table, catching her spilling
hair in the hands cupped to her cheeks. She was trying to
read reassurance from his eyes. But all she saw there were
her own doubts, fears, mirrored.

That *those others were real* she already trusted, believed.
But that *they would keep Angela safe?*

Meg murmured, "Oh, nice. Sure. The happy ending to
the good little fairy tale." She reached out to him with a sad
doubting, smile. "Oh, Tim. Wouldn't that be real sweet to
believe?"

Forty-one

Angela had thought surely she would sleep easily tonight, after this astonishing, so blessed day.

But when she got to her own room and scrubbed her face and brushed her teeth at the wall sink she still felt charged up with thoughts, awakeness. Remembering that look on Dan's face. That way Mary Alice had cried.

She thought it might help make her sleepy if she went right to bed. So she started the undressing briskly, automatically. Like she always did it, top half first, not looking.

Strange panting sound.

In the room.

Looking bewilderedly around her.

Standing on her rug. In her room. In her green nightgown.

Something in her hand.

She lifted her hand, blinking, looking at that thing.

Panties. White panties in her right hand.

Whimpering sound in the room as she moved quickly toward the chair where her gray skirt was spread out. And pushed the panties under it, out of sight.

She turned off the wall switch, and slipped in the familiar dark of that night room into her bed, into those cool welcoming sheets.

Body still trembling a little. Shivering.

She turned herself sideways on the narrow bed, pushing her hand under the pillow, sliding her knees up to her chest.

Aaahhh Sweet Lord she'd thought all that would be *finished now*. Those lost times. She'd been so sure of that.

She pulled back once again those blessed words the judge had said, pulled them around her for comfort.

619

Shivering still. But it *must be* all right, must be safe now.

Sweet loving Lord Jesus everything you asked. Oh please now Lord—enough!

Body twisting, reaching for rest.

Not guilty, he said.

Ahhhhh surely finished now. Enough. Surely—

Done.

Willing, *needing* to go out now.

Willing that blotting surcease into her still tensed, quivering body. Reaching almost angrily for that sleep to take her away from this triumphant day she had earlier wanted never to end.

Tired, so tired.

Enough. Enough. Let me go now.

Finished now.

All that strangeness of theirs.

Safe to go now, sink to that blessed oblivion—

Not guilty he said.

Back to her own life. Herself.

Ahhhhh Sweet Lord let me go.

Yes yes here coming blessed slide to nothing . . .

Smiling. Sliding. Holding to . . .

    not

        guilty

      he

        said.